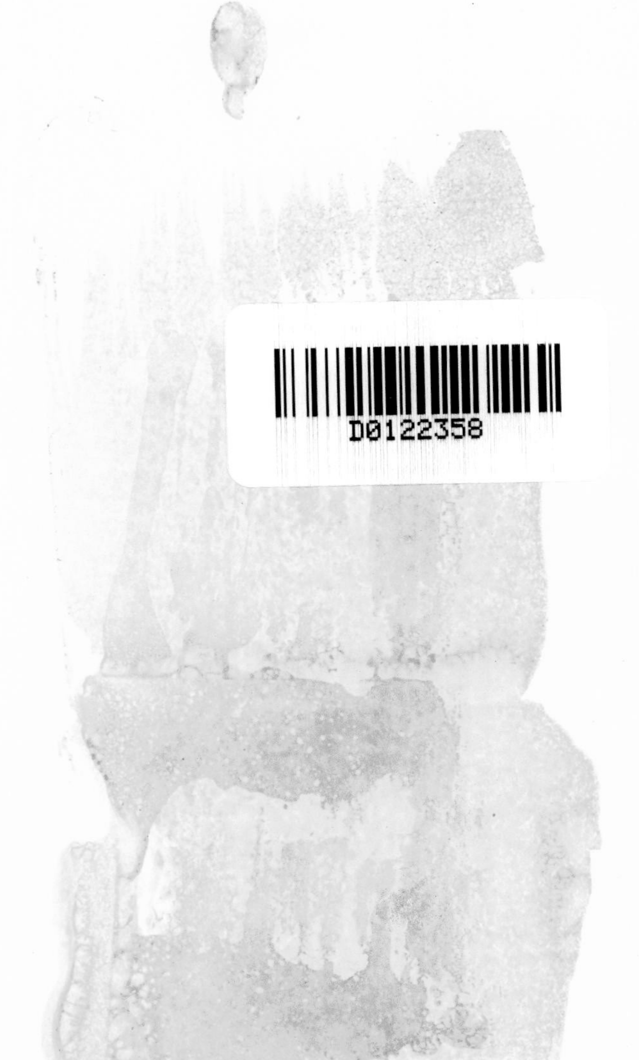

MOTOWN
UNDERGROUND

Also by Doug Allyn

The Cheerio Killings

DOUG
ALLYN

MOTOWN UNDERGROUND

A · THOMAS · DUNNE
BOOK

St. Martin's Press
New York

 For information, address St. Martin's Press, 175 Fifth Avenue, New York, N.Y. 10010

Design by Dawn Niles

Library of Congress Cataloging-in-Publication Data

Allyn, Douglas.
Motown underground / Douglas Allyn.
p. cm.
"A Thomas Dunne book."
ISBN 0-312-08851-5
I. Title.
PS3551.L49M68 1993
813′.54—dc20 92-40796
CIP

First Edition: February 1993

10 9 8 7 6 5 4 3 2 1

TED NUGENT

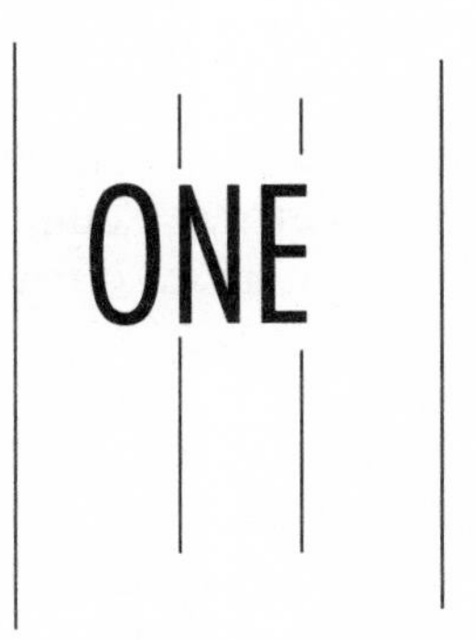

"You believe in full moons, Loop?" Cordell asked.

"Believe? As a bug light for crazies, you mean?" Garcia said.

Bennett and Garcia were cruising the low-rent strip of party stores and secondhand shops that line East Jefferson between the glass towers of the Renaissance Center and the mansions of Grosse Pointe. To have and have not, Motown style. Thanksgiving was still a week away but tinny Christmas carols were already blaring from storefront speakers, rattling down the empty avenue. A pallid moon, bled white by the city glow, ghosted through snowclouds over the Detroit River.

"It ain't no smoke," Cordell said. "I got a buddy works the emergency room at Samaritan, says the body count jumps a third, the full moon."

"Maybe the extra light makes people better targets."

"Or maybe you been on the job too long," Cordell grumbled, turning south into a factory district between Jefferson and the river. A blue-and-white Detroit police prowl car was parked in the lot of an empty warehouse, its roof rack flashers on slow, reflecting off the snow-dusted brick walls of the building. Two uniforms, bulky as Eskimos in their winter jackets, breath showing white in the wintry air, climbed out of their car as Bennett and Garcia pulled up. Garcia recognized Nate Beamon, the pepper half of the salt-and-pepper team: squat, battle scarred, with a Fu Manchu mustache, built like a bowling ball, round, black, rock solid. Didn't know his partner, a tall, horse-faced white guy who looked literally green around the mouth. A bad omen.

"You got any cologne?" Beamon asked through Garcia's lowered window.

"Shit," Bennett groaned, "please don't tell me you got a ripe one, Bea. We ain't had dinner yet."

"We got two victims," Beamon said. "The bodies ain't high but the room's real bad. Gasoline splashed around it, ranker'n hell down there. EMS and the evidence team are on the way but they'll be a while, we're third on the list. Busy night. Always is, the full moon."

"I've heard that," Bennett said, shooting Garcia a look.

Lupe ignored him, popped the glove box, peeled four napkins out, sprinkled them lightly with Old Spice from a small plastic vial, and passed them around. "Let's have a quick look."

"My new partner, Flory Szatkowski," Beamon said, nodding at his buddy, a gangly blond with huge hands, acne scars on his face, bluish and splotchy from the cold. "These two burnouts are Bennett and Garcia, and the fact that they're pullin' weekend swing shift says all you need to know about 'em."

"Speak for yourself, Bea," Bennett said. He was a big man, linebacker size, in a navy car coat, knit watch cap pulled down around his ears. Garcia was slightly smaller, six feet or so, his leather trench coat collar turned up against the wind. Beamon led them up a short stairway to a concrete loading dock, its door battered half off its hinges. Garcia hesitated a moment on the landing, looking across the lot at the river, a frozen, snow-dusted icescape bathed in moonlight. A wind gust moaned over the ice from the Canadian side, sending snow devils dancing and swirling ahead of it. Szatkowski glanced at Garcia questioningly.

"Cold or not, it's quite a picture, isn't it?" Garcia said.

Szatkowski shrugged. "So is what's downstairs."

The raw gasoline stench hit them as soon as they stepped through the warehouse door. Garcia covered his mouth with the napkin and followed Szatkowski down the narrow concrete stairs. A dozen doors led off the basement hallway, all of them kicked in years ago. Beamon led them into a storeroom with a bare concrete floor and galvanized steel heating ductwork overhead. The only light came from the parking lot glare through a row of head-high, steel-meshed windows, most of them broken, that ran the length of the room. Smashed crates and cardboard debris littered the floor like kindling, all of it splashed with gasoline. Szatkowski was right. It was worth seeing.

Two teenagers were seated on cheap metal kitchen chairs facing each other across an upturned wooden crate. One black, one Chicano, both dead. They looked fourteen or so. They'd been stripped to the waist, their ankles lashed to the chair legs with plastic clothesline, wrists handcuffed behind them to the metal spindles of the seat backs.

Their faces were masks of brutality, battered, gashed, painted with crusted blood. Their torsos were bruised, pocked with purplish cigarette burns. The head of the Chicano boy was swollen to nearly twice normal size. Garcia and Bennett eyed the scene in silence.

"What do you guys think?" Szatkowski said at last. "Suicide?"

Bennett glanced at him curiously. "Right. Tied up, beaten to death. Worst case of suicide we ever saw. Lighten up, Ski. We know you're a badass or you wouldn't be workin' the strip. But there's nothin' funny about this."

"No," Szatkowski said, flushing a little, "I guess not. Sorry."

"Killin's can be funny sometimes though," Bennett

said, kneeling to examine the handcuffs. "You remember that go-ahead'n-shoot-bitch we had Labor Day weekend, Bea?"

"A what?" Szatkowski said.

"Pimp killing," Beamon grunted. "You figure 'go ahead 'n shoot bitch' are usually the guy's last words."

"There was this pimp called Greenie," Cordell explained to Ski. "A Rican dude with a Benz, classy apartment. One night he gets loaded, knocks the bejesus outa one of his ladies. So she waits till he's sittin' on the crapper, sticks a .22 derringer in his left ear, and kills him deader'n a coal bucket. No mess, almost no blood. Greenie's just sittin' there with his pants down lookin' totally surprised, you know? Like he can't believe he's dead? And *every*body who saw the dude smiled, evidence team, paramedics, whoever. Couldn't help it. We were layin' bets toward the end that somebody might not crack up, but they all did."

"Unfortunately, we've got the opposite number here," Garcia said. "These kids flat ass paid some dues. Somebody hammered on them a long time for the boy's head to swell like that."

"What do you think about the money?" Beamon asked. A small mound of crumpled bills was piled around a candle stub on the box between the corpses.

"Hell, I don't know," Bennett said, straightening, his face gray, "they damn sure weren't playin' poker. Some kinda ritual, a message maybe."

"For whom?" Garcia asked. "Who'd see 'em down here? Whose turf are we on, Bea?"

"No man's land really, this side of Jefferson. Cobras, Pony Downs, Selby Hood all use the buildings—"

"Hey," Szatkowski said softly, staring at the smaller corpse, "check that out."

Bennett followed his gaze. A small bubble was forming in the blood trickling down from the black kid's broken nose. Bennett pressed a finger under the boy's jaw. "Holy shit, he's got a pulse."

"He can't have," Szatkowski said, "I checked—"

"Fuck that," Bennett snapped, "I can feel a pulse. Get him on the floor, quick." Beamon grabbed the chair back and helped Bennett ease the boy down to the floor. Beamon pressed his ear against the boy's chest.

"Heartbeat," he grunted, " 'bout like a stomped sparrow. He breathin'?"

"No," Bennett said, "not that I can see. He's gotta have mouth to mouth. Anybody got a pocket mask?"

"Ski, get your ass out to the car, get the emergency kit," Beamon snarled. "Haul it!"

"No mask with you?" Bennett said, kneeling over the boy as Szatkowski loped out the door.

"We got one in the car, just hang loose a minute."

"This kid don't have a minute," Bennett said grimly. "Dammit to hell anyway." He tilted the boy's chin upward, clearing his airway, then formed a triangle with his hands and pressed them over the kid's mouth, sealing his broken nose. Bennett pressed his mouth against the ring formed by his thumbs and exhaled a long, slow breath, held his cheek against the boy's mouth to check for respiration, then repeated the cycle. And then again. Beamon reached across and wiped some blood off Bennett's cheek, but Cordell didn't notice, totally focused on breathing life into the boy.

Garcia watched a moment, then turned away. He picked up one of the bills from the table and sniffed it. Gasoline. He dropped it back on the pile.

"Bea, how'd you find these guys?"

"Complaint. Rent-a-cops check the buildings once a shift, drive past, you know? They spotted some cars in the lot."

"Was anybody around when you got here?"

"Just two cars parked on the street, looked like posse wheels. Took off when we rolled up."

Garcia crossed to one of the windows, stood on tiptoe, and peered out. "One of 'em a black Monte Carlo? Jacked in the rear?"

Beamon nodded.

"They're baaack," Garcia said softly, "and I think we might be in a lot of trouble here."

"Got the mask," Szatkowski said, bustling back into the room, paper packet in one hand, his police-issue Remington pump shotgun in the other. "Jesus, Bennett, you shouldn't be—"

"Gimme the damn mask," Cordell snapped, snatching it out of Ski's hand. "I got any blood or spit on my face?"

"No," Ski said, "none I can see."

"Thank you, Jesus," Cordell said. "Now back off, gimme some room." He popped the clear plastic mask open, placed it carefully over the boy's face, and began blowing gently into the nipple.

"What's happening out there, Ski?" Garcia asked.

"Some people are gatherin' around. Must've seen our flashers, come down to check it out."

"Gangbangers?"

"Some. A lot of green jackets, Pony Downs. Some citizens too. I called in, told central to get us an ambulance, code one."

"You ask for backup?"

"Brought some with me," Szatkowski grinned, hefting the shotgun. "Some of the Ponies were gettin' pretty lippy when I moved through."

"But you didn't call for backup?"

"No, why? Evidence team'll be here, EMS. The Ponies'll either spook off or get tired of standin' around in the cold."

"It may not stay all that cold," Garcia said. "Look, they brought these guys down here and beat on them as punishment for stealing, that's why the money's on the table. They sat 'em facing the cash, doused the money and the room with gas, lit the candle, and went outside to wait. The kid was supposed to watch the candle burn down until it reached the bills and boom. Only it didn't happen. Either the flame went out or he blew it out before he fainted. And now we're in the same jam he was. Any Pony Downs near the car when you called for an ambulance?"

Ski nodded.

"Terrific. So they know he's alive. And there's no way they'll let us take him out of here. Is there a back way out of this place, Bea?"

"Not from down here, only the way we came in."

"Kid's breathin' on his own," Cordell said, still hunched over the boy, "but just barely. He's not gonna take a whole lotta shakin'. We gotta get him outta here."

"Him and us both," Garcia said, "only we don't dare take him outside without getting some backup. Bea, help Cordell get the boy out in the hall, air's better there. Ski, you're with me, and bring the shotgun."

Garcia trotted up the basement stairs with Szatkowski close behind. He stopped in the shadow of the doorway, scanning the parking lot. A crowd was gathering around the two cars, thirty, maybe forty people, mostly teenyboppers or early twenties. He could spot only a handful of Pony Down jackets, but there were at least a dozen more young studs in the crowd who were the right age, had the right look. And more were drifting in. Trouble. Real trouble.

"Okay, Ski," he said quietly, "this is how it goes. I'll head for the car. You let me get a third of the way there, then step out on the landing, rack your weapon to draw their attention. By the time they figure out you can't fire into the crowd without wasting me too, I should be in the car on the radio." He pulled his .38 Smith & Wesson AIRWEIGHT from his shoulder holster and thrust it into his trench coat pocket.

"You might make it there," Szatkowski nodded tensely, his knuckles pale on the shotgun stock. "How are you gonna get back?"

"Who's coming back? I'll be down at Tufic's sippin' a brew, checkin' the eleven o'clock news to see how you guys make out. Remember, give me a minute, then show yourself." He was out the door and down the steps before Szatkowski could answer.

He pushed warily through the crowd, not hurrying, just moving along. A cluster of Pony Downs were near his car. A tall, twentyish, fair-skinned black with a weight lifter's build, his hair done in orange dreadlocks, was leaning against the car, talking with four other guys his own age and three younger kids. All of them were wearing green jackets, baseball caps, or had green do-rags hanging out of their back pockets, even the smaller boys. The Ponies draft 'em early.

Garcia might've made the car unnoticed if Ski hadn't followed directions to the letter, stepping out and racking his shotgun. Dreadlocks glanced up at the sound, spotted Garcia coming. He showed no visible reaction to seeing a cop headed his way, or having a shotgun cocked in his vicinity. A bad sign. Still, he apparently wasn't looking for trouble. He nodded to his crew, then coolly sauntered away from the car, followed by the others.

All except one. A younger boy stayed behind in Garcia's path. No more than thirteen tops, he was wearing a Pony green jacket and matching baseball cap, bill sideways, jammed down on his tightly curled hair. Designer jeans, two-hundred-dollar Nike tennies. A serious razor scar on his jaw. Thirteen or not, the kid was a pro. Others in the crowd, sensing the edge in the boy's stance, his hard-eyed stare, began backing away from the car, leaving the kid alone in a cracked concrete arena to face Garcia. No contest. A joke. Except that the Ponies had a history of using teenybop killers who can only draw a juvy hall sentence. This kid was definitely strong enough to pull a trigger. And he was already set in a gunfighter's combat stance, feet apart, knees slightly bent, hand inside his jacket. Just like on TV.

Sweet Jesus. Garcia felt an icy touch between his shoulder blades that had nothing to do with the night wind. A whisper of horror. God, he was only a child. But the two back in the warehouse weren't any older. And this boy had almost certainly been involved in their agony. A lost one, cold as iron, eyes with no more life in them than the dead youth in the basement. But still just a kid. Oh man . . .

It was going to happen here, in this ring of strangers. Garcia could smell it on the wind, in the tense silence of the crowd. His fist was clamped on the revolver in his coat pocket, his eyes locked on the boy's. But he wasn't sure he could shoot even if the kid—the boy's hand moved.

Reflex! Garcia pulled his .38, instantly centering the kid in his sights, two-hand hold, aiming square at the boy's chest from six feet away. The kid's eyes widened, focusing on the gun muzzle, but didn't waver. *"Hold it right there!"* Garcia roared, trying to shake him. "Take your hand out of your coat! Slowly! Now!"

Dreadlocks was grinning. Garcia glimpsed him out of the corner of his eye. Arms folded, he was standing on the edge of the crowd, watching, smiling. But he was too close. If the kid has a gun, Dreadlocks is in his line of fire—the boy jerked a pistol out of his jacket. Garcia flinched, almost fired. But didn't. Christ it was a near thing. Plastic. The kid had a yellow plastic squirt gun. Not even a good fake, some kind of cheap Star Trek crap—

"Folks doowwn!" the boy yelled, grinning, spritzing Garcia with water, then dodging out of his way, ducking into the crush as the crowd erupted with nervous laughter, a few jeers.

"You little bastard!" Garcia yelled after him, anger battling with relief. The kid was already well out of reach, squirming away through the mob. "Okay people, back off, the joke's over."

But it wasn't, quite. His unmarked city Chrysler was sitting on its hubs, all four tires flattened. The prowl car too. Damn. He scanned the crowd. Three or four Pony Downs nearby. Could have been any of 'em.

He unlocked the door, slid behind the wheel, and was greeted by a blast of icy air. The passenger's side window had been smashed in, shards of glass littering the seat. The radio was wrecked, probably demolished by a tire iron. He raised himself in the seat, checking the prowl car alongside. It was in the same condition, window and radio both trashed.

Dammit! No wonder Dreadlocks wasn't worried. With no radio, no wheels, and no backup they were outnumbered ten to one and probably outgunned too. The Ponies could just stall until the tortured boy died, or blow him away when they carried him out to the ambulance, if the damn thing—

Headlights played over the brick wall as a van pulled up to the curb alongside the lot. WKBD TV News. It parked well away from the police cars, keeping the driveway clear. Garcia was out of his car, sprinting for the van before it stopped moving.

"Sergeant Garcia, right?" Stephanie Hawkins, channel 50's street reporter, rolled down her window. "We monitored the squeal on our EMS scanner. What have you got?"

"A killing," Garcia said, "maybe more on the way. We're in a bad situation here. I need to use your mobile phone, now."

She hesitated, reading his eyes, then passed him the phone without a word. Cas Novak, her cameraman, climbed out of the van, minicam on his shoulder, and began filming the crowd, panning across the scene in front of the warehouse as Garcia frantically dialed 911.

"This is Sergeant Garcia, Metro Homicide, badge

twenty-eight forty-one. Request emergency backup at 1316 Montcalm, off Conner. One homicide, a medical emergency, and possible riot situation. Send a fire truck too, we've got a gasoline spill." He listened as the operator confirmed the message and the address, then broke the connection.

"Gotcha, you bastards," Garcia said softly. Dreadlocks was already stalking off, shouldering his way through the crowd toward the street. The rest of the Pony Downs were on the move too, fading away like smoke.

"If you're through with my phone, can you take a second to fill me in?" Stephanie Hawkins said.

"Maybe the good guys just won one for a change," Garcia said, taking a deep breath. "We had a—" Something was wrong. The Ponies were stopping out in the street, holding their ground. Waiting. Novak was filming them, but they weren't paying any attention to him. The building. They were watching the building. . . .

The boy with the squirt gun was crouched in the shadows near the windows. A flicker of light silhouetted him for a moment. What the hell? Garcia glanced down at the silvery beads of moisture on his coat where the boy had sprayed him. He touched one with his fingertips. Not water, some kind of oil or . . . Lighter fluid. Sweet Jesus.

Garcia threw the phone at Hawkins and sprinted toward the building. *"SKI!* Stop him!"

The boy stepped away from the wall, the end of his plastic pistol ablaze, burning like a flare. He dropped into a combat crouch facing a broken window. Szatkowski heard Garcia shout, shouldered his shotgun uncertainly, aiming in the boy's direction. "Hold it!" he yelled at the kid. "Freeze right there!" The boy didn't hear him, or didn't care.

"SKIII! SHOOT HIM! SHOOT THE KID!!!" Garcia slipped, went down hard on the icy concrete. Smiling, the boy spritzed a pissy little stream of flame through a broken basement window. And was instantly blowtorched into a pillar of fire as the building exploded.

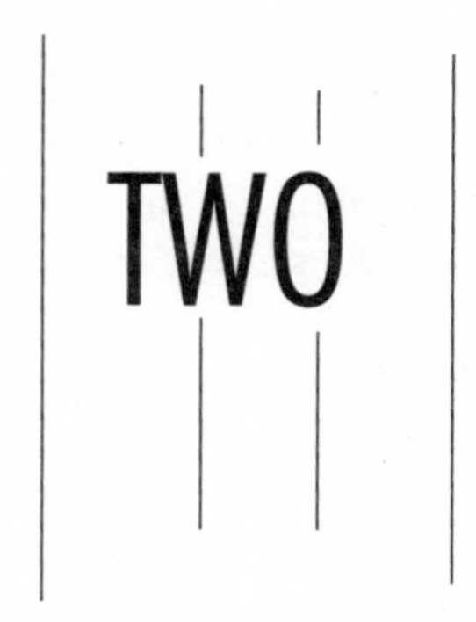

TWO

Garcia drove slowly into the snowy parking lot, checking the mall over. Hall Plaza was a row of one-story shops anchored in the center by a taller three-story red brick building. Developers built the low-budget mall back in the sixties when the Big Three were still hammering out Detroit iron three shifts, seven days a week. Sugartime in Sugartown. Then the auto work moved offshore, to Mexico and Taiwan, stranding the plaza like a dinosaur in winter, blundering along, dying one shop at a time. A few of the businesses were still healthy, a Sam Goody, a Radio Shack, but most had For Sale Or Lease banners in their windows.

The three-story main building, once a JC Penney, was a Chinese restaurant now, the Jade Mountain. The basement nightclub below it had a bold new, eye-stabbing fluorescent green neon sign: Motown Underground. Garcia parked his silver Firebird in front of the club, climbed out, and strode quickly over to the building, head down against the stinging January wind.

He hesitated a moment at the head of the concrete stairway leading down to the club's entrance. Six weeks since the blast, and he still felt uneasy facing basement steps or the stench of gasoline. A drumbeat pulsed up through the soles of his shoes. A band playing at two in the afternoon? Rehearsing, must be. A wind gust nudged him impatiently. He shrugged it off and trudged down the stairway into his past.

He paused just inside the black leather upholstered door, waiting for his eyes to adjust to the dimness, scanning the room for ghosts.

The nightclub hadn't changed—a basement roughly half the size of a football field converted into an industrial-strength rock'n'roll saloon. An honest room, blue-collar proud of its origins, flat black concrete walls splashed here and there with brilliant blazes of color, naked steel girders overhead with multihued rotating spotlights clamped to them that could alter the room's ambience with the twist of a dial, from cool blue to lust rose to belly-rubber purple to a grim-reality white glare.

A Jimi Hendrix clone of a bartender in a tie-dyed magenta shirt and *kente*-cloth headband was bopping behind the bar to the hard rock beat of the band, juggling drinks, bantering with a couple of young studs in biker leathers. A pair of lunch hour lovers were nuzzling in a booth beneath a screaming Bob Seger poster, one of a dozen hometown hero action shots lining the walls: Aretha, the Temptations, Ted Nugent, Was Not Was. A pair of anorexic twin blond flowers with mall-teased hair, neon orange T-shirts, and kneeless jeans were sitting at a table near the stage, sharing a pitcher of beer and listening to the band start and stop and bitch as they fine-tuned a tune. Except for the larger-than-life faces in the wall posters, Garcia didn't recognize a soul.

He ordered a Bud Light from the bartender, carried it to the booth nearest the door, slid in. A wheelchair hummed out of the hallway that led back to the club's office. He idly followed its progress across the deserted dance floor, then swallowed, hard, realizing he was seeing a ghost at last. My God. Danny Kelly. Or what was left of him, gliding toward him in a chrome-and-canvas wheelchair.

Danny was impeccably dressed as usual, wearing a custom-fitted Lord & Taylor jacket that hung on his skeletal frame like death-camp pajamas. His face was ravaged but recognizable, the square Irish features more pronounced, showing a bright mix of humor, curiosity, a hint of brutality. His thick reddish hair, silvered at the temples now, was tied neatly back in a ponytail. Only his eyes were unchanged, intensely alive. Deep Erin green, embers glowing in the ashes.

"Lupe," Danny said, halting the chair beside the booth, "welcome to the Underground, thanks for comin' down. You look like hell, you know that? Man your age oughta take better care of himself."

Garcia nodded, too stunned to retort. He offered his hand, then withdrew it slowly. Kelly's withered claw remained on the chair's joystick, twitching like an idling motor. "So, Danny," Garcia managed at last, "other than the new wheels, how've you been?"

Richie Zeayen eyed the two men in the booth uneasily. The one-way mirror above Danny's battered old desk in the manager's office gave him a panoramic view of the club. He'd noticed the tall Mex in the leather trench coat when he came in, but paid no attention until Kelly wheeled over to talk to him. Friends? Business? Hard to say. The Mexican's face told him zip. Still . . . The two of 'em talking, Danny laughing at something the Mex said. Bad news. Had to be.

He turned down the volume on the PA speaker on the desk, reducing the soundproofed office to silence, then picked up the phone and tapped out a number.

"Find Red for me, get his ass over here." He hung up without waiting for a reply.

"Cancer of the pancreas," Danny said, "kicked in bad in the fall. Surprised the hell out of me, always figured I'd die of heart failure inside some little tulip without ever knowin' her name. No such luck. I was lucky to see Christmas, I won't see Easter."

"That's hard," Garcia said, "I'm sorry for your trouble."

"Rightly so. Since you're partly responsible for it."

"Me? How do you figure?"

"It's possible the cancer was traumatically induced, related to a semiserious thumpin' I got seven eight years back."

"No smoke?" Garcia said. "I didn't know you could get cancer from a beating."

"You never did read enough, Loop. Traumatically induced cancer isn't as common as crabs, maybe, but medical scholars like myself are familiar with it."

"I'm impressed. Where did you read about it?"

"The October issue of Spider-Man, the one where he races the Flash. An unimpeachable source."

"Right," Garcia said, "well in that case maybe I'd better walk. I remember this joint as being fairly rowdy. Don't bother to get up, I'll see myself out."

"You weren't so quick to run off in the old days."

"I was less fragile then. Or I thought I was."

"You look healthy enough to me. By comparison, I mean."

"John Lennon looks healthy compared to you, Danny. My God, how can you joke about a thing like this?"

"Some days it's not easy," Kelly admitted, "but in a way I'm lucky. We all know we're goin', we just don't know when. Okay, I know. All I gotta worry about now is doin' it right. Like Jesus or the Sundance Kid. Question is, do I hang in there sayin' father forgive 'em or drop my guns and shuffle off with my pants down. I'm not sure how I'll handle the moment, you know? And that scares me some. That make sense or should I cut back my medication?"

"I guess it does, which probably means you're putting me on. I never could tell when you were serious."

"Okay, I'll get serious. I saw you on TV back around

Thanksgiving. A warehouse explosion off Jefferson. Ugly business. You come out of it in one piece?"

"Not bad, considering. A concussion, bruised ribs. Nothing serious. I got off a lot easier than the others."

"I see. And your immortal soul?"

Garcia stared at him a moment, then shrugged. "Roughed up a bit," he admitted, "maybe even broken. Too soon to say."

"Papers said you quit the force right after. Resigned."

"I tried. They put me on administrative leave till the end of this month to think about it. It won't make any difference."

"You're getting out?"

"I can't do it anymore, Danny. It's as simple and as complicated as that."

"Understandable," Danny nodded. "So what's next?"

"I don't know yet. Find a job. Maybe go back to school. I don't know."

"I, ah, I may have a job for you."

"I knew it. You need a swamper, right?"

"It is a cleanup job in a way. I'm in trouble, Loop."

"I can see that."

"Nah, not just . . . dyin'. Fact is, the lamer I get, the more curious I am about what's next. I've watched my daughter grow up, made love to a few good women and fucked a lot more. I heard Albert Collins play blues in this very room, and I was only three seats down from Nicholson at the Forum when the Pistons won it all. I'm not afraid, Loop, and that's no smoke. I just hate goin' out without any . . . class, is all. Broke. And stupid."

"Business that bad?"

"No, business is good and gettin' better. Thing is, a few years back when things were really jumpin', I went into hock deep to buy this whole building from the developers. Then when the cancer came on, I put the club up for sale, half a mil. Got a few bites, but they see the shape I'm in, they figure to wait, pick it up for nothin' from Connie after I'm gone."

"Seems reasonable." Garcia nodded. "Not fair maybe."

"I know. Hell, I'd probably do the same. And it's not like Connie and Erin'll be on the street. Connie's working as a receptionist, doin' okay, and Erin's out of school now and doin' even better. Maybe they deserve more for puttin' up with me all these years, but they'll survive. It's my boy I'm worried about."

"What boy?"

"I have a son," Kelly said, looking away. "Born on the wrong side of the blanket to my girlfriend of the month a long time back. He, ah, he was born brain-damaged. His mother OD'd a few weeks after, didn't even leave a note. I was so shook I got my plumbin' remodeled so it couldn't happen again. He's a grown man now, mentally two, maybe three years old, in an adult body. He needs professional care, always will. And it costs, man you can't believe how much it costs."

"Do you have any family left who might help?"

"None. Only my brother the father, and I doubt he'd help even if he could. We've scarcely spoken in twenty years. Havin' a priest in the family's handy for weddin's and wakes, but not for a thing like this. It's not my boy's soul I'm worried about, it's his life, and that's my responsibility. I figured I had to sell the Underground, to get enough for a trust fund. And I fucked up. Big-time. You know a guy named Richie Zeayen? Calls himself Richie Zee?"

"I—remember a guy named Terry Zeayen. Chaldean, I think. In the coke trade. Dead now, though."

"Richie's Terry's younger brother. Cadillac Richie."

"He in the life too?"

"He says not," Kelly said carefully, "but he did offer me a quarter mil for a piece of the Underground."

"Ask you to take a check, did he?"

"Nope, cash. Ah hell, I knew he was on the hustle and

probably couldn't get up all the bread, I was just hopin' to get enough, you know? And it wasn't just the money. The kid had a lotta moxie, and I liked him, I really did. Liked his energy, his enthusiasm. I needed somebody like him. Somebody like you used to be. But . . . He changed. Turned mean, pushy. He's pushing me out."

"And he's stalling you about the money?"

"Right. He gave me thirty thou up front, made his first couple of payments, but . . . like I said, he changed. I guess I should've expected it. He's smart, and it's the smart move, buy in, wait for me to croak, squeeze Connie out. I figured I could handle him, make him come across for enough cash to do me. Six months ago maybe I could have. I just got too sick too fast."

"So get a lawyer. If he's not paying . . ."

"Not that simple. The bastard's got a record, for dope. He can replace me with a front man easy, but if I try to make a fuss I could lose my liquor license for dealin' with a felon. Without a license this place is just another empty building in a town full of 'em. Besides, he's threatened me, Loop, threatened my family. To my face knowin' I couldn't do shit about it. God, I hate being sick like this. I fuckin' hate it."

"With traumatically induced cancer?"

"Hell, I was only jokin' about that."

"No you weren't," Garcia said evenly, "not exactly. You were running a head game on me. A not-so-subtle reminder that you took a beating for me once. Maybe you're right. Maybe I owe you. But it bothers me that you think you have to call in a marker to ask for my help. We never ran games on each other, Danny. It's a little late in the day to start, isn't it?"

"Yeah," Danny said, looking away, watching the band a moment, "I know it is. The shape I'm in, head games are the only kind I can still play, Loop. But you're right, I shouldn't have done that. Sorry."

"No problem. So what do you want me to do, Danny? Lean on this guy?"

"Don't underestimate him, Loop. He's young, but he grew up in the life. He's street smart, and hard. And crazy, maybe even crazier'n you used to be. I think you'll have to kill him."

Garcia eyed him a moment, his face unreadable. "Jesus, Danny, you really are losin' it. I could bust you just for saying that."

"I know," Kelly said, seizing Garcia's wrist with a palsied hand, his eyes flaring with sickly intensity. "I also know you've killed people in the line o' duty. This is no different. The guy's in the trade, he's threatened—Look, I'm not askin' for charity. I got ten large, all I got left of the money Richie gave me. Take it, Loop, please. Don't let him do this to me. Do him for me."

"Dammit, I don't owe you anything like this, Danny," Garcia snapped. "You knew what he was when you got in bed with him—"

"Danny," Richie Zeayen said quietly, "this guy givin' you trouble?"

Garcia glanced up sharply. Two men had sauntered over to the booth. One wore a muted pin-striped suit, a teal polo shirt, no tie. Broad, European features, a sunlamp tan, dark, razor-cut hair. His shadow was much larger, steamroller-sized in a full Cleveland powder blue polyester jumpsuit and nickel-toed cowboy boots. Suety moon face, frizzy, brick red hair, a skimpy red beard that didn't quite camouflage a wine stain birthmark that trickled down his jaw like an open wound.

"Do you mind?" Garcia said. "We're having a private conversation."

"Not private enough," Richie said. "You're spookin' my customers, Jack, and Red here thinks you're hassling my partner. Danny's not a well man. We have to look out for him."

"It's okay, Richie," Danny said, his eyes locked on Garcia's, "he's just a friend from the old days. Used to work for me is all."

"Really? You in the club business?"

"I was," Garcia said. "Not anymore."

"So what do you think of the band?"

"The what?"

"My new band, the Whiteboys. How do you like 'em?"

"From what I've heard, they're fine."

"You haven't heard nothin' yet. They got a Mex chick singer'll knock your socks off. You know what song she sings best? 'Hit the Road, Jack.' I can almost hear it. How 'bout you? You hear it?"

"Maybe I do," Garcia nodded. "Look, we've got no problem here, just give us a couple minutes, I'm history."

"Wrong, you're history already, spick," Red said, seizing Garcia's trench coat collar. "You heard the man, get the fuck—"

Garcia grabbed Red's hand, clawing his ring finger up, bending it back, using the pressure to pull the big man's hand off his collar and slam it palm down on the table. He kept his fist clamped around the finger, holding it upright. "Okay, just cool down. I don't want a hassle, but I've had a bad month—"

"Cocksucker!" Red snarled, trying to jerk his hand free.

There was an audible pop. Red froze, blood draining from his face, his mouth open in a soundless 'O' of shock.

"Jesus that was stupid," Garcia said, wincing in sympathy, but keeping Red's palm pinned firmly to the table. "You ever eat hot wings?"

"What?" Red gasped, sucking air.

"Chicken wings, you know? Like the Colonel sells? Thing is, you just dislocated your finger. Which means it's only attached to your hand by a few tendons now, some skin. You do anything sudden, your finger's liable to tear off. Like a chicken wing. And we're gonna have a real mess here. Get the picture, big fella?"

"Mex," Richie said, flushing dangerously, "you just made the biggest mistake of your life."

"No chance," Garcia said positively. "The way my life's gone lately, this isn't even a three on a scale of ten. So how about we all cut our losses here and back off?"

"Turn him loose, right now."

"No problem," Garcia said, opening his hand. The sudden release of pressure folded Red over in agony, clutching his injured paw to his chest.

"You sonuvabitch!"

"Cool it, Red," Richie said, "for now. Danny, we'll talk about this later."

"You better get some ice on that hand," Garcia offered. "If it swells up before he makes the emergency room they won't be able to set it."

Zeayen eyed him a moment, coldly memorizing his features. Then he turned and stalked off without a word. Red followed, hunched over his wounded hand.

Richie strode behind the bar and through the swinging doors into the small, brightly lit kitchen. He stopped in front of the huge gray commercial ice maker and slid open its Plexiglas door. "Stick your hand in the bin, man, pile some ice over it."

Red complied, flinching as the ice touched his hand. "Spick cocksucker," he hissed, "I'm gonna kill his ass!"

"Good idea," Richie nodded. "How about right now?"

"Now? But—"

"Look, I don't know who this guy is, whether he's one of Echeverria's people or just some muscle Danny's tryna hire, but either way, we can't let him move in and fuck things up. He's gotta go. I know your hand hurts like a bitch, but you got two of 'em. And I got a Mac 10 in my office, silenced, thirty-round clip, full auto. Think you can handle it one-handed?"

"I don't—yeah, fuckin' right I can."

"Okay, then follow him when he leaves, let him get a ways from the club, then blow his ass away. He won't be lookin' for it, figure you're in the hospital. Here," he said reaching into his vest pocket, "pop a coupla these Black Beauties. You'll still hurt but you won't give a shit. What do you say? You up to it, bro?"

"Damn straight I am. Fuckin' hand feels better already." Red grimaced, gulping the pills dry. "Get me the Mac. And bring a plastic bag for some ice, okay?"

"I take it that was your new partner," Garcia said. "Who's the goon?"

"His hardcase cousin. They were both in the D Streets, an Arab gang from Dearborn a few years back," Kelly said. "His real name's Nurredin, Hamid, I think. Everybody calls him Red. You might as well take the money, Loop. They won't let this pass."

"You're really serious, aren't you?" Garcia said, searching Danny's ravaged face.

"You see the jam I'm in," Danny said. "If you won't do it I'll just keep trying till I find somebody who will."

"You shouldn't have too much trouble finding somebody for—how much was the offer?"

"Ten grand, cash. I know it's not enough—"

"For those two?" Garcia sipped his beer. "It's too much. But I'll take it anyway. Give me the money."

THREE

Two hours and three beers later, Garcia walked carefully out of the club to his Firebird. He fumbled his key into the lock, climbed in, then sat a moment, blinking away the fog. Too many brews, too many memories, too early in the day. He gunned the 'bird slowly out of the Hall Plaza parking lot and swung north on Conant.

At the rear of the club, Red Nurredin fired up Richie's black Jeep Comanche wagon, but stalled it as he tried shifting it left-handed. Cursing, he restarted it, stalled again, then jammed the tranny into drive, keeping the pedal on the mat, spinning the 'manche in half a doughnut, roaring across the lot and out onto the street. The first few blocks were touch and go, frantically changing lanes in an unfamiliar ride, trying to keep his right hand buried in the icebag on his lap. Then he slowed, backing off, as he spotted the silver 'bird only a block or so ahead.

No sweat, the spick was just loafin' along, not a care in the fuckin' world. Red popped two more of the Black Beauties Richie'd given him, feeling a rush of energy and exultation tighten his chest, making it hard to breathe. The pain in his hand was still there, ice pick sharp, but sweet agony now, camouflaged by the amphetamines, keeping him pumped up, edgy, alert. He was gonna enjoy this, taste every fuckin' minute of it.

Garcia fished the envelope out of his coat, glanced at it, then tossed it on the seat. Ten grand. Last dollar of a dying man, candy from a baby. Maybe he'd been working the wrong side of the street all along. He cut a quick lane change, then a hard right on Balboa. He almost missed the turn. It had been a while. Seven years? About that. The enclave was pleasant enough, one of the upper-middle-class pockets of prosperity that dot metro Motown like oases. Wide streets, trees lining the curb, lawns broad enough for touch football. Homes, not houses. Honest-to-God "Father Knows Best" homes. He scanned each one as he passed, wondering if he'd still recognize the place.

Red slowed, then stopped, as he watched the Firebird pull over to the curb two blocks ahead. Danny's house. Perfect. He'd whack the spick sonuvabitch right on the crip's front steps. Talk about makin' a fuckin' point. He eased the Jeep to the curb a half block behind the Pontiac and shut it down, watching from behind the Comanche's smoked glass as Garcia crossed the street to Kelly's porch.

Red popped the latch on the briefcase, took the Mac 10 machine pistol out, checked the clip, and racked the action, ejecting a live round. Typical fuckin' Richie, leavin' a piece loaded. Thirty rounds, 9-mm. Even one-handed he oughta be able to nail the Mex with most of 'em. Chicken wing my ass. He was gonna be hamburger—no. Whatta they call it? Fajitas? Somethin' like that. Dead meat either way. He eased the piece down on his lap and settled in to wait. Switched up the tape deck. Risa and the Whiteboys. Like Richie didn't hear 'em enough in the club. Definitely had the bad hots for that chick. But at least he'd quit babblin' about the big plans he had for 'em lately. Bored maybe. Or maybe he finally bored Risa and she was a bum lay. Fat fuckin' chance. Chick looked like she could fuck the Hell's Angels to death, then hump a racehorse for dessert. He toyed with the image for a moment, Risa fuckin' twenty Hells Angels, knowing it was a speeder dream, Black Beauties in action. A rainbow ride.

He groped a doobie out of his shirt pocket left-handed, fired it up, sucking the smoke deep into his lungs, holding it. Allll riight. His busted hand was feelin' better and better.

On the porch, Garcia noticed the peephole wink momentarily as someone checked him out. The door remained closed. He pressed the buzzer again and the door opened a cautious crack. "Yes?"

"Connie? Mrs. Kelly? Do you remember me? Lupe Garcia?"

"Oh," she said hesitantly, "of course. What is it?"

"Well, I'd like to talk to you for a minute. About Danny. Can I come in?"

"I ah—of course," she said, "sorry, I guess I'm getting a little paranoid lately. Come in. How are you? We've been following your—career in the papers. Danny wanted to visit you in the hospital but I was afraid the trip—"

"It's all right, I wasn't there long," Lupe said, stepping in, then hesitating, startled by the living room, as always. The house's exterior was traditional New England saltbox like a dozen others on the street, but inside Danny'd knocked out every single wall on the first floor, leaving only ornate wooden pillars. There was thick plush carpeting in a rich ocher and brown, patterned like fallen leaves. A floor-to-ceiling fieldstone fireplace dominated the room, its flames throwing shadows against gleaming natural walnut paneling. For a moment, Lupe was transfixed, frozen by an image of Danny, the man he'd known, the friend, not the specter in the wheelchair, and the sense of loss stung his eyes, paralyzed his heart. He saw himself and Danny, sitting in front of that fire all night long after closing the club, sipping single-malt Scotch, talking about . . . anything, everything. Connie and Erin would find them there in the morning, semistoned, mellow—

"Lupe?" Connie said, for the second time.

"Ah, sorry," he said, "I was just thinking—dammit Connie, I can't you tell how bad I feel about what's happened."

"Yes"—she nodded curtly—"it's been very hard for everyone. Most of all Danny. He was always so active and—well, you know. Was there anything . . . ?"

He glanced at her, surprised by the edge in her tone, looking at her closely for the first time. Still a very handsome woman, Connie. Heart-shaped Nordic face framed by frosty blond hair, probably tinted now, pale blue eyes. She'd always been controlled, the stable planet in Danny's entropic universe. But she wasn't cool now. She was uneasy.

"No, I ah, just wanted to drop by, to tell you that if there's anything I can do . . ." He scanned the room, seeing it without the gauzy haze of nostalgia. A large room, comfortable, Nat Cole murmuring softly on the stereo, lights low . . . Connie in a sheer apricot dressing gown, middle of the afternoon, her makeup a little smudged? Damn. She was saying they were managing, that Danny's illness was hard but—

"I was hoping to see Erin too," he said. "Is she at home?"

"Erin? Lupe, Erin's been out on her own since she graduated from U of D law school nearly four years ago. She's an associate with Blackmer, Cavanaugh, and Rothman, on Brewer's Square."

"No kidding? Erin an attorney? That's terrific."

"She thinks so," Connie said, again with a faint edge to her tone. "I'm sure she'd love to see you."

"Would she be working today?"

"She works every day," Connie said, pointedly opening the door for him, "and most nights. Tell her to call home sometime, if she remembers the number."

"I'll do that," he said. "Take care of yourself now, and Danny too. And look, I really mean this. If there's anything at all you need, anything I can do . . ." He kissed her cheek, said good-bye, and left. But he hesitated on the steps a moment, trying to place the scent he'd noticed in her hair. English Leather? Brut maybe? So many new brands lately he couldn't be sure. But it was definitely after-shave, not perfume. Damn Danny and his damn troubles. He started down the steps to the street.

FOUR

Red eyed the Jeep's side mirror, watching a gray Jaguar XJ sedan crawl up behind him. Meryl fuckin' Streep. Same long blond hair, flat face. A dynamite chick, dynamite ride. As the Jag crept closer the crotch of his pants began chafing his hard-on. Speeders. Pop a few, get horny enough to stick your dick in a pencil sharpener. Nope, wasn't Meryl, unless Meryl's turned into a twenty-year-old cokehead. The girl looked half stoned, goosing the big Jag ahead in fits and starts, squinting, trying to read house numbers. A fox, no doubt about it. Wide mouth, maxed-out tits—sonuvabitch! The Mex was already across the street climbin' into his damn Firebird!

Red fired up the Jeep, then grabbed the Mac 10 and rested the machine pistol in the crook of his arm. If he could pull alongside the spick he could hose him down, maybe touch off his car too. He gunned the Comanche—then stomped the brakes. The stoner chick in the Jag was blocking him in as she crawled past. And the Firebird was already pulling away—shit!

Leaning on the horn with his right wrist, Red slammed the Jeep into reverse, banging it up over the curb, then gunned it around the Jaguar, roaring down the empty street. The Firebird was nowhere in sight. What the hell? He slowed at the corner, looking for it. Three blocks, four, no sign of it. Couldn't be this far ahead already, must have turned off. Red slowed, looking for a spot to make a U-turn—

WHAM!

The Jeep bucked forward, slamming Red back in the seat. The Jag! Dumbshit broad had rear-ended him. Hammered Richie's ride right in the ass! And the fuckin' Mexican is long gone! Shit! First my fuckin' hand, now this! He piled out of the Jeep and stormed back to the Jag.

Up close the girl looked even finer than he'd thought. And twice as stoned. Not Meryl Streep, more like Jodi Foster only with serious tits. Blond, wearin' an embroidered T-shirt, no bra. Jesus.

Her window hummed open. "I'm real sorry," she mumbled, "I wasn't watching— Are you all right?"

"Hell no," Red snarled, "I got a busted hand here. Look what you did."

"I know it was my fault, but please, don't call the police. I've—had a few drinks. I could go to jail. I can pay for your car, anything you say."

Cops. Christ, this neighborhood, somebody mighta called 'em already. And I got a damn machine gun layin' on the front seat.

"Okay, look," Red growled, "cops come, you're in a lotta trouble, lady. Let's you and me go someplace we can talk, work this thing out, okay?" He caught a whiff of booze on her breath. She'd had more'n a few. A lot more.

"Good," she said, nodding so vehemently he thought her head might fall off. "I'll follow you. I have some money with me. Whatever you think is fair."

"Okay, 'cept maybe I better follow you. Easier to keep you in sight, you know? Go up a ways, find someplace private, pull over. Just remember I'll be right behind you, dig?"

"Absolutely," the girl said. "Thanks. You won't be sorry."

Damn straight I won't. Red stalked back to the Jeep and slid behind the wheel. He refitted the Mac 10 in the briefcase as the chick backed her sedan up and pulled cautiously past. Then she floored it, Michelins howling as she roared off.

"Sonuvabitch!" Red punched the Jeep's gas pedal to the metal, wrestling the wheel one-handed. If she wanted a run, she'd get one. But she didn't. She waved at him gaily in the mirror as he pulled the Comanche close to her rear bumper.

He trailed her for the better part of a mile, leaving the homes behind, entering the commercial district. He was considering waving her over when suddenly the Jag's brake lights flared and Jodie-Meryl cut a hard right into a parking ramp. He followed, staying just a few feet behind as she circled up to the second level, almost rear-ending her when she stopped.

Stone perfect. Nice private spot to get paid and laid both. Broad with a car like that, if she figured she was just gonna get off by tossin' him a few bucks . . .

He slid out of the car, hitched up his belt so his hard-on wouldn't show. And realized the Indian, Tony LaRose, was watching him from the shadow of a concrete post about ten feet away. His greasy hair was combed straight back and he was wearing a seedy black suit that would've embarrassed a wino, with a ratty tan topcoat draped over his shoulders. He flicked the coat open, giving Red a look at a Browning 9-mm automatic with a silencer.

Shit.

"Yo, Red," Tony said, coolly scanning the deserted parking ramp, "how you doin'? Don't gimme no hassle, man. Step away from your car, keep your hands where I can see 'em."

"Look, Tony, you want Richie, not me. Shit, I ain't nothin' but a gofer. You know that."

"That's the trouble with blackout glass on a ride, can't tell who's drivin'. Thought you was Richie. Chill out, Red, nothin's gonna happen, on my honor. Mr. Echeverria wants to talk is all. Just walk in fronta me to that motor home there."

"Anything you say, Tony." Shaking his head slowly, Red stalked over to a twenty-two-foot needle-nosed custom Winnebago, silver with maroon trim. Looked like a damn boat. The back door opened as he approached. A younger guy in a pearl gray suit, café-au-lait skin dusted with coppery freckles, a forked goatee, neatly trimmed. Jesus. Cottler. The Remodeler. Had to be him. Too tall to be anybody else. Looked like Wilt Chamberlin in a bad mood. Stone pyscho . . . Fuck it, be cool. They smell chickenshit they own your ass.

He pushed past Cottler. Inside, the motor home was pimp heaven on wheels, gold plush curtains, gold carpeting, fancy gold-on-cream furniture. The girl from the Jaguar was sitting in an easy chair up front next to a dark-skinned Cuban, his thin face pocked with acne scars. He wore a gold Armani sport coat, black shirt and slacks, Gucci loafers. Echeverria. The Cuban from Windsor. He didn't look so bad. Red stomped guys in the joint twice his size.

The Cuban stared at him a moment, then slowly closed his eyes. *Te Ve.* The words were tattooed on his eyelids. I see you. But it meant a lot more. It meant the Cuban lay quiet while a jailhouse needleman worked over his fuckin' eyelids with soot and spit— Echeverria said something. Soft voice, barely audible.

"What'd he say?" Red asked.

"He wants to know if you speak Spanish," Tony LaRose said.

"Not enough. What is this shit anyway? You guys wanna talk to Richie, why not just come by the club? He ain't hidin'."

"I been by," LaRose said. "He's never in. At least not to me. Look, we had an understanding, you know? And now he don't return calls, he don't stay in touch. We hear he's gettin' into business he's supposed to stay clear of. He's disrepectin' people who helped him, man. Richie's a smart guy, Red, he's gotta know we'd hear. What's happenin' with him, man?"

"Hell, I don't know, he don't tell me—"

"Hey, peckerhead," Cottler said mildly, "I was you, I'd can that dononothin' shit. Mr. E ain't happy."

"It ain't my job to keep him happy. He wants happy tell'im to dust Blondie's twat with coke and tongue her out."

"Don't be pushin' us, Red," Tony said patiently. "We just wanna know why Richie ain't holdin' up his end."

"Okay, okay," Red offered, "maybe it's woman trouble. He brought that band up from Texas to work the club. He's got the hots for the singer but she's married. So maybe he's, you know, a little off his game."

"You sayin' Richie's fuckin' us around over some cunt?" Cottler asked.

"Look, he's young, right? So he thinks with his dick sometimes. It happens, you know? Happened to me about five minutes ago or I wouldn't be here now. But, hell, you know Richie's too smart to jerk you people around. How about I tell him you want him to shape up, maybe set up a meet, make things right. How's that sound?"

LaRose said something to Echeverria, apparently translating Red's offer. The Cuban nodded, then replied in machine-gun Spanish.

"He wants to know what happened to your hand," Tony said.

"Ah shit," Red said, shaking his head. "Danny brought in some outside muscle to help him weasel outta our deal, a Mex dude, old frienda his. He suckered me, busted my finger. I was lookin' for him when Blondie rammed me. So, what you want me to tell Richie?"

Echeverria smiled slowly, flashing a gold incisor. He rattled off a long speech in Spanish and everybody laughed. Even Cottler smiled faintly. A skull's smile.

"What's so fuckin' funny?" Red asked.

"He told a joke, man," Tony said, still grinning. He glanced inquiringly at his boss and the Cuban nodded.

"There's this guy, see," Tony explained, "he's drivin' along, picks up a hitcher. Hitcher sticks a gun in his face, takes his money, makes him take off all his clothes, ties him up and splits, leaves him bareass in the ditch, you know?

"So the guy crawls outta the ditch onto the road, gets all scratched up and shit, next thing, here comes a big fuckin' truck hunerd miles an hour. Guy closes his eyes, hears the tires squealin', truck stops about a foot from his head. Trucker jumps out, says what the fuck you doin'? Guy says, hey, I been robbed, beat up, and left bareass in the ditch. Wow, trucker says, that's too bad, sweetie. I guess today just ain't your day. And he unzips his pants." Tony grinned, waiting.

"That's it?" Red snorted. "That's the big joke?"

"Maybe it's funnier in Spanish," Tony shrugged.

"Okay, great, I'll tell Richie your boss is a funny guy. What else you want me to tell him?"

"Nothing," Tony said, "that's it."

"What's it? The joke? He wants me to tell Richie a joke?"

"No, man," Tony said patiently, "the message is, this just ain't your day."

Suddenly Tony and Cottler pinned Red's arms, jamming him tightly between them. Echeverria eased out of his chair and sauntered over, eyeing Red all the way. He slid a piano-wire noose out of his jacket, slipped it over Red's head, and slowly drew it taut.

Jesus Jesus! The wire bit into Red's throat, burning like a white-hot cable, cutting off his air, blood hammering behind his eyes. He tried to struggle, but they had him jammed, they—

Echeverria said something.

And Red felt the noose slacken, but not Tony's hold, or

Cottler's. They kept him clamped tight between them. "Okay, okay," Red gasped, "I get the picture! Christ, Tony, what's he want me to do? What'd he say?"

LaRose met his eyes, then looked away.

"Nothing, man," Cottler said softly, whispering in Red's ear like a lover. "He just said don't mess up the carpet. Take you into the john, do you in the shower."

FIVE

Brewer's Square is far grander than its name, an ultramodern glass and steel office complex built on the bones of the old Stroh's brewery, upscale uptown Motown. The offices of Blackmer, Cavanaugh, and Rothman occupy most of the fourth floor—thick Prussian blue carpeting, matching drapes, and a silver-tinted view of the city on four sides. Garcia flashed his badge past first-floor security, and again past the smartly turned out male secretary Erin Kelly shared with three other attorneys.

He rapped once on a solid oaken door with an E. Kelly brass nameplate, then stepped in. Wrong office? The woman scanning a file at the chrome-and-acrylic desk bore no resemblance to the perky, mop-topped coed he'd driven to school after all-nighters with Danny, so many mornings ago.

Her hair was a shade darker than Danny's, a rich auburn, cropped almost boot-camp short. She was wearing steel-framed glasses and no makeup, not even lipstick. In her wide-lapelled retro-thirties-style umber business suit, complete with Joan Crawford epaulets, she seemed far too old to be the sparrow of a girl he remembered. She was taller now, and slender, an attractive, almost boyish stranger, until she glanced up and he met her eyes. Honest-to-God Kelly green.

"Have a seat, please, I'll . . . Lupe Garcia. Well. I'll be damned." A grin of genuine delight transformed her like a morning in May. Garcia eased down in the seat, eyeing her across a litter of file folders and lost years.

"M*iz* Erin Shea Kelly." He smiled with mock formality. "All grown up. And every bit as pretty as your mother."

"Do you think so?" she said, her smile fading a bit. "Most people say I look like my grandmother."

"I wouldn't argue the point," Garcia nodded. "A very handsome lady also, as I recall. And in your own *Star Wars* office. I'm impressed."

"You seem to have worn well. Still tall and—the same. But you're not my next appointment, who's due in about three minutes, sooo . . . What can I do for you? Sergeant Garcia."

"For one thing, you can drop the sergeant. I know it's been a while, but we were friends once, sort of?"

"I had a friend once," she said evenly, "or thought I did, named Lupe—Menendez? Isn't that the name you were using?"

"I think so. I used a lot of them in those days."

"My point exactly," she nodded. "I knew a man back then who worked for my father at the Underground. I didn't know an undercover narcotics cop named Garcia. I still don't. But over the years I've read about you now and again, in the *Free Press,* the *News.* So what do I call you now? Garcia? Or Menendez?"

"Lupe will do fine. Look, your father called me the other day, asked me to stop and see him. I've just come from there. I didn't know he was ill. I'm sorry."

"Are you really?" Her smile had vanished completely now. "It's been a very long time."

"I know it has, but it wasn't by my choice. Your father took a risk by letting me work at the club knowing I was a cop. He also took some serious lumps from a couple of Young Boys enforcers and didn't give me up. A few months later, the papers ran my picture and I was through as a narc. If I'd come around after that it could've been dangerous for him, for all of you. You're an attorney now, and even working in an ivory tower like this you must know that's true."

"Perhaps, but the bottom line is, I never *really* knew you at all, did I? So, I repeat, what can I do for you?"

"You can take this off my hands," he said, tossing the sheaf of bills on her desk. "It's ten grand. Danny just gave it to me to—do him a favor. I was afraid if I didn't take it he'd try to hire someone else and buy himself a lot of trouble."

She frowned faintly, picked up the bills, riffled through them. "Ten thousand," she nodded, "and, ah, exactly what kind of a favor do you pay an old friend this kind of money for?"

"That doesn't matter, the point is—"

"My God," she said softly, "it's blood money, isn't it? What did he ask you to do? Put Richie in the hospital? Kill him?"

"What's the difference? He's a sick man, Erin, he doesn't know what he's doing."

"I don't agree," she said coldly. "At this point, I think he's still very much in control of his faculties. Which puts me in a very awkward position, Sergeant. You've just informed me that you're involved in a criminal conspiracy and we have no attorney-client relationship. As an officer of the court, I'm required to report this, or be held culpable myself."

"My, my," Garcia said, "we really have grown up, haven't we?"

"Some of us have," she agreed. "And while I'm obviously not going to inform on my own father, I don't intend to get involved in a situation that could cost me everything I've worked for either."

"Nobody's asking you to get involved—"

"I'd say accepting ten thousand dollars constitutes a fairly substantial involvement, but that's not the point. I've been helping my father at the club since high school, working the gate, booking bands, up until a few weeks ago when—I had problems with Richie. I all but begged Dad to get out of his arrangement with him. He brushed me off. In effect, he made a choice. Richie. I think he hoped he'd turn out to be a kind of pseudoson, or the sort of friend you were once."

"So, he hurts your feelings, you write him off?"

"Don't come waltzing in here after all this time and cop an attitude with me, Garcia, or Menendez, or whatever you call yourself now. I know you think you understand my father, but I doubt you ever did. You see him as some kind of a—free spirit. Very macho, very romantic."

"And you don't?"

"Arrested adolescent might be a more apt description. And he hasn't been abandoned. I see him often, and my Uncle Mick is checking the books weekly, though that's primarily to protect my mother's interests."

"Your mother's interests?"

"When Dad bought the building he used Connie's trust fund as collateral. At this point she owns more of the building and the business than my father does. Odd he didn't mention it, since you two are such great friends. Dad's made it clear he doesn't want me involved, and considering the company he's keeping, he's probably right. I have my own career to consider now. In any case, he didn't ask for my help. He asked you. Since you took his money, Garcia, perhaps you'd better earn it."

"You want me to kill Richie, is that it?"

"Don't be ridiculous."

"Good, at least we're clear on that point. And let's clear up one more. If you've been following my so-called career, you know I was involved in a . . . rough situation a month or two back. My partner's still in the hospital and I'm just out. To be blunt, I've got troubles of my own."

"Then I guess you shouldn't have taken my father's

money. Now, if you don't mind, I have a client waiting. Don't forget your fee," she said, tossing the sheaf of bills to him.

He snatched the money out of midair, considered shredding it into confetti and snowing the pieces all over her trendy new desk. But he didn't. "Funny," he said, rising, "I remember you as being such a perky kid. What happened?"

"Life," she said, showing a ghost of a smile. "I grew up. It happens to almost everybody."

"But not the same way," he said. "I'll see you around campus, Counselor. Oh, just one other thing. I talked to your mother earlier. Excuse me for being so direct, but it occurred to me that she might have someone other than your father in her life now. Are she and Richie friends, would you say?"

"My mother is working as a receptionist at a clinic now," Erin said coldly. "Except for a financial interest, she hasn't been involved in the club business in years."

"That wasn't the question."

"Wasn't it?" she said.

"Two, three, maybe four," Cordell Bennett counted softly on his blunt fingertips, foam lapping gently at his chin as he lounged in the swirling bubbles of the whirlpool bath in the Samaritan Hospital therapy room. "I figure you're complicit in at least three felonies, Loop, plus umpty misdemeanors. Conspiracy to murder, bribery, failure to report all of the above, obstruction, oughta add up to . . . Hell, I need a calculator. Maybe five hundred and sixty years in the joint, minus a few months for good behavior."

"Right," Garcia nodded, "I know it sounds a little . . . crazy, but the guy was a friend, and he's in a world of trouble," Garcia said, rocking back on his heels on the rubber mat beside the tub, hands thrust deep in his overcoat pockets.

"So you figured you'd help him out by divin' in the toilet with him?"

"If Richie hadn't tried to muscle me off, maybe I wouldn't have, I don't know. I guess you just had to be there."

"Wish I had been," Cordell said, "with a videocam. I coulda burned your butt, earned myself a promotion in one shot."

"Hey, if I need someone to tell me getting involved wasn't overly bright, I can just look in a mirror, you know? But I'm in it now, and I could use a little help."

"If you're lookin' for sympathy, Loop, try another pew. I ain't got *beaucoup* to spare, you know?"

Cordell didn't look like he could spare much of anything. His chest was laced with a grid of livid pink surgical scars. His eyes were closed, sunken in the ebon mask of his face, spiderwebbed by pain lines. His raggedly trimmed Afro was suddenly showing a lot of silver. He was barely forty, but looked old enough to be his own father. Garcia gently tugged the plastic privacy curtain open to leave.

"Where you goin'?" Cordell asked, without opening his eyes.

"Home. I thought you nodded out on me."

"Nah, just thinkin'. You sure this guy's dyin'? Could be his wife's ballin' his partner, he wants the dude wasted."

"No, he's dying all right. I thought he might check out while we were talking. As far as the wife, I'm fairly sure she had company. But if Danny wanted something done about that, he'd handle it himself somehow. Matter of honor, or whatever."

"Honor?"

"I know the word's passé these days, but so is Danny. Anyway, he was always straight with me."

"But it's been a while, right? People change."

"Absolutely, but I don't think he has. We sat around, killed a few brews, and it was . . . like no time at all had passed, you know? Sick or not, he's the same man. And he never could lie worth a damn, no aptitude for it."

"Okay, then the way I see it you got maybe three ways to go. For openers, you took the money, can't seem to give it away. Maybe you should just pop Cadillac Richie."

"Very funny."

"Think about it. You're moonin' around ass deep in a midlife crisis, maybe this is the move you been lookin' for.

Especially if you pull it off with style. Buy Richie a two-hundred-buck pair o' Reeboks, bet him he can't jog the Cass Corridor. Won't be enough left of him to bury."

"Tell you what, Cordell, when they furlough you outta here I'll take you over to Danny's, see how your sense of humor holds up."

"Hey, lighten up, it is funny in a way. I leave you on your own for a week, you get all jammed up. On the other hand, maybe Kelly's situation isn't a laugher, so I'll tell you how to fix it. One, it was dumb to take the money, but I can see why you did. If you don't, he keeps tryin' to hire somebody, his partner hears about it and whacks him. Two, you were right not to give the money to the wife on the off chance Cadillac Richie or one of his buddies is her new squeeze, same result as number one. Three, the daughter didn't throw the bread at you because she don't wanna be involved, she did it hopin' you'll help."

"Maybe you're right. So what do I do?"

"Check out the wife first, try to find out who her new playmate is. If it's not Richie, you explain what happened, give her the money, end of problem. Besides, if Danny's comin' unwrapped she's got a right to know."

"And if it is Richie? Or if I can't find out one way or the other?"

"Simple. I get outta here in a couple days, we go to the daughter, I explain that askin' you to help out her old man is like hirin' Charlie Manson for a baby-sitter, give her the money."

"She already turned it down."

"Then maybe I open my shirt," Cordell snapped, "show her what hangin' around you can do for a guy's Medicare premiums. Think that'll do it?"

"Yeah," Garcia said carefully, "I imagine it would."

"Good. That's settled," Cordell said, closing his eyes again and slipping lower in the bath. "So. You done any more thinkin' 'bout what you wanna be when you grow up?"

"Not really. Going into the hit man biz is the first offer I've had. How about you?"

"What you mean how about me?"

"I, ah, heard a rumor that the department offered you early retirement, on a medical."

"They made the offer," Cordell admitted. "I haven't decided yet."

Garcia eyed him for a moment, then looked away. "Damn, Cordell, you're no better at lying than Danny Kelly is. You've made up your mind. So what are you gonna do?"

Cordell blinked one eye open, met Garcia's gaze, then closed it again. "Jesus, you can be dense sometimes, Loop. When a friend bothers to tell you a lie, the polite thing to do is let it lay. Be a helluva world if we couldn't lie to our friends."

"It's a helluva world anyway, and you're ducking the question."

"All right, I'll spell it out for you. When you were in the army, you got real tight with the guys in your outfit, right?"

"Sure. We were like family in a lot of ways."

"Right. And how many of 'em you still see regular?"

"I don't know, not many."

"Not many? How about none? Point bein' when you work with people in tough situations sometimes it's hard to tell if you're friends, or maybe just . . . on-the-job buddies, you know?"

"And that's what you think we are?" Garcia said.

"It don't matter what I think. A deal like this, you gotta do what's right for you, and so do I. If we're friends after, fine. But if one of us makes a bad decision because of what the other does, the friendship's down the tubes anyway, right?"

"Let me get this straight. You're saying it's okay to

discuss minor stuff, like the meaning of life and what women want, but career moves are off-limits?"

"For now, yeah. And I ain't gonna change my mind, so why don't you figure a way to help your buddy Kelly instead of buggin' me? Right now my career's concentratin' on therapy so I can get outta this dump sometime this century. What you got in mind?"

"For openers, see what the Law Enforcement Information Network's got on Richie Zee, check with narcotics, see if they know him. Then maybe I'll take your advice and check out Connie, see what's going on there."

"If this Richie Zee's in the life, Jimmy Hamadi'll know his shoe size and his grammaw's middle name. If you can get to him."

"What do you mean? I'm not off the force yet."

"I hear Hamadi's goin' paranoid. Maybe been workin' the dope scene too long. You know what it's like."

"I remember exactly what it's like. I still dream about it sometimes. But working narcotics, being apeshit paranoid isn't necessarily irrational, you know?"

"True blue," Cordell nodded, closing his eyes again. "Way my head's been lately, bein' apeshit paranoid'd be a major improvement. Go 'way, Loop. Talkin' to you makes me tired."

"Yeah," Garcia said, "I can see that."

SEVEN

The silver-and-blue MichCon van was parked beneath a power-condenser pole on South Jefferson. Garcia scanned the shops as he drove past—a dry cleaners, a bodega, a mom-and-pop drugstore. No way to guess which of them the van was sitting on. A couple of young studs in silver-and-black L.A. Raiders jackets were hangin' on the corner, jivin' each other, but eyeing the traffic too, hawk wary. An RC Cola bottle was beside the lamppost a few feet from them.

Crack, officer? You shittin' me? In that bottle there? Ain't none a mine. Ya'll have a nice day. Nope, the van wouldn't be for two punkass dealers. Garcia tapped his brake pedal twice as he passed the nark ark, then continued on a half dozen blocks to a Dawn Donuts. He bought two coffees, a couple of warm bagels, carried them to a back booth facing the door.

His coffee was barely cool enough to drink when a street-hard dude in a bombardier's jacket and black jeans sauntered in. His dark hair was multitinted on one side, orange and blond, and the diamond stud in his ear was at least a carat. He might as well have worn a sign. Dealer. He gave the room a quick scan, then ambled back to Garcia's booth and slid in. Neither man offered to shake hands.

"Thought you were still in the hospital," Jimmy Hamadi said, scarfing one of the bagels.

"Cordell still is. I got out a couple weeks ago."

"How's he gettin' along?"

"Not bad, for guy who got blown up. He'll be awhile puttin' himself back together."

"Hear you're baggin' the job. Because of what happened?"

"That"—Garcia nodded—"and . . . other things. Sometimes it seems like good people come and go, but crap accumulates."

"Or maybe you think you shoulda shot that kid, or shot at him, 'steada yellin' at Szatkowski to do it? That it?"

"Is that what you're hearing?" Garcia asked.

"I've heard it." Hamadi nodded, eyeing Garcia over his coffee cup. "Mostly from HQ types who never popped a cap at anybody."

"It's in the report," Garcia said evenly. "I had no chance to fire. Parking lot was icy. I fell."

"A Freudian slip maybe? What's Cordell think about that?"

"I don't know. We don't talk about it much."

"What about the Pony Downs involved? You makin' a case against them?"

"Fielder pulled me off it, but there isn't any case anyway. The kid we were trying to save bought it, the shooter bought it, the evidence in the building went up, and everybody faded like smoke. No witnesses, no case."

"And no more Crazy Lupe, the Cisco Kid?"

"Something like that. Anything else you'd like to know, Jimmy? My shoe size maybe?"

"Not yet," Hamadi said. "So what you want, Loop? You didn't buzz by my stake just to bring me up to speed, right?"

"What can you tell me about a guy named Richie Zeayen?"

"Who?"

"Richie Zeayen, Cadillac Richie Zee. Older brother was Terry Zeayen. Chaldeans, in the coke trade, or at least Terry was before he wound up in the trunk of his Caddy, long-term parking out at Metro. Richie's muscling his way into a nightclub called Motown Underground, out near Poletown."

"Kind of a funny thing to ask, for a guy who's packin' it in. What's this Zeayen to you?"

"Not much. A favor for a friend."

"Real plain you ain't been narkin' for a while," Hamadi grunted, wincing at the taste of his coffee. "The captain's put all narcotics information on a need-to-know basis."

"Since when?"

"Since we had a guy get greased up in Toronto. His cover was solid, we still don't know what went wrong, but he's dead all the same. His name was Jase Probert. You know him?"

"No. Should I?"

"He got promoted into narcotics a year or two after you left. Worked undercover mostly. A good man. A friend."

"What happened?"

"He was tortured to death," Hamadi said evenly, looking away. Ugly business. Bad as I've ever seen. So for the time bein' we're heavy into by-the-book procedure, you know?"

"I understand," Garcia said slowly. "How about I lay it out for you, give me what you can?"

"I'm still drinkin' your coffee," Hamadi nodded.

"Six, seven years ago, I was working narcotics, undercover. Got myself hired into the Underground as a bartender. Place was jumpin', lot of Young Boys Incorporated studs hung out there. I hit it off pretty good with the owner, Danny Kelly. He even promoted me to assistant manager. Then one night he tells me he knew I was a cop from day one. And it was okay by him. I made some righteous busts, but eventually the Young Boys got suspicious. Three YBI enforcers pumped Danny about me, beat him half to death. He gave 'em exactly nothing. If he'd talked, I'd be dead."

"So he did his civic duty." Hamadi shrugged. "Good for him."

"Don't give me that crap," Garcia snapped. "I owe him. The department owes him. Now he's got this punk crowding him, and he asked me to help. So what can you give me?"

"Okay, okay," Hamadi sighed, "I can do you a bagel's worth. Don't know much more. Richie was in the trade. Came up through the D Streets, a gang outta Dearborn. Him and two brothers. All with bad-news juvy records. After Terry, the oldest, got hit, Richie wised up, quit trying to run his own game. You ever hear of a Cuban from over in Windsor, a Marielito named Renaldo Echeverria?"

"Name doesn't register."

"He's new. Ambitious though. Heavy dealer, superbad, tight organization. Usually works in Canada. RCMP's never nailed him, or us either. But lately we've been hearin' a few rumbles about him doin' business here. Not necessarily drugs, but somethin'."

"So what's his connection to Richie?"

"Don't know. The Cuban used to work with older guys, ex-cons like himself. Guys he knows will stand up. Tony LaRose is one of his capos."

"Tony I remember. A Cree Indian, right, or half anyway. Chubby? Usually looks like he's been sleepin' in the streets?"

"That's Tony. A badass, but not a crazy. But this side of the line, the Cuban's been recruiting talent out of the gangs, taking their top people, building a new organization. He's got a new enforcer, guy used to be with the Black Counts, a Rican dude named Cottler. Calls himself Hoss, short for *rehacedero.*"

"The remodeler? Funny name."

"Not so funny. He's psycho, as bad as they come."

"You're saying Richie may be linked up with this Echeverria?"

"I'm not sayin' shit," Hamadi said. "I'm talkin' to my bagel, you just happen to be sittin' here, you dig? Only you ain't listenin', Loop. The Cuban's serious bad news. If your friend's mixed up with him, have him file a complaint."

"I wish it was that simple," Garcia said.

"You better make it that simple, Garcia. I'm tellin' you, back off. You piss in the Cuban's punch bowl, you'll get waxed."

"You're telling me? I thought you were talking to a bagel."

"Right," Hamadi said, shaking his head, "I guess maybe I am."

EIGHT

Danny Kelly sat slumped in his wheelchair in his dimly lit office, staring blankly through the large one-way mirror above his battered desk, watching the early crowd drift in. The desk was a huge old oak box from Mumford High, scarred with carved graffiti, gentle epithets from simpler times, carefully preserved beneath six coats of clear lacquer. Richie'd bitched about the desk from day one, wanted to get rid of it. Maybe he would soon, if things didn't work out. Each day it seemed less important.

The club was filling, people streaming in in twos and threes, an occasional larger group. Business was brisk, waitresses bustling through the main room. Tie-dye was bopping around behind the bar in a blouse-sleeved shirt, flamingo pink paisley with matching headband, jiving to the jukebox, juggling glasses, putting on a show, doing more business than any two bartenders who'd ever worked the club. An artist. A pleasure to watch, except that Richie had hired him, which made him a symbol of everything that had gone wrong since.

A light tap at the door. Risa Blades stuck her head in. "Hi, okay if I change in here? Luc and Bailey are hittin' on some honeys in the dressing room."

"No problem," Danny said, "it'll be the high point of my day. Unless you want me to leave?"

"Hell no, I want you to stand guard." She stepped in, a striking contrast in stage makeup and street clothes. Short black hair worn low over one eye a la early Elvis, brown rouge on cinnamon skin, heavy black eyeliner that accented the triangular shape of her face and gave her a predatory look, fierce, sensual. Hawk woman. "I need a favor, Danny," she said, sliding open one of the closet doors beside the floor-to-ceiling liquor racks and choosing an outfit from the half dozen she kept there, a black sequined T-shirt and red leather hot pants. "Some chick laid some bomb weed on Bobby, I figure maybe you could maybe burn some of it for me, lead him outta temptation, you know?"

"You mean smoke it up strictly as a favor for a friend?"

"Absolutely. Stoned, Bobby's not worth a damn, at singin' or anything else."

"Never let it be said I ever turned down a damsel in distress," Danny said. "Care to join me in a toke?"

"Nah, weed's too rough on the throat. It's not fair, guys get raspy, they sound sexy, you know? I just sound like I'm catchin' a cold." She slid a thick, home-rolled cigarette up from the waistband of her jeans, licked both ends closed, and passed it to Danny. His palsied hands could barely manage to insert the reefer between his lips. She watched his struggle with apparent unconcern, then picked up the heavy silver lighter from the desk and held it for him.

"Thanks," he said, sucking the smoke deep into his lungs, fighting off the urge to cough. "Thing is, every time you wander by my hands start to shake."

"So I see. Just maintain, Danny. When Bobby dumps me maybe I'll land right in your lap."

"Right," he said dryly, feeling the reefer buzz spreading out from the smoke knot in his chest, easing the pain in his joints, mellowing him down. "Only waiting for Bobby to do somethin' that stupid might take longer than I've got."

"Bullshit," she said, "you'll dance on my grave. Or I'll by God dance on yours, Kelly. Now turn your back, I gotta get ready for work." She turned to face the mirror, peeled off her top and tossed it on the desk—no false modesty, no brassiere. Her breasts were high and firm and golden, chocolate aureoles nearly as dark as her eyes. Sonuvabitch, he thought, I'm gonna miss all this nonsense. He fumbled at the joystick and swung the chair halfway around.

"That was a nice song you did this afternoon," he said.

"Which one?" She stepped out of her faded blue jeans and slid the red leather hot pants up over her panty hose to her hips.

"The really sad one. Broke my heart."

" 'Aledita'?"

"That's the one. I'd rather hear you sing 'Aledita' alone than hear the Detroit freakin' Symphony play 'Oh Danny Boy.' "

"Gee, if you really liked it, why don't you just say so steada beatin' around the bush? What did your *compadre* think of it? The Latin guy?"

"Loop? I don't know, he doesn't say much."

"Who is he?"

"A friend, from a while back. I told you about him, he's—"

A key rattled in the office door.

"You'd better get your top on," he said calmly, humming his chair over to the door and blocking it.

"Hey," Richie Zeayen said, "what's goin' on? Open up."

Risa coolly slipped on her rhinestoned T-shirt, smoothed it over her hips, then nodded at Danny, who backed his chair out of the way.

"Sorry, Richie," he said, "next time try knocking."

"I don't need to knock on my own fuckin' door," Zeayen said, yanking the reefer from between Danny's palsied fingers, "and I told you before about smokin' dope in here—"

"Hey, lighten up," Risa said, "he was just holding it for me, okay? You want I should smoke it in the dressing room, first place any heat's gonna look?"

"You can take it out in the parking lot, babe, like everybody else," Richie snapped. "Not in my office, understand?"

"Fine," Risa said calmly, "whatever you say—"

"No," Danny said, "it's not whatever he says. And this isn't his office either. Not yet."

"It's not?" Richie said evenly, reading him. "Musta been heavy-duty weed, Danny. Make you feel like a new man, does it? Or maybe you figure your Mex buddy can cure cancer?"

"C'mon, Richie," Risa said, "ease off."

"Get your ass on stage, lady," Richie said coldly, "you're late."

"We don't start for twenty minutes, man. And don't talk to me like that. What's with you lately?"

"Nothing's wrong with me, and you're late when I fuckin' *say* you are," he snarled. "Now move it!"

"Okay, so I'm late," she said, meeting his glare, not backing off an inch, "so maybe you should try dockin' our pay, see what happens. Come on, Danny, Tie-dye's gotta work the door until Red shows, you better spell him or we're gonna have a thirsty zoo out there. Let's go."

"Danny's stayin' " Richie said. "We got business."

"It's okay, Risa," Danny said, "go on. I won't be long."

"Good," she said, folding her arms, "then I might as well wait, right?"

"Why not," Richie snapped, "maybe you'll learn somethin', like who's runnin' the show here."

"What Richie's trying to say is good-bye," Danny said softly. "You see, unless he can come up with the bread he owes me, we're going to dissolve our partnership."

"Pretty bold talk, Pops," Richie grinned. "Figure that

greaser's gonna save your ass? Forget it. He won't be back."

"What's that supposed to mean?"

"Jeez, Danny, you're really losin' it. You think I'd let some guy bust Red's hand and just walk away? Dream on. The guy's history. I warned you about bringin' in outsiders, Danny. Far as I'm concerned, our deal's off. You can go watch the door or whatever, but when you leave here tonight, I want a cash settlement buyin' me out, or papers signin' over your end of the biz. Or your whole damn family'll end up like your spick buddy."

"Chinga, Richie," Risa said, "you can't just roust people like this . . ." Her voice trailed off as she realized Danny was grinning wolfishly, unafraid.

"Somethin' funny, Danny?" Richie said warily. "Or you just smoke too much?"

"You sent Red out after Loop? To hit him?"

"Damn straight," Richie said. "You can't say I didn't warn—god damn it, what the fuck's the joke, old man?"

"You," Danny said, shaking his head ruefully. "Jesus, Richie, when you screw up, you do it big time. Ever see a two-headed coin? Heads you lose, tails you lose? You just flipped one."

"What are you talkin' about? Who was that guy?"

"An old friend. Best manager I ever had."

"He said he's not in the biz anymore. What's he into now?"

"You'll find out soon enough, but I'll tell you up front, if you sent your goon cousin after Garcia, your next family reunion's gonna be one short. Gettin' late," Danny said, checking his watch. "Red should be back by now. If he's coming."

"What are you sayin'? Who was that guy?"

"A friend." Danny grinned. "Used to work for me—"

"God damnit, I ain't fuckin' around, Kelly," Richie said, slapping Danny across the face with his open palm, snapping his head around. "What's with this guy? He ganged up?

Is that it?" He slapped Danny again, bloodying his mouth. Kelly shrank down in the chair, trying to avoid the blows, but stubbornly maintaining his grin like a shield.

"Go for it, Richie, you little pimp! Do me a favor!"

Richie lost control, swinging wildly, hammering Danny with both fists. Risa lunged at him, trying to pull him off, but he leveled her with a backhand slam to the temple, tumbling her into the corner. "How 'bout it, Pops," Richie panted, eyes alight. "Anything to say yet? Who was that guy? What's his—" He ducked as he glimpsed Risa in the mirror charging him from behind, swinging a bottle savagely at his head. He grabbed her wrist but her rush carried them both into Danny's desk. The bottle smashed, spraying booze and glass splinters like shrapnel. They wrestled fiercely for a moment, Richie backward over the desk, twisting Risa's wrist back until the broken bottleneck bit into her flesh and she let it drop.

He thrust his knee up, dumping Risa to the floor, then staggered upright, trying to wipe the liquor from his burning eyes. Risa scrambled up like a cat, snatching the silver lighter from the desk. She thrust it at him like a lance, her hand bloody from the broken bottle, crimson streaming down her forearm.

"Back off, *tu chingada cabrón!* Or I burn you like a match! That's Don 'Q' one fifty-one on you. You'll fuckin' *explode!"* She flicked the lighter and he flinched, eyes wide, a crazed mix of fear and rage.

"Danny, get out of here!" she said, backing toward the door. Kelly nudged the joystick over, hummed the chair to the door, fumbled at the knob with both hands, managed to get it open.

"Hey Richie"—Danny dabbed at his bloodied mouth with his wrist—"since you wanna know about Garcia so bad, I'll tell you. He's a cop, man, a *cop!* If Red waxes him you'll both go down for murder, but I don't figure it that way. I think your cousin's already dead in a ditch, or maybe in jail, and Garcia's comin' back for you. You'd better beat feet, you little pimp—"

"Dammit, Danny!" Risa shouted, "get *outta* here before I fuckin' bleed to death!" She backed out the door after him, keeping the lighter in front of her. "Now cool out, Richie, we can—"

"Bitch!" Zeayen raged, "you're fired! You're all fired! Tell your buddies to pack their gear at the enda the night—"

She jerked the door shut in his face, cutting him off. "Dammit," she muttered, "dammit, dammit, dammit." She dropped the lighter, clutching her savaged hand against her waist.

"I'm sorry," Danny panted, sagging down in his chair, "I didn't mean for you to get caught in the middle o' that."

"Not your fault," Risa said, "it was comin' on anyway, way he's been lately. Come on, let's get back to the dressing room before I need a damn transfusion."

NINE

Five minutes to showtime, Bobby Westover stared into the dressing room mirror, outlining his eyelids with a trace of mascara. Thirtyish, tall, riding crop slender, his barroom pallor and blond-and-fawn rock'n'roll tangled mane made him seem younger, more fragile than he was.

Rey Lucero, the Whiteboys' block-solid bass player, was resting on the sturdy tweed Sears sofa that had served a thousand road bands as a combination one-jump wedding bed and crash couch. The room was neat, functional, nearly indestructible. Beige walls, Plexiglas Tiffany lamp dangling from a ceiling chain, a pair of slab-backed captain's chairs, a Formica dressing table bolted to the wall.

Bailey Reeves, the group's drummer, was leaning against the doorjamb, dark as a mountain and nearly as large. With massively muscled, knife-scarred forearms, shaved head, and mirrored contact lenses, Reeves was the hurricane's eye of the stormy group, settling musical and personal beefs with no more than a glance.

All three men wore variations of black leather—Bobby a Brando jacket and faded jeans, Lucero a black T-shirt and leather pants with narrow red suspenders, laced high-top boots. Reeves was shirtless beneath his leather vest, wearing studded leather wristbands, chartreuse spandex biking shorts, and red Air Jordan tennies.

Bailey checked his biker-band Rolex. Risa was late, nothing new. If Bailey was ever gonna make the big time, this band was the one. Good songs, good people. Still, workin' with a married couple was . . . complicated. Sometimes he wished he was back on the wrong side of San Angelo, playin' gutbucket blues for ten bucks a set and free beer.

Somebody hammered on the door. Bailey unlatched it and Danny Kelly hummed in with Risa right behind. Kelly looked like a train wreck, mouth bloody, face bruised. Risa crossed quickly to the dressing table sink and began rinsing blood off her forearm.

"Christ on a crutch," Bobby said, glancing from Risa to Danny. "What the hell happened?"

"Danny and Richie had a hassle," Risa said. "Richie wigged out, started smacking Danny around. I hit him with a bottle. It busted. And we're fired. End of story. We got any Band-Aids?"

"I got some," Lucero said, scrambling over to the corner, popping his bass guitar case open. He rifled its storage bin, tossing out string envelopes and tuning keys, found a tin of bandages, and passed it to Risa. Outside, a rhythmic clapping had begun, just a few hands at first, but gradually spreading around the room. Showtime.

"What do you mean we're fired?" Bobby snapped. "Dammit, Danny, what's goin' on?"

"The business term is hostile takeover," Danny said bitterly, daubing at his bloody mouth with a handkerchief. "I'm sorry as hell Risa got involved, but she saved my tail and that's a fact."

"It wasn't Danny's fault," Risa added. "I jumped in on my own, so be cool, okay?"

"Hell no it's not okay—"

"Of course it isn't, and we'll straighten it out," Danny

said. "I'll do my best to keep my troubles from affecting you folks, but it won't help if we have a riot in the place on top of everything else. Go on and do your show. Please."

"He's right, babe," Risa said, "let's do the damn gig, unless you wanna refund our cut of the gate. We'll clear this up after."

"Damn straight we will," Bobby said. "Let me see your hand."

"Bobby, it's fine, really. You guys go ahead, cool the crowd down, I'll get cleaned up, be right with you."

"You sure?"

"Go *on,* dammit, feed the zoo. I'll be along." She dried her forearm with a paper towel. Bobby scowled at Danny, then stormed out. Lucero and Bailey exchanged a glance, shrugged, and followed. Danny closed the door after them.

Risa promptly turned both faucets back on, letting them run, wide open. She crossed to Lucero's bass case, took a small .25 auto pistol out of it, and jacked a round into the chamber.

"Listen to me," she whispered, kneeling beside Danny's chair, placing the gun in his hand. "This is insurance. If Richie comes around don't do anything dumb, just back him off, okay? And don't say anything to him you don't want on tape."

"On tape?" Danny said blankly, staring down at the weapon. "What do you mean?"

"Come on, Danny, you know Tie-dye's a narc, right? Hell, he's not even a very good one. Lucero found the bug in the light fixture there the first night we played here. Both johns are bugged too. . . . Jesus, you really didn't know, did you?" she said, reading his face. "I thought you were settin' Richie up—" The opening chord of the Whiteboys' first song thundered through the walls. "Look, I gotta go. Now dammit, promise me you won't mess with Richie on your own. Wait for Bobby and Bailey, okay? Bobby and Richie get along. We'll work it out."

She bent down quickly and kissed his forehead, then hurried out. Danny stared after her for a moment, then at the weapon in his palsied claw. He laid it carefully in his lap, touched the joystick, and hummed the chair over to the dangling lampshade. She was right. A bug. The size of a pencil eraser, antenna slender as a stray hair. The antenna began to waver gently, as though touched by a breeze. The room was shimmering, fading, the walls turning to water. The weed was wearing off and the pain of the beating came smashing through the mellow, jolting his midsection with body punches, doubling him over. Spasms shook his brittle frame. He tried to cling to conciousness, to be ready for Richie, but it was too hard, too hard. The agony carried him down, through the green tile floor, deep into the growling thunder of Lucero's bass guitar.

Richie was slapping him, hard, snapping his head around with each blow. Danny raised his quivering hands to fend off the attack, but Richie punched right through them, each slap a hammer to the temple in perfect time with the thump of Bailey's kick drum booming through the dressing room walls. "Stop it," Danny pleaded, "please. Take anything you want—" A body punch caught him in the belly, buckling him in half. A flood of bile surged in his throat, and reflex snapped him awake, gasping, gagging on the sour stew.

He was alone in the room. His head was pounding, each throb like an icepick in the eyes. But it was the pain of his illness, not Richie's punches. He glanced blearily around, fearfully making sure. No, he was alone, the door was still locked, and for a moment the flood of relief almost washed away the horror and the shame. He'd been crawling, begging that pimp to stop beating him.

And dream or not, it was the truth.

If Risa hadn't driven Richie off, he would have pleaded

like a battered child unable to defend himself or to bear any more. God, he'd gambled one last time that he could force Richie to come up with enough money to bail him out. But he'd lost. And now it was down to this. Cringing in a back room, dependent on the kindness of strangers. And the pain—sonuvabitch! Sonuvabitch!

He doubled over again, racked as though he'd been kicked in the groin. He fumbled in his shirt pocket for his pain pills. Came up empty. Gone. Must've lost them in the scuffle. Jesus, how long had he been out? He checked his watch; after ten, forty minutes, half of the Whiteboys' first set. That's why the pain was so intense, the pills were wearing off. But in a way, he welcomed it. Because it was the truth too. It was real. And familiar. He'd felt it growing stronger over the past weeks, creeping closer, like a tiger circling a dying fire, held at bay by the pills he'd been gobbling like candy. Christ, how much junk was he on now? A handful every couple of hours, plus whatever dope he could score off his friends. A junkie, a stone junkie too snowblind to even realize it. Wrecked, pretending he still had it together, junkie dreams—

Junkie. He swallowed hard, trying to focus on something Risa said before she left. Something . . . Tie-dye. She said Tie-dye was a narc. And she was right. Christ, of course she was right. He was way too good a barman to work a rock joint with a young, blue-collar trade. Kids don't tip. Tie-dye could score more in any Holiday Inn in town. He should have known, should have spotted him the way he spotted Garcia as a ringer all those years ago. . . .

That was it. He stiffened, coldly alert, as though he'd been drenched with ice water. Garcia. He'd begged Loop to hit Richie, knowing the Mex would try to help him somehow, playing on his sympathy, his pity, using a friend's sense of honor to sucker him. But if the band room was bugged, and the johns were bugged . . .

Sweet Jesus.

He clumsily tucked the .25 into his waistband, then wheeled his chair over to the door and fumbled it open.

The club was alive and wired, dance floor packed, people standing between the tables ten deep around the dance area, focused on the stage action. Bailey Reeves was alone, stage center, kicking out the extended drum solo from "Rock and a Hard Place," the audience clapping on the backbeat. Lucero and Bobby were nowhere in sight. Risa was swaying on top of Lucero's monster amplifier, keening above the thunder, a wordless moan that wailed like an electric blues harp from hell.

Danny forced the chair through the people in the aisle, banging ankles and shins, shouting at them to get out of the way, barely heard over the din. Tie-dye was working the door, checking the IDs of a mob of college kids, jokin' and jivin' with them, but keeping them under control. The front booth was empty, no Red, no Richie. Jesus, that was something anyway. If Red had been there— It took Danny all of five seconds to find the bug, a paper-thin PZM plate microphone the size of a credit card taped under the table.

Wired. The whole damned club must be wired. He should have figured it. Richie's connections were no secret, the punk waved 'em under your nose, Cadillac Richie. The cops must have been on him from day one like hawks on a rabbit. Tie-dye had hired on after Richie bought in, and a couple of waitresses, but they came and went so often he'd have to check the books. . . .

No. First he'd have to warn Garcia. Or settle things with Richie himself. Right. Settle it now, if he could. One way or the other. Moving more cautiously now, he threaded the chair through the crowd to the narrow hallway that led to the office and the freight elevator beyond. Locked. He could tell by the position of the key slot. Didn't matter. No chance of surprising Richie anyway. As soon as he opened the door, the club noise would alert him. God. Maybe it'd be better to wait. Wait for Bobby, like Risa said. Or wait for Loop. Just pop a couple of pills, and . . .

Wait to die. He blinked back the throbbing pain behind his eyes, fumbled his key into the lock. He'd made this mess, he'd unmake it somehow. His only edge was that he'd become such a burnout Richie had no respect for him. A helluva lame advantage, the contempt of your enemies. But better than none. He slid the .25 into the pocket of his sport coat, then turned the key and nudged the door open with his chair.

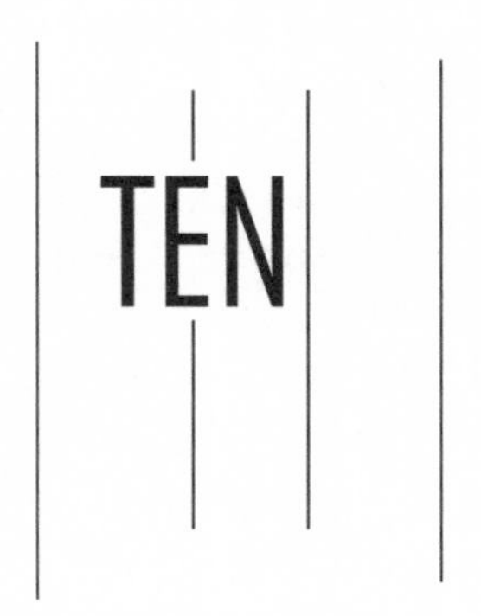

TEN

Garcia drove slowly through the Hall Plaza parking lot, keeping the Firebird in low, scanning the rows of parked cars, occasionally glancing at the note slip with the plate number he'd gotten from the DMV for Richie Zeayen. No luck. There were roughly two hundred cars parked in front of the Jade Mountain–Motown Underground building, but only three Jeeps, none of them a Comanche. He drove all the way down to the end of the building on the off chance Richie'd parked alongside, but there were no vehicles parked there—not surprising, since it'd be quite a hike from there to the club entrance.

He made one last pass in front of the club to check the dead-end alley that led to the loading dock between the Underground and the Radio Shack next door. Empty, except for a few garbage cans. So, Richie's car wasn't here. Was Richie? He considered popping in to find out, decided against it. No point in spooking him. Yet. He gunned the 'bird out of the lot, heading north on Conant.

The lone car in Danny's drive was Connie's red Porsche, but as Garcia cruised past the house he had the uneasy feeling that he was missing something. Couldn't quite recall . . .

He eased to the curb a half block up from the house, where he had a good view of the porch and the driveway. He idly searched his cassette tray, found the Whiteboys tape Danny'd given him, popped it in the cassette slot, reclined his seat a bit, settled in to wait and watch. And listen.

And was pleasantly surprised. The Whiteboys' music was an interesting mix, Tex-Mex and heavy metal, Buddy Holly meets Metallica. And Richie was right, the girl was a dynamite singer, as clear and powerful a voice as he'd ever heard. The third cut was the old Stones song, "Rock and a Hard Place," with a wild, five-minute drum solo added on. A tough act to follow, The Stones, but the arrangement gave the song new energy. Not bad. For Whiteboys.

He idly tapped time on the wheel with his fingertips as he scanned the street. No Jeep Comanche in sight, but . . .

He'd seen one. Earlier today. That was it. When he left Connie he'd checked the street, wondering if her visitor had parked nearby. The only cars around were a parked station wagon, a gray Jag crawling along . . . and a car sitting down the block with its motor running. A black Comanche? Maybe. Possibly a Blazer or a similar car. He hadn't taken special note of it at the time, so he wasn't absolutely sure.

Still if it had been there, what were the odds it would be back? Not good. Give it another half hour.

He settled back to wait, tried to relax, but couldn't. And realized it was the song.

Risa Blades was singing softly, her voice caressing a melody. And something in her tone gradually brought him to a subconcious sensual alert, like a breath of perfume in a darkened room.

The lyrics were in Spanish, so he only understood a word here and there, and yet the song seemed intensely personal, a one-to-one message. "Aledita."

When it finished, he rewound it and played it again. And then once more. The half hour skimmed by. Still no action at the house. The trip had probably been a time waster, but somehow when he fired up the 'bird, his mood had lifted. No rational reason for it, it was only rock'n'roll.

"Aledita."

ELEVEN

The reek of rum rolled out of the office as Danny eased the door open, instantly rekindling his panic so strongly that he almost slammed it again, fearing the pain and the shame. . . . He hesitated, dry-mouthed, hands quivering; then with a silent shudder he jammed the joystick forward, banging his chair into the room.

And it was perfect. Perfect. Richie was at the desk, his back turned, watching the crowd through the one-way mirror. Danny brought the .25 auto up, trying to center the muzzle between Richie's shoulder blades. But sweet Jesus he couldn't steady it! The damned gun was wavering like a bat in a hurricane. Couldn't align the sights, could barely point it in Richie's general direction. His arms were numb from the beating, couldn't— His eyes met Richie's in the inner reflection of the mirror and he froze. His hands spasmed, fumbling the pistol, dropping it to the floor, his gaze locked with Richie's, heart exploding—

Richie didn't turn. Danny stared at him, panting, trying to swallow. . . . And gradually, his panic began to ebb. And he realized Richie wasn't going to react. His eyes were open, staring, but . . .

There was nobody home. No life in them.

Danny cautiously hummed his wheelchair over to the

desk. Richie was slumped in the office chair, his face twisted, ugly. For a panicky instant he thought Garcia'd hit the wrong man, Richie's brother or—

No. It was Richie all right. He just looked so—different. My God, he *was* different. As changed as a person could be. Dead. Beaten to death, from the look of him. God almighty, he'd won. One last time, he'd bet it all and licked the odds. . . .

So where was the adrenaline rush, the high?

Richie just looked . . . abandoned. Where was the bastard who'd roughed him up? The bright-eyed, wired-up hustler who'd conned him into going partners? Not in that chair. Not anymore.

He reached down, groping for the pistol, but the effort brought a stab of pain so powerful he cringed in the chair, trying to hide, gasping. Agony so fierce he thought it wouldn't pass, that it would take him away with it. . . . But eventually it receded, as one wave subsides to build strength for another, leaving him shaken, disoriented.

He scanned the office for his pain pills, spotted the open packet on the floor beside the desk, and guided the chair over to them, grunting with the effort it took to reach down to scoop up a few. He raised them to his lips, his hand shaking so badly he could barely hold them, and then with all the strength he could muster, he forced his fist closed, trapping the pills inside. He lowered the fist to his lap.

No. Not yet. Have to think clearly first. Richie's dead. And so am I. And maybe Garcia too. They've got us on tape talking about the hit as sure as God sees the sparrows fall. Won't matter much to me, a different hospital to die in. Probably never see the inside of a cell. God, the way I feel without pills, I might not see sunup. Not much time, no more'n it'll take for the heat to transcribe the damned tape. Then they'll drag my raggedy tail off to jail or a hospital. A sorry end.

He scanned the office. The room was a mess, but no

more than it was after he and Richie tangled. The kid hadn't given Loop much trouble. Welcome to the major leagues, punk.

The big question?

How much do the police have? Was there a mike in here? He closed his eyes a moment, focusing inwardly, then opened them again. Probably not. Tie-dye might pop in to ask for a bottle if they ran low, but he was never in the room alone. Besides, Richie had the room swept for bugs regularly, and Tie knew it. So maybe all they had was talk, not the killing.

Which left a way out. At least for Garcia. If a man had the belly for it. Aye, there's the rub, as the poet says. One thing to talk tough about havin' nothin' to lose, quite another to throw away what little is left. Still . . .

He glanced around the office, taking stock. God what a small place it really was, this office, the club. My life. He touched the desktop with his fingertips, trying to sense a connection to it, to his past, to feel some of the joy he'd felt in this room as master of the circus, but it already seemed very far away, and fading fast. He fumbled the telephone out of its cradle, painstakingly tapped out a number, waited for the recorded message to finish. When he heard the beep he choked, couldn't talk, had to dial again.

"Ladies. This for you both, the twin lights of my life. I've made mistakes and . . . ah hell, God's truth I'm not sure there's a damn one of 'em I regret. But there are some things I need to explain. . . ." And he did, briefly. He paused a moment, trying to think of a big finish. But he was afraid even now to sound hokey, phony. "I love you both," he said, "I do love you. Remember me kindly. Remember me."

He tried to replace the phone in its cradle, but dropped it. Let it lay. He closed his eyes, trying to focus on the last of the loose ends. It was hard, he felt so . . . distant, as though he were already gone. Not yet. Not quite yet.

He rolled the chair to the liquor shelf against the wall,

took down a bottle of Don 'Q'. It took forever to get the cap off, but he managed, then let it trickle across the carpet as he wheeled the chair back to the desk and emptied the bottle onto Richie's corpse.

The club had gone quiet, an expectant hush as though they were waiting. . . . But it wasn't him they were waiting for. Bailey's drum solo had ended and Risa was alone center stage with her acoustic guitar, strumming it softly. Lucero had moved to the rear of the stage, standing beside Bailey's drum riser, the two of them part of the audience now, as Risa hummed a wordless accompaniment to her guitar. And then she began to sing. "Aledita."

Well. I'll be damned. Danny turned up the volume on the desk monitor speaker and closed his eyes a moment to listen. And felt his resolve begin to waver. No. Time. It was time.

He picked up the silver lighter from the desk, flicked it to life, and held it against Richie's coat. It took a moment to catch, the flames flickering a lovely blue against creamy muslin. Now. Only a few seconds before I'll burn with Richie. One way or the other.

Picked up the pistol, worked his thumb through the trigger guard, then stuck the barrel in his mouth, his teeth clattering against the metal, tasting bitter oil.

His hands were vibrating with tension and palsy and for a moment he wasn't sure he could manage to squeeze the . . .

Onstage, Rey Lucero was leaning against his amplifier stack, watching the crowd, his Fender bass cradled in his arms. Risa's solo was almost finished, and he spotted Bobby moving through the crush, headed back to the stage from the john or wherever he'd been. The song seemed to be goin' over good, Risa had the audience nailed, as usual. . . .

Something odd . . . The mirror on the back wall was glowing, getting brighter, shifting into red. Suddenly it shattered, blown out by a gunshot. Flames flared through the opening. People started shouting, scrambling, trying to get away from the fire as the sprinkler system at the rear of the club kicked on.

TWELVE

Garcia unlocked his apartment door, laying the evening out in his mind. Breaktime. Too much hassle for any one day—Danny, Cordell, Connie . . . even Erin. His head ached, his bruised ribs ached. Call it a night. Maybe heat up some Szechuan rice, crank up Bonnie Raitt on the CD, think things through. . . .

Good idea—good music, good food, maybe a little wine, let it all blow away. Absolutely the right thing to do. He thought so even as he was slipping into his old U of D sweatpants and lacing up his running shoes.

He hit the street at an easy pace, reminding himself to take it easy, doctor's orders. And he did, at first. But after a few blocks, he began lengthening his stride. Too much time in cars and bars and hospital rooms. It was better out in the street, running against the wind, legs seeking the primal rhythm, the perfect pace, the lope that goes on forever.

A fine night to run. An inch or two of snow had fallen, slicking the streets, slowing traffic. The sidewalks were still virginal, unmarked by city soot or footprints. Sane people stayed cozy indoors in the January dark.

Their loss. Snowflakes swirled and danced in the silver streetlight pools, a few leftover holiday lights twinkled in apartment windows, rubber wreaths and plastic Santas in the doorways, ghosts of a Kmart Kristmas past.

He kept his stride loose, his breathing deep and steady, tasting the sharp tang of the night air, diesel fumes, monoxide, the icy bite of the Canadian wind off the river ice. Eau de Troit. And under her gauzy chemise of new fallen snow, Lady Motown looked fine, a vintage beauty after a first-rate facelift.

A cluster of dark figures moved out of the shadows a block or so ahead, stumbling toward him. Young black dudes, four, no, five of them, shuckin'n'jivin', arm-in-arm, holding each other up, obviously plastered, maybe from last night, or even last week. A pang of unease tightened his throat, and for a moment he was outside the warehouse, the kid facing him down in front of his gang buddies. . . .

But these guys weren't bangers. Too well dressed—topcoats, bright silk scarves. Still, he juked between two parked cars and out into the street to give them space.

"Yo, Mama," one of the boys called out as he pounded past, "come on back, have my baby." Two of them broke out of the pack and began chasing him.

He lengthened his stride a bit, but he wasn't really worried. They were drunk, stoned, or both, and he could probably run them into the ground even if they weren't.

They gave it up after half a block, stumbling into one another, sprawling in a snowy tangle of laughter and beery obscenities. Garcia grinned tautly, then picked up his pace by a full third, really turning it on, shutting the boys out, Danny and Cordell out, feeling only the slap of concrete flying under his Snow Joggers, the icy bite of the night wind, and the tart sting of snow crystals kissing his face.

He'd meant to do only a mile, but it felt so good to run, to leave it all, that he kept it up for nearly four miles, pacing himself to catch the lights on green, making a giant circle. And as he neared the Seven Oaks complex, his frustration had burned away, leaving only a single image: the fear in Danny Kelly's eyes when he looked at Richie. Danny afraid of a punk like that. The cancer must be eating more than his bones. Have to do something about that. Lean on Zeayen, threaten him, bust him. Whatever it takes.

Garcia awoke to the sound of J.P. McCarthy chuckling on his clock radio, the morning show, WJR Detroit, Great Voice of the Great Lakes. He felt fuzzy, stiff from the run. But he had a glimmer of an idea about handling Richie. It got clearer under the icy needle spray of the shower. Jimmy said the kid was connected to the Marielito from Windsor, Echeverria. Maybe the Cuban could be persuaded to call him off to avoid trouble this side of the line. . . .

He needed more information. Wrong. He needed caffeine. He pulled on sweatpants and a T-shirt, padded out to the kitchen, and fed the coffeemaker a double helping of custom-ground Colombian beans. He was scrounging in the fridge for a bagel when somebody rapped at the apartment door.

Company at eight in the morning? And nobody'd buzzed from the first-floor entrance, which was always locked. Garcia picked up his .38 AIRWEIGHT from the nightstand and flattened beside the door. "Yeah?"

"It's me, Loop, Al Fielder. Sorry to bother you so early, but we gotta talk."

Garcia popped the latch. Fielder stepped in, a cement block of a man—gray topcoat, slate eyes, salt-and-pepper brushcut, square faced, squarely built with a mindset to match.

"You're a god-awful vision this early, Al," Garcia said, padding back to the bedroom to put his weapon away. "Coffee's on the make."

"I'll drink it if he won't," Jimmy Hamadi said, following Fielder into the apartment, glancing around like a prospective tenant. Hamadi was dressed for the street in his battered bombardier jacket, torn jeans, and biker boots, his dark hair slicked back, double earrings. He looked almost young enough to pass for Fielder's delinquent son, but he'd been head of Metro narcotics for nearly as long as Garcia'd been in homicide. A third man was with them, tall, black, fortyish. Number-two man from the Metro prosecutor's office, an AP named Brownell, primped and ready for court—charcoal topcoat, snow white shirt, red bow tie.

"Grab a seat guys," Garcia said, opening the dishwasher and retrieving four cups. He dealt them out on the table, but the only one who sat was Hamadi. Fielder and Brownell remained standing, cool, wary. Garcia eyed them a moment, then filled all four coffee cups and sat.

"Perhaps we'd better begin by reading you your rights, Sergeant Garcia," Brownell said formally.

"Actually, I'm reasonably familiar with my rights, Counselor," Garcia said evenly. "So why don't I just stipulate that I heard 'em, and you can tell me what you thought you wanted on your way out."

"It's not that simple, Loop," Hamadi said, leaning back comfortably in his chair, sipping his coffee. "Hey, this is good. Colombian?"

Garcia nodded, trying to read Fielder's eyes. Nothing.

"When you stopped by my stake yesterday," Hamadi continued, "you asked about a guy named Zeayen. Why was that exactly?"

"I told you. A friend who helped me out back when I was narking is getting hassled by the guy."

"This friend being Daniel Kelly?"

"That's right."

"So?" Hamadi said. "Did you help him out?"

"I—not exactly, no. I haven't really had time yet. Why? What's this about?"

"You mind telling us where you were last night?"

"Yeah, I think I do. You want to tell me why you're asking?"

"I can tell you this much, Sergeant," Brownell said, "if you refuse to cooperate, we'll continue this talk down at Metro."

"End of discussion, Counselor," Garcia said, rising. "You just jerked the wrong chain. Unless you've got a warrant, I want you out of my place. Now."

"Like I said, Loop, it ain't that simple," Hamadi said regretfully. He fished an envelope from beneath his leather jacket and tossed it toward Garcia. "Hate to bum out your morning, Loop, but you're busted, for conspiracy to commit murder for hire. We've also got a warrant to search for the ten grand Danny Kelly gave you yesterday, and some contraband jewelry. You want to tell me where it is? Save us both the trouble of havin' the uniforms waitin' out in the hall tear your place apart looking for it."

Garcia sank slowly back in his chair, glancing from Hamadi to Brownell, last to Fielder. Al was an easy read, too up-front to conceal much. He was angry, and disappointed. But there was no uncertainty. The situation spoke for itself, and working together didn't mean squat. He looked like a stranger. Maybe he was. "I, ah, don't think I should answer any more questions without the advice of counsel," Lupe said quietly.

"Smart move," Hamadi nodded, "I'd definitely want a lawyer if I was in your situation, Loop. In fact, you might wanna call two or three."

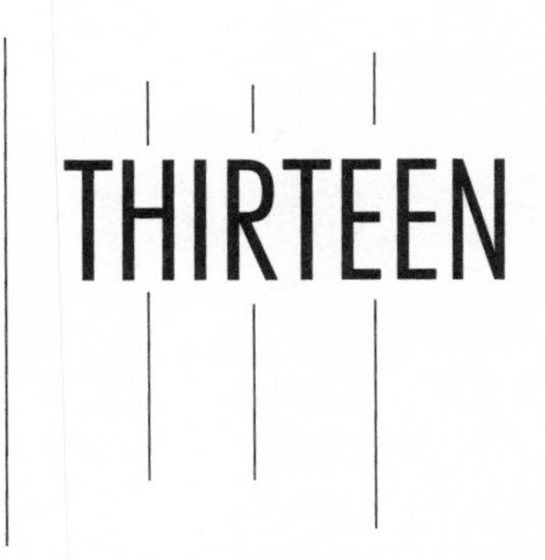

THIRTEEN

At Metro Central station, the booking officer skipped the strip search but frisked him thoroughly, and took his shoelaces and the drawstring to his sweatpants. They put him in a sixth-floor isolation cell usually reserved for jailbait juveniles or psychos. The room was a narrow institutional green concrete box with a steel cot bolted to the wall, a lidless toilet in the corner, a two-inch oaken door with an armored glass slit.

The first hour crawled by like a winter. He forced himself to sit on the cot, to concentrate. He'd been in cells, a thousand boxes, all alike. But not like this. Not like this. Every cop's soul-deep fear, is to screw up somehow, get eaten by the system.

The ride downtown had been silent, Brownell's orders—no questions, no answers. They'd offered him as many calls as he needed, but the only person who might be able to straighten things out was Erin, and she wasn't in her office. He left a message on her machine.

Three hours inched past by the corridor clock.

There was a single rap on the door, the guard opened up, and Erin stepped in. She was taller than she'd appeared at her desk, wearing a black suit with a white collar that made her look like a church school coed. An exhausted one. Hollow-eyed, pale as a vampire's lover.

"Thanks for coming," Lupe said, rising, offering her the cot. "I'm afraid I'm in a bit of a jam. I'd like you to verify a conversation for Lieutenant Fielder."

"Conversation?" Erin echoed, frowning.

"About your father's illness and why I accepted his money yesterday. Unless there's a statute making stupidity illegal, we'll be out of here in time for a late lunch."

Erin eyed him a moment without speaking, then took a deep breath. "Lupe, did they tell you why you were arrested?"

"For conspiracy to commit. It's a crock."

"Is it?" Erin said, sitting on the cot, snapping open her glove-leather briefcase. "I spoke to Brownell before I came up here. He thinks he's got you nailed, and speaking professionally, he may well be right."

"Look, I've already guessed they've got a tape. Hamadi must have a narc working the club undercover and he's got the place wired, so they taped me talking to Danny, but that's all they can have. I only took the damned money to keep him from buying trouble and I tried to give it to you immediately afterward."

Erin eyed him intently for a moment, reading his face. "My God," she said softly, "you really don't know, do you? Okay, here it is. My father and his partner Richie Zeayen were killed last night at the Underground. There was a fire, but the sprinkler system put it out before much damage was done."

Garcia didn't react for a few seconds; then he slowly eased down on the cot beside her. "Sweet Jesus. Did ahm . . . ?"

"What?"

"Hell, I don't know. What happened?"

"Brownell doesn't have the autopsy results yet, but apparently Zeayen was beaten to death. My father's death was either suicide or made to look like it. Pending the coroner's report they're treating the case as a double homicide. My father was physically incapable of killing Richie, so they're assuming both homicides were committed by the same person. You."

"But . . . They can't believe I'd kill Danny?"

"They don't have to *believe* anything. Brownell says he has you on tape agreeing to kill Zeayen, correct?"

"Yeah," Garcia said, rising slowly, starting to pace, his laceless tennis shoes flopping like slip-in mules. "He probably has. But I certainly never intended to do it. And I didn't."

"The money Hamadi and Fielder found at your apartment was the money my father gave you?"

"Right. The same money I tried to give to you."

"It wouldn't have made any difference. It's marked, sting money from a drug buy Hamadi's people made a month ago."

"My God," Garcia said slowly, "from Richie Zeayen?"

"Exactly. They were setting him up for a bust. So they have two killings, they have you on tape agreeing to commit one of them, and the marked money you were paid to do it. They even have a weapon. Can they connect it to you?"

"What kind of weapon?"

"A .25-caliber Sterling automatic."

"No," Garcia said positively, "I've never owned one."

"But if the weapon proves untraceable . . ."

"It could still be mine."

"Exactly. Still think you'll be out of here by lunchtime?"

"No," he said slowly, "I think I'm in a hole so deep I'll have to phone out for sunshine."

"I'm afraid you're right. And under the circumstances perhaps you'd better find another attorney."

"I don't know. . . . I think I'd rather have someone who knows I didn't do this thing. That I couldn't have." She pursed her lips, looked away. "Look, if you'd rather not . . ."

"My father involved you in this," she said, taking a deep

breath. "I suppose I owe you something for that. And in all modesty I'm probably better than any public defender you'll draw."

"I won't need a PD. I'm not a charity case."

"You are now. Brownell's frozen your assets under the RICO organized crime statute as possibly drug related."

"What? He can't do that!"

"Of course he can. You had marked drug money in your possession. Look, you'd better get this straight, Garcia. Brownell thinks you're guilty and he's going to try to take you down, so if you want another attorney—"

"No, not unless you really don't want to do it."

"I'll do it," she said evenly. "For my father as much as for you. So, to business. From this point on, you're mute, you don't talk to anyone unless I'm present."

"Erin, my only chance is to explain what happened."

"Wrong. As things stand, talking won't help. With the circumstantial evidence Brownell has he can't drop the case. You're scheduled for a prelim this afternoon, Judge Bachmann's court. You'll almost certainly be indicted. Brownell will go for no bail, I'll go for recognizance release. For a double homicide Bachmann will set bail somewhere between two to five hundred thousand, so be ready for it.

"The amount's irrelevant since your assets are frozen anyway," Erin continued. "To be blunt, you're going to remain incarcerated awhile, so you'd better make the mental adjustments necessary to get through it. Are you going to be okay?"

"I don't know," he said honestly, "I guess I'll have to be."

"Another thing, Brownell will probably send someone to make you an offer, maybe a friend. Listen, but don't offer anything. You know the game."

"No I don't, not from this side. Maybe I should but . . . I don't."

"Right," she said, rising. "If you don't hear from me for

a day or so, don't be concerned. I have family business and I'll have to reduce my caseload. Anything you want sent in?"

"No. I'm okay. Look, it may not mean much to you now, but I appreciate what you're doing. And I'm very sorry about Danny."

"I know, I . . ." She swallowed hard, shaking her head as though she'd been slapped. And for a moment she didn't look a day over seventeen. But the moment passed.

"Hang in there," she said, gathering herself. "I'll be in touch."

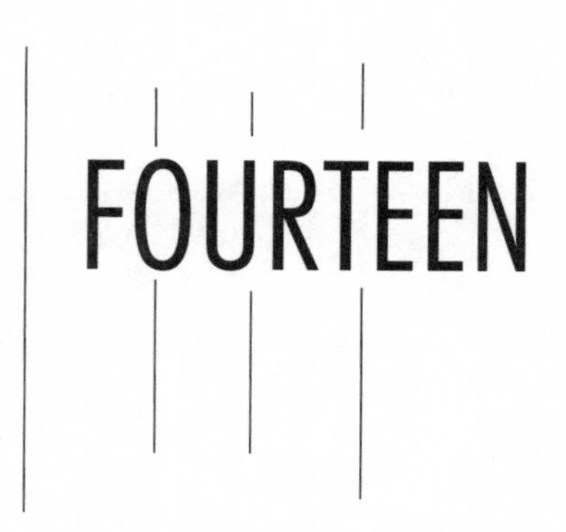

FOURTEEN

A sharp rap, and the oaken cell door swung open.

"Yo, Loop?" Jimmy Hamadi said. "Got a minute?"

"I think I can fit you into my dance card," Garcia said, sitting up on his cot. "This social? Or business?"

"Both," Hamadi said, glancing grimly around as the turnkey locked them in. "Funny, I always figured if one of us wound up inside it'd be me. Heard your bail got set at a quarter mil yesterday. Tough break. Any chance you can make it?"

Garcia said nothing.

"Okay look, I won't screw you around, Loop, Brownell asked me to see if you're interested in talkin' a deal."

"What kind of a deal?"

"Immunity on the Kelly homicide if you'll cop to Zeayen, take the fall on conspiracy. He'll ask for concurrent sentences on whatever you draw. Even with life you could be out in ten years."

"I've already done ten years. Since yesterday. No deal."

"You maybe oughta think about it," Hamadi said, slouching against the cell door, hands in his jacket pockets. "You could offer Zeayen threatening you on tape for mitigation, plus your mental state after the warehouse explosion.

Might not draw much time. Brownell can toss in choice of institutions. A week in Jacktown can be longer than a year in the Thumb or the U.P."

"You know, we're all alone in here, Jimmy, no tape running that I know of. Don't you want to ask me the big one?"

"Which one is that?"

"Like did I do it or not? Jesus, Jimmy, we're not buddies, but we've worked together. Do you really think I did this thing?"

"Straight up?" Hamadi said. "Hell, I don't know. Longer I'm on the job the less I'm surprised by what people are capable of. Especially me. What I think doesn't matter anyway. You're burned, bro, we've got the tape, the money, the bodies. We can place you at the scene—"

"No you can't. I wasn't there."

"C'mon, Loop, don't insult my intelligence. We've got you in a surveillance shot at the scene."

"I drove through the parking lot," Garcia admitted. "I didn't go inside."

"The lot's enough. Even got you checking out the back door."

"The back? You mean the alley? I was looking for a car."

"What car?"

"Richie's Jeep. It wasn't there, so I left."

"Car wasn't there because his buddy Red peeled out in it earlier. Right on your tail, as a matter of fact. So maybe you were looking for it, or maybe you were just checking to see if the alley was clear. That's how you got in, right?"

"I just told you I didn't get in."

"So you did. Trouble is, since we had a man on the front door, and the other doors are alarmed and visible from the lot, Fielder figures you must've used the alley door. There's no lock on it, it just bars from the inside."

"There's also a freight elevator," Garcia said.

"Nope, our guy had the loading dock in view. Nobody

showed, in or out. Had to be the back door. We figure Kelly switched off the alarm to let you in, rebarred it after you left. He musta had stone balls, your friend Kelly. To do what he did afterward."

"What do you mean? What happened exactly?"

"As near as we can tell, he tried to cover the killing by dousing Zeayen's body and the room with booze and touching it off. Then he ate a slug from a .25 auto. He might've pulled it off except that the slug smashed out the one-way mirror over his desk and the sprinkler system killed the fire. A hard way to go."

"Skip the empathy, Jimmy. The man shouldn't be dead. If you'd been straight with me yesterday, he might not be."

"Don't try to lay it on me, Loop. I told you to back off. I did everything but tattoo it on your damn forehead."

"But you didn't tell me you were letting Danny twist in the wind so you could work up a nickel-dime bust on his partner. Dammit, he laid it all on the line for us once. He deserved better than that."

"Look, I'm not happy about what happened to your friend either," Hamadi flared, "but he wasn't exactly a civilian. He was tied in with some of the worst maggots on the damn planet."

"What are you talking about? Richie was strictly a low-rent hustler on the make."

"Right. The bastard was also my only shot at breaking into Echeverria's crew. We had Richie nailed, dead bang. Sure as God he woulda rolled over, given up the others. And I want those guys, Loop, more'n I ever wanted anybody. I spent months setting Richie up. And then you waltz in, blew the whole thing in a day."

"And part of setting Richie up was letting him muscle Danny? Jesus, Jimmy, Kelly was a citizen, one of the people we're supposed to protect. How could you use him like that? What the hell's happened to you?"

"A helluva lot's happened!" Hamadi snapped. "You've been out of the drug scene too long, Loop, you don't know what it's like anymore. They're crazy! This Echeverria is the worst I've ever seen and I had him—shit!" Hamadi slammed his fist into the oaken door hard enough to vibrate the room.

Garcia eyed him for a moment, then shook his head slowly. "You're holding out on me. You were yesterday and you still are. What's so important about this Cuban? Important enough to let a guy like Danny go down the tubes just to get a shot at him?"

"Kelly wasn't the first to go down," Hamadi said. "I told you yesterday we lost a guy up in Toronto. But I didn't tell you all of it. His name was Jase Probert. He was a narc, but he wasn't like us, Loop, crazies who mighta been hoods if we weren't cops. He was young, a college kid, real dedicated. We borrowed him from Cincy two years ago. And then I loaned him to the RCMP up in Toronto to try to penetrate the Cuban's posse. At the time we didn't realize how big it was. Or how bad. We found out. Something went wrong, big-time."

"They made him?"

"I honestly don't know. Maybe he just crossed the wrong guy in the gang. You know how those things can go. All we really know we got from his autopsy. We, ah, found his body in a warehouse. Crucified. They taped his mouth shut, then gave him a couple shots of crystal Methedrine to keep him alert. Didn't want him to pass out and miss anything, you know? And then the bastards nailed him to the wall. Hands and feet both."

"My God," Garcia said softly.

"It gets worse," Hamadi said, swallowing. "They, ah, they cut him, Loop. As bad as a man can be cut. They cut off his penis, nailed it up next to his face. And let him bleed to death. Coroner said it must have taken most of an hour. He was probably concious almost the whole time."

"I'm sorry about what happened to Probert," Garcia said quietly, "but it doesn't justify using Danny Kelly for bait."

"I know it doesn't," Hamadi nodded. "I didn't like it either. But I did it, Loop. And I can live with it. But you know what the worst of it is? It was for nothin'. Probert and Kelly. Even Richie. Echeverria is still building his crew up. And I'm back to square one. And you're in deep, deep shit. All for nothin'. Christ, what a cock-up. So. What do you want me to tell Brownell?"

"Tell him no. I didn't do it Jimmy. I know how it looks, but I didn't. Somebody else did, and Fielder might just fall over whoever it was if he keeps looking. How about it? Is the investigation continuing, or am I already elected?"

"If it was up to me, I'd continue," Hamadi said carefully, "but it's not. You're open and shut for conspiracy, damn near that tight for the rest. You know department policy, Loop, when we have a suspect in custody, we move on. Bottom line, you're it. No other suspects. If you've got anything I can work with, lay it on me. I'll hump it on my own time if I have to. But the way things are you're dead in the water."

"I see. Well, at least I know where I stand."

"Not quite," Hamadi said. "There's this thing you had with Hamid Nurredin? Red?"

"What about him?"

"Good question. You dislocated his finger, right? We got it on tape."

"Actually, he sort of dislocated it himself."

"Whatever," Jimmy shrugged. "Point is he's gotta be hurtin'. Only he hasn't sought medical attention, at least not at any emergency rooms or doc-in-a-box clinics. Last time we saw him, he was hot on your trail. You got any idea where he is?"

"I'm afraid not."

"Afraid's the right word, Loop. Thing is, homicide's

been beatin' the bushes for him since last night, no luck. You better hope he turns up healthy. Or you could be in even deeper shit than you are."

"All due respect, Jimmy, I'm not sure that's possible."

"Sure it is, Loop," Hamadi said grimly. "Take it from a kid who grew up in Beirut. Things can always get worse."

"A funeral home?" Tony LaRose said, slowing the Jaguar sedan a half block back as Erin Kelly swung her mother's Porsche off DeQuindre into a mortuary lot. Tony kept the Jag at a crawl, watching as both women got out and started inside. They looked good, dressed in black, had the figures for it, good legs, one redhead, one blond— Some asshole honked behind him and he had to gun the Jag ahead, lost sight of them.

"Go around the block, pull in," Cottler said.

"Pull in? What for? I don't like these places, man."

"If you'd let me do Richie first insteada his dumb-ass cousin, we wouldn't be here. He woulda given the man what he owed, end of problem."

"Like the dude up in Toronto did?" Tony said, keeping his eyes on the street ahead.

Cottler glanced across at him, then shrugged. "The dude didn't have nothin' to give up. Or he would have."

"Maybe," Tony nodded. "Thing is, seems like most people you talk to never talk to nobody else. Like Richie."

"I never talked to Richie. Place was nuts when I got there, cops all over."

"Right. That's what you said."

"That's how it was. You don't believe me?"

"Nothin' to me one way or the other. Only the man might be wonderin' why you was so late gettin' over there."

"He wants to know, he can ask. Not you, Tony. I don't say shit to you. Any problem with that?"

"I can live with it," LaRose said.

But he didn't like it. Not a damn bit. Tony LaRose had been inside the walls twice, four years at 3000 Cooper Street, Jackson, two at the Thumb. Knew some hard guys, mostly crackhead burnouts'd whack King Kong's nuts for a two-dollar rock. Bad news because they didn't care. Bust you up, kill you over nothin'.

Cottler was harder to figure. Still young, never been inside except for juvy hall. Probably never been jammed up or hurt bad. But he really got off on pain, dealin' it out. A sex thing, maybe.

Tony was afraid of him. And Tony hadn't been scared since he was sixteen, got gangbanged his first night in DeHoCo. The pain, guys gruntin', slobberin on him, standin' in line. Nothing worse, ever. Nothing left to fear. Until the Cuban hired Cottler out of the Black Counts.

Hoss, the Counts called him. Short for *Rehacedor*. Remodeler. Thought it was street jive until the kid made his bones icing the dude up in Toronto. Ugly. In-fuckin'-human. Tony was no virgin. Seen some brutal things but nothing like that. The worst of it was watching Cottler's face. Seeing how much he liked it.

Same with Red. Sure it had to be done, but it shoulda been business. Mr. E. strangled Red in the shower, never broke a sweat, the big guy crying, pissin' himself. Meant less than nothin' to either the Cuban or Cottler. It was like they were in a contest now, to see who had the iron *cojones*.

Cottler went through Red's pockets after, kept the cash he lifted, just shoved it in his pocket instead of sharin' it out. That was the time to push back, with the Cuban there, and the right on his side. But Tony let it slide. Said nothin'. Because truth was, he wasn't sure whether the Cuban woulda backed him or maybe the two of 'em mighta cut him up just for the hell of it.

He circled the block with Cottler shifting in his seat to look the funeral home over. Red brick one-story building, big parking lot maybe a third full. LaRose pulled in and parked a few rows down from Connie Kelly's Porsche.

"Gimme your tie," Cottler said.

"What?"

"Your necktie. I need it."

"What the fuck for?" Tony asked, annoyed, but already loosening his tie, stripping it off.

Cottler turned up the collar of the salmon sport shirt he was wearing under his seven-hundred-buck blazer, neatly knotted the necktie, and checked himself out in the rearview mirror.

"Wait," he grunted at Tony. "If I come out movin' quick, pick me up on the run, otherwise just sit."

"Yassuh boss, you psycho nigger prick," Tony said. But he waited until Cottler'd slammed the door and was halfway to the mortuary entrance before he said it.

Sevum Cottler cautiously eased the main entrance door open. No reason to be careful, just habit. Nobody was manning the gleaming walnut reception desk. A dried-up old woman in a flowered hat, with scrawny, withered arms, was huddled on a parson's bench against one wall. Taking a break from somebody's funeral. Or gettin' fitted for a box of her own. Wouldn't need a very big one. The funeral home was a class act, green carpeting thick as a fairway, flocked tan wallpaper, air flowery scented like a yuppie massage parlor.

"Hey," Cottler said to the woman, "couple ladies came in here a minute ago. Which way'd they go?"

"I, ah . . ." The woman stared up at him, confused, wringing a Kleenex to shreds in blue-veined hands. "I'm sorry. I didn't notice." She looked so stricken, Cottler absently patted her shoulder as he glanced around. He spotted a glass-front directory and wandered over to it, the woman forgotten.

He scanned the directory, frowning, lips moving as he traced the words with a narrow finger. A funeral was in progress down the hall—elevator organ music, flowers stacked around the doorway. Not Danny Kelly's funeral though, he'd still be slabbed down at the morgue. His women would be here to make arrangements. Offices. Right. He sauntered off down the long hallway, coolly opening each door, checking the rooms as he passed. Until he found one that looked interesting, and stepped in.

"You'll find the Briarwood one of our most complete arrangements," Claudio Allessandri said. "It includes a casket with burled walnut inserts, solid brass fittings, a vault. . . ." His voice faded into a hazy drone. Bees on a summer afternoon. Connie Kelly didn't even try to follow the pitch. Instead she tried to remember where she'd seen him before. Young guy, thirtyish, tall, athletic looking, sunlamp tan, well-cut suit. At the club? Unlikely. At the office? She decided she'd never seen him at all. They just look alike, salesmen. Product doesn't matter. They're Friendly. Sincere. Earnest. Slyness behind the eyes. Hazel eyes in this case. Handsome enough, if you like sleek. Probably scored like a goat with the widows and . . .

Widow.

"Excuse me," Connie said abruptly. "I, ah, I need a little air. You decide, honey. Whatever you think . . ." She fumbled at the doorknob, palms suddenly slippery.

"Will you be all right?" Erin asked coolly, making no effort to rise.

"Fine," Connie snapped, jerking the door open. "I'll be in the car."

"Quite a normal reaction," Allessandri said smoothly as Connie slammed the door after her. "Loss affects each of us differently, and—"

"In this case the lady just needs a quick belt," Erin said brusquely. "Look, I'll be blunt. My father wouldn't give a damn whether he was buried in a pyramid or dumped in a swamp somewhere, so just give me the numbers for the last three packages you described and I'll pick one. Then we'll need to discuss the arrangements. They're a bit complicated."

"Perhaps we should wait until your mother—"

"Just give me the numbers. Now. Please."

Allessandri flipped through the brochure, stalling, calculating the odds. The mother would definitely be an easy sale. He'd figured the girl as a college kid tagging along. But the direct way she met his eyes, her tone . . . She was for real. Cut your losses, make the deal. "As you wish, of course," he said, passing her the brochure. "That would be the Blackthorne, the Briarwood . . ."

Connie scanned the hallway, looking for a rest room, a cloakroom, anyplace she could—

"Mrs. Kelly? Could you step this way please?" A tall, well-dressed black man with oiled hair and a neatly trimmed goatee gently took her elbow, leading her into a viewing room.

"I don't—"

"It'll only take a moment. It's important." He closed the door after them and led her up to the dais, where a huge open bronze casket rested on a gold-and-teak catafalque. An elderly man was on display, wearing an old-fashioned double-breasted blue suit, his hollow cheeks carefully powdered and lightly rouged.

"So," the black said, "what do you think?"

"Think?" Connie echoed numbly, "He looks . . . all right."

"I think so too. Looks like he's just takin' a nap, catchin' some z's. They do good work here."

"Look, my daughter's making all of the arrangements, Mr. . . . ?"

"Cottler, my name's Sevum Cottler. Maybe your husband mentioned me?"

"My husband? You mean you don't work here?" She looked at him more carefully now. A striking man. Café-au-lait skin, freckles, handsome in a way. The forked beard gave him an intriguing look. Satan as a male model.

"No, ma'am, I do business with these places sometimes, but mostly I'm in investments. My company invested some money in your husband's nightspot. With Richie Zeayen."

"Wait a minute," Connie said, blinking, "what is this? Who are you?"

"Cottler. Ma'am, like I said, my—"

"Look, I have no idea what you're talking about. If you think you have a claim on my husband's estate, contact his attorneys and get in line," Connie said, brushing his hand off her sleeve. "Now if you don't mind, I'm very tired."

"I only need a minute, and believe me, lady, you don't have anything goin' more important than hearin' me out—"

"Excuse me," Connie said icily, turning away.

"Whatever," Cottler said. He took her elbow as if to help her off the dais, then spun her around. Seizing her collar and the seat of her skirt, he heaved her bodily into the air like a sack of meal and slammed her face down onto the body in the casket, hard, driving the breath out of her. He jammed his forearm across the back of her neck, burying her face in the corpse's throat. She felt her skirt pulled up, his hand thrusting up between her thighs, clamping her groin, a searing white furnace of pain.

"Not a fucking word," he panted, his breath hot against her cheek. "Not one. Just listen. It's like buyin' a new car, a test drive. See how easy this is, you in this box with a corpse? Nobody to hear you? Nobody to help? That's how it'll be.

Like this. Forever. Buried alive with some fuck you don't even know. Now listen up. I'm gonna ask you some things. You yell, or say anything but what I wanna hear, I'm gonna bleed you some, and box you up with gramps here. Understand?" He pinched her vagina fiercely, clamping it with his fist, then eased off. She tried to squirm free, then froze as he squeezed again.

"I asked you if you understand, bitch," Cottler said softly. "Answer me."

Connie tried to nod, couldn't. "Yes", she whispered, afraid to move, tasting the lavender stench of death. "Yes."

SIXTEEN

Garcia was doing push-ups when there was a rap on the cell door and Erin Kelly stepped in, followed by a priest. Lupe rounded off the series and stood up. She looked better than she had her last visit, less wounded, more professional, in a navy Fortune 500-esque suit, with a bit more color to her cheeks. The priest was fiftyish, small, almost jockey-sized, but too well fed to sit a horse—a Pillsburg Doughboy in a clerical collar, with reddish hair gray at the temples and heavily freckled hands and face.

"Morning, folks. Sorry I can't offer you seats. They're a little short on the amenities here."

"Lupe, this is my uncle, Father Kelly."

"Father," Garcia nodded, offering his hand. The priest ignored it. He eyed Garcia straight on, taking his measure. He didn't spit, but looked as though he were considering it.

"The police tell me that my brother may have taken his own life trying to cover your crime," Father Kelly said bluntly. "Or that you may have helped him take it."

"They're wrong. On both counts."

"Perhaps they are. For one thing, my niece believes in you, and she's no fool. For another, you don't look much like a man worth dyin' for."

"I'm not. And I am partly responsible for what happened to your brother. He asked me for help. I blew it. But I didn't commit any crimes, and I wouldn't have harmed him deliberately. We were friends."

"That I do believe. Daniel always had colorful friends. I sometimes do social work in jails so I've met a fair number of Daniel's pals over the years. Not a guilty man in the lot, to hear 'em tell it."

"Maybe not, but if the authorities didn't occasionally blow a call, you wouldn't be wearing that cross, right?"

"True enough," Father Kelly conceded grudgingly. "In any case, I'm not here for a debate. I came because Erin asked me to meet you, size you up myself."

"And?" Erin asked.

"I'm disappointed," Kelly said. "I was hopin' he'd be total scum. Nothin's ever simple, is it? A pity."

"I can go ahead then?"

"You already know what I think, darlin'," Father Kelly said, "and yet here we are. You've inherited Daniel's selective deafness when it comes to my advice. Go ahead, get on with it."

"On with what?" Garcia said.

"A deal," Erin said. "How badly do you want out of here?"

"Is that a trick question?"

"Maybe it is," she said. "My mother's apparently had an attack of concience about your situation. The bottom line is, she may be willing to put up the Underground as surety for a property bond for your bail."

Garcia blinked. Said nothing.

"In return, she wants you to manage the club for us, keep it operating until we can find a buyer."

"Manage the club?"

"It shouldn't be difficult. As my father's executor, Uncle Mick will oversee the accounts. The business is basically the same as it was when you worked there."

"Maybe I'm punchy from being in here, but I'm not following this. If she needs a manager, why not just hire one?"

"She could. But as your attorney, I suggest you not look the proverbial gift horse et cetera. Frankly, it may be a whim. We were at the funeral home making arrangements yesterday when she walked out. I thought she needed an eye-opener, she's been drinking a lot. But when I got to the car she was nearly hysterical. Said she'd been thinking about how you'd gotten involved while trying to help Dad, and we should help you in return. And ourselves. Your name couldn't appear on the license, of course, but we can list you as Connie's assistant without breaking any regulations. We do need a manager. We'll never sell the place if it closes, and we have to sell."

"Why?"

"Constance used her trust fund and their home as collateral when Daniel bought the building from the mall's developers a few years ago," Father Kelly said. "If they can't sell the business as a going concern, she and Erin'll come out of this with less than nothin'."

"I have a mentally handicapped half brother who needs special care," Erin said. "I don't earn enough to pay for his care and have any life of my own. Losing my father is hard enough, Loop. I don't want to lose everything."

"You shouldn't have to. If that's the deal, I'll take it."

"Maybe you'd better think it over. It's occurred to me that Connie may want you there because she expects more trouble."

"What kind of trouble?"

"I'm not sure. Perhaps from Richie's friends."

"I hope she's right. And at least the toilets in the Underground have seats. Where do I sign?"

She shook her head, giving him a ghost of a smile. "Famous last words," she said.

SEVENTEEN

The BMW smelled of new leather and dashboard plastic, plus a faint whisper of Erin's perfume. Garcia sank deep in the seat, trying to forget the stench of jail, the clash of metal doors.

"I don't think I impressed your uncle," he said.

"It was the jailhouse jumpsuit," Erin said. "Orange isn't your best color. Do you want me to drop you at your apartment?"

"I'd rather go straight to the morgue. Richie Zeayen's body won't be there much longer if they haven't released it already."

Erin's mouth narrowed to a thin line, but she swung her BMW hard right, heading north on Woodward. "Will they let you see it?"

"It won't cost anything to ask, which is exactly how much I've got. Which reminds me, can you front me fifty?"

"Why not?" she sighed. "You're now officially worth a quarter of a million. Dead or alive."

"I'm disappointed," Erin said, glancing around the lobby of the Wayne County Morgue. "It looks more like a bank than a—medical facility."

"It is a bank in a way," Garcia said. "Holiday Inn decor,

everything sanitized, high-tech. Next of kin or whoever identify the decedents on an overhead TV monitor, comfortable seats, free coffee. The carpeting on the walls is for soundproofing, but it's not really necessary. People seldom cry here. I can catch a cab from here if you'd rather go."

"And risk losing my investment? I'll wait, thanks." She took a seat, took a notebook from her purse, flipped it open, and mentally disappeared into it. A consummate professional.

He checked in at the long oaken counter, then pushed through the smoked glass door at the rear of the viewing room.

Into hell. Or one version of it. The long, low-ceilinged room was crowded with corpses, more than a dozen of them neatly rowed on gurneys, some draped with white sheets, some not. Shattered bodies, nude, bloodless in the glare of the overhead fluorescent lights, personal belongings in paper bags upright between bare feet. A general assembly of the dead, white, brown, black. But mostly black. And much too young.

Garcia hated this room, the cloying, fecal odor mingled with the piney tang of antiseptic, orderlies wheeling the bodies around like closeout merchandise. It wasn't the grisliness—the mind overloads, blanks out the carnage and vacant eyes after a while. It was what the room might represent. If this was the ultimate reality, he didn't want to know.

Charlie Skowron was hunched over a nude corpse on a metal tray against one wall, muttering into an overhead microphone as he worked. Skow was tall, gangly, his bird face pockmarked with old acne scars, an unlit White Owl cigar clamped permanently in the corner of his skeletal jaw. He glanced up at Garcia, but continued extracting buckshot pellets from the savaged chest of a fourteen-year-old black boy.

"Sergeant Garcia, if that's the proper term of address

these days," Skow said, nodding. "Excuse me if I don't offer to shake hands. Nothing personal."

"I'd be more offended if you did offer, Charlie," Garcia said. "This isn't a social call anyway. I need a rundown on the victims in the double homicide Saturday night, Daniel Kelly, Richie Zeayen. Bodies gone yet?"

"No, they're still here, both autopsies are complete, but I'm afraid that's all I can tell you, Loop," Skowron said, dropping a BB into a metal tray with a clank. "Have your attorney submit an official request for my report and I'll fax it out, but that's the best I can do. I'm prohibited from talking to principals in an investigation."

"Hell, Charlie, I don't have any principles. Ask anybody. Look, I'm jammed up and I need a break. How about it?"

"Well, since nobody's bothered to *officially* inform me of your status, and since I owe you one, I guess you can view the bodies in question. This customer's in no rush. Right this way." Skowron threaded his way through rows of corpses like a tour guide in a wax museum.

"Here we have the late Mr. Zeayen," he said, peeling back a sheet and exposing Richie's upper body, the face charred and reddened, hair scorched.

"Jesus," Garcia winced, "what happened to him?"

"Quite a bit, though the worst of it, the burns, happened after death. The actual *cause* of death was anoxia," Skowron said, eyeing Garcia deliberately. "He suffocated. See this bruised area on his throat? His larynx was fractured. It swelled, and closed off his trachea. There are easier ways to go."

"Fractured how?"

"Result of a beating. Somebody knocked him around pretty thoroughly."

"Any chance a weapon was used?"

"Possibly the proverbial blunt instrument. I doubt I could make a positive ID even if I had it. Edema from the fire is too pronounced. He could have been kicked or clubbed. Nothing with an edge to it, but that's as specific as I can be."

"What's this?" Garcia pointed to a thin red line on the side of Zeayen's neck.

"Laceration. At first I thought he might've been strangled, but the wound's superficial and too high."

"Could two people have been involved, maybe one trying to strangle him—"

"Unlikely. The laceration isn't deep enough, and as you can see here, it doesn't completely encircle the neck," Skowron said. "My best guess is that he was wearing jewelry, probably a chain, and it was ripped off either in the struggle or just after."

"What about these?" Garcia indicated three faint gashes on the peeling flesh of Zeayen's cheek.

"Very astute," Skowron nodded. "They're difficult to see clearly beneath the burns, but they're claw marks. Fingernails I'd say, probably a woman's, though these days you can't always be sure. Not much help to—present company. They were inflicted several hours before his death."

"Before death?" Garcia said sharply. "You're saying Richie was involved in some kind of scuffle before he was killed?"

"Apparently. Getting the timing down is tricky, but the scratch wounds were well crusted over before the decedent was burned, I'd guess an hour or two earlier at the least."

"That's interesting, since he wasn't wearing any scratches when I saw him last. Unfortunately it doesn't help much. Anything else?"

"Not on Zeayen, not until the lab reports come back."

"Kelly then?"

"Kelly's already crated." Skowron re-draped the sheet over Richie's remains. "Body's due to be picked up shortly. What do you need to know?"

"Cause of death?"

"Mr. Kelly died of a gunshot wound, .25 auto, discharged upward at approximately a forty-five-degree angle through the roof of his mouth, exiting through the cranium. Probably self-inflicted."

"Sweet Jesus," Garcia said quietly, turning away.

"Yeah," Skowron said, removing the unlit cigar from his mouth, examining the soggy end. "It wasn't pretty, and that's a fact. If it's any comfort, death must have been nearly instantaneous. And his cancer was so advanced it would only have been a matter of days anyway. Some very bad days at that."

"You said *probably* self-inflicted," Garcia said.

"He was in the last stages of pancreatic cancer, extremely weak, must've been in considerable pain. Wouldn't have been difficult to put a gun in his hand, force him to pull the trigger."

"Any reason to think it happened that way?"

"Perhaps. He'd been beaten not long before his death, much more severely than Zeayen. Had visible lacerations and contusions on his face, arms, torso."

"Somebody roughed him up, then stuck a gun in his hand?"

"Not quite in that sequence. From the lividity of the bruises, I'd say an hour, possibly two passed between the beating and his death."

"At roughly the same time Zeayen's face was raked?"

"Probably, though it's unlikely Kelly inflicted that injury. There was no epidermal tissue under his nails, and I doubt that in his condition he'd have had the strength anyway. Was Kelly a boxer at one time?"

"Not that I know of, why?"

"Scar tissue around his eyes, old fracture lines on the lower mandible."

"He took a bad beating a few years ago," Garcia said quietly, "but he was no fighter. He was a raconteur, and a lover and a barroom philosopher."

"A thoughtful lover, judging from his vasectomy scar."

"He was a thoughtful man in a lot of ways," Garcia said. "Anything else interesting?"

"He'd been smoking marijuana within hours of his death, and there were traces of alcohol, probably rum, on his body, but he hadn't ingested any. Zeayen's body was the same way."

"Are you saying somebody sprinkled the bodies with booze to help them burn?"

"Looks like it. Trouble with that theory is, Zeayen had some glass splinters embedded in his shoulder, probably during the earlier scuffle. I'd say someone either hit him with a bottle or he rolled in some broken glass an hour or two before his death. Which just about covers all I can tell you at this point. If anything shows up in the lab tests or the photographs, I'll give you a call. Off duty of course, and off the record."

"I'd appreciate it, Charlie, I owe you. One last favor—can I take a look at Kelly's body?"

"I can have it uncrated if you don't mind waiting a few minutes," Skowron shrugged. "But, ah, I gather from what I read in the papers that he was a friend of yours, right?"

Garcia nodded.

"Then take some professional advice, Loop. Pass on this one. You really don't want to see it."

EIGHTEEN

The Underground was brightly lit, empty as a stadium before a game. Chairs were neatly stacked upside down on the tables. A skinny black kid in navy blue coveralls, a Sony Walkman wired over his dreadlocks, was running an industrial vacuum cleaner across the dance floor. The bartender (What had Danny called him? Tie-dye?) was wiping down the stock behind the bar, cleaning off the soot. No Jimi Hendrix getup today, just a faded gray Mumford High sweat suit and a red tae kwon do headband.

Father Kelly and Erin were conferring quietly near the office door when Garcia walked up. The area reeked of spilled booze and the acrid chemical stench of charred carpeting. Yellow plastic Police Line—Do Not Cross tapes stretched across the doorway and the blown-out observation-mirror frame.

"Sorry I'm late. The search team kind of rearranged my apartment. Took me a while to find my car keys."

"I'm not sure how much we can do in any case," Erin said. "The police have the office taped off. I've tried calling—"

"Don't worry about it," Garcia said brusquely, stripping

the tape away from the door. "This isn't a crime scene anymore."

"But the tape—" Father Kelly began.

"It's been over forty-eight hours, Father." Garcia wadded up the tape and tossed it in a trash can by the bar. "Every time a furnace kicks on it rearranges the dust, dessicates any organic evidence. If they wanted to preserve it they'd have left a guard." He peered into the office through the empty mirror frame. The room was a mottled mess. A rime of water-spotted soot covered the desk, the small washbasin, and the shelves of liquor against the wall. The red carpet was leprous, splotched with burned patches and oily footprints. The wall safe beside the liquor rack was open.

"Did the police open the safe?"

"No, I did," Erin said. "Connie called me that . . . night, about eleven. She couldn't remember the combination so I came down and opened it for them."

"What was in it?"

"Very little. Some legal papers, licenses. The day's receipts were missing, as well as Richie's lockbox."

"Lockbox?"

"He kept a steel security box of his own in the safe."

"Actually, I hadn't seen the box in several weeks," Father Kelly put in. "I don't think he was keeping it here anymore."

"If the safe was cleaned out, what do we use for operating funds?" Garcia asked.

"The club's bank account had a five-thousand-dollar reserve," Father Kelly said. "I've advised Connie not to invest what little of her own funds she has left."

"Sound advice," Garcia said. "What shape's the stock in?"

"It's okay," Erin said. "The sprinklers prevented any heat damage and the beverage seals are intact. We have about three weeks' reserve."

"One way or the other it should be enough," Garcia said. "What about the books, time cards, all that?"

"I have them with me," Father Kelly said. "Shall we go over them?"

"We'd better call a few waitresses who'd normally be working tonight first," Lupe said. "Ask them to help clean up."

"I'll do that," Erin put in, "I know most of them."

"Good. Better offer 'em a bonus, since they won't be getting tips. And tell 'em to wear grubbies. Father, could you lay out the books in that first booth, please? I'd like to poke around the office a minute."

"Why? The police have already investigated."

"Look, Father, I agreed to manage the club and I will but I need a little leeway. Please?"

"He's right, Uncle Mick," Erin said. "If we're going to salvage anything from this mess, we'll have to work together. Besides, if Lupe manages to get himself off the hook, we'll get our bail deposit back. Plus my fee of course."

Kelly cocked an eyebrow at his niece, then shrugged. "All right, Counselor," he said dryly. "I've already said my piece about this . . . arrangement, but that aside, I'll try to make it work. I'll have the accounts ready in five minutes, Garcia. You can have that long."

Kelly turned, marched stiffly over to the booth, and popped open his briefcase.

"I told you he didn't like me," Garcia said.

"Cut him some slack, Lupe. He and Dad weren't close, but in a way I think it makes all this even worse for him."

"It hasn't been a waltz for anybody," Garcia said.

"Let me put it another way. Lighten up on my uncle, Garcia, and that's not a request. I'll make those calls." She picked up the phone beside the register, pointedly turning her back.

"Right." Garcia opened the office door and stepped in. The stench was much stronger here. Scorched carpeting, and smoke, and booze. And anger. He could almost taste the rage in the air. Or maybe it was his own, just below the surface. He moved slowly around the room, scanning it carefully. He didn't expect any revelations, any pertinent evidence would have been bagged, tagged, and carried off by the investigating team. They seldom missed much. Still . . .

A friend of his had died here. By his own hand? Garcia tried to relate to that. It wouldn't come. It ached like an old wound. And rightly so. The truth was, the man who died in this room wasn't really Danny, his friend and mentor from all those years ago. He was only a shadow of that man, and now he wasn't even that. Maybe he was better off.

Richie Zee? Yes. There was something of him in here. A smoke-smudged photo of Richie kneeling beside Danny's chair, his arm draped over the smaller man's shoulder, both of them smiling at the camera. There were also splinters of glass on the carpet. From a broken bottle, Skow had said. One with a lot of booze in it. Which meant that Danny hadn't swung it at Zeayen. He could barely manage a cigarette. And Richie hadn't hit Danny with it either, no glass splinters on him, only booze. No need for Richie to use a bottle anyway. Danny was too weak to defend himself. No, somebody else had swung that bottle.

Who? Not just someone who'd happened by, the office was always locked. So, someone with a key, or who belonged here. Richie's buddy Red? Maybe. Where was he anyway? Spooked off by what had happened? Or just waiting for things to cool out before he drifted back to see what he could scavenge?

He slid open the closet door. A couple of Danny's spare jackets, slacks. And several items of women's clothing, halter tops, spandex tights, a leather skirt. Erin's? He lifted a halter top. Sequins on black silk glistened like a patch of night sky. Frederick's of Hollywood. Definitely not Erin's. English tweeds would be more her speed.

Whose then? Danny'd always been a ladies' man, considered it a duty never to miss an opportunity, and the club was an ideal hunting ground. He was always discreet, never balled the same one twice, never got involved, emotionally or financially. But in his condition? Hardly. One of Richie's women maybe.

Lupe rehung the halter top and closed the closet door. The desk drawers were empty, cleaned out. He took a last glance around the room. Still no sense of what had happened here. But unless he could change his luck, his future would look a lot like this room. Or worse.

NINETEEN

"When you set up shop, you really set up," Garcia said, sliding into the ID check booth opposite Father Kelly. The table was immaculate, ring binder ledgers perfectly aligned, an oval magnifying glass, a pocket calculator, two pencils, and a Clic eraser arrayed alongside like a place setting. A gold-framed photograph stood upright in the corner, a Kelly family portrait, Mick, Danny, their mother, Erin, and Connie smiling at the camera.

"Force of habit," Kelly said, "no pun intended. I'm more bookkeeper than priest these days, assigned to the chancery office on Washington Boulevard. I handle the accounts of the entire archdiocese, which is not unlike the proverbial Chinese fire drill. Keepin' my own little corner of things organized helps."

"What does the chancery think about your handling the books for the Underground?"

"I've never actually *kept* them, it wouldn't have been appropriate. Constance asked me to check the figures now and again after Daniel refinanced his loans to buy this building. I've been checking them weekly for the past several months."

"Since Richie bought in?"

"Exactly," Kelly nodded. "Connie was afraid Zeayen

might manipulate the accounts. Daniel didn't like the arrangement, resented the implication that he couldn't cope even ill as he was. But he agreed, to keep peace in the family."

"So? Did Richie try to cook the books?"

"I never caught him at it, and in all modesty, I'm a good accountant. Richie was a sharp young man in many ways. Too bad he didn't put his talents to better use. He could do sums in his head as quickly as I could with a calculator."

"Crack trade," Garcia said. "You get sharp when mistakes can cost you a kneecap. How was he as a manager?"

"From a financial standpoint, excellent. Business picked up after he bought in, nearly doubled in the past fiscal quarter. Daniel had no share in the increase, of course. The arrangement was that Zeayen would keep all profits above a certain figure, and pay Danny the difference if receipts fell below it."

"You say business doubled in three months? Can I see the P-and-L ledger?"

"Of course." Kelly pushed it across and Garcia scanned it quickly, riffling through the pages of the bound notebook, tracing the figures with his index finger.

"Here," he said, "first two weeks in November, there's a dip, then a steady increase afterward. What happened?"

"That was when Richie changed the entertainment. Hired a new band, the Whiteboys. From Texas, I believe."

"Texas? Long way to go for a band."

"I gather he knew them. Apparently he spent time down there."

"Probably made the trip twice a month muling coke up I-75," Garcia said. "Question, with the business doing this well, why was Richie stalling on his payments? With the kind of money he was making, he could have made them easily."

"I wouldn't know," Kelly said, "I just oversaw the books. I tried to warn Daniel about Richie, told him he was ganged up—"

"How did you know that?"

"This collar doesn't cut off circulation to my ears, sonny. I work with young people at St. Aloysius and Holy Trinity, which means I meet a fair number of bangers. Word was Richie was connected to the D Streets and movin' up. Daniel wouldn't listen. Typical for him, choosing to deal with the devil rather than accept failure and work things out with his creditors. He always took the easy way."

"Not always."

"No? How well did you know my brother, Mr. Garcia?"

"Quite well. At one time."

"Really? You were aware then, that his principal hobbies were fornication and drugs? That he was a draft evader?"

"I was aware he wasn't perfect. Isn't part of being a friend accepting people, flaws and all? He never smoked dope around me, and having an eye for available ladies isn't a capital crime yet. As for ducking out to Canada, it's kind of a cheap shot to carp about who did what when you stayed home and watched it on TV."

"It might be, if that's what I'd done," Kelly snapped. "But when Daniel skipped, I volunteered. In effect I served in his place."

"Not quite," Garcia said evenly. "Since chaplains don't kill people, Father, you weren't exactly faced with the same choices, were you? Serving your country is one thing. Killing for a cause you don't believe in is something else again."

"Still, Daniel's actions show a sorry pattern—"

"Not to me they don't," Garcia said. "Whatever failings Danny had, he stood up for me when it counted. I owe him for that. And frankly, it seems to me that a man in your business ought to be a little more charitable, remember his strengths and forget the rest."

Kelly looked away, visibly controlling his anger. "Perhaps you're right," he said tautly. "I know I'm not handling this well. Are you a Catholic, Garcia?"

"I was. A lifetime ago."

"Then maybe you can understand. I believe in mother church. She's been my life. Some days it ain't much of a life, but it's mine own. Daniel made choices. Did things that I can't forgive without . . . spittin' on everything I hold dear. A better man than I probably could. I can't. It makes all this very hard."

"I suppose it would."

"But the worst of it," Kelly said, leaning forward intensely, "is losin' the fight. I always thought in the end he'd come home. Find his faith again, make his peace with the church. And with me. But he didn't. Instead, at the end he threw away his life and his last hope of salvation. For you. And that's tough for me to accept, mister. It makes me angry, and maybe a bit jealous. To be honest, I'm havin' a helluva time just bein' civil to you. Nothin' personal, but there it is."

"That's straight enough, Father," Garcia said. "No offense taken. But Erin was right. If we're going to salvage anything from this, we'll have to work together. So. Suppose we just stick to business? Do you have the wage statements in the cost-accounting ledger?"

"Wage statements?" Kelly frowned, riffling through the folder. "Right here." He passed a logbook across to Garcia. "Richie wasn't padding it if that's what you're wondering."

"Nope," Garcia said, scanning the ledger, "I'm just looking for . . . really good workers. Like this one. Willie J. Torrance. Do you know him?"

"I believe he's the bartender, the one cleaning up now."

"Thought he might be"—Garcia nodded—"the one they call Tie-dye? Tell you what, Father, we'll need new carpeting in the office, and a new observation mirror. Since I presume you want to hang on to the checkbook, would you mind trying to get some repairmen down here ASAP. Tonight, if possible."

"Tonight?"

"Or first thing tomorrow. I've been out of the club

business for a while, but I know this much. With all the negative publicity the Underground's gotten, if it doesn't reopen by this weekend it never will. People will assume it's folded and we don't have enough advertising cash to change their minds. Also, I'd better contact the band. Do you have a number for them?"

"Constance mentioned that they called, said they'd be down to get paid and pick up their gear around seven. They're quitting."

"One crisis at a time. First, if you wouldn't mind, try to get us some carpet. And send the bartender over, please."

Kelly hesitated, eyeing Garcia as though seeing him for the first time.

"Something wrong, Father?"

"Not exactly. It's just that . . . never mind. I suppose this is why Connie hired you. I know a couple of parishioners who might install the carpeting tonight as a favor. I'll see what I can do." He slid out of the booth. Garcia quickly began scanning the P-and-L ledger.

"You wanted to see me?" the bartender said.

Garcia continued tracing figures with his fingertip. "Sit down, Mr. Torrance. I've just been looking over your work record."

"Yeah? So how'm I doin'?" Close up, he was a bit older than Garcia'd thought. Narrow face, aquiline nose, startling blue eyes beneath black brows. A dark smear of soot across the chest of his Mumford High sweatshirt.

"You're a good worker, Mr. Torrance. Hope we can keep you."

"I can use the job," Torrance said cautiously. "But call me Tie-dye, okay? I hear Mr. Torrance, I start lookin' 'round for my ole man, you know?"

"No problem, Tie. Tell you what, why don't we save each other some hassle? I know the club's wired, it's how I got in the jam I'm in. Which means a narc's working here undercover, and after checking the books, I figure it's you.

You hired on a week after Richie bought in, haven't missed a day since, always on time. Word of advice, don't be so punctual your next assignment. People in this business tend to be a little flaky."

"Man, you got me wrong, I don't—"

"Save the smoke, Tie, I've got no beef with you. You were just doing your job. But I'm wondering why you're still here."

"I don't know what you talkin' about."

"It's simple. You hired in here to keep Richie Z. under surveillance. He doesn't need watching anymore. You could've pulled the bugs out anytime during the past few days and moved on to your next gig with your cover still intact. But here you are. Which means you've got a new assignment, right? I'm guessing it's me. How am I doing?"

"Hamadi told me you were sharp," Torrance said, glancing around warily. "So now what? Am I fired?"

"Not yet. But nothing in life's free, bro. According to your time card, the night Danny and Richie bought it, you were working. Tell me about it."

"Why? So you can get your story straight?"

"No, so you can keep your job. I'm not asking about your operation, just tell me what you saw."

"Yeah, well it won't take long," Tie-dye said, chewing his lower lip. "Red was late so I was working the door, checkin' IDs and collectin' cover charge. Club was jumpin', I was hustlin' my ass off. No reason to think anything was up. Didn't see anything unusual."

"Like me, for instance," Garcia said.

"No, I didn't see you. But like I said, I was busier'n hell. Parking lot surveillance camera saw you though, so I know you were here."

"I drove through," Garcia admitted. "I didn't stop."

Torrance just looked at him, said nothing.

"Fair enough," Garcia said. "What was going on when the hit actually went down?"

"That's just it, nothing, man. I noticed Danny at the front booth for a minute, thought he was gonna work it, but then he headed back to the office. After that, I didn't see anything until the one-way mirror blew out. Couldn't see much anyway. The club lights were out."

"What do you mean they were out?"

"Well, not completely out, but dimmed way down. Risa was singin' that slow song from their album, the one she does by herself. I dim the houselights for that one. So I didn't spot you at the back door, if that's what you were wonderin'. And that's about all I can tell you. So, you gonna fire me or not?"

"No way. I want you working here. I even want the bugs to stay. Know what else I want? I want the office cleaned up, top to bottom. It's a dirty job, but a devoted worker like yourself won't mind, right?"

"Yassuh, bossman," Torrance said, sliding out of the booth and back into character. "Only doncha think maybe you oughta be keepin' on my good side? Seems to me a man in shit up to his eyeballs might need a friend."

"I had a friend once," Garcia said, turning back to the ledger, "and now I'm in shit up to my eyeballs. Just get the office clean, okay?"

TWENTY

By six thirty the cleanup was already well under way. Three waitresses came in and Erin put them to work wiping down the tables, chairs, walls, anything with soot on it, which meant nearly every surface in the room. The kid with the Walkman proved to be a steady worker, marching his vacuum cleaner methodically around, swaying to the beat of his own private drummer. Garcia spent half an hour wandering through the club, getting reacquainted. Not much had changed. There were new barstools and computerized cash registers, but otherwise things were much the same as when he'd worked here. There was something depressing in that. A helluva world when the most stable thing in your life is a rock'n'roll saloon.

The carpet men showed up just before seven, two Jamaicans complete with sunny island accents, orange coveralls, good humor, and ten rolls of carpet in the back of a battered van. Erin chose a sturdy berber pattern, but in dark blue, not red, to redo the office. Garcia left the financial arrangements to Father Kelly, and was helping Tie-dye horse Danny's battered old desk out of the office door when the stage lights flickered on and a couple of guys in scruffy denims began shifting equipment off the bandstand and onto the dance floor.

"Now what?" Garcia grunted, easing the desk against the wall.

"The Whiteboys," Tie-dye said, straightening. "Clearin' out looks like."

"Get the kid to help you finish up here," Garcia said. "Duty calls. Hey guys, wait up a minute."

The two men on the dance floor lowered a huge PA speaker to the floor and straightened. The larger one, a black with a shaved head, iron pumper's build, stepped forward to intercept Garcia. The other one, a blocky Latin with a spade goatee, shifted a bit to one side, getting the angle on him. Stone street fighters, both of them, no question. Garcia slowed midway across the dance floor, keeping his hands in plain sight.

"Somethin' you want?" the black said.

"Yeah, I'm hoping I can save you some trouble."

"No need," the Latin said. "We can handle any trouble you got."

"I don't doubt it. That's not what I meant. My name's Garcia, I'm the new manager here. Who's the leader?"

"We're a democracy," Bobby Westover said, stepping out of the shadows at the rear of the stage into the light. Tall guy, rangy, shaggy mane of shoulder-length blonde hair, wearing a faded blue Van Halen sweatshirt, jeans. "But I'm the president. What's on your mind?" He was holding a three-foot chrome-steel microphone boom casually in his left hand, not threatening, but not hiding it either.

"Well, I hope you're not set on pulling out. As you can see, everybody's working hard to get things back to normal. Could we sit down and talk about it?"

"Mister, we're a long way from home with miles to go before we sleep," Westover said. "You want to talk, go ahead on."

"Bobby?" The singer, Risa, moved up beside Westover. She was dressed in grubbies, frayed jeans and an olive drab T-shirt, her short ebon hair a tangle, eyes hard and dark as lodestone and just as magnetic. "That's him," she said warily, "the guy that was talkin' to Danny that day."

Westover glanced sharply at Risa, then back at Garcia. "Let me get this straight. You're the guy they busted? And now you're running this place? That's very heavy. Out on the road you hear stories about Motown, Murder City, all that jazz. Maybe I shoulda listened. Okay, so what's on your mind?"

"Your job. There's no need for you to pack up. The Underground will open Friday night, business as usual. If you stay on, we'll pay the face value of your contract, a full week's salary for only two nights' work. Fair enough?"

"I don't know, man," Bobby said uneasily. "This gig looks shaky to me."

"Maybe you should look a little closer," Garcia said mildly. "I've read your contract, Mr. Westover. Your deal is with the club, not the management, and the club's still here."

"I got a flash for you, jack," Westover said, stepping down from the stage, moving toward Garcia, slapping the microphone boom against his palm. "Lincoln freed the slaves a while back and if I say we're goin', we're gone. If you wanna sue us, lotsa luck. You got anythin' more direct in mind, bring it on."

"Dammit, Bobby, cool out," Risa snapped, grabbing his arm and stepping between them. "This could work out. We got nothin' to run to, we can maybe make a new deal, the record's getting airplay, why not stay?"

"If you're concerned about your safety—" Garcia began.

"Hermano," Risa interrupted, "we've played joints back home make this place look like a nunnery. We can take care of ourselves. Why don't you take a walk, let us talk this over?"

"I, ah, sure." Garcia nodded. "Whatever you say. Ma'am. I'll be in the office."

* * *

"Funny," Risa said from the doorway, "it almost looks like . . . nothin' happened."

"That's the general idea," Garcia said. He was on his knees on the new carpeting, replacing the liquor stock on the bottom shelves. "I take it you've decided to pull out?"

"Maybe. Maybe not."

"I noticed you've already moved most of your equipment offstage."

"Insurance," Risa said, stepping into the office and glancing around. "If our little *palabra* here doesn't work, we'll have the gear in the van and be down the road in twenty minutes flat."

"I see. So why are you here? Why not your . . . president?"

"You two didn't seem to hit it off, you know? I thought I might have better luck. You got a problem talking business with a woman?"

"Not at all. Some of my best friends are women."

"Somehow that doesn't surprise me. Okay, straight up, we didn't get paid for last week so you already owe us eighteen hundred. We want it up front."

"I see," Garcia said. "Anything else?"

"Yeah. Since the situation here don't look too stable, we want this week's money in advance."

"I've heard you sing," Garcia said, rising, dusting his knees. "Danny gave me your tape. You're very good."

The girl shrugged, said something in rapid Spanish.

"I'm sorry," Garcia said, "I didn't follow that. *No hablo.*"

"No? I thought you were Chicano."

"I am, but I grew up in Detroit, never learned Spanish well, just bits and pieces. What did you say?"

"Maybe it's better you don't speak," Risa said, smiling faintly. "To . . . summarize, it's nice you like the music. What about the money?"

"Suppose we say eighteen hundred now, another five hundred when your equipment's back on the stage, five more in your hand before your first set Friday night. Sound fair?"

"We'll take it."

"You sure? Shouldn't you talk it over with the others?"

"I said we'll take it. Give me the eighteen."

"Be a slight delay. Danny's brother, the father, is settling up with the carpet layers. He's got the checkbook."

"I'll wait."

"Good, I wanted to talk to you anyway."

"Yeah? Well I'm not so sure I wanna talk in here. Doesn't it bother you, being in here after what happened?"

"I'm not crazy about it," he said, straightening the last of the liquor stock. "Danny was a friend of mine, just like Richie was a friend of yours."

"What makes you think Richie was my friend?"

"Like the man said, you're a long way from home."

"In rock'n'roll you go where the work is. We were playin' gigs around Austin, Richie saw us there, made us an offer."

"And you traveled fifteen hundred miles, just like that?"

"Not just like that. You meet jive artists in the clubs all the time, gonna take us big-time, wanna talk it over in my motel room. Richie wasn't like that, he was all business. Showed us pictures of the club, the recording studio. Deal was we work the club, he puts up money for the record, promotes it, pays all our expenses up front. He seemed like a right guy. Had a lot of ideas, lot of . . . enthusiasm, you know? But all business."

"So you weren't friends?"

"You think I'd be here talkin' to you if we were? Richie was okay, at first, but playin' on the road, you learn not to get close to people. Kinda like the hit man business, no?"

He glanced up at her sharply. She had wide, dark eyes and a small scar on her forehead that disappeared into her hairline. An intriguing face. He couldn't tell if she was kidding or not. "I wouldn't know," he said. "Maybe it is."

"You don't know about bein' a hit man? Funny, the cops that grilled us half the night kinda hinted you might."

"Well, I don't. What did you mean Richie was okay at first? Did you have trouble with him?"

"Wasn't our trouble," she said brusquely. "Just didn't like the way he treated Danny is all. Danny was special."

"Yes," Garcia agreed, "that he was."

"I guess you musta thought so," she said, giving him a quzzical look. "Know somethin'? Even if you did what the cops said, maybe I've got no problem with it. Danny was due for a break. Wasn't for bad luck he wouldn't've had any at all. I better get back or the guys'll wonder if you did me in too. We'll start putting the equipment back onstage. But I expect to see our money real soon, no?"

"Yes, ma'am," he said. "A pleasure doing business with you."

"Not so bad," she nodded. "You know, this might turn out to be a real interesting gig. We start the usual time Friday night?"

"I sure as hell hope so," he said.

TWENTY-ONE

A key rattled in the office lock, followed by a gentle rap on the door. Garcia glanced up from the inventory list.

"Hi," Erin Kelly said, "am I interrupting anything?" She was wearing a black suit, shoes, and gloves and was carrying a small duffel bag. Her coppery hair seemed to glow like a banked fire against her pallid, almost translucent complexion.

"No, ma'am, I was just doing some homework. Take a pew, you look like you've had a long day," he said, offering her the chair at the desk.

"I'd . . . rather not," she said, glancing around. "At least not in here, and anyway I've been sitting all day."

"The funeral?"

"It . . . wasn't as grim as I thought it might be," she said. "My God, Loop, there must have been a thousand people there. Holy Trinity was jammed, people standing in the street outside. They had to put the service over the loudspeakers. And it was so . . . funny. You wouldn't think a funeral could be funny, but it really was. They played a video of Abbott and Costello doing 'Who's on First,' the pastor delivered the eulogy wearing a beanie with a propeller on it, a biker from the Detroit Outlaws told a story about my dad cooking up a road-killed raccoon to win a five-dollar bet. Musicians, comics—you forget over the years how many people got their start working here. But they didn't forget. They all came, Bob Seger, Mitch Ryder, Ted Nugent. Alice Cooper sent a bidet full of flowers. Quite a show."

"I'm not much on funerals," he said, "but I'm sorry I had to miss this one. You said pastor. Your uncle didn't deliver the eulogy?"

"He couldn't," she said simply. "He tried, but . . . And you were right to stay away. The press was all over the place, camera crews from Two, Four, and Seven, the *News,* the *Freep.* If you'd been there it might've turned into a feeding frenzy instead of the . . . celebration it was. God, I still can't believe he's gone. Even the way he was at the end, he was more alive than most of the people I see every day." Her voice was thinning, getting shaky.

"If you want to cry, go ahead," he said, "you're entitled. And you're among friends."

"No," she said, taking a deep breath. "I'm too mixed up to cry. How can you wish somebody back who wanted to . . . go. To die?"

"I don't think he wanted to. He just felt he was out of time."

"But what about us? He cheated us, you know. No chance to say good-bye, or I'm sorry or I love you. No . . . anything.

"Know what I missed most?" she continued, as much to herself as to him. "My turn at the all-night bull sessions you two had by the fireplace. He never sat up like that with anyone else. I thought eventually just he and I would but . . . it never happened."

"They weren't really that big a deal."

"Of course they were. I used to eavesdrop, you know."

"Eavesdrop?"

"Absolutely. I'd sneak downstairs and sit in the dark on the landing, listening. It's a rare thing when people say what they truly think to each other, but you two did, didn't you? Life and death and love and money. Quite an education for a teenybopper."

"It wasn't intended to be. It was just a way to blow off steam. We were both under a lot of pressure at the time and usually half stoned."

"That just made it more interesting. In weedo veritas. I learned more from those sessions than I ever got from the nuns at St. Cecilia's, or my legal ethics classes at Wayne, or from my parents for that matter. For instance, I learned that my everlovin' dad who wouldn't let me date until I was seventeen, was a lecher, that he'd screw anything that moved and even some who couldn't. Do I recall comments about him balling a paraplegic once? Ironic, isn't it, considering how things turned out."

Garcia said nothing.

"His playing around didn't bother me so much, but I really hated the hypocrisy. He didn't trust me with the truth. He'd tell it to you. And lie to me. Different rules for men and women."

"For men and women? Or just for fathers and daughters? You were seventeen, remember? Cut him some slack, Erin. You're not seventeen anymore."

Her glance flicked up like a whip. "You're right," she said. "I'm not. I feel more like fifty. Sorry. I'm just so damned angry. At him. At this whole mess. I forgot you have troubles of your own. You've, ah, you've done wonders with the club, I thought we'd be closed for a couple of weeks at least, but instead you've gotten it up and running almost overnight. Maybe my mother's idea wasn't so crazy after all. I'd better get ready for work, it's nearly seven."

"For work?"

"Don't look so surprised. I'd rather be here than sitting around the house with a lot of relatives I barely know wailing and moaning. Besides, since this place'll take me with it if it goes under, I intend to keep an eye on things."

"I assumed that would be your uncle's department."

"Uncle Mick? Hardly. The church isn't quite that liberated yet. I was surprised he agreed to check the books when my mother asked him to. He and my father weren't close."

"We talked about that," Garcia nodded. "It's odd they didn't get along better. They're really a lot alike."

"Flip sides of the same coin," Erin agreed, smiling wanly, "on opposite sides of everything since Vietnam, I swear. I never understood it."

"Feelings about the war ran pretty high. On both sides."

"So I gathered, over the years. It doesn't seem so important now, does it? In any case Uncle Mickey Mouse wouldn't blend with the decor down here. Most of our customers never owned a suit and use neckties to hold their jeans up. Speaking of which, I'd better change."

"Would you like me to step out?"

"No need, I'll just use the ladies' room."

"You don't usually change in here then?"

"In here? No, why?

"Because somebody did." He slid open the closet door. She frowned, lifted a pair of slacks off its hanger, held them against her hips. They were too short, barely reaching to midcalf.

"Hot stuff," she said, "very flashy. My guess would be one of Richie's girlfriends. Or maybe Risa, the girl in the band."

"Was she one of his girlfriends?"

"Possibly, he liked the ladies. A lot. It's one reason I quit working here."

"He hit on you?"

"A bit more than that. We saw each other for a while. Nothing heavy, just a few dates. He could be charming when he wanted to be."

"So what happened?"

She cocked her head, eyeing him oddly, and for the first time it truly registered how far from seventeen she was. He'd been seeing her only as Danny's little girl grown up. But she was more woman than girl now, very much a person on her own. And one he really didn't know very well.

"He turned out to be a bit too much like my father," she said at last. "I don't mind competition, but not against an army. If my father and Uncle Mick hadn't given me so many lectures about Richie I would have stopped seeing him sooner than I did."

"I see. And how did Richie take it?"

"I doubt he noticed I was gone. And to be honest, I had mixed emotions about that. He was an . . . intriguing guy. Magnetic. But apparently it was out of sight, out of mind for him. And a girl has her pride."

"Thank God for that."

"There," she said, smiling, "that's the Lupe I remember. My long-lost big brother. Or something. I'll get changed and set up in the front booth to take care of the meet, greet'n'seat. And the gate receipts."

"Maybe I should do that."

"No, if we have trouble you'd better be free to handle it. To be blunt, that's why you're here. The crowd is rougher than it used to be, and some of them were Richie's buddies, so keep an eye on things from here as much as possible," she said, indicating the replacement one-way mirror. "If I have any problems I'll flash the red light above the booth."

"I doubt you'll have to," he said. "I don't expect much business tonight."

"Want to bet lunch on it? I think we'll be packed."

"After all that's happened? No way. You've got a bet."

"You haven't been listening to the radio today, have you?" she said, hesitating in the doorway.

"No, I've been busy, why?"

"The jocks on both heavy metal stations have been playing the Whiteboys' record, making jokes about what a 'killer' band they are, how people are dying to see 'em."

"My God."

"Don't knock it. It's free advertising and Dad would've loved it. And you're going to owe me lunch."

Erin won her bet early. The club was two-thirds full before nine. She called in three extra waitresses and kept busy as a dervish herself, checking IDs, seating people. Garcia stayed in the office or the hallway just outside, watching for problems. Crowds have personalities of their own and this one was an edgy mix, working-class kids, bikers, yuppie couples, college kids from Wayne and U of D. Even the entertainment editor from the *Free Press* dropped by to check out the action.

A minimob of a half dozen gangbangers wandered in, wearing colors. Garcia thought they might be trouble, but Erin stood her ground, made them leave their gang jackets in their cars. He kept an eye on them as they moved through the crowd. There was something familiar about the leader. Tall white kid, hair in a bleached blond, braided ponytail, aquiline face. Somebody he'd busted? Maybe. Face didn't register, but the guy was definitely familiar. They ringed a table near the dance floor, eyeing it until the couples seated there decided they'd be more comfortable farther back.

The Whiteboys showed twenty minutes before showtime, and it struck Garcia how much they looked like a gang themselves: Bobby Westover wearing leather riding pants, jacket, no shirt, Lucero in a black T-shirt and jeans, and Bailey Reeves, the drummer, in a muscle shirt and running shorts, his shaved head gleaming like an oiled ball bearing. They moved through the crowd like street royalty, a smile here, a word or two, an autograph. Risa was electric, obviously enoying herself, joshing with the men, drilling the women with a five-hundred-watt smile. One of the gangbangers, a muscular blond kid, his hair done in cornrows, intercepted her in front of the dressing room and said something. She glanced toward their table, shook her head. He scowled and seized her wrist, but Reeves moved in, whispered something in the guy's ear, and he let her go. The band disappeared into their dressing room. The banger stalked back to his table.

Garcia took an envelope out of the desk, made his way warily through the crush to the dressing room door, and rapped once. It opened a crack, and he could see himself reflected in Bailey Reeves's mirrored contact lenses. Eerie.

"What's the password?" Reeves said.

"Password? How about payday?"

"Close enough," Reeves nodded, letting him in. Bobby Westover and Lucero were tuning up their instruments, Risa was touching up her makeup at the table, eyeing him in the mirror. "Sorry," Reeves rumbled, "thought you might be somebody else."

"The kid with the cornrows? A problem?"

"Nothing we can't handle," Bobby said. "You got our money?"

"Cashier's check for five hundred, as agreed," Garcia said, passing him the envelope.

"Our record's been getting a lot of airplay, good publicity for the club," Bobby said. "If you want us to play next week, we'll need a raise."

"Let's see how the weekend goes," Garcia said, "then we'll talk. I'm a reasonable guy."

"Sure you are. I'll ask Richie about that next time I see him. Now, if you don't mind? We're on in ten minutes, and we've got some talking to do. In private."

"No problem," Garcia said, "break a leg."

"Or you'll break it for us right?" Risa said blandly, arching a brow at him in the mirror. Bailey Reeves opened the door for him, and followed him out.

"Yo, Garcia? That kid with cornrows, he ain't trouble for us. Might be for you. Keep a eye on 'im, hear?"

"Why for me?" Garcia said, but Reeves was already gone.

Garcia gave the bunch at the table a closer look on his

way back to the office. Gangers for sure. Still couldn't place the leader . . . but it would come. He was sure of it.

Tie-dye, ablaze in a gold silk shirt with matching headband and wearing black shades, intercepted him at the office door. "Man, this bunch is drinkin' like the end of the world. I'm already low on Jack Daniel's and Bacardi. Gonna be a helluva night."

"Yeah," Garcia said, glancing back at the gangbangers. "One way or another."

TWENTY-TWO

The Whiteboys were late. At twenty to ten the table of gangbangers began a rhythmic clapping that quickly spread through the crowded room, a rumble of contagious impatience that could quickly turn ugly. Garcia had hurried out of the office and headed for the band's dressing room when he noticed the red strobe light flashing above the ID check booth. Damn!

Everything seemed normal as he approached. Erin was waving a yuppie couple toward seats in the rear of the club. No apparent trouble. Still the light was on. "What's up?" Garcia asked.

"The cover charge," she said, sliding a cashbox toward him. "We've already taken in about twelve hundred, too much to keep out here. Better put it in the safe."

"Hang on to it a minute, the band—" He was drowned out by a roar from the audience. Risa and the Whiteboys had stepped up onstage, and Tie-dye killed the houselights.

"What?" Erin said, "I can't hear—"

"I said I'd better put the cash in the safe," Garcia shouted.

"Good idea," she yelled back, smiling, "glad you thought of it," and for a moment the years fell away and their old, bantering relationship clicked back into place, filling an emptiness he hadn't known was there. The moment was blown away by a clap of thunder from the stage as the Whiteboys kicked off their first set with Led Zeppelin's "Black Dog," metal power chords hammering the room like an auto crusher, Risa wailing a storm warning above the din. The dance floor filled immediately, mostly the younger set, punkers mixing with retrohippies, dyed hair, shoulder-length earrings on both sexes, clad in a mix of eye-stabbing neon reds and yellows, and two-hundred-dollar tennis shoes with dragging laces. Slam-dancing couples bouncing like kangaroos, banging into each other chest first. Nope, Garcia thought, the old days weren't quite like this.

The first hour passed in a blur as he made goodie runs, taking Tie-dye more liquor, backing up Erin at the door when three college kids from U of D tried to bully past her with fake IDs. So far, so good, a typical Friday night at the Underground, action on the edge of chaos.

He was transferring some gate money into the safe when suddenly the club went very quiet. Now what? The Underground was standing room only, roughly seven hundred wall-to-wall bodies, and a sudden silence . . .

He slammed the safe closed, crossed to the one-way mirror, and scanned the room for trouble. Nothing obvious, he could barely see anything at all. The Tie-dye had dimmed the houselights and the stage had gone dark, save for one blue spotlight, on Risa Blades. She was sitting on a barstool, stage center, cradling a black acoustic guitar, stroking it quietly, crooning a wordless melody, a mother singing to her instrument child. Or her lover. "Aledita." The ballad that was getting all the airplay around town. Garcia was as transfixed as the rest of the crowd, watching her from the dark as she sang her story in Spanish, the loving tongue, no translation necessary, a message passing soul to soul.

He'd seen it a few times before, the blues singer Albert King, and Motown's rock prince, Bob Seger, but neither of them had ever held an audience any closer than Risa was doing now. Magic time, Danny called it. Crystal blue moments that made all the hassles of the club business worth it.

The moment passed. The song ended, the audience erupted with a roar of approval and then it was kick out the jams time again as the Whiteboys closed the set with Bailey Reeves's spectacular drum solo grafted onto the Stones' "Rock and a Hard Place." Hey Ma, Garcia thought ruefully, they're playing my song.

Lupe was updating the Liquor Control Commission logbook when he glimpsed Risa through the mirror, talking to the young gangbanger she'd brushed off earlier. Something in her look . . . He felt a shiver between his shoulder blades, someone stepping on his grave. He closed the ledger and hurried out into the club.

He moved warily through the crowd. Risa was apparently just batting the breeze with the bangers, five young white dudes in studded denims, typical punk regalia. They looked hyped, and ready for Freddy, but not openly hostile. Yet there was something in Risa's face. . . .

"Everything all right here?" Garcia asked.

"Who's the asshole?" the husky blond kid with cornrowed hair asked Risa. "He your dad?"

"I'm the manager, sonny, so cool out or say good night." Risa was trying to tell him something with her eyes—

"You're the one'll be sayin' night night, taco," Cornrows snapped. "But first say hello to your new boss." Cornrows jerked a thumb at the tall, narrow-faced kid Risa'd been talking to—Richie! That's why he looked familiar. The tinted hair had thrown him off, but up close he looked enough like Richie to be . . . his brother.

"This is Aziz Zeayen, Mr. Mendez," Risa said hastily, "we were talking about the record deal—"

Too late. Zeayen's eyes met Garcia's, locked, and widened with recognition and shock. "Motherfucker!" He lunged out of his chair with a roar, swinging a beer pitcher at Garcia's head, crashing headlong over the table as Risa gave him a sharp push from behind. The pitcher exploded into glass and foam and the table toppled over hard, carrying Aziz and two of his buddies down with it.

No time for finesse, grab ass and pray. Garcia leveled the ganger closest to him with a forearm smash to the temple, threw a vicious right cross at Cornrows, who was charging up from the tangle. The punch caught him on the shoulder, barely slowed him at all. Cornrows slammed into Garcia waist high, tackling him, the force of his rush carrying them into the next table, where two business suits and their dates were frantically scrambling to get out of the way. Cornrow's hands clamped around Lupe's throat like a noose, cutting off his air, going for a kill. Then he suddenly let go with a gasp as one of the business suits kicked the kid hard in the rib cage, folding him in half. Garcia hit Cornrows a brutal shot across the bridge of the nose, feeling the cartilage crumple, seeing the guy's eyes roll back as he tumbled off, stunned.

Garcia staggered to his knees, then dove for the floor as Aziz swung a chair at his head. He jabbed Zeayen a straight shot to the groin and pulled him down, the two of them entangled with the chair and each other. No room to swing, and Aziz was berserk, teeth bared, clawing at Garcia's eyes. Lupe rolled hard, desperately trying to get out from under. He jerked his head back, avoiding a kick, taking it hard in the shoulder. His left arm blazed into agony as though it had suddenly caught fire. Aziz grabbed his shirt, tearing it, groping for Garcia's throat, then collapsed, sagging down in a heap as Bailey Reeves, the Whiteboys' drummer, dropped him with a single short clip to the jaw. And that finished it. Cornrows, Aziz, and the kid Garcia'd hit first were all down and out, and Bobby Westover and Lucero had the other two backed up against the dance floor railing with chrome-steel microphone booms.

Garcia stayed on his knees a moment, head down,

holding his numbed shoulder, trying to contain the surge of pain and fighting rage, trying to keep from going over the edge as Aziz had, battling the urge to hammer the dazed punk through the floor. A close thing. Very close. He stumbled painfully to his feet, glancing around. The scuffle had gone down in under forty seconds, camouflaged by crowd noise and dancers gyrating to the din of the music system. Only the customers in the immediate area were even aware of it.

"You and you," Garcia snapped at the two gangers Lucero and Bobby had cowed, "pick up your buddies and book. If your boss thinks he owns anything, tell him to hire a lawyer. Move it!"

No argument. The two gangers helped Aziz up, Cornrows and the one Garcia'd leveled managed to stand on their own, and the lot of them stumbled off toward the entrance like walking wounded. The Whiteboys faded into the crowd, headed for their dressing room. The business suits and their dates had fled. Tie-dye sauntered up, eyeing the wreckage.

"You all finished here, boss? I got a party of five at the bar waiting for a table."

"You sonuvabitch," Garcia said. "You could've helped."

"Hey, I ain't drawin' combat pay on this gig, baby, and that's no way to talk to an em-ploy-ee neither," Tie said, righting the table, picking up dumped glasses and debris. "If I file a complaint with the N-double A.C.P. you'll find out what reeeal trouble is. And go get changed, man. Your jacket's got blood on it, shirt's torn. This is a class joint and you look like a wino recruitin' poster."

TWENTY-THREE

In the dimly lit office, Garcia eased out of his jacket and draped it across the back of the chair. His shoulder was throbbing, bone-deep pulsing ache. He stripped off his torn Underground T-shirt and checked out the wound. A deep gouge in his left shoulder, blood oozing slowly up through the bruised welt. Damn. Somebody rapped on the door. He opened it a crack.

"I got a beer shower in the hassle," Risa Blades said. "I had some clothes in the closet here, they still around?"

"Sure, come on in. I wanted to thank you for trying to cover for me, and for the help."

"Hey, we just didn't want him trashin' the place just when things are pickin' up." She stepped past him, glancing warily around the office. She was wearing a short leather skirt, knee-high boots, and a wet black T-shirt that clung to her like a second skin. She slid open the closet door. "Scary isn't it, Aziz lookin' like a white-haired, leaner, meaner version of Richie? *Fantasma.*"

"What?"

"That's right, you're the Chicano *que no habla.* Sorry. It means like a—ghost, you know? Like Aziz is Richie's ghost. Damn, these clothes smell like smoke."

"Sorry. If I'd known they were yours I'd've sent them out."

"Yeah, well at least they're dry. Turn your back, okay? And you better rub some Absolut into that ding on your arm."

"Absolute?

"What, you don't speak Russian either?"

"Oh, you mean Absolut vodka? What the hell, why not? You, ah, want me to drop the blinds—no, I guess not." Risa had already stripped off her top and tossed it on the desk. Garcia turned his back, and was pointedly busying himself popping open a bottle of vodka when the office door opened.

"Are you okay, Lupe?" Erin said. "Tie-dye said—"

"Shut the door," Risa snapped, stepping into her pants. "You ever hear of knockin', lady?"

"I'm—what the hell's going on here?" Erin said, glancing at Risa, then Garcia.

"Damage control," he said, wincing as he dabbed his wounded shoulder with vodka. "We had trouble."

"You seem to be on the road to recovery," Erin said acidly. "And I don't want anyone in this office who doesn't belong here, understand? You're supposed to be managing the club, not—" She stalked out, slamming the door after her.

"Sorry about that," Risa shrugged, smoothing her toreador pants over her hips. "That was Danny's daughter right?"

"That was Erin, yes."

"Thought so. She was workin' here when we first got here. She was Richie's main squeeze then, or thought she was. When she found out he was spreadin it around they had a major hassle about it and she quit. Danny used to talk about her a lot, real proud of her, you know? Hope I didn't mess up your love life."

"Nothing to mess up. We're just helping each other out."

"Right, that's why she put up the club for your bail."

"Wrong again," Garcia said, slipping into his shirt, buttoning it up. "Her mother put up the bail."

"Really?" she said, arching an eyebrow. "I'm starting to wonder what I'm missing."

"It's really not like that. We were all pretty close at one time, like family."

"So maybe the ladies are into incest. Don't be so defensive, it never hurts to get along with the people you work for."

"No, it doesn't," Garcia said. "How well did you get along with management before?"

"Great," she answered, smiling. "We got along good, had some laughs. Even in the shape he was in, Danny could always laugh."

"I didn't mean Danny. Richie was the one who actually hired your group, wasn't he? And put up the money for the record deal?"

"I told you that was strictly business."

"Who actually made the deal. You or Bobby?"

She hesitated a moment, then shrugged. "Bobby handles the business end of things. He may not look like the executive type, but there's a lotta hard-nosed Texas oil patch in Bobby."

"And yet here we are."

"We're here because I got beer on my outfit," she said coldly, "and because Bobby knows I can take care of myself. I gotta go, the guys are already onstage and I sing the first song this set."

"Stay just a minute, please. There are a couple of things I'd like to ask about. They can do another song."

"Another song? Even if they wanted to they couldn't, man. Our sets are sequenced."

"Sequenced?"

"You know, sequencers? Synths? Like computers?"

Garcia shook his head. "I've been out of the business awhile. What's a sequencer?"

"Maybe I'll explain it to you sometime, but right now I gotta go. I'll catch you later, Garcia."

"I look forward to it."

"Yeah," she said, eyeing him in frank appraisal, "I think I do too."

TWENTY-FOUR

The rest of the evening blurred past like a VCR on fast forward—supplying Tie-dye, backing up Erin at the door, hustling out customers who'd had their limit. And waiting.

Each time the Whiteboys took a break, Garcia was in the office, waiting for Risa. She didn't come. The group spent their breaks at a table near the stage, apparently doing an interview with the *Free Press* music critic. Occasionally Risa would glance toward the office from the stage, and their eyes seemed to meet above the crowd, but it was an illusion. From the stage she could only see her reflection in the mirror.

The Whiteboys got a standing ovation at the end of their show and had to do two encores before the audience let them go. Garcia spent a hectic last half hour, cooling a push-and-shove, easing the crowd out the door.

By 2:20 the place was empty, glasses cleared away and washed, chairs upended on the tables, the stage dark and deserted. Except for the litter on the floor and the smoke hanging in the air, the night might never have happened.

"Nearly three grand at the gate," Erin said, dropping the cashbox off at the office. "Not bad for a place going broke. How did we do overall?"

"I don't know yet," Garcia said, "I'll figure it out after I finish up the Liquor Control Commission logs."

"You mean tonight? Why not leave them till morning?"

"Can't risk it. The prosecutor's office may ask the LCC to spot-check us to try to get me out of here. I'm making double sure everything's in perfect order before I leave tonight."

"Do you want any help?"

"No, but thank the girls for me, they did a good job."

"Yes, they did. . . . Look, Lupe, I think I owe you an apology."

"For what?

"For overreacting when I found what's her name in here, half dressed. It was none of my business. I was just . . . surprised."

"Why don't we talk about it over lunch?"

"Lunch?"

"Our bet about the crowd, remember?"

"God, you're right. It seems like a million years ago."

"Go home, Erin, you've had one helluva day."

"Yes," she said, "so I have. I'll tell Tie-dye to check the doors before he goes."

"Thanks. For everything."

"Yeah," she said, gathering herself, giving him a last, unreadable look, "right."

He was sitting at Danny's old desk finishing up the books when he noticed a flare of light in the darkness. Someone had lit a cigarette near the stage. But everyone had cleared out an hour ago. He killed the office lights, eased through the doorway to the house lighting control panel in the hall outside, and switched on the whites.

He'd half expected to see Risa, but it wasn't. Two men, Latins from the look of them. One was tall, looked like a Spanish grandee, neatly trimmed forked goatee, sharkskin suit, coolly smoking a thin cigar. The other man was shorter, chunky but solid, wearing a rumpled, off-the-rack Kmart sport coat. Not a Latin, an Indian. Tony LaRose.

"Gentlemen, you're gonna have to hit the door," Garcia said, walking over to their table. "The club's closed."

"Yeah, we noticed," LaRose said. "Pull up a chair, Garcia, we need to talk."

"You won't be staying that long. How did you get in here?"

"My name's LaRose. That mean anything to you?"

"I've seen the name." Garcia nodded. "On a rap sheet. You two were here earlier, weren't you? When the fight broke out, you booted a guy off me."

"No charge. Like I said, we need to talk."

"At three in the morning? About what?"

"For openers, about jail. See, my friend Cottler here's the guy who talked Danny Kelly's widow into bailin' you out. And if we don't hear something we like in the next few minutes, he may change her mind back again."

"Why?"

"Why what?"

"Why any of it?" Garcia said, easing down on a seat opposite LaRose. "Why did you get me out of jail, for instance?"

"Simple. I wanted to talk to you. I don't like jails. So here you are."

"Even if I buy that, and I don't, same question. Why?"

"Because Richie Zee had a . . . arrangement with certain people. We put up money to set him up in business. A lotta money. So when you took him out, you fucked us up, *hombre.* You waxed one of our people, messed in our deal, and cost us some serious cash."

"If you mean the money Richie was supposed to buy this place with, all he ever made was the down payment, thirty grand. He was weaseling out of the rest. That's why Danny called me. If Richie owed you thirty, file a claim against his estate."

"The thirty K was Richie's money. It's what he brought to the deal, that and a lotta bullshit. He was a helluva salesman, Richie, big ideas. He sold the people I work for, they invested in him, and since you fucked up our investment, you're stuck with the tab."

"What kind of investment? Blow? Couple bales of weed?"

"C'mon, man, show some respect. I know this place is wired. All I'm sayin' is, you're on the books for our investment with Richie. You're gonna have to make it right."

"How much?"

"I'm not exactly sure, since we don't know what shape it's in now. But if you come across a hundred large worth of anything, you know who it belongs to. And you'd better come across it soon. Richie was behind in his payments, so you're already late."

"And if I don't see it that way?"

"We seen you in action tonight," LaRose shrugged. "You looked pretty good, prob'ly think you're even better. Hard guy, stone *vato.* And maybe with this jam you're in, you think you got nothin' to lose. But you're wrong. There are worse things than bein' dead, like bein' lamed up, and doin' double life in the joint. You do right by us or you'll be in the house of many doors till you choke to death on some spook's dick."

"Funny, you don't strike me as a guy with a lot of leverage with judges, LaRose." He glanced at Cottler. The taller man was toying with a book of matches on the tabletop, ignoring them.

"We got leverage, Garcia. Red. The guy you had trouble with the day you waxed Richie? You busted Red's hand for him, no? People saw you. And if there's one thing I know about, it's the rules of evidence. Say his body turns up, outside your apartment? You'll be back in the slam five minutes later and you'll never see sunshine again, man, ever. You know it's true."

"Maybe, maybe not. Why should I believe you?"

"Hey, *cabrón,*" Cottler said suddenly, "do you smoke?"

"Smoke?" Garcia said. "No." And suddenly he was looking down the muzzle of a 9-mm auto. Cottler pulled the piece so quickly Garcia barely saw the move. He eased the hammer back with an audible click and pressed the muzzle against Garcia's cheek, just below his left eye. Held it there, waiting for a reaction.

"You're wrong," Cottler said at last. "Everybody smokes. Everybody." He flipped the book of matches open with his thumb, folded one down, and flicked it alight, then held the book just below Garcia's chin.

Lupe felt the bite of the flame, but didn't move. Cottler's eyes were aglitter with madness. One twitch and spade-beard would splatter his brains all over the floor. The match burned slowly down, then suddenly ignited the others, flames searing Garcia's chin before Cottler dropped the book.

Cottler blew gently on his fingertips, cooling them. "See? You smoke, man. You'll even cook like Richie and your buddy did if you get too close to a fire. And you're too close right now, *comprende?* Don't let fat boy here give you the wrong idea. We're serious people. You do like you're told. Get the money up, prick." He eased the hammer of the Browning down, sliding the piece under his jacket in a single fluid motion. He ground out his cigar on the tabletop, rose, and sauntered off toward the door.

LaRose shrugged. "You see how it is, man. You got a week to turn up our stash. After that we write this thing off as a bad deal, you with it, payback for fuckin' in our business. I'll be in touch."

"Hey, Tony," Garcia said quietly, "it doesn't matter how hard your psycho buddy pushes. I didn't kill Richie. I don't know about his stash."

"No?" LaRose said, staring down at him, showing a faint, tiger's smile. "Too bad. For you. Tell you what, Garcia,

I'll toss you a freebie. The man I work for's got no particular hard-on about you greasin' Richie. He was in deep shit with us anyway. You find our stuff, maybe we can work somethin' out, get you off the hook for Richie. You don't and you're gonna wish you could swap places with him." He strolled over to the front door, pushed the crash bar. It didn't move. "Hey, wanna let us out?"

"You don't have a key? How did you get in here anyway?"

"Just waited in the john till everybody split. Security here sucks, you know that?"

TWENTY-FIVE

It was nearly four when Lupe updated the last of the logs and closed the office. Vaseline from the first aid kit eased the sting of the burn on his jaw, but the throbbing was a constant reminder. A danger signal. He did a final tour of the dimly lit main room, checking the emergency exits and the freight elevator, then let himself out the front door, locking it behind him.

He paused in the shadows at the top of the stairwell, scanning the parking lot. There were a half dozen cars parked in front of the club, including his own. Nothing unusual in that, there were always a few cars that wouldn't start, or whose owners scored a newest truest love or got too trashed to drive. He watched the lot for a good ten minutes, looking for movement, a cigarette glow, steamy windows, anything. Nothing. It looked as dark and empty as he felt. He raised his collar against the night wind and strode briskly across the lot to his Firebird. And heard an engine rumble to life.

A car gunned out of the shadows at the far end of the building, a black Dodge Charger, blackout glass, jacked rear end, howling toward him full bore, motor screaming, pedal to the metal. He jerked his car door open, leaped in behind the wheel, slammed the door, fumbling his key into the ignition. Too late. No time. The Charger was coming too fast, almost on him, smoked windows rolling down—

He scrambled across the seat and out the passenger door, dropped to the icy pavement on his belly, and squirmed under his car just as the Charger shrieked to a halt alongside his Firebird and opened up with a shattering broadside of gunfire. Three weapons, maybe four. Pinned beneath his car, barely able to breathe, Garcia tried to focus on the voices of the guns—shotgun, a couple of handguns, some kind of a full automatic machine pistol, 9-mm, Uzi or a Mac 11. Nothing that could shoot completely through a car body, maybe. But when they got out to check . . .

He thrust himself a few inches farther under the car, then a few more, wriggling beneath it toward the driver's side, feeling the weight of two tons of icy metal grinding into his shoulders. He could barely squeeze below the dual exhaust pipes, chill steel forcing him down, rasping his face against the icy concrete.

He was only inches from the edge of the 'bird's rocker panels now, the Charger's front tires clearly visible a foot or two away, parallel to the Firebird's. The crazy bastards were still firing, the roar and flash of gunfire was blinding, deafening, empty shell casings rattling down on the pavement beside him. Seconds, he only had a few seconds left, while the shooters were still flash blind. Do it, dammit! Now!

He squirmed out into the open between the two cars, belly-crawling the scant yard or so, cringing, expecting the hammer of lead against his flesh at any second, and then he was under the Charger, slithering back between the jacked rear wheels and out the far side, scrabbling crablike on his knees, then shambling into a crazy-legged sprint across the slippery concrete toward the alley between the Underground and the Radio Shack—

He almost made it. The dark maw of the alley was only a few yards away when the firing stopped, then somebody shouted and fired off a couple of hasty rounds that spanged off the bricks near his head. Two steps into the alley he stumbled over a garbage can in the dark and pitched headlong, skidding on his chest in the icy grime. And probably saved his life as two rounds of double-ought buckshot scythed the walls above him chest high, splintering some empty crates stacked farther down. Behind him the Charger's tires screamed as the driver cut a doughnut in the parking lot and howled toward the alley mouth.

Dead meat. No exit. The alley was a cul-de-sac, deadending at the freight elevator loading dock, a steel door barred from the inside, no entry. He was trapped like—

Fire escape. A single metal stairway threading up the side of the building. He scrambled to his feet, sprinted for the ladder, jumped—and missed the bottom rung by a foot, falling back to the pavement, wind knocked out, his left elbow a white blaze of pain. No way he could jump it, footing too slippery. Desperately he grabbed an empty crate, jammed it against the wall, clambered up on it, and leaped again, banging into the cold iron ladder in the dark as the Charger thundered into the alley, pinning him in its headlights momentarily, then fishtailing past beneath him, trashing the crate to kindling, bumper grinding sparks off the bricks. Garcia pulled himself up to the landing, then clambered up a flight of steel steps midway between floors as the Charger's doors banged open, spilling the gunmen out in the alley below.

Aziz Zeayen was first, fumbling shells into the loading gate of a shotgun, eyes wild, platinum hair a tangle, trench coat whipping in the wind. The kid with cornrows had an Uzi machine pistol, holding it waist high like a movie Dillinger, blazing away up into the darkness above, bullets chewing into the bricks a few feet beyond Garcia's perch. The car had skidded to a halt too far into the alley. Garcia was out of the light beams and they were still flashblind from the headlights and gunfire. But as soon as the driver realized it and backed up—

Lupe clambered up into the shadows on the next level of the fire escape. The last level. The damn thing didn't lead to the roof, it ended at the third floor windows of the Chinese restaurant. Armored glass, steel grilled. He kicked frantically at the window, cracking it, then smashing it in. A burglar alarm began to blare like a warship at battle stations, but the steel mesh inside held, locking him out. Couldn't break through. Damn it!

He scanned the narrow balcony for something, anything, to punch through the grillwork. But there was only a snow-crusted aluminum lawn chair, a long, narrow flower box wired to the railing, a half dozen clay flowerpots on a shelf below it—nothing. Sweet Jesus, he was jammed up here, nailed to the cross.

He snatched up the lawn chair and hurled it over the railing, filling the alley with a hazy cloud of powdery snow as it clattered down. The firing stopped as Aziz and his buddy cringed at the racket. Garcia started grabbing flowerpots and raining them down, not aiming at anything, just trying to buy a few seconds—and got lucky. One of them smashed through the Charger's rear windshield, exploding it into diamond chips, another shattered at Cornrow's feet, close enough to startle him and make him jump back. But only for a moment, and Garcia was out of things to throw. He clawed at the flower box, desperately trying to wrench it off the railing, when a distant siren scream began to overpower the whoop of the burglar alarm.

Aziz and Cornrows cut loose with one last fusillade from below, but they still weren't sure where he was, and the rounds hammered wildly off the bricks several yards beyond the fire escape, whining up into the night sky. And then they were all scrambling as the Charger began backing out of the alley, banging off the walls, the driver trying to control it in the slush. He spun it out of the alley mouth, mashed the pedal, and they were gone. A few seconds later a blue-and-white prowl car roared past in hot pursuit.

Garcia gave up on the flower box and slumped to his knees beside the shattered window, chest heaving, arctic air searing his throat. He tried to slow his breathing to collect himself. Too much. It all happened too fast. Couldn't think. And the damned burglar alarm blare didn't help—

The alarm. Unless he wanted to spend what was left of the night answering questions or getting booked for vandalism . . . Time to go.

He rose slowly to his feet, took a deep breath, climbed unsteadily down the fire escape to the lowest level, and dropped the last four feet to the bricks. He hesitated at the alley mouth, checking over the lot. Silent and empty as the last time. No sign anything had happened. Except for his car.

Son of a bitch.

Garcia walked somberly to his Firebird, circling it like the bier of a friend. The windows were jagged patches of shattered glass, the driver's side door, hood, and rear deck were bullet dimpled, punched through like a doily. The 'bird was atilt, its rocker panels almost touching the pavement, resting on flattened tires. Garcia swallowed, remembering how tightly he'd been jammed beneath the car. If the tires had blown while he was still under it . . .

A siren approaching in the distance snapped him out of it. He absently patted the car's wounded flank, saying a last good-bye, then raised his collar against the wind and trotted off in search of a gypsy cab.

TWENTY-SIX

The Haitian cabby didn't seem to notice the grunge smears on Garcia's face and coat. But he drove with one hand inside his jacket all the way to Seven Oaks. On a gun butt? Or juju beads? Garcia was too whipped to care. Battered, body and spirit, he barely had enough energy to climb out of the cab.

The elevator door shushed open at his floor, but he didn't step out. Risa Blades was sitting on the carpeted hallway floor outside his apartment. She was wearing a flower-embroidered black denim duster, faded jeans, and western boots; her hair was a dark tousle against the door-jamb. Her eyes were closed. They blinked open at the sound of the elevator.

"Hi," she said, uncrossing her legs, getting effortlessly to her feet. "Nice you could drop by."

"What are you doing here?"

"Waiting for you. I came over to see if you wanted to go out for breakfast, maybe talk some business. Only unless you're a real bad housekeeper, I think somebody trashed your place."

"What?" He strode past her. His apartment door was ajar, the lock jimmied professionally, barely a mark on it. His living room looked like a tornado had touched down in it, everything piled in the center, furniture slashed, carpet torn up, light fixtures dangling like entrails from the wall. He stepped carefully through the debris to the bedroom, the bathroom. Both gutted. Risa stood calmly in the doorway, watching.

"How did you know where I lived?" Garcia asked, turning abruptly to face her.

"Tie told me."

"I see. And how did you get up here?"

"I just waited till somebody came, went in with them. I thought I'd knock on your door quiet, if you don't answer, I split. But when I saw how it looked, I figured I'd better wait in case you asked around, found out I was here. Wouldn't want you to get the wrong idea. I'm sorry about your place. Looks like it was nice. Before."

"I liked it," he sighed. "Let me get this straight. At four in the morning, you just dropped by?"

"Hey, I'm night people, Garcia. I'm always wired after a show, usually stay up till five or six. Sometimes I'd go over to Danny's, make him some breakfast and talk. He said you used to do the same thing so I thought you might be up. You gonna call the cops?"

"No, not tonight."

"Well look, you can't stay here, man. If you want, I've got a couch you can crash on."

"What about Bobby? Won't he mind?"

"Not likely, since he's prob'ly shacked up with some honey he picked up at the club anyway. We don't live together, Bobby and me, haven't for a while. He's a great guy, but the only time we really get along is when we sing. Hey, you mind if we talk on the way? This place is depressing, you know?"

The cab wheeled to the curb in a deserted block of four-story brick buildings in East Pointe, lofts built in the boom years when Hank the First was turning out a Model T

Ford a minute. The only business left was a tiny mom-and-pop deli, its name written in English and Arabic.

Garcia paid the cabbie and followed Risa up two flights of swaybacked steps lit by a single forty-watt bulb at each landing. On the top floor, Risa plugged her key into the latch of a gunmetal gray door, and Garcia stepped from a squalid corridor into wonderland.

The room was billowed and draped like a harem tent lifted from the Arabian Nights. Swirls of red and orange parachute silk spun down from the center of the ceiling to the walls, then flowed to the floor like taffy twists. A couple of futon mattress chairs, a Sony boombox, a few Turkish rugs on the gleaming hardwood floor, and a minirefrigerator in one corner were the only furnishings in the room. She'd totally transformed an empty studio flat with soap, elbow grease, and accessories that would probably pack into a single suitcase with room left over for twelve beers.

"Nice," he said, glancing around. "Very . . . imaginative. I like it."

"On the road, Holiday Inns get old," she said simply, "any place of your own is better. If you want a drink, I got a couple Heinekens and some orange juice, but I'm afraid that's it."

"Thanks anyway. It's either too late in the day or too early. Look, I really appreciate your putting me up."

"Mi casa, su casa, such as it is," she said with a grin, hanging her coat on a hook by the door. "It's the least I can do for a Mexicano a long way from home."

"I'm not a long way from home," he corrected, "I am home." He eased down on a futon chair. It felt surprisingly friendly.

She poured herself a glass of orange juice and sat cross-legged on the floor on a rug facing him. "You always lived in Detroit?"

"Not always. My uncle had a farm up north, near Thunder Bay. I spent summers up there. I bounced around the world in the army but I missed Motown. The music and the soot and the snow."

"You picked the right town for snow. Ever visit Mexico at all?"

"Sure. Ever see an old Marlon Brando flick, *One-Eyed Jacks?* Or *Bandido* with Robert Mitchum?"

"Who?"

"Robert—before your time I guess. Anyway, it's set in Mexico, and when I was a kid I used to see those movies and pretend I was there."

"And you wanted to be a bandido when you grew up? Or a cop?"

"In those old movies it wasn't always clear which was which."

"Not so different from now, right?"

"No," he said, "not so different. You mentioned wanting to talk business?"

"Why? You don't like talking about yourself?"

"It's old news to me. I'd rather hear your story."

"It would take longer than we've got." She smiled. "Thing is, it's like I already know you in a way. Danny tells me stories about you, then you show up and . . . boom!"

"And is that good or bad?"

"I'm not sure," she said honestly. "Maybe it turned out good for Danny. To go out in a blaze of glory. Better than dyin' wired up to machines in a hospital. But Richie? That's more complicated. I liked him at first, but lately he was a real slime, roughin' Danny up, pushin' people, includin' me. But from a biz standpoint, I don't know. See, our deal with him wasn't just to play the club. He put up the money to record us at the old Motown studio. He was supposed to get us local airplay, build our rep, then go national."

"And now?"

"That's the funny part," she said, nibbling her lower lip. "Maybe you did us a favor. Richie wasn't keepin' his end of the deal anyway. It was like he had somethin' more important goin'. Even talked about sellin' our contract to a major label."

"Was that bad?"

"Might've been good. A guy from RCA was supposed to check us out this week. When the trouble came down with Richie and Danny, we figured it's over for us up here, we better head south. But now things look different. You handle the club okay, business is even better than before. And since our record's gettin' heavy airplay now, maybe we still got a shot at breakin' big up here. I know you and Bobby didn't hit it off, but unless you're already figurin' on makin' changes, we'd like to stay on. What do you think?"

"I think it's only fair to tell you it may not be safe for you to stay. There was more trouble at the club after hours, and it may not be over. Real trouble, the kind where people get hurt."

"We've seen trouble," she said evenly, "the real thing. We've worked too hard to back off now. We want to stay. How about it?"

"Fine, the best news I've had all day." He blinked hard, trying to focus on her.

"You're half asleep," she said, "maybe two-thirds. You're sittin' on your bed, just unfold the futon, wrap yourself up in a rug, and sweet dreams. Sorry the accommodations are so crude but I don't do a lotta company."

"It'll be fine," Garcia said. "The shape I'm in I could sleep on a railroad track."

"Bathroom's down the hall. My, ah, bedroom door hasn't got a lock, but don't sleepwalk, okay?" She rose effortlessly, graceful as a dancer, and stood looking down at him, a magnetic hawk of a woman. "I'll see you in the morning. Not before. *Comprendé usted, hombre?*"

"I look forward to it," he said.

Sometime during the night he heard her softly strumming her guitar, singing, her voice clear and delicate as crystal, so different from the hardcase image she presented onstage. He lay there in the warm dark, nestled in the futon beneath the billowed silk in a room that smelled faintly of sandalwood. Dozing, comfortable, content for the first time in months. He wondered if the song was an invitation, a subtle siren call. The thought brought him a bit more awake. Her voice faded and he realized he'd been dreaming.

He tried to doze again, chasing the dream, but it was gone. Instead, he was back in the fight, wrestling with Aziz Zeayen and his goons, smelling the rank heat of Cornrow's breath as he clawed at his throat. Cornrows was strangling him, and he was helpless, dying, when suddenly Robert Mitchum kicked the kid off him. And snapped Lupe awake.

He sat up, panting, swallowing past the bruises on his throat as though they'd happened moments before. He checked his watch: 6:40. Dawn soon. And something else. Some wisp was lingering from the dream, something about the song or the fight, something that mattered. Robert Mitchum . . . Whatever it was, he was too tired to focus. . . .

He awoke from a blackness so deep it took several minutes to climb back to reality. The billowing Arabian Nights decor didn't help. Risa's. He was at Risa's, sleeping on a futon. Alone.

He'd half hoped she might come to him in what was left of the night. She hadn't. And maybe it was better she hadn't. He felt like he'd been bungee jumping off the Renaissance Center with a loose noose. A half dozen complaints were phoning in from different time zones—bruised knees, a midriff stiff as a railroad tie. Too much noise, smoke, too little sleep. He checked his watch. After nine. He thought about nodding out, dreaming away the morning. The idea seemed even sweeter as he eased his pants on over his aching knees and padded to the refrigerator.

The tiny box was set to one degree above freezing and

the orange juice was so cold and tart it took his breath. He sipped slowly—and saw one punch. He blinked hard, trying to hold the image. A fist, a black fist, in the background. Bailey Reeves, the drummer, had nailed Aziz Zeayen with a punch that barely traveled six inches. And put the guy's lights completely out. A professional punch, so short and quick Aziz never saw it coming. A punch that could fracture a brick wall. Or a larynx. Richie promised us a record deal, Risa said, but then he lost interest. . . . And how would a guy like Reeves react to that?

"Good morning," Risa said sleepily, blinking from her bedroom doorway. She was barefoot, wearing a floor-length unbleached muslin shift with a chain of daisies embroidered at her throat. He tried not to gawk, but couldn't help it. She looked like a different person. Minus her stage makeup and high heels, she seemed smaller, scrubbed and slender, like her own much younger sister. And even more attractive. He sipped the orange juice slowly, letting it soothe his bruised throat.

"Hi," he managed at last. "Sorry, I didn't mean to wake you."

"You didn't," she said, smiling wanly, "I'm still asleep. There's a chocolate doughnut and instant coffee in the cupboard."

"The orange juice'll do fine. Thanks for letting me stay the night."

"You say that like you're leaving."

"I have to get my own place straightened up, take care of some business. Your drummer, Reeves, is that his name? Where would I find him?"

"Bailey? I'm not sure. He met a chick a couple weeks ago, I think he's staying with her now. Why?"

"He helped me out last night in the scuffle, I'd like to thank him."

"Well, between ten and noon you can catch him at the gym. He works out every day."

"Which gym?"

"I don't know"—she frowned—"it's got a funny name, Crank's or something. It's downtown."

"Kronk's?"

"That's it," she nodded.

"I take it he used to box?"

"Yeah, I guess he was pretty good. How did you know?"

"Kronk's is for fighters only. Maybe I'll stop by."

"I'd offer to help shovel out your place, but I'm not quite up to it yet. Bring some Chinese when you come back, we'll do lunch."

"I—don't think you should count on that. I'm not sure how long all this will take."

She glanced up at him, a bit more awake. "Sure," she said, "I understand. Look, it's still the middle of the night to me. I'm goin' back to bed. Lock up when you go."

"Okay, but let me say thanks—"

"Forget it, you're welcome—"

"—and that talking with you last night was the nicest thing that's happened to me in a long time. Thanks for that too."

She eyed him a moment, a wary combination of vulnerable kitten and feral cat. "That's not bad," she said at last, showing a narrow smile. "If it's just smoke, don't tell me. I'd rather not know. But the bottom line's the same. You're goin' out and I'm goin' back to bed. I'll see you around, Garcia." She closed the door with no lock, very firmly indeed.

God. It was worse than he'd thought. By the light of day his apartment looked as if a dumpster had been hit by a train in the middle of his living room. Every record in his collection snapped in two. His grandfather's guitar smashed to kindling. Might be better off just tossing a match—

A muted gurgle sounded from somewhere in the trash pile heaped in the center of the floor. Booby trap? He warily nudged a slashed sofa cushion aside with the toe of his shoe. The sound came again, clearer this time. He knelt, groped in the debris, and came up with his portable telephone, cracked, but obviously still serviceable.

"Garcia."

"Lupe? Is that you? I can barely hear you."

"I'm having a little trouble with my phone, Erin. What's up?"

"What's up? My God, Lupe, what happened? Lieutenant Fielder called me at five this morning trying to locate you. He said your car had been shot to pieces, the Jade Mountain broken into—are you all right?"

"More or less. There was a hassle in the club parking lot last night. What did Fielder say exactly?"

"For openers, he said that if you didn't contact him by

noon he'd have the prosecutor move to revoke your bail."

"Then I guess I'd better talk to him. Look, I'm sorry he woke you up—"

"Dammit, Garcia, don't be obtuse, I don't care about that. What happened?"

"Somebody took a shot at me in the parking lot. Richie's old street gang, I think. His brother's running things now."

"Fielder said the local police have them in custody on half a dozen charges. I don't understand. If you know who shot at you, why didn't you call the police?"

"I didn't want to spend the night in a police station."

"Fielder also said your apartment had been ransacked."

"Yeah. All in all, not a night I want to relive during my golden years. I'm pretty sure my apartment was worked over by a guy named LaRose, Tony LaRose. Name mean anything to you?"

"LaRose? Not offhand, why?"

"Mr. LaRose says the people he works for put up the money Richie invested in the club and then some. They want it back."

"Do you think this—LaRose may have killed Richie?"

"He's capable of it all right, and he's got a friend named Cottler who'd do it on a bet. Stone pros, both of 'em. But that's the trouble. They wouldn't have done Richie without getting their money first."

"How much money are we talking about?"

"A hundred thousand. And it may not be cash. He kept referring to it as assets."

"A hundred? Are you serious?"

"Dead serious. LaRose'd never make it as a comic."

"But if Richie had that kind of money, why was he defaulting on his payments for the Underground?"

"Maybe he blew it somehow, though considering where he got it that would have been terminally stupid and people keep telling me what a bright guy Richie was. I take it you haven't seen an extra hundred large laying around?"

"Of course not."

"Me either. How about your Uncle Mick? Since he was overseeing the books, he's the guy to ask, problem being that we aren't exactly saddle pals, your uncle and me."

"A situation that isn't likely to improve, considering the Chiangs called him first thing this morning screaming about a burglary. He's over there now cooling them off and having a new window installed."

"Good for him. Look, if you're not busy this morning, I, ah, don't suppose you could give me a lift to the Club? My car's running a little rough. And you do owe me a ride or two, right?"

"I suppose I do at that. What the hell, it's too late to go back to bed anyway. Will an hour be all right?"

"Fine. It'll give me a chance to make a dent in this place."

"And, Loop, call Fielder. Now."

"Right. That too."

"You're a bit subdued," Garcia said, "something on your mind?"

"A number of things," Erin said, concentrating on the road. They were in her white BMW, threading through traffic on the Chrysler Freeway. Even after the long night, she looked crisply impeccable, dark power suit, minimal makeup, auburn hair in perfect order. Turn around and they're sixteen, turn around and they're grown. . . . "For openers, what did you do to your chin?" she asked.

"I singed it. Shaving. I definitely need a new razor."

"I should think you'd be used to close shaves by now. What did Fielder want?" she asked.

"That I'm in a lot of trouble, which isn't exactly news. The prowlie that ran down the D Streets last night only found one weapon in the car, they apparently dumped the others, but with the gun, reckless driving, failure to stop, et cetera, they'll be on ice for a while. Tell me about the Chiangs."

"The Chiangs? A Chinese family, a clan really, lots of uncles and cousins. Must be twenty of them working in the restaurant. The grandmother, Nana, runs things. They had a small place in Greektown and were barely scraping by until Uncle Mick convinced them to lease the building over the Underground. They've done very well there. When Dad got sick Nana offered to buy the building, for roughly a quarter of what it's worth."

"Did they get along with your father?"

"Hardly. Nana complains constantly, but Uncle Mick's been taking most of the heat. As Dad's health failed my uncle gradually assumed the duties of landlord, complaint department, you name it. My mother could have handled it, it's her building after all, but she distanced herself from my father early on, like cancer was contagious."

"Have the Chiangs ever had trouble with the police?"

"Not that I'm aware of, why?"

"Because an alarm went off last night when I kicked in one of their windows, but Fielder said they refused to file a complaint."

"Sometimes minority groups are reluctant to get involved with the police."

"So they are. And I still think something's bothering you."

"It's—nothing really. When Fielder called this morning, he said your apartment had been ransacked and you were missing. I said I had no idea where you were, but I'm fairly sure I did know. You spent the night with her, didn't you? The girl from the band?"

Garcia glanced at her. She kept her eyes on the road, and didn't seem particularly interested in his answer. "I crashed on her couch," he said, at last. "Everybody's got to be someplace. Why?"

"Just an old habit," she sighed. "I used to try to keep track of my father's girlfriends. Not names, or types, just numbers. I quit around sixty or seventy I think. Too depressing. No wonder you two were such great buddies."

"We were friends for a lot of reasons, but that wasn't one of them. Funny, I always thought your dad handled things fairly well for a guy with that . . . hobby. Always discreet, nobody seemed to get hurt. I guess that wasn't quite true, was it?"

"It wasn't even close," she said grimly. "Ask my older brother sometime. But don't be surprised if he doesn't answer. He can remember his name, and mine, but that's about all."

"Older brother? I thought he was younger?"

"No, he's three years older. And technically he's only my stepbrother, but he's still family and blood's thicker than water."

"Not always," he said.

The decor of the Jade Mountain was a study in scarlet and gold, deep red carpeting, red-and-gold flocked wallpaper in a dragon design, gold filigreed oriental lanterns hanging from redwood beams. The restaurant wasn't open yet but the room was abustle. A small army of waiters, waitresses, busboys, all oriental, uniformed in black slacks and white shirts, were arranging tables, dusting, putting out silverware, each setting complete with chopsticks sealed in cellophane. The air was rich and mysterious as a Shanghai marketplace, whispers of ginger and coriander mingling with a dozen subtler spices.

Nana Chiang was seated at a large table at the rear of the main room. But for the snowy hair neatly coiled in a prim bun at the nape of her neck, Garcia wouldn't have had a hint of her age. Forty-five? Seventy-five? Her face was lightly powdered, but almost unlined, her black silk cheongsam looked like it had been stitched on in one piece. A small, square-faced oriental, the dark brush of his hair cropped GI short, was seated at her right, apparently translating an ongoing stream of complaints for Father Kelly who was seated across from her in rumpled shirtsleeves, looking harassed, wispy hair askew. A pudgy, sumo-sized giant of a boy, barely eighteen from the look of him, stood directly behind Nana, arms folded across his chest. There was something odd about his eyes, the shape of his shaved head. . . . Down's syndrome. His oriental features camouflaged it, but from the vague focus of his eyes, the moist droop of his mouth, Garcia guessed he was at least semiretarded. And very, very big.

Mrs. Chiang broke off her speech, eyeing Garcia as he and Erin approached. Father Kelly glanced over his shoulder, grateful for the interruption.

"Sorry to interrupt," Garcia said, "I'd like to talk to you when you have a minute."

"Gladly," the priest sighed. "Have a seat. You're the subject at hand."

Mrs. Chiang said something to her interpreter. "My mother says she is most sorry about your father," brushcut said to Erin. "He was a good man, a good friend."

"Thank you," Erin said formally. "Tell your mother we're very sorry about the window being broken this morning. We'll pay for it, of course, or rather Mr. Garcia will."

"The window's the least of our problems," Father Kelly said. "Mrs. Chiang says she's afraid the publicity about the club will ruin her business. Their offer to buy the building still stands, but if we don't accept, she'll have to break the lease."

"So much for condolences," Garcia said, easing stiffly down into a seat after holding Erin's chair. "Can she do that?"

"The lease still has a year to run," Kelly said. "They'd have to go to court, but I think a judge might well allow it, considering the situation."

"Did you explain what it would mean to us if she vacates?" Erin said. "It'll be almost impossible for us to find a buyer for an empty building."

"That I did," Kelly said dryly. "Roughly translated, her reply was business is business."

"So it seems," Garcia said, glancing around the bustling room. "Bad publicity or not, it looks like she's expecting a busy day."

"I believe they do quite well here," Mick said with a nod. "Still, they might do just as well elsewhere."

"Maybe." Garcia nodded. "Tell your mother I'd like to thank her," he said to the interpreter.

"Thank her?" brushcut said, confused.

"For not calling the police about the broken window this morning. It could have made trouble for us."

Nana said something in Chinese, then nodded at Garcia, inclining her head in a curt bow.

"My mother says you are welcome. She wishes to make no trouble for the Kelly family. Their luck has been bad."

"Too true," Garcia said, returning her bow. "Still, it was good to leave the police out of it. I appreciate it. And tell your mother I'll return the favor. I won't ask immigration to run a check on how many of your employees are illegals. Unless I hear any more crap about breaking the lease."

Chiang the Younger hesitated. Nana eyed Garcia coldly for a moment, then spat a rapid fire epithet, rose, and stalked off to the kitchen, followed by her interpreter. The Mongoloid hesitated, confused.

"It's okay Li," Father Kelly said gently, "go along now." If the giant understood, he gave no sign. He kept staring at Garcia with the intensity of a frog eyeing a fly. Then he frowned, as if he'd forgotten why he was angry, and shambled off.

"Right," Father Kelly sighed, shrugging into his overcoat, "I guess that wraps things up here. For now."

"What did she say?" Garcia asked.

"I couldn't say, but I doubt she was wishing you a long life and a smooth road. On the other hand, I don't think we'll hear any more about lease breakin' for a while. How did you know she'd be afraid of immigration?"

"Educated guess. This place doesn't need anywhere near this much staff unless they're working awfully cheap, and work's not that hard to find in this town."

"Guess or no, it worked," Mick nodded. "I don't think you impressed Li too favorably though, and he's bad to be crossways of. Keeps order in the family for his mother. Saw him carry a refrigerator up here for her once. Didn't bother with the freight elevator, just picked the damn thing up, hauled it up the stairs on his back like a bag o' laundry. If you see that boy comin', head the other way, Garcia. Don't bother trying to talk him out of anything, I doubt he understands much Chinese, to say nothing of English."

"I'll keep it in mind. You mentioned the freight elevator. I know it opens out onto a loading platform, but it also operates between floors, doesn't it? Could someone have used it to get into the Underground from the restaurant? Say someone like Li?"

"No, there are different keys for each floor. Each business has its own. The Chiangs couldn't open the elevator door to the Underground, nor could Daniel open theirs," Father Kelly said. "Besides, the Chiangs had no reason to harm anyone, especially since apparently the last thing they want is trouble with the law. Now, what was it you wanted to see me about, other than reimbursing them for a broken window, that is."

"Money," Garcia said, "a hundred thousand dollars. Small change compared to a broken window, I'll admit."

"Maybe not, the way the Chiangs keep books. What about this money?"

Garcia waited until they were on the steps outside the Jade Mountain. "I had a visitor after the club closed last night, a gentleman named LaRose. He claimed to have invested over a hundred thousand with Richie Zeayen. Do you know him?"

"No," Kelly said, hunching against the cold, "and I doubt very much that his story's true. Connie asked me to run a credit check on Richie when Daniel was considering taking him on as a partner. For a young man with no visible means of support his rating was fair, but he was making payments on a twenty-thousand dollar car, owed Kuppenheimer several thousand for tailored suits. I'd bet the thirty thousand he put up was every dime he had and this LaRose character is just on the hustle."

"Unlikely. LaRose is definitely not the con man type," Garcia said, rubbing the reddened burn on his jaw. "Could Richie have had assets that wouldn't turn up in your check?"

"Absolutely. I only got a credit profile and I committed a sin of omission for that."

"Sin of omission?"

"The credit bureau presumed he was a parish employee and I failed to enlighten them. In any case, stocks, bonds, real estate wouldn't be in his credit rating unless he listed them in applying for credit, but frankly he didn't strike me as a good risk for a ten-cent loan to say nothing of a hundred thousand."

"In LaRose's circles the hundred may not be all that much. But say Richie had it, where would it be?"

"At his bank, I suppose."

"No, the marked money he gave Danny was still intact so it had never been deposited. You mentioned a lockbox he kept in the safe?"

"He kept it there at one time," Father Kelly said. "I've not seen it for several weeks."

"Maybe he stashed it somewhere else. Was he involved in any other businesses that you know of?"

"He had a small percentage of a recording studio, no more than a few thousand. Perhaps he kept the money at his home."

"The police report showed him as living with his family, and I doubt Richie left anything where his brother might find it. Maybe you're right, and LaRose is just blowing smoke. Still, if you happen to stumble across a spare hundred thou . . ."

"I'll phone you from Tahiti," Father Kelly said dryly. "Anything else, or can I go home to breakfast?"

"Well, I did do the accounts last night, they're on my desk if you'd like to take a look while you're here."

"Perhaps I'd better do a once-over," Mick sighed, "just to make sure the i's are dotted." He held out his hand palm open. Garcia glanced at him questioningly.

"I'll need your key to the office," Mick said, "I don't have one."

"Right," Garcia said, handing him the key, "sorry, it slipped my mind."

"Did it now?" Kelly asked, eyeing Garcia with a trace of a smile. "Somehow I doubt that."

"Can I drop you someplace, Loop?" Erin put in quickly.

"Sure, if it isn't too much trouble. Kronk's Gym, downtown?"

"A workout? After the fun you had last night?" Kelly said. "Ah, the energy of the young. Better save some for your job, Garcia. Be a pity if you lost it."

"Amen," Garcia said.

TWENTY-EIGHT

The weight room at Kronk's was at the rear of the gym, fully equipped with Nautilus units, chromed sets of York barbells and free weights. A black businessman-type the size of George Foreman, his paunch staining the seams of his Everlast sweat suit, was puffing mightily with each step up the stair climber. Bailey Reeves was the only other trainee. He was doing sit-ups on an inclined abdominal board. Clad only in purple spandex stretch shorts, a free weight in each hand, his heavily muscled body coiled and uncoiled effortlessly as an assembly-line robot. His face and chest were gleaming with perspiration, but except for the *huh* of expelled breath with every third repetition, he showed no hint of strain.

"You're lookin' good," Garcia said, "how many you up to?"

"One ninety," Reeves grunted, "almost done, don't fuck up my count, okay?"

"No problem," Garcia said, kneeling beside Reeves as the big man continued to pump. "Wanted to thank you for helping me out last night."

"One ninety-one, no charge, just makin' sure you'd be in one piece come payday. Ninety-two."

"You dropped that guy with one shot. Helluva punch."

"One ninety-three, sucker punch. Ninety-four. No big thang. Ninety-five."

"It looked pro to me."

"Ninety-six. I can punch. Ninety-seven. Used to fight some, ninety-eight, went forty-four and six, semipro. Forty—fuck! What was my count?"

"One ninety-nine," Garcia said. "Two hundred now. How many you goin' for?"

"Two twenty-five."

"Two oh one now," Garcia said, "how'd you get from being a boxer to a drummer?"

"You beat on drums, two oh two, they don't lay for you after wid' a ball bat, two oh three, or burn yo' ass up. Oh four."

"Burn you? By tossing gasoline in your cell you mean?"

"Oh five. Yeah, in your cell. Oh six. I learnt fightin' in the joint. Oh seven. Like you didn't already know. Oh—what's my count?

"Oh eight. And I didn't know."

"Oh nine. So now you do. So what? You wanna try me out? Two ten. Maybe spar a few rounds?"

"After seeing you in action? No chance. No, I wanted to ask you about Richie. Guy at the desk said he worked out here too."

"Lotta guys work out here. Two eleven. Place is famous. Two twelve."

"It's also pretty much restricted to fighters, and since Richie wasn't, I figure he probably worked out with you."

"He tried for a while, thirteen, wanted to learn to fight. No belly for it, gave it up."

"He gave up on a lot of things," Garcia said. "Like your record deal?"

"The music biz runs on busted promises. Two fourteen. He was tryna sell our contract, talkin' to RCA, Warners, couple other major labels. Fifteen. RCA was supposed to see us this week. We woulda been better off if Richie'd closed the deal before he got dead, but with the record cookin' like it is, we might still get a deal. And since I was onstage when it happened in front of about five hunert witnesses, if you lookin' for somebody to hang, keep lookin'. I had no beef with Richie. 'Cept for the same one you had."

"That I had? How do you mean?"

"With his goon, Red. Sixteen. You got lucky with him, man, took him by surprise. The dude was serious trouble."

"Trouble for you, you mean?"

"He tried to be. Seventeen. Guys like him think they bad, hear I used to fight, get nervous. Get to wonderin' how bad I am. Eighteen. Gotta try you on or turn you out. Red start ridin' on my ass, trash-mouthin' me, nineteen. I asked Richie to cool him, don't want no hassle. Instead, Richie he lays down two large says I can't take Red in five. Two twenty."

"So what happened?"

"Hey, for two thousand bucks I'd go five rounds with Tommy Hearns wearin' a blindfold. Twenty-one. Besides, Red's white, looked slow to me, figured I could handle him."

"You fight here?"

"No, man, at the house. Wild scene. Two twenty-two."

"What house?"

"Richie's place. Out in Mount Clemens. Twenty-three."

"I thought he lived in Dearborn."

"Nah, his folks live there I think. He had his own crib, big sucker. Right on the river. Twenty-four."

"So? Was Red slow?"

"You oughta know. You tried him on."

"Sort of," Garcia nodded, "but not in the ring. Inside the ropes is another thing."

"Two hunert and twenty fuckin' five. Hoooooeee." Reeves lay all the way back on the inclined board, arms outstretched, then started bringing the chromed weights slowly up from the floor, curling them to his chest, slowing his breathing, cooling out. "You say that like you done some ring time."

"Some," Garcia conceded, "not like you. Police Athletic League when I was a kid, then in the army."

"Figured you had, watchin' you last night. You covered up good, kep' movin'."

"With a little help from my friends. What happened with Red?"

"Man, it was unreal. Dig it, this house is a mansion, like *Gone with the Wind* or somethin'. I bet I was the first black face on the block wasn't a gardener. Place had a lotta rooms, musta had a dozen bedrooms. Beds is about all it had, though."

"How do you mean?"

"Wasn't no furniture, not like somebody lived there. Nice though, real fine crib. So on the big night we go over there after the club closed—"

"We?"

"The band, Lucero, Bobby, Risa. Needed somebody on my side, make sure I get my money. We make the scene and musta been a hunert people there, all stoned to the bone. Most of 'em looked like players, you know, nice threads, stone fox chicks. We go down to the rec room, and Richie's got it all fixed up with a ring, not a real one, only 'bout ten, twelve foot square, but with real ropes, canvas, posts, the whole shot, all them people packed in there, motherfuckin' DJ with a giant boombox pumpin' out jams loud enough make your ears bleed, reefer smoke so thick you get half blowed away jus' breathin'. Wild."

"Sounds like it."

"That wasn't half of it, man. I get taped up, get in the ring, fuckin' Richie comes out in a tuxedo, got a microphone just like a real ring announcer, you know? Makes a big deal outta introducin' us, doin' it up proper. Then he tells everybody about the bet, says he prove he ain't jivin', starts countin' out the money, two grand in twenties, dealin' it out like cards, man, tossin' it on the floor. Money all over the mat. Next fuckin' thing, everybody's doin' it, throwin' cash into the ring, tens, twennies, fifties. It's like a fuckin' green carpet. Winner take all.

"I'm lookin' at Red, he lookin' at me, an' we both lookin' at all that money, knowin' this thing ain't no joke no more. Somebody gonna pay some dues, pick up all that cash.

"So firs' roun' me an' Red get to it. He comes on real strong, throwin' heavy leather, wild, not much control. Fucker can punch though. You been in the ring, it ain't like the movies. You get a dude that big, don't matter whether he can box or not, he land one big shot, he can take out fuckin' Godzilla.

"So I'm cool, you know, playin' it careful, ring's slippery cause of the cash, so I'm coverin' up, hookin' him to the body when he come in, checkin' out his style, which wan't easy since he don't have none. He jus' kep' comin, throwin' leather.

"Las' minute of the round, hammer time. I got his timin' figured, so I come on strong, nail 'im with some heavy shots, tryna take him out. But it ain't happenin'.

"We get to warrin' in the middle of the ring, both of us whalin', he's missin' mosta his, I'm landin' mosta mine, but we comin' out even 'cause I'm feelin' it and he ain't. I catch him with a right cross shoulda laid out the Statue o' Liberty. But he takes it, drills me with a counter so hard rings my fuckin' bell. My legs go rubber. I clinch him, hang on. And I see his eyes up close. Nothin' there. Lights are on but nobody home. Fuckin' Red's higher'n a kite on coke or crank and I'm in a shitstorm, 'cause I just nailed him with my best shot an' the fucker din't even feel it. Steada droppin' he damn near punched my lights out.

"Between rounds, the place goes crazy. Richie's pumpin' up the crowd in his fuckin' zoot suit, money's flyin' all over the place, like one o' them parades in New York, you know? They throwin' dope too, nickel bags, pills, you name it. And I'm for sure Red's high 'cause the fucker grabs a bag off the floor, snorts five lines o' white lady right there in his corner, gettin' even more wired up while I'm tryin' hard to remember my fuckin' name, what year it is, you know?"

"Sweet Jesus," Garcia said softly.

"You got it, man. I been in a few jams, but this is big-time. I'm mixin' it up with a guy thinks he's King fuckin' Kong an' wouldn't feel it if I shot him in the head with a forty-five. And it ain't like I can win this thing on points, you know? It's his crowd. If he drops me them people are so hyped they likely to stomp me to death for laughs. Only chance I got is take Red all the way out, but I'm still so wobbly I can barely find the fuckin' ring."

"What happened?"

Reeves opened his eyes a moment, looking at Garcia, but still seeing that room, tasting it. The executive type on the stair climber was frozen, listening. Bailey's face split into a wide, slow smile. "Richie saved my ass," he said.

"Richie?"

"Oh, he didn't mean to. Thing is, he's in the ring hypin' the crowd, it's snowin' money an' dope, then some drunk blond chick tosses her bra in, gets a big hand for it, so she peels off her top, throws that in too. Starts dancin' aroun' half naked, shadowboxin'. Place goes absolutely nuts. Richie's screamin' it ain't right me an' Red are the only ones with no shirts, everybody get topless or get the fuck out. Man, I thought there was gonna be a fuckin' riot.

"Mosta the people're so blowed away they go right along with him, start shuckin' their shirts, then some hassles break out with the ones who didn't, chicks gettin' their clothes tore off, people scufflin'. Musta been five, ten minutes before things gets settled halfway down. Crowd's even crazier'n before, all them women bare tit, screaming at us to get it on. Wild, man.

"By time second roun' starts, I got my head screwed

back on straight, know what I got to do. You done some boxin', ever hear what Joe Louis said 'bout knockin' people out?"

"If the body falls, the head goes with it," Garcia said.

"You got it," Reeves nodded, grinning at the memory. "Still it wasn't no walk in the park. Red was throwin' some heavy shots, fucker could really punch, man. He wasn't in top shape, carryin' too much weight, but with the coke he was snortin' between rounds, he wasn't gonna run outta gas neither, so I had to play him real cautious. Not too cautious, though. Way I figured it, wadn't gonna be enough just to beat him, I had to win the crowd over too if we wanted to get outta there in one piece.

"Doin' coke shut down his pain. I couldn't hurt him, but it was takin' away his game too. He was throwin' a lotta leather, looks like a helluva fight's goin' on, but his acc'racy was off. He wasn't hittin' me with nothin' solid. I risked doin' a little showboatin', Ali shuffle, shit like that, got some o' the people cheerin' me, faked like I was hurt once, got a little sympathy. But mostly I just worked his body, wearin' him down. Dropped him once at the end of the fourth. Fifth round I knocked his honky ass clean out. Got the best parta six grand."

"And, ah, where was Risa during all this?"

"What you mean, where was she?"

"You said all four of you were there, what happened when everybody started peeling off?"

Reeves's eyes scanned Garcia's face a moment, then closed again as he continued slow-curling the free weights. "She gettin' to you, right? Not surprisin', chick look like that, sing like that. We're buddies, me'n Risa, and she even gets to me sometimes. She's one fine lady, every way there is. She's also Bobby's wife. You know that."

"I understand they're not living together."

"Don't matter. She still his wife. They're a pair, those two, him writin' and her singin'. Thing is, no matter what their situation is now, Bobby's a south Texas redneck stone through. You mess with his ole lady you maybe buyin' into more shit'n you can handle. I been workin' with Bobby awhile an' I'll tell you somethin', man, he ain't nobody I'd cross. Knew guys like him in the joint. Not so big, I got him by forty pounds and I could prob'ly drop him in a round or two. But if I did, I'd hafta stomp him to death right then. Or be lookin' over my shoulder for the resta my life, watchin' for him to come settle up."

"I'll keep that in mind."

"Sure you will. But you still wonderin' about Risa, right?"

"Yes," Garcia said, "I guess I am."

"Well, tell you the truth, Garcia, I ain't sure. I was kinda busy at the time, you know? After the fight I was scramblin' aroun' pickin' up the money. I give it to Bobby an' he cleared out and I don't remember whether Risa was still there or not. Place was crazy. I got stoned, got laid three times, woke up with two chicks I never saw before. Thought it was just a wild night because of the fight, but it wasn't. The place was that nuts most times."

"What do you mean?"

"Ball parties, man. Richie used to do orgies there 'bout once a week after the club closed. Downstairs when you come in, people be drinkin', tootin' coke, whatever, upstairs, shit. Had to shuck all your clothes to go upstairs, everybody fuckin' everybody, doin' daisy chains, eatin' one another out. Heavy scene. I tried it on a couple times."

"Just a couple?"

"Well man, I never really figured the group sex thing was all that great," Reeves said evenly. "Maybe I'm gettin' old, but seemed to me it's like drinkin' or smokin' dope. Coppin' a nice buzz on somethin' fine is one thing. Gettin' trashed outta your tree on whatever shit's handy, that's somethin' else. No class to it. 'Sides, I was the only gentleman of color there, you know? Felt like I was on loan out of a zoo. 'Bout that time I met Loreen at the club, college kid, Wayne State. We hit it off good and I remembered how fine it is when you with the right one. I quit goin' out there. Didn't miss much. Heard Richie called things off not long after."

"Why did he do that?"

"Dunno. Maybe Richie's the kinda guy starts things up, not so good on the follow-through, you know? Like with our record."

"That how he struck you?"

Reeves hesitated a moment, the weights suspended in midair. "No," he said, resuming his curls, "I don't think so. He was a real go-getter when we met him down home. He talked us into comin' up here, and it ain't like he was the first bullshitter I ever met. Nah, somethin' happened, month, six weeks back, took his mind off his game. Some kinda trouble."

"Why do you say trouble?"

"Acted like a man with a lot on his mind. Got real edgy, short fuse. Started pushin' Danny around. I liked Richie when I met him, lotta hustle, street dude on the make, you know? Figured he could do us some good. But lately he was turnin' into a first-class prick. You did the world a favor, man."

"I didn't do Richie," Garcia said.

"Whatever," Reeves said. "Look, I got a date this afternoon, gotta hit the showers, soo . . . Anything else you wanted?"

"Just one. The house, do you remember the address."

"Ain't likely to forget it, considerin'."

"No," Garcia said, "I suppose not."

TWENTY-NINE

Erin was leaning against her BMW in Kronk's parking lot, arms folded across her chest, waiting less than patiently. A striking contrast, a tall, fire-haired gazelle loden green leather coat against a concrete backdrop dusted with dirty snow. "Have a nice chat?" she asked, straightening.

"Very," Garcia said. "I thought you were going home."

"I was, but since sitting around my condo wondering if I'll be evicted didn't seem like a great way to spend the afternoon, I decided to do something constructive. Where to next?"

"Look, I really appreciate the offer, but maybe I'd better cab it from here on."

"Why? Where are you going?"

"Beaufort Gardens in Mount Clemens. House hunting."

"You're thinking of buying a place in Mount Clemens?"

"More along the lines of breaking and entering."

"In that case I'd definitely better drive. You'll need a lawyer and I need the business."

"Good point," Garcia said.

Beaufort Gardens' main thoroughfare was sheltered by

century-old elms, offering occasional glimpses of the Clinton River between the multistory estates set amid snowy lawns broad enough for polo. The address Reeves gave Garcia was for a home that was large even by the enclave's standards, a huge modernist structure, glass-walled levels stacked unevenly on an artificial hillside, with long, swooping concrete ramps connecting the sections of the house. Erin followed a long driveway bordered by cedar shrubs to the rear parking area, a half acre of concrete facing a six-car garage.

"My God," Erin said softly, climbing out of the car, eyeing the house. "This place is Richie's? Maybe I gave up on him too easily."

"I doubt he owned it," Garcia said, stalking up the ribbed concrete ramp to the rear door, "but apparently he had the use of it. Only in America. Turn your back please, Counselor, you don't want to see this." He worked on the lock with a small set of picks for less than thirty seconds. The door opened with a muffled click.

Empty. He could sense it the moment he stepped in—no life, no movement. They'd entered through a marvelously equipped kitchen, with copper pots, skillets, and colanders suspended above a preparation area worthy of a five-star restaurant. It was deserted now, refrigerator doors left open, no scent of cooking from the half-acre ovens, only the acrid odor of stale Pine Sol. White dustcover sheets draped the dining table in the next room like shrouds. Garcia lifted a sheet on one of the chairs. Early American, cheap oak veneer, stiff twill fabric. Motel standard. "The furniture doesn't belong here," Garcia said. "Probably rented."

"What are we looking for?" Erin asked, glancing around.

"I'm not sure. Richie's lockbox, drugs, I don't know."

"What about the house itself?"

"No chance. A hundred K would barely make the down payment on this place."

"Decor's not Richie anyway," Erin said, "no Elvis on black velvet paintings."

"We haven't seen it all yet."

The living room was similarly draped, dustcovers over everything in a basketball court–size room dominated by a massive sandstone fireplace at one end, a winding staircase at the other.

"Funny, Reeves described this place as a party palace," Garcia said. "I don't get any sense of that. It just feels . . . abandoned."

"I don't like it," Erin said, hugging herself against a psychic chill. "Can we hurry things along?"

"Fine, let's split up, you want upstairs or down?"

"I'd better take the upstairs. Younger legs."

"True," Garcia said, "but undeserved."

"Be grateful you don't always get what you deserve," Erin said, starting up the stairs. "Meet you here in ten minutes."

Movie set. *Laura, My Cousin Rachel,* or any Barbara Stanwyck film from the forties. Garcia couldn't shake the feeling as he moved quickly from room to room on the ground floor. Paintings, statuary, a huge library, but no sense that anyone ever read in it, or that anyone ever lived here at all. There was a wall safe behind a painting in the library, open, a light sheen of dust in it. Richie'd apparently quit using the place, probably hadn't left anything of value behind.

Only the rec room looked lived in. It had been cleared, the furniture stacked atop a billiards table jammed in a far corner. There was an echo of energy here, cigarette ashes ground into the carpet, spots from spilled drinks. Through half-closed eyes Garcia could almost see Bailey Reeves fighting Red in this room, cash littering the ring, the half-nude, totally stoned crowd screaming for blood. . . . He shrugged off the image and moved on.

The six-bay garage was as barren as a defunct dealership, not a tire mark or a grease spot on the inlaid tile floor. The large combination workshop-storeroom attached to it was more interesting, with a fully equipped oak-topped workbench as immaculate as an operating table. The Peg-Board above the bench was better stocked with tools than most hardware store displays.

A Maytag washer and dryer, commercial-size, stood beside a large upright freezer against the far wall. The white enameled shelving above them held nonperishable housekeeping items, Bounty towels, toilet tissue, king-size boxes of Tide.

He opened the room's other door and found himself back in the kitchen. But as he closed the door behind him, he heard a faint click from the storeroom.

Frowning, he flicked the lights back on and looked around. Nothing. As empty as before, and as silent, except for the faint hum of the upright freezer in the corner. The noise had been the freezer switching on. Garcia began to close the door again, then hesitated. The refrigerators in the kitchen were open and unplugged. So? So probably nothing. He sauntered over to the freezer and opened the door.

Marijuana. The freezer's lower racks had been removed to make room for a single oversize gray plastic garbage sack, standard packing for hundred-kilo bales of weed. But with the price of reefer sky high, why would Richie leave it here? Garcia untwisted the plastic tie at the top, jerked the bag open. And stiffened.

Hair. Red hair, rimed with frost. Swallowing hard, he warily tugged the bag further open, being careful not to tear it.

God. It was Red. Eyes bulged, face purplish, tongue protruding, neck deeply creased by the wire line of a garrote. Jesus, Jesus, Jesus. Garcia took a step back, instinctively breathing through his mouth though there was no stench of decay. Then he swallowed and forced himself to examine the body more closely.

Strangled to death apparently, a single reddened line around the throat, no other visible wounds. The corpus was frozen nearly solid, icy as a glacier. Which meant that forensics couldn't pinpoint the time of death closer than a few days.

Wincing, Garcia reached farther down into the bag, forcing it open a bit more. Red's right hand was deeply bruised, his ring finger swollen to the size of bologna. No cast, not even a bandage. So he'd been killed before he'd sought medical attention for his hand, probably within an hour or two after his finger'd been broken. My God. Double life. LaRose was right. If Red's body turned up now after the hassle they'd had at the club with no way to ascertain how long he'd been dead . . . He glanced around, trying to remember what he'd touched. The doorknob, the freezer. He picked up the wire tie, carefully pulled the bag back up over Red's face, tied it off again, and closed the freezer door. He stood there, staring at the cool white enamel for what seemed like a very long time.

Erin was nowhere in sight when he found the living room again. He gave a piercing split-fingered whistle and she appeared on the upstairs landing.

"You rang, James?" she asked, mincing languidly toward the stairway, her fingertips brushing the banister. He smiled in spite of himself.

"Vivien Leigh, right?"

"Bette Davis. Any luck?"

"No, probably nothing to find. The people Richie owed money to have access to the house, so I doubt he stashed anything here. You find anything?"

"Not really, it's all bedrooms and baths up there. One's locked though."

"One what's locked?"

"A bathroom, I think. In one of the master bedrooms."

He hesitated, anxious to be away. Damn. "Show me."

* * *

"There are six bedrooms up here," Erin said. "Two are larger than the others, but they all seem to be laid out the same way. Which makes this the door to a bathroom, right?"

"Seems like it," Garcia said, glancing around the bedroom. It was large, twenty by thirty or so, plush salmon carpeting, the walls pearly pink damask, a walk-in closet on one side and what was probably a bath on the other. The only furnishing was a king-size water bed, bathed in the glow of the crystal chandelier above it and matching rose-bulbed sconces along the walls. A framed poster of Marilyn Monroe's nude calendar pose hung beside the walk-in closet, a large, ornate ormolu mirror was on the outside of the bathroom wall opposite.

Garcia eyed the mirror a moment, then quickly circled the room's perimeter, examining the carpet. He paused briefly to examine Marilyn.

"Were there any posters in the other bedrooms?" he asked.

"No, just this one."

"Right"—Garcia nodded—"and Marilyn's hanging from a nail. Richie strike you as an art lover?"

"Hardly. Maybe she's here to get people in the mood."

"From what I've been told, they didn't need much help. The lock on the bathroom door doesn't match the rest of the fixtures, which means somebody changed it, probably Richie. And he hung the mirror and the picture at the same time."

"I don't understand." Erin frowned. "Why do you think the picture is significant?"

"I'm not sure it is. Unless it's already doing what it's supposed to do. Lie down the bed."

"I beg your pardon?"

"Just for a second. Please."

Erin hesitated a moment, then sat warily on the edge of

the bed. Garcia crossed to the mirror. "Can you see yourself in the mirror?"

"No, the angle's too high."

"Not even from the, ah, missionary position?"

Erin raised an eyebrow, then stretched out, deliberately languid. "No, the angle's still wrong. What's your point?"

Garcia didn't answer for a moment. Somehow the image of Erin stretched out on the bed in a leather coat struck him as far more sensual than Marilyn in her nothings. She read his glance, and sat up slowly. "You were saying?"

"Um, right. The mirror's too low to dress by, and too high for . . . recreation. I'm guessing Marilyn's here to do what she did best, to draw attention to the poster and keep it away from the mirror. . . ." He trailed off, feeling around the mirror's frame with his fingertips. The hell with it. He grasped the top and yanked the frame out of the wall. And found himself staring into the lenses of two cameras, one video, one Polaroid, mounted on tripods and focused on the water bed through a hole sawed crudely through the bathroom wall.

"What is it?" Erin said, getting to her feet.

"Showtime," Garcia said. He stretched an arm through the opening and unlocked the door from the inside.

The bathroom walls were papered with Polaroid snapshots, Scotch-taped to the tiles. Action shots showing couples and groups on and around the water bed, nude or in costumes. Some were body-painted, some in leather bondage. Nuns and tigers and Little Bo Peep entwined in sweating tangles, mouths slack, eyes glazed. Garcia scanned the first dozen or so quickly, then began searching the rest of the room, the medicine chest, the cupboards under the sink.

"My God," Erin said softly, brushing past him, "what is all this?"

"Richie Zee Enterprises at work," Garcia said, kneeling and rifling the shelves. "Look at the faces."

"What about them?"

"Nobody's looking at the camera, not even edgewise. They didn't know they were being photographed." He rose, popped the door of the linen closet in the corner, and found a plastic rack holding a dozen or so videotapes. "My guess is Richie was using the club to recruit heavy party types, then using the house parties as a cover to get some very special guests into this bedroom. He was going into the blackmail business." He riffled through the tapes, scanning the jackets. Numbers, no names.

"You could be right," Erin said, moving slowly down the room, examining the pictures. "A lot of these are of older men, younger women—my God, Harvey Neubauer, the Ford dealer. A couple of attorneys . . ." Her voice trailed off. Garcia glanced up, alerted by the edge in her tone. Erin sat down slowly on the edge of the tub, the color draining from her face.

"What's wrong?"

She started to reply, then suddenly she was on her knees at the bowl, gagging, losing her lunch. Lupe dampened a paper towel in the sink and passed it to her, then scanned the photographs taped to the tile beside the tub.

There were a half dozen naked action shots of a man and woman in a number of sexual positions. Richie Zeayen, and Connie Kelly. He eyed them a moment, lips pursed, then began peeling them off the wall.

"What are you doing?" Erin coughed, sitting up, wiping her mouth with the towel, her face ashen.

"Maybe defusing a bomb, I don't know," he said, stripping off more pictures, making a stack. "I take it you didn't know about your mother and Richie."

"I—wondered if something was going on between them," Erin said, her voice shaking. "It's why I quit seeing Richie. But I didn't think . . . it was anything like this."

"Look, we've got to get out of here. Help me find the shots of Connie—"

"Leave them!" she said fiercely. "I don't care."

"Dammit, sort out your family tree on your own time. You want Richie's crew to find these?"

She glared at him, her eyes molten iron. "All right," she said, snatching a pair of photos off the wall. "Maybe they'll come in handy if—what was that?"

They both froze, listening. Someone was moving around downstairs. Garcia crossed quickly to the bedroom door, eased it closed, and locked it.

"Police?" Erin said.

"Not unless they're driving a gray Jag sedan," Garcia said softly, glancing out the window. "Getting arrested could be the least of our problems. Do we have all the pictures?"

"I think so," Erin said, glancing around, "but—"

"Then let's go," he said, raising the window sash and beckoning to her. "Quietly."

THIRTY

Erin clambered through the open window to the snow-covered garage roof beyond. Garcia followed and they cautiously made their way across the snowy slope to the edge. A metallic gray Jaguar sedan was parked beside Erin's white BMW fifteen feet below.

"How do we get down?" Erin whispered.

"Over here." Garcia moved warily to the corner of the roof and knelt at the edge. "Come on, I'll lower you down to the snowbank."

She hesitated a moment, reading his eyes, then nodded, grasped his hand firmly, and lowered herself over the edge without a word. Straining to hold her, Garcia gradually eased her down until his chest was resting on the rim of the overhang.

"Ready?"

Erin glanced down, then nodded. He released her and she dropped the last five feet, plunging to her thighs in the snowdrift. She barely had time to scramble out of the drift as Garcia slid off the roof, clung to the gutter for a moment, then dropped down beside her. "Go! Go! Go!"

She sprinted to the car and slid behind the wheel, with Garcia piling in only a step behind. She fired up the BMW, backed away from the garage, then slammed it into drive and gunned across the parking area. Sevum Cottler burst out of the back door, clawed his automatic from beneath his overcoat, and ripped off two quick shots as they rounded the corner of the house.

"What the hell?" Erin gasped. "He shot at us!"

"Right," Garcia said grimly. "Do you have a weapon?"

"Sure, a can of Mace in my purse," she snapped. "Hang on!" The BMW rocketed down the driveway and skidded broadside onto the street on two wheels, tires howling. The Jaguar roared out of the drive only a few blocks behind them.

"Which way?" Erin said.

"Take Gratiot into the city and keep the hammer down. With luck maybe we'll get nailed for speeding."

"Dream on," Erin said, cutting hard left down a side street, followed by a neck-snapping right turn. "You never find a cop when you need one. I don't think I can outrun a Jag but maybe I can lose them."

"Maybe you can," Garcia acknowledged as she snapped a quick right, skillfully weaving between a parked UPS van and an oncoming V-dub Beetle. They were in Roseville's business district now, blocks of shops whizzing by. The Jag flashed into view a second later, a half block farther back than before, but it quickly began closing the distance again, Cottler driving, LaRose riding shotgun.

Erin downshifted and swerved across the centerline, barely dodging an orange Men at Work barricade in the right lane. Garcia twisted in his seat, quickly scanning the construction site in the middle of the block. A MichCon truck with its cherry picker elevated was working on the building's electrical mast. Plumbing and electrical wiring contractors' trucks were parked behind the barricades.

"Right at the next corner," Garcia snapped. "Go down a block, hang right again."

"Around the block?"

"No, turn into the freight alley in the middle of the

block. There'll be a loading area that services all these stores. Drop me there, then blow on through the alley."

"Why? What are you going to do?"

"I don't know," he said. "Something."

"That's not an idea, it's a hormone." But she was already cranking the wheel hard to the right.

In the Jag, Tony LaRose was clinging to the door latch, half hoping Cottler would wipe out the car and have to explain it to Echeverria. No such luck. The kid was a good driver, good reflexes and too psycho to tense up.

"Get ready," Cottler grunted, throwing the car into a power skid around the corner as the BMW disappeared into the alley halfway down the block. "We catch 'em in there, we whack 'em. No more fuckin' around."

"The Cuban didn't say anything about—"

"Fuck you, LaRose," Cottler snarled, stomping the brakes, turning hard into the alley. "You can jerk off and watch if you wanna, but they're gone, dig?"

"Whatever you say," Tony said, bracing himself as Cottler gunned the car down the alley, pedal to the metal. The BMW was closer than he expected, less than fifty feet ahead. Too close.

"Hey, wait a minute—" LaRose began.

He never finished. A man stepped out a scant car length ahead of them, silhouetted against the alley light, arms upraised, holding a cement block above his head.

"Shiiit!" Cottler screamed, instinctively swerving the car to the right as Garcia hurled the block straight at the Jag's windshield and dove clear.

The block bounced off the roof but the car smashed nose first into the side of the building, metal shrieking against brick, then slammed to a dead stop as the rear end snapped around, jamming the Jag broadside across the alley.

Tony's head bounced off the dash and back into the

headrest, a one-two punch that crushed the cartilage of his nose. Blood gushed instantly down his mouth, soaking his coat. Cottler looked dead, slumped over the wheel. Tony began fumbling at the seat belt. Got to get out. Car might burn . . .

Suddenly the driver's side window exploded inward, spraying him with glass. Tony gaped, too dazed to react as Garcia jerked Cottler upright in the seat and yanked the automatic out of his shoulder holster. Even with his head still ringing from the crash, Tony heard the quiet *snick* as Garcia eared back the hammer of Cottler's 9-mm.

"Don't do it, man," he said, his voice sticky with his own blood. "Please."

Garcia didn't answer. He kept the muzzle of the Browning Hi-Power centered on Tony's forehead as he pressed a finger against Cottler's throat, feeling for a pulse.

"Dead?" Tony asked.

"Not yet," Garcia said, letting Cottler sag back against the headrest. "Straight up, Tony, did you two trash my apartment?"

LaRose almost lied, but caught himself. A wrong answer could kill him, he could read it in the Mex's eyes. "We were lookin' for Richie's stash," he admitted. "Nothin' personal, I swear."

"Don't swear, just listen. I'll only say this once. I didn't kill Richie. I don't have his stash. You tell the Cuban the way I see it, I lost a friend, he lost some money. We're dead even now. Cut your losses, Tony. Walk away. Understand?"

"Yeah, only . . . I can't promise you nothin' about what he'll do, man. And that's the truth."

"I know. But you better be clear about something. If anybody bothers Danny's family again I'll take it personally. I'm jammed up, Tony, I've got nothin' to lose."

"I understand." LaRose nodded. "I'll tell him." A car pulled into the alley behind them. The BMW. Garcia glanced at it, then leaned into the car, rifled Cottler's pockets, and came up with a matchbook. He snapped a match alight with his thumb, holding it beneath one tip of Cottler's forked goatee until it began to smolder, filling the car with the acrid stench of burning hair.

"I'll be damned," Garcia said softly. "He's absolutely right. Everybody smokes."

THIRTY-ONE

"Shouldn't we notify the police about what happened?" Erin asked. They were in her BMW on Grand River, headed back into the city.

"Not now. They could use it as an excuse to revoke my bail, hold me as a material witness or whatever."

"You may not need bail much longer anyway." He glanced at her. She was taut as a wire, her knuckles white on the wheel.

"Why not?"

"Why? Surely you realize what these pictures mean?"

"I don't know. What do you think they mean?"

She cranked the wheel hard to the left, barely avoiding a van in the right lane. A light snow was falling, slicking the pavement. "There's a cassette in the glove compartment," she said. "Give it to me."

She took it from him, jammed it savagely into her tape deck, switched it on. Background noise, the Whiteboys finishing up "Rock and a Hard Place," then Danny's voice. "Ladies, this is for you both, the twin lights of my life. I've made mistakes and . . . ah hell, God's truth I'm not sure there's a damn one of 'em I regret. But there are some things I need to explain. Sorry I won't be able to say good-bye in person, but I've finagled myself into a helluva mess, and worse, I've pulled Lupe in with me. He's . . . done more for me than I had any right to ask, and now I have to try to salvage what I can."

Garcia could feel his heart freezing as the tape played. "Remember me kindly. Remember me," Danny finished softly. The clatter of the telephone falling followed, then the click of Erin's machine switching off. Her eyes were swimming, twin silver tracks streaming down her cheeks. She was unaware of them, coolly concentrating on the snow-dusted street. And at this moment, when she was vulnerable, most like the girl he'd known all those years ago, he could see how much she'd truly changed, how strikingly lovely she'd become. For a long time the only sounds were the hum of the highway and the sweep of the wipers on the windshield.

"You've had this tape all along, haven't you?" Garcia said at last. "You believed I killed Richie for your father?"

"He believed you did," she said, swallowing. "He died believing it. To tell you the truth, I've been so . . . destroyed. . . . It never occurred to me that he could have been wrong."

"And now?"

"Now I know he was. The pictures prove it."

"All the pictures prove is . . . well, the obvious."

"What's obvious is that my mother was being blackmailed, which gives her one helluva motive. Opportunity? Considering how . . . intimately they knew each other, Richie would have opened the door for her."

"Why would she bail me out of jail?"

"Guilt. She knew you didn't do it. She's no cold-blooded killer, she's just a drunken slut. She can plead a combination of justifiable homicide and alcoholic impairment and might not serve a day."

"That's coming down on her a little heavy, isn't it?"

"Why should you defend her?" Erin snapped.

"I owe her," he said simply, "but beyond that, I think you're overreacting."

"But you've no objection to clearing up the matter?"

"No, and in a way I hope you're right. But while we're clearing things up, that tape is evidence in a homicide investigation. You could be disbarred for withholding it. So why did you?"

"I . . . to tell you the truth, I'm a little mixed up about that myself. Maybe it was because . . . we were lovers once, Garcia. You didn't know that, did you?"

He glanced at her. "I'm not sure what you mean."

"Lovers. At least to me. I was in high school, remember? A Catholic school. Still a virgin. And you were . . . the tall, dark, mysterious stranger who drove me to school, met me for lunch sometimes. My girlfriends were positively green. They were so sure you were . . . introducing me to all of the mysteries. And I let them think so. I had a lot of fun with the situation."

"It was a joke, you mean?"

"Maybe it started out that way. The problem was, you treated me like . . . someone special. An honest-to-God woman grown."

"You *were* special," he said. "You were a bright light in a dark time for me, and I liked you. A lot. You were also the very young daughter of a friend."

"Eighteen isn't so young. And you were what? Ten years older? Not so much."

"The life I was in at the time, it felt more like a thousand. And what you're describing was just a schoolgirl crush, right?"

"Or perhaps first love," she said. "I was too young and ignorant to know the difference then. Or maybe there isn't so much. But I've had lovers in my life since. The real thing. And I know the difference now." She eased the BMW over to the shoulder of the road, let it roll to a stop, then turned to face him. Her eyes were aglisten, from tears or a trick of the light. She cupped his cheek with her palm, and kissed his mouth, gently at first, then with rising, surprising intensity.

"A schoolgirl crush?" she asked quietly.

"No," he breathed. "Definitely not."

"The timing could be better though," she said, gathering herself, slipping the car into gear.

"Right again. Maybe we should . . ."

"What is it?" she asked, glancing at him.

"You know, there's something funny about that tape."

"What do you mean?"

"I'm not sure. It's not what Danny says, it's . . . the background. The band is finishing a song called 'Rock and a Hard Place,' a Rolling Stones jam from a couple of years back. And Risa's beginning 'Aledita' when the tape ends."

"What's odd about that?"

"Nothing, that's the problem. That's the order they play them on their tape. But they didn't play them in that order last night."

"Why should that matter?"

"Maybe it doesn't. But when a group releases a new tape, they usually play the songs live in the same order to build audience recognition. And Risa told me that they couldn't change their sets, something about them being . . . sequenced. Do you know what that means?"

"I know it's some kind of electronic equipment bands use. I'm not sure what it does. But considering how busy you were last night, are you certain they changed the set?"

"I'm sure."

"Yes," she said, concentrating on the road again, "I suppose you would be."

Erin parked on the street in front of Danny's home. A full-size Buick station wagon was in the driveway, its tailgate open. A heavyset man, blond, fortyish, stockbroker-soft in a Christmas cardigan sweater, came out the front door carrying a suitcase in either hand as they approached.

"Hello," Erin said, blocking his path to the car, "I'm Erin Kelly. What's going on?"

"I, ah, I'm helping your mother move," Christmas cardigan said uneasily. "I'm Jerry Margolin. Connie and I work together."

"Right," Erin nodded, "she's mentioned you."

"Connie's inside," Margolin said. "Excuse me, we're running late." He brushed past and began loading the cases into the Buick.

"Who is he?" Garcia asked.

"Jerry Margolin. He's my m—he's Connie's boss. And obviously a lot more." Erin stalked into the house, Garcia followed. Connie Kelly was in the living room, wearing faded Calvin Klein jeans and a pink cashmere sweater, pacing. She looked haggard, drained, clutching her highball glass as if it held the last drink on earth.

"Mother?" Erin said. "Going somewhere?"

Connie glanced up, startled, ashen. She stared at them a moment, then shrugged. "I'm going to Europe," she said warily. "I was going to call you."

"When? In mid-Atlantic? Why the rush? What's going on?"

"Everything," Connie said, knocking back a serious belt of her drink. "Too much. I've got to get away."

"I guess I can understand that. Still, the timing could be better. The club business is—"

"We're out of the club business," Connie said bluntly, "as of Monday. The Chiangs upped their offer by a quarter. I'm taking it."

"You can't do that," Erin said.

"It's already done. I've given your uncle Sean power of attorney to handle the transaction so you needn't worry about getting your share. He'll set up a trust fund to pay for your stepbrother's care and divide the rest between us. I'm sorry, Lupe, but I'm afraid you'll have to make other arrangements to continue your bond. I've asked Sean to—there are two more bags in the upstairs bedroom, Jerry."

Margolin hesitated in the doorway, clearly curious

about what was happening. "The flight's in an hour—" he began.

"Then you'd better hurry," Connie snapped. "Please." Margolin flushed with annoyance, but shrugged it off and trotted obediently up the stairs.

"Jerry's going with you?" Erin asked. "I thought he was married."

"He's leaving his wife, and yes, we're going together."

"Well, you're certainly not wasting any time replacing my father. But then there's no reason why you should, since you've been shopping for a while." Erin took the sheaf of photographs out of her purse and tossed them face up on the coffee table.

Connie stared at the pictures, transfixed, what little color she had draining away. "Christ," she whispered, "that bastard. It's never going to stop, is it?"

"Connie?" Margolin paused halfway up the stairs. "Are you all right?"

"I'm fine, Jerry, please, just get the car loaded and let's get out of here."

"Maybe you should tell him to unload it instead," Erin said. "I don't think you're going anywhere."

"No?" Connie said. "Why? Because of these?"

"They're no surprise, are they? You've seen them before," Erin said.

"Once," Connie admitted. "Richie showed them to me. Or some like them."

"Why?"

"He thought he could pressure me into helping him squeeze your father out of the business."

"You must have felt very . . . threatened."

"Threatened? By these? My, you really don't understand, do you? I couldn't have cared less if Richie'd shown them to Danny. In fact, at the time, I rather hoped he would."

"I . . . don't follow you," Erin said. "What are you saying?"

"What the hell, Erin," Connie sighed, "once the club is gone we may never see each other again, so we may as well clear the air. We were never a match made in heaven, your dad and I. He made an honest woman of me and I did my best for you both. When the business started going downhill, I loaned him every dime I had, went to work, turned over my check, never complained. I welcomed it. After all these years he truly needed me."

"But then he got sick," Erin said coolly, "was that it?"

"Partly"—Connie nodded—"but not the way you think. When he knew he was dying, he didn't reach out to me, or anyone else. He closed up like an armored car. Went into business with that pimp to try to win one last game. And when I tried to tell him how lost I felt, he shut me out. Said I shouldn't waste any tears, that he'd been cheating for years with women he picked up in the club. The funny part of it is, in his way, he thought he was being kind, trying to keep me from grieving. But it didn't work out that way. I refused to believe him, so he gave me details, lots of details. A good memory, your father. There must've been a hundred of them, sometimes two at a time. And you two knew about it, didn't you? You must have known, working at the club."

"I knew," Erin admitted. "I guess I assumed you either knew or didn't want to."

"It doesn't matter now, and for what it's worth I probably wouldn't have believed you if you'd told me. Anyway, I couldn't handle it. I fell apart. Started drinking, tried to get even with Danny by balling every man on the planet. Richie picked up on what was happening and came on to me. He invited me to some parties, and I went. And he, um, he took some pictures. Not these, though," she said, frowning. "In the ones he showed me, I think I had two partners—"

Erin slapped her, hard, the crack of it sharp as a gunshot. Connie staggered, blinked, but otherwise seemed unaffected. "I'll be damned," she said, rolling her highball glass slowly over her reddened cheek, "I think that's the first honest exchange we've had in years. Too bad it's so late in the day. Feel any better? I think I do. It clarifies things. I really tried with you, you know. Sometimes relationships just don't develop no matter how badly you want them to. But it wasn't all my fault. You were always hard, Erin, even as a child. Too much of your father in you I guess. But if you think Richie frightened me with these pictures, or that you can, you're wrong. I don't give a damn if you run them on the front page of the *Free Press.*"

"And Jerry? How would he feel about it?"

"He's seen them. Says he finds them . . . stimulating."

"Well," Erin said, drawing a ragged breath, "you're right about one thing. I don't think we'll see each other again. Let's go, Loop, I wouldn't want the *lady* to miss her flight."

"Just one question," Garcia said. "Did Richie's buddy Cottler give you the okay to sell?"

Connie sank slowly down to the sofa, shaken, swallowing. "I, ah, no, he doesn't know. For God's sake, he's the reason I'm running. Please, don't say anything to him. Please."

"No, of course I won't, but he may find out anyway. He seems to be pretty well informed. Still, I can't say you're doing the wrong thing, Connie. When you get to where you're going, keep your head down. And thanks for doing what you could."

"I'm sorry about this," Connie said, looking up at him. "God, I'm sorry about everything."

"Right," he said, "me too."

THIRTY-TWO

"What are you going to do?" Erin asked, keeping her eyes on the road ahead. Neither of them had spoken since leaving the house.

"Go to work, I guess," Garcia said. "Can you drop me at the club?"

"No problem," she said, checking her mirrors before changing lanes, "but . . . if you want me to drop you at the airport, I will, no questions asked."

"Skip, you mean? I'll admit it's crossed my mind. I'm not crazy about going back to jail. Still, I've got until Monday before—by the way, who's your uncle Sean? I thought Father Kelly was handling the business."

"He is. He's Uncle Sean."

"But you call him Mick. He change his name when he joined his order?"

"Nothing so dramatic. Sean's his given name. I started calling him Uncle Mickey when I was very small, Mickey Mouse actually. And I just never stopped. You know how things like that go."

"Why Mickey Mouse? Granted he's not very big, but—"

"Size had nothing to do with it. He has a tattoo of Mickey Mouse on his arm."

"Of Mickey Mouse?"

"Well, maybe not Mickey exactly, more like an army mouse, wearing a helmet. But when you're three or four, all meece are Mickeys." She turned into the Hall Plaza lot. The area in front of the Jade Mountain was nearly full.

"Thanks for squiring me around this afternoon," Garcia said. "I'm sorry things turned out, well, the way they did. If you don't feel like working tonight—"

"And miss the Underground's last big night? You must be kidding. I'll be back at eight. See you then."

Tie-dye Torrance was a vision in pink, blouse-sleeved gypsy shirt, matching headband. He glanced up from pre-fabbing lime and orange slices and gave Garcia an exaggerated salaam. Garcia let himself into the office, stripped off his jacket and his shirt, and splashed some cold water on his face over the basin. He found a pack of Bic throwaway safety razors and a travel can of Foamy in the cabinet above the sink, lathered up, and was shaving when someone rapped on the door.

"It's open, Tie."

But it wasn't Tie. A short, portly black man he'd never seen before stepped in; mid-fiftyish, round chocolate face, salt-and-pepper goatee, brown leisure suit, red Hawaiian shirt open at the throat, porkpie hat.

"Mr. Garcia?"

"That's right."

"My name's Blackjack Markham. My band Blackjack and the Blue Flames plays here on Sunday nights."

"Sure," Garcia said, offering his hand, "the blues band, right? Excuse the lather, what can I do for you, Mr. Markham?"

"Just stoppin' by to see what's haps. We still got a job?"

"Tomorrow night's a go, but I'm afraid you'll have to make other plans after that."

"You givin' the Whiteboys our night," he said. "Don't

blame ya. They hot right now, gettin' played all over the radio."

"It's not that at all, Mr. Markham. I understand you've been doing a fine job. Thing is, the club's being sold. The Chinese restaurant upstairs is going to expand into the space. Does your contract say anything about severance pay?"

"Nah, we never had no contract with Danny. Just a handshake."

"I think Danny's handshake should cover an extra week's pay, considering the short notice you're getting. Can't promise, but I'll try to get it for you."

"Do what you can." Markham shrugged. "Crazy business, ain't it? I been up an' down in it, but never quite this fast. From seven nights to none in one flop."

"Seven nights?" Garcia echoed. "I thought you only played here on Sundays."

"We was. Been doin' okay but nothin' to write home to Mama about. The seven-night thing never did make no sense, 'specially with the Whiteboys so hot."

Garcia paused, staring into the mirror, the safety razor poised in midstroke. "Mr. Markham? Would you care for a taste?"

"I wouldn't say no," the old man smiled. "You buyin'?"

"Absolutely. Pick your poison out of the rack, pour us a couple." Garcia toweled off the lather, accepted a shot glass of Southern Comfort. "Tell me about the seven-nights thing."

"Not much to tell. Crazy Richie called me las' Friday night, told me to get my group together, we'd be takin' over the gig the nex' night, seven nights a week."

"What time was this?"

"I dunno, eight, maybe nine o'clock."

"Did he say why he was making the change?"

"No, fact is, he wasn't makin' a lotta sense, definitely

freaked about somethin'. Figured he musta had trouble with the Whiteboys, maybe they hit him up for a raise or somethin'. Hadda be somethin' like that."

"Why?"

"He wouldn'ta replaced 'em otherwise, not with us. Mind, it ain't like Sunday nights been a bomb, we usually get half a house, mostly gays. Gay bar up the street closes Sundays so they come down here. But we ain't been drawin' near the crowds them Whiteboys do. I stopped by a few minutes las' night, and the club was the jumpin'est I ever seen it. That girl sure can sing, can't she?"

"Yes she can," Garcia agreed. "You've been in to hear her before then?"

"Oh sure, I stop by now an' again. And Bobby, he comes by on Sundays, sits in with us sometimes, or jus' hangs out, gets trashed. Used to be musicians'd sit in and play together, but all them electronic gimmicks they use nowadays, sequencers and like that, you can't do it no more. Too hard changin' things around."

"How do you mean?" Garcia asked. "And what the hell is a sequencer anyway?"

"Sequencer? It's sort of a cross-breed tape deck and computer. Like the Whiteboys don't have no keyboard player, right? So Bobby can punch the keyboard parts into the sequencer and it'll play 'em back along with the band, kinda like a player piano. Whiteboys got their whole show programmed like that. It's why they sound so big with only the four of 'em."

"I see," Garcia said. "So how do they change things, add songs or whatever?"

"No big deal, jus' gotta reprogram the unit. It takes a little doin' but Bobby's good with it."

"I'll bet he is. One last thing, Mr. Markham, on Sunday nights, is Bobby just hangin' out? Or cruisin'?"

Blackjack eyed him a moment, then knocked back the last of his drink. "You wan' know 'bout Bobby, you best talk to Bobby. Thanks for the drink. You let me know 'bout the money."

"I will," Garcia said.

"You know, it's too bad, this place closin'," Markham said, hesitating in the doorway. "Not many rooms lef' in this town for blues. Soup Kitchen Saloon downtown, the CanUsa 'cross the river. Years ago they was blues rooms all over Deetroit. Maybe it's the times. People don't wanna hear no blues when they livin' 'em."

"I know the feeling," Garcia said.

THIRTY-THREE

"Walk away," Echeverria mused, "that's what he told you?"

"I don't think he meant disrespect," Tony LaRose said cautiously. "If he wanted trouble, he coulda popped me and Cottler both. For a minute there I thought he was gonna. It was a near thing." They were in an eighth-floor suite at the Ponchartrain. The Cuban and his coke-eyed girlfriend were in the third course of a room-service candlelight dinner when LaRose and Cottler stumbled in, bloody and disheveled. Cottler's face was seared, slimy with burn ointment, half of his beard burned away.

The Cuban didn't say shit. He just closed his eyes for a minute, like he was meditating, showing the *te ve* tattoos. Then he sent the girl out. Tony expected a tongue-lashing, maybe even to get slapped around for wrecking the car. Instead, Echeverria told Sevum to get cleaned up in the john, then listened to Tony's story without interrupting. Just stared out the window, checkin' out the view like a fuckin' tourist.

"How much?" Echeverria said suddenly.

"How much what?" Tony said, confused.

"Money, Tony. How much money am I out? This *maricón* says we're even. How much does he figure this Kelly was worth? Way I see it, I'm out the hundred K we had with

Richie, we got no piece of the Underground anymore, he knows about the house in Beaufort Gardens, probably knows about the setup there so we can't use any of the film we got, an' we'll have to get the stiff outa there—*chinga!* I need a bookkeeper to figure it up. But I know this much, we ain't close to even. I could chop his fuckin' mother into dogmeat, sell her for a grand a pound and we wouldn't be even. Still, sometimes in business you gotta suck it up, take a loss on a deal. You think this is one of those times, Tony?"

LaRose hesitated, knowing his life depended on his answer for the second time in as many hours. He'd looked past a gun muzzle into the Mex's eyes and seen his death. Bad as that was, Echeverria with his back turned, talking soft, was worse. At least a bullet would be quick. "I don't know," Tony said at last. "What do you think?"

Echeverria glanced at him. "That's a pussy answer," he said, not bothering to conceal the contempt in his tone. "You're second rate, Tony, I knew that when I took you on. But you," he said, shifting his gaze to Cottler, who'd just stepped out of the john, "I expected better from you. *El rehacedero,* the remodeler, the Counts called you. You do okay when a guy's nailed to a wall, not so good when he's loose, *mano a mano,* eh? You're the one got remodeled this time."

Cottler blinked and said nothing, but he was close to blowing, Tony could smell it coming. Jesus, they'll kill each other, maybe me too. "Okay," LaRose said quickly, "look, we fucked up, we know it. The guy blind-sided us. It won't happen again. What do you want us to do?"

"I think we do some advertising," the Cuban said quietly.

"What?"

"Advertising. It's important in business, Tony. Even fuckups like you two must know that. The way I see it, this Mexican fuck's blown our deal. So what we do is try to turn a profit on the situation. We lose our piece of the Underground? Okay, then nobody gets it. We take it out. Big-time. And the next time we want a piece of a business, we don't have to threaten nobody. All we gotta do is whisper Motown Underground to 'em, and they bend over and drop their pants. Understand?"

"I like it," Cottler said with a zombie's smile. "And Garcia?"

"He's yours," Echeverria said. "I give him to you, payback time. Just remember this town ain't Toronto. People get killed here every day. Do him with style. Remodel him. So people remember it."

"They'll remember," Cottler said.

THIRTY-FOUR

Risa Blades opened the dressing room door a crack at Garcia's knock. "Hi," he said, "we have to talk."

She hesitated, then stepped back. "Sure." She was wearing her hawk woman look again, rouged cheeks, heavy eyeshadow, her dark hair combed Early Elvis and sprayed hard as a helmet, black T-shirt, leather hot pants, thigh-high boots. For a moment he tried to picture her as she'd been that morning, barefoot, in bleached muslin. Couldn't. She was two people, both of them magnetic. Bobby Westover was sitting at the makeup table, touching up his eyes. No sign of Lucero or Reeves.

"What's up?" Risa's tone was neutral, and yet he sensed a warning in it.

Westover glanced at Garcia in the mirror, then continued his task. Shirtless, in leather jeans with a metal studded belt, he looked leaner, harder than Garcia would have guessed. Nobody to mess with, Reeves said. Garcia believed it.

"There's no way to sugarcoat this," Garcia said. "The club's being sold. You'll have to make other plans."

"We heard," Bobby said without turning. "Blackjack

Markham stopped by a few minutes ago. How much time we got?"

"Almost none. We'll be closing after this weekend."

"You musta been born under a bad sign or somethin', Garcia. You been nothin' but trouble since you showed up. Anything else?"

"A couple of things. For openers, I think your wife's a very attractive woman."

Bobby froze a moment, glancing up from the mirror; then he shrugged. "You and half the bozos in the club on any given night. I'm kinda fond of her myself. So what?"

"Maybe nothing," Garcia said, "except that it seems to me the only way a guy could be married to Risa and leave her alone, would be if he wasn't into girls at all. And you're not, are you?"

Westover stood up slowly, casually loosening the buckle on his chain belt. "I wouldn't jerk that belt," Garcia said. "There's no room to swing it in here anyway."

"It's only gonna take one," Bobby said, his fist still locked on the buckle. "What kind of a game are you runnin', man?"

"I'm not running a game, Bobby, you are. Your marriage, for instance, that's a game. A front."

"A front for what?" Bobby said. "This isn't the fifties. Gays are out of the closet or haven't you heard?"

"Maybe in the theater and the arts. But in the music biz? Get real. Metal rock'n'roll's as homophobic as the Ku Klux Klan. There's no way a major label would risk signing your group if they knew. And a contract means a lot to you. Risa said you've been playing dives and hustling for years, hoping for a break."

"So has every other band in the business."

"So I wonder how it felt to be so close, and then have Richie threaten to blow it? He was going to, wasn't he? First he backed out of the management deal so he could sell your recording contract, then you had some kind of a hassle in the office the night he was killed and he fired you, called Blackjack and offered him your job. And there went your big chance. A record company won't sign a band it can't see, and Richie could've blown any deal you made by telling them you were gay. Blackmail was his business, he would have known about you."

"You've got it wrong," Risa said quietly. "Bobby didn't tangle with Richie that night. I did. He was half out of his tree because Red was late, started slapping Danny around. I tried to stop him, got decked for my troubles. Besides, we've got a fairly solid alibi, you know? We were onstage when Richie bought it."

"You were," Garcia said, "because you sing every song. But Bobby? From the beginning of 'Rock and a Hard Place' to the end of 'Aledita,' there's no guitar work for nearly fifteen minutes, and the house lights are dimmed."

"Wrong again, Garcia," Bobby said warily, "we don't play 'Hard Place' till the end of the set."

"You mean you do now," Garcia said. "The night Richie was killed you did it in the same order it appears on your album. Don't bother blowin' smoke at me about it. I heard it on tape."

Westover shook his head slowly, running his fingers through his rock'n'roll mane. "You were right, *chica,"* he said to Risa, "the dude's sharp. Okay, Garcia, suppose we talk a deal?"

"What kind of a deal?"

"Simple. I *was* offstage, even went back to the office, and maybe you can jam me up about that. But I can bury you, man."

"How do you figure?"

"For openers, you can't hang Richie's killing on me. It just won't fly. No way I would've killed him. I needed him. Alive and in one piece."

"Even after he welched on your contract?"

"Contract?" Bobby echoed bitterly. "The damn contract

is the least of my problems, man. Check this out." He leaned back on the dressing table, pulled up his pant leg, and tugged his boot down. A narrow plastic band attached to a microchip the size of a postage stamp encircled his ankle. "You know what it is?"

"An electronic tether," Garcia said slowly.

"That's right," Bobby said. "I'm on a leash, monitored twenty-four hours a day. If I get more'n two blocks off course between the club and safe house where Lieutenant Hamadi's got me stashed, I go straight to the slam. You were right, I wanted a record deal bad. I wanted it so bad that when we were half done with the album and Richie said he needed somebody to make a goodie run to Toronto for a load, Risa and I agreed to go."

"And you got busted?"

"They had us nailed from the git. Ten minutes after we made the pickup we were wearin' cuffs in an RCMP office with Hamadi and a Mountie explaining the facts of life. The only thing that kept us outa jail was they wanted Richie's boss so bad they were damn near frothin' at the mouth."

"A Cuban. Echeverria," Garcia said.

"Right." Bobby nodded. "Deal was, we go through with the delivery, report what we see at the club, pump Richie for what we can get, and maybe, just maybe, we can walk away when it's over."

"But you didn't tell them about going back to the office, did you? And you changed your set to conceal it. Why?"

"Hell, everything was a botch the night it happened. I went back to talk Richie outa firin' us, office was locked and nobody answered my knock. Then after I got back to the stage all hell broke loose. Hamadi hauled me in right away, but I could tell from the questions they didn't know I'd been back there, so I dummied up. Figured he might need a fall guy to take the rap for you, you bein' a cop and all. And after they nailed you for it, I decided I'd best stick to my story. If

Hamadi found out I held out on him he'd burn me sure as God made the little green apples."

"Why should I believe you?"

"I don't much care whether you do or not. I didn't kill Richie, he was the only thing keepin' us out of jail, and if you lay it on Hamadi that I was back there, I'll bury you. See, I know about the missing piece in their case. How you got out."

"And you think you know?"

"I know I do. The freight elevator, man. I heard it runnin' as I came down the corridor."

"Are you sure about that?"

"Hey, if there's one thing I'm an expert on, it's sound. I heard it all right, so back off, Garcia. Way I see it, we're all neck deep in shit so let's not make any waves, okay?"

"A Mexican standoff," Risa said dryly.

"Yeah"—Bobby nodded with a thin smile—"something like that."

"Question," Garcia said. "After Richie was killed, why did Hamadi turn you loose, even with a tether?"

"The same job as before," Bobby said evenly, "to keep an eye on the club manager and find out what we could."

"I'm sorry about that," Risa put in, meeting his eyes squarely. "I didn't like it. But you see how things are."

"We all do what we have to sometimes," Garcia said. "No problem."

"So," Bobby said, "we got a deal?"

"Like you said, I've got no reason to make waves. And for what it's worth, I hope you get out from under. I like your music. Good luck tonight."

"Garcia," Bobby said as Lupe opened the door. "It was all for nothin' you know. Waxin' Richie."

"What do you mean?"

"He was gettin' out anyway. That's why he was sellin'

off our contract, stallin' everybody about money. He was puttin' enough cash together to run."

"Run from what? I thought he had everything going for him."

"Not quite. His life kinda kicked back on him, man. Every time he looked at Danny he was seein' his future. Richie was feelin' down a couple months ago, and got tested. He was HIV positive. AIDS."

"How do you know?"

"He told me. Hell, who else could he talk to? The mob he was in with, you're in for life. No retirement, no insurance. He figured the Cuban would whack him as soon as he found out. His only chance was to get a stash together and split. He just waited a little too long."

"How much did he have?"

"A lot, maybe two hundred K. He'd been dealin' dope in the club, turnin' it over as fast as he could. As soon as he'd collected for our contract he'd've been gone. You killed him for nothin', man. Nothin'."

"I didn't kill him at all."

"Whatever you say, man," Bobby said, rebuckling his chain belt. "But if you did, I hope he kissed you good-bye."

THIRTY-FIVE

The club was filling early. A few dancers were already on the floor shakin' it to a Jeff Beck CD on the sound system. "I'm Goin' Down." And maybe I am, Garcia thought, pushing through the crush, scanning the room. Saturday night crowd, a little older, better dressed, with enough college kids and street hustlers to make an interesting mix.

Erin was on duty at the entrance, coolly elegant in a simple white blouse and black skirt. An emerald green scarf at her throat highlighted her eyes, not that they needed it. She was checking the IDs of a restless line of college kids that stretched out the front door and up the stairway. A lady in control, radiating quiet authority, efficient, collected. And he could recall the taste of her mouth without even closing his eyes.

She sensed his gaze, glanced up, gave him a barely perceptible nod, a fainter smile. But he felt it, and thought she did too. Subliminal communication. An elemental wavelength. Heart to heart. Or something. He turned and headed for the office.

No sign of LaRose or his psycho sidekick. And with Aziz and his top shooters in jail the D Streets should be too disorganized to cause trouble over the weekend. After that it wouldn't matter. By Monday night he'd probably be sharing a cell with Aziz.

Father Kelly was sitting at Danny's old desk in street clothes, a navy blue blazer and plain white shirt, his well-padded frame concealed by the back of the chair. He was watching the crowd through the one-way mirror when Garcia stepped into the office. And for a moment he could have been Danny. There was a strong fraternal resemblance in the tilt of his head, the set of his shoulders.

"Hello, Father. Seeing how the other half lives?"

"I wish that's all it was," Kelly said, swiveling the chair to face Garcia. "The club accounts have to be updated by Monday and since Sundays are busy for me, I'll have to do it tonight. I hope you don't mind."

"Would it matter if I did?"

"Not a whit," the priest said cheerfully. "And I wanted to talk to you anyway."

"About what?"

"The sale of the Underground. For what it's worth, I'm sorry things are working out badly for you. You understand I'll have to revoke your bond Monday in order to clear the club's title for sale?"

"Why should you be sorry? You were against the idea from the start."

"True enough, but there was nothing personal in that. You've worked hard and done a good job and . . . anyway, I'm sorry."

"Then why do I have the feeling that the Chiangs' new offer was more than a happy coincidence?" Garcia said, resting a hip on the corner of the desk. "You talked them into upping their price, didn't you?"

"A case of striking while the iron was hot," Kelly admitted. "You'd already spooked them. It didn't take much persuasion. Again, nothing personal. It's best for Daniel's family."

"I can't argue the point. Still, since it's going to inconvenience me a bit, I wonder if I could ask a favor?"

"What kind of favor?"

"Clarification of a religious matter."

"I wasn't aware you were a religious man, Mr. Garcia."

"Sad but true. That's the problem. Correct me if I'm wrong but as I recall my catechism, a lie is a venial sin, right?"

"Unless it's a particularly vicious lie which causes grievous harm to another. Such a lie might be deemed a mortal sin."

"I see. And deliberately allowing someone to believe something untrue? Is that the equivalent of a lie?"

"Not quite. Failure to correct an untruth would be a sin of omission, less serious than an outright lie, which is a sin of commission. Why are you asking all this?"

"Lies are my business," Garcia said simply. "One of the hardest things you learn as a rookie is that people lie to you. They look you in the eye, swear on their mother's graves, and lie their buns off. Sometimes they even lie when they'd be better served by the truth. When you work undercover, you learn to lie too. I got good at it. Probably too good. Still, occasionally a lie will surprise me. Like yours, Father."

"You think I've lied to you about something?" Kelly asked, unoffended.

"Lie is too strong a term. More like a sin of omission. That first day, when we were arguing about Danny avoiding the draft, I said you had no right to judge him because chaplains don't face the same moral choices as soldiers. You should have corrected me. You weren't a chaplain then. Erin told me you got your nickname because of a tattoo, Mickey Mouse, wearing a helmet. I saw a few of those in Nam. The men who wore them were tunnel rats. Little guys, about your size, who'd go down the VC spider holes with a forty-five and a flashlight, never knowing what they'd find. Rats were some of the bravest men who ever wore a uniform. So

I'm curious, Father. Why commit a sin of omission about being a hero?"

"Don't flatter yourself that I sinned for your benefit," Kelly said dryly. "It's just that Nam isn't one of my favorite topics. If you're curious, I went down more'n a dozen holes, got blown to flinders by a ten-year-old kid with a grenade in the last one, spent two years in and out of VA hospitals afterward. It was the worst time of my life."

"Mine too," Garcia nodded, "which is why I can't believe you were on the outs with Danny all these years because he dodged the war. There was a lot more to it, wasn't there? What was his sin, Father? What did Danny do that you couldn't forgive?"

A doubleboom of drumthunder from the stage interrupted him as Bailey Reeves kicked off the Whiteboys' first set, laying down a heavy fatback beat, his muscular arms crossing his chest with every stroke, a gleaming ebony rhythm machine.

"Y'all ready to party down?" Bobby roared at the crowd, strutting across the stage, his guitar slung low as a gunfighter's holster. Garcia switched off the office monitor speaker, reducing the sound from the stage to the muted thump of Bailey's kick drum vibrating through the walls, the Underground's hard rock heartbeat.

"Whatever trouble there was between Daniel and me," Kelly said coldly, "was buried with him. It's over."

"No," Garcia said, "it's not. It's still going on, and it's getting worse."

"For you, perhaps."

"For all of us. Father, Richie wasn't stalling on his payments to squeeze Danny out. He was putting together a bankroll, getting ready to run."

"To run?"

"From his life," Garcia said simply. "He'd tested HIV positive. He had AIDS."

Kelly stared at him a moment, reading the truth, then

slowly closed his eyes. "Holy Mary, Mother of God," he whispered. "Connie."

The smaller man's face was too painful to watch. Garcia glanced away, out into the club. A busy night. Danny would have loved it.

"You know, don't you?" Kelly said at last.

"That you took Richie off? I wasn't sure until a moment ago. Maybe it's my upbringing, but it was hard for me to consider the idea, and anyway I didn't think you were physically capable of handling a guy like Richie. Until Erin told me about the tattoo. Even then, I didn't understand why. You wouldn't have done it for Danny. But it wasn't about Danny, was it? It was about Connie. And so was the trouble between you and Danny. He took them from you, didn't he? Connie, and Erin?"

"Constance was my—love first," Mick said softly, "and my first love. Then Daniel moved in. When he got his draft notice and fled to Canada, he took her with him. Erin was born five months later. Meanwhile I'd volunteered and was in Nam trying my best to become a dead hero. I almost made it."

"Erin's your daughter, not Danny's?"

"Daniel only had one child, a boy born brain-damaged several years before he met Connie. He had a vasectomy afterward. Erin is my child. And Connie's."

"And that's what triggered this, isn't it? You saw the photographs, didn't you? Of Richie, and Connie?"

"I think Richie deliberately left them in the desk for Daniel, but I came across them first." He said, taking a ragged breath. "Seeing them was bad enough, but worse, I knew the vicious bastard was dating Erin too. It was more than I could take. More than anyone should have to. So I, ah, I decided to drive him off. I'd heard rumors that he was dealing drugs in the club. I thought I could threaten to expose him, or . . . Hell, I don't know what I thought.

"Since I'd become de facto landlord for the building,

Connie'd given me her keys, including a master key for the freight elevator. I came in that way to avoid meeting Daniel. But when I got here the office was a shambles, liquor splashed all over the place. Richie was in a rage. When I tried to talk to him he cut me off, tried to throw me out. He, ah, he slapped my face. And I—exploded. I attacked him.

"I'm not even sure what happened. Old reflexes I guess, from hand-to-hand combat training. I thought I'd forgotten it all long ago. In the scuffle I hit him in the throat. He sat down hard in the chair. And never got up."

"Why didn't you call the police?"

"I wasn't thinking all that clearly. I wanted to protect my family and the church. And myself. And I panicked. I grabbed his lockbox off the desk, ripped off his gold chains. I hoped the police would think it was a robbery. God knows we have enough of them in this town."

"And when they didn't? When I was arrested?"

"To be honest, I was relieved," Father Kelly said bluntly. "From what I read in the papers, you were a rogue cop who'd taken blood money. I didn't know you, or owe you a thing. It seemed like poetic justice."

"And now?"

"I don't know, I—what's wrong?"

"I'm not sure," Garcia said uneasily, switching the monitor speaker back on and peering out into the club. "The dance floor lights went out and the band quit in the—Cottler! My God, Cottler's out there! Stay here!" He wheeled, heading for the door.

"Lupe!" Risa's shout of warning cracked over the PA system like a lightning strike, followed by a thunder blast that hammered the walls like a steel fist, smashing Father Kelly out of his seat as the observation mirror exploded into the office.

Stunned and deafened, Garcia staggered to his feet, gasping at the sting of water on his face as the sprinkler system kicked on. Through the twisted frame of the mirror, the club was a shambles, flames licking at the office walls, bodies scattered like jackstraws near the bar. The dance floor was a writhing, wailing tangle, people trying to stand or crawl away, screaming, crying. The bandstand was in total darkness, he couldn't tell if—

"Garcia? Help me, please. I can't see." Father Kelly was on his knees, fumbling at the overturned chair, trying to get to his feet. His face was a crimson mask, blood streaming from a dozen glass shards from the shattered mirror embedded in his skin.

"Don't move," Garcia said, "stay where you are." He stumbled to the basin, grabbed a hand towel, drenched it with cold water then carefully removed Kelly's thick horn-rimmed glasses and began blotting the blood from around his eyes. "I think you're okay, your glasses didn't break, thank God. Open your eyes slowly. Any glass in them?"

"I . . . no, I—don't think so."

"Okay, your face is lacerated and bleeding pretty freely, but it's not serious. Take this towel, keep the blood out of your eyes. Can you get up?"

"What happened?" Kelly said, staggering to his feet, holding the towel to his forehead. "Grenade? Oh my God, Erin?" He fumbled his glasses back on and stumbled to the desk, peering out into a smoking, screaming hell.

People were dazedly getting to their feet. Only those closest to the office seemed to be badly injured, but the others were already dissolving into a panicked, roiling mob, pushing, scrabbling over each other toward the exits. Then, for a heartbeat everything stopped.

"Cool out! Cool out now!" Bobby Westover shouted, thundering like the voice of Jehovah over the PA system cranked all the way up. "Everything's gonna be okay! The sprinklers will handle the fire, just be cool, we'll all get outta this. Now everybody look around you, help the people up who can't stand on their own, and start walking to the

nearest exit. Don't push. There's another exit over there—*Look at me, Goddamn it!* You think I'd be up here if I thought we were gonna fuckin' *die?* Now look at me and listen up!"

Bailey Reeves plugged a tape into the sound system, dialing it low, background music under Bobby's voice. And gradually, incredibly, it began to work. The panicked rush didn't stop outright, but it slowed, and those in the rear quit trying to blindly claw their way toward the front door, following Bobby's directions to the alternate fire exits.

"I've got to find Erin," Father Kelly said, wrapping the bloody towel around his forehead like a turban. "If anything's happened to her—"

"She was next to the front door, away from the blast, she should be all right," Garcia said, yanking hard at the doorknob, "but I'm not so sure we are." The steel office door opened a few inches near the bottom but that was all. It was twisted, jammed in its frame. "Give me a hand here," Garcia said. "Grab one of those shelves to pry with."

"The hell with that," Kelly said, climbing up on the desk, kicking the shards of the broken mirror out of the way. "We can get out through here—"

"No, don't!" Garcia shouted, grabbing the back of Kelly's jacket, pulling him away from the opening as a blast of gunfire exploded from an overturned table near the bar. Buckshot ripped through the mirror frame, scything into the office walls, catching Garcia full in the back, hurling him across the room, hammering him down. Into a Lions-Jets game at the Silverdome, Thanksgiving Day. Barry Sanders breaking away for a long gainer, the crowd roaring like a great beast, howling . . .

THIRTY-SIX

The floor was shuddering, rumbling like a train. Train? I'm on a train. Screams, noise, people shouting. Garcia tried to open his eyes. Too hard, couldn't manage. Smell. The train smelled . . . spicy. Chinese. Ginger. That was the smell. Ginger. The train lurched to a halt. Chains rattling as the car door—

"Garcia? Can you hear me?" Danny whispered. Jesus God.

"Danny?"

Garcia opened his eyes slowly. Father Kelly was kneeling in front of him, his face blurry, only inches away. Garcia tried to look around, but couldn't seem to move his head. He was numb, leaden. "What happened?" he said.

"You've been shot," Kelly panted. "People in the club went crazy, panicked, climbing over each other like—Mother of God, it's awful, awful." His eyes were swimming, pink trails streaming down his gore-spattered face, his head still wrapped in a bloody turban. "I pried the door open, dragged you back to the freight elevator."

"Where are we?" Garcia asked.

"Kitchen of the Jade Mountain. We've got to get out of here. Can you walk at all?"

"I don't know. I can't feel anything. Where am I hit?"

"In the back. Buckshot, I think. It's—bad. Very bad. I'm afraid to drag you any more, you're bleeding too much, and I'm just not big enough to carry you. Come on, try to get up, I'll help you."

Kelly grasped Garcia by the lapels, pulling him up. Lupe groaned and crumpled to his hands and knees, tried to crawl, right hand, left, slide a knee forward, head down, dragging himself like a smashed slug, leaving a crimson smear across the white tiled floor. His spine was shattered. Had to be to hurt this much . . . Everything went suddenly white. The floor. His face was on the tile floor. Must have fallen . . .

He felt himself being lifted again. Kelly trying to haul him up . . . "Aaahhh! *God,* no!" The priest stumbled and they both went down in a tangle.

"I'm sorry," Father Kelly panted. "I just can't—I'm sorry."

"It's okay," Garcia gasped. "Look, just help me sit up, lean me against the counter. C'mon." Mick knelt in front of him, shifted him as gently as he could. Garcia slumped against the cupboard door, arms limp, useless at his sides, legs out in front of him.

"Better?" Kelly asked.

"It's good. I can breathe. Thanks."

"How long before the police get here?"

"Probably on their way now," Garcia said swallowing. "May be too late though. It'll take 'em awhile to sort out the mess downstairs. Cottler may guess where we are before then."

"Erin. I've got to see to Erin."

"Yes, you'd better. . . ." Garcia nodded, dazed, his mind wandering. Danny? Is that you? Father Kelly's face was shrinking, fading to black. . . .

Garcia's eyes blinked open, startled by the slam of the freight elevator gate. As the cage disappeared down the shaft in a rattle of chains there was a crash of breaking glass from the front of the restaurant.

Sevum Cottler burst into the kitchen a split second later, his StreetSweeper shotgun waist high, his eyes Methedrine wide and wired, scanning the room like hyperactive radar. He'd shaved off the remains of his beard, but a livid burn mark still remained. In black fatigues and combat boots, kamikaze headband, a combat bowie knife in a shoulder sheath, he looked like a Rambo fantasy figure, strung out on speed, dressed to kill. But the weapons were real, the smell of death on him was real.

"Where's the other guy?" he hissed at Garcia. No answer. Garcia's eyes were closing, the kitchen fading again. . . .

"I said where *is* he?" Cottler snarled, kicking Garcia hard in the pit of the belly with his steel-toed boot.

"Gone," Garcia gasped, sagging forward, doubling over, "God, he's gone."

"Holeee shit," Cottler said, sidestepping cautiously closer, glancing hastily down at Garcia's blood-soaked shoulders, then around the kitchen again, his eyes flicking back and forth like heat lightning. "Damn near blew you in half, didn't I? Glad I didn't. 'Cause we got some shit to settle, you and me, Garcia. Paybacks are a bitch, motherfucker, an' it's payday."

He slung the shotgun over his shoulder, stepped quickly over to the kitchen counter. "Hey, check this out, spick, place got more gadgets'n Toys 'R' Us. Sharp ones. Couldn't be fuckin' better. You still got some blood left, right?"

He jerked open a silverware drawer, pawed through it, cursed, dumped it on the floor with a crash, tried another. Came up with a salad fork. "Whaddya think?" he said, testing the tines against the back of his hand. "No way, not sharp enough." Tossed the fork aside. And found an ice pick. He held its tip up to the light, frowning. "Yeah, right. You checkin' this out, cocksucker? Wonderin' what happens next?"

He rattled his hand through a line of utensils hanging from a wall rack above the chopping block. Picked out a heavy oriental meat cleaver. Laying the shotgun aside, he knelt in front of Garcia and slammed the meat cleaver down, burying it in the floor beside Garcia's left thigh.

"C'mon, wake up," Cottler hissed, slapping him sharply across the face, hard, back and forth. "C'mon, Goddamn it, you don't wanna miss this." Garcia raised his right hand, feebly trying to ward off the blows. Cottler seized his wrist, holding it as easily as a child's. "This hand still works some, huh?" He twisted the wrist savagely, forcing Garcia's palm down on his thigh.

"Forgot the rope, can't tie you up," Cottler panted, grinning. "But we can improvise." He lifted the ice pick, waving it back and forth in front of Garcia's face, waiting until Lupe's eyes began following the gleaming tip involuntarily, then gradually brought it closer, until the point was brushing his right eyelash, making it blink. . . . And then he suddenly swept the blade down, piercing the back of Garcia's hand, pinning his palm to the muscle of his thigh.

"Aaahhh!" Garcia's pupils flared with shock, his face instantly beading with perspiration, his arm quivering with a thousand-volt surge. Cottler rocked back on his haunches, watching as Garcia tried to bring his left hand across to the ice pick. He couldn't. The hand lifted a little, then fell back, twitching like a broken bird.

"So," Cottler said, leaning forward, his face only inches from Garcia's, his breath Methedrine rank, eyes aglitter, "how 'bout it, greaser? You wanna say anythin'? Like how sorry you are you fucked with me? No? Well you will. I'm gonna remodel you, stud. Make a new man outta you. Or a new somethin'. You dig what I'm sayin'? The man said to do you so people remember it. I'm gonna do you up proud. You ready?"

He jerked his bowie knife out of its sheath, held it in front of Garcia's face a moment, twisting it so the light reflected off the blue steel blade, the saw-toothed, deeply serrated back. Then he slowly lowered the knife to Garcia's thigh, slid the tip through the fabric of his jeans, and thrust it slowly forward toward his groin, slitting a shallow, bloody line in his skin. Then up to his belt, slicing cleanly through the leather. Cottler's breathing had gone shallow, his eyes locked tautly on Garcia's, wide, unblinking.

"Got the picture yet?" he whispered, his voice hoarse, the words almost a caress. He lowered the blade to Garcia's right thigh an inch below where his hand was impaled with the ice pick, then followed the same path with the blade, up through the beltline, the razor-edged blade hissing through the denim like tissue paper. Cottler was blinking rapidly now, swallowing. He reached down, peeled the slit flap of Garcia's jeans forward, exposing him.

"Well, well, what we got here? Looks like a limp dick." Garcia's face was a bloodless gray, dripping, taut as a wire. Cottler grasped him gingerly, uncertainly, then clamped on, hard, teeth clenched, nostrils flaring, steeling himself. "Ready, greaser? C'mon, say somethin'. Tell me you're sorry, maybe I'll use the blade instead of the cleaver. No? Then fuck you, man—"

"Nooooo!" The howl startled Cottler, freezing him, as Mick Kelly exploded through the kitchen doorway, launching himself, catching Sevum head high. Garcia screamed as the two men came down hard on his ice-picked thigh, then rolled off, writhing, clawing at each other, Kelly clinging desperately to Cottler's knife wrist with both hands. But the younger man was quicker and stronger. He thrust a knee into Kelly's stomach and bucked him over. Kelly managed to hang on to the wrist, but Cottler scrambled on top of him

and began hammering the priest's bloodied face with his free hand.

Garcia tried to move, couldn't, no feeling in his back or legs. He couldn't lift his left hand, but managed to make it crawl along on its fingers across his naked waist like a smashed tarantula, then down his thigh to the ice pick.

Kelly's grip on Cottler's wrist was slipping, sliding down the wrist toward his elbow, gradually losing his hold. Mick's face was a crimson mask now, blood streaming, unable to defend himself from Cottler's fist. Garcia managed to grasp the handle of the ice pick with his left hand. He drew his knee up a few inches, and dropped it, clutching the handle, pulling the blade out an inch, then repeating the process, until the ice pick blade came clear of his thigh. He tried to yank the pick out of his right hand with his left. The pain was incredible, but he was so dazed he was barely aware of it. The blade wouldn't budge. His left hand hadn't the strength to pull it out.

Cottler was sitting astride Mick now, grinning crazily, toying with him, slapping him around openhanded, snapping his face back and forth.

Garcia closed his eyes, concentrating; then slowly he pushed his right palm down to the floor, forcing the ice pick out.

Tiring of the game, Cottler suddenly jerked his knife hand up and out of Mick's grasp and slashed the smaller man across the chest, once, twice, swept the blade up, then hesitated.

He blinked rapidly, more in surprise than pain. He dropped his knife, began scrabbling frantically at the hilt of the ice pick protruding from his armpit. With the last of his strength Mick clubbed Cottler in the temple with his fist, knocking him off. Cottler sprawled face first on the floor, splintering his teeth on the tiles. It didn't matter. He didn't know.

Kelly lay on his back a moment, covering his eyes with

his forearm, his breath coming in sobs. Then he rolled over, forced himself up to his hands and knees. He crawled to Garcia, peered intently into his face, then gently pressed a fingertip at the base of Lupe's jaw, feeling for a pulse. Garcia tried to focus on Kelly's face, couldn't manage it. He was wavering, flowing like water into darkness. . . .

"Garcia, can you hear me? I don't think you're going to make it. Would you like to make an act of contrition?"

"No." Garcia's voice was scarcely a whisper.

"Lupe, please. I've seen men go in combat. You're almost home."

With the last shreds of his will, Garcia forced his eyes to open, to concentrate. "You're not going to go for help, are you?"

Kelly looked away. "I came back because I couldn't . . . leave you to be slaughtered by that pig, but . . . I can't help you now. It's too late. For the both of us."

"Mick, don't let me die here. Please."

Kelly glanced at Cottler a moment, then back at Garcia. His face was battered, bleeding, tear-streaked. He got unsteadily to his feet, his mouth a grim, narrow line. "I'm sorry," he said, "I can't. It would destroy my family."

"Mick," Garcia called after him, "I won't talk. I give you my word."

"No," Kelly said without looking back, "you'd have to. To save yourself."

"Do you want to keep Richie's money? Is that it?"

Kelly hesitated, then turned, blinking as though he'd been struck. "I don't give a damn about the money. I wish to God I'd never seen it."

"Then I can save us," Garcia said, his voice fading, "both of us. At least listen to me."

"No," Kelly said, "I don't believe you."

"You don't have to believe me," Garcia whispered, his eyes closing. "Father, do you believe in money?"

THIRTY-SEVEN

Jimmy Hamadi looked sharp, clean shaven, wearing a cashmere topcoat, tailored slacks, and Nunn Bush tasseled loafers. His thick, dark hair was neatly parted a few degrees off center, combed down to camouflage his multicolored punker streaks. He drove absently, one hand on the wheel, the other toying with his Camaro's radio dial, ignoring the programmed search-and-destroy functions.

"You didn't have to dress up for me you know," Garcia said quietly. "I would've settled for a corsage."

"The suit's not for you. Fielder's called a meeting of department heads at four. Damage control."

"So sorry," Garcia said.

"Far as I know, your name's not officially on the agenda," Hamadi said, "but I think there's a fair chance it'll come up. Mostly it's gonna be about the shooting at the Windsor Tunnel last night. It's lookin' a little shaky. The Cuban's bimbo girlfriend is telling the press it was a hit, that LaRose and Echeverria were gonna surrender."

"Were they?"

"The Mountie in front of the car had the best view. He says they reached for weapons. Even if he fired first it doesn't matter. Both men were armed, both of 'em fired, and both of 'em were DOA at Samaritan. The girl's lucky to be alive. She's a Canuck. They've already filed for extradition and we're going to comply. Once she's in a Canadian lockup, her memory might improve."

"I wouldn't be surprised."

"And since we're on the subject, we might as well clear the air about something, Loop. When you got messed up in the sting I had runnin' at the Underground, it bothered me. I never really believed you took that punk off, and a lot of people thought Brownell went after you too hard with what we had. But in a way you were better off then. You looked guilty, but at least people could understand you tryin' to help a friend. Now you look dirty."

Garcia glanced at him, said nothing.

"The setup was too crude," Hamadi continued. "Some junkie turns Fielder on to a body hangin' in a basement and surprise, surprise, it's Zeayen's buddy, Red, complete with a suicide note confessin' to killing Richie. 'I can't live with the death of my cousin on my conscience.' Problem bein' that Nurredin was a stone psychopath, wouldn't know a conscience if it bit him on the ass."

Garcia shifted uncomfortably in the seat. His left arm was in a sling beneath his leather overcoat, his chest and shoulders tightly bandaged. "What do you want from me, Jimmy?"

"I'm just sayin' you look bad the way things are. You ought to make some kind of a statement."

"You mean like the truth?" Garcia said. "Okay, here's a truth. If I hadn't asked Echeverria for something in exchange for Richie's stash, he wouldn't have gone for it. And we're both damned lucky he decided to cut his losses and do a deal. If he hadn't you wouldn't have taken him dirty at the border. True?"

"Maybe," Hamadi conceded.

"Here's another truth. I didn't kill Richie Zeayen. Or Red Nurredin. And what happened to Cottler was self-defense and then some."

"That's not what I mean and you know it. People aren't stupid, Loop. If you let things stand the situation's got fix written all over it."

"And they think I fixed it? From the intensive care ward at Samaritan?"

"No." Hamadi shook his head. "That's why you come off lookin' so bad. They know somebody else set it up. And it doesn't take a mental giant to figure it was probably the Cuban. You're gonna take a real hammerin' in the papers, you know."

"And in the department?"

"There's talk," Hamadi admitted. "A lotta guys think you just rolled over and traded us Echeverria for a get-out-of-jail-free card."

"If that's what they think, nothing I say will change their minds. The way things stand, you've got Nurredin for the Zeayen killing. If I admit I traded Richie's stash to the Cuban for setting Nurredin up you'd have to reopen the case, and I'd still be the prime suspect, right? No thanks. If it comes down to doing time with friends thinking you're innocent or walkin' free and having them wonder, which would you choose?"

"You wanna take the heat, fine, dummy up. You got into this jam tryin' to protect somebody, and I think you still are. I hope it's worth it, Loop, because you're gonna pay some heavy dues for it. I'll do my best to cover your butt at the meeting this afternoon, but nothin' in life is free, you know? Sometime down the line, homeboy, you're gonna tell me all about this. Just you and me and a pint of Johnnie Walker Red."

"Could be," Garcia said, turning away, "but I doubt it."

THIRTY-EIGHT

Garcia could feel a pulse thumping up through his calves as he stepped carefully down the Underground entrance stairway. Not music. Hammers, and wrecking bars, and the banshee howl of a power saw. Inside, the room was barely recognizable. Work lights blazed down through the naked steel ceiling framework, casting a skewed checkerboard shadow on the floor. The carpet had been ripped up, and rough gray concrete showed through the scabrous patches of foam padding and contact cement.

Tables and chairs were piled haphazardly against the back wall, a jagged mountain of furniture shrouded with paint-spattered drop cloths. Sawhorses stacked with raw lumber and new paneling were stationed around the room. A half dozen denim-clad carpenters in safety goggles and breathing masks were stapling up a lathwork matrix for insulation, anonymous as Martians.

Danny's office was already gone, the walls obliterated as though they'd never existed. Two workmen were installing plumbing beneath a stainless steel salad bar where his desk had been. The corridor wall beside was pitted. Grenade fragments? Hard to say now.

Garcia walked slowly across the dance floor, taking in the changes. It'll be just another empty building in a town full of 'em, Danny'd said. And so it was, if only temporarily.

He stepped up on the empty stage, glanced up into the overhead spotlight racks, barren but for a single glowering work light. He tried to imagine what it would be like to play on a stage, the thunder of drums, the smell of the crowd.

"I have a forwarding address if you'd like it," Erin said from the dance floor. She was dressed for the winter streets, a stylish Hudson's Bay trench coat in black leather, knee-high boots to match, a green tam perched smartly atop her auburn hair. Even more cool and professional than usual.

"Address?" Garcia said. "Oh, for the Whiteboys you mean? I already have it. The, ah, happy couple stopped by to see me before they left for L.A., record contract in hand. A talented bunch. Hope they make it."

"I came by to see you too," Erin said. "Twice. You were asleep both times."

"Why didn't you wake me up?"

"You looked like you needed the rest. You still do. Should you be out and about so soon?"

"I wrote myself a pass. I've done all the hospital time I can stand and I wanted to see this place while there was still something left of it. Father Kelly said the Chiangs were gutting it. He wasn't kidding."

"He told me he'd seen you, which surprised me a bit. I didn't think you two hit it off that well."

"He thinks there's hope for me."

"An incurable optimist, my uncle," she said, glancing around. "God it's hard to see the Underground go. I grew up down here. It was a magic place to be a kid, but after all that's happened . . . I'm glad it's going. It was my father's playground. It wouldn't be the same without him."

"No," Garcia said, "I guess not. Have you heard from Connie?"

"Just a note. She's in Spain. Barcelona. She checked herself into an alcohol rehab clinic there. The best part is, when she was admitted, she tested negative for HIV. It's too soon to be sure, of course, but maybe she got lucky and dodged the bullet."

"I hope so. I think the lady's overdue for a break. By the way, I don't suppose you know what the Chiangs did with Danny's old desk?"

"Absolutely," she said, brightening a little, "they moved it to my office. Sorry, Loop. Snooze and lose."

"That's okay, I was just . . . Your office? Doesn't the desk clash with your high-tech decor?"

"Contrast is the word. Retro-reality chic is the very latest thing, you know. Or at least that's what I told my boss. Speaking of bosses, I have to get back. Can I drop you somewhere?"

"I'm—not sure," he said. "My apartment, I guess, if it's no trouble."

"Your apartment? I thought it was still pretty well messed up."

"I'll have to start on it sometime."

"In the shape you're in? Bad idea. Why don't you stay at the house instead? Connie's in Europe, the place is empty. You can redo your apartment at your own pace, and house-sit for us meanwhile. What do you say?"

"I, ah, sure. That would definitely work for me if you're sure it's all right."

"It's not all right, it's perfect," she said briskly, taking a last look around. "Tell you what, after you get settled in, maybe I'll pick up a pizza after work some night, and we can munch in front of the fire. And talk. About everything. The way you and my father did."

"Man to man, you mean?"

"No," she smiled, "that's not what I mean at all."

"I'd like that. A lot. As long as you don't build up your hopes too much. They say you can't go home again."

"I've heard that," she said. "I'm not sure it's true."

"I hope not," he said.

A Bit on the Side

By the same author

THE DOG IT WAS THAT DIED
ALL EXCEPT THE BASTARD
THE SANITY INSPECTOR
GOLFING FOR CATS
THE COLLECTED BULLETINS OF IDI AMIN
THE FURTHER BULLETINS OF IDI AMIN
THE LADY FROM STALINGRAD MANSIONS
THE PEANUT PAPERS
THE RHINESTONE AS BIG AS THE RITZ
TISSUES FOR MEN
THE BEST OF ALAN COREN
THE CRICKLEWOOD DIET
BUMF
PRESENT LAUGHTER (Editor)
SOMETHING FOR THE WEEKEND?
BIN ENDS
SEEMS LIKE OLD TIMES
MORE LIKE OLD TIMES
A YEAR IN CRICKLEWOOD
TOUJOURS CRICKLEWOOD?
ALAN COREN'S SUNDAY BEST
ANIMAL PASSIONS (Editor)

For children

BUFFALO ARTHUR
THE LONE ARTHUR
ARTHUR THE KID
RAILROAD ARTHUR
KLONDIKE ARTHUR
ARTHUR'S LAST STAND
ARTHUR AND THE GREAT DETECTIVE
ARTHUR AND THE BELLYBUTTON DIAMOND
ARTHUR v THE REST
ARTHUR AND THE PURPLE PANIC

A Bit on the Side

Alan Coren

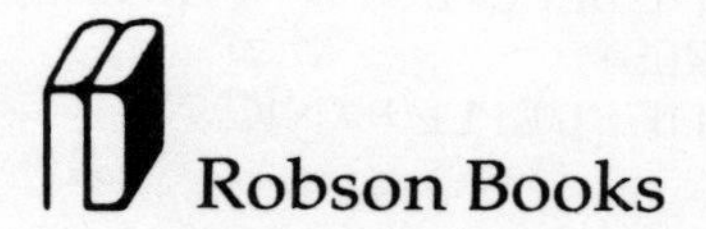

First published in Great Britain in 1995 by Robson Books Ltd, Bolsover House, 5–6 Clipstone Street, London W1P 8LE

British Library Cataloguing in Publication Data
A catalogue record for this title is available from the British Library

ISBN 0 86051 990 2

Typeset by Columns Design and Production Services Ltd, Reading.
Printed in Great Britain by WBC Book Manufacturers Ltd, Bridgend, Mid-Glamorgan.

Contents

A Bit at the Front

I was once passing through the offices of *The Times* on my way to an important business meeting with, as I recall, the coffee machine, when I overheard a sub-editor describing my copy for that Wednesday's paper as "a bit on the side".

Having always prided myself on the cannily oblique stance I take when dealing with major world issues – the piece in question was a searing exposé of a man who had come to my door in a flagrant attempt to sell me a pullet – I was of course delighted by this perceptive analysis of my life's work, and stopped to tell him so.

"A bit on the side, eh?" I said. "More so than usual, would you say?"

He looked at me.

"No," he said, "it's always a bit on the side."

"Well," I said, "I do my best, and it's nice to know that someone . . . "

"Wednesdays, Simon Jenkins does a major piece in the middle of the page, and you do a bit on the side. I was just telling Brian. He's new."

"I see," I said. "Hallo Brian."

"Hallo," said Brian.

No, But I Saw the Movie

For five Sundays past, many of you will have sat sighing before your fireside tubes while Dick Lester's series *Hollywood UK* celebrated 1960s British cinema. You were sighing not only because the resonant clips of *Room at the Top, Whistle Down the Wind, Saturday Night and Sunday Morning* and many another gritty monochromatic corker will have reminded you of the quondam splendour of our national cinema, but also because, even as these disparate gobbets unspooled, similarly spasmodic sight-bites will have been playing elsewhere in your head. As, 30 years on, you once again watched Albert Finney asking Shirley Anne Field to meet him outside the Odeon, you simultaneously will have seen yourself outside the Odeon to meet the date you were taking inside to watch him asking it. At least, you *think* you will have seen yourself.

I wonder. I have just finished watching a 1963 British masterpiece in its entirety, and although I knew exactly what I was doing on the day it was shot (as one is supposed to with 1963), it transpires that I do not have the remotest idea. But first, the film. It is major. It manifests all the stunning innovatory techniques of that golden era, often to the point of impenetrability. Quite how it escaped Lester's meticulous trawl I do not know, unless it was because I possess the only print. I myself, mind, had not watched it for nigh on 30 years; but since tomorrow is its anniversary and it occurred to me to celebrate this with a private showing to a small, select audience, I dug it out today to ensure that it remained in projectable nick.

It is called *The Wedding of Mr and Mrs Core*. That is just one of the things I had forgotten about it. The film was waiting for us when we got back from our honeymoon, and I always meant to ring the *auteur* about the missing *n*, but I never got round to it. As the title was composed by sticking red magnetic letters to what looks like a fridge, it is possible the *n* was less magnetic than its siblings, but we shall never know, now. The title fades to reveal a garden gate, which opens mysteriously, or would do if you couldn't see an ear sticking out from behind it, and the camera then lurches down a path towards the front door of the future Mrs Core's pre-marital house, whereupon an unidentifiable figure darts from the garage, so briefly that we are not immediately sure whether we have seen him or not. This, remember, is a full three years before Antonioni pinched the idea for *Blow Up*.

Suddenly, we are inside, where the future Mrs Core and her mother, who are dressing, are telling the camera to go away. Since this is a silent movie, only lip-readers, sadly, will recognise the language as a milestone in cinema frankness. The scene now returns to the garden, and a front door opening fairly mysteriously to allow the future Mrs Core to exit just in time for a gust to lift the bridal veil prematurely from her face and snag it on a rose bush brown with seasonally shrivelled buds, a symbolic coup so daring that, had Bergman seen it at the time, he would undoubtedly have chucked in the sponge.

And, suddenly, a hundred drunks are dancing. Cunningly flouting the convention of showing the Cores emerging from the ceremony by the masterly trick of leaving his camera in the car, the *auteur* cuts straight to the reception. The question is, whose? Watching it now, I am unable to recognise a single player among all these sideburned men and beehived women: we seem to have stumbled into an Englebert Humperdinck and Lulu lookalike contest, though the *leitmotiv* is maintained by their silently shrieking insistence that the camera go away. Clearly, this is a brilliant metafilmic device, just like the subtle *hommage* to Mack Sennett represented by the motionless figure of Mr Core, standing pitifully alone in his baggy morning suit and staring at a cake on which he and his bride are depicted in miniature unity, even as, ironically, she dances by animatedly with a leering character in fashionable flares.

It goes on like this for an hour, until the poignant closing sequence of people stretched senseless on a lawn, which both evokes and trumps *Gone with the Wind*'s epic pan across the Atlanta dressing-station. A great film, then, and one for the cineaste's canon: but, to make my point, of what I myself was doing at the time I have no recollection whatever.

Red Badge of Courage

It can only be a matter of time, and a very short time at that, before Wilson want their socks back. Worse yet, they will in all probability dispatch a man to Brondesbury Lawn Tennis Club to get them. I shall be serving at match point (not, of course, mine), and the wonky door at the end of the court will suddenly creak open, and the man will stride on and hold up his hand – possibly, even, blow a little chromium whistle – and I shall turn, and he will say, "Good morning, Mr Coren, I am Norman D. Simmonds of the Wilson Hosiery Division, here is a company cheque in full refund for your socks, would you take them off please?"

I shall say, "I'm sorry, I don't understand, is there anything wrong?" and he will cry *"Is there anything wrong?* You are playing Mr Ian Millar, who is not merely ten years older than you, but has recently had a new knee fitted, and you are 1–6, 1–5 and love–40 down, and you ask me if there is anything wrong? We at Wilson sold you those socks in good faith, they are emblazoned with our logo, a mark of quality wherever discerning sports persons forgather, and the statement they are supposed to make is that people perform better in Wilson socks, but you are playing, if that is the word, in such a fashion as to bring our great name into disrepute and jeopardise the jobs of our entire workforce. By the way, is that also a Wilson ball you were about to throw up and hit into the net with the rim of your racquet?"

At this, there is a shout of "No, it isn't!" The shout comes not from me, but from another man who has insinuated himself onto the court. He carries a smart briefcase bearing the legend Slazenger (Balls Dept) Ltd, which he now snaps open in order to serve an injunction restraining me from causing further distress to his company. He also has a petition signed by 16 householders who live adjacent to the club, inquiring why it is only Slazenger balls which fly over their fences at a height of 60ft, thereafter causing serious damage to windows and hydrangeas and, in one tragic case, irrecoverably reducing a ginger tom to a vegetable. Even while he is explaining this, I become aware of a strange sensation at my left breast, and look down to discover a tiny Lacoste seamstress deftly unpicking the little green crocodile from my shirt: pressed, she confides that a recent shareholders' meeting expressed concern over the company's ability to survive another year of that unique cross-court running backhand I do where I bounce off the side netting and reduce the umpire's chair to matchwood, an observation which prompts a mutter of "Yes, but have you seen his forehand volley?" from a Dunlop executive who has sprung out of the courtside shrubbery, snatched my Dunlop racket, thrust it into my Dunlop bag along with the Dunlop tracksuit I had incautiously hung on the net-post, and is now awaiting the first opportunity to unlace my Dunlop shoes so that the various pieces of embarrassingly escutcheoned kit can be totted up against a credit note allowing me to purchase any other Dunlop item, provided it is in no way connected with tennis, what about a nice new tyre, sir, or is there something I should know about your driving?

Yes, it is an iffy business, badging. While it is one thing to have Pete Sampras publicly endorse your range of sporting goods, it is quite another to have it demonstrated equally publicly that it is not your range of sporting goods that made him Pete Sampras. Nor does it stop at sporting goods: in the sweet lang syne, King George VI could run around Wimbledon unencumbered by a slogan on his flannels testifying that Robertsons were jam-makers by royal appointment, but these days the more illustrious the competitor, the likelier it is that he will turn up looking like the window of a village shop, decorated *cap-à-pied* with the iridescent decals of everything from potted shrimps to patent blackhead salve, which is all fine and dandy as long as he is at the top, but misery for countless marketing departments as age or luck or injury or sheer ineptitude begin to shuffle him down the computer ratings. Which brings me to Monday. On Monday, I watched the Ashes go. They went to a team with XXXX on their shirts. The shirts of the losers said Tetley's Bitter.

I'll bet he is.

A Word in Private

Here I am, after midnight, at the warehouse door. That is my shadow thrown on the door by the streetlight behind me. The shadow sports a fedora with the brim turned down and an overcoat with the collar turned up. The door is a grey steel door, with big hemstitched rivets; it has a bell-push and a shuttered slot. I poke the one, the other snaps open. There are these eyes.

"Yeah?"

"The Wop sent me."

"What did the Wop have on his feet?"

"He had these two-tone Wop brogues."

"Any facial hair?"

"A typically thin pencil moustache, and typically long sideburns."

The slot shuts; the door opens; I go in. There is a hat-check girl with fishnetted thighs sleek as two trawled dolphins; as she reaches up to shelf my fedora, her embonpoint bids to bifurcate her *bustier*.

I say: "You ought to take something for that chest of yours."

She says: "You are a silver-tongued bastard, and no mistake."

I say: "I was going to make a crack about basque separatism, but it would have been over your pretty little head."

She says: "No, this is the kind you step out of."

I say: "Careful, that was so dumb it was almost smart," but I push a tenner into her cleavage anyhow, because if degradation comes cheap, how is a man going to feel superior? I walk into the joint; it has a lot of red-checkered tables and a little stage. On the stage, a minstrel with a straw hat and a banjo and lips like a white quoit is telling his mammy he'd walk a million miles for one of her smiles. I sit down at a table, and a waiter with a fez and jellaba shuffles up and offers me a cocktail menu.

I study it.

"I'd like a white lady," I tell him.

"Wouldn't we all?" he says.

I nod and stick a fiver in his sash. It was a good riposte. It is what I came here for. It is what everyone comes to The Speakeasy for. That is why it is called The Speakeasy. It was opened the day after the Political Correctness Act was passed and prohibition came in. It was opened by Sam

Rosenberg and Nat Levy who, it is generally agreed by the club's membership, have a nose for business. They knew it wouldn't be easy for bigots to kick the habit.

The waiter shuffles back with my drink. I tip him 10p. He looks at it. He spits on it, rolls his eyes, wrings his hands, ululates briefly, and finally says:

"What are you, some kind of Scot?"

"I'm sorry," I say, "I'm a bit short."

"I notice. Where's the law that says that midgets have to be stingy? Which reminds me, I haven't seen your brother in here lately."

"He's been feeling a little queer," I say.

"There's no answer to that," says the waiter, and I give him a pound, because that was exactly the answer there is to that. Then I give him a fiver, but it is not for him, it is for the cockney comic who has replaced the minstrel and is asking for requests.

"You want the one about the stammering Irish vegetarian and the one-legged Bengali cross-dresser again?" inquires the waiter.

"No," I say, "I'd like the mad cow disease one."

"Any particular woman politician in the payoff?"

"I'm happy to leave it to him," I say.

So he tells the joke, which is a really good one, because this time it is about MI5 boss Stella Rimington and how she can not only never keep a secret, but also never find her gun because she has so much other stuff in her handbag. I am laughing so heartily that when my table is visited by a hostess wearing nothing but a fox's brush, who is taking the hat round for the Quorn on the grounds that if more foxes were killed the price of fur coats would come down, I give her my last fiver. Not that it matters. You can always get a free lift home from The Speakeasy. Half the members are cabbies.

Those Barren Leaves

It is not generally known (ie, I have just found out) that what Barnes Wallis actually invented was the bouncing conker. It is, of course, altogether right and proper that it should have been: has any military engagement ever sprung more patently from the pages of the *Boy's Own Paper* than the dambusters' raid? The dear old school in trouble, a madcap scheme which might just work, a dotty boffin, a daft invention, the fresh-faced chums of Lancaster House slipping from their dorm after lights-out, a breathless hush in the Ruhr tonight, and Guy Gibson hurtling in from the Wuppertal End to fling his short-pitched stuff at Johnny Hun – is that not how we have ever regarded it?

If so we have been working, I now discover, from a slightly skewed scenario: the game which was afoot that night was not quite the game we had imagined. For the weapon we had always thought of as scattering the Möhne stumps was not the world's biggest cricket ball at all, it was the world's biggest horse-chestnut. In evidence of which (since I am blessed with a sort of sixth sense when it comes to an audience's mistrust), I cite that impeccable authority, Kew Botanical Gardens.

This is the place you telephone if you have planted a horse-chestnut tree and it has not borne fruit. You planted it only to get the fruit. It is the best fruit there is. Who can ignore a fresh-fallen conker, not pick it up, stare at it, fondle it? From the glorious colour, the rich patina, the silken texture, conkers might not be new-born veg at all, but 200-year-old offcuts of mahogany, whittled and buffed in their tea-breaks by Sheraton's more talented apprentices. Do you know how much you would have to pay for conkers if they were sideboards? That is why I wanted a tree of my own; that, and the fact that the only practical point of conkers – they could not be converted into cutlets or sweets or liquor or poultices – was to wizen into free kids' toys, representing a considerable saving on minor gifts should I ever have grandchildren.

So I bought a nursery sapling eight years ago, and each year it grew sturdier, and each year it blossomed, and each year I waited for the blossom to do the stuff that blossom is supposed to do; but each year nothing happened, so this year I looked at what was by now a pretty big tree, and I telephoned Kew and the man went to get his conker book, and when he came back, and before we could get down to cases, he informed me that horse-chestnuts, contrary to what I had always believed about their practical valuelessness, were a prime source of dimethyl ketone, without which high explosive devices would be unable to go bang. Get off, I said, straight up, he replied, and went on to explain that during the Last Lot, thousands of tons of horse-chestnuts were harvested by the Land Army to be pressed, quite literally, into pyrotechnic service. This, as you can imagine, tickled me no end; we major philosophers are ever on the *qui vive* for succinct exemplars of life's little ironies, and the proposition that war's abominable folly could be reduced to so pertinent an absurdity as a game of conkers could not be allowed to go unsavoured

But that wasn't why I'd rung him. What of my tree? Why was it barren? Why would it not produce offspring so that my offspring's offspring would have something to put on a string and lash out with until they were old enough to find a proper battlefield to fight on? Ah, he said, what you almost certainly have there is a sterile cultivar. Surely not, I said, it cost twelve quid, a nursery would not stay long in business if a capital investment of that order did not cough up an annual dividend. On the contrary, he said, the sterile cultivar is what customers favour these days, they do not want acorns and beech-nuts and sycamore seeds converting their lawns into bonsai forests, and they particularly do not want trees full of conkers likely to encourage passing boys to chuck things up to bring them down. I strained to catch a nuance of judgement in his voice (surely a botanist must be on the side of fecundity, if only in the cause of job-security?) but he was merely an information desk, partiality was not his brief.

It's mine though. I do not relish the prospect of a landscape in which conkers no longer fall. To say nothing of our being totally defenceless when the Next Lot breaks out.

Nu Reedrs Bigin Hear

Rupert Murdoch thros hat in air, Rupert terns cartweel, big beem spreds acros Rupert's rugdly hansem fase! Sudnly *Th Times* is 10 per sent bigr, it is 10 per sent betr valu, yet, "Stoan th flamin cros!" crys Rupert, "it is stil th same *fizcal* size, we ar lookin at a flamin mirakl, fone this Coren bloak rite away, tel him he is on a 10 per sent rize, wate, make that wun per sent, no sens chukin all these sudn profits down th flamin drane, get me Nu York, get me Brisbn, get me Markt Harbro, wares mi flamin helicoptr?"

It is tru. This colum is but th ferst puf in th imnent tifoon:

wot yu, deer reedr, ar gettin today is th same lenth as yu got last Wensdy, but it is pakt with 10 per sent more stuf, thanx to Mr Leo Chapman of The Simplified Spelling Society. Becos Mr Chapman has just ritn to tel me about Cut Spelling, a startlin nu sistem of not only streemlinin spellin but also choppin out unnesry letrs wich, and I kwote, "cuts wuns time at th keebord by 10 per sent and also reduces th amount of spase needed in a nuspapr, thus allowin about 10 per sent more editorial to be fittd in". Ferthrmor, his teem has calclated that of th 28 milion British werkfors, 10 milion ar ilitret or semilitret and cant evn reed a nuspapr; to kwote th mastr wunce agen, "ther is a hole nu constituency watin to be tapt by simplifyin spellin". Now, is this or is this not musik to Mr Murdoch's eers?

But th mirakl dus not stop ther: let us look at th chaptr "Furthr Advantajs" in Mr Chapmans amazin leeflet, ware it tels how th sistem "saves time and trubl for evryone involvd in ritn text, from scoolchildren to publishrs, from novlists to advrtisrs, from secretaris to grafic desynrs". We lern how they wud not only save time by ritin 10 per sent less, thus offrin freedm to persu othr displins (wot? simplified Rushn, cut jomtry, streemlined brane sergry?), but also benfit evrythin from producshn costs (eg smallr books etc) to th envirnmnt (eg chukin away smallr books etc). It wil also be eesier to get into universty (no dout becos dons wil no longr think "Hear is an ilitret doap," they wil think, "Hear is sumwun hoo wil get thru th corse 10 per sent kwikr, even longr hols for us, bluddy grate, giv him a skolship!") and, in a fasnatin exampl of th sosity's infnit wisdm, "public syns and notises cud be ritn larjr," in othr werds (kwite litrly), thos with 10 per sent mor time as th result of cut spellin hoo wontd to, eg, spend that time in Hide Park wud be in no dout, from th nu big notises, that it wos an ofens to chuk rubish about or widl on th flours, thus avoidin hevy penlties.

"Incredbl!" yu wil probly be shreekin at this point. "Wot a boon this nu spellin is, sudnly th hole kulchr is lookin at brord sunny uplands, Britn will be grate agen, opn th bubly!" But ther may be, I hav to tel yu, a slite snag to al this; at presnt, it is but a litl cloud on th horizn only 10 per sent bigr than a mans hand, but it bothrs me a trifl, becos I hav had a few trys at ritn difrnt tipes of stuf in th nu stile, and I think I may hav spotd wot mite be a teknikl hich wich has for sum reesn, God nose how, escaped Mr Chapman and his sosity.

Considr these hedlines: "Chansler Sez No Nu Taxes: Reed Mi Lips"; "Man Nifes Gard In Bank Rade"; "Desprit Plite of Hoamless After Leeds Fludds"; "Athton Struk On Hed By Beemer, Tuch And Go Sez Surgn." Now, can yu gess wot I am slitely wurried about? Rite, I am slitely wurried about th fact that it is abslootly impossibl to take enythin seriusly if it is ritn in th nu spellin. It cannot be dun. I do not no wy this shud be, all I no is that if I open *The Grate Gatsby* or *War and Peas* or *The Mare of Casterbrij* at randm and attemt to tern just wun singl paragraf into Mr Chapmans remarkabl orthogrfy, pritty soon I am rolin helplesly about on th flore, coffin and spluttrin, and this is almost sertnly not wot these majr riters intended.

But yes, since yu rase th point, ther is indeed a persnl ax been ground heer. Becos sudnly evrywun hoo evr rote enything is about to becum a bluddy humerist, and these days it is hard enuf erning a krust as it is, without evrything from *The Brothers Carry Mats Off* to *Pair O'Dice Lost* gettin in on th act.

Lost Horizon

While you are staring at this, I shall be staring at an insurance claim form. I know that that is what I shall be doing, because it is what I have been doing for some time past, and it is what I shall be continuing to do for some time to come; I have stopped doing it now only for long enough to tell you what it is I am doing, because it is important for you to know. Important, that is, to me. It doesn't matter a damn to you. You haven't just waved goodbye to a million pounds.

If that's what it was. I have no way of assessing exactly what it was I waved goodbye to, which is why my days are spent staring at a claim form. Nor did I wave goodbye to it personally, since I was a thousand miles away when it went; if I had not been, it would not have gone, because the bastard who last week put a jemmy to the shutters of my little French bolt-hole and sheared off its little French bolts would have been working his night shift at some other, unoccupied, target.

What, then, was nicked, and why do I not have the remotest idea what it was worth? Well, what was nicked was the familiarly nickable, a television set, a VCR, radios, binoculars, phones, a few other bits and bobs, and a computer. Hang on, you will mutter, what is he going on about, that's never a million quid, he must know what that stuff's worth, he is a man of the world, why doesn't he just jot it on his claim form and bang it off to his insurers, so that we can all get some peace? That is because you do not know what was on the computer.

For the past year, I have been cobbling a novel. And do not ascribe that description to the bogus humility with which hacks pretend to dismiss their worth: cobbling is precisely what I have been doing. Since subsistence duties leave me no time for fiction, it is only when I take French leave of them that I am able to knock out the odd narrative chunk and nail it on the end of the one I did on the previous trip; or possibly on the front of it, because you can do that, with a computer. Thus, by these spatchcock means, the novel had lurched its way to some 20,000 words, many of them different, but all of them inscribed on the hard disk of my Apple Macintosh. Which, a week ago, fell onto the back of a lorry. My God, you cry, I thought we said he was a man of the world, did he not have the sense to copy this book of his onto back-up floppies? Yes, he did, and he also had the sense to place the floppies next to his computer so that he would know where to find them; for which the bastard with the jemmy will have been extremely grateful, since you do not wish to waste precious time on broken and entered premises poking around for the box of disks which will make a nicked computer even more saleable.

To whom? Need you ask? This is Provence we're talking about: by day the cicadas are inaudible in the rattle of typewriters, by night the glow-worms are upstaged by the flicker of VDUs, for the hills are alive with the sound of expatriate hacks shrieking that they could be the next Peter Mayle, all it takes is one good idea. Well, there is one good idea on the loose there, now, and when I reflect on the obvious customer my thief will seek for an Anglophone word-processor, my heart plummets bootwards. The recipient could well find himself sitting on a goldmine.

Just how good an idea it is, mind, I cannot know, which is why I can't fill in the claim-form box about the compensation I can't assess. Are we talking hardback blockbuster, tabloid serial rights, gilt-embossed transglobal paperback? Are we talking Spielberg, John Thaw, T-shirts, arcade video spin-offs, eponymous fried-chicken outlets? Or are we talking remainder shelves, dog-ears, wonky piano legs?

I may never know, but if I do, I may not want to. Because while I don't have the stomach for a fresh start, whoever inherits the computer won't need one, and if there turns out to be a million in it, it'll be his. Unless, that is, I can sue it off him, which is why I began by telling you how important you were. I don't get much time for reading, and I need your help: should you one day find yourself snuggling into your airline seat with a bestseller beginning: "At 4.20 on the chill morning of 9 January, Her Majesty Queen Elizabeth II slipped a .38 Smith & Wesson into her reticule, and left Balmoral via the laundry-chute," tip me the wink.

Dem Bones, Dem Bones, Gonna Fall Aroun'

In my younger days, I used to wonder what my skeleton looked like. I can even pinpoint the spark which detonated this speculation: I was studying *Hamlet* at the time, or at least hitting Gerald Finch over the head with it, because he sat in front of me for O-level English, and Mr Hoskins, to whom Lady Luck had dealt Finch and me from the bottom of her deck, inquired why I had struck my colleague with a cornerstone of our culture, and rather than bring up a girl's name, for these were gallant days, I replied that we had been having an argument about the play. Oh really, he said, because he had not been born yesterday, what kind of argument, and I said I wanted to know how Hamlet knew the skull was Yorick's, all skulls look the same, and Finch said the clown told him, sir, and I said why would Hamlet believe a clown, I wouldn't sir, I might believe a clown if he told me how much water got poured into the average trouser, but would you believe anything a clown said to you in a cemetery, sir, and Mr Hoskins said not necessarily, and that is an interesting point, Coren, well, fairly interesting, I shall try to find out whether skulls look different from one another, Mrs Gibson might know, her brother was in the RAMC.

He never got back to me, and it was *Guy Mannering* the week after that, but the question of what skulls looked like remained inside mine for some years. Nor only skulls, but the entire osseous sub-frame: it bothered me that I should never see mine, except in X-rays, where it always appeared hilarious: there were all these little grey bones, apparently not joined together, one serious sneeze and your entire infrastructure would fall to the bottom of your legs, leaving you to spread across the floor like a deflating blimp. I don't know why skeletons should be funny, perhaps it is nature's way of palliating *timor mortis*; a few years ago I fell off a horse and the osteopath I went to see had a skeleton dangling from his ceiling, pretty comical in itself, but when he hit it with a stick to indicate which vertebra I had damaged it started dancing, I laughed till it hurt, ie, immediately, and the poor quack said to my wife, is he always like this or could it be concussion?

He said it because she's a doctor, which brings me to the 5 June issue of the *British Medical Journal*, a comic she regularly passes on to me in the forlorn hope of bridging the marital gap, but for once it contained an article worth the unequal struggle. Entitled "A prospective study of alcohol consumption and bone mineral density", by Troy Holbrook and Elizabeth Barrett-Connor of the University of California, it concluded that heavy drinkers had stronger skeletons than teetotallers. Even better, while drinking strengthened bones, exercise weakened them; ie, provided you eschewed jogging in favour of slumping in front of *Cheers* with a large Scotch, you could advance happily into old age knowing you contained a skeleton on which Eiffel himself could not have improved.

Not surprisingly, this lifted the spirits no end (oh, please, today's is a scientific treatise, if you want puns come back next Wednesday), especially since I could not remember the last time my lifestyle had received anything but an admonitory caning from the medical establishment: it is normally impossible for me to open a paper without reading that everything I do is lopping years off my life, unless I start fell-walking and eating a daily stone of bran I shall not see Christmas, so you may imagine my joy at learning that tipsy inertia was good for you.

And my wretchedness at subsequently discovering that it was not. For Troy and Elizabeth, canny as any hack, had saved the twist for the tail; arriving at their closing paragraphs and poised for statistical evidence that these strong bones of ours were proof against geriatric breakage, I found all hope summarily dashed. Can you guess why? Of course. "Studies of fractures and alcohol consumption are confounded by other risk factors, including increased likelihood of impaired vision and falling."

Alas, poor Yorick! A' may have pour'd a flagon of Rhenish on your head once, he always liked a drop, he had bones like pikestaffs, but a fat lot of good they did him the night he walked right off the Elsinore battlements. Thought he saw a ghost, they say.

Floral Tribute

There is, I swear, no personal rancour behind the hereinunder. The fact that over the next few days the hereinunder will be used for wrapping rhizomes is of no greater account to me than the fact that it is at all other times used for wrapping haddock, for both are facts of the hack's life, and are, furthermore, no small help to him in nurturing that salutary scepticism on which the practice of columnism depends. That the days of man are but as grass is nowhere more evident than in a newspaper office; or, rather, in the chip-shop next door.

No, today's is proxy rancour, directed on behalf of those unable to direct it themselves, and towards those who will be wrapping it around their rhizomes. Or scrunching it up to buffer their potted bedders, or folding it carefully to swaddle their cultivars, or perhaps just laying it in their carboots to sop up spillage. For they are the jerks driving home from the Chelsea Flower Show, who, having swooned before the world's most beautiful blooms, have stopped off to buy the wherewithal to replicate them on their own premises, and *The Times* is what they had the pernickety foresight to bring with them to shield the Volvo's carpet.

Whether they or their Royal Horticultural Society mentors deserve the greater rancour, mind, I cannot decide. I am appalled by the Chelsea Flower Show. I find its *Weltanschauung* inexcusable. How can an enlightened era allow something so politically incorrect to flourish? For what the show does is celebrate and reward beauty, and it does so, moreover, as if beauty were not simply a virtue, but the highest virtue of all. Dear God, even the ghastly Miss

World Contest requires the paragon bust to commit itself to international peace, and the prodigal buttock to devote at least part of its career to those less fortunate than itself; nor can any candidate simply shimmy on expecting to end up weeping beneath the rhinestone accolade without first getting her speedwriting or her winebar-management up to snuff.

But it is enough, apparently, for a peony to be just a pretty face. Nothing more of it is required than the mien and carriage of a floral bimbo, simpering this way and that in the Royal Hospital breeze, flashing its exemplary parts, exuding its egregious scent, and hinting at such eager pollinative promise as to make the more susceptible judges rubber-legged with excitement. All other, nobler, qualities are ignored: dedication, courage, service, integrity, caring, are of no account; what is celebrated and rewarded here is pulchritude alone.

You have, I guess, already twigged on whose behalf I speak: that brave, misshapen, horticulturally challenged fellowship of all those born to blush unseen, and waste their sweetness on the Cricklewood air. Beauty they may not have, not at any rate your common or garden beauty (in my case neither common nor garden, as a matter of fact), but they none the less have virtues which far outshine mere flashiness. I have roses which each season struggle, thanks to a gritty commitment the England middle-order batsmen would do well to emulate, to find some floral form more winsome than the wizened brazil nuts for which they are annually mistaken, I have delphinium, if that's the plural, not that you'd notice, which continue to bud (almost, indeed to bloom) despite being pinned permanently to the earth in the bindweed's grapple, I have dahlias prepared to spend their entire working lives underground, save for the odd malformed digit poked selflessly out to feed the ants, I have hydrangeas hideously pocked with blights which have sent visiting shrub consultants scuttling home for an antiseptic shower, I have pinks which have never known the meaning of the word, and clematis with less allure than Clem Attlee, and hanging baskets which have so lost their appeal they might have been strung up by Albert Pierrepoint, yet all of these and countless more battle gamely on, year after year, in their pitiable eagerness to please the gardener and waylay the bumble-bee, against what annually prove to be the insurmountable odds of thrip and greenfly, scab and canker, rust and mildew, slug and mite. In a decent world, such virtues would not be put to shame by meretriciousness. But in ours, whatever the colour, Chelsea is the game.

Osric the Hedgehog

There could well be a knighthood in this. For is not my voice broken, my wind short, my chin double, my wit single and every part of me blasted with antiquity, and will I yet call myself young? Add to this the fact that I was born about three o'clock in the afternoon, with a white head and something of a round belly (both of which, interestingly, I seem to be getting back), and you will, I am sure, be hard put to come up with a candidate better qualified to hurtle down to his local job-centre this very minute and offer himself for the position of drinking companion to the Prince of Wales, specialist subject the works of William Shakespeare 1591–1613.

Is there a vacancy? Is there ever. Because, despite the fact that our beloved heir is girt round with all manner of advisers, mentors, boffins, coaches, gurus, tutors and other consultant sycophants ever on the *qui vive* at the end of a cellphone should HRH's brow begin to furrow, he appears to have nowhere to turn when it comes to solving the problem of his offspring's indifference to the Bard. I learned this from the speech he made on Monday when inaugurating his new Shakespeare School at Stratford: "I know," he confessed, "that if I tried to drag my children here, they would say they didn't want to come, that it would be boring, that they'd far rather play with their computer games."

The heart bleeds. A picture materialises, does it not, of our deeply caring monarch-in-waiting, tilter at carbuncles, sworn opponent of all he deems to be meretricious, ephemeral, or just plain tacky, leaning on a lectern at the corner of the Highgrove nursery and attempting to interest Prince William in the fact that he, too, will one day be given the latchkey of this earth of majesty, this seat of Mars, this other Eden, demi-paradise, this fortress built by Nature for herself against infection and the hand of war, but is William listening? Is Henry? Are they hell, their eyes are glued to two enormous screens, their fingers are twinkling across two keyboards with all the unsettling dexterity of the contemporary young, they are hermetically absorbed in the pressing business of getting out of the dungeon and across the drawbridge before the Terminators climb out of the moat and eat them, they do not give a damn for their old man's fervent declamation of England's top iambs, they like things that go tink-tink-tink and bleep-bleep-bleep.

Very well, then. That is why, this morning, I offer my liege lord my sworn service. I have the answer, and I have it after a mere two hours' fiddling with my Macintosh software, for that is all the time that was required to devise *Hamlet: Prince of Nintendo*. Now, press this key: see, a rudimentary oblong battlement has materialised, with a little Lego-like bloke standing on it. He is called Bernardo. He squeaks, "Who's there?" A multiple choice now appears: *(a) Postman Pat, (b) Francisco, (c) A Ninja Turtle*. Press the key again; if you have got the right answer, Francisco, Horatio and Marcellus appear. They are all scuttling about and squeaking like mad. What have they seen? *(a) Tyrannosaurus Rex, (b) Gazza, (c) A ghost*. If you select Gazza, Horatio explodes, preventing the game from continuing.

The choices, of course, become progressively trickier, particularly if you have selected correctly from *(a) Walked under a bus, (b) Martian fell on him, (c) Got murdered by someone pouring poison in his ear*, because you have now qualified to enter Part Two of the game, which concerns what Hamlet is going to do about it. If, for example, you select *(b) Put on a cape and run Claudius over in the Batmobile*, you will have to start again from the beginning, whereas should you choose correctly, you will arrive at the interesting teaser that neither you nor Hamlet knows what he is going to do about it, at which point the little Lego-like figure in the black outfit will ask you what you would do in his position, thus moving the game into its interactive phase, where you will be able to do anything you want, provided, of course, that everybody ends up exploding, as Shakespeare intended.

This, then, is what I am offering to HRH. He can only say "I know thee not, old man: fall to thy prayers", but he is a sensitive cove, he surely wouldn't want to see a Prince of Wales make the same mistake twice.

Softly, a Word or Two

Odd, how a buried memory may be dislodged by the unlikeliest jolt. I met a bloke on the north face of the Eiger once, it must have been, what, 30 years ago, and I haven't thought about him from that day to this, but then something happened on this day and now I can't think about anything else.

I say met, but I exaggerate, of course; you know me well enough not to have imagined your correspondent, even in his youth, vertically spreadeagled against the world's most terrible rock and sharing an ice-flecked pemmican butty with some other grappled madman. The truth is that only he was on the outside; I was inside, trundling snugly upwards on the Wengenalpbahn which climbs through the middle of the mountain, occasionally emerging to allow the weedy the unnerving view of those who are doing it the hard way. So there we were, I swaying in my seat, he dangling on his rope, and as we passed, so help me he waved, and I waved back, which took a lot of guts because it left me holding the seat-rail with only one hand, and if the train had lurched I could easily have sprained something. And I remember thinking, his is only one way to climb the Eiger.

But why do I remember it, on this day? I remember it because of a news item to the effect that something called Crossword Genius has just been launched; it is a computerised phone helpline which gives the answers to all the clues in all the crosswords in all the national papers, and it gives them from the very dawn of the day on which they are published. It does this by having the first editions delivered at midnight to packs of young Oxford academics straining in the slips to polish the puzzles off by 6 am.

Them I do not blame. Times are tough these days along the Isis, and if a few extra bob may be turned in the flicker of the midnight oil by those capable of cracking *Animal often found on mat (3)*, then I for one rejoice that a liberal education can still be more than its own reward. My complaint is directed not at them, but at Andrew Chapman, their employer and the founder of this appalling enterprise, who, like many an opportunist before him, claims to be answering a need when what he is actually doing is creating one.

For who that calls himself a crossword enthusiast would dream, when stymied, of picking up a telephone and unstumping himself? That is not what crosswords are about; they are about the doing, not the having done, their solution is merely an end to a means, and a literally wondrous means it is, since we can never quite know what it is: some days you have it, other days you don't, which is to say that some days you grope and gnash and struggle to reason, other days some synaptic miracle occurs whereby rational analysis is bypassed and everything you ever read or heard or experienced is suddenly all there for the instinctual exploiting, you do not have to think at all, the solutions self-select from a billion far-flung cerebral crannies to come flashing full-blown from the pen, it is like being David Gower.

But even on the really good days, there is generally a clue or two that eludes, and if you are lucky this may lead to the best days of all; when, cast aside and seemingly superseded by life's other pressures and demands, the unsolved clue, much later and quite arbitrarily, proves to be not dead at all but sleeping, and what's more dreaming as it sleeps, marinating, as it were, in its own possibilities, until suddenly it leaps awake, in the middle, perhaps, of dinner or *Fidelio* or the M25, and you have it, not even realising that you were still after it, and joy is unconfined.

It is this joy which Mr Chapman threatens; and he threatens it, I fear, from the certainty of that same canny acumen which gave the world Polaroid cameras and bottled suntan and Pot Noodles, because the world wanted everything now, it could not hang about, it had to be somewhere, it had people to see, it had things to do, it had bridges to build and papers to sign, it might have a window between 3 and 3.15 but it wasn't promising. It is a world which will jump at the chance of having its crossword done for it, while it's flying over the Eiger.

Now Read On

Even were the world not split into those who think it is *Paddy Clarke Ha Ha Ha* by Roddy Doyle and those who think it is *Roddy Doyle Ha Ha Ha* by Paddy Clarke (with not a few still unconvinced that it mightn't be *Roddy Clarke Ha Ha Ha* by Paddy Doyle, or indeed . . .), it is clear that these are uncertain times for fiction. Cock an ear on any Cricklewood street corner where two or three long-faced literati are gathered together, and you will have it roundly confirmed that nobody knows where the novel is going.

That is why we are currently so besotted with where it has been. Cruising my local fiction hire outlets for National

Library Week, I was intrigued to discover not only that the two novels most in demand were Alexandra Ripley's *Scarlett* and Susan Hill's *Mrs de Winter*, but also that the most keenly ordered newcomer, published next Monday, was William Horwood's *The Willows in Winter*. Since all three are sequels to earlier blockbusters, it is evident to the merest clod, not to say publisher, that readers are falling over themselves to have their blocks busted in the same old way; and while, admittedly, the three in question are so resonantly middlebrow that serious money might well attend an agglomerative fourth starring Rhett Toad of Manderley Hall, I see no reason why the principle should not be applied to more upbrow fiction. As the literary novel lurches into the Valley of Death, cannon to the left of it, cannon to the right, it is all too clear that someone has blundered; the reading public, we hear at every turn, is on the side of the cannon.

Very well, then; here's my plan. Sadly, it can be no more than that, since I am an 800-word man and unable to capitalise on a demand for 800 pages, but I am more than happy, in the cause of culture, to sit here on Pisgah and direct the prolific towards the promised royalties.

I cannot, for example, be alone in wondering what happened to Ahab after we left him lashed to Moby Dick and bucking through the spume until he was no more than a waving dot. What of his future jolly adventures? Did he, beyond the blue horizon, open a profitable Marineworld, found a cats' meat empire, meet a sloe-eyed Chanel *parfumière* who had spent her life dreaming of a seafaring man with one leg, a stovepipe hat, and an endless supply of top-of-the-range ambergris?

And what of Connie Chatterley? We left her, you will recall, with a divorce in the pipeline and a new knot waiting to be tied, but do we not yearn to eavesdrop the subsequent domestic life of *Mrs Mellors' Hubbie*? Now that the couple have exchanged the hurly-burly of the forget-me-knot for the deep peace of the steak and kidney, will they live happily ever after, or will Ollie get her into another fine mess? Similarly, with dear Jane Eyre, which of us would not enjoy curling up before the roaring logs with a kilo of Black Magic and a fat book that began "Reader, I married the bastard!", wherein the ghastly Rochester, now so recovered from his blindness that each of his eyes is able to rove independently, rediscovers his youthful fancy for big Creole women and drives his enraged wife into torching his elegant Balham love-nest?

I am even keener to discover whether Gregor Samsa finally got himself sorted out; because anyone who has ever tried to kill a cockroach will testify to their resilience, and I for one would be fascinated to read how Gregor recovered fully from the apple and went on to a major career with Hammer Films. For, apart from anything else, I have always felt death to be a terrible waste of good characters, and if popular demand can pluck Sherlock Holmes, dripping but unbowed, from the Reichenbach Falls, I see no earthly reason why, say, the guillotine should not stick, to allow Sydney Carton to go on, in, perhaps, *The Tale of Twelve Cities*, to become the eponymous father of modern packaging, with outlets in every major European capital, nor why the wrong sort of leaves on the line should not delay the train under which Anna Karenina planned to chuck herself so that she can be spared to review her life, come to her senses, and run away with Levin.

Which Levin, you ask? Not for me to say. If fiction is going to be any good, it has to be left to the imagination.

Knotty Problem

Like Bethlehem and Kittyhawk before it, like Agincourt and Los Alamos and Gdansk, like Gettysburg and Darlington and Yalta and Khartoum, another quondam unsung and unlikely spot has woken up this morning to find itself famous. It has become a *locus in quo*. Posterity will trek to Isleworth and goggle.

For it was here, through a hole in the ceiling of the LA Fitness Club, that Clio smiled down and invited history to change its course. Where that course will henceforth run I cannot say; I know only that when the shutter fell between those humble Isleworth joists, the constitutional implications of its quiet click echoed round the world. Because the *Daily Mirror*'s tacky snaps have succeeded in doing what none of the Princess of Wales's own titanic efforts has managed to do: they have united the nation behind her. Where yesterday she might have enjoyed the sympathy of only some, today she basks in the empathy of all.

How has this happened? It has happened because, in catching her at her physical jerks, the camera freeze-framed our collective nightmare. For we are never more grotesque and pitiful than when we are struggling to become more fetching and admired, and the horrible thought that some unspeakable ratbag with a Brownie might be lurking to capture us at our risible worst – with a view, moreover, to making his private exposure our public one – not only starts the heart pounding and the sweat springing as no mere workout ever could, it grapples us to Her Royal Highness with hoops of flab.

For we have all been there, and we have been there for a very long time. We were there as tiny babies, dangling in our daft elasticated bouncers while cackling relatives inquired how long it might be before our legs were strong enough to corroborate Darwin; we were there as infants, our pipe-cleaner limbs tangled in the gymnasium ropes as we hung aloft, turning like wind-dried sausage, too petrified to climb either further up or down, while cross-legged classmates rolled about, helplessly sniggering, below; we were there as seven-stone weakling pubescents, rigid with the Dynamic Tension which Charles Atlas would post us in return for fifteen bob and which made only our temple veins bulge, never our muscles, leaving us to wonder how many 12-stone sand-kicking bullies would be put off by rippling blood-vessels; we were there when the chest-expanders flew back and rearranged our teeth and the Bullworkers shot shut and dislocated our shoulders; we were there when the Royal Canadian Air Force Exercise Manual had us jumping on the furniture and falling into the grate (why in God's name did Canadian pilots need to be so fit, were they required to pedal their planes, did they need to flap their arms auxiliarily?); we were there when isometric gurus tried to convince us that just by squeezing the telephone or tugging the Tubestrap, the trivial round, the common task would furnish all we ought to ask.

And we were also there when whatever we had managed to make of ourselves began to unmake itself again. So, in middle-age, we jogged by night, that none should see our sagging bellies swing, we trotted to lunchtime gyms but slunk more slowly back to allow the betraying purple to drain from our capillaries, we checked in at health farms under assumed names and told Selfridge's to be sure to wrap the rowing machine nicely, because it was a present for a friend; and while I cannot authoritatively speak for those who did all this as girls and women, I have good reason to believe it was the same for them – with the ghastly additional burden of musical aerobics – as all personkind, in the pursuit of perfection, both faced the disappointment and risked the ridicule that imperfection brings.

You will have heard that the Beast of Isleworth expects to make a million pounds for rolling back his rug and poking the knot from its knothole, and you will no doubt, as decent people all, have fulminated at his treachery. But calm yourselves with the fact that there was far more in this than met his eye: it may well be that, though it must perforce be left to history to determine exactly what, he has done the state some service.

Crumpet Involuntary

On Monday's late, chill afternoon, even as our great prime minister was nodding dramatically into his cheval-glass and rehearsing the goose-pimpling tropes of the Guildhall speech with which he was about to exhort us to so brace ourselves to our duties that things might perhaps one day turn out to be quite agreeable, I myself was also addressing the momentous matter of getting back to basics.

Further yet, even as his devoted consort struggled, in the shadow of his bobbing chin, to tie his white bow in a manner adequate to the variant demands of yesterday's conventions and today's lens-bites, my own fingers were engaged in the no less fraught (nor metaphorically less significant) effort to come to terms with that uneasy yoking of tradition and innovation which lies at the core of all this island race's present banes. I was trying to open a bubble-pack of Mother's New Crumpets.

It was a time for crumpets. The first frost had lain upon the lawn all day, pocked by squirrels scuttling to garner their hibernal tucker and blackbirds bravely drilling the adamantine sod for one last worm, and, as the misty gloaming settled upon Cricklewood, I too felt the old need come on for that little winter something which has been, for centuries, the Englishman's exclusive treat. So I wrapped up warm, and I jogged up the hill through my own pluming breath to Quality Family Foods, where I inquired, and he pointed.

"No," I said, from beside the shelf, "what I want is crumpets."

"Those *are* crumpets," he insisted, from the till.

I looked at the packet. I picked it up. I brought it into the brighter light beside the till. The nine things inside the packet were oblong, roughly five inches by one.

"Crumpets?" I said. You'll guess my tone.

"*Finger* crumpets," he said, with, if I judge aright, a tactical hint of embarrassment shrewdly calculated to ensure that I did not henceforth take my business elsewhere. "They are new from Mother's Pride."

"I'm sure they are," I said. "Have you got any round ones?"

"No," he said.

Time passed. I could hear his cat scratching, in some further aisle.

"The thing about a round crumpet," he said after a bit, "is that the butter runs down your chin. Down your arm, sometimes."

"Yes," I said, "that is exactly the thing about a round

crumpet. Butter from a round crumpet has been doing that for several hundred years."

"But the thing about these," he said, gamely, "is that they fit the mouth. You bite from one end. No mess."

"Do they, perhaps," I said, "conform to some new EC standard or other? Has Mother been compelled to knuckle under before some bloody Brussels directive? Is what we are looking at nothing more nor less, in fact, than a Eurocrumpet?"

"I don't think so," he said. "I think it's more a matter of marketing progress. They have always moved with the times, up Mother's Pride."

"Oh, have they?" I said. "Oh good. And the times are clamouring for oblong crumpets, are they?"

He shrugged.

"All I know is," he said, "they're selling like . . ."

"Don't say it," I warned. He looked disappointed, and my heart went out to him: as a toiler in that same waggish vineyard I know how rare such opportunities are. So I bought a packet, and left, and walked down the hill again, wondering if, perhaps, Gibraltar's apes might not be chucking their bits and bobs into suitcases, now, or the Tower's ravens revving their wings for exile; because there was a new straw in the November wind, and it might just be the last one.

Back home, I wrestled with the packet, and a little later I toasted the oblongs, and then I ate them, spotlessly, and not so long after that the prime minister stood up and said: "This is not nostalgia. I have no reason to be nostalgic. It is the future that concerns me. In fashioning policy for a world that is swiftly changing, we must have an eye to the underlying instincts with which, as a nation, we are comfortable," and I thought, Oh yes, John, indeed, how very true, most sensible, fat chance.

Four Wheels Bad

I knew the noise, last midnight. Who that lives on T-junctions does not? First there is the rasping slew of braking tyres, then the clunk of mutually indenting coachwork, next the poignant clatter of a hubcap rolling wonkily away, and, finally, after a bit, the oaths and squeals of recriminative rage. So I threw on a coat against the falling snow, quickly checked in the cloakroom mirror that no smugness betrayed my solicitude, always a risk, and popped outside.

An enormous Toyota Landcruiser, which had been belting incautiously in one direction, had collided with a huge Chrysler Jeep-Wrangler which had been belting incautiously in the other. You could tell they had been belting incautiously by the fact that the anti-freeze from both fractured radiators was now commingling to produce hissing green channels in the frozen slush, which does not happen to cars that have been driven sensibly. So, then, do I blame the drivers? To an extent. But what I blame mainly is the cars.

I blame them for not being cars at all. What they are, and what they are inordinately proud of being, is off-road paramilitary vehicles, and there are more and more of them about, but they are not driven by off-road paramilitary people. They are driven by ordinary folk who are not entirely averse to letting it be thought that they might be off-road paramilitary people. They drive Range Rovers, but they do not rove ranges in them. They rove suburbia, praying to find a parking space large enough to accommodate their unnecessary bulk. They drive Vauxhall Fronteras, but they do not boldly go in them where none has gone before, they go to Waitrose and Bejam and Sainsbury's. They drive

Isuzu Troopers, but not towards the sound of the guns, only towards the sound of pre-school rotas shrieking on metropolitan pavements. They drive Nissan Patrols, but not into No Man's Land, only into everyman's clogged side streets designed for something considerably less wide. They drive Ford Mavericks, but not to herd steers or pay out barbed wire, merely in order to drop the old man off at the railway station.

They do not need four-wheel drive, or 12 gears, or cross-country tyres, or cow-catchers, or banks of quartz halogen search-lights, or tow-bars, or clamps for shovels, theodolites, jerrycans, rocket-launchers. All they need is to convey the impression that they do; that when the long, dull week of advocacy or executive marketing or gynaecology or whatever is over, they are off across uncharted and inimical terrain to plough and stalk and brand and abseil, and that their holidays are spent not in some chic Riviera hotel or staff-crammed Tuscan villa, but in negotiating the virgin depths of the Matto Grosso or mercy-dashing through Serbian shot and shell.

Fine. Save for a little selfish gas-guzzling and the occasional side-swipe in a narrow road, they do no harm to anyone. But then it snows; and when it snows these folk suddenly find themselves in a position both to vindicate and to amortise their preposterous purchase. It is the only chance they get, and they grasp it gleefully. They do not chuck a fresh log on the fire and curl up, they dash out into the muck, for no other reason than that it is there; because a need for the unnecessary has created itself. Last weekend, forced to drive to Ware on glazed and fogbound roads, I found the world to be exclusively theirs. They hurtled maniacally past me, to left and right, as if to cry, "See? *See?* Look at my chunky tyres, look at my big lights, eat my wake, who is the dingbat now?" And when I pulled into a layby to wait for the snow, perhaps, to stop, a Land-Rover Discovery ploughed into the drift behind me, and the driver leapt out excitedly and asked if I was stuck, he had a rope, he had a power-winch, he could tow anything out of anywhere, and when I said thanks but I'm not, I could see at once that I had unmade his day. If you have a car like that, you want to show that it is a car like that. That is why I blame cars like that for last night's shunt.

After which they came in and phoned first for the AA, then for a cab, and when the cab arrived, I apologised to its driver for the fact that my road was icy. "No problem," he said. I couldn't look at them when he said it. My heart bled.

Aux Armes, Citoyens!

I blame myself. I know this government by now, I know that it wakes up every morning with a wonderful new idea, I know that over the boiled egg its wife murmurs, Coo, beloved, what a wonderful idea, I know that it gets into its car and is reassured by its driver about the new idea, I know that it tells everyone about its idea all morning, and they all go, Oh yes, wow, my word, that is a corker and no mistake, so it announces its wonderful new idea, and someone says, Hang on a minute, and then the government goes away and has a bit of a think, and pretty soon it is tinkering with the idea and soon after that the idea is all over and there is nothing for it but to hit the sack and come up with another wonderful new idea for the next morning, so you can see why I blame myself.

Because, early last week, I was sitting opposite the Home Secretary at dinner, engaged in the innocent social commerce of persiflage and quip, and all the time the spare capacity of that remarkable brain was cobbling together the next day's wonderful new government idea, for it was his turn; and although I didn't know it was his turn, I might have made a smart guess, since he hadn't announced one for at least a week and the next morning there it was, and the next evening there it wasn't, and if only I had asked him whether he had a wonderful new idea, I could have dragged him from our host's table to the cupboard under the stairs and told him how to make the new idea, for once, work, instead of allowing it to go off at half-cock as a flash in the pan; and if you think two ballistic clichés are a bit much, even for me, let me defend their aptness on the grounds that we know a bit about musketry in the 17th/21st Cricklewood Volunteers.

Yes, that is the wonderful new idea it is; or was, before it became the terrible old idea. It was announced the following day as Mr Howard's plan for organised street patrols, and hardly were the words out before my exhilarated neighbours and I were on the mutual blower, discussing the relative merits of knobkerry and pick-handle, was it better to have hard hats for safety or black balaclavas for terror, should we march mob-handed down the middle of the roads or skulk the hedges in covert threat, how many did karate, who knew semaphore, could we muster enough mountain bikes for a decent cavalry unit, where could we get a bull-horn, an Aldiss lamp, a Mace spray, a Rottie?

But hardly had we rung off and gone our several ways to

make our delegated inquiries in preparation for that evening's inaugural moot before the Home Secretary's nervous temporising started. Under pressure from senior coppers, caring wets, Opposition timeservers, and moaning media minnies of every sort, the climbdown began: not only could patrols not bear arms, they were not even to be allowed uniforms (I, ever the traditionalist, was already at work on a fetching combination of jodhpurs and epauletted flak-jackets, particularly after the bloke next door had put in a claim for black Lycra which might easily have misled civilians into thinking we were merely delivering Milk Tray), and as for our giving suspects a bloody good hiding and manacling them (or, more sensibly, vice-versa), this was totally out of order. All a patrol could do was mince about with poserphones and, on spotting something suspicious, ring Plod, who, when he had finished his jam-roll, would amble round and take down a statement for subsequent typing and filing.

Oh, would that I had had the nous to buttonhole Michael when I had the chance! For he does not have the first inkling of the mood out here in the suburbs, where his core electorate grows more fugitive by the hour not simply because his government does either nothing well or everything badly, but because whatever is done is done so ineffably dully. We are disaffected because we are bored, and, last week, a banner began to unfurl behind which we would have been thrilled to march, and then it was furled again. It is not that we want justice, or even revenge, we just want to have fun, we want to form fours and whistle Tipperary in descant to our rhythmic hobnails, to make big maps and stick little coloured flags in them, to honk klaxons, vault fences and flash big torches, to debrief one another over enamelled mugs of rummy tea. In short, a bit of National Service would do us the world of good.

Hard Cheese

Had they had any inkling, the milling Heathrow mobs, of who he really was, this glistening athlete jinking between them on his headlong dash for Gate 19 and France, they might have been less grudging. Had they twigged his gallant buccaneering mission, they might have watched the wall, my darlings, while the gentleman ran by. But how could they know these things? With his hot hat askew, his beaded bubbles winking at its brim, his tie-knot wedged beneath his ear, his boarding-pass flapping in his teeth, his leading hand frenziedly cleaving his passport through the human thicket while his trailing one banged his plastic bag against their knees, he looked like any other sophisticated jetsetter: how were they to guess, as they oathed his plucky bids to jump the security queue, that the line he truly stood in stretched back down all the arches of the Anglo-Gallic years to the very eve of Agincourt itself? How could they know that he was bringing the tennis-balls back, to fling them in mortal challenge at the Froggies' feet?

Even if they had peeked into the plastic bag, they would not have known. The tennis-balls did not look like tennis-balls, they looked like a cheese; but even then, they looked like a cheese only to those who knew what a cheese like this looked like. To the ungrocered eye, it was a black-waxed drum, eight inches in diameter, three inches thick and six pounds in weight. Even for the security man, it was a whole new experience.

"A what?"

"Look at the label. It says 'Mature English Cheddar', it does not say 'Mature Czech Semtex'."

He picked up a long-bladed instrument, and hefted it. I pulled the cheese away.

"It was given to me," I cried, "by Lord Archer! Of," I added crisply, "Weston-super-Mare!"

He faltered, as a lifetime's training struggled with the urge to invite this one to be pulled, on the grounds that it had bells on. And lost. It may have been that I struck him as a man to whom peers give cheese, it may have been that no liar in his right mind would ever dare a provenance as preposterous as Weston-super-Mare, who knows? All that matters is that, a few minutes later, the cheese and I were bound for France.

I have never known why Jeffrey sends people giant cheddars every New Year's Eve. Could be some arcane custom culled from his anthropological browsings, could be an adroit covert pun offered in witty consolation to those who have not made the Honours List to which he is doubtless privy, but whatever its purpose, the hard cheese is always welcome. And never more so than this year. This year I had for it a purpose of my own.

Ever since we set up hut here in Provence, I have been locked in contretemps with our local *fromager*: since he is not merely a major cheesemonger whose shelves creak with a hundred exemplars of top curdling from cow, goat and sheep to, for all I know, mare, vole and cat, but also the president of the regional *association fromagère*, I have for years sought to persuade him to import British cheeses. However, as you know, when it comes, in France, to British comestibles, the market grows suddenly uncommon. The French have a phrase for it: "*Ça n'existe pas*." Worse, no matter how vauntingly comprehensive a *fromager*'s advertised claims, he will tell you not merely that British cheese does not exist, but that even if it did it would be inedible. That is why I was acting as gauntlet-bearer to the Black

Cheddar of Somerset on its noble challenge to French hegemony. I would cut the *fromager* a chunk and watch his eyes water, for Jeffrey gives cheddar so mature that it could doubtless make wiser decisions than any member of the government its donor so loyally serves. Once tasted by my cheeseman, it would surely, henceforth, be ordered in bulk.

He is an honourable man, and did not, this morning, dissemble. His eyes rolled, his lips smacked, his entire mien compromised his patriotic stance. So will he now, I asked, be ordering it by the tonne? He looked at me. Dear God, how is it that I am so much less mature than my cheese? How could I have been so naïve as to imagine that a Frenchman would give house-room to a cheese so demonstrably superior to his own?

Thus it is that the best-laid schemes of mice and men gang aft a-gley. French mice will never know what they have missed.

'Ullo, John, Got a New Motto?

Why is there confusion over what these basics are? Put another way, can I really be the only man in Britain who knows exactly what it is that John Major is talking about?

Here is what happens when you go back to basics. You wake up in the morning because a cheery milkman has shouted "Milk-O!", and when you draw the curtains, you see that Mr Foskett from across the crescent is following the Express Dairies float with his little bucket and shovel. Mr Foskett is very proud of his roses. They are his pride and joy. They are what he fought Jerry for.

After you have opened the window and taken three lungfuls of healthy fresh air, you fold your blue-striped Sea Island cotton pyjamas carefully, draw on your cream Winceyette vest and pants, button their respective flaps, step onto the Ruberoid mat beneath your Armitage corner washbasin, clean your teeth with Wisdom bristles dipped in Eucryl toothpowder, wash your face with red Lifebuoy soap, and address your Culmak shaving brush to your stick of Erasmic, not too little, not too much, but just right, as their chirpy advertisements in *Lilliput* enjoin. Shaved, you touch your styptic pencil to a seeping nick, dab a smear of palmed Brylcreem into your hair, and gloss it with the two silver-plated Finlay's brushes you have taken from their oval leather case. Then you slip on your checked Viyella shirt and your grey Meaker's flannels, knot your tartan Tootal tie, horn your Dunn's-socked feet into your Cherry-Blossomed brown Barratt brogues (so that you may walk the Barratt way) and go downstairs, where Mother is cooking breakfast.

Mother is your wife. She is a jolly good sort. She has filled the Ideal boiler with Coalite, and waxed the lino with Linowax, and Vimmed the enamel-covered drop-flap of the eau-de-nil Easiwork cabinet so that nothing will stain the folded *Daily Express* you are about to prop against the Daddy's Sauce bottle while you eat your egg, bacon, fried bread, tomato and (since it is Saturday) sausage, and she has hung the chamois on the side of your galvanised pail and placed the Simoniz tin next to it, so that no time may be wasted – after the teaspooned Syrup of Figs has performed its clockwork way with your bowels – in bringing an enviable sheen to the Morris Eight, which she would also have driven out of the garage for you, if she were allowed to.

And she is there, too, when the AA badge gashes your buffing thumb and Dettol and Germolene are called for, just as she will be there after you have returned in the glinting Morris from the Rat & Cockle, your appetite whetted by your Saturday mild-and-Mackeson's, with Spam fritters and mashed Pom, and spotted dick for afters, smothered in Monk & Glass's custard, and a cup of Bev to top it off, because no one should do topiary on an empty stomach. It is coming along, your privet duck, it will have a beak any year now, even Mr Foskett will comment favourably. And when gloaming dulls your Spear & Jackson shears, inside you trot for a glass of Wincarnis with your high tea and Henry Hall on the Ferguson, for tonight is his guest night (your two pink-scrubbed boys, wearied by the day's bob-a-jobbing, are tucked up in bed with a bag of Clarnico jellies, listening to *Variety Bandbox* on their cat's whiskers), and afterwards, while Mother darns her cheery way through a mound of cardigans, you may smoke a Park Drive or two over your *Reader's Digest* condensed H.E. Bates, before the chime announces the arrival of the Fosketts for a hand of rummy and a soothing Horlicks in front of the Magicoal, because Horlicks know a thing or two about sleep.

And now it is 10.30, bong goes the Gamage's bracket clock, crackle go the Fosketts' departing Pakamacs, oink goes the Brassoed stair-rod on the seventh step, sizzle goes the Steradent in the bedside tumblers, click goes the light-switch on the Ediswan. Soon it will be Sunday, the *Empire News*, your navy-blue Horne's worsted, a lusty chorus of *Jerusalem*, a shilling in the plate, and, to follow, Mother's matchless steak-and-kidney pudding (the secret is Atora).

And that is all there is to say about John's notorious

slogan. Except, perhaps, that it was an advertisement for something which itself had never really been anything more.

Asking For It

As the first plucky harbingers of spring push their little heads up through my lawn in order to get their little necks broken, I find myself much cheered by the news that Mr Eric Robson has been given the chair of *Gardeners' Question Time*.

I am cheered because he is not a professional gardener. After all the hysterical press speculation which had bandied about umpteen amateur names as variously diverting as the Bishop of Durham and the Prince of Wales but had then rejected them on the grounds that celebrity was not an adequate qualification, I had begun to fear that the hottest job in British caring would once again go to a rosette-hung boffin obsessed with botanical minutiae, rather than to some sturdy layman with a firm grasp of horticultural reality. But yesterday brought reassurance: the puff of white smoke floated up, at last, from the Corporation potting shed, Eric Robson wellied out to inherit the earth, and declared that he was just an ordinary bloke who liked mucking about in gardens.

Great news indeed! All my gardening life I have had

nowhere to turn when the big questions sprouted from the cracks in my geoponic knowledge, those problems which beset all dabblers but get short shrift on a *Gardeners' Question Time* more concerned with producing paragonic plots that cry out to be photographed for major jigsaws than with the blighted Flanders salients on which so many of us toil and sob.

Do you, for example, know what my opening paragraph is about? It is about wood-pigeons stepping on snowdrops. I do not have that many snowdrops to start with, binoculars are a help, and even then you'd be hard-pushed to distinguish the flowers from the droppings left by the pigeons stepping on them, and what I want to know is how to stop this happening, especially as it also happens when the crocus comes out. The answer is not next door's cat, because next door's cat does not eat pigeons, it eats only fish, thereby nicely bracketing gardener's questions 2 and 3, ie, how do you stop the things you edge-planted to make the pond ornamental spreading unornamentally into the pond to allow a cat to walk into it and eat the fish? The answer is not next door's dog (from the other side), because next door's dog does not frighten off next door's cat, it merely hurls itself at the fence until the featherboarding loosens and the trellis falls off.

Which is the best glue for repairing fences, Eric? I know you will not advise nailing, because you are just an ordinary bloke who knows that when you try to hammer a nail into one board on a busted fence, six other boards fall out. Trellis cannot be nailed at all, which is why I now have rambling ground cover, interesting in its way, but does the panel think one should have to get down on one's knees to sniff honeysuckle?

A hammer is best reserved for wall-nails, isn't it Eric? Hammering a wall-nail is the surest way of getting it to fly back past your ear, leaving you staring at a big hole in the brick. No matter, you wanted wall-nails only because the experts said it was how to train wisteria, but you had a drainpipe handy and it was simpler to train the wisteria up that; the wisteria liked this, Eric, it liked it so much it got big enough to shove the drainpipe off the wall, what do I do now, panel?

Why does the spring on secateurs stop working the day after you buy them, Eric, so that you need two hands to work them, and a third hand to stop the things you cut off with them falling on your head? How do you find out when it is *not* going to rain, so that you can treat your lawn with fertiliser whose label warns you not to apply it if it *is* going to rain?

Why do corms stored in the garage for the winter die? Is it because they have an adverse reaction to being run over, Eric, or because the frost came through the window you didn't notice had been cracked by the flying wall-nail you lost track of after it had gone past your ear? Why is a big stone tub always in the wrong place only after you have filled it with enough earth to make it impossible to move it to the right one?

And can I just ask you another 300 questions like these, Eric?

Busy Going Nowhere

You know Argos of course. He had eyes all over his body, which was not only why he was also listed as Panoptes in the Olympus phone-book, but also why he was selected to look after Io after Zeus had changed her into a heifer. A lousy job, but someone had to do it, and when you reflect that Io not only named the Ionian Sea while swimming through it as a woman but also named the Bosporus while swimming through it as a heifer (*bos* = ox, *poros* = ford, as anyone who read Greek at Bosporus will tell you), you can see why Argos needed eyes in the back of his head. He nevertheless enjoyed the job (it is said he clocked on every morning singing, "Io, Io, it's off to work we go!"), but since he was subsequently slain by Hermes for no better reason than that Hera needed a boxful of eyes to customise the tail of her new invention, the peacock, you can understand why, in his next incarnation, Argos decided to come back as a chain of cut-price retail outlets; shrewdly retaining no exposing hint of his former caring self other than the motto on the cover of his mail-order catalogue, "Argos takes care of it".

Which brings us, though not for a bit, to the pressing contemporary issue of what video games are doing to the constitutions of British children. The bit finds me on a bicycle, pedalling towards Shanghai. That it is no ordinary bicycle will be clear to anyone who knows my true feelings about the Gobi Desert, in the middle of which I should now be if it *were* an ordinary bicycle, but since it is not, I am still in the middle of Cricklewood, though with calves like rugger balls and arteries down which a corpuscle may sprint without once banging its head from start to finish.

This is because my bicycle is an unwheeled exercise number bought at Argos five years ago, from the odometer of which it may be seen that my subsequent heart-cleansing half-hour a day now tots up to 8,340 miles, putting me, as it were, within a week's hard pedal of Ulan Bator's delightful outskirts. Furthermore (something else I shall return to after a bit) within one volume of the end of *A Dance to the Music of Time*; since throughout the same five years I have also, thanks to the hands-off option immobility affords, been reading a daily half hour of Powell, which I certainly couldn't have done had my bicycle been wheeled: they're barmy drivers the Kazakhs, and as I was deep in *Casanova's Chinese Restaurant* at the time, I might easily have wound up finishing it while plugged supine into an iffy Tselinograd drip, holding the book above my head with my good hand.

And yes, I do realise this isn't the shortest route to Shanghai, but as the alternative was trans-pedalling the Himalayas, I think I made the right choice. I wasn't born yesterday. We shall come to those who were, but not until we have addressed the last bit of the bit; for it is now time to introduce you to the Mini Stepper.

This is yet another cardiophiliac gem from Argos, and I bought it last week because, combined with their bicycle, it will make me live even longer. The Mini Stepper is two hydraulically operated steel footprints: when you place your own feet on them, you can walk as far as you like, on the spot. It is nothing more nor less than a titchy personal road, and I have already done 20 miles on it; indeed, I like the exercise so much that there is a grave risk of my ending up using it more than the bicycle, and may thus not only never pedal into Shanghai, but, around 1998, pass myself on foot just outside Nanking. Never mind: either way, I shall be as fit as a flea.

Which finally brings me to those who were born yesterday; ie, to the British Heart Foundation's present fear for the cardiac destiny of tots who spend their lives in front of video games, never taking any exercise, to offset the chance of their atheromic arteries snapping like pipe-stems before they're 50. What, cries the BHF, is to be done?

What is to be done is our old chum, parental choice. Parents must choose to buy either an exercise bike for 60 quid or exercise feet for 30, stick their infants aboard, and then pop the whole ensemble in front of the screen. Where, as they pump, the kids may simultaneously play all the video games that ever were or will be, to their hearts' content.

The Princess and the Pea

You know how it is, when you are idly scanning a length of text in which you have hitherto had only the merest interest and suddenly a shibboleth springs out of it to strike the retina with such force as to make thy two eyes, like stars, start from their spheres? And how, furthermore – when it is a really top shibboleth – thy two spheres, having finally got their eyes back, themselves continue for some considerable time to roll around like marbles in a soup-plate?

Come with me, then, to last Sunday morning and the

hurly-burly of a chaise-longue bearing the unstable spoil-heap of Sabbath newsprint in the middle of which I am rustling, like an insomniac dormouse in its winter nest, trying to find something of import.

Which, at first glance, the Princess of Wales's parking saga unquestionably isn't. You will recall that our next Queen, of a mind to tie on the lunchtime bib at San Lorenzo on Saturday, fetched up in Beauchamp Place at 1pm in her nice new Audi, only to discover that there was nowhere to put it. To her, enter two constables; who, softly gazed at, I have little doubt, from beneath those famously lowered lids, instantly broke out in a muck sweat generated by assorted devotions too complex to unravel, and scribbled a note for the royal windscreen to the effect that the nice new Audi was on the fritz, and must not be ticketed, clamped, towed or even given a nasty look. Whereupon the Princess happily twinkled off for her spag bol, lowering the curtain, you would imagine, on as unmomentous a comic playlet as you could shake a slapstick at.

But you had reckoned without Mr Bob Cryer, Labour MP for Bradford South. For Mr Cryer was waiting in the wings, *diabolus ex machina* that he is, to spring on and open Act II. Nor was he waiting patiently. He was jumping up and down. He was foaming at the chops. He was gnawing the curtain, the better to persuade it of his view that so gross an abuse of privilege had occurred that there might well be nothing for it now but to herd the entire royal family into the Buck House basement and whistle up the marksmen. Now, we might feel this to be a bit strong, particularly if we believe that in the war between motorists and meterists no holds are barred and that the Princess's coup was therefore one for our side, but we feel it only because we have not yet clocked what was really upsetting Mr Cryer. So let us, since he has now bounded onstage, look at his actual words to the groundlings: "It is outrageous that the police should devote several man-hours to guarding a royal person's car while she is having a slap-up lunch."

A slap-up lunch? *A slap-up lunch?* Oh, my *Dandy* and my *Beano* long ago! Do you remember the slap-up lunch? It was what the toffs and the nobs always went to, at the Hotel de Posh, and they went in shiny top hats and shiny big cars with number-plates that read URA1 and RU12, and it consisted of a mountain of mashed potato with a dozen bangers poking out of it, gobbled in the fawning company of wing-collared waiters endlessly firing corks at chandeliers. Was there ever a more potent class-war signifier than the slap-up lunch?

Not, I bet, to Mr Cryer. You can tell. You do not have to be a dab hand at subtexts and hidden agendas to see what has really got up Mr Cryer's nose, nor how far up it it has got. What has made the irradiating core of his rage go critical is not that a royal person's car was parked where it shouldn't have been, but that the royal person parked it so that she could tuck into San Lorenzo's towering mash and enormous bangers in the company of other toffs and nobs, while all that Keyhole Kate and Dennis the Menace can do is press their hapless poverty-stricken noses against the window and dream their futile gastric dreams.

So that was what made me sit up and take notice last Sunday. For I had rather hoped that all that foodist nonsense lay behind us, back in my far, class-ridden youth; but seemingly not. I note that Mr Cryer is to ask the Home Secretary about it in the Commons, so God alone knows how many man-hours he himself wishes to have further devoted to the matter. If only the Princess had told the Old Bill she was just going to see if the Knightsbridge job centre had anything for an unemployed single parent, none of this would have happened.

Rogue Mail

I need your help. I have to contact a couple of people, and I have to contact them urgently. I do not have a physical description of either of them, but I have a pretty fair idea of their age and their lifestyles, I have the city they live in, and I have a name. Their name is Corem.

The city they live in is London, but there are no Corems listed in the London phone book. My guess is that they are ex-directory rather than phoneless, since I know them to be well-heeled, with, what's more, taste: they will have several telephones, of a design evoking the great days of Edwardian telecommunications, almost certainly in best onyx, with a smart gilt dial which cannily belies the leading-edge technology beneath. These probably stand on neo-Jacobean tables, scattered from their original nests throughout the elegant Corem premises. I deduce all this from the fact that Mrs Corem loves ropes of Victorian-style cultured pearls and Regency-type cruet sets, while Mr Corem would not be seen dead without a traditional pigskin briefcase, but only one updated with six-digit combination locks and a zippered cellphone pocket.

The Corems, I should stress, do not actually have these, at least as far as I know; they would just like to have them. And they could get them too, and in a trice, if I could only find out where they live, for there is a company desperate to give them to the Corems for nothing. I know this because I have, God forgive me, been reading their mail. It has been arriving, by some mischance, at my address for some months now, and while I of course popped the first letters back in the postbox marked "not known here", this did not stanch the flow. There is clearly a glitch on the mail-mode of a computer otherwise so remarkably well-informed as to be able to make such precise observations as, "I am sure, Mr Corem, that a man in your position has often felt that his life would be enhanced by a luxurious holiday home away from the London bustle," and "I know, Mrs Corem, that this fully-fitted vanity case would be just the thing for those weekend breaks".

The vanity case is free, too. It was offered to Mrs Corem in the course of a somewhat tetchy letter noting that she had not come to collect her pearls yet. Or the cruet. Or a hairdryer with a thing on it for enclosing Mrs Corem's whole head. As for Mr Corem, by letter five, his free brief-case, though cavalierly ignored, was now lying next to a free trouser-press and a free crocodile wallet with a calculator in it no thicker than a credit-card. You can understand why the company was getting tetchy: not only was the Corems' stuff piling up in its Hitchin office, the ingrates had not even had the grace to explain why they hadn't been down to take it off their hands. Despite the fact that the company had thoughtfully, in every letter, sent a map, with a useful calendar on the obverse, telling the Corems how to get there.

With letter six, I became seriously agitated. The company had demonstrated itself to be so forgiving as to offer the Corems the chance of a free Vauxhall if they would only come down and take their presents away, and a free Vauxhall is a major item. I had thus been put in an intolerable position. I was the only link between the Corems and what were clearly their increasingly frantic benefactors, for the tone of the letters had become so pitifully solicitous ("I cannot understand why I have not heard from you," etc.) that I feared the sender would do something silly if his generous attempts to spread a little happiness through this bleak world received such short shrift.

And he did, even though I rang his office and explained matters to a very nice girl eating a boiled sweet of some kind, who said she would pass the message on to her woss-name. The silly thing he did was ignore the message and send a seventh letter (written, by its tone, on his knees) informing the Corems that he now had £250,000 for them. All they had to do was show up and listen to him telling them about undiscovered Spain. The Corems do not even have to buy a ticket, scratch a card, pick eight draws. Just go to Hitchin. From wherever they are now.

If you have any idea where that is, for God's sake let them know.

Pole Position

At a loss for the exact size of Hoboken? Unable to sketch a spider's genitals? Never dawned on you that Robert Maillart might just be the father of Swiss concrete? Baffled as to why the Aral Sea is shrinking? Embarrassed when the cocktail chit-chat turns to feedback loops or ophi-cleides? Well, here's a handy tip for the harassed auto-didact: why not buy a sturdy 4ft length of common pine, a handsome MDF oblong offcut slyly veneered in bogus afrormosia, a 2ft length of beaded ash lipping, an iron thing the uninventive use only for sticking a Christmas tree in, and build yourself a lectern to grace any snug or den?

Our story begins on the morning of 25 December, when the thing for sticking a Christmas tree in still had only a Christmas tree stuck in it, beside which lay, or rather towered, a tinselled carton with my name on it. This I carried upstairs – gratified that it weighed little more than the average hatchback, if slightly concerned that the country's surgeons might be too busy sectioning poultry to turn out just to suture a hernia – and excitedly unwrapped.

Inside was *The Columbia Encyclopaedia*, the biggest book in the world; it contains seven million words, and, says its fly-leaf, was called by John Updike "an incomparable one-volume omnifactotum", probably when describing it to his osteopath. A present from my wife; who, though she had somehow guessed that among its million facts might well lurk a few with which I wasn't already familiar, did not herself know one with which I was, *viz.* that I didn't have a shelf large enough to accommodate *Columbia*, and even if I did, I should not be able to lug it thence to my desk without having a bit of a lie-down afterwards, and even if I did that, I should not be able to put it on my desk without taking everything else off it first. Thus, the boon she had so thoughtfully believed she was offering a deadlined hack stuck for the population of Lutsk or the gestation period of the weasel, seemed insurmountably offset by the time and effort needed to look such things up. It would be simpler to phone Lutsk, or (there must be one) Weaselworld.

It was not until two days later that the solution hit me. I would buy a lectern. Nothing fancy, no brass eagles, no ormolu acanthus, just an honest wooden stand with a sturdy angled shelf on which my encyclopaedia could rest, open, on the constant *qui vive* should I need urgently to know anything from the cubic capacity of Nuvolari's helmet to the dietary quirks of the Vorticists.

So, for a fortnight, I approached every imaginable outlet from conference convenors to suppliers of sundries to the sacerdotal trade, without a nibble, save for a Kensington antiquier's offer of a nice 18th-century example which, thanks to the recession, he might be prepared to let me wrest from his grasp for only two grand. It was then that I looked again at the sketch I had roughed out for faxing to putative lecternmongers, and realised that if I ran round to Cricklewood Timber with it, they might be able to provide the wherewithal for me to knock one up myself. So they lathed a length of 4 × 4 into a smooth pine pole at only £41.50, threw in the offcut and beading, and sent me home to lip the shelf, screw it to the upright at a pre-cut 45-degree angle, coach-bolt the ensemble into the vacated iron tree- stand, and set it vertical.

Or, what's the word, off-vertical. Not by much; just enough to ensure that when the world's biggest book was put on it and opened, it continued, if you let go, to turn its own pages, with a gentle *flop-flop* sound.

So did I rage? Did I weep? Only at first; because after a bit, I saw that I had, quite fortuitously, invented a remarkable educational tool via which the process of investigating one thing invariably led to the learning of two things. For example, I should never have known of the shrinking of the Aral Sea had I not been reading about Andropov, turned away, and turned back to find that *Columbia* had flopped itself 31 pages on.

There could be big money in the Wonky Lectern. Because while it is one thing to have a big book which enables you to look up things you do not know, it is quite another to have a big book which enables you to look up things you did not know you did not know. Just think, if Updike had owned a screwdriver, he'd be a millionaire by now.

Punch Up, Punch Up, and Play the Game!

Last Saturday I watched a really cracking football match. One of those matches you walk home from thinking, "Yes, that is what soccer is all about." Fourteen fouls in the first ten minutes, fists flung, throats elbowed, eyes poked, shins hacked, shirts ripped, hair pulled, enough ballistic saliva to fill a trainer's bucket, and a richer variety of air-blueing oaths, I'll wager, than Mary Whitehouse has been able to net in a lifetime's trawling.

Utterly professional. Totally committed. Prodigiously physical. Impressively cynical. Above all, unstintingly competitive, and not a player on the field over 12 years old.

God only knows how it went after the first ten minutes. I had to get home to gut the duck, and Clitterhouse Playing Fields are supposed to be a short cut back from the butcher's; hang around for the first fractured skull and you might as well have taken the paved route. That is why I have never watched a whole match between the teams of small Cricklewood boys who regularly assemble here to bash each other about. As a sports fan, I have missed much. Those with time to stand and stare have probably seen exposed bone.

And these matches are friendlies. They are not for the sake of a ribboned coat or the selfish hope of a season's fame, they are not fought for school or club or community, they are played between scratch teams who have convened simply to knock seven bells out of one another. A fact-finding Martian could be forgiven for transmitting to mission control his conclusion that the object was not to win but to take apart.

Which was why, as the duck and I strolled home, one of us found his thoughts inevitably turning to Mr Iain Sproat. For our great sports minister, desperate to come up with a basic of his own to get back to, believes that Old Albion could be steered towards moral redemption if only competitive sport were returned to the nation's schools. He thus takes his place in the team picture of that dimwit governmental *galère* which seeks to establish nostalgia as policy, ignoring not only L.P. Hartley's shrewder vision of time, but also its inescapable obverse: the present is a foreign country, Mr Sproat; they do things differently here.

For sport has changed, and competition has changed, and it is too late to change either of them back. We live in an age which has introduced the head-butt to international squash and the crowbar to Olympic ice skating, so that soccer icons like Cantona or Gazza need not feel ashamed of garnishing their genius with brutality, nor Courtney Walsh shrink from dismembering Devon Malcolm; an age when the captain's hand cannot smite anyone on the shoulder to exhort them to play up, play up and play the game because the captain's hand has been punched through the dressing-room door and he has been ambulanced away to the stitchers, leaving Middlesex without him for much of last season; a particular pity, since Mr Gatting is Cricklewood's only local sporting hero, so how are the Clitterhouse kids to behave when the year turns them from soccer to cricket? Might we not much prefer them to stay indoors and watch Vinny Jones's *Hard Men* video?

So then, how smart a move would it be to re-introduce competitive team games to our schools? To invite our youth to model itself upon its heroes, so that fair play and honour and selflessness and respect for rules and disciplined behaviour may shape their social character and instil some moral structure in their lives? Think on't, Mr Sproat.

And while you do, spare perhaps a brief auxiliary reflection as to why the goalposts may have shifted on our unlevel playing fields. Consider, that is, the possibility that our irritatingly jocular practice of making sport a metaphor for the national condition might be sidetracking us from the recognition that it isn't a metaphor at all. Put another way – and selecting your favourite core text to put it – suppose that Rugby School had been given into the stewardship not of Thomas Arnold but of Margaret Thatcher: who would have ended up with the Victor Ludorum cup on his mantelpiece, Tom Brown or Harry Flashman?

Chickening Out

Any day now, you may be shot of me for good. Any day now, I may toss my quill into the wastebin, sink a thimbleful of the editor's brown sherry, shake his hand, tuck Rupert's valedictory bracket-clock beneath my arm, and march off to start a whole new life. For that is what I have just been offered, and since opportunities to start whole new lives come rarely down the pike, I am considering it very seriously indeed.

At a little after nine o'clock this morning, I answered my

doorbell to a small wiry man with a flat cap, a donkey jacket, and a chicken. The chicken was cradled in his arms, darting its head this way and that in tiny spasmodic jerks, not unlike a punch-drunk flyweight, but otherwise keeping its own counsel. It was the man who said: "We are in the area."

Now, as you know, many doorstep conversations start that way, but they usually go on to involve gravel, glazing, politics, roofing, or God. Not this time: this time, the man and the chicken were in the area to talk about men and chickens. Nor did they plan to let empty etiquette delay their mission: the man did not raise his hat, he raised his chicken.

"Most people," the man began, "do not realise that a chicken like this lays an egg a day – which comes to 30 dozen a year, call it £40 up Tesco – but costs less than a tenner per annum to keep. Work it out. I am in a position to offer these fine English hybrids . . ." he nodded at the chicken, which nodded back ". . . at only a fiver the brace."

"Brace?"

"You need two, minimum. They encourage one another."

"I don't need any at all," I said.

The man and the chicken exchanged a second look.

"You wish to go on chucking money down the drain?" inquired the man. "Never mind eating month-old eggs that taste like a fish laid 'em?"

"I don't have the space," I said.

"Don't have the space?" cried the man. "Show us round the back!" I hesitated. "I am doing you a favour," he said, but it was not this which settled it, it was the chicken's sudden squawk. When it comes to double acts, I am a pushover for good timing. I led them through the side door. The man put the chicken down, and looked at the garden. The chicken pecked at the lawn.

"She likes it here," said the man, firmly. "And don't talk

to me about no space, that is 400 square metres, give or take, do you know how many hens you could get on this?"

I shook my head.

"Ministry regulations state seven birds per square metre. You could get 2,000 birds in here and still have room for cooping, what is 2,000 times 30 dozen, or should I say times 30 quid clear profit? Work it out."

"The council would never . . .'

"Ring 'em up. Me and her'll be all right out here."

"There are no restrictions as to numbers," said Barnet Environmental Health Office, "provided your neighbours don't object."

"They won't," said the man, when I went back into the garden, "you wouldn't credit how much people in towns like a bit of clucking. Also feathers blowing about. It is deep in all of us, that. And if they do complain, you can bung 'em a few eggs."

The chicken walked into the middle of the lawn. It looked good. If you narrowed your eyes, you could see 2,000. The man had stopped talking. Had he, knowing as he did what lies deep in all of us, sussed out that vulnerable spot in men of a certain age for whom, if they are to ride ramrod on 2,000 head of prime chicken clucking along the Chisholm Trail from the Rio Grande to Abilene, it is now or never?

"Sixty thousand pounds a year, eh?" I said.

He cleared his throat. "Minimum," he said.

"I'll start with two," I said, "and see how it goes from there."

So I gave him a fiver, and I put the brace on the lawn, and I came up here to the loft to type what could well be some of my last few words. Unless, of course, there is anything in the fact that, as I type, I can see next door's cat sitting on the wall, staring at the 60 grand.

A Personal Statement
by
Richard Gere and Cindy Crawford

For some reason unknown to us, there has been an enormous amount of speculation in Europe lately concerning the state of our marriage. This all stems from a very crude, ignorant and libellous "article" in a French tabloid. We both feel quite foolish responding to such nonsense, but since it seems to have reached some sort of critical mass, here's our statement to correct the falsehoods and rumours and hope it will alleviate the concerns of our friends and fans.

We got married because we love each other and we decided to make a life together. We are heterosexual and monogamous and take our commitment to each other very seriously. There is not and never has been a pre-nuptial agreement of any kind. Reports of a divorce are totally false. There are no plans, nor have there ever been any plans for divorce. We remain very married. We both look forward to having a family. Richard is not abandoning his career. He is starting a film in July with others planned to follow.

We will continue to support "difficult" causes such as AIDS research and treatment, Tibetan independence, cultural and tribal survival, international Human Rights, Gay and Lesbian Rights, ecology, leukaemia research and treatment, democracy movements, disarmament, non-violence and anything else we wish to support irrespective of what the tabloids try to imply.

Now, that said, we do feel we have a basic right to privacy and deserve to have that respected like everyone else. Marriage is hard enough without all this negative speculation. Thoughts and words are very powerful, so please be responsible, truthful and kind.

A Personal Statement

For some reason unknown to us, there has been an enormous amount of speculation in Europe lately concerning the state of our marriage. This does not stem from a very crude, ignorant and libellous "article" in a French tabloid, unfortunately, because if it did, we should sue the French tabloid for every sou it had, since there is nothing like a few million francs to shore up an iffy marriage, if we had one, which we haven't; in our case we should blow the money like two people who are very much in love and share everything, ie, I would buy a Ferrari Testarossa and Mrs Coren would get something suitable for pottering about in, she would only drive the Ferrari into the gate and give rise to an enormous amount of speculation in Europe concerning the state of our marriage: you know neighbours, it is impossible for two people who are very much in love to scream at one another without Europe jumping to conclusions. We both feel quite foolish responding to such nonsense, but since it seems to have reached some sort of critical mass, here's our statement to correct the falsehoods and rumours in the hope it will alleviate the concerns of our friends and fans.

We got married because we love each other and we decided to make a life together. People did that in 1963, because if they just lived together not only was there no tax benefit, but Mrs Coren's father, if she hadn't been turned into Mrs Coren, would have come round with a baseball bat and there would have been an enormous amount of speculation in Europe. Whether we would have got married in the subsequent days when people just living together could get tax relief on two mortgages I cannot say, but it would have been a hell of a poser for Mrs Coren's father. Not that he was a mercenary man, his main fault was opening two clubs when he had only ten points, a genetic glitch inherited by his daughter, but I always let bygones be bygones, after a year or so, because if I ran off with the blonde up the road she might well turn out not to be a bridge player. She might also turn out not to be a blonde, according to Mrs Coren.

We are heterosexual and monogamous and take our commitment to each other very seriously. Watch one of us talking to, for instance, a blonde up the road and you will see just how seriously the other one takes it. And vice versa, if one of us ever catches her at it.

There is not, and never has been a pre-nuptial agreement of any kind. If there had been – regarding, say, hot dinner on table when required, lavatory seat left up/down, ERM, smacking children, responsibility for turning off gas, uselessness of UN sanctions, being out of gin, Loyd Grossman, MCC/Garrick excluding women, geraniums put in too early, turn to worm cat, private schools, getting drunk with Waterhouse, Greenham Common, leaving partner vulnerable to opponent's lob, well I thought it said black tie, and so on – we should have had so little to scream about that there would have been an enormous amount of speculation in Europe, *je ne l'aime pas, Tonto, c'est trop tranquil!*

Reports of a divorce are totally false. There are no plans, nor have there been, for divorce. After 30 years, we now own 18,352 things: had there ever been plans for divorce, Europe would have spotted tea-chests stretching round the block. We remain very married. We both look forward to having a family. We may have one any day now, should they deign to drop in, do they even bloody phone, do they hell, sometimes we wonder why we had them in the first place, but there you are.

We shall continue to support "difficult" causes, such as the Lifeboat Fund, the Distressed Gentlefolks' Association, the Donkey Sanctuary, the Cricklewood Festival, and anything else we wish to support, irrespective of what the tabloids try to imply. As to Tibetan independence, while he supports it, Mr Coren wishes to point out that he is not a Buddhist, he is merely a bit thin on top.

That said, we do feel we have a basic right to privacy. That is why we have taken so much space in *The Times*. Whether, when Mrs Coren finds out we have taken it, the consequences will give rise to an enormous amount of speculation in Europe, is nobody's business but ours.

On the Other Hand

I address, this morning, the common weal. Oh, good, you will say, for good is what you take the common weal to be, but that is because you have forgotten my penchant for puns. I, on the other hand, cannot forget my penchant for puns, because the common weals I received as the result of it still hurt in wet weather. Where they hurt is on the other hand.

You have now, at a guess, had enough of my being too clever by half. You are sick and tired of my showing off. You think I do it just to draw attention to myself. I suppose I think I'm funny. Well, these observations are not new to me. As a matter of fact, I was waiting for you to say that the way to deal with boys who think they are smart is to make them really smart, until I remembered that none of you was Mr Clayton. Mr Clayton could not only trade pun for pun, Mr Clayton had the edge when the punning had to stop: he had a cane to stop it with.

It was about all he had in common with Mr Chenevix-Trench, the dead head of Eton whose relish for raising weals is currently receiving so much *brouhaha*, following the publication of Tim Card's history of the school. (Why Mr Card should have dwelt on flogging I cannot say, I know only that if my name had been Card, it would have been a hostage to fortune that none of my teachers would have been able to resist, so there may be a measure of revenge in Mr Card's motives, if he was once too clever by half.) For Allan Clayton was a humane soul who derived no unseemly frisson from swish, thwack, or yelp; when, limbering up, he would mutter that he did not know what to do with me, it was expressed as a confession and, even as he swung, his face would fill with the gloom of professional failure.

Why, then, did he do it? He did it because all heads did it, then; which is why it strikes me as singular that so much attention is lavished on the history, the psychology, the social significance etc. of corporal punishment in public schools, but none on whacking in the genuinely public sector. For mine was a local grammar, which together with all the other state secondary schools made up 90 per cent of the nation's cane-fodder, and you would therefore think that when it came to speculation upon the role of bamboo in the manufacture of the national psyche, some attention might reasonably be addressed to the overwhelming majority.

Why is this not so? It is not so because, while common folk were caned on the hand, toffs were caned on the buttocks. And buttocks, it is argued, are a bit special: they are not only more fun to write about than hands, but stinging assaults on them may well give rise to an unwholesome taste for anything from humiliation and agony to, well, buttocks.

So what, I say, if a mere tenth of the nation is involved? What about the myriad consequences on those of us who were caned on the palms? Starting, of course, with the humiliation of not being caned on the buttocks, like gents, and therefore being put firmly in our lower-class place. Whether this punishment has given us any particular sexual needs or fancies I cannot say, but what I can is that our humiliation was even greater, because, unshielded by the trouser, our malefactions were on display to all. Worse, countless of my schoolfriends would, unable to conceal their welts, receive a supplementary domestic clip round the ear for, quite literally, their pains. Happily, my own father not only shunned this, but also took some pleasure in remarking that the artisan class got caned on its hand because that's what it worked with, which was why the upper class got caned on its bum.

He wasn't wrong, either, *vide* that reference to the other hand, this being what dear old Clayton used, in his concern, to insist on. You would hold out your right, but he would indicate the left, because he didn't want any excuses about not being able to do your homework, the lower classes were here to improve themselves, that was what grammar schools were all about.

And was the cane an aid to that improvement? Did it never do me any harm? We shall have to await the boom in the sociopsychology industry I trust I have just generated. Only then will we know whether it taught me not to show off.

In Like Flint

Among all the excited analysis generated by that osseous sliver from the Boxgrove pit, and all the even more excited speculation, there lurks a dispiriting but ineluctable truth which none has, until this morning, addressed. It is that, though he may be quite interesting now, Boxgrove Man, some half a million years before he became a monument, was a monumental bore. Indeed, it would surprise me if subsequent truffling among the remnants of vole and mink and rhino and all the rest of the frail palaeolithic gubbins with which the famous shin was surrounded did not suddenly throw up, any day now, the hind leg of a donkey.

"How," you understandably query, "do you know this? Yours is not a household name where archaeologists forgather, you do not even have a proper trowel, where do you get off putting in your two pennorth?" Precisely because I do not have a proper trowel, is where: those of us who, faced with the need for a bit of ad hoc trowelling, reach for the kitchen spatula, know what Boxgrove Man was like, all right. Because one line stands out, for us, among all the reams of expository prose which attended his resurrection: "Not only was this hominid familiar with sophisticated tools, he was also able, through his rudimentary voice-box, to communicate that expertise."

Astonishing, is it not? Half a million years ago, the barely humanised world was already divided between those who could talk about tools and those who did not have the faintest idea what those who could talk about tools were talking about. We are looking, here, at nothing less than the birth of humiliation.

Let us move forward down the long arches of the years and fetch ourselves up at, for argument's sake, the front drive of a house that has awoken to a somewhat unsettling smell. Set into this front drive is a manhole-cover which the householder has been attempting to lift; in half a million years' time, archaeologists will be able to divine this from the surrounding detritus of broken screwdrivers, sheared garden-fork tines, kitchen spatula fragments, and, if their eyes are good enough, bits of fingernail. As the householder sits on his wall, staring bitterly at the immovable iron slab, enter to him a passer-by: Cricklewood Man.

"Yes, werl," says Cricklewood Man, "what you need there is a four-and-a-half Whitworth flat-head lip crow."

"What?"

"The one with the elbow. Slip the head under the lid-lip, liver it on the elbow, and double it up as a brace while you're rodding out."

The scene now changes to the trade counter of Cricklewood Building Supplies. Standing in a line of dungareed men cheerily swapping arcane anecdotes of plumb-bobs and sash cramps is a householder; his lips are moving, too, but silently. He is struggling to remember. Finally, it is his turn.

"You what?"

The householder repeats his request. The men in dungarees fall about. Eventually, the householder brokenly explains what it is that he wants four halfs of a Molesworth fat-face something or other for, creeps out with his purchase through the helplessly gasping dungarees, and at last manages to lift the manhole-cover. It is while he is waist deep in the manhole frantically trying to retrieve the cricket bat which has somehow unSellotaped itself from the broomhandle and begun its gradual but inexorable subterranean passage towards Barnet Sewage Works that Cricklewood Man reappears above him, invaluably to inform the householder that what he should have used was a 9-bore Sefton flexible bi-pole reamer with a Cambridge reverse spiro-claw attachment. At this point, the householder levers himself out, takes three baths, and phones a 24-hour cowboy millionaire so that he can be asked who the prat was who has been down here already.

Let us, therefore, not be beguiled by all the anthropological flim-flam seeking to impress us with both the dexterity and the articulacy of Boxgrove Man. Let us instead spare a thought for Boxgrove Man-Next-Door, gamely attempting to build himself a front wall with a flint kitchen spatula and a yak-bone teaspoon, when a rudimentary voice-box behind him grunts: "You don't want to do it like that, what you need is a . . .'

Birdman of Cricklewood

You know that unsettling feeling of being watched? And when you look up, you are being watched? And what is watching you is standing on your table?

Oh, you don't know that one? Then you certainly don't know how it feels when what is standing on your table watching you suddenly jumps on to the rim of your bowl of Shreddies and sticks its uninvited face in your breakfast. How it feels is complicated.

Certainly, it felt complicated on Monday morning when, having ported the Shreddies into the garden for a bit of peace and roughage, I found that I was to have neither because (*a*) all these complicated feelings were to ensue, and (*b*) you do not want to eat Shreddies that have had a budgerigar poking about in them. It is not just a question of what you might catch off a budgerigar – psittacosis minor perhaps – it is also a question of what else a budgerigar might have been poking about in before it got to your Shreddies, ie, there is the even more imponderable question of what you might catch off a worm.

If, mind, this were the only complication, I should have been able to cope. I should simply have shouted at the budgerigar and it would have flown off, probably to practise this new shout it had learnt on somebody else. I should have heard my shout echoing up and down the road. But because it was not the only complication, expulsion wasn't an option: the second complication was that this was not my budgerigar. I am not the sort to keep a feathered homunculus on the premises, hopping about and badgering visitors with coy queries about its prettiness, so the complication of its not being mine was, of course, that it was somebody else's.

What, then, was it doing here? Had it been evicted? Had it escaped? Or was it, rather, a trusty, whose impeccable behaviour in chokey, never a little ladder unscaled, never a little bell unrung, had earned it day release? Would it dutifully hurtle back when the vesper tocsin clanged for banging-up?

I need to know these things. One has to, these days, now we are all one caring world. Indeed, all those possessive pronouns I have been so thoughtlessly chucking about are themselves well beyond the pale of political rectitude: budgerigars, in 1994, do not belong to people, they share their lives with them. They are always there for one another. But this one wasn't there for them any more, it was here for me.

What I needed to do was debrief it: even were it prepared to divulge only name, rank, and serial number, that would be something. I could then stick a note on the gate or put an ad in *Cage and Aviary Birds*, especially if it had an uncaged section. The budgerigar was now walking about in the milk, but it stopped when I asked it what its name was, and looked at me. It spoke, however, not a word.

So I said: "Joey?" Then I said: "Polly?" It continued to

look at me – most sane people would – but, after a moment or two, it began walking about in the milk again. In the old days, I could have frogmarched it to the basement and let the *Untersturmbannführer* have a go at its toenails, but these are the new days, and I am a new man. I am such a new man, indeed, that I now began to wonder whether I ought to contact its owner at all: what if it had been ornithologically harassed, abused, forced each Christmas to recite *The Green Eye of the Little Yellow God*, while sozzled in-laws pelted it with dates? Suppose it had tunnelled its way out, seeking a safe house, a new identity, the Swiss border?

And even if none of this were so, should birds be caged at all, and this one's owner count himself fortunate I do not come round in a balaclava and set light to his wife's fox tippet? But then again, should those that have decaged themselves be left to tackle the wild? They are a rough crowd, the starlings of Cricklewood, and if anything polychromatic minced up to them and inquired who a pretty boy was, they would give it a right seeing-to. What do I do? It is still there. I shall go into the garden in case it's decided to speak. What I want it to say is goodbye.

To Boldly Go, Plus 17.5 Per Cent

For all those doomed to plough the lonely furrow to which, this morning, I yet again address my battered coulter, the first cleft is ever the toughest. It is the very sod to turn. Because that opening sentence has to be a corker. It is the hook from which, and on which, all else depends. It has to grab.

That is why it is a truth universally acknowledged, that a single man in possession of a good fortune, must be in want of a wife; that is why all happy families resemble one another, but each unhappy family is unhappy in its own way; that is why it was a bright cold day in April, and the clocks were striking thirteen. And that is why, when HM's Customs & Excise sat down to compose *VAT Notes No 1, 1994*, they first pumped the keywords "Austen", "Tolstoy" and "Orwell" into their very smart computer in the earnest hope that it would come up with an opening sentence which would not only synthesise the major VAT themes of solvency and unhappiness, but also make our neck hairs rise in illimitable dread.

They were not wrong. I knew this the moment I read it, for *VAT Notes* is a single-leaf pamphlet, and when, a mere nano-second after the eyes have scanned one of its really top opening sentences the fingers holding it start to tremble, *VAT Notes* itself begins to flap and wobble. If you thought only Heineken could do this, you erred: you had forgotten that it is the very *raison d'être* of HM Customs & Excise to reach the parts others cannot.

Here, then, is the opening sentence I read this morning: "Customs & Excise are developing a strategy to take VAT into the next century, determining the principles that will shape the organisation and management of the tax, and our aims across the entire VAT spectrum."

Take it in. Tremble. Does it, perhaps, not remind you of a fourth great curtain-raiser? Let me help: "These are the voyages of the Starship VAT. Its ongoing mission: to boldly go where no tax has gone before." Now do you feel, with me, that blast of intergalactic chill which is the unique iciness of deep fiscal space? Do you not see, as the imminent millennium dawns, the enormous VAT complex accelerating to Warp Factor 17.5 in its ambition to deploy as comprehensively as possible those sharp-eared inspectors from whom all sentiment has been deleted to leave only the untrammelled capacity for cold calculation which is the Vulcan watchword?

They have never needed a warrant, but, oh look, now they do not even need a doorbell. Thanks to this newly developed strategy of theirs they can beam themselves into your premises at will, rematerialise inside your filing cabinets, note that you have illegally claimed exemption for chiming onyx doorstops, marzipan pelicans exceeding 8 cms in girth, and replica Ben Jonson folios bound within rexinette covers *not* imported from signatories of the Brest-Litovsk Laminate Declaration, and beam themselves up again, leaving you with no indication of their visit until the Fraud Squad fronts up at your holiday beach-hut and throws a blanket over your head.

Do not attribute my fulminations to anything ulterior. What I think about VAT is irrelevant; my concern is expressed in all our names, because that riveting opening sentence says everything about them and nothing about us. What is the strategy? What are the principles? What is the organisation and management? What are their aims? What is their spectrum? *VAT Notes* does not go on to say. It goes on to say only: "If you would like to help us develop the strategy, please send your comments to Paul Riley, Liverpool L74 4AA. We shall be grateful for your input but please forgive us if we do not manage to reply individually."

That is the final sentence, proving that final sentences can be just as unsettling as opening ones. Of what we are all in for, there is, between the first and last sentences, nary a word, If the object is to creep the flesh, it has worked a treat. For I hear in my head, as the nation's fingers rip open their demands of 2001, a dreadful, if familiar, cry: "This is taxation, Jim, but not as we know it!"

The Once and Future Jeff

It is not every day that a man can plunge his hand into the lexical brantub and pull out 800 words which, when arranged in roughly the right order, will simultaneously save the throne, the government, European civilisation and the MCC, but this Wednesday is one of those days. The last time we had one was 74 years ago, but since I was then unfortunately not around to sort things out, they remained unsorted, with the result that things went from bad to worse on all four fronts.

I refer, of course, to that moment in 1920 when Albania, seeking as its king "an English sportsman with £10,000 a year", pressed this suit on C.B. Fry. Tragically, Fry declined, whereupon the post was offered to the man soon to become famous only as ex-King Zog, due, no doubt, to a tendency to flash at short rising balls outside off-stump.

And now history has repeated as much of itself as makes no odds. This time, Estonia wants a king, and she, too, has flatteringly sought him among English ranks, to wit, Prince Edward. So far, Buckingham Palace has yet to reply formally, and we must all of us pray that it does so negatively (but nicely), since for Prince Edward to accept and make a go of it would be as bad as for him to accept and make a pig's ear of it, for reasons which I trust do not need spelling out to close observers of the current state of our monarchy and its succession.

Yet, lest outright rejection so offend Estonia that British businessmen currently beavering away at emergent markets are given the bum's rush from the whole of Eastern Europe, we have to offer someone in his place, and quickly. I have thought hard about this, and, having ruled out, as it were, not only our royalty but our aristocracy too (the old are clapped out, the young spaced out), I have concluded that since it would insult Estonians to palm them off with anything less than a noble peer, we could offer them no finer king than my old friend and, according to some literary critics, mentor, Lord Archer of Weston-super-Mare.

Not only is he an English sportsman with possibly as much as £12,000 a year, he fulfils the regal bill in every Baltic respect: a fine public speaker fit to grace any palace balcony, whose words, I'm sure, would lose little in translation, an irreproachably natty dresser for whom gilt epaulettes, swagged frogging, plumed helmets, and iridescent Orders of this and that would present no sartorial challenge to which he could not effortlessly rise, a prodigious fundraiser capable of seeing off the Estonian national debt with two gala auctions and a car boot sale, and a man so dedicated to pursuing high office that not even the prospect of leading one-and-a-half million Estonians would daunt him, despite the vast extent by which they outnumber current Tory voters.

He is as much a writer as a sportsman, a happy synthesis of, say, Vaclav Havel and Gubby Allen; just the ticket, I'd have thought, for a recently unsettled culture seeking, now, to have its disparities bonded in one mighty monarch capable of being all things to all men. His queen? Is she not radiant? And yet, while that is what we ask of queens, is she not also smart as a whip, so adept at both alternative energy and television management as to be uniquely qualified to offer the fortunate Estonians a dozen terrestrial channels run off two solar torch-batteries and a child's windmill, for a licence fee under five kroon?

I yearn for King Jeffrey. I see him now, trotting his lads onto the Lord's pitch for an Estonian Test likely to restore, albeit briefly, some *amour propre* to the English team, I see him ushering monarchs, ministers, tycoons past the palace portraits of all the ancient Estonian kings from whom he has discovered he is obliquely descended, as he does his uttermost for Estonia, and of course Britain, I see volume after bestselling volume issuing from his reinvigorated nib . . . as for the British government's loss which is Estonia's gain, is it not possible that their common grief will unite them as never before?

There will be those, mind, who fear that, given Jeffrey's susceptibility to destiny's more melodramatic quirks, there is a risk of his not ascending the throne. A lookalike, a sleeping draught, a villain from Hentzau . . . but what of that? With one bound, I have no doubt, Jeffrey would be free.

Travel Sickness

Given the season, a fair number of you will, I know, be reading this newspaper on holiday. An even fairer number, however, will be wearing it, and you will be wearing it precisely because you are fairer: some of you will have fashioned it into a hat, others will merely have scissored a neat little cone from it to place over your nose, and there may even be those among you, the fairest of all, who are completely dressed in it, having hung a brace of Business News broadsheets fore and aft to form a rude tabard, wound a couple of sports pages around each leg, cobbled a sola topi from the obituaries, and gummed this column to your face with four coats of Factor 96, leaving nothing of your skin exposed except the hands required to hold the Court Circular, which is all you have left to read.

You have done this because you do not want to go brown. Going brown, which used to be one of the main reasons you took holidays, could kill you, given what is now falling out of the sky. But won't covering yourself in newspaper be a mite inconvenient when you go for a dip? Only if you're crazy enough to go for a dip. Going for a dip, which used to be one of the main reasons you took holidays, could kill you, given what is now falling into the sea.

And since eating or drinking anything, these days, could also kill you, it would clearly be a fatal mistake to rustle your way gingerly towards that nice little local taverna, bistro, trattoria, weinstube, or even Olde Copper Kettle, which used to be one of the main reasons you took holidays. As for that box of duty-free corona-coronas, or those invigorating brief encounters, both of which used to be . . .

There is therefore nothing for it, you have concluded, but to swaddle yourself in lengths of what is now quite literally a snip at 20p, and, doing absolutely nothing at all, wait for the dread fortnight to run its minatory course.

But you are wrong, as those who are smart enough to be reading the rest of this column before Sellotaping it to the backs of their necks are about to discover. There are still many safe things to do.

In the Algarve, for example, it is the high season for evening classes. Few of these will kill you, but steer clear of making wickerwork donkey heads, since the rushes rarely conform to EU safety standards, and do remember that home-brewed port may explode without warning. Always wear rubber gloves when handling sardines.

On the Riviera, the additional risk of fires makes it dangerous to go out at all, especially if you are wrapped in *The Times*, but as both evangelists and national lottery sellers are prepared to make house calls, your days need not be without interest. Burn any lottery tickets you buy, of course, since they are a notorious target for muggers. Looking for rabid dogs through a telescope is also fun, but beware of inadvertently pointing your lens at the sun. Many tourists have gone blind.

For those holidaying in Spain, both bullfights and flamenco dancing can be unforgettable experiences, particularly if the crowd has anything contagious. Instead, why not see if the British Consul plays Scrabble? All diplomats are required to keep their inoculations up to date, and are also useful contacts should coffins have to be shipped home cheaply.

For those reading this in the Greek islands, and, unnerved by the fact that the sea appears to be wine-dark, do not fancy sailing anywhere to look at the antiquities, remember that many Greeks are only too happy to bring the antiquities to you. You will find their phone numbers in the book, but do not be surprised if, say, the Parthenon is somewhat smaller than you had imagined, and plays *Never On a Sunday* when its roof is lifted: unlike the larger example on the Acropolis, big bits of this one will not fall on your head, and you can also keep Lomotil in it.

As for readers on Italian vacations, RAI, under the brilliant new management of Snr Berlusconi, is currently showing *Till Death Us Do Part*, conveniently dubbed to enable British lip-readers to pick up a working knowledge of the Calabrian patois. Do not watch this in your hotel room, mind, as sitting too close to cathode rays could kill you. Stand, in the shade, across the street from the window of a TV showroom. If you are near Vesuvius, keep one eye on that, too. You never know.

Where Was I?

I see that Professor Curt Johansson, the Swedish psychologist, or perhaps merely a Swedish psychologist, I do not know how eminent he is. I should have to phone Sweden to find out and it looks like being another scorcher. I cannot sit sweating here for hours listening to Swedish directory inquiries entertaining me with a medley of Hugo Altven favourites while they trawl their files for the right Curt Johansson, I do not have his address, I do not even have his town, and since it is a pound to a penny that 31 per cent of all Swedes are called Curt Johansson, the odds on finding him at all are extremely remote, especially in view of the fact that Sweden has more psychologists per head of population than any other European country; if, mind, it *is* a fact, at the moment it is only a sort of feeling I have, generated by the Swedish predilection for suicide, ie, if the heads of population are chucking themselves under trams all the time, it is only reasonable to assume that many young Swedes will plump for psychology as a career, there is clearly a bob or two in it. Unless, of course, patients tram themselves before settling their bills.

Then again, it could be that all that suicide is down to not having enough psychologists, in which event there may be only one Prof Curt Johansson listed by Swedish directory inquiries, but I should still prefer not to risk it, given that Hugo Altven succeeded in composing only one favourite, which probably means that their tape-recorder just plays *Swedish Rhapsody* over and over again, and you would not be able to listen to that for very long before you found yourself running into the street to look for a tram.

Not that you would find one in London. The last time I was on a tram in London was in 1948, a No 31 going from Manor House to the Embankment, and my grandmother said stop doing that, people are looking.

Alternatively, might Swedes be killing themselves not because they have too few psychologists but because they have too many? The psychologists may be no help at all to patients who had seen them as a last resort. The last stop, as it were, before the tram terminus. It may be an overcrowded profession. If it is an overcrowded profession, of course, it could even be that it is the psychologists themselves who are swelling the suicide statistics.

I see that I have not completed the sentence which began "I see that Professor Curt Johansson . . ." and you will therefore have no idea what I have seen about him, unless you saw it too. It was in most of yesterday's papers, but you would have had to have got to the end of the articles to see it, and very few of you will have done that, according to Professor Johansson. You will have begun wondering, perhaps, what happened to Ingemar Johansson, Sweden's only ex-world-heavyweight champion, is he now, indeed, ex-world altogether, or is he currently living somewhere peaceful among the permafrosted firs, surrounded by gleaming trophies and rapt grandchildren who never tire of hearing how he took Floyd Patterson in 1959, is he punchy, is he paunchy, does he own restaurants, as so many fighters do – you may even have gone on to try to list all those catering fighters, unless you found yourself wondering: "Curt Jurgens, is he still with us?"

I didn't. By the time many of you arrived at Curt Jurgens, I had begun considering the return of the trolleybus. I can see why it would be a headache to bring trams back, the chaos involved in digging up roads, the risk to traffic-flow represented by Swedish tourists grown irreparably glum at the cost of ice-cream and the absence of the royal standard over Buckingham Palace, but might it not be time for the back-to-basics lobby to consider the return of the silent, unpolluting, friendly trolleybus? Would this not be something of a coup for Dr Mawhinney as he slides into his nice new seat at the MOT, especially if combined with the reappearance of those wooden ticket-holders that went ding?

I see, by the way, that Professor Curt Johansson has warned that the present heatwave is a threat to thinking. "Over 75 degrees, it is impossible to concentrate on anything." He is quite wrong. Over 75 degrees, you concentrate on everything. You do it a little more briefly, that is all.

Talking Point

On 10 March 1876, in a small back room in Boston, Massachusetts, the words "Watson, come here, I want you!" were signally uttered. At which, no less signally, the wanted Watson, who was in a small front room, duly came. And what, of course, made all this so signal was the signal that made it, for those six little words comprised the very first message ever to be transmitted by telephone.

I have always cherished them. Indeed, in the great roster of Victorian opening remarks to assistants called Watson, they come, in my view, second only to: "You have been in Afghanistan, I perceive." What I cherish them for is their sheer telephonic quintessence: here are two discrete men separated by one concrete wall, and they need to make contact; one dials, the other picks up the phone, but there is no spendthrift taradiddle about "Hallo, is that Small Front Room 1, my name is Alexander Graham Bell, I was wondering if I might perhaps have a brief word with . . ." or "Good morning, thank you for calling Small Front Room 1, this is Daniel Farrar Watson speaking, how may I help you?", there is just a bark and an instant response. Right there on day one, telecommunication was as good as it was ever going to get. After that, it would be downhill all the way.

Quite how far down that hill I find myself this morning, I do not know and cannot guess. I know only that British Telecom wants to bolt a personal stereo to my head and fly me to Sydney in a kimono, and I guess that what it wants in return for doing this is me to spend money. I have come to these conclusions notwithstanding the claim by BT that what it wants is me to save money, because, well, call it a feeling.

I have received a letter from Mr David Duxbury, BT's marketing director, announcing "a new way for our most important customers to enjoy even greater benefits". My chest having finished swelling, I noted that the new way was entitled PremierLine; but despite the fact that long experience has taught me that any neologism with a capital letter in the middle of it exudes a warning whiff of dodginess, I nevertheless read on, since being most important confers certain responsibilities. Thus I learnt that PremierLine offers a 15 per cent discount on calls for customers who use the phone a lot. If I cough up £24 per annum for PremierLine, every time I subsequently dial I shall, according to BT, be saving money: even though, according to me, I shall be spending it.

No matter: I am the last person to complain about the manipulation of language for cash. I am, however, the first person to complain about the proliferation of language for it; there is already far too much language about, and most of the too much is the direct responsibility of the telecommunications market: the exponential burgeoning of phones, faxes, mobiles, telexes and all the rest has ensured a Parkinsonian footnote which declares that chit-chat expands so as to fill the apparatus available for its completion. BT knows this, and knows that PremierLine will incite subscribers to spill more language for more money, if less purpose. We shall all be talking more and more, saying less and less.

Especially if we want to fly to Sydney in a kimono, nodding our heads to Dire Straits. For, as if the 15 per cent discount were not enough to persuade us to dial[2], PremierLine will also bring us TalkingPoints. When you join, you receive 500 free (*sic*) TalkingPoints, and the more you talk thereafter, the more TalkingPoints you clock up; which, when you have enough, may be exchanged for both air miles and "exclusive free gifts for all the family, from kettles to kimonos, tumblers to torches, pens to personal stereos".

I do not know how long you would have to talk to get to Sydney in a kimono, but I do advise you to find out, it would be ghastly to be stuck in, say, Kowloon, clutching only a tumbler, when another 23 hours of needless natter would have brought you up to fully intercontinental chic. If, indeed, 23 hours would do it. It's a fair old distance to Australia. Though not, perhaps, as great as the one separating us from the days when you could pick up a phone, say: "Watson, come here, I want you!", and have done with it.

A Better 'Ole

I missed a great opportunity on Sunday. A caption in Monday's *Times* told me so. Beneath a charming snap of two old dears lolling on picnic chairs between the ranks of glinting Rollers, the legend ran: "More than a hundred hearses were on display at an exhibition at the Beaulieu Motor Museum yesterday by the British Institute of Funeral Directors. Visitors were given the chance to test-drive the latest models."

Test-drive? It cannot be that after the two old dears had polished off the last of the bloater-paste, they were invited to slip behind the wheel of an M-reg hundred-grandsworth and hurl themselves round Hampshire. Going for a test-drive in the latest hearse can surely only mean lying supine in the business section, possibly with a brace of pennies on your eyes and a nodding lily between your folded hands, while a bloke with a melancholy mien drives you slowly over gravel. That is the only way to find out whether or not a hearse is any good.

Which I need to know, if am going to end up lying next to His Imperial Highness the Grand Duke Michael Michaelovich of Russia. The grandson of Tsar Nicholas would not, I feel, take kindly to his new neighbour fronting up in any old banger. Nor would his wife, Countess Sophy von Merenberg. More yet, the glittering couple donated a diving-board to Highgate Pond, and would unquestionably be miffed to think that their old, as it were, haunt was repaying their generosity by allowing parvenu stiffs to get themselves delivered on the cheap, lowering the tone of the place irrecoverably.

The place? Fortune Green Cemetery, a furlong from my gate, three respectful minutes in a Phantom V, a bit longer in a clapped-out back-firing Humber, and the eternal rest-home into which Mrs Coren and I are booked, dates to be confirmed. Regular readers may recall my recent discovery that Marie Lloyd was buried here; what they do not know is that the discovery alerted me to the irresponsibility of dilly-dallying on the way, since our local graveyard is filling up at a hell of a lick, and I should not wish when the time comes to have my coffin, unable to find a spot within, propped against the wall of the next-door Nautilus Fish Bar whither my grief-stricken legatees have repaired to consider, over a nice bit of haddock, whether the simplest course wouldn't be to cab me round to the Royal Free and donate me to the student scalpel.

We have, then, a double hole-in-waiting; what we do not have is any idea of where to have it dug, and we should probably not have addressed the matter at all had the Camden History Society not just published a little guide to the cemetery, since when we have addressed little else. For this will be our last move, and we shall be there a long time, the Archangel Gabriel and Lady Porter permitting, and the quality of one's neighbours is, I fear, a prime suburban preoccupation.

Should we, then, try to wedge ourselves in beside the imperial couple? Or next to George Careless Trewby (1839–1910), who built the Constantinople gasworks? "Note his unusual second name," says the booklet, leaving it at that. So, stands the Constantinople gasworks where it did? One would not seek the eternal company of a cowboy gasometrist. But how about Laszlo Biro, illustrious inventor of the ineradicably stained breast-pocket, or Dame Gladys Cooper, or Charles Hengler, "too tall for tightrope dancing, but became a successful circus proprietor, and riding instructor to the royal family"? Toney company all; were we to be entrenched next to any of them, might it not perhaps implore a better passing tribute than a sigh from impressionable posterity?

Maybe. But you know me, friends, I save the best till last, and never more so than when the last is my own. I have not yet broken it to my wife, but I know where I want to be. "Arthur Prince was the first ventriloquist to perfect talking and drinking at the same time. His dummy Jim, who cost £3 15s, is buried with him. They appeared at the first Royal Command Performance in 1912."

Lay me next to Arthur and Jim. To hell with cutting a posthumous dash, I want to be there when the Last Trump honks and the pair of them spring from the earth beside me, calling impeccably for a gottle of geer.

King of the Road

I took only the one A level this summer, and I have just had the result. My hands are still trembling. My mouth is still arid. My little heart is going pit-a-pat. Beads of aftershock wink on my pate. It is exactly the same as the reaction I had after I heard the O-level result in 1956. Almost exactly. The beads of aftershock did not wink on my pate, then, because I did not have a pate for them to wink on.

Not only was the pate covered with hair, the hair had a school cap on it.

It had to have. It was an offence not to wear your school cap on the street, even if the rite of passage you had just negotiated by securing this particular O level was a right of passage which conferred, more than any mere homophone, adulthood. I did not wear the school cap, mind, while I was negotiating it; I stuffed it into my pocket before I stepped into the exam room, because the exam room was an Austin A35 and I did not wish to offer the examiner a hostage to fortune. If you wanted to be taken seriously as a driver, putting away childish things seemed a smart move. I hoped he would notice the grown-up nicotine stain on my forefinger.

Thirty-eight years on, driving towards the Institute of Advanced Motorists in Chiswick, I hoped that he wouldn't. Rather, that he wouldn't notice the spot where the stain had been before the forefinger had been pumiced to the bone. That had seemed a smart Advanced move. It went with polishing the ashtray, so that it declared: here is a motorist who does not distract himself by smoking. I also detached the detachable radio and replaced it with the replaceable trim. I thus hoped to compensate for the seriously negative signals given off by the rest of the car, for the rest of the car is a red BMW convertible, ie there are three major things wrong with it if a middle-aged driver wishes to be taken seriously as a grown-up. It should have been a black Volvo saloon.

Should it have been clean? Who could say? I had thought long and hard about this. Did a shiny car bespeak the right or the wrong priorities? Would the examiner ask me to lift the bonnet to check whether I was as assiduous about its innards? Might he turn pale and stagger at the sight of a grubby grommet, cry "Call that Advanced?" and throw away his clipboard? What about dress? Would it be more Advanced to front up in a flat cap and string-back gloves, or in a black homburg and a three-piece grey whistle? Not only did I not know any of this, I did not even know what was required in the driving line. What, precisely, was Advanced driving? Was it about skill, or about knowledge, or about caring, or perhaps about all three, would I be asked to take the car through a rain-soaked Druid's at 120, strip it down and rebuild it with only a nailfile, and then kiss a flat hedgehog back to life?

When I arrived in Chiswick, I discovered that it was tougher even than that. It was about satisfying Ted Clements MBE. Why in God's name had the IAM assigned me their Chief Examiner? This was merely an A level, it was not a B.Mot., it was not a D.Driv., why should it demand the scrutiny of a banana so top as to have inspected himself into the Honours List? Had the IAM been alerted that a driver of such ineptitude was about to put his head on the block that nothing but their most illustrious executioner would adequately serve the occasion?

I did not know, and do not still, I know only that our 90 minutes together from Chiswick to Windsor and back have changed my life so radically as to have persuaded me to write this piece solely in order to invite you to change yours. For miraculously, I have before me as I write a length of vellum testifying to my having become a member of the Institute of Advanced Motorists, and it has had the remarkable effect, at a stroke, of making me what it says I am.

For, truth to tell, the past 38 years have been far from Advanced. There has been many an occasion, indeed, when an Institute for Retarded Motorists would have been inscribing parchments by the quire. But all that has changed, simply as the result of my having been vouchsafed a criterion to justify. I cannot believe my driving now. I am a paragon. The very dogs on zebras bless me. My MBE can be only a matter of time.

Post-Modellism

Check the snapshot shimmering on the cover of this book. That forthright conk, brazen almost, set off on either side by winsome crinkle-cut pouches, the cunningly asymmetric grin offering a glimpse of teeth arranged with breathtaking nonchalance, the bold chin beneath, the somewhat shyer chin beneath that . . .

It has something, this face. It could be next year's Face. Men seeing it with a hat on will rush out to buy the hat. Women seeing it with a tie beneath will rush out to buy the tie to give to the men who have rushed out to buy the hat. Quite who will rush out to buy the suit to go with the tie and the hat, mind, rather depends on what the Face does with the body beneath it. Will it be next year's Body?

Could be. I have just minced briskly up to the long cheval-glass in the corner of my bedroom, twirled virtually without stumbling, and minced briskly back again. I do not, of course, know what the body looked like when it minced back again, but it looked pretty good mincing up. Music would have helped, though: something foxy, like, say, *Any Old Iron?* or *Bring Me Sunshine*, some street-smart rhythm meet for the style of the suit, and the man super-modelling it.

Yes, you have caught the drift. You know now that supermodelling the suit was the second thing I did this morning. The first thing I did this morning was answer the door to a dispatch rider who had brought me a press-hot copy of Naomi Campbell's first novel, *Swan*. One glance at the cover told me that this was a major piece of fiction, for Naomi's face is very literary indeed. I speak as one who has seen the faces on the Booker shortlist, and I am here to tell you that Naomi's will, beyond any question, outsell all six of them put together.

That is why she received an advance of £100,000. Over the past 30 years, I have had many a lunch with publishers who claimed to be interested in a novel from me, but none of them was a tenth as interested as Naomi's publisher was in a novel from her. The reason was that I never came up with a good enough idea for a novel, but I have come up with one now. It is not, sadly, as good as the novel ideas Ivana Trump and Martina Navratilova came up with and for which each of them has been offered an advance of $1 million, but since there is little chance of my becoming a trophy husband, and even less chance, thanks to this dodgy knee, of my winning a string of Wimbledon titles, I am in a position to offer neither option to a publisher.

I do rather think, however, that I could hack it on the cat-walk. I have, in the line of business, attended a number of male fashion shows, and it is quite remarkable how few of the models even remotely resemble the men you see trying on grey flannels in John Lewis. Their shape excludes them from any consumer-response save pity at the time and money squandered in gyms and health farms which could have been spent in restaurants and pubs. Nor can I recall ever seeing a trilby hat, let alone one worn with anything like sales-boosting *élan*, and as for the flair which a suitably built model of the right vintage could bring to the striped cotton pyjama or the bottle-green cardigan, the wasted promotional potential is nothing short of profligate.

Well, I am determined to change all that. I would have changed it all years ago, if only some caring publisher had told me that that was the kind of novel idea he wanted. But it is not too late. This morning's deft shimmy across the bedroom floor convinces me that it is only a matter of very brief time before I am indeed the glass wherein the noble middle-aged do dress themselves, at which point top fiction publishers will begin falling over themselves to beat a path to my door.

"Oh," you will protest, "come on, we have seen that clip of Tolstoy shuffling up and down the Astopovo platform. We wouldn't be caught dead in an overcoat like that. We have seen that photo of James Joyce with his trousers at half-mast, never mind the one of Marcel Proust in that ghastly nightcap. You do not have to be a natty dresser to get on in fiction." But those, I have to tell you, were very different days. It is a capricious Johnny, literary fashion.

With One Bounder

It is more than 30 years ago, now, but I have never forgotten the suit. I have never forgotten the suit because I have never forgotten the placard that was selling the suit. It was selling it to the French, and it was doing it in the window of Louis Guerin, the swishest tailor in that swishest of tailoring streets, the Rue du Faubourg St Honoré.

The suit was a three-piece number in Prince of Wales check. It comprised a deep-vented jacket with egregiously flapped slant pockets, an unnecessarily lapelled double-breasted waistcoat and a pair of sponge-bag trousers which could have contained both legs of a substantial man in each leg of their own. More yet, the jacket had been swung open to reveal a lining of azure silk counterpointed by a scarlet pocket handkerchief tumbling beneath a matching carnation *boutonnière*, which in turn matched the dominant stripe of the dummy's fake-regimental tie.

And the placard said: *Très snob – presque cad!*

That, moreover, M Guerin's establishment stood bang opposite the front gate of the British Embassy should not be ignored. The placard was thus simultaneously a cocked snook and an irresistible sales-pitch; for slice him where you will (as young men in spats were once wont to chortle to one another in the Drones), a Froggie is always a pushover for that unique brand of English chic which goes with bounderhood.

Now, while I may never have forgotten the suit, I did not recall it until yesterday, when the national press suddenly filled to the gunwales with the doings, if such they were, of Major James Hewitt. And to help with the filling, since pages and pages and pages were required to teem with the stuff if dishonour was to be satisfied, there was pressed into service a vocabulary which I had feared had long passed from the earth: Major Hewitt was a cad, a bounder, a rotter, he was a snake in the grass and a viper in the bosom, a ne'er-do-well and a good-for-nothing, a blackguard, a scoundrel, an out-and-out rogue – and he had (oh, joy!) Brought Disgrace to the Regiment.

How very odd, then, that so many commentators, in so many media, should have bemoaned this latest addition to the royal gallimaufry as a nail in the coffin of British honour, the final, and the most damning, piece of evidence of our irreversible national decline. What piffle, tosh, balderdash, tommyrot (please insert your own aptly retro term here) that is! Did none of our enormous band of jeremiad hacks twig that the very wealth of epithets they suddenly found at their disposal only stood testament to the wealth of precedents for which they were minted? From Sir Launcelot and Lord Darnley to Harry Flashman and Terry-Thomas, from Sir Francis Dashwood and Lord Byron to Captain Grimes and Major Ferguson, the cad has straddled our culture, in fact and fiction, as he has straddled no other; look on this tabloid picture and on this, and tell me that James Hewitt, with his ratting cap, his polo stick, his two-seater, his rhinestone tie-pin, his iffy majority, his riding instructorship, his cheesy smirk, his jettisoned inamorata, his desperate need for a few bob to tide him over till his postal order arrives, tell me that he does not stand heir to a lineage that extends far further back than that of any other heir he may have cuckolded.

Which is why all true patriots should relish his emergence. He is part not of England's arguable decline, but of her unarguable web and woof; just because a tradition isn't honourable, that doesn't stop it being a tradition. More yet, James Hewitt is not, as at least three newspapers insisted, the one thing the monarchy doesn't want right now; he is the one thing it does. Up until now, the populace has had no clear field of fire on the targets it needs if it is to slake its irritation; it has throughout this sorry mess been forced to yield the easy moral judgements it would prefer to clouding argument and counter-argument; it has been compelled not only to take sides, but also to change them with each new revelation, and to lower its shotguns undischarged.

We now have someone we can empty both barrels at. We have flushed out an absolute shit. And I for one am very grateful. If I knew where that suit was now, I'd buy it for him.

Burning Question

When, in the murky gloaming, the doorbell rang, I tiptoed up and offered the spy-hole a chary eye. A householder cannot be too careful, these days: life is harsh, money tight, scruple rare, and there are desperate men ever on the *qui vive* for the incautious lifting of a latch. You could be double-glazed, loft-lagged, and culinarily refitted before you knew it.

The fish-eye lens offered two huge heads, as fish-eyes will, but low down. Children, then, possibly midgets, and with a pushchair between them, but its occupant so far beyond the spy-hole's range – you do not get a lot for £6, and, if you fit it yourself, you end up with even less – as to be unidentifiable. As far as I and my wonky Securiscope could see, however, they carried no order book, no sample mullion, pipe, or worktop, no suitcase poised to snap open on a tea-towel, peg or *Reader's Digest* subscription, no clip-board waiting to jot me down for sponsored potholing @ 50p a foot to save the whale, no Bible pressing me to witness. I opened the door.

It was the pushchair which first caught my eye. There was a terrorist in it. It was a bit early in the year for terrorists, true, but I knew the signs; if, as the nights draw in, you run across a bin-liner in a tatty old jacket, with a teddy-bear's head, a black cardboard moustache, a clay pipe and a baseball cap, you immediately recognise it as the insurrectionist who once crept beneath the Mother of Parliaments' skirts with a view to giving her a nasty turn.

"Penny for the Guy," said the larger boy. Ten, perhaps. "Remember, remember, the fifth of November," said the smaller one.

"It's the tenth of October," I said.

"You have to start early," said the larger one. "It's two pounds for a proper rocket."

"You're not supposed to go round door to door," I said. "You're supposed to stand on a street-corner."

"We did that," said the smaller one, "but nobody gave us nothing."

"Well, he's not a lot like Guy Fawkes," I said.

They both looked at the bear's head.

"We had a Stan Laurel face to put on him," said the taller one, "but the elastic bust."

"It would have helped," I said. "Just out of interest, do you know what Guy Fawkes did?"

Why do I give kids a hard time?

"He blew the king up," said the smaller of the two.

"Near enough," I said. I bent and straightened the bear's moustache. "Is he just for show, or are you going to burn him on the night?"

"Burn him. With bangers inside him and caffrin wills in his ears."

"We're going to make a hole in his head," said the smaller one, "and stick a rocket in it so's it goes off when his face catches fire." So I gave them the wherewithal for the *coup de grâce*, and I watched them trundle their victim down the path, and it was only after I had closed the door again that it suddenly occurred to me, I'm ashamed to say for the first time, how astonishingly unsavoury, how politically incorrect, how altogether unacceptable a business it is to which the nation annually addresses itself with such grisly relish.

For here we all are struggling against the lengthening odds to inculcate tolerance, understanding, non-violence and all the caring rest into our offspring, yet every year we leap about with them in the cheery glow of a burning Catholic freedom-fighter, pausing only to pluck the potatoes roasting in his pyre. How very odd. Why should Guy Fawkes remain the one dissident in British history unredeemed by caring hindsight? Just how comfortable would you be if your kids sat on street corners with an effigy of Jomo Kenyatta, what if they tugged the sleeves of passers-by, begging a penny for the Mahatma, suppose they stuck a paper fez on a clapped-out teddy bear and called it Nasser?

Never mind the incalculable ramifications if, every 4 July, Britain commemorated the Declaration of Independence by setting fire to ten thousand Thomas Jeffersons with bangers inside them and caffrin wills for ears.

Where There's No Will

The curse of the alarm-clock radio is not only that it plunges the startled waker *in medias res*, but also that it plucks him *ex medias res* in order to do it. One moment you are crawling on all fours after a bus from the platform of which George Bernard Shaw is throwing ukuleles at you, the next moment Jim Naughtie is telling the Home Secretary to pull the other one. The third moment is thus spent in psychic limbo.

At 6.59 on Monday morning, I was sealed in some kind of suitcase and bobbing on an unseen sea, when a sudden voice cried: ". . . will be here to talk about the start of National Will Week." Then the news came on. I did not listen. My head was still echoing to the remnant gobbet. Had I heard it in the suitcase, or on the radio? Was National Will Week my subconscious invention, or the government's conscious one? The latest slogan, perhaps, of the Blue Water initiative, urging Britain on to new nosed grindstones and shouldered wheels, tote more barges, lift more bales, write more columns? Do, in short, more bit?

I ran the bath. The news concluded. And now a man was indeed there to talk about National Will Week. But he was not a Smirk of State from the Department of Codswallop exhorting us all to snatch up our shovels and hi-ho into the broad sunlit uplands, he was a lawyer exhorting us all to make our wills. For that, it transpires, is the National Week it is.

As my body sank into the suds, its heart sank lower yet. It does that when its ear hears "will". Not because the word reminds it of mortality, but because it reminds it of immortality, which is far harder for a heart to handle: dead, we live on in the junk we have accumulated, and how we posthumously distribute that junk may well be how we are remembered. That is why, however much it hurts me to think of lawyers going short of a little gravy to dip their bread in, I have never commissioned a will.

Suppose I simply bequeathed everything to my wife. Free of taxes, it would be the most sensible thing to do. "What did he do?" the world would inquire. "He did the most sensible thing," it would be told. "Yes, typical," the world would respond, "that was him all over. Dull bugger." Leave it to my children? "Did you see that his son has just wrapped a Ferrari Testarossa round a lamp-post?" "Doesn't surprise me, the man never had the first idea about family responsibility. I understand his daughter is currently walking home from Las Vegas."

More fraught yet are the wider bequests a will invites: if their values, whether commercial or personal, differ, all but one of my legatees will feel dissatisfied, slighted, or both; if their values are identical, even the one will feel it. A pecking order of affection will be posthumously set up, and may, indeed, result in the miffed inheritors pecking one another. "I only got his bloody watch, who got his car?" "I got his car, but the steering's shot, who got his Regency desk?" "Regency? *Regency?* Mid-Victorian, and one iffy leg at that, he was either a liar or a fool, Sotheby's told me to try a boot-sale, I didn't know where to put my face, sooner have had his car, who got his books?"

Did my old college get my books? And did its librarian shriek, "My God, he had a complete set of Archer signed first editions, can we take his degree back, how did he get in here in the first place?" Leave my old school a memorial bench? "Ungrateful bloody tightwad, where'd he have been without our A levels, we need tennis courts, we need computers, we need a staffroom snooker table."

Endow, perhaps, an annual prize? So that, on current

form, *Snot* can win the award for fiction, *Cat's Head on Stick* the palm for art, Pol Pot the gong for peace, leaving gleeful public derision to spin me in my grave? I should better serve my memory by leaving everything to the Flat Earth Society, even if it meant an enraged Oblong Earth Society aerosoling my tombstone.

"Whatever you do," begged Monday's spokesman as I towelled, "don't go to your grave intestate, leaving problems behind for your loved ones." Why not? leaving problems behind is one of the best reasons for going.

An Apple for the Teacher

So, then, it is hats off to Professor David Barron of Southampton University! Not to say mortarboards, though his own students will not be doing this personally, of course, they will be doing it only after they have poked the MacCeremony program into their desktops and tapped the appropriate keys so that, many miles distant, their huzzahs, backslaps and Latin encomia can appear on Prof Barron's screen and bring a lump to the pedagogic throat, even while it negotiates its morning Kellogg.

For the great educator has just pulled off a double first which, in his own words, "means that the students do not have to come and meet in a lecture theatre, and the teacher does not have to spend time standing up and talking". What does? Southampton's new BSc course in Information Engineering, is what: for it is the first in Britain to be conducted via computer link-ups on the Internet. Henceforth, instead of creeping like snails unwillingly to campus, undergraduates will sit at home in front of their PCs and download lectures and essay assignments alike; they will even be able to attend electronic seminars where members, of the group will log on simultaneously in order to hold on-line discussions.

Now, old codgers among you will doubtless react to this wonderful breakthrough by gnashing a denture and moaning that there is more to education than study, ie, a university is not a university unless you can climb up it with a chamberpot, but you manifest in this only your own lack of knowledge: for the electronic superhighway extends exponentially with each passing day, and as it runs, cities of dreaming terminals spring up shimmering on either side, and there is absolutely nothing that tomorrow's students will not be able to do in them. Should they, to press your question, wish to relax after a long day's keying by sticking a po on a spire, they will have only to select MacPissed and in less than a nanosecond the screen will offer them anything from Tom Tower to the Eiger, with, at its foot, Sonic the Student poised to stagger to its summit; in return, moreover, for points which may subsequently be converted into either course credits (if, say, they are minoring in Physical Education), or air miles (if, say, they have purchased their PCs on their American Express cards).

Ah, you codge, but they will not have a Boat Race Night on which to do it, will they? You clearly know nothing about Internet: its wondrous interactive boons would allow eight strapping holograms from the University of Amstrad to fight it out with their Macintosh College rivals up the grey-green greasy Limpopo, down the Swanee, or wherever else the electronic fancy took them, while their nationwide supporters leapt up and down in snug bedrooms safe from towpath sleet, waving their scarves, hollering themselves hoarse and, in the dandier cases, bouncing their dear old teddies Aloysius on their kimonoed knees.

And, yes, all this may sound a trifle Oxbridgist, but why not? The superhighway rolls over such superannuated distinctions; the discrete homebased undergraduate may cobble together whatever environment he chooses, and it surely cannot be long, now, before Homebase itself responds to the new market need for hardboard panelling, stonette fireplaces, and stick-on mullions beyond which back-projection offers rolling Cam or Isis according to choice; or indeed, for those with less archaic tastes, a vista across some glinting science park from a bedsit mock-eyrie lined with post-modernist glassbrick.

Ah, but will there be long evenings of furious contention and helpless laughter, political bicker and literary consort, *ad hoc* string quartet and hip-hop band, chess and five-card stud? Think not, and you betray just how little you know of the Internet culture: you clearly have scant inkling of how, even today, notation can speak unto notation, still less of the imminent bits at which tomorrow impatiently champs. As for sex, which so often pitilessly eluded yesterstudent, the interdating modem has transformed the highway into an electronic Reeperbahn.

Truly, the professor has laid out a university prospectus to rejoice in! It wants for nothing but the resonant tag to which such masterplans are always entitled. If it were up to me, I should call it the Barron Future.

Top Floor

I am sitting on a goldmine. You can't see that it's a goldmine, of course, because like all good goldmines it lies far below the surface; almost a full inch, at a guess. In order not to have to guess, you would need to pick up the carpet, and if you did that you would find yourself standing on the gleaming ore itself, and get into no end of trouble. English Heritage heavies would have you out of there so fast your feet wouldn't touch the ground, because the ground they risked touching is very precious to English Heritage. The ground is lino.

The scene now shifts to Newcastle-upon-Tyne's Trinity House, where the Brotherhood of Mariners, charged with keeping the place shipshape and Bristol-fashion, wants to do a spot of redecorating. This involves taking the old lino up, because it is full of holes and little casts a bigger blight on maritime knees-ups than having honoured guests suddenly going down by the stern during a hornpipe; but it cannot be taken up, because English Heritage has slapped a preservation order on it. For this is not any old lino, it is rare old lino, and "historic decoration", says EH's Andrew Saidi, "is no less important than bricks and mortar".

Tell me, do you catch that unmistakable whiff of worm which tells you that a can of them has just been opened? Can what we are looking at here be anything less than a watershed in the history of domestic refurbishment? Are we not standing at the crossroads of doing-up? Beneath the carpet on which I am jotting this lies the stuff we covered 20-odd years ago, original to the house 50 years before that, a fetching ochre base patterned, as I recollect, in blue and red rectangles, very Mondrian, very Bauhaus, a prime example of 1920s Art Lino: were it to turn up (any day now, if I know my canny BBC) on the *Flooring Road Show*, the experts would turn cartwheels. And I have three concealed floorfuls of similar vintage. Should I not be a happy man?

I am a petrified man. If EH finds out, I am done for. They will be round here with a restore-or-die warrant in a trice, they will have my snug Axminster off, they will leave me with floors you stick to in summer, freeze to in winter, and break your neck on when hurtling between bath and phone. But that is not the half of it, for if lino has come into its inheritance, can lincrusta be far behind? To save you trawling the OED, its etymology is *linum* (flax) + *crusta* (rind), but that is not because, in 382, the Romans did their premises out in tasteful flax-rind, it is because, in 1882, a Mr Walton, not content with inventing linoleum for floors, went on to invent lincrusta for walls, so that when my house was built some 40 years later it could be lined with an embossed paper so impervious to the chisel that the only course open to those not wishing to live with mud-brown Maltese crosses was to overpaint or overpaper; but never so successfully that an English Heritage prodnose could not spot its subcutaneous ghost, list it, and insist that it be stripped back to pristine funereality

He might suffer a crux, mind, in the one room where the lincrusta has been hidden, thanks to the strips of polychrome hessian gummed to it in 1972. Hessian was very big, in 1972. It was everywhere. It was what wall-covering was all about. Strip it off, and a mural era would be expunged from the heritage. So there is a nub, here, is there not? Can any of us ever confidently redecorate again? It is not merely a matter of thinking carefully before we crassly bang in low-flush suites when it means enskipping lofted cisterns, their charming chains, their jolly squashball grips, or fill fireplaces with slimline radiators, or replace stone kitchen sinks with aluminium, or conceal halogen pin-points in bare ruin'd ceilings where late the sweet bulbs hung, or perpetrate any of the other ravages involved when progress supervenes tradition, it is also a matter of thinking carefully what we do when yesterday's progress becomes today's tradition, and then tomorrow's Grade I listing. How long will it be before it is an offence to remove a satellite dish?

There is a gum-tree here, and English Heritage is perforce stuck in its branches. I have no answer, but my heart bleeds for those who go down to the sea in Newcastle: for they occupy their business in greater waters than they could ever have imagined.

Ducking Out

A man from the East has sent me a duck. I do not know if he is a wise man, because what I know about the mail-order duck business you could put in your eye, but his own eye is certainly on Christmas, which is why I did that stuff about a man from the East. I also know he is not a king from the East, because he has signed the duck Sam Ho Lee, and if he were King Sam Ho Lee that is how he would have signed the duck, since Sam does not strike me as the sort of man who would miss a trick like that. You do not need to know much about the mail-order duck business to know that a royal endorsement would be worth an extra bob or two. You will, by the way, be relieved to hear that I do not intend, despite the seasonal sub-text, to make anything of the fact that Sam is called Ho Lee, or to draw attention to the fact that if he had indeed been one of three wise men they could well have been called Ho Lee, Ho Lee, Ho Lee.

I say signed the duck, but what I mean is he has signed the label wired to the duck's leg. This puzzled me somewhat when I opened the box, because you know what split-seconds are, a lot can happen in them, and my first thought was that the duck was called Sam Ho Lee and wore the sealed label on his leg because it was some kind of homing duck which, since it was dead, had tragically failed to home and been put in a box by a well-wisher. I did not wonder why the well-wisher had then sent the dead homing duck to me, because the split-second was by this time all used up, and my attention had moved on to the letter lying beside the duck. I should tell you here, so that you have a clear picture of the scene, that this was an entire duck, head, legs, wings, lacking only feathers. Instead of feathers, it appeared to be dressed in a tight-fitting shiny brown cat-suit. I did not discover it was actually dressed in a tight-fitting shiny brown duck-suit until a little later, when I took it out of its box, and it crackled.

That was after I read the letter. The letter explained that this duck had been sent to me by Sam Ho Lee Enterprises of Kowloon, in the hope that I would publicise his Flying Duck Service in time for Christmas. The dead duck in the box was a review copy; I would eat the duck, do a column about what a terrific duck it was to eat, and *Times* readers would then beat a path to Sam's door, or at least their credit card numbers would, with the result that dead boxed ducks would swarm out of Kowloon to grace Yuletide boards throughout Britain. They also made wonderful presents, said Sam, adding the usual guff about imagining the faces of friends and relatives lighting up with joy when . . .

He also – for the benefit of those who were in fact imagining the faces of friends and relatives staring sightlessly at the ceiling from pennied eyes – assured me that this was a wind-dried duck, and could not go mouldy and kill people. It was, indeed, guaranteed not to do that, I had Sam's word for it. It is a word I shall have to take, because I do not know what wind-dried ducks are or how they get that way: if they just hang on clothes-lines all over Kowloon, I can't see why that should stop them going mouldy or, come to that, why Kowloon's ants don't get to them before Sam Ho Lee does. Maybe he hangs them up indoors and leaves the window at either end of the premises open so that the wind can do its stuff, who can say?

Whichever, it answered, albeit without my understanding how, any queries as to why, if Sam was trying to corner the Christmas market, he hadn't gone in for turkeys. Wind-dried turkeys would be out of the question. You would need two men to lift each one onto its hanger. Labour costs would be prohibitive.

Is this, then, the column about eating the duck? I'm afraid not. I cannot eat it. It is not fear of wind-dried bacteria which stays my bib, nor irritation at Sam's judgement of me as a man to go to if you need to shift stiff poultry, it is the fact that this isn't meat at all, it is a duck. Rigid, yes, glazed, perhaps, but by these very tokens Pompeiian; caught perfect, in its terminal throe, forever quacking and forever young. You can't go at a little chap like that with a knife and fork, especially at Christmas. It would be like eating Tiny Tim.

Too Hot to Handle

I pray to God, for all our sakes, that by the time you read this the heatwave will be over. As I write, it is still a broiling 12° C here in the Cricklewood Wadi, but my sweat-soaked Walkman has just brought me, albeit faintly through the sunspotted static's freak crackle, the parched voice of a hero who has braved dehydration and carcinoma alike to crawl along the Met Office roof towards his sizzling pine-cone, and I think he said that a cold snap might just be on the way.

It cannot come too soon. The hottest November since 1659 has been intolerable. What, of course, has made it intolerable has been people not just talking about it, but asking unanswerable questions about what it means; because while for unfathomability the weather's possible consequences have left Bosnia, *Finnegans Wake*, and Shane Warne's wrong'un at the post, that has not stopped the entire population seeking snap solutions to the manifestly insoluble, and seeking them, moreover, from those least likely to have the first bloody idea.

What do I know about thin hedgehogs? My next-door neighbour asked me a day or so ago if I had seen any. I said no. This was not enough: he then asked me whether, if I did see any, I would think it was a good idea to leave bread and milk out for them. I asked him why, and he said that he normally had hedgehogs, and this was the time of year they hibernated behind his shed, but they weren't there because the warm weather was encouraging them to keep running around looking for food, which was now in really short supply, and the combination of running around and the lack of food they were running around after would result in their not having enough fat to insulate them against the cold when they finally did hibernate, but if you left bread and milk out for them, mightn't it be got to first by birds which migrated to look for food, and now wouldn't? And while he was on about it, he had noticed that a blackbird was making a nest in his maple but there wasn't any protective foliage on it now, so if the bird laid eggs would the squirrels, which haven't hibernated either, spot them, and what would be the ecological consequences of that?

I asked him, God help me, whether he meant that he was worried the squirrels would then hibernate on eggs not nuts and what this might mean, and he said, no, he was worried that if the eggs were eaten now, there mightn't be any new blackbirds next spring to eat the bugs they were supposed to, God alone knows what effect that will have on my magnolias even if it does represent more jobs in the pesticide industry, but the nut question was well-raised, might it mean there would be more new trees, and I said never mind all that, have a butcher's at my pond, I may not know what a thin hedgehog looks like but I know what a fat newt means, it means it's pregnant, where will that lead, and he said I don't know, but have you got British Gas shares, because if nobody turns the heating on, there won't be much of a dividend, is Cedric Brown laughing on the other side of his performance-related face now, won't he have to give the 200 grand back?

Funny you should bring that up, I said, only this morning a cabdriver asked me whether I thought that people would use the money they saved on gas bills to buy lottery tickets. Interesting, said my neighbour, what effect do you suppose that'll have on subsidised theatre, are we going to get a lot more experimental rubbish? Hard to say, I said, but given that the warmth has almost certainly ensured both thriving fleas and new strains of flu, it always does, you probably wouldn't want to go to the theatre anyhow, would you? Or the cinema, he said. A pity, I said, now that cinema attendances are finally growing; I suppose people will go back to waiting for the video to come out, but it won't, because if they don't go to the cinema, the money won't be there to make new films in the first place, will it? I've no idea, he said, but do you think the bottom's dropped out of thermal underwear, and I said, ha, ha, it's good to see the old ones coming back, it's an ill wind that blows nobody any good. And he said: are you absolutely sure about that?

Serving Us Right

Oh, look, there's a basic! What's more, we appear to be going back to it. And what's most, perhaps, is that its basicity is, for once, unquestionable: it is not founded upon the controversially shifting sands of class, or gender, or marriage, or race, or faith, it is not concerned with the disputed desirability of maintaining aitches or rattling off the nine-times table, it does not require the nation to wear a tie, cut its hair, and place all litter in the receptacles provided, it advances no opinion as to whether constables should salute, doctors make house calls, or members of the royal family embody hope and glory, it is both dis- and uninterested in televised copulation and tabloid mendacity alike, it does not even demand that our elected representatives should, once the long day's business is done, go home to their own beds.

The basic is about none of this; it is about shopping. It is about the news that the department store is making a comeback, because customers are coming back to the department store. After a decade of retail flightiness during which they have been seduced into countless brief encounters by each flashy new high street gigolo that cared to wink its neon at them, British shoppers have at last come to their senses. They are returning to the sort of shops that Celia Johnson knew were the best, really. They are flocking back to Selfridges and Harrods and Debenhams and D.H. Evans and John Lewis and all the rest, enabling them, at the eleventh hour, to cheat that bourne from which no Hollingsworth returns.

Nothing, in these harrowing days, could make me happier. For not only have I remained faithful to the department store through thick and thin, I have subjected that loyalty to fine-toothed scrutiny, and am, I submit, in a better position to account for this revival than all the business analysts presently truffling for more arcane explanations.

My earliest view of a department store was diamond-shaped. The year was 1944, the store was Selfridges, and I was looking at it through one of those rhomboid peep-holes Mr Churchill had thoughtfully cut into the green mesh designed to stop the Luftwaffe blowing bus-windows all over us. After we got off the bus, my mother, as was her attentive wont, spat on her hankie in order to remove from my face any detritus likely to upset floor-walkers, but for once I did not shrink as my cheeks were shoved this way and that. I stood stock still. Not just still, rapt. Selfridges was the biggest thing I had ever seen. It wiped the floor even with items I had seen only in *The Big Boy's Book of Big Things*, where Arthur Mee had stood a Cunarder on end to show how far up it Nelson's Column came. And this was a *shop*? Hitherto, a shop had been a small dark place with a cat snoozing on the bacon-slicer, or a woman saying they only had grey wool due to U-boats everywhere; but here was a shop from one end of which you couldn't see the other. Had I read *The Big Boy's Book of John Keats*, I should almost certainly have felt like some watcher of the skies when a new planet swims into his ken, or like stout Cortez when with eagle eyes he stared at the Pacific.

And then we went inside. The inside was bigger than the outside. That is what happens with magic. It had to be big because there were a trillion things for sale; but most astonishing of all, they were different sorts of thing. I had been only in serial shops before: you bought a cabbage in one, then you crossed the road to another one to buy a scarf, and if you wanted a kettle, you had to go into a third one. But Selfridges sold everything there was in the world to sell, and you got to it by going up on electric stairs and coming down in electric rooms. More amazing yet: after my mother had duly bought this and that, we went to another part of Selfridges and had beans on toast. I was eating in a shop!

Dear God, so much plenitude in a time of austerity, so much possibility in a time of circumscription, so much fun in a time of dejection – is it any wonder that that lenitive glow in the infant psyche should have retained a glimmer to be fanned, in an emergency, by adult need? Like good old Watson, the department store is the one fixed point in a changing age.

Shock Move for Rolling Stones?

At a point in this island's history when each day's fresh crop of drear domestic news serves only to plummet the patriot heart further still and faster yet, what a joy it was to fall, quite unprepared, on Monday's *Times* headline, "Stonehenge dating dispels icesheet theory".

There is no theory I would rather have had dispelled. Ever since its first triumphalist mooting by Flash Harry geologists in 1971, it has sunk my spirits whenever, in the lonely watches of the night, it has returned to mind: I smell the cold snap in the Pleistocene air, I hear the nascent glaciers crackle on the bluestone slopes of far Welsh hills, and then I see, bit by monolithic bit, the enormous slabs of kit-form Stonehenge shear off and start their peristaltic trundle eastwards to Wilts, there to thaw out, ready for simple assembly an æon or so later when neolithic ramblers out on some serendipitous lope cry: "Hallo, these look nice, give us a hand!" and, in more or less a trice, stand them up.

What a downer that theory was, as flat, cold, monochrome and cheerless as its epistemological nub! Compare it with every Briton's hitherto cherished conviction that these great big lumps from the astoundingly distant Preseli Mountains had fetched up 4,000 years ago on Salisbury Plain only because our sturdy Beaker ancestors had schlepped them there! More yet; beyond mere technological mystery or historical romance, the Great Stone Pull was Britain's membership card to the International Culture Club: it was not only our Anabasis, our Exodus, our Kon Tiki, it was our Sphinx, our Jus Romanum, our *Oresteia*, it was the big one we pulled out whenever anyone accused us of gormlessly running around in woad until Caesar turned up with income tax and central heating. It showed we were *somebody*; it showed we were a *contender*.

And as of yesterday, it shows it still, thanks to some nifty Chlorine-36 dating by Prof David Bowen proving the stones fell off their mountains a scant 14,000 years ago, 400 centuries too early to catch the last glacier out of Wales. What we always believed, prior to 1971, is true: they just lay there until the Beaker expedition turned up and, spotting that these were just what was needed to cobble a heliopolis, girded their loins, and tugged them back, miraculously, to Salisbury Plain.

How they did this, mind, remains unknown. While each

of us has his own queries – did they push from behind or pull from the front, did they inveigle oxen, did they invent the wheel expressly for the job and subsequently jettison it because it had served its purpose (one henge being enough for anybody), did they, as I like to imagine, get under each slab in tough little droves and port it on their backs, much in the manner of ants rhythmically marching off with Donald Duck's picnic basket? – we may never get the answer to how this extraordinary thing was done.

Unless, that is, we go out and do it. For, like everyone else, I have been cudgelling my brains in the hope that one of my few fleeting cells might come up with a fitting way for Britain to celebrate the imminent millennium, and it occurred to me, the moment I spotted the icesheet rebuttal, that we could do very much worse than dismantle Stonehenge and throw open a national competition to get the 123 bluestone megaliths back to Wales, using only neolithic technology.

There would surely be no shortage of candidates for the 123 teams: who at, say, Cornhill Insurance, Burger King, the *Sun*, Barclays Bank, Greenpeace, The Really Useful Company, Virgin, CAMRA, Crinkly Bottom, or any other such great national institution would not jump at the highly profitable opportunity of celebrating AD 2000 by demonstrating, with appealing symmetry, that Britain still had what it took in 2000 BC?

Using, of course, only a notched stick, I have calculated that if they set off on 1 January, each team would have to move its stone a mere 192 yards per day to get it to Preseli by New Year's Eve 2000, and this sounds to me to be so much of a doddle that I see no reason at all why even *The Times* should not manage to front up a credible equipe. I fully intend to be down at Wapping first thing tomorrow, selecting biceps.

It Could Be Who?

I have never yet taken anything to the European Court of Human Rights – it would mean hanging around for months in Strasbourg, a stolid place enlivened only by the noise of geese having things poked down them to swell their livers (if a European Court of Poultry Rights is ever established, Strasburghers will have a lot to answer for) – but given the extraordinary concatenation of the past week's most momentous events, I may now be left with no other course. I seek clarification.

The first momentous event was that a man who years ago bought a painting at a flea market, took it home, and, according to all newspaper reports, "immediately threw it in his attic", has just discovered it to be worth £20 million. That is because it is by Van Gogh. You can tell this by looking in the lower right-hand corner, since that is where Vincent signed it, in huge red letters, and while you might argue that that doesn't prove anything, I would argue that it should at least be enough to exercise the curiosity of somebody who went out to buy a painting in the first place. If you or I did that, and saw the most unmistakable signature there is, I cannot believe that our first move would be to bung it immediately in the attic. Come to that, I cannot imagine why anyone would buy anything to bung in the attic immediately, unless, of course, he was barking mad – oh, look, beloved, a worthless painting, that will go very nicely with my tea-chest full of mouldy shoes, it will look terrific propped against your rusty Mickey Mouse tricycle, it will set off our pile of old *Reader's Digests* a treat, pass me my chequebook – but what is even odder is that, many years later, he went back into the loft, looked at his picture again, and for some reason decided, this time, to ask Amsterdam's Van Gogh Museum to authenticate it. Whereupon he was informed that it was as far from worthless as worthlessness ever gets.

Leaving us with umpteen questions of our own. For this lucky bastard has just realised one of mankind's most pervasive dreams: he has gone up a loft-ladder broke and come down it with £20 million, and we, who share that dream, want to know all there is to know about it. We shall, however, discover nothing; for he is, we were told, "exercising his right to remain anonymous".

I was still seething over this when the week's second most momentous event fortuitously collided with it. It was another of mankind's most pervasive dreams. It was the one about going into a newsagent's broke and coming out of it with £20 million. We, who share that dream, wanted to know all there was to know about it. We shall, however, discover nothing; for the National Lottery winner is, we were told, "exercising his right to remain anonymous".

Oh really? What right? There are 50 million of us out here, we have rights, too, what's so special about his that it should so cursorily disenfranchise ours? No man is an island, sunshine, you have realised your dream in all our behalves, we have the right to know who you are and what it is like to be who you are at this seminal moment, we even have the right to dog you for the rest of your days to see what happens, will you rise further, will you plummet, will you be happy, will you go mad? Lifelong scrutiny is the price for those who realise other people's dreams, it comes with the territory: you cannot just stick £19,880,003 in the Woolwich and slide back into snug obscurity, you do not have rights, what you have is obligations, what you have is duties.

National ones, what's more. So take a lesson from one

who has ever appreciated what that means: for last week, incredibly, the third of mankind's most pervasive dreams was also realised, the one about finding a fortune buried in the garden. But unlike the wimp with the Van Gogh or the poltroon with the jackpot, this lucky winner did not flinch from the limelight's myriad threats. She exercised no specious right, cobbled to serve a selfish end and leave poor dreamers gnashing their teeth over the withheld identity of "a Windsor woman who yesterday discovered that oil under her castle lawn could be worth £100 billion". She stood up and was counted. She was, as always, an example to us all.

The Rime of the Ancient Plumber

Amid all the miles of newsreel footage pressed into heartrending service over the *QE2* fiasco, one fleeting telephoto shot stood out in poignancy, for me, from all the rest. The moment I glimpsed it, my welling empathy – for chapfallen revellers, bewildered oldies, sobbing newlyweds, unhinged glitterati, disconsolate teddy-clutching tots, and all the other pitiful Cunard bumpees cheated of their Yuletide, nay lifetime, dreams – I switched sides. I wept only for this poor jerk, framed in a porthole, slumped against an unconnected downpipe, four spanners sagging his dungaree marsupium, and a cellphone to his ear.

I knew whom he was ringing. He was ringing his wife. I knew what he was saying. He was saying: "We've run into a bit of wossname, don't wait up, could take days." I knew what he was thinking. He was thinking: guess who'll cop it for this cockup.

My father was a plumber, too. Were he still around, he would have picked up his own phone the moment the story broke, and his first word to me would have been: "Typical." I would have asked him what was typical. He would then have read me out the headline: "PLUMBERS FAIL TO MEET QE2 DEADLINE." I would then have gone on to say that the thing with bloody civilians was that they didn't have the first idea about running water, and he would have replied that it was too true, spot on, dead right, running water was a living thing, you took liberties with it at your peril.

Astonishing that Cunard, of all people, should not have known this. Have they that go down to the sea in ships and occupy their business in great waters no inkling of the capricious habits of their medium? If not, then now that the Cunard board, as Psalm 107 goes on, "reel to and fro, and stagger like a drunken man, and are at their wits' end", they have only themselves to blame.

They are, however, blaming the plumbers. They are blaming them for not meeting deadlines, but it is Cunard's fault that deadlines were set. You cannot set deadlines for plumbers, any more than for poets: though the craft aspires to discipline, its craftsmen must, willy-nilly, go with the flow. I, a quondam part-time plumber's mate who once stopped cocks, eased gate-valves, rodded out, primed blowlamps, boiled white metal, wiped smoking joints with moleskin and went to ring my mother to say we'd run into a bit of wossname, don't wait up, could take days, I know these things.

We would be called to flooded premises, where tenants ran around distraught. They would shriek: "What is it?" My old man would say: "Could be anything." They would beg: "Can you fix it?" He would reply: "It all depends." And add: "You cannot rush water."

We would turn everything off, drain everything down. My father would then call for absolute silence, produce a stethoscope, and percuss the walls, sometimes murmuring: "I thought as much", sometimes sniffing hidden pipework like a drug-hound, sometimes laughing the knowing laugh of a man on whom water has once more failed to put something over. Sometimes he would cry: "Clear the premises, that ceiling could go at any time!" Sometimes we would pump out, but not before he had sectioned off a square of pavement behind a big, hand-painted sign that roared: EMERGENCY! KEEP CLEAR! He was a plumber's plumber.

He never gave estimates. He gave rough ideas, because there might be unforeseen circumstances. They were the same circumstances that made him refuse deadlines. If a client insisted on having his circumstances foreseen, my father would offer the name of another plumber, thus: "He's quick, and he's cheap. He bloody has to be."

But he accepted that plumbers were doomed always to bear the blame for everything. You could do nothing about that: it was typical. Certainly, he would have made no complaint had Cunard pressganged him along with all the rest currently sailing to New York, plumbing as they go. I see him lashed to the taffrail shouting, "Emergency! Keep clear! That funnel could go at any time!" with half the running water in the world rolling beneath him. He would be, quite literally, in his element.

Sleazy Does It

Though mine may not perhaps be a household name wherever theologians forgather, I am nevertheless emboldened by recent events to take a crack, this morning, at a spot of exegesis which could well leave a number of top hermeneutical bananas tugging their earlobes, scratching their tonsures, gnawing their lower lips, and murmuring "Blimey!"

You will recall that in the First Epistle of the Andrews Sisters to St Timothy, Patti, Maxine and Laverne were of one harmonious voice in declaring that money was the root of all evil. This observation, having the authentic ring of a universal truth, was an immediate winner; and ever since, we have all walked around smugly citing it whenever a mail-train went on to an unscheduled stop in Parkhurst, a big gun turned up in a crate marked "Drainpipes", a newspaper proprietor fell off a boat, or any one of a thousand other come-uppances occurred to console the scrupulous poor. As universal truths go, therefore, it has done a workmanlike job. However, I have, as I say, been taking a close look recently at how the world turns and have arrived at the conclusion that it is not half as universal, if pedants will forgive me, as what I am now convinced were the words as originally written: whether the error was caused by an inadequate grasp of Aramaic or botany, I cannot say (it may even be down to primitive recording equipment), but it is quite clear to me that what the Andrews Sisters should have observed was that money was the *fruit* of all evil.

For is it not the case that whenever anyone does anything naughty these days, even if his or her original motive was not greed, profit will come of it? Worse yet, that profit will not be illegal. The naughty will not end up in Parkhurst, they will end up in Antibes. Let us suppose you wish to compete successfully in the Olympic Games, to which end you dispatch your pit bull terrier to lunch off rival calves. Do you know what will happen? Publishers will claw one another's eyes out in the bid for your memoirs, that's what will happen. Should you, on the other hand, be a shrewdly international terrorist with a caring agent adept at cobbling together a Hollywood auction where not only eyes will be clawed but bespoke Raybans ripped off and trodden underfoot to get at them, then enough may be generated from film rights to snap up both a safe house on the Acapulco beachfront and a fighter-escorted Learjet to whizz you to production conferences and back.

But even if you are only a minor politician on a small salary per annum with no thought of becoming a major broadcasting star on an enormous salary per annum, you will find to your astonishment that this transition may be speedily and effortlessly accomplished by nothing more than a brief encounter on sensibly indiscreet premises with any accommodating person (except, that is, the mother of your children), whereafter, this time, those clawing one another's eyes out will be television producers. And even if you are merely any accommodating person, then newspaper editors will be the ones doing the clawing, as they vie for the exclusive rights to your anecdotes of this, that, and, of course, the other.

Should you be a top accommodating person, mind, your anecdotage income will be substantially supplemented by glossy international weeklies and monthlies in clawing need of ten colour spreads depicting you gambolling in the Jacuzzi wing of your Hampshire shooting lodge or whacking balls across its croquet lawn the better to display the gussets of your own-label sportswear, the success of the diet available in all major video outlets, and the ability of your endorsed maquillage to withstand anything Mother Nature can throw at it.

Good news, eh? But how are the rest of us to cash in? What must someone like me do to end up backstroking across the gravy? Take a baseball bat to Bernard Levin's wrist, set up a Popular Front for the Liberation of Wags, slip off in my Range Rover to a bugged Cricklewood love-nest to make profitable tryst with a soubrette, a prop forward, a merino sheep? I haven't yet decided, but be assured that I shall decide very soon; because it is, as the Andrews Sisters elsewhere observed, nice work if you can get it.

Just Not My Day

Dear W.H. Smith: Every year for the past 31, Santa has brought me your Day-to-a-Page Pocket Diary. That is because Santa knows what I want. He has been spoken to firmly by my wife and put unequivocally in the diurnal picture. He knows that I require nothing of a diary save that it has a day to a page and fits into a pocket. He knows that while you produce any number of specialist diaries to suit all sorts and dispositions of men, from lepidopterists and cobblers to sous-chefs and balletomanes, in sizes so various that the smallest easily fits into an ear and the largest barely fits into a Volvo, and discretely gobbeted with arcana as disparate as early closing day in Surinam and the optimum bore for shooting peccary, I want none of any of this. I want only a different date at the top of each page, and room beneath for exactly 100 longhand words. That is what I expect to find in the toe of my stocking every Christmas morning, just below the walnut whip and just above the tangerine, and for 31 years I have not been disappointed.

Which is why I am writing to you now. Especially as you have invited me to. You have done this on the flyleaf of my new 1995 diary, where there is a tiny detachable questionnaire explaining that you have, this year, made a change and would like my opinion of it. And since it is so tiny that I had room to write only "My opinion is that you have buggered the diary up completely", I thought I would take this opportunity to elaborate, in order that it should come as no surprise to you, when you return to your Swindon HQ from your festive break, to find a man standing in the forecourt chucking bricks through your windows.

For the change you have made is the wanton introduction of adages, maxims, saws, bromides, canons, axioms – all those gee-gaws which sound as though they come from a Victorian dentist's toolbox, and might as well have, for all the pleasure they bring. What they in fact bring is ruin to a vast amount of what, without them, might be quite decent pottery, embroidery, calendars, pokerwork, and similar artefacts, and now, and most irritatingly of all, to your Day-to-a-Page Pocket Diary.

Look at the page for 1 January. In 1994, it told me only that it was 1 January. In 1995, it tells me: "Seize the day: trust the morrow as little as possible. HORACE (65-8 BC). Roman poet." It tells me it, moreover, in print so microscopic that I first read it as "trust the marrow as little as possible", and was, I admit, briefly diverted by its imponderability, until I put my glasses on. Now, having at last deciphered this handy Horatian tip, what am I supposed to do with it, except rage at the room it has taken up which might far more valuably have been used to jot: "Take 2 copies of Alan Bennett back to Hatchards, send thank-u notes to all 3 donors, get haircut"? Should I instead sit mulling the hoary aperçu, perhaps act upon it, rush out and seize 1 Jan by the scruff, come home again in good time to start dreading 2 Jan? Or flip on to 15 Jan, and ponder: "Better three hours too soon than a minute too late. WILLIAM SHAKESPEARE", an apophthegm useful only to those seeking comfort in the fact that the national hack had his off-days, too, but that can't be why you put it in, Smith. Unless, of course, you were the Mr W.H. who was the onlie begetter of the ensuing sonnets, and were simply repaying the acknowledgement; a mite unlikely, given that the last time I asked for poetry in one of your outlets I was told that you might have some somewhere, try behind that box-file display.

Shall I check my birthday? Oh, look, "Rain before seven, fine before eleven. PROVERB", that's good to know, I shall write beneath it: "Get up late, leave brolly in stand, smear sunbloc on nose"; how lucky I wasn't born on 10 September: "Life consists of what a man is thinking of all day. RALPH WALDO EMERSON", I should have to spend all day trying to think of what the old fool might have been banging on about.

This is a bad business. A diary is not for other people's thoughts. So since you have a fancy for the potted sooth, let me offer, in answer to your plea for feedback, this from dear old Chesterton: "Chuck it, Smith!"

A Matter of Will Power

You are, I know (and rarely a genuflecting bedtime passes when I do not offer up heartfelt thanks for it) as literate a readership as any show-off hack could wish. And yet I wonder whether even you realise how momentous is the date which stands just to the north-east of this column. I wonder whether you know that 4 January 1995 marks the 400th anniversary of the day on which William Shakespeare wrote the line: "And thus the native hue of resolution is sicklied o'er with the pale cast of thought."

He did not, of course, incorporate it professionally for a good five years: I know that you know that until he stumbled across François de Belleforest's *Histoires Tragiques* early in 1600 he had no inkling of the existence of a melancholy Danish procrastinator for whose temporising lips this corking observation might have been minuted, thus enabling Shakespeare to build a major showstopper around it. On 4 January 1595, the line had come into his head for no other reason than that he had just (*a*) started smoking again, (*b*) come off his diet, and (*c*) gone back on the sauce, after only three excruciatingly resolute days. And four centuries on, we sympathise. We understand just how it happened. We know the inevitable fate of resolutions after they have come under pressure from thinking.

Here is Shakespeare on New Year's Eve 1594, just finished *Romeo and Juliet* against a murderous deadline, and coughing his lungs to tatters on his fifth pipe of the night, doubtless cursing Raleigh for importing the muck in the first place. Remember, too, that smoking was even nastier than it is now, since this was long before the invention of the cigarette (otherwise Christopher Marlowe's celebrated curse on those "who love not tobacco and small boyes" might well have read "fags and small boyes" and got an even bigger laugh), and involved a crude frangible pipe which time and again either stuck to the lip or broke in the teeth – and furthermore, if the latter, ignited the crotch – so that smokers despised themselves even more than they do today.

That Shakespeare was also grossly overweight is beyond contention; everybody was, for which they again had Raleigh to thank. The average Elizabethan consumed ten pounds of fashionable spuds a day, sluiced down with enough booze to provide Shakespeare with more references to it than to anything else in his concordance. Ignore, therefore, the First Folio frontispiece, which was for gentle Shakespeare cut, wherein the graver had a strife with nature to outdo the life; that was just Ben Jonson blurbing for an easy groat beneath a cosmetic publicity snap. Shakespeare in fact weighed a Falstaff-and-a-half, much of it liver.

Which was why, 400 years ago last Sunday, he simultaneously forswore food, drink and weed; a regimen which worked fine for perhaps two hours. He then, as adumbrated hereinabove, began to think about it. For having just been signed up by the Lord Chamberlain as both actor and dramaturge, he was contractually obliged not only to turn out twice nightly in that season's panto as Gammer Gurton's daft son Jack, but also to get cracking on his *Richard II* script, a project as you know, singularly close to Elizabeth's heart.

Picture it. William sits in his icy dressing-room, straw in his hair, an idiot grin chalked over his miserably quill-chewing mouth, and the eyes crossed in readiness for Jack's first entrance, staring inaccurately at a pile of blank paper on which the trembling hand is expected to scribble a real belter to keep the monstrous virgin sweet. But his throat is dry, his stomach rumbles, the ghost of nicotine past flits mischievously across his tongue; and these are all he can think about.

Until, next day, he thinks: a little snort of sack would get me going, a nice fat hare would give me strength, a puff or two of shag would clear the head no end; my work needs them. But resolution holds. Until, next day, he thinks: this is not me, I am a cakes-and-ale man, my smoke-rings set the table on a roar, they loved me then, but who will love me now? Yet still the will, in punning loyalty, remains intact. Until day three. Day three he thinks: what, live for ever? Better to pop a happy clog at 52 than dodder on, sans teeth, sans eyes, sans taste, sans everything. Day four didn't stand a chance. It rarely does.

If I Had a Talking Picture of Me

Of all the exhibition joints in all of the towns in all of the world, you would not want to walk into the Las Vegas Convention Center. That is because you might run into Snappy, and Snappy could do you a serious mischief. For Snappy is one of 41,000 cutting-edge gadgets currently being demonstrated at the 1995 Consumer Electronics Show, and what Snappy could do is star you in *Casablanca*.

According to *US Computer Monthly*'s review of the exhibition, Snappy could do this for only $200. It is a gizmo which, plugged into your personal computer, "allows you to manipulate video images so that, for example, you can place yourself alongside Bogart and Bergman at Casablanca airport, walk the street with Gary Cooper at high noon, dance with Gene Kelly in the rain . . . in short, for $200 you can fulfil everyone's dream of playing in just about any movie ever made."

Oh really? Are dreams so easy to fulfil? I think not. The record on dreams generally proves that they are somewhat easier to shatter, and it is my guess that if Snappy's own dream is to retire on the proceeds of physically inserting us into celluloid worlds we have hitherto only spectated – however metaphorically transported we might have been while spectating – then Snappy's dream will prove to be as fragile as ours. And I set aside here the collateral damage done to the film itself: while *High Noon* may never be the same for having a denouement in which, with the clock showing 11.55, a grinning man from Cricklewood in a baggy cardigan suddenly walks through a wall into Main Street, or *Singin' in the Rain* be hard-pressed to recover from a scene in which the remarkable new star of *High Noon* reappears in order to slosh about asynchronously in the gutter while Gene Kelly twinkles on the sidewalk, the destruction of a seminal work of art is not the issue here. The issue here is the extent to which the interloper can integrate, for only thus may he realise the dream that Snappy maintains everyone has of becoming a part of the whole iconic shebang.

So picture this. Synthetic fog swirls about the *Casablanca* set. In the background, as fateful aero engines cough alive, Bogart and Bergman stand for their parting moment, so that Bogie can pass on to her his considered view that the problems of three little people in this crazy world don't amount to a hill of beans. But Bogie has not noticed that they have been joined by another. This other has worked hard to prepare himself for the part. He has shed his baggy cardigan and donned a nice creased Burberry and a wide-. brimmed trilby, set at a rakish angle. A cigarette slants from his lips, which, at this point, are pressed into further service. The lips say: "Make that four little people."

But neither Bogart nor Bergman responds. This is not because they do not know who this fourth hat is who has unexpectedly materialised from the pea soup to throw in his lot with them and Paul Henreid, or what part he might have played in the plot which has brought them to this bank and shoal of time, it is because they do not know he is there at all. They cannot see him. As if to emphasise this, when Bogie now says "Here's looking at you, kid," there is only one kid he is looking at.

Because the reality, as opposed to its virtual simulacrum, is that the man from Cricklewood, jiggle his keyboard however he may, is as doomed to be no less a bystander at these proceedings than he was when he first watched them from the one-and-nines. Worse, his pitiful attempt at inclusion serves only to exclude him further now than then, for it is one thing to identify with Bogart, but quite another to attempt unsuccessfully to replace him. Oh, look, he has pushed a new button, he has made himself a head taller than Bogart, he has stopped smoking, he is talking Swedish, but Bergman none the less continues to ignore him, because she can do nothing else, she must get on the plane with Henreid. All the dreamer can do is stand there and mutter: "We'll always have Cricklewood," which nobody hears.

For you must remember this, Snappy: you can put the movie into the boy, but however much time goes by, you cannot put the boy into the movie. The fundamental things apply.

A Bout de Sifflet

Those of you with nothing else to think about will recall that last week's column found me unable to attract the attention of Humphrey Bogart. This week's column, by contrast, is much more serious. This week's column finds me unable to attract the attention of Mrs Humphrey Bogart. What makes this much more serious is that whereas last week I was only a hologram, this week I am a man. Or rather, mostly a man: because between this week and last, I have lost one of the major items which makes a man a man. I have lost my whistle.

Which means that were I to run into Mrs Humphrey Bogart in, say, some cheap Caribbean flop-house, and were she to lean sinuously against my door-jamb murmuring: "If you want me, all you have to do is whistle, you know how to whistle, don't you?" I should have to say no, I don't. Even if she went on to explain that the trick was just to put my lips together and blow, my answer would, tragically, remain the same.

And that is why this week's column is much more serious than last week's, since Lauren Bacall, unlike her late husband, is not late. Far from it: for those men of my generation whose concupiscent lot it has ever been to hanker after older women, she is just about the only older woman left who can still raise a serious hanker. It is therefore a major blow to realise that, should the opportunity ever arise to attract her attention, the major blow required to do so would be beyond me.

It used to be a great whistle, mine. Not only did it enjoy a range and a timbre which enabled me so to handle the Bach Double Violin Concerto as to startle bus passengers into searching the upper deck for both Oistrakhs, it had a pitch which could summon cabbies from six streets away while leaving dogs undisturbed (or, by the subtlest adjustment of a cheek, vice versa), and, following a Les Ferdinand goal, alert the whole of West London to the fact that Queens Park Rangers were still a force to be reckoned with.

But last Friday morning, in the Middlesex Hospital, it was surgically removed. It was not removed deliberately (eclectic though this great institution may be, no Department of Whistle Surgery is flagged upon its indicator board), it was simply, when I woke up minus a tooth which had been removed deliberately, not there. I did not realise this immediately, mind, I realised it only after I had recovered from the anaesthetic and gone out to hail a cab. A cab came up Mortimer Street, I put my lips together and blew, there was the noise of an unknotted balloon hurtling around a room, and the cab went by, forgivably ignoring a man standing on the pavement wiping his chin.

And five days on, things are incalculably worse. In what should have been a cheering sequence, the wound has healed, the stitches have gone, the gums have deflated, the twinges have quietened, yet each recovery serves only to focus on the greater incurability. It is not merely the loss of sway over dog and cab and barman, it is not just the inability to lead the mob in approval or derision, or, when someone asks how something goes, impeccably flute a few identifying bars, it is not the realisation that, should the upcoming celebration of VJ-Day require it, I should not be able to contribute one single note of *Colonel Bogey*, it is not even the passing of the dear dead days when I could whistle while I worked, sloshing emulsion onto ceiling or adverb onto screen with a gusto of which *Pedro the Fisherman* was somehow both a diversionary descant and a contributory boon to concentration, it is more than any of these: it is about no longer being able to do what blokes are supposed to be able to do. Knowing how to whistle was the first rite of passage. In my primary school, it was what separated the boys from the infants.

So, since you have forked out the 20p which entitles you to demand of a columnist that he bang on not just about himself but about issues of burning topical note, let me close by buttonholing Nottingham council, which has just set up a Considerate Roadworks Hotline designed to give counsel to women upset by men whistling at them in the street. Is it unreasonable to hope that the same political correctness might spare a small caring spot on the switchboard for any men who can't?

Soaring Taxation

Strive as I might, and always do, to be as unconvoluted as possible, there really is no way of approaching this morning's topic without going via Benjamin Franklin. He is enmeshed in its every ravelled thread. His ghost perches on my shoulder as I tap, now pointing this way, now that. And though my prime commitment remains, of course, to you, there is no question but that, today, this one is also for him.

I have always loved old Ben. Who that has any relish for life's hilarious heterogeneity could fail to love a man who invented the glass harmonica, sought to identify the presence of electricity in lightning by standing in a thunderstorm with a kite, and lurched around in two pairs of spectacles, one on the bridge of his nose, one on the tip, until crying to hell with this, and inventing bifocals? It would be hard to think of anyone in whom dottiness and wisdom combined to more productive effect, and it is thus altogether fit and proper that he should be riding shotgun for me as I face down Her Majesty's Customs & Excise on the burning issue of hot-air ballooning.

Especially as it was he who made the two keynote remarks on the subject: the first in 1783, when, posted to Europe as his fledgeling nation's plenipotentiary to negotiate the Treaty of Paris, he witnessed the Montgolfier brothers whizzing over that city in the first journey made by men hanging on to a big bag, and murmured: "Whether science has embarked upon a fresh source of human joy or of human folly, I dare not speculate," and the second six years later, in his letter to M. Leroy, when he wrote: "In this world, nothing is certain but death and taxes."

Which finally brings me, as readers registered for VAT may already have twigged, to the new edition of *VAT Notes*, that merry little quarterly which keeps us abreast of all those swingeing innovations which give the lie to Treasury claims that taxes are not going up. As a publication, mind, it is a mixed curse, in that it does reveal all manner of wondrous items I would otherwise never have known existed, eg chiming non-ferrous ornamental ptarmigans, or showerproof bridal accessories (except hand-wound rayon horseshoes), or all the millions of other arcane gew-gaws which have been truffled out by sniffer dogs trained to catch the whiff of anything not yet carrying 17.5 per cent, and run panting with it to the Chancellor's feet in the hope of a pat and a chocolate button.

And look what they have found now! "From 1 April 1995, services relating to entertainment or recreational activities that include passenger transport will become wholly standard-rated. This includes 'fun' or historic rides, specialist train rides and other forms of transport within theme parks, and hot-air balloon rides." I particularly savour the inverted commas they have placed around "fun". Can we not see the meeting at Dracula House, following the discovery of what they had hitherto been missing 17.5 per cent of? "Fun, eh, we'll give 'em bloody fun!"

Was there ever a more horrible levying? Did any impost ever bespeak a flintier heart? Could any piece of legislation distance more irretrievably the feelgood factor its legislators are so desperately seeking?

I rang the VAT Führerbunker. Was there now VAT on dodgem cars? Yes. Ferris-wheels? Of course. Big dippers? No question. Ghost trains? Definitely. "While public transport in its usual sense will continue to be zero-rated," I was told, "public transport *where the purpose is entertainment* will now carry VAT." I cannot say whether the italics are theirs or mine, but it does not matter. What matters is that this is not merely a levy on fun, it is a levy on the fun of those whose fun is likeliest to be circumscribed by it, for the diversions thus hammered are unquestionably those of the nation's harder-up.

Is the Treasury so strapped for cash that hot-air balloon rides must be pressed into fiscal service? How much will they bring in, do you imagine? And since you ask, I have not turned to the ghost on my shoulder to ask him whether he has now, after two centuries, reached a conclusion as to whether balloons are a source of human joy or of human folly. I dare not. He is probably furious at me for having so incautiously mentioned glass harmonicas. They are just the sort of item the VAT people might up till now have missed.

Unsafe as Houses

First thing we do, let's ring all the lawyers. That is what Dick the butcher would cry today, four centuries on, were he, say, to find himself looking at a rasher of thumb atop 8oz of fresh-laminated gammon. His immediate thought would be to sue the manufacturers of his bacon-slicer, his next to sue the company whose passing bus had backfired his concentration, his third to sue the customer for exposing him to risk when she could have chosen a nice pullet, and so on. He would cry it because there are no accidents any more. There is only liability.

Which is why I spent a gloomy weekend. For Friday's newspapers had reported the case of Phillip Marsh – or, rather, the two cases, since Mr Marsh, having become a backache case as the result of falling down front steps belonging to Mr Stefan Kirwin, had brought a court case against Mr Kirwin for having the sort of steps you could fall down. The steps were icy. They had got this way as the result of the sub-zero temperature in which Mr Marsh walked up them. Partly up them. Now, there are those who would say that even had his frozen conk not alerted Mr Marsh to the possibility of slipperiness underfoot, the presence of snow on the lawn on either side of the steps might have done the trick, but those who would say that are not lawyers. Lawyers would say that for Mr Marsh to be adequately alerted, Mr Kirwin should have put up a big illuminated sign saying: "Watch out, Mr Marsh, you could fall over on these icy steps and cost me £100,000 in damages!"

But he did not, so that is what it cost him.

It was a tale to make the blood run cold (and, yes, the newspapers responsible for telling it should know that my lawyers are at this very moment consulting top cardiac opinion as to the long-term effects of suddenly cooled blood) in every householder, and thus the cause of my weekend gloom.

My house, I now see, is nothing but a litigation-trap, a mountain of liabilities waiting only to be converted into red-ribboned sheaves and trucked round to the High Court to be met at the door by Gravy Bar QCs holding big chunks of bread; and this realisation has changed forever not merely my relationship with my home, but with anyone I might be incautious enough to invite into it. For it is an old house, and we have lived in it a long time, with the result that it is now an outstanding example of *Art Negligé,* that great decor tradition which eschews the meretriciously shipshape in favour of the lived-in charm of snapped sash-cords, loose light-switches, missing stair-rods, warped doors, wonky chairs, footloose tables, and rare old rugs where a heel caught in the kind of delicate antique hole-work you never find in modern fitted shagpile can send an admiring visitor surfing across the uneven floor-boards into a magnificent ear-height mantelshelf above a fireplace so huge it takes two paramedics to pull you out of it.

We have, down the long arches of the years, done much entertaining here, and not a little bandaging, but, after Marsh *v* Kirwin, dare we ever have guests again? To select but one fond memory from countless, when I was strolling our meticulously unspoilt garden on Sunday I recalled the day when a senior politician, somewhat the better for gin and having already measured his length on the prettily lichened terrace, leant on our sundial and was pitched into the pond, a cause of much good-humoured banter, then, and not even a dry-cleaning bill. These days, you'd be looking at the wrong end of half a million.

Dinner parties? Be serious! Never mind the juridical

menace posed by dodgy chair-legs, self-detaching knife-blades or serrated goblet-rims, think of all the warnings with which the table would have to be girt: "Caution! The soup is hot and may cause blistering!" or "While every precaution has been taken to fillet the haddock, guests are advised that the risk of the odd bone sticking in the gullet cannot be ruled out", or "This wine contains alcohol, and could result in your walking into a door, losing your driving licence, or waking up in a foul mood."

I tell you, when Burke wrote "Laws, like houses, lean on one another," he didn't know the half.

Numbers Racket

By the pricking of my thumbs, something wicked this way comes. More precisely, by the pricking of my fingers. My fingers know they are about to be asked to cope with a whole lot of new stuff, and they know they are about to be found wanting. They know this because they have been watching television, clutching the armchair to still their trembling, and they know that what is coming is PhONEday. That is how it is advertised, because BT want to engrave on our memory the fact that the figure 1 is to be added to all our phone numbers and, fearless of irony, they know that the way to engrave it is not with a number but with a word. We can remember words: you all have my introductory quote by heart, but if the Second Witch had chosen instead to rattle off her Access number, who now could summon it effortlessly to mind? The only way BT could have fixed 1 as a number would have been to flash up Ph1neday and back its iffy graphic with a tape of Kiri Te Kanawa trilling *One Phine Day*, laying coloratura emphasis on the one, and if you think I am rambling you are dead right, that is what blue funk does.

Once upon a time, life was a doddle for fingers. If they wished to dial someone, they referred to a brain stocked with words – ENTerprise, JUNiper, GLAdstone – to which a mere four digits were attached. The brain could store hundreds of these. It had no need of a personal organiser, to be carried at all times, on which a minimum of ten digits had to be stored for each phonee, the phonees themselves codified numerologically, so that if the fingers needed to look up their number, the brain had first to remember the number under which the fingers had stored it.

Had, mind, the brain wanted to buy a personal organiser, or anything else, it would have obtained the requisite cash by going to a bank where its fingers would write a cheque. It would not have stood in the sleet outside the bank, as today's brain does, struggling to distinguish between its cashpoint number, its PIN number, its car radio locking code, its personal number for the keypad on its office door, and the number of the combination lock of the briefcase in which it planned to put the money for the kind of really safe keeping you get when you cannot subsequently remember the number of the combination lock; only to realise, when its fingers had tapped the cashpoint numbers out and the machine had eaten the card, that the number they had tapped was in fact its video club membership number, though for which of its three video clubs the brain could not, as it were, put its finger on.

That the brain did not write any of these numbers down goes without saying, since the whole point of codes, see OED, is that they are a system of signals designed to ensure secrecy, though not necessarily from the brain inside the head currently banging itself on the wall of the bank, knowing that the only way to get at its own money is to write to the bank so that the bank can, after a week or so, issue a card with a nice new number for the brain to forget.

Some brains, though, do write these myriad numbers down, but they do it very cannily, by jumbling the numbers, eg middle digits reversed, outer digits increased by one, so that all the brain has to do, when asked to give its account number at, say, John Lewis (if its John Lewis card is inextricably locked inside its briefcase) is look at the account number on its personal organiser (if it can remember the number under which it was stored), remember exactly the system by which the digits were jumbled, and then wait for John Lewis to call the police.

This need not be a major problem, as the police will allow the brain to make one telephone call, to its solicitor. It becomes a major problem only if its solicitor's number is inside the briefcase which the brain has to explain to the desk sergeant that it is unable to open, in which event it is possible that the brain may find itself with a new number it has, for once, no difficulty in remembering, since it is stitched on its shirt.

No wonder, then, that the fingers prick at the imminence of PhONEday. More yet, the eyes weep to remember the words which follow that introductory quote of mine: "Open, locks, whoever knocks." It was a terrific system.

A Thought for Your Pennies

The last thing I need is another *memento mori*. Indeed, I have the occasional startled dawn awakening, these days, when a reminder that I am still *vivus* would not come amiss, hang on, is that a ceiling I am staring up at or a lid, so I have decided to look on the bright side of last Sunday's discovery and regard it as a signal not of my impermanence, which was my first reaction, but of my perpetuity.

As a matter of fact, last Sunday's discovery has two bright sides, now that I have had a go at it with the vinegar. One side shows the Emperor of India, and the other Britannia – a brace of identities currently so ideologically explosive that it set the gooseflesh crackling to note, once the vinegar had done its deoxydising trick, that the date of their joint minting was only 1944. Strange, how a mere half-century can render the old penny so politically unacceptable that if it happened to fall from your pocket in a roomful of 1995 right-on uniglobers, they would probably tear you limb from limb before you had the chance to shriek that you had just dug it up in your garden and were carrying it ironically.

But that's history for you. Strata. When I first started turning over flower beds, in about 1960, there was little in them but bits of blue-and-white china. I never inquired why this should be, preferring to assume that at some critical point in the late-Victorian vogue for this particular crockery – could have been Krakatoa erupting, could have been a meteorite shower, could have been a rash of Anarchist bombings, could have been a spontaneous nationwide outburst of domestic mayhem brought on by too much booze or too little sex – it all got smashed. And I used to reflect, as I dug, that that was how future archaeologists might be disposed to characterise the 1880s: an era of flying soup tureens and chamber pots, and citizens running through suburban gardens with their hands over their heads.

I don't come across blue-and-white shards any more; no doubt they have all sunk, thanks to the peristaltic nudges of Time's ever-rolling subsoil, to a level below the depth of spades, to await the excited speculations of future Carters and Schliemanns. What I get now is headless tin grenadiers, Zambuk lids, rusted clockwork, old fountain pens, Dinky wheels, two-pin plugs, bent Meccano girders, Boys' Brigade belt-buckles, ribbed brown bottles embossed with the signature of Dr J Collis Browne, cap-gun barrels, flat-trodden kazoos, Bakelite knobs and, as of last weekend, superannuated coinage – all the pitiful detritus, in short, of my own infancy.

I do not know how the penny got into my border, any more than I knew how the Victorian potsherds used to. Whether, new-minted, it was blown there by one of Cricklewood's three doodlebugs or, outdated, tossed irritably away when decimalisation came in, or merely prey to some lesser cataclysm between, I cannot guess. I know only that it moved, fiscally, from life to death, and thence to history. The d was dead, long live the p.

A friend came over for a drink last Sunday morning, after I had finished gardening, and brought his ten-year-old son with him. The boy, poking about as boys will, spotted the penny descaling in its saucer, and wanted to know things. So I told him that, once upon a time, there had been twelve of them to a shilling. He is a smart kid, but had great difficulty in taking this on board. He thought I was winding him up. When I went on to explain that a pound once contained not only 20 such shillings, but also 960 farthings with little wrens on, he fell about. He is, as I say, smart. He wanted to know how our calculators used to cope. They must have been enormous.

After the pair of them had gone, I looked at the penny and realised that it had not passed into history alone. It had taken me with it. This was my stratum. That was my era. Clockwork, Bakelite, Platignums and, more resonant yet than all of these, a big copper Emperor of India you could poke into a slot machine which would swap him for a bar of Fruit-and-Nut.

Museum stuff, now. Highly collectable. Much prized. Archaeological stuff, next. Not ephemera at all. Life after death.

Oscar Victor Bravo

At three o'clock on Tuesday morning, at the very moment that a front door in temperate Cricklewood opened to admit a major pizza, extra ham, no anchovy, a distant cuckoo in the lightless lee of Greenland's icy mountains sprang 12 times from its little premises to alert its nodding owner to the fact that it was time to chuck another fir-trunk into the grate and another elk-pelt over the knees, for it was going to be a long cold night.

On India's coral strand, however, it was going to be a

long hot morning, so at 9am, in countless millions of coast-to-coast teapots, vast quantities of sustaining char were being put on to brew against a parching ordeal scheduled not to end until the noonday gun. Afric's sunny fountains, on the other hand, had only recently begun to roll down their golden sand, and at 6am the buttons atop millions of alarm clocks were cool to the disconnecting touch; while, away to the east, the spicy breezes blowing soft o'er Java's isle were at that selfsame moment bearing the reverberations of a far mellower tocsin, as countless temple bells struck 11 to call the faithful to their television sets.

And all because it was 6pm in Hollywood, signifying that one billion inhabitants of Planet Earth were about to glue themselves to the 67th Academy Awards Ceremony. *One billion!* I know this figure to be accurate, because, within seconds, tuxedo after smirking tuxedo was bouncing on to the rostrum to tell me so, as if constant reiteration would somehow save the imagination from collapse.

It did not work. Yesterday, between 3am and 6, the imagination sat gobsmacked, not by the glutinous maunderings of this glittering prizewinner or that, or by the triumphal snippets entered in evidence of their genius, but by the fathomless speculation which each announcement generated – a condition owing not a little to the fact that the room in which the imagination was sitting had a television set in one corner and a large globe in the other, and I very soon found that I could not stop my eyes flickering nystagmically between them, attempting, willy-nilly, to cope with the idea that two thousand million other eyes had simultaneously seen what they just had.

What in God's name could they have made of it? What did David Letterman's already esoteric Tinseltown wisecracks sound like in Hungarian subtitle? How many Uzbeks could with any confidence distinguish between all these megastar triumphs of the orthodontist's art caught in ring-twisting aspiration at their tables, when even buffs like me were flummoxed?

Who among the Sarawak viewership even knew what second-unit direction was? Was anyone in this rapt Borneo longhut or that Hezbollah gunpit in a position to explain to the others with any authority why Alan Bennett had been sidelined or Nigel Hawthorne robbed? As for Ulan Bator, the last time it had stayed up all night was for the World Cup final, and there had been no problem there, they had all kicked a ball about a bit, but how many Mongolians could take a convincing stab at guessing why the make-up team on *Ed Wood* should have won the right to thank its uncles and aunts and second cousins twice removed for everything, when the make-up team on *Frankenstein* had been left with no option but gamely to bite its cheated knuckle?

The truth, I fear, is that all these minutiae are globally irrelevant. The majority of my fellow-billion will have switched on for no better reason than that this was a competition with winners and losers. That is the kind of thing people want to watch, whether it is the Eurovision Song Contest, the Booker Prize, or indeed the Belgian Synchronised Swimming Final and the by-election results from Llandrindod Wells. It is not necessary to have any understanding whatever of what is being contested: we mark not how they played the game, but that they won or lost.

So do not be downhearted that Britain's principal achievement was for Best Song Sung by a Drawing. A billion viewers will have thought we did rather well. Oh all right, nearly a billion.

Turkey Trot

Picture this. It is fetid midnight in a flyblown backstreet shebeen in old Ankara, pungent with the variegated miasma of rotgut, hashish, boiled offal, stale pomade, periodontal ruin and old dog. At one end of the cellar, on an oildrum dais, an ageing belly-dancer arrhythmically shifts her various lumps about, as if a hummock of dough were being kneaded by invisible hands, to the tinny cackle of a wind-up gramophone and the contrapuntal click of worry-bead. Above the dozen rickety tables, sporadic glow-worms seem to flicker, but they are only the wonky gold teeth of the barrel-bodied patrons, catching, as they grin, the scant ochre light of bottled candle.

What are they grinning at? They are grinning at a demure blonde Welshwoman standing at the bar and nervously thumbing her phrasebook in search of the Turkish for a small pot of Earl Grey and a toasted teacake. They are grinning because she has a red rose in her lapel, and when a woman wears a red rose in Turkey it means, as all sophisticated travellers know, only one thing. But she is not a sophisticated traveller: she is wearing the red rose because she is the Labour member for Cynon Valley, and goes nowhere without it. That is Ann Clwyd's way.

It will not help her here. Already, the barman is nervously taking down his mirror, muttering, "Of all the arak joints in all the towns all over the world, she had to walk into mine," because he knows that Clwyd, though he could never pronounce it, spells trouble. The clientele is pushing back its chairs. Some are tossing coins. Some are drawing lots. Several are wrapping their beads around their enormous knuckles.

But stay! Suddenly, the entrance's hanging plastic strips fly apart, as through them strides a riveting cynosure. Beneath his sola topi, strong spectacles jut; from the pocket of his bush shirt poke four nasty-looking ballpoints; in his right hand he carries, deceptively loosely, his service clipboard. For this is none other than Indiana Cousins MP, known by every lowlife from Tangiers to Macao as a former member of Wallsend Borough Council. He cups Ms Clwyd's trembling elbow in his strong pink palm and, as the ragged curtains of black moustache drop sullenly over the glow-worms, bears her through the cheated mob to freedom. It is only when they are outside that he murmurs: "You crazy little fool, you might have got us both killed!"

Why do I invite you to picture this? Because that is precisely what Mr Cousins invited, after yesterday's tragic sackings. "I could not leave Turkey without Ms Clwyd," he declared, in defence of his scorning of the Whips. "I felt obliged to protect her in a dangerous part of the world."

And, in so declaring, brilliantly – dare one say mischievously? – he left his sacker staring into an enormous can of worms. For what was this if not the very cleft itself of New Labour's dichotomy? Its leader had just embarked upon perhaps his only affirmative action, *viz.* positive discrimination in favour of female Labour candidates in order, some might say undemocratically, to rig the House of Commons in distaff favour, against the ambitions of many aspirant male Labour candidates. Yet here was a prominent member of the unreconstructed Left steadfastly maintaining that all those women MPs couldn't be left to wander this horrid world without a big strong chap at their side.

Now, under what pass in politics for normal circumstances, this would be settled with no more bloodshed than Mr Cousins's: the sacking would have the twin benefit of asserting the leader's grit, while simultaneously mollifying outraged feminism. But New Labour is a bipolar beast, a Push-Me-Pull-You desperate to close its other set of teeth gently but firmly over the neck of Middle England and, growling support for traditional values, carry it off to its lair. And what could more appeal to back-to-basics fans than the notion that New Labour was a home fit for heroes prepared to stand up to all that Johnny Turk could throw at them to protect the honour of British womanhood?

Mr Blair has been set a problem. And whether Jim Cousins has helped him restore the Lost Ark to his wilderness party or consigned it once more to the Temple of Doom, who dares with any confidence predict?

Soft Options

I do like evolution. It creates faith. If there were a God, and if he, or perhaps He, had a right hand, Darwin would be sitting at it.

Let us now get out our microscopes and take a close shufti at what is wriggling on our slides. It is a declining species. Do you know why it is declining? It is declining because of its external genitalia. Is it, you ask, declining because they are shrivelling? On the contrary: look, you can see them quite clearly, and they are egregiously prominent. They are also, if we are any judge, in full working nick. How can it possibly come about, then, that with genitalia like this, the species to which they are attached – and which, clearly, is deeply attached to them – can be threatened with extinction?

It is because the species is homo politicus. Yes, we are looking at members of parliament, not because we are bent and twisted journalists who find cheap puns irresistible, but because we are straight and true scientists who are deeply concerned that the country will become ungovernable if all it has to govern it are members unable to govern their own. If not a day goes past without a member chucking in the sponge because he has been getting back to the kind of basics which the electorate is encouraged to regard with disfavour, then not many days will pass before the electorate is left with no members at all.

Worse yet, how will they find any new ones to elect? That is the anguished cry we hear in every pub and club and cab, after the cackling has died and faces compose themselves to say, "But seriously . . ." For if the prime criterion for office is to be sexual probity, where shall we find such men? Is it not tragically probable that, through his very oestrus, homo politicus is doomed to become extinct?

No. The thing with evolution is that as one door closes, another opens. I should now like you to put away your microscopes, and open that nice new book on your desks, hot from the Boston University Press. It has what it thinks is a harrowing tale to tell, but that is because it does not give a fig for politics, preferring to donate all its figs to what it describes as the evolution of the New Sportsman. And if I tell you its title, you will quickly see why it thinks the tale it has to tell is harrowing. The book is called *Blunt Trauma: The Pathophysiology of Haemodynamic Injury Leading to Erectile Dysfunction*.

As a top scientist, I of course read many such books, and I have to tell you that this one is what we call a little cracker. It examines the rise of the New Sportsman, and concludes that that is the last thing you should call it. For the New Sportsman, as familiar over here as he is over there, is the fitness-freaking paragon of the professional classes – lawyer, doctor, broker, what you will – whose every non-professional moment is spent striving for physical perfection, on horse and mountain bike, trampoline and parallel bar, water-ski and martial-art mat; but what he actually achieves, as the result of damage to the blood-vessels of the groin, is impotence.

It is, we read, a major problem for the modern achiever. But only if we read it that way. If we read it another way, and I know you're ahead of me, you're a bright class, it is the salvation of democracy. We would seem against all the apparent odds, to have found such men. And there are thousands and thousands to choose from.

Here we are in the committee room of the Rottenborough constituency party. The door opens, but the doorway itself remains filled, for this is a big candidate, barn-door shoulders, rippling pecs, seam-busting biceps, topped by a fatless head not only bronzed and sparkling-eyed, but containing the 162 IQ points which made him, what, a consultant at 30, a QC at 35, a billionaire at 40? And now he wants to be the candidate for Rottenborough. The selection committee catches its breath: were they to adopt him, a landslide would be a formality, a ministry inevitable, and everything beyond merely a matter of very brief time.

There is only one thing they need to ask; but he is ahead of them, for it is his way always to be ahead. He strides across the carpet with his lithe athlete's stride, smiles his winning smile and places on their trestle table, between the jug and the ashtray, a note from his doctor.

After the Fox

I have taken up foxhunting. I know the grisly risks I run in disclosing this intelligence but I am unable to withhold it. Though I have become unspeakable – in pursuit, ironically, of what is now the only love left which dare not speak its name – I can speak of little else. It is in my blood. Oscar would finally understand. I am no longer my own master. I am master of the Cricklewood Hunt.

Before the more caring among you reach for your balaclavas and pickhandles, allow me a few words. It is just possible they may be enough to avert a civil war, and that is a better use for a few words than to elegise one. Think of today's column as the Cricklewood Address.

Sunday night was balmy, and balm being precisely what one needs after the spirit-riddling enfilade of the Sunday papers, I took a turn around the garden for that springtime propaganda, of hopeful regeneration disseminated by the waft of the wooing blossom and the burp of the rutting frog. And as I sat with soothing fag and tumbler beneath the pear tree beside the pond, I grew gradually aware that l was not alone: first a rustle, could have been a toad, then a sniff, could have been a hedgehog, and finally, when I turned, two yellow eyes. Could have been a cat – until my own irises, adjusting to the dark, suddenly revealed, much in the manner of those magic eye pictures, the outline of a fox.

We looked at one another for a bit. It raised its head slightly, and sniffed again: but – whether because there was too little wind for me usefully to be down of it or because the fox lacks humankind's topically prissy objections to Silk Cut and Vat 69, I cannot say – it did not move.

This was unsettling: I had been led to believe that foxes were more afraid of us than we of them, which has always seemed plausible given that foxes did not congregate in reinforced toppers and red-tailed coats to set about lone citizens engaged on an innocent rural potter; but possibly that was then and this was now. The new urban fox might be a nastier evolution and, in the absence of the ducks and rabbits which elsewhere formed the vulpine diet, fancy a nice bit of man.

So I stood up. But the fox merely trotted, unhurriedly, across the lawn towards the narrow gap between houses which gives access to the road. It gives it, mind, only after, if you are not a fox, you have covered yourself in muck and left half your shirt on a wall-nail and half your ear on an air-vent. But damage is the huntsman's lot. We do not stop for pain.

Out on the street I saw my quarry turn the corner. It was making for the playing-fields opposite. I urged myself into a canter. The fox went under the perimeter fence. The huntsman took it at a bound. A bound and a scrabble. A bound and a scrabble and a pratfall on the other side. But no matter, we were both in open country, now, the fox at a lope, the huntsman at full gallop, a fine serendipitous sight, in the moonlight, for any townies setting an alarm-clock or flossing teeth, and one glimpsed hitherto only on biscuit tins. I wished, for their sakes, I had a hunting kazoo to blow. For my own, I required only the rushing wind on my face, the sweat springing on dewy grass – the thrill, in short, of the chase.

For the fox's, however, it went at last to earth, which is what we countrymen call Cricklewood Trading Estate, a place full of floodlit security men going "Oy!" from which even the bravest spirit shrinks, so I reined in, and turned for home at a steady limp, there to pull off my muddied clothes, Elastoplast my sporty wounds, quaff a stirrup cup and lie exhilarated and exhausted together, at one with Jorrocks's stout opinion that 'unting is all that's worth living for, all time is lost wot is not spent 'unting, it is the hair we breathe!

But wondering (I promised a solution for our divided culture) why foxhunting demanded *dead* foxes. Why not simply gallop after them? Behind, if required, muzzled hounds? That, surely, is where the fun is, if we are not ourselves beasts, and it would be bound to preserve the sport by spiking its opponents' only genuine gun. I do believe I shall try it down here in Cricklewood. All I need is a horse and a decent tailor.

Correct Diet

In a moment, we shall attempt to consider the freshness of barns. But before that, let us take a little trip back to July 1974, and to a house in Gloucester Crescent, NW1, then as now the epicentre of ideological rectitude for those in a position to afford it, where a face not entirely dissimilar from the one on the cover of this book is framed in the open sash of an elegant Regency window.

Its only dissimilarity, give or take the odd footmark testifying to 20 years of passing crows, is that the mouth is not grinning. Indeed, it scarce resembles a mouth at all. It is more like the backside of a cat. It is as pursed as a mouth can get, and it does not know what to do with the contents pursing it. It would spit them through the open sash, but there are hydrangeas out there, and if my host awoke next morning to find them shrivelled, he might recall my standing by the window. So, at last, I swallow. I shall not describe the next few seconds, other than to observe that those who think retsina is something boxers wipe their feet in may not be wrong.

For this was a party thrown to celebrate the fact that the Greek junta had just been given the elbow, to the boundless delight of what later came to be called the chattering classes, who had not permitted themselves to drink anything Greek since 1967. I, who had never drunk anything Greek at all, could only wonder, as my entrails puckered, how great a sacrifice to democracy theirs might have been.

Sardines, though, were a different kettle of fish. There is nothing like a Portuguese sardine, but who could eat them while their country toiled beneath the fascist yoke? That is why 25 April 1974 was such a big day for us anti-fascists: with the fall of Caetano, what a joy it now was to wake up peckish at 3am! Not, mind, if you fancied a South African grapefruit, or a goblet of Spanish sherry, for these delights were yet to be, along with countless other foodstuffs from benighted nations whose cellars then teemed with jack-booted apparatchiks oiling pliers.

Nor, given the volatility of politics, was spotting these always easy. It didn't take much to put a *Guardian* subscriber off his tucker, and even if you were planning only an informal little supper you would be wise to read the paper's every word before going into Sainsbury's to spend an hour scrutinising labels for countries of origin, since a shift to the right in, say, some Danish by-election could, if you had not noticed it, mean a nice bit of boiled gammon ending up all over the dinette wall.

But then, suddenly, everything was all right. All the regimes which stood between liberals and a great night out had fallen, you could guzzle anything from anywhere to your conscience's content, and the anxious host no longer needed to be on the *qui vive* for every political tremor.

This golden era lasted for about ten minutes: for the thing with ethics is that they abhor a vacuum, and that is why we must now address the freshness of barns. I refer of course to Monday's Co-op report which declared that 60 per cent of shoppers were concerned about "ethically unsound food". The capacity, furthermore, of this unsoundness appears illimitable: it is, it seems, not enough to be told that a free-range egg is "barn-fresh", it is also essential to know how fresh the barn itself was. (I can only pray that caring readers will forgive me if I admit that upon reaching this point in the Co-op narrative, I found myself wool-gathering a movie entitled *Barn Fresh*, in which Elsa the chicken, having been raised by Joy Adamson from an egg, is at last, to heart-wrenching musical accompaniment, returned to the wild, to lay eggs of her own.)

This ethical commitment does not of course stop at chickens: the upbringing of anything edible must apparently conform to the exacting standards of that majority of the populace who need to know their dinner was living the life of Riley up until the moment they sank their teeth into it. It will thus not be possible for the rest of us to invite anyone over ever again. Forgive me, but, asked whether a sardine went into its tin to serve the interests of a repressive regime, I can offer a pretty confident answer. Asked, however, whether it was happy to do so, I fear I shouldn't have the faintest idea where to begin.

REBEL TALENT

REBEL TALENT

Why It Pays to BREAK THE RULES at Work and in Life

FRANCESCA GINO

An Imprint of WILLIAM MORROW

HarperCollins books may be purchased for educational, business, or sales promotional use. For information, please email the Special Markets Department at SPsales@harpercollins.com.

FIRST EDITION

Library of Congress Cataloging-in-Publication Data has been applied for.

ISBN 978-0-06-269463-8

18 19 20 21 22 DIX/LSC 10 9 8 7 6 5 4 3 2

To Alexander, Olivia, and Emma

In the real-life version of my favorite improv comedy game, you are the "Three Things!" that make life really matter.

CONTENTS

INTRODUCTION

MARCIA!

You don't let tradition bind you. You let it set you free.
—MASSIMO BOTTURA, OWNER AND CHEF, OSTERIA FRANCESCANA

"*Marcia!*" Upon hearing this command, which means "Gear up!" in Italian, I hustled from the hushed dining room back to the bright, boisterous kitchen to pick up the next dish—called, of all things, "The Crunchy Part of the Lasagna" (*La parte croccante della lasagna*). Spoonfuls of ragù and béchamel rested under a sheet of pasta that looked like the corner piece of a lasagna—all carefully assembled to take on the appearance of a lightly scorched Italian flag. I followed the lead of another waiter, Pino, as he picked up his dish and then walked to the dining room. My hand trembled as, in unison, Pino and I placed our plates in front of a famous Italian couple who were celebrating their wedding anniversary. On the walls, painted light blue and gray, hung a world-class collection of contemporary art, one of many unusual touches at Osteria Francescana, a restaurant in Modena, Italy, that holds three Michelin stars and took first place in the World's 50 Best Restaurant awards in 2016. It was the first Italian restaurant in history to reach the top of the list.

Back in the kitchen, Pino and I picked up another signature

dish, "*Bollito non bollito*"—quite literally "Boiled Meats, Not Boiled." Bollito misto is a classic northern Italian stew largely composed of boiled meat. Traditionally, the dish consists of various parts of the cow, such as the tongue and other off cuts, served with the broth and a *salsa verde* (green sauce) and sometimes a few other piquant condiments. Although the dish is comforting on a winter day, it is not very pleasing to the eye, and the process of boiling the meat strips it of its flavor and color. Yet this is simply how the dish is done. Italian cooking follows an extremely stringent set of rules: Short pasta goes with meat sauces, while long pasta goes with seafood sauces. Time-honored recipes are not to be polluted with substitutions. From cooking and folk dances to festivals celebrating saints and a day off for La Befana, a night in January when a good witch on a broomstick delivers candy, Italian culture cherishes its traditions.

Massimo Bottura, the owner and chef behind Osteria Francescana, wanted to challenge the traditional way bollito misto is cooked. After much experimentation with his team, Bottura discovered that the taste and texture of the meat were far superior if he used *sous vide*, a cooking technique where food is placed in a vacuum-sealed plastic pouch and immersed in heated water to be cooked at a precise, consistent temperature for hours. In *Bollito non bollito*, six different cuts of meat are cooked *sous vide* and then shaped into cubes. Each block is then placed on the plate in a line, alongside a second line of bright green parsley, smoked red and yellow gelatin made with peppers, a few capers and anchovies, onion marmalade, and some apple mustard. The dish, I learn, is inspired by New York City, where Bottura worked when he was a young man. In a nod to Central Park, the meat cubes rise like little skyscrapers above green foam trees, and the red and yellow gelatin makes a lawn with little anchovy people mingling on it. *Bollito non bollito* leaves you speechless; the cubes melt in your mouth like anxiety after a first kiss, bursting with waves of intense flavor: meaty, fatty, and sumptuous, yet buffeted by the light herbaceous foam and the gelatin.

Two orders of *Bollito non bollito* for Table 8 were ready in the kitchen. I carefully adjusted my plate until it matched Pino's, watching for his approval. I followed him out of the kitchen, matching his movements, and taking care to protect the delicate dish.

What was I, a Harvard Business School professor, doing in the heart of Italy's Emilia Romagna, serving food in one of the world's top restaurants? I was as surprised as anyone to have ended up there. But I had written two Harvard Business School case studies of fast-food chains, and I decided that it would be interesting to see how restaurants work at the other end of the spectrum. I contacted Bottura, and he told me that to understand his business, I would have to spend a full day in the kitchen and another in the dining room. No problem, I told him: On-site visits are a typical part of HBS case studies. Plus, being a native Italian, I always take any excuse I can to visit Italy.

I showed up early on the morning of my first day. As I entered one of the restaurant's three dining rooms, I saw a tall man chatting with the staff—Giuseppe Palmieri, the restaurant's longtime maître d' (called "Il Direttore" at the Osteria) and sommelier. Seeing a new face, he welcomed me with a smile. Everyone calls him "Beppe." Beppe introduced me to Pino, who was apparently going to try to keep me out of trouble. Just a few minutes later, I was polishing dishes and glasses with Pino. Next, we took care of the silverware and then the *mise en place*—getting the tables ready. A few other activities followed, including checking that there were flowers in all the appropriate places, and helping to set the table for the staff meal. As we prepared for our first customers at noon, it dawned on me that Bottura planned to have me do everything, including serve customers, during my time there. I had worked in various low-key restaurants in Italy and in the UK when I was younger, but Bottura did not know this. Putting a novice out in the dining room of a top restaurant—my hands trembling as I placed dishes on the table—seemed a rather odd move, and not one I imagine other owners of fancy restaurants would make.

It was classic Bottura. Many of Bottura's management decisions can seem impulsive. In 2005, two head chefs had joined Osteria Francescana: Kondo Takahiko, known as Taka, had lunch as a customer and, not long after, was cooking in the kitchen; Davide di Fabio had just started the process of sending out applications when he received a phone call from Bottura, offering him a job without even an interview. Bottura first met Beppe while he was working at a big two-Michelin-star restaurant close to Bologna, a place where Bottura and his wife used to dine. On his way home from dinner the first night they met, Bottura called Beppe with a job offer. Many of Bottura's hires happened this way: fast, almost as if by accident.

The second youngest of five children, Bottura grew up in Modena, not far from Osteria Francescana. His mother spent most of the day cooking, alongside her own mother, to feed the children, her husband, a sister-in-law and a brother-in-law who were living with them, and everybody's friends. As a five-year-old boy, Bottura often watched his mother and grandmother cook, curious about the rolling pins they used to make pasta and the interesting tortellini shapes. When his brothers got home from school, they would chase him around the kitchen, using any makeshift weapons they could find. Bottura would hide in his safe spot under the kitchen table, ready to eat the bits of pasta dough that ended up on the floor.

Bottura didn't go to culinary school. His career as a chef was an act of defiance. He had gone to law school to please his father but dropped out after two uninspiring years. In 1986, the Campazzo, a trattoria on the outskirts of Modena, came up for sale. The restaurant was falling apart, and Bottura, twenty-three at the time, had no restaurant experience. But he thought—*why not?* After all, he had done plenty of cooking. When he was still in high school, he and his friends would often find themselves back at Bottura's house after a late night of studying or partying, and he was always the one at the stove. He remembers taking a beach vacation near Salerno, in southern Italy, when he was eighteen. He would use a megaphone to call down to the water, asking what kind of pasta his friends wanted for dinner, carbonara or amatriciana.

Bottura is in his fifties, thin and bearded, with graying hair. He wears chunky, modern, black glasses and comfortable jeans, cuffed at the bottom. His hands are in constant motion. I was with him when a supplier dropped off fresh *mozzarella di bufala*, and he immediately opened the box, carefully lifting out a large, white, creamy ball of mozzarella. A staff member came in with a fork and knife so that he could taste it, but Bottura was already taking big chunks off with his bare hands. "This is simply divine," he said, handing me a piece. "You've got to taste it."

I once asked Bottura who inspired him, and he named the Chinese conceptual artist Ai Weiwei. Trained in the West, Ai combines different traditions, particularly minimalist and conceptual art. One of Ai's performance pieces was *Dropping a Han Dynasty Urn*, in which the artist smashed a two-thousand-year-old historic vase. "Why break thousands of years of history in an instant?" Bottura asked me. "You see, as I came to understand later, Ai's destructive gesture was actually a constructive one. A beginning. Break, transform, create."

MOST BUSINESSES ARE ALL ABOUT FOLLOWING THE RULES, NOT BREAKING THEM. Whether they are standard procedures on how a job needs to be done, a detailed chain of command, or even the dress code on the job, rules can be found everywhere in organizations. Disregard the rules and it will lead to trouble. Even chaos. Rebels are grudgingly tolerated, or, if they become too annoying, they are shown the door.

Bottura was different. In a context where rules had been cemented by centuries of tradition, he could seem utterly reckless—yet, somehow, it all worked in his restaurant, and spectacularly well. In fifteen years of studying businesses, spending time in the environments where people do their work, and talking to executives, I have occasionally run across characters like Bottura: People who are not afraid to break the rules when the rules are holding them back. People who question their own assumptions and strongest beliefs, as well as the widely accepted norms around them, to identify more creative, effective ways of doing transcendent work. People who are "deviants," but in a positive and constructive way.

For years, my academic work led me to study why people cheat on exams or tax forms, or tell lies on speed-dating websites, or don't stop at red lights. I had become an expert on people who break the rules and, rightly so, end up in trouble. But over the years, I also saw how much rule breaking is associated with innovation. I followed stories of corporate corruption and misconduct, yes, but also stories of courage. These were stories of rule breaking that brought about positive change and, in ways big and small, made the world a better place. I found myself wondering, what might we all learn from these people? What are their secrets?

At around the same time that I became curious about these questions, I had also begun to explore another phenomenon. At many of the companies I studied, work was not something that most people enjoyed. I saw the same pattern again and again: Employees would become disengaged after a certain amount of time at a job and would use more and more of their time unproductively—and in ways that made them unhappy and frustrated. Why was this the case? Or, to put it another way: Why does work suck?

On a visit to the Harvard Coop, a local store in Cambridge,

these two ideas came together for me. I was browsing the bookshelves, a cup of coffee in my hand, when a book caught my eye. Its appearance was somewhat unusual (it was large, and merlot in color, with thick gold lettering on its cover), and so was its title: *Never Trust a Skinny Italian Chef.* It was a cookbook, but not a typical one. It was filled with beautiful color photos of unusual, playful dishes, like *La parte croccante della lasagna*, and each was accompanied by the unusual tale of its origin. This is where I first learned the story of Massimo Bottura and how he had sought "to break with tradition and make way for a new Italian kitchen." I know well how Italians value their traditions, and so it was immediately clear to me that Bottura was a rebel. But I also recognized how much he loved his work. This connection—between rule breaking and passion for one's work—was not one I had made before, and yet it seemed powerful. The two so often go together.

I teach at Harvard Business School, but my work is grounded in psychology. Across borders, and between industries, organizations differ in so many respects. And yet they all share one thing: *People* work in them. The confluence between organizations and psychology is fascinating because it allows me to make sense of behaviors that, on the surface, seem to make little or no sense at all. Looking inside an organization raises all sorts of questions—from why we avoid difficult conversations to how we work effectively in teams. To answer them, at a basic level, we need to understand how our minds work—the psychology behind our decisions. This psychological perspective was essential as I sought to understand rebels and the organizations in which they work.

I have found rebels in many places over the last few years, from a Ducati Corse motorcycle racetrack to call centers in remote, rural parts of India. I've traveled the streets of Milan, raced through the desert in the Middle East on quads, and walked the floors of various manufacturing plants. I've talked to musicians, magicians, surgeons, sport coaches, CEOs, and pilots. I've gone behind the scenes of improv theaters and sat through welcoming and training sessions at a professional services firm. I traveled to Pixar in San Francisco, to Valve Software in Seattle, to Goldman Sachs in New York, and to Morning Star in California.

The rebels I met in these organizations came from all walks of life, and each struck me as unique. But all of them have the quality that I have come to call *rebel talent*. In my observations, I have also come to identify five core elements of rebel talent. The first is *novelty*, seeking out challenge and the new. The second is *curiosity*, the impulse we all had as children to constantly ask "why"? The third is *perspective*, the ability rebels have to constantly broaden their view of the world and see it as others do. The fourth is *diversity*, the tendency to challenge predetermined social roles and reach out to those who may appear different. And the fifth is *authenticity*, which rebels embrace in all that they do, remaining open and vulnerable in order to connect with others and learn from them.

As this book progresses, I will explore each of the five elements of rebel talent in more depth, and I will show you how to combine them successfully, like executing a great recipe. Rebellion, as you'll see, is an approach to life and work that we can all embrace. Rule breaking does not have to get us into trouble, if done correctly and in the right doses—in fact, it can help us get ahead. To see this in action, we'll journey to some surprising stages of rebellion, from a Tennessee drive-through of a fast-food chain with a giant hot dog on its roof to Italy's first typewriter factory in the foothills of the Italian Alps. We'll visit rebels at work in high-end hotels, tomato fields, consulting firms, and a Hollywood movie studio. We'll learn from rebels who are willing to be their most vulnerable in front of twenty thousand–plus basketball fans. And I'll ultimately share the eight principles rebels live by, and how we can all be agents of positive change by embracing them. Every one of us, no matter our innate personality or where we are in our career, can be a rebel.

One of the biggest surprises in my research has been the discovery of how important, and meaningful, rebel talent can be in one's personal life. I began this project by trying to understand rule breaking in the workplace. But breaking rules, as I discovered along the way, enriches every aspect of our lives. Living life like a rebel is energizing. I've tried it myself, and it's opened me up to a world of new experiences. As a result, I now drink milk in all sorts of colors for breakfast, wear red sneakers on formal occasions, and am always on the lookout for positive ways of being in the world that may at first feel wrong, or possibly even destructive. My hope is that this book will help you discover your own rebel talent and allow you to help others to do the same. There are strong habits that pull us toward the familiar and comfortable. We need to learn to "break" these habits, like so many Han dynasty urns. Only then will we be ready to transform them—and, ultimately, to create our own success.

1

NAPOLEON AND THE HOODIE

THE PARADOX OF REBEL STATUS

It's not rebels that make trouble, but trouble that makes rebels.
—RUTH MESSINGER

"Forward! Remember that from those monuments yonder, 40 centuries look down upon you." The French soldiers, despite being tired, thirsty, and hungry after marching for twelve hours under the hot Egyptian sun, felt energized by these words from their leader. The Great Pyramids were faintly visible on the horizon, some ten miles away. More clearly visible was the enemy army, waiting for them on the left bank of the Nile.

It was July 21, 1798. Under General Napoleon Bonaparte, the French army was approaching the fortified village of Embabeh, eighteen miles northwest of Cairo. Earlier that year, Bonaparte had proposed invading Egypt, knowing it would provide a new source of income for France and deal a blow to his nation's main European opponent, Britain: Controlling Egypt meant blocking the Red Sea, a major British access route to India. A French invasion might even benefit the Egyptians themselves. The country was ruled by the Mamelukes, descendants of Muslim slave soldiers. The Egyptians had endured the Mamelukes' oppressive rules for centuries and believed the French could save them. Having already secured Alexandria, Bonaparte hoped to next capture Cairo, which would decisively claim the prize of Egypt.

On the enemy side, an estimated six thousand mounted Mameluke soldiers, supported by forty cannons and a small Turkish contingent, were ready for battle. The soldiers' horses pranced and snorted in the heat of the day. Riders were armed with muskets and pistols; javelins made of sharpened palm branches; whatever battle-axes, maces, and daggers they could attach to themselves or their saddles; and short, curved swords made of black Damascus steel. Soldiers had dressed in turbans and caftans for the glory of battle and carried precious jewels and coins. Closer to the Nile and the Embabeh village, some fifteen thousand fellaheen-peasant levies stood, armed mostly with clubs and spears or long-barreled muskets. On the Nile's east bank was a force led by Ibrahim Bey, who, along with Murad Bey, was one of the two Mameluke chieftains. (*Bey* translates as "chieftain.") Under Ibrahim Bey's command were thousands more Mamelukes and about eighteen thousand fellaheen-peasant infantry. On the Nile itself waited a small Mameluke flotilla manned by Greek mercenary sailors. All told, the enemy had over forty thousand troops.

The Mameluke forces clearly outnumbered the French, who had deployed about twenty-five thousand men in five divisions, supported by artillery and a few cavalry troopers. But because of the Mamelukes' position, Bonaparte believed he had an advantage. By placing his troops on the left bank of the Nile, Murad had made a strategic mistake: He saved the French from having to cross the river under fire to attack him. Ibrahim Bey would have to cross the Nile to help Murad Bey if something went wrong. Given this advantage, Bonaparte decided to engage in a decisive battle. After allowing his troops just an hour to rest, he sent orders for each of his divisions to advance on Murad's army.

This wasn't the only advantage Bonaparte saw. He had witnessed the Mamelukes' primary tactic, a cavalry charge, in other battles. After trying to intimidate the enemy with parade maneuvers, the Mameluke cavalry would rush the enemy en masse, often repeatedly, attacking from the flanks or from the rear. The horsemen in these mass cavalry charges, known to be highly skilled in close fighting, approached very close to one another, like a moving wall.

Bonaparte had created what he thought would be an effective countermeasure: the massive divisional square. The square was actually a rectangle—the front and rear faces of it consisted of the division's first and second demi-brigades, while the two sides consisted of the third demi-brigade. The French soldiers lined up in a hollow formation with the artillery and supplies in the center. The army could rotate as the Mamelukes attacked, picking off enemy fighters. An hour into the battle, the French emerged victorious. The Mamelukes had lost about six thousand men; the French, only thirty.

The victory had many legacies: the eviction of the Mamelukes, the liberation of the Egyptians, further expansion of the French empire into the East, and increased French domination of mainland Europe. And thanks to the 150-plus scientists, engineers, and artists that Bonaparte brought on the journey, the victory spurred an exploration of Egypt's past and present. The birth of Egyptology revealed the secrets of the pyramids and the society that built them. In addition, Egypt was influenced by its new relationship with France and its culture, as seen in its later adoption of the Napoleonic Code.

Bonaparte's brilliant strategies have formed the basis of military education throughout the Western world. When planning a campaign, determined to be thoroughly prepared and to avoid the errors of previous generals, he would read books about his opponent's history, geography, and culture. Always, he strived for surprise. Sometimes that meant striking a decisive blow when the enemy was off guard. In an era when armies tended to march against each other in an orderly, gentlemanly formation, Bonaparte led his troops into position at a very fast speed, surrounding the enemy before they even realized he was there.

Bonaparte revolutionized warfare by introducing the corps system, which rendered the tactics of other countries virtually obsolete. The corps system organized troops into mini-armies, allowing them to separate when marching, but always to come together when it was time to fight. The corps would move within a day's march of each other; each changed into the rearguard, vanguard, or reserve quickly, depending on what the situation demanded and on the enemy's movement. Since France's defeat in the Seven Years' War in 1763, military strategists and theorists had been struggling with how the country could improve, and Napoleon was France's new savior. The military expedition to Egypt that he led in 1798 cemented the growing belief in his abilities and would serve as a springboard to power for him. Thanks to a coup he engineered in 1799, at just thirty years of age, he became First Consul of the Republic. Even as his political career advanced, Bonaparte continued to carefully study the works of successful generals, tacticians, and officers and put their ideas to practical use on the battlefield. For instance, the core idea behind Bonaparte's strategy of the central position came from Pierre de Bourcet, a chief of staff who was part of the royal armies in various wars, including the Seven Years' War. The strategy involved splitting numerically superior enemy armies into parts so that each could be attacked separately. Another tactic Bonaparte often used was the *ordre mixte* formation: He mixed line and column formations so that a battalion in line was supported on each wing by an infantry battalion column. Though Bonaparte did not invent these concepts, he perfected them, and his radical, strategic mind heralded the birth of modern warfare.

Bonaparte also fought in the trenches alongside the troops, which was highly unusual. Historians believe that his men nicknamed him "the little corporal" during the Battle of Lodi in May 1796, after he took over the sighting of one of the cannons himself, a job typically performed by a corporal. When his army faced direct fire, he was usually in the thick of it. At a critical moment on the first day of the Battle of Arcole in November 1796, for instance, Bonaparte rallied his troops by seizing the colors of one of his battalions and exposing himself to intense Austrian fire until one of his officers dragged him away. When the fighting was over and the enemy's guns fell silent, Bonaparte would generally rise up sweaty, dirty, and covered in gunpowder. He also made an effort to remember his soldiers' names and visited their campfires before battle, chatting with them about home and expressing confidence that they would triumph over the enemy. In Bonaparte's army, soldiers from humble backgrounds could rise through the ranks to become officers, as Bonaparte himself had done.

This same spirit guided his political reforms. At the time of the French Revolution, laws were often not applied equally to all people, and they were not even codified. By introducing the Napoleonic Code, Bonaparte created a legal system based on the idea that everyone was equal before the law. The code forbade birthright privilege, granted freedom of religion, and indicated that government jobs should be awarded based on merit, not rank. Dozens of nations around the world later adopted the code. Bonaparte ensured that the tax system applied equally to everyone. And, recognizing the importance of education, he introduced reforms that served as the foundation of the educational system in France and much of Europe today. He also implemented various liberal reforms to civil affairs, from abolishing feudalism and establishing legal equality to codifying religious tolerance and legalizing divorce. Bonaparte's contributions to the institutions of France and to Europe were large and long lasting.

Historians have often portrayed Bonaparte as power hungry and driven by hubris. But British historian Andrew Roberts in the biography *Napoleon: A Life* makes a compelling case for why this interpretation of Bonaparte's story is misguided, arguing that his downfall was caused not by a big ego, but by a few mistakes that led to significant defeats. Others disagree with this interpretation. There is no doubt, though, that when it came to battle strategy, Bonaparte was an outlier. Europe's other monarchs adhered to a strict military hierarchy in which recruitment and promotion were based on wealth and noble titles rather than qualifications and skills. Many of Bonaparte's contemporaries kept their distance from the troops, sending their generals out to lead while they spared themselves the fight. Bonaparte did things differently: He threw himself into the fray.

ON A COLD FEBRUARY MORNING IN BOSTON, I STRUGGLED THROUGH A HEAVY SNOW-storm on my walk to work. In my classroom at Harvard Business School, 110 eager executives, all with quite remarkable résumés, were unbundling themselves and taking their seats, ready for a session on "Managing Talent." I'd be teaching them about Morning Star, the largest tomato-processing company in the world and the subject of a case study—a ten- to fifteen-page article based on intensive research and interviews—I had written. The case focused on the company's unorthodox operations. There are no bosses or job titles at Morning Star. The company's employees decide for themselves how their skills can best help the company and then develop their own mission statements, which they discuss with colleagues before making them final.

Morning Star employees do not need to run upgrades by managers. Instead they go to the experts: the employees who would be working with the new equipment. Though the company has no R&D department, strong incentives exist to encourage innovation. Employees who successfully innovate earn the respect of coworkers, in addition to financial compensation. One of the dilemmas presented in the case was the decision to introduce a new compensation system, and whether it was consistent with the core philosophy the company was founded on.

Class began, and though case discussions generally open with a question about the challenge a protagonist is facing, I instead led the executives in a short free-association exercise. What comes to mind, I asked, when you hear the phrase "rule breaking"?

"Chaos," said the CEO of a global restaurant chain. "Disorder," shouted another student. I wrote these words on the blackboard. Some of the students' answers were positive: innovation, creativity, flexibility. Most, however, were negative: crime, rebellion, rejection, loss of reputation, misconduct, illegality, dissonance, penalty, punishment, fights, and deviance.

Terms like *rule breaker*, *nonconformity*, and *deviance* make us think of subversive, even dangerous, individuals. One student brought up Wells Fargo, where employees had created millions of fake savings and checking accounts in the names of real customers. After clients discovered they'd been charged unanticipated fees and issued credit and debit cards and lines of credit they hadn't asked for, regulatory bodies had fined the bank $185 million and the bank had fired more than 5,300 employees.

Another student mentioned Bernie Madoff, the financier who had persuaded thousands of investors to trust him with their savings. With his creative rule breaking, Madoff had made more than $20 billion disappear in a Ponzi scheme that presented itself as a hedge fund. He's now serving a 150-year prison sentence for running one of the biggest frauds in U.S. history.

Most of our decisions are governed by well-defined institutional arrangements with pre-specified obligations and rights. Some of these arrangements are relatively straightforward, like signing an apartment lease or hiring a babysitter. Others are more complex, like our relationships with government and corporations, which come with explicit rules. For instance, organizations use company handbooks to establish policies ranging from vacation time to codes of conduct. We generally expect people to obey these rules and codes of conduct. But this was not the case at Wells Fargo, where employees had betrayed their duty to act in the best interest of customers, or with Madoff, who had filed false regulatory reports and lied to his clients.

We also adhere to social norms—unwritten rules about how to behave in a particular culture, society, or social group, ranging from a friendship to a work team to a nation. For example, we expect students to arrive to class on time and complete their work. We expect people to be silent in libraries, to not interrupt us when we are talking, and (at least in most groups) to wear clothes in public. Social norms provide order and predictability in society and have played a critical role in the evolution and maintenance of cooperation and culture over centuries. Children as young as two or three years old understand the rules governing many social interactions. Usually, we internalize social norms so effectively that we don't even consider the possibility of violating them. To do so would be embarrassing or distasteful. Violators tend to be punished with gossip, derision, and rumors—all of which are powerful corrective measures that influence how we behave. In colonial America, a person caught breaking social norms, such as stealing or committing adultery, was confined to the stocks or pillory in the center of town. These long confinements were uncomfortable, but even worse was the realization that everyone you cared about would know what you did.

Shared rules make society run smoothly. In the military, recruits are taught from day one to follow orders, immediately and without question. In fact, those who enlist in the U.S. military, active duty or reserve, solemnly swear to obey the orders of their officers. For thousands of years, military leaders across the globe have maintained a strict hierarchy to keep order under the stress of battle.

Bonaparte ran things a little differently. In 1793, as a twenty-four-year-old captain, he was given the opportunity to take control of the artillery during the Battle of Toulon. The city was a key port, occupied at the time by antirevolutionary British forces. If the French revolutionaries did not triumph, they would not be able to build a navy to defy Britain's dominance of the sea. Suffocation of the French Revolution would follow.

One battery in particular was critical to the bombardment due to its elevated terrain. But it was also the most vulnerable to counterattack, thus making it the most dangerous to operate. Bonaparte's superiors informed him that no soldier would volunteer to man the battery. Walking through camp in contemplation, he spotted a printing machine, which gave him an idea. He created a sign to hang near the battery: "The battery of the men without fear." When the other soldiers saw it the next morning, they clamored to earn the honor of operating that cannon. Bonaparte himself wielded a ramrod alongside his gunners. The cannon was manned day and night. The French won the battle; Bonaparte won acclaim.

To break the rules is not necessarily to become an outcast. Madoff, of course, deserves to be in jail. Wells Fargo deserves its fines. But Bonaparte broke the rules and, rightly, earned status and respect. He is a prime example of how a rebel can be a hero.

BACK IN THE NINETEENTH CENTURY, THE WEALTHY POPULATIONS OF EUROPE AND the United States typically adorned themselves in diamond-studded jewelry and overindulged in rich foods and potent drinks. In the United States at the time, middle-class extravagance often went even further, including things like bathtubs cut from solid marble, waterfalls installed in dining rooms, and garden trees decorated with artificial fruit made of fourteen-karat gold. From an economic perspective, this behavior made little sense. People in the middle class were spending as if they were rich.

The behavior caught the attention of the Norwegian-American sociologist and economist Thorstein Veblen, who is known for challenging many of the economic theories of the era. Veblen concluded that this kind of spending demonstrated that the buyer was able to "waste" money and that the real point of it was to enhance status. The lavish spending of the rich "redounded to their glory, and now the middle class was using its newfound wealth to purchase elite status." Veblen famously dubbed this phenomenon "conspicuous consumption": choosing and displaying obviously expensive products—such as sports cars, expensive watches, and luxury clothes—rather than their cheaper, functional equivalents. Conspicuous consumption signals to the world our financial success, even if the success is mostly on loan.

As it turns out, we engage in this kind of costly signaling all the time. Many of the personal qualities that we want to convey to others are not directly observable, such as commitment, dedication, cooperativeness, or persistence. As a result, you may spend hours in yoga classes not because you really take pleasure in yoga, but because you want to show your partner that you are a disciplined person. Similarly, you might choose to attend an expensive business school to communicate your prestige, smarts, and persistence to future employers.

Signals such as fast cars, fancy suits, and jewelry share an important feature: They aren't cheap. And even absent financial burden, those yoga classes we secretly dread rob time and effort from activities we actually enjoy. Signals can also involve personal risk. Wearing expensive jewelry can attract thieves as well as admirers, and signaling toughness through gang tattoos might catch the eye of the police.

This type of public grandstanding is common in the animal world, too. Israeli ethologist Amotz Zahavi noted that animals often engage in showy and even dangerous displays of courage to attract mates and raise their status. Male peacocks show off their gorgeous plumage in part to demonstrate to females that they can support the heavy weight, an evolutionary disadvantage. (Large tail feathers translate into slower running and a reduced ability to hide from predators.) Antelopes often engage in *slotting*: They leap acrobatically straight into the air when hungry cheetahs are pursuing them, even though sprinting straight for the horizon is the better move. The animals' dangerous waste of energy conveys strength, telling the cheetah, "Don't even bother trying." Similarly, guppies swim right under their predators' noses before darting away. In evolution, it seems, survival of the fittest only captures part of the story.

From one perspective, Bonaparte's decision to join "the battery of men without fear" seems foolish. He was, by the social rules of the time, working beneath his level. He was also risking his life. But by taking these burdens on himself, for all to see, he was sending a costly signal—that his talent allowed him to break the rules, to serve, and to lead his charges to victory. This is an important insight of the rebel mindset.

ON MAY 7, 2012, A CROWD OF PAPARAZZI GREETED A BLACK SUV AS IT ARRIVED AT the Sheraton hotel in Manhattan's Times Square just before one p.m. Facebook's cofounder and CEO, Mark Zuckerberg, stepped from the car and was escorted into the hotel by security guards. For Zuckerberg, it was the kick-off event of a cross-country initial public offering roadshow: a presentation to potential institutional investors, a prelude to any IPO. CFO David Ebersman and COO Sheryl Sandberg joined him onstage to discuss the deal. About 50 bankers and 550 investors, most dressed in suits, packed the hotel and formed a snaking line around the block, watched by police, clipboard-carrying staffers, and members of the press. The stern-looking security guards ensured that only invitees would hear the presentation.

Facebook's was perhaps the most anticipated IPO in the history of the tech industry. The company had experienced rapid growth in recent years. In 2012, it was responsible for 56 percent of all shared content online, far surpassing email, which ranked a distant second with 15 percent. By taking the company public, Zuckerberg would cement his place in history, reward the investors who had backed him, and firmly establish that, among the many failed social networking sites of the era, he alone had found the right formula to create a lasting online powerhouse.

The meeting lived up to expectations, introducing what turned out to be the biggest technology IPO to date, with a peak market capitalization of over $104 billion. Interestingly, though, one of the big headlines from that day concerned Zuckerberg's attire. Like Steve Jobs and Albert Einstein before him, Zuckerberg didn't waste any mental energy on the trappings of fashion. Instead, he appeared onstage in the casual, fashionless uniform of the typical software engineer: gray T-shirt, black hoodie, comfortable blue jeans, and simple black sneakers. The entire ensemble had probably cost less than $150.

"Mark and his signature hoodie: He's actually showing investors he doesn't care that much; he's going to be him," Michael Pachter, an analyst with Wedbush Securities, told Bloomberg TV. "I think that's a mark of immaturity. I think that he has to realize he's bringing investors in as a new constituency right now, and I think he's got to show them the respect that they deserve because he's asking them for their money."

In fact, Zuckerberg was not the first tech whiz whose wardrobe choices at key business meetings raised eyebrows. When a young Bill Gates was about to take Microsoft public back in 1986, the story goes, a PR consultant nearly wrestled him to the ground to force him to swap his patented floppy sweater for a tailored suit. Steve Jobs initially made concessions to sartorial tradition, but after Apple made so many people rich, he went back to his trademark black mock turtlenecks. For these leaders, dressing down meant flouting social norms for proper business attire. They weren't oblivious to corporate dress codes, but they intentionally decided to defy convention.

We generally have a clear sense of how to match behavior with context. For example, we expect the audience to be quiet at the symphony and loud at rock concerts, for executives to wear relatively formal clothing at meetings, and so on. Rules and norms in organizations and, more broadly, in society instill order and predictability. But as with conspicuous consumption and public generosity, something very powerful happens when we act in ways that are unconventional or unexpected.

If you were to stroll down New York's Fifth Avenue from one luxury boutique to the next, you'd expect to see well-dressed shoppers carrying bags filled with thousands of dollars' worth of merchandise. This would fit your expectations of relevant social norms. But, as it turns out, those who subvert these expectations may be more likely to attract our admiration, my research shows.

Rome is the capital of Italy, but Milan is the country's fashion capital. Postcards of the northern city generally depict its classic Gothic cathedral, the impressive shopping mall Galleria Vittorio Emanuele II (the oldest in the world), and the well-known opera house Teatro alla Scala. But when I visit the city, I always like to take a stroll down the "fashion quadrilateral," which consists of Via Manzoni, Via Monte Napoleone, Via della Spiga, and Corso Venezia. Along these four streets you can find luxurious boutiques, both

Italian and foreign, from Bottega Veneta, Armani, Valentino, and Prada to Chanel, Burberry, Dior, Kenzo, and Hermès. No matter what you are wearing, it is easy to feel underdressed as you pass the store windows. Nearby, imposing houses with high, ivy-covered walls, lattice doors, miniature fountains, and beautiful courtyards help make this one of the noblest areas in the city.

In 2012, when I traveled with colleagues to Milan to conduct an experiment, we homed in on the fashion quadrilateral, knowing we were in the perfect place to learn more about the signals that clothing sends. For our research, we asked shop assistants working in luxury-brand boutiques to respond to a survey. Each read one of two versions of a vignette in which a woman about thirty-five years old entered the boutique. In one version, she had a dress on and a fur coat; in the other, she wore gym clothes. The shop assistants rated the woman's promise as a client by answering questions about how likely it was that she would make a purchase. They were also asked to rate the likelihood that the woman was a celebrity or a VIP. We used these surveys as measures of the potential customer's perceived status.

Contrary to what you might expect, the elegant woman in fur projected less status than the woman in gym clothes. The shop assistants had the strong suspicion that the dressed-down customer was intentionally deviating from the norms of appropriate behavior. "Wealthy people sometimes dress very badly to demonstrate superiority," one shop assistant said. "If you dare to enter these boutiques so underdressed, you are definitely going to buy something." Context is everything. When we presented a similar scenario to people at Milan's central train station, they said the dressed-up woman, not the dressed-down one, had higher status.

This is not just a high-fashion phenomenon. We surveyed American college students and asked them to react to a description of a professor teaching at a top-tier school. For some students, we described the forty-five-year-old professor as wearing a T-shirt and having a beard. For others, we described him as clean-shaven and wearing a tie. The students rated the professor in a T-shirt as having higher status. The perception that an individual is consciously *choosing not to conform* is critical.

To signal status, deviations from the norm must demonstrate one's autonomy to behave consistently with one's own inclinations and to pay for the cost of nonconformity. In another study, we found that participants perceived a guest wearing a red bow tie at a black-tie party at a country club as having higher status—and even being a better golfer—than a conforming club member wearing a black bow tie. The man in the red bow tie was not seen as clueless, but as a master of his domain—a rebel.

A FEW YEARS AGO, I WAS ASKED TO TEACH TWO BACK-TO-BACK, NINETY-MINUTE executive education classes at Harvard Business School for ICIC, the Initiative for a Competitive Inner City. I was intrigued by the opportunity. Founded in 1994 by HBS professor Michael Porter, ICIC is a national nonprofit organization that conducts research and advisory work on the economies and businesses of inner-city neighborhoods in the United States. The organization focuses on neighborhoods with poverty rates of 20 percent or higher, and with unemployment rates greater than those found in metropolitan areas. About a hundred business, government, and philanthropic leaders from more than a dozen cities would participate in each of the two sessions, hoping to refine their negotiation and influence skills. This is a topic I regularly teach at the executive level, and one that participants generally find valuable, as the applications to real-world settings are easy to see.

For those teaching executive-level classes at HBS, expectations are always high. As a professor, you are well aware of the students' time being especially precious, and you certainly don't want to waste it. Often, they are a tough crowd to please, clock-conscious and deeply experienced. In addition to wanting my students to learn, I also want their respect; after all, if they see me as influential and high in status, they will be more likely to listen closely and remember what I teach. The class I was about to lead typically requires hours of preparation. I needed to be clear, professional, direct—and properly dressed. Not being a big fan of skirts, my dress code for executive teaching consists of a conservative suit over a blouse or dress shirt, and a pair of dressy leather shoes.

But the back-to-back sessions I would be teaching to two sets of ICIC students were exactly the same, so I decided to use the day as an opportunity for a little experiment on the effects of attire on status determinations. Specifically, during the break after the first class, I slipped off my leather shoes and laced up a pair of red Converse sneakers. Just imagine: I was wearing a dark blue Hugo Boss suit, a white silk blouse, and a pair of very red, very non-dressy shoes. Colleagues gave me strange looks as I made my way back to the classroom.

It is often difficult to tell whether students are engaging with the material and enjoying your classes. But I could sense a tangible difference between the two classes that day: The red-sneakers class seemed more attentive and thoughtful, and they laughed more. Part of the difference, I realized, was likely due not only to the sneakers, but to the effect they had on me. I didn't feel more self-conscious, despite the reaction of my colleagues. Rather, I felt more confident. Even though I was teaching brand-new material, I felt more certain about its effectiveness, more poised when leading discussions, and more adept when making transitions.

At the end of each session that day, I asked the students to complete a short survey assessing my professional status and competence. For instance, I asked them to guess at my status within the school and how likely my research was to be featured in the *Harvard Business Review*. Interestingly, the students viewed me as having greater status when I wore the red shoes. They also thought my consulting rate was higher. All thanks to a pair of red sneakers.

After the second session, I bounced back to my office thinking the red-sneakers test was worth expanding on. So I devised an experiment in which I invited college students to complete a task that most of us would view as stressful (at least, without a few beers): singing the Journey song "Don't Stop Believin'" in front of an audience of peers. Before the performance, I asked half the students to wear something that they agreed would make them feel uncomfortable—namely, a bandanna wrapped around their heads. (The bandanna, I expected, would serve as the nonconforming behavior—the headgear version of my red sneakers.) The other group did not wear a bandanna. With help from the karaoke machine, I measured note-hitting accuracy, as well as heart rate and confidence. The bandanna-wearing students sang better, had significantly lower heart rates, and also reported feeling more confident.

We all have opportunities to boost our confidence through nonconforming behaviors. In another study, I recruited a few hundred employees from different companies and asked some of them to behave in nonconforming ways at work over the next three weeks, such as voicing their disagreements with their colleagues' decisions, expressing their true ideas or feelings rather than those they were expected to have, or proposing ideas that colleagues might find unconventional. I asked others to behave in conforming ways for three weeks, such as staying quiet and nodding along even when they disagreed with a colleague's decision. And then I asked another set of individuals, the control group, to behave as usual during this time. After the three weeks had passed, members of the first group indicated that they felt more confident and engaged in their jobs than members of the other two groups. They were also more creative when completing a task I gave them as part of a three-week follow-up survey, and their supervisors rated them higher on both innovativeness and performance.

Nonconformity can enhance not only our professional lives, but our personal lives as well. When hanging out with friends, we've all found ourselves nodding along during a discussion, even when we seriously disagree with the argument being made. And at times, we may express emotions we don't feel just to please those close to us. Or we might dress to fit in with a group, or order the same dish as our date even if we'd rather have something different. In research similar to my field study on employees and conformity, I asked a large group of college and MBA students to behave in ways that were conforming or nonconforming in their personal lives outside of work for a few weeks. The results of engaging in nonconforming behaviors were equally beneficial in the students' personal lives. Nonconforming behaviors (such as expressing true preferences in social circles rather than going along with the majority opinion) improved their happiness in their day-to-day interactions. Interestingly, the participants had predicted just the opposite.

Despite our differences, we all share the desire to be happy. What my research suggests is that we can actually bring more joy into our lives by being rebels: by behaving in ways that defy conformity. And something as simple as a pair of red sneakers might make all the difference.

A MAN, LIKELY IN HIS THIRTIES, SITS AT A SMALL TABLE OUTSIDE A CAFÉ IN AMsterdam. Behind him, two picture windows reveal some of the life inside the café—menus on the walls, a large espresso machine, and waiters bustling to bring drinks and food to customers. This man is the protagonist of a short video clip that University of Amsterdam psychologist Gerben Van Kleef and his colleagues created for an experiment. Two versions of the video were shot. In the first version, the man violates what we would all probably agree are norms of proper public behavior: He puts his feet on another chair and flicks his cigarette ash to the ground. After consulting the menu, he doesn't return it to its stand. And when the waitress asks for his order, he brusquely answers, "Bring me a vegetarian sandwich and a sweet coffee." He does not reply when the waitress says, "Right away." In the second version of the video, he behaves politely, crossing his legs and using the ashtray on the table. He also carefully returns the menu to the stand. And when the waitress asks for his order, he replies with a much more polite, "May I have a vegetarian sandwich and a sweet coffee, please?" and then thanks her when she says, "Right away."

Imagine how you'd feel if you were waiting on the man in the first video. Having worked as a waitress when I was younger, I can say with confidence that he would have annoyed me. After all, being polite and respectful doesn't require very much effort. Nor does sitting properly in a chair. Unfortunately, all of us encounter such irritating rule-breaking behavior on a regular basis. Someone puts their package on the only vacant train seat, so that you have to ask them to move it to sit down. Your boss walks abruptly into your office without knocking, interrupting your private phone call. A loud conversation in the movie theater distracts you from the film. A friend looks at her cell phone constantly during dinner. In these cases, rule breaking has gone too far, from the realm of the admirable to the realm of the annoying. But even if these norm violators drive us crazy, we still view them as powerful, research says.

In Van Kleef's experiment, participants were divided into two groups, with half being asked to watch the first version of the video and the other half being asked to watch the second version. After watching, each participant answered a few questions about their reactions to the man depicted, including how powerful they viewed him to be. The result? Participants who watched the man violate norms in the first video were more likely to see him as powerful than those who watched him conform in the second video.

Power is typically associated with lack of constraint, and we think of powerful people as generally having the freedom to behave as they wish. Indeed, as you may have noticed in your own professional and personal life, people *in* powerful positions and those who *feel* powerful often act without fear of negative consequences. In one study, people who felt powerful were more likely than those who felt less powerful to switch off an annoying fan while working on a task that required concentration—they were less concerned about what the experimenter might think. Whether power is real or simply perceived, it leads us to take more risks, express stronger emotions and views, act based on our natural inclinations and impulses, and ignore situational pressure.

We perceive people who interrupt others as more assertive than those who don't interrupt, and those who express anger as mightier than those who express sadness, a more socially acceptable emotion. As people gain power, they feel greater freedom to defy conventions. Paradoxically, these violations may not undermine their power but instead augment it, thus fueling a self-perpetuating cycle of power and rule breaking that can go too far, as with people like Bernie Madoff. The link between nonconformity, power, and status leads us to a deeper question: How should we use the power and status that we gain throughout our careers?

IT'S EARLY MORNING AT VIA STELLA, 22, ON A PICTURESQUE COBBLED STREET IN the center of Modena, Italy. There is a discreet coral-colored façade, and the only indication that one has arrived at Osteria Francescana is a small brass sign bearing its name. The scene gets more lively around nine a.m., when the staff starts showing up for work. Noise from the engine of a black Ducati motorcycle fills the street: Bottura arriving not long after his team. Within minutes, he has put on his white chef's coat and grabbed a broom to start sweeping the pavement outside the restaurant.

Bottura regularly takes on tasks that other chefs couldn't be bothered with. It's Bottura who waits for the cargos of fresh produce, fish, and meat. He is the one who jumps onto the back of the truck, opening up the big boxes to inspect the produce and ask the deliverymen about it. When his questions are answered, he helps unload the truck. This is part of the excitement of working at Osteria Francescana. Everyone at the restaurant knows that there are no pre-defined roles that will box them in. Everyone is free to work on tasks that in other restaurants would be assigned to a particular individual. At most places, only the delivery person unloads the produce from the truck, and only the pastry chef prepares the desserts, but at Osteria Francescana this is not the case. Everyone is free to experiment with ideas and to challenge their "leader" with a unique perspective. And Bottura himself shows little regard, maybe even contempt, for the idea of tradition-bound roles. Right before service, he joins his staff for a meal. In between services, he is either helping with cleanup or playing soccer with the staff outside of the restaurant. None of this is typical chef behavior. Bottura's troops are so devoted because they have seen him on the front line, and they are inspired to greatness.

2

THE DOG NAMED "HOT"

A TALENT FOR NOVELTY

The first kiss is magic. The second is intimate. The third is routine.
—RAYMOND CHANDLER

A man steps to the center of a small stage, pulls up a brown leather chair, and sits down. He is wearing a sleeveless white shirt and loose-fitting jeans. I'm sitting offstage with my husband, Greg, and a group of about a dozen other people. We're in a large room, used by a local public school during the day, and in one section there are different areas set up for children's activities—drawing and painting, reading, LEGOs. The lights are dim.

The man extends his hands, as if gripping an imaginary steering wheel, and starts to drive. I rise from my seat and step onto the stage, pull up another chair, and sit next to him. "Welcome to the *Enterprise*," he says. "Did you hear about the new uniform-making machine?"

"Yeah," I say. "I was disappointed when I heard about it. After our last meeting, I was hoping that we would focus on another product to launch our business. Didn't we think striped underpants would be the next big thing?"

Laughter.

Another woman, Rachel, rises from the audience and taps my shoulder. I return to my seat, and the scene continues. "I wasn't sure what to say," I whisper to my husband, "but somehow people found it funny."

Greg smiles. "You didn't get it? You totally missed the reference. That was *Star Trek*. Eric was doing Captain Kirk. So you took the scene in a pretty different direction." Eric wasn't driving a car—he was commanding the USS *Enterprise*.

Greg and I were in Central Square, Cambridge, not far from where we were living at the time, at a beginner's improv comedy class I had signed us up for—two-hour sessions across ten consecutive Mondays. That night we were playing an improv game called "actor switch," in which one player starts a scene and is soon joined by another. New players step in one at a time, tapping the shoulder of someone already onstage to replace him or her, building on the original story and characters. Nothing is decided in advance, but after only a few seconds, the group has cooperatively established a basic dramatic frame. By the end of the scene, we've managed to develop a rather complex (and pretty funny) scene.

In improv, you go with the flow. Maybe you're not crazy about the choices of the person who came before you, but you accept the terms of the scene and then add to it, rather than contradicting it. So, if the first player says "This is an apple," you shouldn't reply "No, it is a rather small melon." That might buy you a laugh, but it would kill the scene. It's much better to follow the "yes, and" principle that lies at the heart of improv: "Yes, and we can fill it with poison before we offer it to the queen." The story I've just told wasn't the first (or last) time I completely missed a classmate's cultural reference. (I have yet to watch *Star Trek*.) But if I hadn't been willing to miss these cues and go with it, I wouldn't have had as much fun.

Improv is all about performing without preparation and without a script—responding to others in the moment, listening to your inner voice, and bursting out with whatever comes to mind. The British-Canadian director, playwright, actor, and improv pioneer Keith Johnstone once noted that improvisation is like steering a car by looking through the rearview mirror: You don't know where you're going; you can only see where you've been.

The improv experiment was a Christmas present I gave to Greg in 2011, before parenthood made it harder to go out on weeknights. I thought it would be a good gift since we would spend some time together on a regular basis, involved in a totally new activity—one that consisted, in my mind, of just making fun of ourselves and laughing a lot. But that wasn't my only motive. Recent research suggests that if we inject novelty into our romantic relationships, we'll stay more engaged in them and experience greater satisfaction in the long run. Greg and I were happy. From the first time we met, in the security line at Logan International Airport, our relationship had always felt natural and easy, even when our different cultures—I'm Italian, and he was born in Warner Robins, Georgia—introduced differences of perspective. But I knew how easy it is for marriages to suffer the grind of routine. What, I wondered, would happen if we had a weekly date with the unexpected?

IT HAD ALL BEEN DECIDED: ON JUNE 27, 2009, GREG AND I WOULD GET MARRIED IN Tione di Trento, my hometown of three thousand people in the mountains of northern Italy. Picture a warm summer afternoon, the perfume from daisies and roses hanging in the air as a gentle fresh breeze dances between the vaulted ceilings of an old church, its main door open, waiting for the guests to enter. A little orchestra of clarinets, trombones, and flutes plays softly as the groom waits nervously for his bride . . .

We were excited. Maybe even more excited was my mum, who

would finally see a church wedding for one of her three children, complete with all the important traditions. My brother had decided against marriage, though he had settled down with his partner and two children. My sister and her husband had tied the knot at City Hall.

Months before the wedding, I bought my white wedding dress. I also bought a garter, following a tradition that dates to the fourteenth century, when it was thought that the guest who departed with a piece of the bridal trousseau would be blessed with good luck. The groom had his own rituals to honor, including supplying the bridal bouquet as a final gift to his girlfriend before she became his wife. And then there would be the *bomboniere* with *confetti*: wedding favors with sugared almonds for the guests. For a traditional Italian wedding, the almonds must be coated in white sugar, and the number given must always be odd. Why? Because marriage unites two people, and the amount must never be divisible by two. With the wedding over, we would go on a *luna di miele*, or honeymoon—so named because in ancient Rome, newlyweds would spend an entire phase of the moon eating a portion of honey at every mealtime.

Of course, respect for tradition is about as uniquely Italian as a bride in a white dress. In Indian weddings, couples recite seven vows and aren't considered legally married until they've taken seven steps around a holy fire, after which seven married women greet them. In Vietnam, families of the bride and groom avoid the number seven at all costs because it brings bad luck. Throughout Latin American, a *quinceañera*, the coming-of-age celebration for a girl's fifteenth birthday, often involves fathers changing their daughters' shoes from flats to high heels. In Japan, during the traditional coming-of-age day, Seijin no Hi, parents present their daughters with a pair of flat zori sandals.

From celebrating religious beliefs to mobilizing political action, rituals and traditions have a long history across societies. Today they are ubiquitous forces, from our family lives to the workplace to the locker room. Notre Dame football players walk an identical route from the university basilica to the stadium before kickoff, while employees at companies such as Walmart and New Balance begin the day with chants and stretches. Such rituals, my research shows, improve group performance. For instance, in a scavenger hunt that my colleagues and I organized through the streets of Boston, groups who practiced rituals together during the event performed better than those who didn't. Another study, this one of over two hundred people working in many different types of jobs across industries, found that they were more satisfied by their jobs when they regularly engaged in meaningful workplace rituals—including playing their own version of Bingo with their colleagues and, when they worked on a Saturday, regularly shouting out "half time" about halfway through the day and doing a "happy dance."

One of the main purposes of rituals and traditions is to impart and nourish values. At home, daily family prayers emphasize the importance of faith; nightly bedtime stories affirm the value of education, reading, and lifelong learning; and regular family dinners or activities strengthen our most cherished bonds. In time, shared values gain the power of treasured memories. On the flipside, given the meaning and closeness that traditions reinforce, broken traditions can give rise to disappointment.

Nearly a year before our perfect Italian wedding, Greg and I learned this lesson firsthand. It was a sunny morning in early September in 2008, when we were living in Chapel Hill, North Carolina. While sipping coffee on our porch, we finally agreed that it was time to call my family. Almost two weeks earlier, on August 20, Greg and I had gotten married at City Hall to address some of the legal issues related to an Italian marrying an American in the United States. I still hadn't told my mum. I knew she'd be very upset at the news, even furious. She would probably yell at me for breaking from such an important tradition.

"It's not a big deal," Greg reassured me. Our real wedding—the traditional one we had so carefully planned—was still set to take place in Italy the following summer. I dialed my mum's phone number. As soon as she picked up, I said: "Mum, I have some wonderful news to share."

"You are pregnant?"

"No," I said. "Greg and I got married!"

Click. She had hung up.

When I finally got her on the line again, days later, she did yell at me, as I'd expected. She was furious that there hadn't been a single family member present to celebrate one of the most meaningful moments in her child's life. There were no wedding-themed pictures of the family, no memories she could cherish. In time, though, she got over it; I had my Italian wedding with my family all around us, and all turned out well.

Rituals can bring us together and imbue life with deeper meaning, but often they also rob us of something equally valuable—the experience that comes with making difficult decisions. Planning my Italian wedding was rather easy, as most of my choices were already made for me. (The hardest decision we faced was picking a date.) But the process was also short on opportunities to challenge and surprise myself. In the grip of tradition, we miss out on novelty—and therefore the excitement of working without a script. Boredom, or something worse—any kind of mindless complacency—can creep up on us. The rebel—always trying new things, the way Greg and I did with improv—fares better.

We stick to traditions and old ways of doing things because, at least in part, we figure there must be a good reason for them. In one study, for instance, a team of Yale researchers found that children model themselves after adults so faithfully that they even copy their mistakes. In one of the study's exercises, a group of three- to five-year-old children could see a dinosaur toy that had been placed in a clear plastic container. A researcher followed different steps to retrieve the toy, some of which were useful, such as unscrewing the lid, and some of which were not, such as tapping the side of the container with a feather before removing it. The children had to indicate which steps were silly and which made sense, winning praise when they identified the former. This was done to show that the adult could not be trusted and that the unnecessary steps he had used could be safely ignored. Later, the children watched adults as they took a toy turtle out of a container using needless steps. When they performed the task themselves, the children still over-imitated, squandering time and effort in the same way that the adults had. In fact, when children see an adult taking a prize from a container by a method that both adults and chimpanzees can easily identify as both inefficient and clumsy, they seem to lose the ability to figure out how to open the container "correctly." In other words, watching an adult do something wrong prevents kids from figuring out how to do it right.

Experience would seem to be the cure, but on the contrary, studies show that over-imitation actually increases as we age, with adults performing irrelevant actions with higher levels of fidelity than preschoolers. Hard to believe? Ask yourself the following: When trying to understand some new, complicated device, like a computer, how often have you followed on faith the instructions of an expert? If you're like me, the answer is very often, as you may (or may not) find out later when someone else points out a simpler way to operate the device. Much of what we "know" is really only trust in someone else's knowledge. After all, we conclude, if a practice has been around for a long time, there must be a very good reason for it, right?

In one study examining this phenomenon, I brought groups of four participants into a room where a team of paid actors was folding T-shirts. Some groups saw teams using an efficient process to fold T-shirts, while other groups saw teams adding a few irrelevant actions to the process, such as stacking the T-shirts in piles of three before folding them or folding and unfolding the sleeves. At the beginning of the study, when participants received information about the task they would complete, they were told that they would be paid based on the number of T-shirts they folded in the allotted time. (Adding unnecessary steps obviously slows down the process.) The participants watched the paid actors fold T-shirts for a couple of minutes and then took their spots. They folded T-shirts individually for ten minutes, until another group came to watch them for a few minutes before taking over the work. This pattern was repeated six times with groups of four participants.

Among the participants who watched teams fold inefficiently, 87 percent simply imitated the actions of the initial group of actors, and thus walked away with less money than those who were part of the groups that observed the efficient process. Those who watched an initial group of actors fold inefficiently for just a few minutes perpetuated this behavior across time to many other groups. Of the 336 people in the study, only three explicitly asked questions or raised concerns about inefficiency. As often happens in real life, most team members accepted the nonsensical process without protest.

The traditions and rituals you encounter in your organization and in society often endure out of routine, rather than as the result of thoughtful deliberation. Psychologists and economists alike have a name for this phenomenon: the status quo bias. William Samuelson and Richard Zeckhauser first demonstrated this bias back in 1988, in a study in which they presented participants with a series of decision-making problems that either included or did not include the choice of sticking with a status quo position. Participants tended to favor the status quo when it was offered to them, even as an objectively inferior choice.

Too often, we take deeply ingrained rituals and traditions for granted. When we become comfortable with the current state of affairs, we experience any diversion from the status quo as a loss, and we weigh these losses much more heavily than the idea of potential gains. In fact, when offered a bet with an equal probability of winning or losing, the average person requires a gain that's twice the value of the potential loss before accepting. If only we could put aside the fear of losing, we might jump at the chance to win. But instead, the fear holds us back, chaining us to the status quo even when change is clearly in our best interest.

STUDYING THE LONG HISTORY OF IMPROV LED ME HOME. THE MOST DIRECT ANCES-tor of the art form is thought to be the Italian Commedia dell'Arte. In Europe in the 1500s, performers would travel from town to town with their troupes, performing shows in public squares. Improvised dialogue within a set "scenario" would serve as the framework for these performances. From the beginning, their craft broke with the traditions of mainstream theater, demanding of players an unusual ability to react in the moment.

Long after the Commedia died off, improv was reinvented in the 1950s by British-Canadian playwright Keith Johnstone and American acting coach Viola Spolin. The two made separate, spontaneous contributions to improv. In their own ways, both brought novelty to the stage. Believing that live theater had become pretentious and catered only to intellectuals and the upper class, Johnstone—who was writing plays and teaching acting in London—wanted to create art for everyday people, those whose favorite forms of entertainment were ball games and boxing matches. His answer? A new acting method, "spontaneous improvisation," and a hybrid form of entertainment called Theatresports in which features of sports—like teams, judges, scores, and competitions—were adapted to improvisational theater. Teams would compete for points that judges would award them, and audiences would be encouraged to cheer for scenes they enjoyed and mock the judges ("Kill the umpire!").

When working with actors, Johnstone tried to help them be

more responsive and alive in their work. Informed by his own childhood, he had come to believe that the educational system was blunting creativity. Flipping the notion of children as immature adults, he viewed adults as atrophied children. Johnstone wrote down a list of "things teachers stopped me from doing" and told his own students they should do just the opposite. His unconventional approach and strategies were highly successful in helping actors become more spontaneous.

In her native Chicago in the 1920s and '30s, Spolin had the same passion as Johnstone: theater for the masses. Her approach to teaching adults was based on the insight that children enjoyed learning to act when lessons were presented as a series of games. She had instructed immigrant children in drama as part of a public works project and realized that the same techniques could be used to stimulate creative expression in adults. Spolin's son, Paul Sills, built on this insight in the mid-1950s, helping to spearhead an improv movement centered around the University of Chicago. The group that sprang from Sills's work, The Compass, eventually led to the development of the famous improv theater company Second City, where Tina Fey, Bill Murray, and many other comedy greats got their start.

In the third week of my improv adventure with Greg, the teacher asked all of us to sit in a circle on the floor. We were going to play the game "one-word story." The teacher would provide the title of the story and then pick a person to say the first word. The person to their left would say the next word, and so on, continuing around the circle. The point of the game is to tell a coherent, original story, one word at a time, as if a single narrator is speaking at a normal, conversational pace.

"Here is your title," the teacher began. "A furry dog sits on a stove."

And then we were off: "A—dog—named—Hot—enjoyed—sitting—on—a—red—and—yellow—stove.—One—day—he—

did—not—realize—the—stove—was—on—so—his—butt—felt—warmer—than—usual . . ."

The story kept going, ending with a parrot yelling "butt—on—fire!"

In improv, we are trading in the currency of unpredictability. We don't know what our partners will say next, how others will react, or even when a scene will end. The other players may bring up topics that we know nothing about. That's okay. The goal is to always react purely in the moment. Consider the strategies required in two popular games, chess and Ping-Pong. When you play chess, you need to think ahead. You focus on following your own strategy, as well as anticipating your opponent's. By contrast, when you play Ping-Pong, you need to react in a split second. You can try to anticipate the next volley, but a better bet is to focus on where the ball is moving in the moment. The same goes for improv: You can't "pong" until the other player has "pinged."

Even as it makes us anxious, this unpredictability fuels our need for novelty, which runs surprisingly deep. In the 1860s, German zoologist Alfred Brehm placed a covered box of snakes in a cage with several monkeys. When the monkeys lifted the lid, they were terrified, as any monkey (and most humans) would be. But then the monkeys did something rather odd: They lifted the lid again to get a second look at the snakes. Since Brehm published these findings, scientists have examined the reactions of more than a hundred species of reptiles and mammals to things they've never seen before. No matter how frightening the sight, the animals cannot resist the pull of novelty, and they take another peek.

Novelty compels both humans and animals to engage with the unfamiliar. Indeed, our strong desire for novelty has evolutionary roots, improving our survival odds by keeping us alert to both friends and threats in our environment. As new parents quickly learn, when given a choice, babies consistently look at, listen to, and play with unfamiliar things. One of my favorite moments from early parenthood was when I watched my infant son notice his hands for the first time. His discovery stands out as a metaphor for learning: His interest in what those strange, wonderful appendages could do was his first step toward controlling them. The preference for novelty is an efficient way for immature cognitive systems to process information, helping babies cope with changes to their environment before unleashing their inner explorer.

Interestingly, in human genetics, a preference for novelty has been linked to the migration of early humans to the far reaches of the earth. Recent studies have shown that human groups that migrated the farthest from Africa had more of the genes linked to novelty seeking. That is, the people who traveled the farthest from home may have had some biological propensity to experience mysterious new places. And yet, while we are born with a strong drive to seek novelty, this drive fades over time. As we grow older, other desires take over, like wanting more predictability. The organizations we build and join reflect this reality: paychecks at the same time each week or month, evaluations according to established processes, jobs that involve a known set of activities.

The thrill of novelty—running into an old friend in an unfamiliar city, buying a new car, accepting a promotion—can instill a sense of delight and wonder at our good fortune, but not for ever after. You and your friend eventually part; the car loses its new car smell and starts to seem ordinary; the promotion brings the stress of new responsibilities. In time, we grasp a difficult truth about emotional experiences: their intensity fades.

PAL'S SUDDEN SERVICE IS A FAST-FOOD CHAIN WITH TWENTY-NINE STORES IN northeast Tennessee and southwestern Virginia. Most are boxy, eleven-hundred-square-foot double-drive-thru restaurants topped with statues of burgers and fries. Speed is a key factor at Pal's, and employees are trained accordingly: A typical order of two sandwiches, two sides, and two drinks takes about forty-three seconds to fill. The work is highly standardized: Whether taking orders, grilling, toasting bread, or preparing hamburgers, employees learn to follow the process with zero errors, even during peak times. Responsibilities are split between fifteen different stations. Employees get to work on one of them only after taking a test, and the only passing score is 100 percent.

All businesses face the same conundrum: To stay profitable and competitive in the marketplace, they depend on the work of their people, but people always need new challenges. Pal's is the kind of place where tedium is a constant threat. But the owners have come up with a clever way to fight the tedium of highly standardized work: Not until employees arrive at work for their shifts do they learn the order in which they'll move through the stations. The first task on a Monday may be making shakes, followed by French fries; on Tuesday it may be biscuit production and order delivery. As a result, workers are less likely to shift into autopilot and more likely to up their game. Novelty is a stimulant.

Pal's has achieved impressive numbers: They average one drive-thru order filled every 18 seconds (competitors need minutes), one mistake in every 3,600 orders (the average in the industry is one every 15 orders), scores of 98 percent for customer satisfaction, and above 97 percent for health inspection. Turnover at the managerial level and on the front lines is very low. The sales numbers are similarly remarkable: about $2 million a year per store. In fact, despite operating in a highly competitive industry where global giants like McDonald's, Burger King, and Wendy's dominate the market, Pal's performs remarkably well financially. On most measures—from revenue per square foot and gross margins, to return on sales or on assets and customer satisfaction—Pal's beats the competition.

As this fast-food chain demonstrates, there's room for variety in even the most rote job. My colleague Brad Staats (of the University of North Carolina, Chapel Hill) and I analyzed two and a half years of data from transactions of employees who processed applications for home loans at a Japanese bank. The mortgage line required each employee to engage in seventeen different tasks, activities like scanning applications, comparing the scanned document to the original, inputting application data, comparing that data to underwriting standards, and conducting credit checks. After a worker completed a task, the system automatically assigned him or her a new one. We found that when workers were assigned a greater variety of tasks across a few days, their productivity (as measured by processing time) improved. Variety acted as a motivator.

Novelty increases our job satisfaction, our creativity, and our overall performance. It also increases how much we grow in both confidence and ability. In research conducted by psychologists Brent Mattingly (Ashland University) and Gary Lewandowski (Monmouth University), participants were asked to read a list of facts. Some participants were provided with facts that came across as interesting, novel, and exciting ("Butterflies taste with their feet"), while others were given information that was duller ("Butterflies begin life as a caterpillar"). Reading interesting facts made participants believe they were more knowledgeable than reading mundane ones did. All of a sudden, they felt more like masters—and more confident in their ability to accomplish new things in the future. When presented with new tasks, they worked harder on them.

Part of the explanation is that, in our brains, novelty and pleasure are deeply entwined: Novelty generates surprises, and surprises lead to pleasure. In a series of studies led by Tim Wilson at the University of Virginia, the happiness people experienced after an unexpected kindness (such as a gift) lasted longest when the act was anonymous. In another study, researchers had participants watch an uplifting film based on a true story. They were then given two passages describing what happened to the main character after the events depicted in the film—one true, one fictional. Both passages told positive stories, but their details differed slightly. One group was told which story was true, the other group was kept in the dark. Members of the uncertain group stayed in a more positive mood for much longer after seeing the film. The uncertainty of the situation increased their pleasure rather than detracting from it.

Another factor serves as a powerful source of novelty: excitement. In a now-classic study published in 1993, psychologist Arthur Aron and his colleagues had fifty-three upper-middle-class, middle-aged couples fill out questionnaires asking them about the quality of their marriages. They were also given a list of sixty activities that couples could engage in together, such as dining out, going to a movie, attending concerts or plays, skiing, hiking, or dancing. For each activity, each member of the couple individually rated how exciting and how pleasant they thought the activity would be to share with their partner. In some cases, ratings varied widely. While one person may highly anticipate the new episode of a favorite show, the other may be bored by the prospect of another night in front of the TV. Similarly, one half of the couple may love to ride roller coasters, while the other person practically has a panic attack just contemplating the idea.

Next, couples were randomly assigned to one of three treatments. In the first condition, they were asked to engage in an activity they both had rated as "exciting" but only moderately pleasant, just once a week for ten weeks, for ninety minutes at a time. In the second condition, the couples chose a weekly activity they both had rated as "highly pleasant" but not as exciting. In the third condition, couples were not asked to engage in any special activities. The researchers found that engaging in highly exciting but only moderately pleasant activities dramatically improved relationship quality. But for the couples in the other two conditions (pleasant activities or no special activities), there was no change. For an experience to be exciting, psychologists have learned, it needs to be more than novel—it also needs to be challenging.

A more recent study of one hundred couples found that those who engaged in activities that both members deemed exciting for at least ninety minutes per week for four weeks reported higher levels of happiness and relationship satisfaction. The effect lasted at least four months. In fact, research that has followed couples through time has found remarkable benefits in novel activities—and dire consequences in their absence. Insufficient novelty makes us feel that the relationship is boring, which takes a toll. One longitudinal study found that among married couples, lack of novelty predicted especially strong declines in satisfaction nine years later.

Even very brief novel activities, such as reading through a new recipe to try, watching a movie trailer together, trying a tango move, or picking a subject at random to talk about—have been found to increase relationship quality. A study of 274 married people in the United States found that 40 percent of those who had been married more than ten years reported still being "very intensely in love," a state that was linked to the fact that they shared novel activities. Interestingly, when we engage in exciting activities together, we view both our partner *and* the relationship as exciting. What this research suggests is not that you and your spouse should learn hang-gliding. Seeking novelty may involve simple activities such as walking in a part of town you're not familiar with, checking out a new restaurant, or giving improv a try.

Surprisingly, novelty is even more important than stability. In a study I conducted with a group of three hundred new employees, I found that the more frequently they experienced novelty in their work in the weeks that followed (because they learned new skills, met new colleagues, or felt challenged in their tasks), the more they felt satisfied with and energized by their jobs, and the longer they were interested in staying with the organization. Stability, by contrast, did not seem to bring these benefits. When employees reported that their job felt "more or less the same every day," their satisfaction suffered, and they were more eager to move on.

In another study, I enlisted about five hundred workers across a wide range of U.S. organizations to take part in a six-week study inspired by Arthur Aron's research on novelty and romantic relationships. I randomly assigned each employee to one of three conditions. In the novelty condition, I asked participants to carve out some time at work (at least once a week) to engage in novel or challenging tasks, such as reaching out to a colleague in a different division, learning a new skill, or working on a project outside their comfort zone. I sent them a reminder once a week for five weeks. For participants in the pleasant condition, I asked them to make some time at work to engage in tasks they enjoyed, to the extent possible. In the control condition, participants did not receive any instructions.

At the end of week six, I asked everyone to complete an online survey on job satisfaction, engagement, commitment to the organization, and innovative behaviors. I also sought permission to ask their supervisors about their performance. Just as in the romantic relationships Aron studied, boosting novelty produced the highest scores on all the measures I assessed. I found the same results for employees in a large retail organization in India and for a large sample of European workers. The value of novelty at work (and in relationships) seems pretty universal.

At Pal's, managers regularly set up new challenges. One manager liked to make weekly deals with his employees, such as the following: He told a worker at the order window that if she could correctly predict the orders of one hundred drive-thru customers in the next hour, she would receive a $100 gift card. As the employee told me the story, she recalled thinking initially that the task seemed impossible. And I agreed. But then she told me that most of Pal's customers are repeat customers, people who drive in to get lunch or dinner three to five times a week. "After a while, you recognize their faces and the order they always seem to make, almost out of habit," she noted. She claimed her prize.

WHEN GREG FIRST OPENED THE BIG BOX TIED IN RED RIBBON THAT I HAD PUT UNder the Christmas tree for him in 2011, I could tell he was disappointed. Being a bit of a tech geek, he was probably expecting me to get him some exciting new gadget. What he found instead was a lot of empty space and a printed-out description of our improv class, something he'd never considered doing on his own and clearly wasn't interested in. I was convinced he was wrong—that he would love it as soon as we started. But after the first session, he told me that he'd hated the class. He'd felt uncomfortable being so vulnerable in front of strangers. Worse, he didn't think he was funny.

The second class didn't do much to change his mind. I can perfectly picture his face during an exercise called "three things!" The group stood in a circle chanting "three things!" while bouncing our fists, as if pounding a table. The rules are simple: One person starts the game by turning to a neighbor and naming a category: "three things you'd find at the back of your closet!"; "three brands of cereal!"; "three terrible excuses for showing up late!" As quickly as possible, the neighbor has to call out three responses with authority. The group chant starts up again, and the next person gets a category. Sometimes the answers fit the category "appropriately"; other times, they don't, but that's okay—whatever comes to mind is the right answer. The idea is to generate and celebrate a quick response.

I was standing right across from Greg in the circle. A person in the group shouted, "Three things you could hide in your nose if you had to!" while turning to Greg, who had no quick answer. After hesitating a few more seconds, and getting encouraging smiles from others, he stopped biting his lips and said, "my finger, a raisin, a penny." At the end of the class, as we walked out of the building, "three things!" was still on his mind. "It was so awkward," he told me. He was miserable.

But soon, things began to change. Greg learned to get the most out of class without worrying what others were thinking. He embraced being in the moment and surprised himself with his own reactions. He was fascinated, as I was, by the lessons and experience each exercise unlocked. He came to truly enjoy improv. Our delight in a particular session would carry into the next day, and the day after that. We started to share our enthusiasm with friends, describing the scenes or jokes we surprised ourselves with. And if Greg giggled after a cultural reference sailed right over my head, I usually joined in.

Another funny thing that eventually happened to both of us: we felt we were good at something new. We never became great actors, but we learned how to put ourselves out there, to be more comfortable with both our strong and weak points, and to support each other. We had no problem making fun of ourselves afterward. And when we played "three things!" again in later classes, the answers flowed with no hesitation. We'd become masters of producing answers in seconds, and the only safe prediction was that we'd end up laughing.

Psychologists call this kind of experience "self-expansion." When we engage in novel activities and acquire new skills, our sense of who we are expands, as does the number of traits we use to describe who we are. This, in turn, heightens our confidence that we can accomplish our goals, even when we're outside of our comfort zone, and it also increases our commitment to reaching our destination, no matter how tough the road. Aron initially wrote about self-expansion as a side effect of being in rewarding relationships. By getting closer to our partner, we learn something new from them, and we ourselves "expand," broadening our knowledge and interests.

Before we took our improv class, neither Greg nor I thought we were very good at being funny on the spot. And while we don't fool ourselves into thinking we're ready for *Saturday Night Live*, our sense of who we are has expanded: We now know that we are capable of being silly, and thus vulnerable, in front of strangers. We grew closer to each other by sharing in this sometimes frightening experience and seeing each other in a new light. Aron wrote about self-expansion as a natural desire to grow and change. When we challenge ourselves to move beyond what we know and can do well, we rebel against the comfortable cocoon of the status quo, improving ourselves and positioning ourselves to contribute more to our partners, coworkers, and organizations.

The third week of improv class, we warmed up with a game called "hot spot" that made me intensely uncomfortable. We all stood in a circle. One person entered the center and began singing a song. In no particular order, other players took turns singing in the center. The first time I sang, I felt huge discomfort. I've never been much of a singer, and my voice sounded soft and thin. But the beauty of the experience was that I didn't really have time to focus exclusively on my own discomfort. Rather, I needed to focus outward and support my classmates, helping them look good as they suffered through their own discomfort in the center of the circle. I learned that by smiling at them, singing along, or taking their place quickly when they were struggling, I could help. As I took the spotlight in the weeks that followed, my nerves dissolved and I found myself focusing on the excitement that came with singing new songs. My voice became stronger and more assured—even if I was still completely out of tune.

Improv teaches that it is OK to be uncomfortable. Comfort is overrated. It doesn't make us as happy as we think it will. With too much comfort, we miss out on the anticipation of what's going to happen next. It's so much better to go through life like a child dreaming of Santa Claus, wondering what gifts the future holds.

3

THE VANISHING ELEPHANT

A TALENT FOR CURIOSITY

Look at this life—all mystery and magic.
—**HARRY HOUDINI**

When New York City's Hippodrome Theater opened in 1905, its builders touted it as the largest and grandest theater in the world. Spires and American flags adorned the roof, giving the Hippodrome the appearance of a grand castle. Inside, seats for crowds of more than fifty-six hundred fanned the stage in a three-tiered semicircle. In popular magazines of the era, the theater was referred to as a "mammoth show-place on Sixth Avenue," "supreme in size and extravagance."

On January 7, 1918, the famed illusionist Harry Houdini walked across the stage, dressed all in black, with the eyes of the sold-out crowd upon him. For over two decades, the Hungarian-born escape artist and magician had been traveling the world, astonishing audiences with his death-defying escapes from handcuffs, ropes, straitjackets, and chains. He was particularly known for extricating himself from locked containers—from prison cells to milk cans to airtight coffins. One of his best-known escapes is called the "Chinese water torture cell." To perform the trick, Houdini began by dangling upside down with his ankles locked into a frame, before being lowered headfirst into a tank of water. If he couldn't escape within two minutes, an assistant standing by with an ax was prepared to break the glass—but that was never needed: Houdini broke free every time.

Houdini's exploits went beyond remarkable escapes. One of his tricks involved swallowing a hundred needles and twenty yards of thread with nothing more than a drink of water as a chaser. After showing the audience his empty mouth, Houdini would then reach in and pull out every single needle, fully threaded together and sometimes spanning the length of the stage. Often enough, his audiences were too dumbfounded to applaud right away.

At the Hippodrome that winter, the crowd was expecting him to perform the world's most incredible illusion. Houdini stood in the middle of the stage next to a giant wooden box on wheels, about eight feet square. "Ladies and gentlemen," he cried. "Allow me to introduce Jennie, the world's only vanishing elephant!" Jennie, a full-grown Asian elephant, came walking out onto the stage, standing eight feet tall and weighing over six thousand pounds. She raised her trunk in greeting, a baby blue ribbon tied around her neck. "She is all dressed up," Houdini said, "like a bride."

Twelve attendants turned the wooden box in a circle, opening all the doors to show the crowd that there was no way to escape. The doors were then closed, and the trainer marched the elephant slowly around the box before leading her inside. Houdini closed and sealed the doors, confident in his every movement.

He had been a trickster from the beginning. As a child, young Harry learned to open the locked cabinets in which his mother hid the pies and sweets she had baked. Growing up, he helped supplement his family's modest income by shining shoes and selling newspapers, but when he wasn't working, Houdini was drawn to athletics and practiced acrobatic stunts. He held his first performance at age nine, calling himself "the Prince of the Air"—wearing a pair of red socks his mother had made for him, he would swing on a trapeze hung from a tree. He launched his professional career when he was seventeen, performing magic shows in front of civic groups, at sideshows, inside music halls, and at the amusement park on New York's Coney Island, where he had as many as twenty shows a day. Fascinated by locks and handcuffs, he became an expert on them. Whenever he traveled to a new town, Houdini would offer $100 to anyone who could produce a pair of handcuffs from which he could not escape—but he never had to pay.

At the Hippodrome, a loud, dramatic drum roll filled the air, followed by the firing of a stage pistol. Then, the stagehands flung open the doors of the box at both ends. Poof: the giant pachyderm had vanished. "You can plainly see, the animal is completely gone," Houdini announced to rapturous applause. And for over ninety years, long after Houdini's death, the trick's secret remained a puzzle that even other magicians could not solve.

THE EIGHTEENTH-CENTURY SCOTTISH ECONOMIST AND MORAL PHILOSOPHER ADAM Smith is commonly regarded as the father of modern economics for having articulated the tenets of capitalism. However, Smith also made some interesting, lesser-known observations about the experience of wonder, writing that it arises "when something quite new and singular is presented . . . [and] memory cannot, from all its stores, cast up any image that nearly resembles this strange appearance." According to Smith, wonder is associated with a specific bodily feeling: "that staring, and sometimes that rolling of the eyes, that suspension of the breath, and that swelling of the heart."

In ancient times, people felt a sense of wonder and awe when the sun was blacked out by a solar eclipse. And even in the modern era, when we know what causes an eclipse, when to expect it, and exactly how long it will last, the phenomenon continues to beguile. For the total eclipse that crossed North America on August 17, 2017, many thousands of people traveled to spots within the "path of totality" to see the moon completely cover the sun and briefly instill darkness during the day. The sight drove some to tears and left many speechless. The natural world is a common source of wonder: the birth of a child, the sight of lions and elephants on a safari, or even watching the progression of an inchworm across one's finger.

Infants and children, who are experiencing everything for the first time, are likely the creatures most filled with a sense of wonder—as I'm reminded whenever I'm with my four-and-a-half-year-old son, Alexander. Lately, one of his favorite words is "Why?" As in: "Why is the sky blue?" "Why do you get receipts when you pay for things?" "Why can't we keep on playing?" and "Why do we wear clothes most of the time?" Every time I am confident I've given him a thoroughly satisfying answer, he pelts me with another string of queries. Like most other young children, he doesn't assume he has everything figured out or feel embarrassed about not knowing something. He takes time to puzzle over issues and doesn't dismiss ideas that might be outlandish.

This youthful sense of wonder was a central part of Houdini's personality, and it remained so throughout his life. When Houdini was seven, a traveling street circus passed through his hometown of Appleton, Wisconsin. What most captured his attention was not the clowns and acrobats, but the man in tights who climbed twenty feet into the air to a small platform and then walked across a taut wire stretched between two poles. As the crowd cheered, Houdini wondered: Why was the man risking his life? How long did he have to train to be able to walk the wire? When the man suspended himself from the high wire by his teeth, Houdini asked himself, How did he do it? How many times had he performed the trick before? What if he failed? Did his teeth hurt?

All these questions needed answers. Houdini rushed home that afternoon and found some rope to tie between two trees. Balancing on the rope was not easy: the first time he tried, he fell to the ground. But with perseverance, he learned to walk the tightrope. As for his attempt to replicate hanging by his teeth, it failed, as he did not realize that the man from the circus had used a mouthpiece. "Out came a couple of front teeth," Houdini remembered. Curiosity has its costs.

IN THE EARLY 1900S, HENRY FORD, FOUNDER OF FORD MOTOR COMPANY, WAS DEtermined to find a way to lower his production costs in order to create a car for the masses. On October 1, 1908, Ford realized that vision by rolling out the first Model T. The car had a twenty-two-horsepower, four-cylinder lightweight engine, could drive as fast as forty miles per hour, and ran on either hemp-based fuel or gasoline. The company's engineers had developed a system of interchangeable components, which not only saved time and reduced waste, but also made it easy for workers to assemble the cars, no matter how skilled (or unskilled) they were. This approach was far ahead of the rest of the auto industry. Ford's single-minded focus on efficiency and minimizing costs for the Model T turned out to be a remarkable success, and by 1921, the Ford Motor Company was responsible for 56 percent of all the passenger cars produced in the United States.

But in the late 1920s, as the U.S. economy rose to new heights, consumers began to thirst for greater variety in cars, not to mention a closed-body design (that is, a roof!). Competitors like General Motors saw an opportunity. In 1924, Alfred Sloan Jr., GM's president at the time, came up with a new market strategy: He divided the U.S. car market into different segments by price range and by what he called "purpose." Cars in the different segments would have different features and looks, depending on what consumers wanted and how deep their pockets were. Ford, instead, remained fixated on improving the Model T. Ford's competitors surged ahead while the Motel T started running out of gas. By the late 1920s, Ford had lost its lead position and GM had the largest share of the market. In the years that followed, Ford continued to lose market share to GM and was criticized for not understanding what customers wanted in a car. "The old master," GM's Sloan was happy to observe, "has failed to master change." Ford remained a follower in terms of the look and style of his cars, even when launching new models such as the Mustang, Maverick, and the Pinto. Despite some successes along the way, Ford ultimately lost in head-on competition with GM, and to this day, Ford has not regained its former position.

This brings us back to Harry Houdini. If you are trying to run a company efficiently, someone like Houdini might not be your first choice for an employee. But when we look closer, we see that unlike Ford, but like Ford's competitors, Houdini allowed his sense of wonder to guide his thinking. He may have lost a few teeth in the process, but he was always elevating his craft.

Even as I criticize Henry Ford, I'll admit that I personally often have the same inclination. Take a common early morning at my house. It's 6:30. The sun rose not long ago, but my fifteen-month-old daughter, Olivia, rose before it. I am half-asleep and still in my pajamas, making coffee. Meanwhile, Olivia is full of energy. She opens one of the cabinets in the kitchen and finds the colander; soon she's wearing it as a hat, then as a mask. Before I know it she's on the other side of the kitchen, opening another cabinet and moving jars of spices to a new location. Next, she fixates on a tall plastic canister containing rice. She sits on the floor and shakes it. "How can I get these small white pieces out of this container?" she seems to be asking. Next, my son, Alex, is up and ready to join in. The kids are both giggling as they find buttons to press and drawers to open.

I have to stop myself from picking Olivia up and putting an end to all this opening and closing of cabinets, all this fun exploration. Children absorb information like sponges, and they learn at a rapid pace. But as they grow, they become more aware of how others—adults in particular—see them, and they begin to rein in their curiosity. Curiosity, research suggests, typically peaks around age four or five. With age, self-consciousness increases, and so does our desire to make a show of expertise. But rebels learn to hold on to this childlike curiosity, and they never stop asking "why."

One recent morning, Greg poured Alex some cereal and milk for breakfast. Alex was sitting on his stool at the kitchen counter, and he seemed to be thinking hard about something. "Daddy, remember the food coloring we bought for Easter? When we colored eggs? Do we still have it?" Greg went over to the cabinet with the baking supplies, fished out the food coloring, and put the box next to Alex's bowl. "Here it is," Greg said. "What are you going to do with it?" Alex informed us that he was going to use the food coloring in his breakfast. Greg looked at him, confused. "Alex, we don't use food coloring in our milk."

"Why not, Daddy?"

Greg turned to me. "We just don't do that. Right, Mommy?" Meanwhile, Alex had taken the cap off the little red bottle, and soon his cereal swam happily in pink milk. Greg frowned. As he sipped his coffee and kept quiet, he seemed to be struggling with the same urge I'd felt seeing Olivia exploring the kitchen. He was resisting the impulse to put the cap back on the bottle of food coloring and pour our son a fresh bowl of cereal. While at the same time asking himself, Why, really, *shouldn't* the milk be pink? And, perhaps, what other colors could breakfast be?

IN 2000, THE BRITISH BROADCASTING CORPORATION, KNOWN ACROSS THE GLOBE as the BBC, was facing challenges on many fronts. Established in 1922 as a private company, it initially broadcasted programs to radio owners. Its first director-general, John Reith, had a clear vision for the BBC: "to educate, inform, and entertain" British people. In the years that followed, the BBC grew and developed television broadcasting. It also entered the news business and, later on, it started offering digital services like the twenty-four-hour BBC news service and the BBC Online. The company became one of Britain's best-known global brands.

But in the late 1980s and 1990s, the marketplace started to change, and the media industry went through a seismic shift. The nineties saw the arrival of a new digital broadcast technology known as cable, which gave consumers many more choices—twice as many channels as compared to analog technology, better quality of services, and Internet access. The commercial channels risked losing audiences and, with that, advertising revenues. Yet the BBC had no clear vision or strategy for how to adapt. To compound the problem, the BBC itself was going through some tough struggles internally. It had lost its vitality, and the quality of its content was suffering. There were 168 different business units all operating within the BBC, and complexity and confusion had taken over what had once been a well-organized workplace. A group of employees had come up with a three-word description for the BBC: "despondent, down, and dismayed."

In 2000, the company brought in a man named Greg Dyke to be its new director-general. Dyke had begun his career as a journalist, eventually entered broadcasting and became director of programs for London Weekend Television in 1987, and then served as the company's group chief executive. In 1995, he joined Pearson Television as CEO. Over the years, Dyke developed a reputation for being a charismatic leader with a remarkable track record in television. Early on in his career, for example, while working as program director of a new morning TV franchise at London Weekend Television called TV-am, Dyke rescued the channel by promoting a puppet called Roland Rat to a regular slot every morning and introducing cartoons for younger viewers. If children liked Roland and watched the show, Dyke predicted, then their mothers would keep the channel on. The ratings went up, and so did the number of people who watched the channel, from about 200,000 when Dyke started to 400,000 people just one month after his arrival, to 1.5 million by the end of his first year in charge.

The BBC presented a different kind of challenge for Dyke. It was much larger than his previous employers and had a deep connection to the public sector. Though the BBC operated independently from the British government, there were strong ties between the two entities: the government signed off on the BBC's long-term charter, and it also appointed the chairman of the BBC Trust. Dyke came up with an interesting transition plan. He overlapped with his predecessor, John Birt, by five months, and spent that time getting to know the BBC. Birt had developed a reputation for leading the BBC from his office in London. Dyke, instead, began traveling all around the United Kingdom, from Wales to Northern Ireland to Scotland, from the well-known BBC facilities to the most remote ones. He visited every major location and traveled to offices that had never received a visit from a director-general in the past. At each location, he met with the entire staff. Confounding employees' expectations, he didn't give a lengthy presentation about what he planned to change. Instead, he asked a simple question: "What is the one thing I should do to make things better for you?" Then Dyke would sit down and listen to the responses. After that, he asked a follow-up question: "What is the one thing I should do to make things better for our viewers and listeners?"

Dyke's first move in one of the most powerful jobs in British broadcasting was remarkable. People generally fear that asking questions will make them look foolish, especially when they are asking for help with large problems that have been around for some time. Aren't leaders supposed to provide answers? Management books are filled with guidelines on how leaders can make long-lasting first impressions by communicating their vision right from the start: Make clear who's in charge, for example, and delegate when appropriate. CEOs joining organizations are expected to start implementing their vision, not to spend time asking others how they can be most helpful to them. Many leaders in Dyke's position, brought in to fix the problems of a deeply troubled organization, would have *talked* rather than ask questions. And most of us would have the same impulse.

When Dyke made his visits, he didn't have lunch in the executive dining room. Rather, he'd often grab a tray in the cafeteria with the staff and keep asking them questions. Dyke learned that employees were frustrated by the many top-down changes Birt had put in place without asking for input. They felt unmotivated and disempowered. Many believed the BCC had lost its creative spark; they also complained that facilities were badly in need of updating.

By Dyke's first official day in the job, when he formally addressed the staff, they were eager to hear his plans for the future and to work with him to implement them. Dyke explained that he wanted to shift the BBC's goal from being "the best-managed organization in the public sector," as his predecessor had suggested, to being the "most innovative and risk-taking place there is." As a signal for the change he wanted to create, Dyke distributed yellow cards that looked like the penalty cards that soccer referees hold up when they're cautioning a player. He encouraged the staff to use the cards to "cut the crap and make it happen." If anyone saw or heard someone trying to block a good idea, they should wave the yellow card in the air and state their case.

Dyke's unconventional approach paid off. Within a year of his arrival at the BBC, ratings increased for both BBC1 and BBC2, and audience satisfaction with the BBC increased overall from a 6 out of 10, just before Dyke arrived, to a 6.8. In July 2002, ratings for the flagship station BBC1 surpassed those of its main competitor, ITV, for the first time in many years. BBC radio reached record audiences. The BBC also dramatically reduced its overhead, allowing it to put an additional 270 million pounds into new broadcasting programs. And the upgrades that the employees wanted were also put in place.

The way that we typically think about the effect of asking questions—especially when we are in leadership positions—is just plain wrong. We fear that others will judge us negatively for not having all the answers, when in truth it's just the opposite. When we interact with others by asking questions, our relationships grow stronger, because we are showing genuine interest in learning about them, hearing their ideas, and getting to know them more personally. As a result, we gain their trust, and our relationship becomes more interesting and intimate. If you are worried that by asking a question you may come across as incompetent, you have that wrong also: People think of us as being smarter when we ask questions than when we don't.

To demonstrate the value of asking questions, my colleagues and I recruited a group of 170 students. We sat them down in front of computers and told them that they would be matched with another person taking the study, who would remain anonymous. What they did not know was that their partner was a computer-simulated actor. As a cover story, participants were told that the study was about understanding how instant messaging influences performance on a brain teaser. Participants then had to solve the task under time pressure, and they learned that their partner would also be completing it later in the study. They were told that their performance mattered, as they would be paid a bonus for each of the five problems in the brain teaser that they solved correctly.

To make sure the participants had no doubts that their partner was a real person, we gave them the opportunity to send an instant message to their partner at the beginning of the study. The computer-simulated actor did not provide a direct response to the message but simply sent one to them that said: "Hey, good luck." Once they had completed the brain teaser, the participants received another message from their partner. Depending on the condition they had been randomly assigned to, they received one of two messages: "I hope it went well" or "I hope it went well. Do you have any advice?" Participants could respond to this message after they received it knowing they would not hear back. They then evaluated how competent they thought their partner was and reported on how likely they would be to ask their partner for advice on a similar task in the future.

Participants who had a partner who asked them for advice rated the advice seeker higher on competence. They also indicated that they would be more likely to turn to their partner for advice. Thus, contrary to what we tend to believe, asking for advice *increases* rather than decreases how competent we are perceived to be. We underestimate how flattering it is to be asked for advice. By asking questions, we give others the opportunity to share their personal experience and wisdom, thus stroking their ego. Curiosity is a way of being rebellious in the world. Rebels fight their fears and are willing to push past the discomfort of showing others that they need their help. It may feel scary, but it brings about all sorts of benefits.

Curiosity is related to both greater positive emotions and greater closeness when we interact with strangers for the first time. In one study my colleagues and I conducted, we had college students engage in conversations with a peer where they were instructed to ask many questions or just a few. Students liked their partner more when they received more questions, we found, simply because that gave them the opportunity to talk and disclose information about themselves. People who ask more questions are better liked, our research shows, and speed daters who ask more questions get more second dates. In another study, undergraduates who didn't know each other were instructed to either engage in a conversation with a peer designed to generate intimacy, asking questions like "For what in your life do you feel most grateful?" or they engaged in casual small talk. Those who had an intimate conversation reported feeling closer to their partner and happier than those who engaged in small talk. Yet we are usually reluctant to ask more probing questions like this, believing we're getting too personal and that we should mind our own business instead.

Research has also found curiosity to be associated with greater satisfaction and a greater sense of social support in existing relationships. When arriving home after a day of work, you'll feel more connected to your partner if you show you are curious about how their day went. In a newer relationship, you'll have a more enjoyable date, and you'll be more excited to have another, if your partner asks questions that lead you to share more about yourself. When you show curiosity by asking questions, others share more, and they return the favor, asking questions of you. This sets up a spiral of give and take that fosters intimacy.

When we open ourselves to curiosity, we are more apt to reframe situations in a positive way. Curiosity makes us much more likely to view a tough problem at work as an interesting challenge to take on. A stressful meeting with our boss becomes an opportunity to learn. A nerve-racking first date becomes an exciting night out with a new person. A colander becomes a hat. In general, curiosity motivates us to view stressful situations as challenges rather than threats, to talk about difficulties more openly and to try new approaches to solving problems. In fact, curiosity is associated with a less defensive reaction to stress and, as a result, less aggression when we respond to a provocation. In a diary study conducted each day over four weeks, people who had higher tolerance for uncertainty indicated that they had conflicts with friends less often, fewer passive-aggressive reactions, and were more willing to excuse transgressions. Curiosity, in short, translates into greater engagement with others and with the world, thanks to the exploratory behavior and learning that it inspires.

How we express our curiosity has its roots in childhood and can be shaped by the lessons we are taught as we grow up. In one study, researchers showed eight- and nine-year-olds a school science project called "The Bouncing Raisins," which involves adding raisins to a mixture of vinegar and baking soda and watching them bounce up to the top of the glass. After the activity, the experimenter responded to the children differently. For half the children, she asked, "I wonder what would happen if we dropped one of these [picking up a Skittles candy from the table] into the liquid instead of a raisin?" To the other half of the children, she simply said, "I'm just going to tidy up a bit. I'll put these materials over here," as she cleaned up the work area.

In both scenarios, the experimenter then left the room, saying, "Feel free to do whatever you want while you are waiting for me. You can use the materials more, or draw with these crayons, or just wait. Whatever you want to do is fine." Children in the first group, who had seen their guide deviate from the task so that she could satisfy her own curiosity, tended to play with the materials much more, dropping raisins, Skittles, and other items into the liquid. Children who instead had seen her tidy up were more likely to simply do nothing. A teacher's behavior has a powerful effect on a child's disposition to explore. Similarly, a manager's actions can influence the curiosity and creativity of those in their organization. At Intuit, when curiosity results in innovations that are particularly creative, it is recognized with a Scott Cook Innovation Award. But there is also the "Greatest Failure Award," which celebrates curiosity that did not lead to a good result but still offered an important learning opportunity. The award comes with a "failure party."

The same researchers then flipped the Bouncing Raisins study to measure how teachers would respond to children's displays of curiosity and exploration. The teachers who volunteered were asked to do the same experiment with a student, whom the experimenters had instructed to behave in a certain way (unbeknownst to the teachers). Half of the teachers were told that the focus of the lesson was to learn about science. The other half were told that the focus of the lesson was filling out a worksheet. The teachers began by showing the children the Bouncing Raisins experiment, as before; this time, the students were instructed to stray from the instructions and put a Skittle into the glass. If the teacher asked the child what she was doing, the student was trained to reply, "I just wanted to see what would happen."

The results were striking. Teachers who believed that the goal of the lesson was learning about science responded to the diversion with interest and encouragement, saying things like, "Oh, what are you trying?" or "Maybe we should see what this will do." But those teachers who had been encouraged to focus on completing the worksheet said things like, "Oh, wait a second, that's not on the instruction sheet" or "Whoops, that doesn't go in there." How we react to the exploration and experimentation of our colleagues or subordinates is likely to directly influence whether they feel comfortable exploring their curiosity. A workplace with failure parties is going to yield a lot more creativity than one where efficiency is celebrated above all else.

As in the case of the production of Model Ts at Ford Motor, or the urge we feel as parents when we want to stop our children in their messy explorations of the world, I fear that schools may be too focused on perfecting skills or preparing for tests in ways that are detrimental to curiosity. While checking out schools for Alex's pre-K year, I saw a teacher in one of the classes teaching children how to draw perfect triangles, squares, and circles and then color them. She seemed particularly interested in having the shapes be "properly" drawn, and when the children colored, she continually reminded them "NOT to color outside the lines!" Focusing on teaching students to avoid making mistakes, to perform well on standardized tests, or to be well behaved may lead teachers to forget what education is about, at least in my mind: the beauty of fueling and nurturing their natural curiosity so that they will keep asking questions about the world. I also fear that workplaces are not that different in their approach to curiosity: By following rules and orders in executing the work, employees lose the sense of wonder that could lead them to approach the job differently.

Massimiliano (Max) Zanardi is a manager who knows how to tap into his employees' curiosity, and his own, to run a better business. He likes to introduce himself as "100 percent Italian, and 50 percent Turkish." He was born in Italy but spent many years living in Turkey. Like many Italians, Zanardi talks in an animated fashion and uses lots of hand gestures. He was the general manager of the Ritz-Carlton in Istanbul for several years, playing a key role in the hotel's opening and working hard to improve customers' experiences. In 2015, the hotel was voted Turkey's Best Luxury Hotel in the prestigious *Business Destinations* Travel Awards, and *Business Destinations* magazine praised the hotel as standing out for its innovation, unparalleled facilities, and the passion of its employees for the work they do. Standing in the lobby, you will enjoy the subtle fragrance of the hotel's bespoke perfume, and throughout public areas in the hotel, carefully selected contemporary music inspires you to smile or even do a little dance.

The hotel's employees attribute their passion to the way that Zanardi encouraged them to always ask questions. As general manager, Zanardi regularly challenged employees to redefine luxury by asking "Why?" and "What if?" For example, each year employees were used to planting flowers on the terrace right outside the hotel's restaurant. One day, when it was time to fill the pots and choose what to plant, Zanardi asked staff members, "*Why* do we always plant flowers? How about vegetables? What about herbs?" This conversation eventually led to a terrace garden full of herbs and heirloom tomatoes that were used in the hotel's acclaimed restaurant, Atelier Real Food. All of this from asking a few simple questions.

ON OCTOBER 29, 1908, IN A SMALL PICTURESQUE TOWN IN THE FOOTHILLS OF THE Italian Alps, Camillo Olivetti founded Italy's first typewriter factory as a family business. A gifted and eclectic engineer, Olivetti had been inspired by a visit to the United States to import typewriters to Italy, and then, later, to manufacture them. Olivetti started with twenty employees, who assembled about twenty machines per week. Under its founder's direction, the company, called simply Olivetti, grew rapidly; by the early 1920s, it had 250 employees and was producing more than 2,000 machines a year.

In 1924, Camillo's son, Adriano, joined the family business after graduating from college. He started as a production worker on the factory floor. Adriano noticed the monotony of many of the tasks employees completed day after day and the tough working conditions—there was not enough light inside the factory, nor enough time for breaks. Workers were also too isolated from one another, he thought, with each person handling a different step of the production process, and their hours were too long. Adriano was struck by the fact that, as workers completed routinized and simplified tasks in the style of Fordism, they stopped thinking. Work, Adriano believed, should not be passive or negative. Rather, it should provide joy and have a noble purpose, leading people to a better life. In Adriano's mind, companies have a moral obligation toward their workers; after all, it is through workers' physical and intellectual contributions that companies grow. Adriano believed that companies should not only provide their employees with economic rewards, but also promote cultural and social initiatives that would help them and their families flourish alongside the firm.

The management scholar James March first wrote about this trade-off between efficiency and innovation in 1991, highlighting the contrast between "exploitation" and "exploration" in organizations. Exploration, or looking for and identifying new ideas and ways of doing things, involves risk taking, experimentation, flexibility, play, discovery, and innovation. Exploitation, in contrast, involves improving and refining existing products and processes through efficiency, selection, implementation, and execution. These two activities, March argued, require substantially different capabilities, processes, and cultures. Groups organized around exploration tend to have flexible structures and are associated with improvisation, autonomy, chaos, and emerging businesses and technologies. Meanwhile, those organized for exploitation are more often associated with routine processes, control and bureaucracy, and stable markets and technology. Exploitation, March noted, often crowds out exploration.

Departing from the single-minded focus on efficient processes that characterized Ford's methods, Adriano Olivetti was able to get the balance between exploration and exploitation just right. He became the company's general manager in 1932 and its president in 1938. Under Adriano's leadership, the firm adopted a much more efficient production system, thus following in Ford's footsteps. But unlike Ford, the company also invested in its workforce—in ways that were rather unusual, especially at that time. In the northwest Italian town of Ivrea, new factory buildings were built almost entirely of glass, so that the workers could see the mountains and valleys, and those outside could see what was happening inside. Cultured, sophisticated, and community-minded, Adriano was an engineer fascinated by art, design, and architecture, and he drew on these interests in his corporate role. Under Adriano, Olivetti's design strategy became integrated into the product-development process. In fact, in 1937, the company was one of the first to integrate a graphic design department into its corporate structure. Rather than limiting designers to fashioning the appearance of products only after engineers had developed them, Olivetti's designers were equal partners from the start.

In the 1940s, Olivetti launched creative new products into the market, like its Divisumma electric calculator (launched in 1948), a ten-key printing machine capable of division, which became very popular. In 1969, Olivetti's Valentine typewriter turned what was once a utilitarian machine into a must-have of the day. Using modern materials, a new manufacturing process, and a clever design, the portable Valentine typewriter created a new mass-market product category. The company also started to diversify—specifically, into the production of the first mechanical calculators and a highly innovative electronics division. Thanks to the fact that designers were so involved in the process, Olivetti's products became known for being highly functional but also aesthetically unique. For instance, the Valentine typewriter had smooth lines and punchy colors—it came in red, white, green, and blue—making it fun, and adding personality to an area that had long taken itself too seriously: the office. At the same time, Olivetti expanded internationally, opening subsidiaries across Latin America and Europe. The company grew from a factory with fewer than nine hundred employees in its early years to a multinational firm with about eighty thousand workers at ten establishments in Italy and eleven abroad. By the 1970s, Olivetti had become "an undisputed leader in industrial design," a phrase Steve Jobs would use a decade later when talking about what he wanted his company Apple to be.

Though initially impressed by the production efficiencies he saw at Ford, Adriano believed the intensive work schedules overly stressed employees and could, in the long term, alienate them. He not only paid Olivetti workers more than other companies did at the time, but he went to great lengths to ensure that they remained engaged, curious, and exposed to knowledge and culture from different disciplines. Under Adriano, new factories included playgrounds for workers' children, libraries filled with tens of thousands of books and magazines, and rooms for film screenings and debates. (Tech companies like Google and Facebook offer similar perks these days, but they were rather uncommon at the time.) He also hired writers, poets, and other intellectuals. During the 1950s, for example, the novelist and psychologist Ottiero Ottieri oversaw recruitment, and the poet Giovanni Giudici ran the firm's library (which Adriano referred to as the "factory of the culture"). Workers were given a two-hour break for lunch: one hour to eat food, the other to "eat" culture—by reading books from the library, or attending concerts and talks by famous intellectuals Olivetti had invited. Mechanical engineers received lessons on the history of music or the French Revolution. For Christmas, management gave employees special editions of books that were considered classics, or custom-made calendars with reproductions of famous artworks or illustrations made by emerging artists. The company also sponsored the renovation of various masterpieces, including Leonardo da Vinci's *The Last Supper*.

Adriano had no data to support his approach to management, and other executives often thought he was "wasting time" with all these activities and initiatives for his employees. But he was clearly spot-on with his intuition: By investing in workers' well-being and curiosity, his company kept innovating and putting successful products on the market. In addition to the traditional typewriter, Olivetti developed products that allowed the company to expand into new markets, including, eventually, the first personal computer in the world, Programma 101 (P101), in 1964.

By making innovation the core of his company's production strategy, Adriano Olivetti fostered a highly creative environment for his staff. He believed that the success of Olivetti products was about much more than the processes; it was about what he did for his people. He gave workers much more ownership over the manufacturing process, invested in their well-being, and encouraged them to be curious. Olivetti is the oldest technology company in Italy, and it has also become the largest. In the mid-1990s, it was the second-largest computer maker in Europe. Its great design and innovation are the key sources of that success, together with the company's vast range of products, from the first mass-produced personal computer and typewriters, to fax machines, cash registers, and inkjet printers.

In a similar manner today, design and consulting company IDEO seeks to hire what are known as "T-shaped" employees. (This terminology apparently originated at the management consulting firm McKinsey & Company in internal hiring conversations.) The vertical stroke of the "T" in "T-shaped" employee refers to the depth of knowledge and skill an employee relies on to add her contribution to the creative process. The horizontal stroke of the "T" refers to an employee's inclination for collaboration across functions, which consists of two aspects: empathy and curiosity. Empathy is what allows people to take another person's perspective when considering problems and to listen actively. Curiosity refers to an interest in other people's activities and disciplines, an interest so strong that an employee may start to practice them. Adriano hired prestigious designers to design Olivetti's typewriters—people who clearly had deep skills—but he also assured that the workplace was structured to nurture their empathy and curiosity. Like IDEO's leaders, he believed that people perform at their best not because they're specialists, but rather because their depth of skill is accompanied by an intellectual curiosity that leads them to keep exploring.

Research evidence for a link between curiosity and innovation abounds. Spencer Harrison, of the INSEAD business school in France, and his colleagues examined this relationship in the context of an e-commerce website where people sell handmade goods. Over a two-week period, the artisans answered questions about the level of curiosity they experienced at work. Their productivity was then assessed by counting the number of new items each artisan listed over a two-week period. Curiosity was associated with a greater creative productivity; a one-unit increase in curiosity (e.g., moving from a score of 5 to 6 on a 7-point scale) was associated with a 34 percent increase in productivity.

Curiosity produces performance benefits in all kinds of jobs. Take the case of call centers, where jobs are heavily structured. As a result, turnover is generally high. To make matters worse, calls are often monitored, and employees' performance is evaluated based on the speed at which they handle each call. Harrison and his colleagues asked new employees from ten different call-center organizations to complete a survey that measured their curiosity before they started working in their company's call center. Four weeks into the job, the same employees reported on different aspects of their job, such as how well they were learning and whether they were seeking information by reaching out to other colleagues. The most curious people the company had hired were those who sought the most information from coworkers, and they were the best able to use that information in a way that allowed them to be creative and perform at higher levels. Some of them, the researchers learned in follow-up interviews, saw their jobs less as "an assembly line in your brain," in the words of one employee, and more like a puzzle in which they had to figure out new ways to use the prescribed system to benefit customers. It was these people who became the highest performers.

My own research finds that curious people often end up being star performers in their organizations for several reasons: they have larger networks; they're more comfortable asking questions; and they more easily create and nurture ties with others at work—ties that are critical to their career development and success. The organization also benefits, as these curious employees are more connected to others who can help them overcome work challenges and are more motivated to go the extra mile.

When Adriano was the CEO of Olivetti, one of his workers was caught leaving the factory with a bag full of iron pieces and machinery. The colleagues who caught him accused him of being a thief and suggested the company fire him. The employee protested that he wasn't stealing, but rather taking the parts home to work on a project over the weekend because he didn't have enough time to do it at work. When Adriano heard the story, he asked to speak with the worker directly. At their meeting, the worker explained that he had a plan to build a new machine, a calculator. Intrigued, Adriano put him in charge of the production process for the new machine. Not long after, the new electrical calculating machine was built—the first of its type on the market. The Divisumma offered automatic calculation with all four basic mathematical operations. In the 1950s and 1960s, Divisumma became a popular product across the globe and was a dramatic, lucrative success for Olivetti. Adriano promoted the worker to the position of technical director. Rather than firing the employee, Adriano gave him the opportunity to play with his curiosity, with astounding results.

HIGHWAY 101 RUNS FOR OVER FIFTEEN HUNDRED MILES ON THE WEST COAST OF the United States, through the states of California, Oregon, and Washington. Back in 2004, an anonymous billboard made its appearance on the highway south of San Francisco, in the heart of the Silicon Valley. The billboard had a strange ad on it: "{first 10-digit prime found in consecutive digits of e}.com." Across the country, in Cambridge, Massachusetts, a similar mysterious banner appeared at the Harvard Square subway stop.

The message contains a challenging math puzzle. As I found out after a bit of searching online (since I couldn't remember this from my math classes), *e*, the base of the natural system of logarithms, has a numerical value of 2.71828. The number actually goes on forever, but eventually you will get to the first ten-digit prime found consecutively within it. (The correct answer is 7427466391.com.) If you were curious enough to solve the problem and then go to the website, you would have found another equation to solve, an even harder problem. Eventually, if you were a determined enough problem-solver, you would have found yourself at a Google webpage asking you to upload your résumé. From there, the few remaining contestants landed an interview at Google headquarters.

Tech companies have relied on mathematical and logical puzzles for quite some time, at least since the 1950s, in their attempts to recruit the most curious candidates. For instance, Microsoft, which popularized this hiring method, posed the following problem to candidates in first-round interviews: "Imagine an old-fashioned clock with two hands on it. When it is at twelve o'clock, the minute hand is directly on top of the hour hand. The question is, how many times a day does it happen that the minute hand is right over the hour hand, and how would you determine the exact times of the day that this occurs?" (You can find the answer in the Notes section of this book.) Other companies use more obvious methods to find curious employees, from explicitly encouraging curious people to apply in job postings to asking candidates about their interests and hobbies outside of work.

With its billboard recruitment plan, Google was looking for people who are "geeky enough to be annoyed at the very existence of a math problem they haven't solved, and smart enough to rectify the situation," according to an official blog post written by Googlers in 2004. If engineers were curious enough to pursue answers to the problem, they had a quality the company was looking for. Curiosity encourages new ways of thinking, challenges long-held assumptions, and fuels transformative change. As Google

CEO Eric Schmidt has commented, "We run this company on questions, not answers."

Recruiting creative people is certainly important, and finding them can be challenging. But by far the biggest challenge that organizations and their leaders face comes after an employee is hired: How do we keep people creative? The curiosity we all naturally had as children does not express itself as easily when we become adults. And as we enter new relationships, whether at work or in life, we all face the risk of seeing our creativity decline because we stop asking questions. In one survey, I asked about 250 people who had recently started new jobs with various companies about their level of curiosity when they started. Although they started off at different levels, after six months passed, their curiosity level had dropped by more than 20 percent, on average. Why? We ask too few questions when approaching problems. We work to finish assigned tasks without questioning the process or asking about overall goals. And, rather than celebrating curiosity, our leaders often discourage it. They see its value, but their actions often tell an alarmingly different story.

In another survey, I asked over three thousand employees from several industries to answer a few questions about curiosity. Most of them (92 percent) credited curious people for bringing new ideas into teams and organizations, and viewed curiosity as a catalyst to job satisfaction, innovation, and high performance. Yet only a minority, about 24 percent, reported feeling curious in their jobs on a regular basis. And about 70 percent reported facing barriers to asking more questions at work, like the pressure to execute their work at a rapid pace, the reluctance to take risks, fearing some sort of punishment in the case of failure, and the unwillingness to question existing procedures.

We all differ in how curious we are by nature. But no matter our natural level of curiosity, in organizations, curiosity can be fostered. Leaders can encourage it throughout their company by first being more inquisitive and curious themselves. Curiosity needs champions, and that needs to start at the top. Whether in brainstorming sessions or in regular firm meetings, leaders can set a good example by asking "Why?" and "What if?"—just as Zanardi did at Ritz-Carlton and Greg Dyke did at the BBC—and by encouraging others to do the same. As the sense of curiosity grows in a workplace, some good answers will likely follow. Outside of company meetings, leaders can stress the importance of curiosity in other ways. For instance, Facebook CEO Mark Zuckerberg publicly sets new personal learning goals for himself each year, inspiring others inside the firm to do the same. In the last few years, Zuckerberg's goals included learning Mandarin, reading a book every other week, meeting a new person every day who doesn't work at Facebook, and visiting and meeting people in every state in the United States.

Organizations can also foster curiosity by encouraging their employees to explore their interests. When Adriano Olivetti was presented with a "thief," he recognized a talent who needed the time and resources to explore a great idea. Other successful leaders and organizations have done the same kind of thing. Since 1996, the manufacturing conglomerate United Technologies (UTC) has provided up to $12,000 in tuition per year to employees seeking advanced degrees on a part-time basis, no strings attached. Employers are often not in favor of training staff, fearing they might find a job with a competitor and leave the firm with their expensively acquired skills. But Gail Jackson, UTC's vice president of human resources, thinks differently about this. "We want people who are intellectually curious," she notes. "It is better to train and have them leave than not to train and have them stay."

Another way leaders can foster curiosity in employees is by acknowledging the limits of their own knowledge with a simple "I don't know—let's find out," or by highlighting the inherent ambiguity of a decision the company is facing. At one company I visited, employees were asked to come up with "What if . . . ?" and "How might we . . . ?" questions about the firm's goals and its plans. As a sign that questioning was not only encouraged but also supported and rewarded, employees and management chose the best of these questions to display on banners on the company's walls. Maintaining this sense of curiosity is crucial to creativity and innovation in an organization. Think of the story behind Polaroid: The inspiration that led to the instant camera was born out of a question that the three-year-old daughter of its inventor, Edwin H. Land, asked in the mid-1940s. When her father snapped a photo, she found herself waiting impatiently to see it. She learned that the film had to be processed first, but as her father explained this to her, she wondered aloud, "Why do we have to wait for the picture?"

There's a good management lesson to learn in the way parents respond when their baby comes across something new. First a baby will express surprise, and then look at the parent: If the parent makes a sad face or a face that evokes negative emotions, then the child's surprised expression turns negative. If the parent expresses pleasant excitement, on the other hand, then the child does as well. Similarly, at work, we'll continue questioning and exploring only if we are part of a group or organization characterized by what researchers refer to as "psychological safety"—a shared belief that members can take risks. If a workplace does not feel safe, a person is reluctant to ask questions or even to bring up problems that would clearly make the group better off. When Harvard Business School management scholar Amy Edmondson studied medical teams in various hospitals, she discovered that the best teams were the ones that were psychologically safe: Team members were not afraid to admit to errors and discussed them openly with their colleagues. In a group that is psychologically safe, you would not fear being embarrassed about raising unorthodox questions, ideas, or doubts.

Think of one of the most beloved characters in children's literature: Curious George. The little high-energy monkey who lives with the Man with the Yellow Hat dives into every experience he comes across, eager to explore and experiment. The Man with the Yellow Hat is always ready to bail George out of the sticky situations he gets himself into (for instance, flying by in a helicopter just when George floats too high on a bunch of balloons). Fortunately for George, he benefits from his curiosity, enjoying new experiences and discoveries, because he's never punished for getting into trouble. Too often, there is no room for Curious George characters in the workplace. People who explore and end up with unsuccessful experiments or, even worse, create a messy situation, are usually punished for it. Rarely are they praised for championing the value of experimentation regardless of outcome.

There are many ways that leaders can let employees know they value curiosity. When Satya Nadella joined Microsoft in 2014 as the new CEO, for instance, he changed the criteria in the firm's performance review so that they would include an evaluation of how well employees learn from their colleagues, share ideas, and apply their new knowledge. Ed Catmull, who cofounded Pixar Animation Studios and is now its president, worried that Pixar's success would lead new hires to be in awe, to the point that they would not challenge existing practices. To address his worry, during onboarding sessions when new employees are welcomed to the firm and get socialized into it, he shares examples of how the company has made certain bad choices in the past. He stresses the simple but often overlooked fact that we all make mistakes and that Pixar is not perfect. His unusual candor gives new recruits the license they need to be curious.

Training can also foster healthy questioning. Recently, an organization approached INSEAD's Spencer Harrison for advice on encouraging curiosity in its employees. With his colleagues, he created two versions of an online training program for the firm. Half of the company's employees were taught what the researchers called "the grow method," which explained that success would come from following existing processes. The other half received a modified version, called the "go back method," which asked employees to go back and question the common assumptions we all tend to hold about goals, roles, and the organization as a whole. As an example, employees learning the "go back method" were told the story of a scientist who was trying to help people with diseases that caused their extremities to shake, which made it difficult for them to complete certain activities, such as eating cereal for breakfast. Initially, the scientist was focused on the idea of creating a drug that would stop the shaking. But as he thought more about the goal of stopping the tremors, he came up with a mechanical solution: attaching a gyroscope to a spoon so that the spoon would absorb the tremors.

Weeks later, managers at the company rated the employees who went through the "go back" training as more creative and innovative than those who received the more traditional training (without knowing who had engaged in which program). Harrison and his colleagues also examined the type of connections people created at work by looking at the emails they exchanged with one another. They found that people who went through the "go back" training changed how they engaged with their colleagues: they expanded their networks, sent more emails, and, as a result, gathered more information, which allowed them to be more creative in their jobs. When we ask questions about aspects of our job and organization that we generally take for granted, we build relationships with colleagues more easily, and our ideas get more interesting.

ARE YOU STILL WONDERING ABOUT HOW HOUDINI MADE THE ELEPHANT DISAPPEAR? Researchers often use the Vanishing Elephant trick to trigger curiosity and study its effects on people's behavior. For instance, doctoral student Lydia Hagtvedt of Boston College and her colleagues divided participants into two groups, and asked them to read different versions of a news article on the Vanishing Elephant trick. For one group, the article described the Vanishing Elephant trick as an industry standard and included an explanation of exactly how Houdini accomplished it. Participants were asked to describe how they would feel if they were watching in the audience and how they thought Houdini did the trick, which had already been explained to them. They submitted their responses via computer. After a short delay, they were informed that their answer regarding the solution to the trick was correct.

For the second group, the experiment's "curiosity condition," the article did not include any clues about how the trick worked. After reading the article, the participants had to describe how they would feel if they were in the audience watching and how they thought Houdini did the trick, and, as with the other group, they submitted their responses via computer. But in this case, it appeared as if their answer to the question about how the trick worked was being compared to a correct answer in a database; in reality, this was simply a time delay in the program. After a few seconds, participants were told that their answer was close but not fully correct. In this way, participants in the second group remained curious about how the trick was accomplished, while those in the control group were led to feel confident that they knew the nature of the trick.

Next, all participants moved on to a different task: generating additional ideas for magic tricks. They had to imagine that they were Houdini and were hoping to perform a trick better than the elephant one. Professional magicians with over twenty years of experience evaluated the creativity of the participants' responses. In addition, independent coders read participants' answers and rated the degree to which their magic-trick ideas moved beyond the core aspects of the original Vanishing Elephant trick. So, for instance, a response such as, "I would put the curtain over the box with the elephant in it and then make the box disappear leaving just the elephant," received a low score because the idea involved the three core aspects of the Vanishing Elephant trick: disappearing, elephants, and boxes. But a response like "I would perform a trick where it looked like I was levitating" received the highest possible score because it did not contain any of the core aspects of the original trick.

Participants in the curiosity condition generated ideas that the professional magicians evaluated as creative significantly more often (69 percent of the time) than those in the control condition (34 percent of the time). Their ideas were also less fixated on core aspects of the Vanishing Elephant trick. Curiosity led participants to generate ideas that experts judged as more creative and that diverged more dramatically from the status quo.

Throughout his career, once Houdini had mastered one escape, like freeing himself from locked handcuffs, he would quickly move on to mastering a new challenge, like having the local police in a town he visited restrain him, and managing to escape. Once he'd mastered each of these situations, he decided to try jumping into rivers while handcuffed and chained. Houdini was constantly looking for new ways to challenge himself. He pushed himself relentlessly and trained hard for his various difficult feats. When we realize that we don't have an immediate answer to a puzzle or problem that confronts us, our mind fills with creative ideas, if we let it. Every single day we can choose between focusing on what we know or what we don't know. When we do the latter, we engage our curiosity and are more likely to see the world as Houdini did.

Houdini inspired awe in his audiences through his magic, Greg Dyke took the helm at the BBC by asking questions rather than providing answers, Google found rare talent by making potential job candidates wonder, and Adriano Olivetti created an almost magical workplace where he used various tricks to broaden his employees' interests. Although tough and competitive at different times and in different contexts, all these players were able to instill curiosity in those they interacted with, and remained curious themselves. Their inquisitive nature and sense of wonder was contagious.

As it turns out, the vanishing trick was not actually invented by Houdini. The credit for it goes to Charles Morritt, a hypnotist and illusionist from Yorkshire, England, whose trick the Disappearing Donkey was a precursor to Houdini's Vanishing Elephant. For the donkey trick, Morritt would usher the uncooperative animal into a wooden chamber on wheels, and the audience could see that there were no trapdoors being used. As Morritt closed up the sides, the audience could hear the sound of the donkey's hooves pounding the wood of the chamber that held him prisoner. Unbeknownst to those in the audience, the chamber had been specially designed, and when Morritt opened it up again, the donkey had "disappeared." Audiences loved the act, which eventually brought Morritt to Houdini's attention.

Despite his inventive genius, Morritt's ability and charisma as a performer were lacking. Morritt also needed money, so he sold Houdini the secrets to many of his best and most carefully guarded illusions, including the Disappearing Donkey. The switch from donkey to elephant was Morritt's idea as well, a suggestion he made to Houdini to make the stunt even more memorable. Here is how the Vanishing Elephant trick actually worked: When Jennie entered the box, her trainer hid the elephant behind a large mirror that extended on a diagonal from the corner of the box that was closest to the audience to the center of the doors at the back of the box. When the doors were reopened, the audience saw a seemingly empty box, not realizing that they were actually viewing only one half of the box's interior and its reflection.

Though Houdini did not invent the trick, he brought his amazing showmanship to it, and he constantly pushed to make it better. The fact that audiences remained amazed by the trick for decades, and that no one could figure it out until one of Houdini's prop engineers divulged the secret to *Modern Mechanix* magazine in 1929, was due in large part to how well Houdini performed and perfected it. For the stunned audience, Houdini's Vanishing Elephant magic trick raised a question with no clear answer—and it inspired the curiosity of generations.

4

THE HUDSON RIVER IS A RUNWAY

A TALENT FOR PERSPECTIVE

There's a literal freedom you feel when you're at the controls, gliding above the surface on the earth, no longer bound by gravity . . . Even at a few thousand feet, you get a wider perspective.
—CAPTAIN CHESLEY SULLENBERGER

On a January afternoon in 2009, US Airways flight 1549 took off from LaGuardia Airport in New York, headed for Charlotte, North Carolina. The weather in New York was cold, about 21 degrees Fahrenheit. The winds coming out of the north were not too strong, and the sky was mostly clear with only scattered clouds—it had stopped snowing earlier that morning. The plane carried 150 passengers and five crew members; only one seat was empty. For the crew, this was the final leg of a four-day trip. Captain Chesley Sullenberger, an experienced pilot known as "Sully," shared the cockpit with Jeff Skiles, a first officer with whom he'd never worked before.

Less than two minutes into the flight, Sully looked out of the cockpit's front windows to see birds—massive ones, their long wings extended horizontally—flying headlong toward the plane. The plane was climbing above 3,000 feet, the engines whining with the effort, at just over 230 miles an hour. "Birds!" Sully shouted.

At the same moment, the sound of something similar to a very bad storm filled the cockpit and cabin, as if the plane were being pelted by hail or heavy rain. The birds began to hit the plane just below the windshield, smashing against the nose, the wings, and the engines with a series of thuds. Then a loud screeching noise came from the engines, followed by severe vibrations, as if the engines were protesting the sudden disruption. A pungent charred smell entered the cabin, and then the engine noises subsided—an eerie quiet. Everyone heard a "rhythmic rumbling and rattling, like a stick being held against moving bicycle spokes. It was a strange windmilling sound from broken engines," Sully said. The Airbus A320-214 has two engines, and both had failed.

With so little altitude and both engines destroyed, there was little time to act. If the plane had lost one engine rather than two, the pilot and first officer would have been able to maintain control of the aircraft. They would have declared an emergency and, with the air traffic controller's help, found a nearby airport where they could likely land safely. But without any working engines, the plane had become a very heavy glider, loaded with fuel.

"My aircraft," Sully said, and took control of the plane. "Your aircraft," Skiles responded. He pulled out the aircraft's Quick Reference Handbook, found the checklist for loss of thrust in both engines, and got to work. "Mayday, mayday, mayday," Sully called out to Air Traffic Control. Patrick Harten, the air traffic controller sitting at his radar position at the New York Terminal Radar Approach Control located on Long Island, didn't hear the mayday call. At the same moment Sully was calling out for help, Harten was making a transmission of his own—to Sully himself, giving him routine direction for the flight. When Harten released his transmit button, he caught part of Sully's emergency message: ". . . hit birds. We've lost thrust in both engines. We're turning back toward LaGuardia."

In his ten years on the job, Harten had worked many thousands of flights and had never failed to help a plane in distress get safely to a runway. He had worked in many emergency situations in the past, from assisting jets with failures of one engine to helping airplanes hit by birds. Controllers guide pilots to runways: that's their job. Harten offered Sully LaGuardia's runway 13, which was the closest to the plane's current position. He immediately contacted the tower at LaGuardia, asking them to clear all runaways. "Cactus fifteen twenty-nine, if we can get it for you, do you want to try to land runway one three?" he asked, getting the flight number wrong in the stress of the moment.

Looking out the window, it was clear to Sully that there were few good options. The 150,000-pound plane was gliding at a low altitude, at low speed, with no engines, and it was descending rapidly. The jagged architecture of the nation's largest metropolis was all too clear through the windshield. There was no major interstate nearby without heavy traffic. Nor were there any long, level farmer's fields. Turning back for the airport they had left just minutes earlier would eliminate all other options. Given how densely populated the area surrounding LaGuardia is, choosing to turn back needed to be a sure thing rather than a probable bet. Even if they made it back—which wasn't looking likely to Sully—missing the runway by just a few feet would mean a torn-open airplane, engulfed in flames.

"All right, Cactus fifteen forty-nine, it's gonna be left traffic for runway three one," Harten said to Sully.

"Unable," Sully responded. He had made the decision: LaGuardia was not an option. As the plane kept dropping, the synthetic voice of the Traffic Collision Avoidance System issued a warning inside the cockpit: "Traffic. Traffic."

Harten offered another runway at LaGuardia.

"I'm not sure we can make any runway," Sully responded. "What's over to our right? . . . anything in New Jersey, maybe Teterboro?"

On his radar screen, Harten could see that the plane was now about nine hundred feet above the Manhattan side of the George Washington Bridge, which stretches across the Hudson River from New York City to New Jersey. Teterboro was no closer than LaGuardia, but Sully was considering all possibilities. Working with the Teterboro controller, Harten quickly arranged for the plane to land on the arrival runway—the one easiest to clear of traffic. But Sully could see the area around the airport moving up in the windscreen—Teterboro, he realized, was also going to be too far away. That left the Hudson River.

Sully had been flying airplanes for forty-two years, since he was in high school in Denison, Texas. He'd gone on to attend the Air Force Academy and began his career flying a Vietnam War–era fighter, the F-4 Phantom. In his many years of flying, he had never experienced an engine failure. Nor had he ever tried to land in a body of water. But from his perspective, the river was long enough, wide enough, and smooth enough to serve as a landing spot. Outside, it was just 21 degrees, the wind-chill factor was 11, and the water was about 36 degrees. Rescue boats or helicopters would take at least a few minutes to arrive at the scene to help. Hypothermia posed a serious risk to passengers even if the plane made it into the river intact. But the choice seemed to be the best option, for the simple reason that there were no buildings on the Hudson.

Sully made a cabin announcement: "Brace for impact."

Skiles had tried multiple times to relight the engines with the standard clicking igniters, but it hadn't worked: The engines had banged and flamed and lost thrust on the right and almost completely on the left. They had both swallowed dozens of Canada geese, but they hadn't exploded or thrown shrapnel into the fuselage. They were simply not restarting. Skiles stopped trying and focused instead on helping Sully as they were heading into the Hudson.

Without any thrust, the only control Sully had over the plane's vertical path was the raising and lowering of its nose—that is, the pitch. His goal was to maintain a pitch that would give the airplane an appropriate glide speed, not too fast, not too slow, so as to land in the water as gently as possible. The airspeed indicator was still working, so every time Sully thought he was slower than he needed to be, he lowered the nose of the plane slightly. And when he felt the plane was traveling too fast, he raised the nose.

". . . turn right two eight zero," Harten told Sully. "You can land runway one at Teterboro."

"We can't do it."

"OK, which runway would you like at Teterboro?" Sully was the one inside the plane, Harten knew, and had a better sense for the situation.

"We're going to be in the Hudson," Sully responded.

"I'm sorry," Harten said, ". . . say again?"

He continued to offer options to Sully, trying to find a solution that would keep the plane out of the water, but there was no answer. "Uh," he said, "you still on?"

Sully was focusing on the task at hand. The plane was less than twenty-two seconds away from impact. From the cockpit, the water was moving faster and faster toward the plane.

"Brace, brace! Heads down, stay down!" the flight attendants shouted. They had no eye-level windows, but some of the passengers could tell that the plane was headed into the water. One passenger called out from the back of the plane, "Exit row people, get ready!" A man sitting mid-plane asked the woman sitting next to him if he could brace her baby boy for her. She gave the child to him. Other passengers began to pray.

Back in the cockpit, the automated ground-warning alarm

kept going off: "Too low. Terrain. Caution, terrain." Another automated callout from a different warning system kept repeating the same message: "Terrain, terrain. Pull up. Pull up," as if it were hoping someone could change how the event was unfolding. Sully and Skiles worked to slow the plane by extending the flaps on the plane's wings. At 200 feet, flying at about 180 miles an hour, the plane was still on its glide.

Sully lowered the nose slightly in the last few seconds before the plane touched the water. This put the aircraft at a more favorable angle and at a speed of less than 140 miles an hour. The impact tore away the left engine and ripped open the plane's belly toward the rear. The plane skimmed to a stop. The Hudson's dark green heavy spray made the passengers sitting near the windows think they had gone underwater.

The plane was floating on the river, but there was no time to waste. Water rushed in from the tail of the plane, making the rear exit doors unusable. The doors at the front of the aircraft and those over the wings, all of them still above the waterline, were opened, and emergency rafts inflated when they did. One after the other, the passengers evacuated the airplane, climbing onto the wing and entering escape slides. Sully and Skiles helped the flight attendants assist passengers and hand out life vests. At the rear, the floor had buckled, and a beam from the plane had broken through, causing water to rise almost as high as the chests of the passengers and crew waiting to evacuate. As they made their way out, some were disoriented, stunned to realize they had landed in the Hudson.

In just three-and-a-half minutes, everyone had evacuated the plane. Sully and Skiles, with the help of some young male passengers, gathered blankets, coats, jackets, and life vests from inside to hand to those standing on the plane wings, shivering from the cold. Water rose to the ankles of some and almost up to the waists of others. One passenger jumped into the river and began swimming toward New York but, deterred by the frigid water, swam back to the plane; other passengers helped him get into a raft. One passenger slipped off the wing and into the water, and two others pulled her back, risking falling into the river themselves. On the plane's wings, on inflated slides, and in the emergency rafts, passengers and crew members awaited rescue.

Within four minutes, the first of the rescue boats arrived. Sully was the last to exit the plane and board a boat: He walked in the deep water of the cabin multiple times to make sure that no one had been left behind. There were no casualties. From the moment the flock of migratory Canada geese hit the plane to the moment Flight 1549 touched down onto the Hudson River, only 208 seconds had passed.

FOR MANY PILOTS, FLYING CAN BECOME A FAMILIAR ROUTINE, WHICH INCLUDES sticking to a scripted series of steps like checking the flight plan and fuel volume before departure, or working through the preflight checklists. Even in the case of an extreme emergency, pilots are trained to carefully follow standard operating procedures. After all, as any experienced pilot will tell you, it is much safer to work through a checklist than it is to frantically do the first things that come to mind.

Flight 1549 was no different. Captain Sully called for the Quick Reference Handbook (QRH) about thirteen seconds after the bird strike. First officer Skiles already had the QRH out and open to the appropriate page—the "Dual Engine Failure Checklist," which identifies steps to follow when both engines of an Airbus fail. The handbook is full of technical shorthand (e.g., FAC 1, OFF then ON; ENG MODE Selector, IGN) and directions that only experienced pilots would understand ("Add 1° of nose up for each 22,000 lbs above 111,000 lbs . . .").

Airbus designed its checklist under the assumption that dual-engine failures would only happen at cruising altitude and that the crew would have plenty of time to run the multipage list. But those were not the conditions that Skiles and Sully found themselves in. Nonetheless, they started to follow the plan. Various decision paths were built into the QRH. For instance, Step 1 concerns fuel. "If no fuel remaining . . ." has eight sub-steps to complete before going on to Step 2. "If fuel remaining . . ." is even more complicated, with guidance based on type of aircraft, ability to reach Air Traffic Control, and the results of trying to relight the engines. The longest path in the QRH has fifteen sub-steps. The crew of Flight 1549 worked through much of the checklist, including an attempt to relight the engines, but ran out of time and could not execute Step 3: preparing for ditching—that is, an emergency water landing.

When you face a stressful situation—a car veering into your lane, your boss asking you to speak up in a meeting on a topic you know little about, your partner lashing out after you forgot to do something important—your body responds by making sure you've registered the threat. Your heart pounds. Your palms get clammy. And your mind is affected as well: You focus on the immediate threat, to the exclusion of the world around you. Your thinking and attention narrow. Although this evolutionary trait, known as "fight-or-flight response," served humans well when they were facing threats in the wild, it leads to poor decision-making in the modern world. Under stress, we tend to scan a few alternatives quickly and overlook the bigger picture.

In a crisis, when we think about what we *should* do, we focus on the most apparent courses of action, often those we relied on when making similar decisions in the past, whether we are following a checklist or not. Paradoxically, though, it is at these moments of extreme stress that taking a step back would be most helpful. When we think about what we *could* do, our thinking becomes much broader: We imagine and explore a much larger set of possibilities before making a final decision. Considering what we *could* do shifts us from analyzing and weighing options that we assume to be fixed to generating more creative options.

The different outcomes of "should" and "could" thinking apply beyond our reactions to extreme emergencies. In all aspects of our lives, whenever we face an important decision, we naturally ask ourselves "What should I do?" But this framing constricts the answers we will come up with. When we instead ask ourselves "What could I do?" we broaden our perspective.

Imagine how easy it would be to fall into "should" thinking when you are flying a modern jet, with all of its automation and strict procedures. Sully avoided this fate, thanks in large part to his commitment to lifelong learning. For him, as he told me during an interview, that meant making each flight a learning experience and each one better than the previous one. By considering what he could learn every time he entered the cockpit, Sully remained open to the possibility that the flight would provide some new knowledge or insight he had not considered before. It's also essential, Sully told me, to be aware of the tunnel vision that threatens to engulf us in stressful situations, and to learn to broaden our perspective so that we are in a better position to evaluate a range of options, including novel ideas—such as landing in the Hudson River.

Once we get comfortable with a job, it is natural to perform many parts of it without much thought. By forcing himself to continuously learn, Sully was able to fight the tendency to succumb to routine and assume that every flight is the same as the previous one. This aspect of his rebel mindset kept him open to new perspectives, and saved the lives of everyone on the plane. In our own jobs, we might not be facing life-or-death situations, but we do face stressful situations.

Imagine you are on your way to be a top performer at B&B, a medium-sized investment bank. When it comes to organizational loyalty, B&B has an almost cult-like culture: Those who choose to stay there accept that company loyalty comes before their health, family, and friends. One of the main projects you have been working on involves orchestrating a leveraged buyout for one of B&B's clients, a company called Suntech. B&B provides short-term financing, put together bank financing for the deal, and it also acquired most of Suntech's assets. One of the banks that was involved in underwriting the loan for the senior debt was Universal, and you know one of the Universal team members who worked on the project well: She is your roommate, Sandy.

You come home one day after work and find Sandy in tears. She tells you that your conversation needs to be confidential, and you agree, assuming she's having a personal problem. But then she tells you that Universal is dissolving its capital finance group, which means that not only is Sandy out of a job, but the deal with B&B is now in jeopardy. Here's your dilemma: If you do not share this news with your boss at B&B right away, then the public might hear of it first, making potential investors in Suntech turn their attention to other opportunities and putting both B&B and the client at risk. But you also promised Sandy that you would not talk to anyone about this confidential situation. You face an almost impossible choice between breaching your loyalty to your friend and risking serious damage to your employer and one of its clients. This is a moral dilemma in which the competing principles of duty to your friend and to your firm and client are both important. There's no obvious "right" answer.

I framed this story as a fictional one, but it's based on the real-life experience of a former student in a leadership and accountability class taught by one of my Harvard Business School colleagues. This all transpired while this student was in my colleague's class, and he had reached out for advice. As part of a study, my colleagues and I presented a similar set of dilemmas to a group of study participants. We asked some of them, "What should you do?" We asked others, "What would you do?" And we asked yet another group to answer the question, "What could you do?" Approaching a dilemma with "could" thinking led participants to examine it from new and fresh perspectives, and to generate many more possible solutions. They realized that they did not have to concede one set of moral imperatives for another to resolve a dilemma. For example, one could-thinking participant wrote, "I would keep my promise to Sandy, but would line up alternative financing for the senior debt. If I could pull this off, I could spin the loss of Universal's role in the deal as a positive for other banks who would profit from Universal's defection." The solutions that "could" thinkers generated were more morally insightful than those of "should" or "would" thinkers: they went beyond choosing one side of the dilemma at the expense of the other. (In real life, following advice from my colleague, the former HBS student convinced his roommate to allow him to broker a meeting between the Universal and B&B team members, where the news inevitably came out, avoiding disaster.) When you open your mind to considering a seemingly impossible situation from a new perspective, a solution may come to you.

EVERY YEAR, CARDIOLOGISTS PERFORM HUNDREDS OF THOUSANDS OF ANGIOPLASties, procedures that restore blood flow through the coronary artery, with the insertion of a small wire cage called a vascular stent. After being introduced in the 1990s, stents became the treatment of choice due to their ability to relieve pain and because they are a far less invasive (and cheaper) treatment than bypass surgery. Doctors and patients started to believe that stents also saved the lives of patients with stable angina (a painful condition caused by poor blood flow through the blood vessels in the heart), though there was no solid evidence of that. In the early 2000s, a new device called a drug-eluting stent came along, which slowly releases a drug to prevent the artery from closing again, something that could happen with the bare-metal stents. These stents were welcomed with much enthusiasm from both doctors and patients because they were more effective in keeping the blockage from coming back, but were considered just as safe, if not safer, than the bare-metal stents.

In late 2006, however, medical studies suggested that drug-eluting stents were being used in cases not approved by the U.S. Food and Drug Administration (FDA), including cases where patients had been diagnosed with more complex conditions, and that these "off-label" uses likely increased the risk of blood clotting and even death. As a result, in 2006, an emergency FDA advisory panel issued a warning about the dangers of such off-label use. In its announcement, the FDA advised physicians to use caution, particularly when treating off-label cases. Over the next several months, the market share of drug-eluting stents fell from over 90 percent to about 60 percent.

My colleagues and I wanted to understand how cardiologists reacted to the FDA's announcement and what role expertise might play. We gathered data on 147,010 angioplasty procedures performed by 399 cardiologists over a six-year period. There was a surprising pattern: Cardiologists with *more* experience were more likely to continue to use drug-eluting stents, despite the obvious dangers highlighted by the FDA. We saw the same thing with doctors who were surrounded by experienced cardiologists, independent of how long they'd been in the field. We all tend to modify our behavior as a result of pressure from those around us. For the doctors in our sample, this translated into following the choices of more experienced cardiologists, not realizing that the effect of experience was to obscure what was best for patients.

We generally think of experience as a good thing. With experience comes knowledge, skill, and expertise, after all. Sully, for example, wouldn't have been able to land his plane in the Hudson River without all those years of experience. When we face problems that we believe we've encountered in the past and that we have the proper knowledge to solve, we feel a sense of comfort and confidence. This feeling, psychology research tells us, often leads us to approach situations mindlessly rather than thoughtfully. Fighting this feeling was another way that Sully was exceptional.

Sully studied psychology at the Air Force Academy and then served as a fighter pilot for the U.S. Air Force for five years. "Flying a jet fighter is the pinnacle of tactical military aviation," he's said. "It's like driving a Formula One racer on steroids—in three dimensions, not just two." He often used his spare time to teach other cadets to fly airplanes and gliders on his weekends and after school. He went on to become a training officer and a flight leader after that, and then a commercial airline pilot—a position that led to thousands of additional hours of flying. Sully also enjoyed investigating past airline accidents and understanding the mistakes of other pilots as a pilot's union safety volunteer and accident investigator. He learned about cases where standard procedures did not produce the desired outcomes, and about cases where human judgment failed under pressure. To broaden his education, he completed two master's degrees: one in public administration from the University of Northern Colorado and one in industrial psychology from Purdue University. It's hard to imagine anyone having more expertise in the cockpit.

But Sully viewed expertise not as something to achieve, but as a process that must be kept alive. "I have been making small, regular deposits in this bank throughout my life of education, training, and experience," he told me. "When we were suddenly confronted with a tough situation that day, the balance in that account was sufficient that I could make a sudden withdrawal." He had never practiced a water landing before, as the simulators did not even allow it. But he had gained much experience from all sorts of different situations, which reminded him that there is always something more to learn and that every choice can be approached from more than just one perspective. And as he acquired more and more flying hours, Sully found a simple way to fight the feeling of knowing: Though flights are almost always routine, every time the plane pushed back from the gate, he reminded himself that he needed to be prepared for the unexpected. Before each flight, he would ask himself, "What can I learn?"

Our understanding of human psychology suggests that Sully's mindset was crucial. When we frame work around *learning* goals—such as developing our competence, acquiring new skills, and mastering new situations—we perform better than if we frame work around performance goals, such as hitting results targets. When we are motivated by learning rather than performance, we do better on tests, get higher grades, reach greater success in simulations and problem-solving tasks, and receive higher ratings after training. When Air Force–enlisted personnel received a challenging performance goal about the number of planes to be landed, the specific goal *decreased* rather than increased their performance landing planes. And in another study, sales professionals with a performance orientation performed worse than those who had learning goals.

The danger of the feeling of knowing is that it leads us to rationalize our prior views and decisions—and the urge gets stronger with more experience. "Like a totalitarian government," writes psychologist Joachim Krueger of Brown University, "the ego has been said to shape perception in such a way that it protects a sense of its own good will, its central place in the social world and its control over relevant outcomes." Experience should open our minds to the fact that the same decision or task can be approached differently. And yet, when the feeling of knowing intrudes unchecked, it closes us off instead. In one study, for instance, my colleagues and I asked participants to choose between two hypothetical investment options. Next, we made one group of decision makers, and not the other, feel like experts by having them answer an easy version of a general-knowledge test. The easy quiz had questions such as: "In what North American country is the city of Toronto located?" The quiz we gave to the other group included more challenging questions, such as, "Who is credited with inventing the wristwatch in 1904?" Once they completed the quiz, participants were shown the correct answers so that they could see how well they'd done.

We then presented everyone with bad news about the outcome of their investment choice and asked whether they wanted to change their decision. We wanted to see if those who felt like experts would be less open to a shift in strategy. And that is exactly what we found: As in the study of cardiologists, decision makers who felt a significant sense of expertise—even though it was founded on very little and unrelated to the area they were asked to judge—were unwilling to listen to important negative information.

Power aggravates the problem. As we climb the organizational ladder, our ego inflates, and we tend to feel even more threatened by information that proves us wrong. If we're not careful, being in charge can, over time, close us off to what others have to offer. When teaching the Harvard Business School cases I've written, I often invite the main protagonist to come in to class so that he or she can hear the class discussion and, during the last fifteen to twenty minutes of class, engage in a Q&A session with my students. A few years ago, I noticed an interesting pattern: the guests, usually high-level executives in the firm, typically said they were eager to learn from the students. But during the class, many would spend the time talking *at* the students, and in some cases even pontificating, rather than listening to the students' questions and being open to learning from them.

The gap between what many guests had told me they wanted to do in class and what they actually did was both puzzling and interesting, so I decided to investigate. My colleagues and I found that the executives in my classes were in fact exhibiting a more widespread behavior: When we (whether "we" are top executives or college students) feel powerful, we are less open to the perspectives of others. In one study, for instance, we induced some of our participants to feel powerful by asking them to write about a time when they had power over other people. When making decisions, those participants listened to their own opinions more than those of a more informed advisor. In another study, team leaders who were induced to feel powerful dominated the team discussion by taking most of the airtime. As a result, they missed out on learning critical information that other members of the team had. Their teams performed worse than those of leaders who were not induced to feel powerful, and team members enjoyed the experience less and felt less engaged. When Bob Nardelli was CEO at home retailer Home Depot, between 2000 and 2007, he used a brash communication style that didn't leave a lot of room for others' perspective. This lowered employees' morale, alienated workers, made stockholders angry, and led many executives to leave the company. After a few years at the helm, Nardelli came under fire and eventually resigned.

When we take too much "airtime," we demotivate those around us. In high-pressure environments, when leaders work with people who are highly talented and skilled, this lesson is especially critical. I saw this play out in a fascinating study I conducted while attending cardiac surgeries at a large teaching hospital in Boston. My colleagues and I observed fifty-eight operations and conducted thirty-four interviews with members of surgical teams, including surgeons, nurses, physician assistants, and anesthesiologists. The teams where everybody seemed to enjoy the work, in spite of challenges (from standing for hours on one's feet in a very cold room to the attention needed for coordination), were ones where the surgeons were approachable and not dictator-like in their style, inviting team members to contribute whenever appropriate. But other teams had a more difficult time working effectively together. The surgeons who led those teams, we found, had trouble trusting others. Their leadership style was more autocratic, and they especially struggled when they felt their authority was being threatened. Our observations supported other research on surgical teams, which has found that when a surgeon is inaccessible or has an autocratic style, the surgical team's performance suffers—often to the detriment of patients. Less autocratic surgery teams, by contrast, communicate and coordinate better, and achieve better outcomes for patients.

Rebels recognize that it is more important for the team to work well and get the job done than it is to display their power or respect some formal hierarchy. Once when Sully and his crew were preparing for a snowy flight out of Minneapolis, a baggage handler came up to the cockpit and told Sully that he had seen what looked like oil dripping from the right engine. Sully thanked him for his report. With the help of the first officer and a maintenance technician, Sully figured out that on the previous stop, a technician had put too much oil in the engine, and some of it had overflowed. But Sully wanted to thank the baggage handler for his effort, and rather than summoning him up to the cockpit again, Sully put on his overcoat and went down to find him. Even though there hadn't actually been a problem, Sully told the baggage handler, it was important to rule out this possibility. "You potentially saved us all a lot of trouble," Sully told the baggage handler. "I hope that, on another day, on another flight, if you notice something out of the ordinary, you will tell the crew again."

Too often, power is viewed as a license to raise one's voice without listening to the voices of others. When we feel powerful, research shows, we are more inclined to express our attitudes and opinions in groups, and we also come to devalue the perspectives, opinions, and contributions of others. As a result, we feel entitled to dominate these interactions. Leaders know all too well the power they have over their followers. In fact, "playing deaf" is a dysfunction I often observe in leaders: they disregard the views of others and pay attention only to their own. If they got to the top, they seem to think, it is because they know best.

At Osteria Francescana, with its three Michelin stars, there is always the risk that the fame that accompanies those stars can lead the whole team to become arrogant and inattentive to the needs of their customers. But as we were waiting to open the doors for dinner one night, maître d' Giuseppe Palmieri told me a story illustrating that this was anything but the case at the restaurant. A few months earlier, a family of four had booked a table for both Friday and Saturday nights. On Friday, all four family members—mother, father, and two sons, who were about eight and fourteen—ordered the thirteen-course tasting menu, called Sensations. On Saturday night, Palmieri and the rest of the front-of-the-house team welcomed them back. "We'll go with Tradition in Evolution for four," the father happily stated when it was time to order—another tasting menu, this one with ten courses. Palmieri smiled as he recounted the story to me. "I saw in the face of the kids a clear message, as if they were desperately thinking, 'Please, I don't want to eat that.' But they were being quiet about it. So I turned to the youngest boy and asked, 'What would *you* like to have?' And he told me, 'I would like to have a pizza.' "

Palmieri ran to the phone, called the best pizzeria in Modena, and ordered a pizza. It arrived not too long after, via taxi, for the kids to enjoy. "I am pretty sure those two children will never forget us for the happiness we brought to them that evening. It simply took a change of course, and one pizza."

WE ALL TEND TO PROCESS INFORMATION IN A SELF-SERVING MANNER. WE UNCRITI-cally accept evidence when it is consistent with what we want to believe and call for more data, or disregard the evidence, when it isn't. Harvard psychologist Dan Gilbert observed that the way we consider evidence resembles how we react to data from our bathroom scale when we weigh ourselves. If the scale gives us bad news, we get off and then step back on a second time, so that we can be sure there was not an error on the display, or that we weren't standing in a way that put unnecessary pressure on one foot. But when the display shows us good news, we proudly smile and then get into the shower. We get stuck in our own point of view and invested in just one type of thinking: our own.

Here's a more scientific example of how this tendency works. Two psychologists, Peter Ditto (of the University of California, Irvine) and David Lopez (founder and CEO of iAnalytics Statistical Consulting), told participants that they would take a test to determine whether they had a dangerous enzyme deficiency. For the test, participants had to put a drop of saliva on a strip and then wait for the results. Some learned that the test strip would turn green if they had the deficiency; others learned that green meant they did not have the deficiency. The strip wasn't a real test—it was simply a piece of paper that never changed its color. The result? Participants who hoped to see the test strip turn green as evidence that they didn't have the deficiency waited much longer than those who hoped not to see it turn green. That is, people waited more patiently for data when they believed the data would reassure them than when they believed it would scare them.

In another experiment, the two researchers asked participants to review information about a student one piece at a time so that they could evaluate his intelligence, the same way experts would during college admission decisions. The information was quite damning, and participants could stop examining it once they felt they had all the evidence they needed to reach a firm conclusion. Participants also received a picture of the student and some other information, allowing them to form a quick impression of the applicant. When participants liked the student, they kept turning over cards, searching for information that would allow them to evaluate him positively. But when they felt less fondly toward the student, they only turned over a few cards, enough to confirm the negative feelings they had for him.

Fortunately, there are ways to combat our self-serving tendencies. One powerful technique is suggested by the 1998 film *Sliding Doors*, in which Gwyneth Paltrow's character, Helen, rushes to catch a train in the London Underground. The film then follows two storylines: one in which Helen makes it through the sliding doors and onto the train, and one in which she misses the train. This seemingly minor moment ends up having a dramatic effect on Helen's life. The film prompts viewers to think about how events large and small might have changed how their lives have unfolded. Though we usually don't know how things might have gone differently if we'd made a train or caught an elevator, most of us, at different points in our lives, have probably found ourselves wondering, "What if I had . . . ?" Certain moments stand out to us as turning points that lead us to reflect on how life might have been different, for better or worse, if they hadn't occurred. For example, what if you had skipped the party where you met your romantic partner, accepted a different job, or approached a conflict with a coworker differently?

This "counterfactual thinking" is a powerful way to forget what you know and consider a situation from a fresh perspective. There are usually an infinite number of alternate worlds to all choices we make or problems we face, but most of the time we do not consider them unless we think counterfactually. When we do, we can feel more grateful for the jobs we have and happier in our relationships: we just need to think through alternatives that used to be available to us and that would have turned out to be quite undesirable.

When employees think counterfactually, their commitment to the organization and their coworkers rises, as does their happiness at work, research has found. In one study, for instance, a group of participants reflected upon the origins of their organization and then described how it might not have existed had certain events not occurred. Another group of participants also reflected upon the origins of their company, but then were asked to describe these events in more detail rather than thinking through counterfactual possibilities. Participants then indicated how committed they felt to the company and assessed whether its trajectory was positive or negative. Counterfactual reflection resulted in an increase in participants' commitment to the company as well as their optimism about its future. Recognizing that the organization might never have existed incited feelings of commitment that amplified what people liked about their organization.

Counterfactual thinking also prompts us to make positive changes. Thoughts such as "If I had worked harder, I would have performed better on the exam" or "If I were more patient, I would be more contented with my partner" make us more inclined to do better in the future.

Part of the reason we fall out of love with work and life is the common tendency to neglect information that contradicts our views or preferences and to instead focus on data that confirm them. Imagine that you change careers and aren't very happy at your new job. As a result, you feel regretful and think you made a mistake, even to the point of disregarding positive signs that things will get better. Counterfactual thinking should help you broaden your perspective: "What if staying in my old career ended up becoming a boring routine?" When we consider how things might have unfolded differently, we become more sensitive to the unpredictability of life. As a result, we consider decisions more systematically and approach life with a more open mind.

Counterfactual thinking can also instill a sense of meaning. In one study, a group of participants was asked to reflect upon an event that was pivotal in their lives. Some of the participants were also asked to consider how this event could have turned out differently. These participants, as compared to those who did not consider a different path, viewed the event as more meaningful. In another study, half of the participants were asked to reflect upon events that could have prevented them from ever meeting people who became their best friend. The other half, in the control group, instead were asked to reflect upon details of the time they first met their best friends. Participants who entertained counterfactual thoughts perceived their friendship as more meaningful.

Thinking counterfactually takes the focus away from just our own view, a troublesome tendency that is unfortunately compounded as we gain experience. One of the problems, it seems, is that we forget the experience of being *in*experienced. When we become experts, we have trouble remembering memories of our experiences as novices. We are also prone to the so-called hindsight bias: Having knowledge of an outcome leads us to assume that we knew the information all along.

This "curse of knowledge" leads us to overestimate the amount of knowledge that others have. If you've ever felt bewildered as a mechanic rattles off what's wrong with your car, or while a doctor rushes through an explanation of what's wrong with your body, the problem may not be your lack of expertise but rather the expert's failure to recognize what you probably don't know. When interacting with novices, people with more expertise often fail to account for the fact that novices don't have access to their specialized knowledge, and they also underestimate the amount of time it would take for novices to learn complex tasks.

Ting Zhang, a postdoctoral fellow at Columbia University, sought to determine whether experts can overcome the "curse of knowledge" and better communicate with and relate to novices by rediscovering the feeling of inexperience. In one study, she recruited expert guitarists with at least three years of experience playing. She asked some of them to flip their guitar around so that they were strumming using their nondominant hand (right hand for lefties, and vice versa); of course, the hand that they normally used for the fingerboard was reversed as well. She asked others, those in the control condition, to play as they normally would for a minute.

Next, all of these expert guitarists watched a video clip of a beginner guitarist who struggled to play a series of chords. The experts were asked to give advice to the beginner, to evaluate the beginner's potential, and to rate how similar they felt to the person. Zhang also recruited a separate group of guitarists who had played for less than one year to rate the experts' advice.

Playing with their guitars reversed proved difficult for the expert guitarists. They felt (and sounded) more like beginners than did those who played the instrument traditionally, suggesting that the change in how to hold the guitar was effective in allowing experts to rediscover inexperience. Guitarists who played nontraditionally also saw more potential in the novice than did guitarists who played traditionally. And, interestingly, novices rated the advice of experts who rediscovered the feeling of inexperience as more helpful than advice from those in the control condition. In this domain, at least, behaving like a beginner helped experts to more successfully take their perspective. Rediscovering the experience of inexperience is a way to counteract the misleading—and potentially life-threatening—feeling of knowing.

FOR DECADES, DIAMONDS WERE CUT USING MECHANICAL MEANS, LIKE SAWS. IN the 1970s, this started to change, thanks to the development of powerful, relatively cheap lasers. But this didn't necessarily simplify the process. When diamonds are cut, whether with a saw or a laser, this can create new fractures that are not visible to the naked eye, but which reduce the diamond's value. Diamond manufacturers wanted to come up with a technique for splitting diamonds along their natural fractures without creating new ones. They found a solution in a surprising source: food companies and the humble green pepper. When food companies need to deseed peppers, they place them in a special chamber and increase the air pressure, causing the peppers to shrink and fracture at the stem. Next, the pressure is dropped rapidly, which causes the peppers to burst at their weakest point, and the seed pod ejects. Diamond manufacturers figured out that they could submit diamonds to a similar process, which results in crystals splitting along their natural fracture lines with no additional damage to the stones.

At times, all of us face problems, whether at work or in our personal lives, that we're unable to solve on our own. Sometimes we can gain the knowledge we seek from an expert—a financial advisor for help managing our money or an experienced recruiter to help us jump-start a new career. Though experts can often help within their domain of expertise, there are times when we might try consulting someone who could offer a truly fresh perspective. Rebels understand that different perspectives can lead us away from stale assumptions toward deeper, more powerful thinking.

When a young man named Alph Bingham was attending Stanford as part of his PhD in organic chemistry, his chemistry professor assigned weekly projects. On the due date, the professor would start class by having five students stand up and defend their work on the project. Interestingly, Bingham noted, class after class, the students had very different solutions to any given problem. He concluded that the unique perspective we bring as students, by virtue of our different backgrounds and experiences, may be more important than what we're taught in class. Our freshest ideas and solutions come from our own unique approach, not from the tools we're given.

Bingham eventually became a scientist who worked for Eli Lilly. In Waltham, Massachusetts, in 1998, Bingham cofounded a start-up, InnoCentive Inc., with two other Lilly scientists, based on his insight from chemistry class: If a firm can't solve a problem on its own, it should make good use of the Internet and its reach to see if someone else has the solution. So InnoCentive works with companies called "seekers" that post their challenges on the company's website. "Solvers" are charged with coming up with answers and can win cash prizes the seekers offer. InnoCentive believes this approach of posting online challenges can work for problems in all types of fields, from engineering, chemistry, and computer science, to life sciences, business, and even economic development. Some challenges are narrowly focused, such as the request for a method for measuring the thickness of thin polymeric films, while others, such as increasing social and community acceptance of renewable energy, have a broad scope. Between 2001 and 2016, more than 1,600 challenges were posted on the InnoCentive website, with more than $40 million awarded to some of the over 300,000 registered solvers.

The problems posed on the InnoCentive site often seem to require deep domain expertise—yet winning ideas regularly come from outside the problem's domain. One challenge Bingham often talks about came from the field of polymer chemistry. The company that initially posted it was pleased with the variety of solutions that had been submitted and awarded five of them with cash prizes. The people who received those awards were an industrial chemist (no big surprise here), a veterinarian, a small agribusiness owner, a drug delivery system specialist, and an astrophysicist.

Harvard Business School professor Karim Lakhani and his colleagues analyzed four years of data from InnoCentive on 166 challenges successfully solved and found that people whose domain of expertise was six degrees removed from the domain of the problem were three times more likely to solve the problem than people whose domain of expertise was closer to the problem. Nonexperts were actually better problem-solvers than experts.

InnoCentive collaborated with another team of researchers, Oguz Ali Acar of King's College London and Jan van den Ende of Erasmus University, on another project. They collected data from 230 problem-solvers registered on the site. The researchers asked them to rate the degree to which they had chosen problems from their own field of expertise and how much they used a wide range of resources to figure out a solution. The respondents also indicated how many hours, in total, they'd spent on the project and how many people they'd contacted while developing an answer. Their analyses revealed that breakthrough solutions are more likely to be the result of investments of time and effort than of expertise in a field. Insiders, who already had quite a bit of knowledge about their own field, came up with solutions that were more creative when they used a more diverse set of outside resources. Meanwhile, the odds of outsiders developing a prize-winning solution were much higher when they dug deeply into the problem's field.

It can be easier to approach problems from fresh perspectives when we are *not* experts. Unfamiliar or unpleasant arguments, opposing views, information that disproves rather than affirms our beliefs, and counterintuitive findings—rather than familiar arguments and evidence that confirms our views—cause us to think more deeply and come to creative and complex conclusions. And that's where outsiders have an advantage over experts: They are less rooted in, and defensive of, existing viewpoints.

In 1500, Bayezid II, the Sultan of the Ottoman Empire, felt compelled to unite what today we know as "old Istanbul" with the nearby neighborhood of Karaköy. There was only one thing standing in his way: an estuary of the Alibeyköy and Kağıthane Rivers, which separated the two areas with twenty-five hundred feet of water and marshland. This inlet was better known as the Golden Horn, and it was thought to be impossible to build a bridge across it. Expert bridge builders struggled to come up with an effective design for a potential bridge, as its span and length posed some serious design challenges. The Sultan knew that a connection with Karaköy would only help both zones to flourish, and he needed the sort of bridge that even the Romans, despite their bridge-building prowess, had never attempted. He enlisted the help of Leonardo da Vinci, who at the time was much better known for his paintings than his engineering and seemed an unlikely source for a breakthrough. But the Sultan felt that Da Vinci's twenty-odd years of research into and study of self-supporting bridge designs might be exactly what was required. Despite the fact that Venice and the Ottoman Empire were at war, Da Vinci put his mind to the task, and using three well-known geometrical principles—the parabolic curve, the pressed-bow, and the keystone arch—he proposed a novel and elegant solution for the Golden Horn: a single-span 240-meter-long and 24-meter-wide bridge. Had Da Vinci's bridge been built, it would have been the longest at that time, and it would likely be the eighth wonder of our modern world today. But the Sultan studied Da Vinci's design carefully and, ultimately, rejected it as an impossibility. It could not possibly work, he believed.

Three hundred years passed before the engineering principles underlying Da Vinci's bridge became widely accepted. In 2001, engineers in Norway finally decided to build a bridge based on Da Vinci's design. The 328-feet-long, 26-feet-high wooden bridge was constructed in Aas Township, about twenty miles south of Norway's capital, Oslo. The bridge, which opened in 2001, is a pedestrian crossing, with railings made of stainless steel and teak. Outsiders can bring a fresh perspective to new and old problems. But it may take years, or even centuries, to recognize their brilliance since, as experts, we are often too focused on our own points of view.

TO WORK WITH CHEF BOTTURA IS TO BE CONSTANTLY REMINDED OF HOW DIFFER-ently people can see the world. For instance, he sometimes asks his staff to create dishes based on a piece of music. "I had been here for just a couple of months, and I was getting used to [Bottura's] style," Canadian-born chef de partie Jessica Rosval told me when we were cleaning up at the end of a day. "With all of his energy, he burst into the kitchen one day and said 'Okay, everybody: new project for today. Lou Reed, "Take a Walk on the Wild Side." Everybody make a dish.' And I was just like, 'Oh my gosh, where do I even start?' "

"We created a wide variety of dishes," Rosval said. "Some people focused on the bass line of the song. Some people focused on the lyrics. Some people focused on the era in which the song was written. We had this diverse array of different plates that were created from this one moment of inspiration when Massimo had been listening to the song in his car."

For Rosval and the rest of the staff, the assignment was challenging, but it also encouraged them to play in the kitchen, and that's unfortunately too rare in our jobs. Challenges like this one make work more playful and open our eyes to something we can easily forget: that our view of the world is incomplete. It's always good to be reminded that our knowledge and skill set can be expanded. This, in turn, increases our motivation as well as our humility. Tenelle Porter, a postdoctoral scholar in psychology at the University of California, Davis, writes about the importance of intellectual humility, or the ability to acknowledge that what we know is sharply limited. In Porter's research, higher levels of intellectual humility are associated with greater willingness to consider views that don't align with our own. People with higher intellectual humility also perform better, whether in school or at work. And intellectual humility makes us wiser: We are more apt to see that the world we live in is never still, that the future will likely be different from the present. Wisdom means rejecting the feeling of knowing.

With his Lou Reed challenge, Bottura also made his staff realize how the same problem can lead to a variety of solutions, similar to what Bingham saw in his Stanford chemistry class. Bottura's lifelong habit of thinking this way yields surprise after surprise. Take his dish *Camouflage: Hare in the Woods*, a rabbit stew that is served spread out on a plate like a canvas instead of in a pot: the bottom layer consists of cream of hare stew, toasted with dark brown Muscavado sugar, like a crème brûlée, which is then arranged in a camouflage design using variously colored mineral and root powders. The intensely savory hare liver morphs into a chocolaty, coffee-laced cream with the addition of crème royal. The dish was inspired by a story that Bottura heard about Gertrude Stein and Picasso back in 1914. While walking along Boulevard Raspail in Paris one evening, they encountered one of the first camouflaged military trucks. "We invented that!" Picasso reportedly burst out. "That is cubism!" As Bottura thought about this story, he had the idea of a hare wearing camouflage.

What we see in any situation—in a painting, in a three-Michelin star dish, or outside the cockpit window of a plane that's lost power—depends on our perspective.

5

UNCOMFORTABLE TRUTHS

A TALENT FOR DIVERSITY

The difference between a lady and a flower girl isn't how she behaves. It's how she's treated.
—GEORGE BERNARD SHAW, *PYGMALION*

One evening in early February 2016, writer and filmmaker Ava DuVernay, forty-four, was sitting in the waiting area on the second floor of what is known as the Team Disney building, the company's 330,000-square-foot corporate offices in Burbank, California. Despite the imposing size of the building, it's hard not to smile when you see it: sculptures of the iconic Seven Dwarfs from *Snow White* stand tall on the façade, acting as de facto columns that hold up the roof. The nearly twenty-foot dwarfs are a whimsical reminder that the company is built on the magic of animated classics.

DuVernay, best known for her Oscar-nominated 2014 film *Selma*, was scheduled to meet with Sean Bailey, president of Motion Pictures Production at Walt Disney Studios, and Tendo Nagenda, Disney's executive VP of production. Bailey and Nagenda, who have worked together at the company for almost eight years, are tasked with keeping productions organized and on track, and choosing writers and directors for films that Disney is interested in producing.

The pair wanted to explore whether DuVernay would be the right person to direct an adaptation of *A Wrinkle in Time*, Madeleine L'Engle's beloved science fantasy novel. First published in 1963, L'Engle's book tells the story of thirteen-year-old Meg, who journeys with her younger brother and a close friend through time and space in search of her father, a gifted scientist who has disappeared. As a film project, it seemed daunting. *Wrinkle* is a science fiction story, but not the familiar Hollywood kind with lasers and spaceships. Meg travels to other dimensions by way of a tesseract, a cube that extends into the fourth dimension (time), which would have to be rendered visually. In both cost and scope, it promised to be a much larger film than anything DuVernay had done before. Also challenging was the very idea of a big-budget Hollywood movie whose protagonist was a cerebral thirteen-year-old girl wearing glasses.

There was a time when DuVernay could not have imagined such a meeting. She was raised in the city of Compton in Los Angeles County. Compton has a reputation for being a rough neighborhood, but for DuVernay it was a beautiful place where she was surrounded by family and friends. The oldest of five, DuVernay grew up watching her mother go to school at night, then move up from a job as a bank teller to a position in hospital administration to a role as the head of an HR department. Her aunt introduced her to films, taking her to the movies and talking with her about what they'd seen, and about the cinema more generally. As a child, she aspired to become a lawyer. In eighth grade, her grandmother Charlene bought her a briefcase, and she felt a few steps closer to her dream. DuVernay attended an all-girls Catholic school for twelve years, where she became the first black homecoming queen and student body president.

After graduating from UCLA, where she studied African-American history, DuVernay worked in journalism before starting her own film publicity company, and spending fourteen years as a Hollywood marketer and publicist. As someone who'd always been interested in movies, she relished having a role in the industry. She found herself on many sets and having long conversations with directors during plane rides to press junkets and premieres. "As a publicist, I was always around filmmakers," she told *Interview Magazine* in 2012. "I started thinking, 'They're just regular people, like me, with ideas. I've got ideas!' "

Even so, acting on these ideas would mean a delayed start in a field already overcrowded with extraordinary talent. At first, DuVernay hesitated. "But I started to realize that being so close to great filmmakers and watching them direct on set and the experiences that I did have, although different from film school, were still super valuable," she said in *Interview*. "I coupled that with some very intentional study and practice—picking up a camera—and just started making it." She was thirty-two when she directed her first short film.

On the path to Hollywood success, DuVernay faced several challenges as a woman in a male-dominated industry. Having men invade her personal space and question her leadership made her think carefully about her appearance on the set, including how she dressed. She often wore a hat to avoid unwanted "hair-touchers"—people interested in touching her locks—and glasses so that nobody would mistakenly get the impression that her eyes were welling up during a particularly moving scene, when in fact she was simply having trouble with her contact lenses. "You don't want to get caught up with the glistening," she told an audience at the LA Film Independent Forum. "Especially as a lady director, that's when the grip is going to walk by and say, 'She was crying.' It's just not worth it."

Her lack of industry connections, or, as she put it, "a rich uncle," increased the odds against DuVernay, and it sometimes stung to imagine where she might have gotten with some well-placed help. But then one day it hit her: "All of the time you're spending trying to get someone to mentor you, trying to have a coffee, all of the things we try to do to move ahead in the industry, is time that you're not spending working on your screenplay, strengthening your character arcs, setting up a table reading to hear the words, thinking about your rehearsal techniques, thinking about symbolism in your production design, your color palette . . . All of the so-called action that you're doing is hinging on someone doing something for you."

Her first two features were small-budget films, including one she financed with her own savings. Then came *Selma*, the story of the 1965 voting rights campaign that Martin Luther King Jr. led. The film was "bold and bracingly self-assured," according to A. O. Scott of the *New York Times*. "Even if you think you know what's coming, *Selma* hums with suspense and surprise," Scott wrote. "Packed with incident and overflowing with fascinating characters, it is a triumph of efficient, emphatic cinematic storytelling." *Washington Post* critic Ann Hornaday described DuVernay's film as "a stirring, often thrilling, uncannily timely drama that works on several levels at once . . . *Selma* carries viewers along on a tide of breathtaking events so assuredly that they never drown in the details or the despair, but instead are left buoyed: The civil rights movement and its heroes aren't artifacts from the distant past, but messengers sent on an urgent mission for today." In addition to the Oscar recognition—*Selma* was the first film helmed by an African-American woman to be nominated for best picture—DuVernay earned a Golden Globe nomination for best director.

After *Selma*, DuVernay showed no signs of slowing down. *Queen Sugar*, a series she created for the Oprah Winfrey Network, became a critical success, praised for its clever storytelling, strong sense of place, and thoughtful depictions of characters rarely glimpsed in pop culture—African-American farmers in the rural South. DuVernay decided to recruit only female directors for the series, thinking it would be "quite a radical statement." Instead of using typical Hollywood channels for hiring, she sought filmmakers whose work had inspired her over the years, in some cases connecting with them via Twitter. She also scouted independent films.

DuVernay was responding in part to challenges she herself had faced, some subtle. In interviews, journalists asked her about her background as an African-American, about being a woman in the film industry—about everything but making films. She was black, a black woman, a black director—but rarely just a director, seldom asked strictly about her vision for a film, or how she approached rehearsals. These were questions for white male directors. And so DuVernay fought back. Along with seeking out unsung talent, she hosts a podcast, *The Call-In*, in which she invites African-American filmmakers to discuss their writing, shooting, and editing in detail. Her questions skip over race and identity, and instead she asks her guests to zero in on the technical and creative process behind the work.

Arriving at Disney, DuVernay was able to put all these issues and frustrations out of her mind. She knew Bailey and Nagenda, who had already made clear how much they admired her work. "In that particular room, for the first time, I was able to walk in and tell my story," DuVernay said in an interview with *Vice*. She walked into the office, she said, "like a white man does." It did not take long for the Disney pair to realize that DuVernay was the right person to adapt *A Wrinkle in Time*. In follow-up discussions, DuVernay suggested that Meg could come from a mixed-race family, and that the film, in part, would be about how Meg became more comfortable in her own skin. Bailey and Nagenda thought the idea was brilliant, and the job was hers. A different studio might have pitched DuVernay another *Selma*-like project, but Bailey and Nagenda had a broader conception of her potential. They saw her for her talent, not her race, and DuVernay responded. When she sat down to talk with the Disney producers that February evening, she was just a filmmaker, ready to trade ideas about the work she was passionate about.

"All of the other stuff and baggage," she said, "was not there."

AT NINE O'CLOCK ON A SPRING MORNING IN CAMBRIDGE, MASSACHUSETTS, I WAS IN my office, anxiously checking my phone. Given where I was headed, I was cheered, at least, by the blue sky after days of heavy rain. I wasn't teaching, so I had dressed in business casual—blue cropped pants, a short-sleeved gray sweater, and flats. A colleague from Harvard Business School had offered to pick me up and take me to the Registry of Motor Vehicles, where I had finally scheduled a driving test after years of living in the United States without a license. I had passed a driver's test in Italy many years ago, but I was still a bundle of nerves. Failing in front of my colleague would be humiliating. Plus, he was lending me his car for the test, a BMW six-series. A little scratch could translate into a large bill.

My colleague's text pinged on my phone, and I zipped up my backpack and headed to our meeting point, where I found him dressed in a gray pinstriped suit. "The outfit is not to celebrate your American driving license," he said, smiling. "I'll be teaching later today." Soon we were in the parking lot of a Watertown mall, awaiting my turn behind the wheel. My friend listed common mistakes to avoid during the test, from rolling stops and improper lane changing to driving too slowly. He was interrupted by a tall DMV officer in dark sunglasses who called my last name.

"You can get into the driver's seat now," the officer told me as we approached the BMW, "and your dad can sit in the back and come with us, but he'll have to stay quiet."

I tried to stifle a laugh, while my colleague, who was only about fifteen years older than me, climbed in behind us. I was sure the officer didn't mean any offense; he'd just made a quick judgment based on our appearance—my colleague's suit, my backpack. After all, he must have been quite accustomed to dads riding along on driving tests.

Stereotypes, sets of attributes we associate with particular groups, are rooted in the fundamental mechanics of human thought. We make links and abide by them: thunder and rain; gray hair and old age; daughter and father showing up together for a driving test. In a world where the fittest survive, animals have evolved to make snap judgments about predators. Some chimpanzees instinctively attack chimps outside of their group. Certain fish go after their own kind simply because they weren't hatched in the same lake. We humans also distrust outsiders. To distinguish friend from foe, we have evolved to judge people using easily observed criteria, such as age, weight, skin color, and gender—as well as educational level, disability, accent, sexuality, social status, and job.

Stereotypes can help us make sense of the world. But because they are mere generalizations, they can also stir up a great deal of trouble. Irritating behavior, like the officer calling my colleague "your dad," is the least of the threat. When we buy into stereotypes, we can sometimes end up perpetrators of cruelty and discrimination, often without even being aware of it. Rebels, by contrast, realize that stereotypes are blinding and that fighting the tendency to stereotype produces a clearer picture of reality—and a competitive advantage. Rebels do not thoughtlessly accept the social roles and attitudes that society promotes. They challenge such roles and attitudes, never missing an opportunity to prove them wrong.

When we're not careful, stereotypes act like firewalls, blocking new information from penetrating our thoughts and preventing us from changing our minds unless something truly dramatic happens. In the 1999 film *Beautiful People*, which is set in London during the Bosnian War, there is a scene in which a young doctor brings home a Balkan War refugee who has recently arrived in the city—someone whom she, and the viewer, knows nothing about. At the dinner table, the doctor's conservative upper-class family comes across as a group of patronizing snobs, while the refugee appears to be unsophisticated and uneducated. And then the refugee sits down at the family's piano and starts to play *Souvenirs d'Andalousie for Piano*, a romantic piece by American composer Louis Gottschalk. He plays masterfully, and in the process catapults both the family and the viewer out of stereotypical assumptions so that we can view him, and maybe others like him, through a new lens.

Whenever I talk about stereotypes in the classroom, I give my students a little test. On a big screen, I flash words like "desk," "kitchen," and "computer" one after another, and I ask them to shout out whether each word belongs to a category shown at the top left of the screen (such as "career") or a category on the top right (such as "home"). My students always perform well when matching work-related words such as "desk" and "computer" to "career," and home-related words such as "kitchen" and "children" to "home." They also have no trouble matching typical male names like "Brian" to the category "male" and typical female names like "Katie" to the category "female." To make the task more difficult, I then have a round where the words flashing on the screen include both first names and words related to either career or home. The students need to shout out "left" or "right" to indicate whether the word that appeared on the screen belongs to one of the two categories "male" or "career" on the top left or to one of the two categories "female" or "home" on the top right of the screen. When this is what the task calls for, they rarely falter.

The trouble comes when I ask them to switch these orientations, having "female names" and "career" as the two categories listed on one side of the screen and "male names" and "home" as the two categories listed on the other. Now, all of a sudden, they stumble, performing half as fast. Right then, their bias sinks in: Men belong with work and the business world, and women at home. It hardly matters that the students, as they are quick to remind me, do not hold overt biases against working women—in fact, many of them *are* working women. We associate men with work more quickly because we are more used to seeing men in the workforce.

This kind of thinking surfaces early in life. By ten months, when shown faces of men and women, infants begin to make stereotypical associations with gender-typed objects such as a hammer or a scarf, telling us that even babies can form primitive stereotypes. By about age three, children exhibit a capacity to understand sex differences that have to do with adult possessions (shirt, skirt, tie), toys, roles, physical appearance, and activities. Children at about the same age also identify abstract associations related to gender (e.g., softness as female; hardness as male). When researchers examine the spontaneous associations children make regarding girls and boys, they find a consistent pattern in which children from preschool through fifth grade view girls as soft and nice, wearing skirts or dresses, and playing with dolls, and boys as being rough, having short hair, and enjoying active games.

Parents set the scene for gender stereotypes even before their children are born—decorating boys' rooms with airplanes and trucks, for instance, and girls' rooms with princesses and stuffed animals. And the fairy tales children hear at bedtime or watch on TV and in movies can affect how they see themselves and others. These stories often portray weak female characters who succeed only when a man intervenes. Think of Prince Eric providing Ariel with a life of luxury on land in *The Little Mermaid,* or Prince Charming helping Cinderella out of rags and into riches. Although Disney has lately strived to reduce stereotypical story lines in its films (as in *Frozen*, *Moana*, and *A Wrinkle in Time*, which feature strong female characters), most entertainment continues to conform to old ideas about gender.

Once learned, stereotypes and prejudices are hard to shed, even when evidence contradicts them. They are reinforced over time by the comfortable feelings we experience when interacting with others like us—people of the same gender, race, ethnicity, or political leaning. When we feel similar to others, we tend to think of them the same way we think about ourselves, and we also tend to assume we'll get along. Through adolescence and into adulthood, we continue to gravitate to people just like us. Conversation and cooperation feel easier when preferences, habits, and views are basically the same. Meanwhile, dealing with people who are dissimilar can cause friction, which feels unsettling or unproductive. Research on romantic relationships shows that, contrary to the old adage "opposites attract," we are attracted to people similar to us. And we feel more comfortable in groups in which we're surrounded by the like-minded, segregating ourselves accordingly from an early age.

Those who dare to violate stereotypes often experience a backlash, researchers have found. For women perceived as successful in masculine fields, the backlash can be especially strong. In a study in which women were portrayed as competent employees in a stereotypically masculine field, such as finance or construction, research participants rated them as being just as competent as their male counterparts, but less likable. When it was left ambiguous whether women were qualified in such a field, participants perceived them as less likable *and* less competent than their male counterparts. As a result, participants believed the women should receive lower salary offers and fewer promotions and resources than men with the same qualifications.

"I don't have a traditionally female way of speaking," former Canadian prime minister Kim Campbell once said. "I'm quite assertive. If I didn't speak the way I do, I wouldn't have been seen as a leader. But my way of speaking may have grated on people who were not used to hearing it from a woman. It was the right way for a leader to speak, but it wasn't the right way for a woman to speak."

THE INITIAL RISE OF WOMEN IN THE WORKPLACE WAS DUE TO EXTERNAL CIRCUM-stances. In the United States, during both World War I and World War II, women were needed to fill factory jobs, replacing men who had been killed or injured in battle. During wartime, many women joined the military, working as nurses, driving trucks, repairing airplanes, or performing clerical work so that men were freed up for combat. Others flocked to civil service jobs, while some worked as engineers and chemists, developing weapons for the war. Though many women had to relinquish their roles to returning veterans after both wars, the wars solidified the notion that women were in the workforce to stay. As professional opportunities expanded, women weren't the only ones who benefited. There were gains for the companies they joined and for the economy more broadly.

Those gains are no less a reality today. A recent report by management consulting firm McKinsey & Company used proprietary data on 366 public companies across a wide range of industries in the United States, Canada, the United Kingdom, and Latin America, and found that firms belonging to the top quartile for gender diversity are 15 percent more likely to experience financial returns above the median of their respective national industry. The organizations where women lead show better financial performance. An increase in female participation in the labor force also accelerates economic growth. In fact, increasing the number of women in the workforce can boost a country's GDP by as much as 21 percent.

But change did not happen without resistance. When women initially entered the workforce, venturing into factories and offices during the Industrial Revolution, men typically viewed them (along with the rise of machinery, for that matter) as a threat to their status, and many women were criticized for taking jobs from men—even if this wasn't the case. For women with husbands and children, the backlash was even stronger. Working mothers took the blame for increases in juvenile delinquency. And, unlike men, women faced the double bind of juggling work outside the home with caring for their families.

We now understand the psychology behind the resistance women have faced. We think of women as communal—other-oriented, modest, affectionate, helpful, gentle, pleasant, sensitive, and nice—while men are considered "agentic," or independent, strong, forceful, self-focused, competent, and competitive. As a result, we expect men to pursue their career goals while women stay at home as caretakers. These expectations shape the way we view men and women in the workplace. An authoritative male worker is "the boss," while an authoritative woman is "bossy." An assertive man is "persuasive," an assertive woman "pushy." And so on.

Entrenched gender views lead to bias in hiring, performance reviews, and promotion decisions. In one field study, two female and two male college students were recruited to apply in person to work at sixty-five restaurants in Philadelphia categorized as low-, medium-, or high-priced. The students' résumés made clear their similar personal histories and experience. The job they applied for was also the same: being a waiter or waitress. Most of the job offers made by high-priced restaurants went to men (eleven out of thirteen), and most of the offers made by low-priced restaurants went to women (eight out of ten). Earnings would be substantially higher at the high-priced restaurants; thus, the apparent hiring discrimination resulted in gender-based differences in earnings. But it also would harm the restaurants by depriving them of the best employees.

When women are hired, it's harder for them to get ahead. A 2014 study using data from 248 performance reviews across 28 companies found that 59 percent of the reviews of men had critical feedback in them as compared with 88 percent of the reviews of women. Both men and women received constructive feedback, but women were more likely to be criticized based on their personalities, often being told to be less loud or abrasive, to take a step back to make room for others, and to be less judgmental.

In August 1982, thirty-eight-year-old Ann Hopkins was proposed as a candidate for partner at the accounting firm Price Waterhouse. Since joining the firm four years earlier, she had brought in an estimated $40 million in revenue, more than any other partnership candidate. She had also billed more hours in 1981 and 1982 than any of the eighty-eight other candidates. In the nominating proposal prepared by her group, Hopkins was praised for her "outstanding performance." Yet various male partners evaluated her as being too "macho" and in need of "charm school." More than half the nominees were promoted to partner, but Hopkins, the only woman, wasn't one of them.

One partner who supported her promotion told her about the feedback from the voting partners: She was, according to them, "overly aggressive," "unduly harsh," "difficult to work with," "impatient with staff," "overcompensated for being a woman," and "universally disliked." Another partner advised her to "walk more femininely, talk more femininely, dress more femininely, wear makeup, have her hair styled, and wear jewelry." The praise she received was grudging: One partner said she had "matured from a tough-talking somewhat masculine hard-nosed manager to an authoritative, formidable, but much more appealing lady partner candidate."

It was true that Hopkins was an unconventional woman for the era: She swore like a sailor, drank beer at lunch, smoked, rode motorcycles, carried a briefcase instead of a purse, and wore little makeup or jewelry. Then again, she was allergic to makeup and, even if she weren't, she thought it'd be difficult to apply, given her inability to see much without her trifocals. She found that putting everything she needed in a briefcase was easier than having to also carry a purse, especially when she was managing a suitcase. In any case, she didn't understand what such trivial matters had to do with her job.

Price Waterhouse had given Hopkins one year to demonstrate "the personal and leadership qualities required of a partner." But just four months later, she was informed that she was unlikely to be promoted. In December 1983, she received some unexpected news: She would not be re-proposed for a partnership even if reviews of her work were, on balance, favorable. Meanwhile, the nineteen men who had been placed on hold along with Hopkins fared much better. Fifteen of them were promoted to partner that year. For Hopkins, it was the last straw: Four days before Christmas, she resigned.

Although Hopkins had these experiences in the eighties, women continue to be underrepresented in top management positions today. In 2017, only thirty-two Fortune 500 firms had female CEOs, in part because both men and women believe that effective leadership requires masculine traits. Research suggests that, in our minds, good managers are typically male. Women are often perceived as less competent and as having less leadership potential than men, and thus are more likely to encounter skepticism and backlash when they behave aggressively in the workplace and go for top positions. And other women are as likely to discriminate as men. When women are in charge, both men and women criticize them for being bossy, cold, bitchy, or aggressive—all attributes at odds with traditionally "feminine" features such as compassion, warmth, and submissiveness.

More often, women are found toiling behind the scenes. When teaching at the MBA level, I often ask students to complete group projects in teams of four or five. Though not a favorite among students, these projects are an effective way to teach both the class materials and teamwork. Still, I usually find myself spending many hours dealing with the same issue: One student ends up doing most or all of the work, while everyone on the team earns the same score.

And often, I find, it's a female student who ends up picking up the slack for the rest of the team.

Research suggests that this pattern is common in groups. Women carry at least as much of the load, if not more, than men, but the men get more credit. When male employees bring ideas forward, their performance evaluations are higher; when women propose the same ideas, managers' perceptions of their performance do not change. Similarly, when executives speak up rather than staying silent, they receive competence ratings that are 10 percent higher when they are male, but when the executives engaging in the exact same behavior are female, their ratings suffer: They are 14 percent lower.

This is bad not just for the women who carry the weight of their groups, but also for their organizations. Think of how much potential is yet to be tapped. If some members are slacking off just because they know someone else will step up to the plate, the team won't live up to its potential, and the organization won't either. It is hard to overstate how much there is to gain when everyone contributes.

IN JULY 2010, LESS THAN A MONTH AFTER BEING PROMOTED TO ASSOCIATE PROFESsor at Harvard Business School, I had to teach my first executive education class, part of a one-week program designed for leaders from all sorts of businesses across the globe. I was initially a bit nervous about telling a group of almost ninety experienced executives how to be effective negotiators, but by the end of the week, I felt good about how things had gone.

Later, the chair of the executive education program came by to tell me that he was about to send out the student feedback from the course. There was, he warned, one comment that would probably upset me. He was giving me a heads-up in the hope that I would read it and then move on, without dwelling on it. About an hour later, the email came. The ratings were good, overall, but as my colleague had warned, one comment stood out: "Professor Gino should wear less well-fitted clothes. This would allow the students in her classes to pay more attention to what she is saying rather than being distracted by her clothes."

Had I worn a slinky, low-cut dress? No. I had worn a dark, conservative pantsuit. Yes, it was cut for a woman, but it was not tight or revealing.

A few years later I taught another executive class. This time I had more experience under my belt, and I also had a larger belly—I was eight months pregnant. Before the start of the session, a male executive approached me to say that pregnant women are known for tiring easily and that I probably should have asked somebody else to teach my class. I didn't know how to respond. "Good luck, though," he said, breaking the awkward silence. "We'll see how it goes."

Once the class began I looked around at the executives, most of whom were men. I couldn't help but imagine that they were wondering why they did not have a more experienced, thinner professor leading the class—someone not at risk of passing out from exhaustion or suddenly going into labor. They were leaning back in their chairs, as if signaling that they were not interested in what I had to tell them—as if they doubted my teaching skills. Were my perceptions correct, or had the student's comment rattled me?

Moments like this have stuck with me over the years. Sometimes they come to mind when I'm preparing for an executive education class or a consulting meeting, or running a training session in the field. They make me wonder what expectations my audience might have based on my female first name—and then, after I enter the room, what additional assumptions they make. Women in my classes often relay feedback they have received in their own organizations, comments that they doubt male colleagues get: observations about their dress, criticisms of their assertiveness, and other remarks that have nothing to do with their actual work.

The effect of such judgments is truly insidious. Imagine, for example, that you are a woman (likely easier for some of you than others!). You walk into a meeting and see that all the other participants are male. Before anyone speaks, you feel less confident than the men about how you will come across, so you find yourself hesitating before speaking. That's when one of the men jumps in and proposes an agenda. You try to argue a certain point, but your voice betrays your nervousness. Detecting your insecurity, the men dismiss your concerns. Their dismissal leaves you shaken, and you fall silent. Too bad, because the subject under discussion is one you know well. When you speak up again, you have trouble holding the floor to present your view. The final decision suffers the absence of your expertise.

This is common. Especially when outnumbered, women are frequently interrupted, talked over, shut down, and penalized for speaking out. Men, research consistently shows, dominate both conversations and decision-making processes in corporate offices, school boards, town meetings, and government. In fact, the more power men have, the more they talk—which is not the case for women. Similarly, men who show anger at work are rewarded with more respect and authority, but angry women are seen as incompetent and unworthy, and are penalized. These experiences, in turn, affect confidence, expectations, and future behavior. For instance, the sexist comments I received in my executive classes made me nervous about teaching or even interacting with executives in the future.

Psychologist Claude Steele refers to this phenomenon as "stereotype threat," or the tendency to "choke" and underperform due to the fear of bias. Consider the stereotype that female students are naturally inferior in math and science. In a study in which women were reminded of their gender before taking a math test, they scored lower than equally qualified men who took the same test. The women's performance suffered because they were worried about confirming negative stereotypes, the researchers found. However, when reassured of equal ability before the test, the women matched the performances of men. Similar results have been found for African-American and Latino students: Stereotypes predict they will underperform in academic pursuits relative to whites, and they do underperform when primed to think about race. Reminders can also be visual: Studies have shown that women score higher in math when surrounded by other women than when testing in a mixed-gender group.

The consequences of stereotype threat go well beyond poor performance on tests; we can also find ourselves closed off from others, less ambitious, and disengaged from our work, unable to fulfill our potential as leaders, negotiators, entrepreneurs, and competitors. Of course, the consequences hurt not only those who experience the threat, but also their organizations. And a vicious cycle develops: When women experience stereotype threat, their mental energy is taxed as they work to disprove the stereotype, leaving them with less mental energy to perform the task at hand. This creates more stress and lower performance—thus maintaining the underrepresentation of women in the workplace, especially in leadership positions. All of us are part of some group that can be affected by negative perceptions, and we know we may be judged by it. No one is immune to stereotype threat.

But here's the good news: Expectations can influence results. This insight has been demonstrated for years through the use of medical placebos. In one study, patients received intravenous injections of morphine over the course of two days to reduce the pain created by dental work. On the third day, the same patients received an injection of saline that they thought was a powerful painkiller. Patients who received the placebo tolerated the pain much better than what one would normally expect even from people given morphine.

Outside of medicine, the same phenomenon holds. The simple

fact of knowing that I'll soon be in a meeting with a potential client, working on a joint project with new colleagues, or in a class full of executives leads to expectations of how well I think I'll do. The interaction proceeds accordingly: If I expect to do well, I'll feel more comfortable and excited. As a result, I'll not only perform better, but I will also be judged, research shows, as more competent and even wittier.

In a similar way, we can shape our expectations about the behavior of *others*. For instance, when looking over the roster for my executive class, I might tell myself that I expect my students to make particularly clever comments and to do well in even the most challenging exercises. Once my expectations are set, research shows, I'll behave differently toward my students in a way that confirms my positive expectations.

A story from Greek mythology has inspired much research on the topic of how expectations influence behavior: Pygmalion. According to the story, told most vividly in the ancient Roman poet Ovid's *Metamorphoses*, Pygmalion was a talented sculptor from Cyprus who had become disgusted by some local prostitutes and as a result had lost all interest in women. Dedicating himself to his work, he spent long hours crafting a beautiful statue of a woman, Galatea, out of ivory.

When he finally put his chisel down, he was captivated by the woman he had created. She was so perfect that Pygmalion, despite his professed disdain of all women, fell deeply in love. He began to bring the statue gifts, such as beads, seashells, songbirds, and flowers. Pygmalion prayed to the goddess Aphrodite to bring Galatea to life, and she granted his wish. In a sense, though, his expectations were what had brought her to life.

The story of Pygmalion has resonated across the centuries. In George Bernard Shaw's 1912 play *Pygmalion* (which was later turned into a 1956 Broadway musical and then into the popular film *My Fair Lady*), Professor Henry Higgins works hard to transform an uncouth cockney flower girl named Eliza Doolittle into a refined young lady, becoming besotted with her in the process. Psychologists have studied what they call the "Pygmalion effect," in which a person's expectations of another person turn into a self-fulfilling prophecy. Evidence of the effect emerged in 1965, when students in a California school completed a test that was described to them as one that would identify "growth spurters," students who were poised to make strides in their academic journey. Teachers were given the names of elementary school children who allegedly had great intellectual potential. Although these children were chosen at random, they showed a larger gain in performance than their peers when they were tested again at the end of the year. The only significant difference between them and their classmates was in the minds of the teachers.

These days, I find that I often benefit from the Pygmalion effect in my own teaching. When my colleagues—usually male and older than me—introduce me to my executive education classes now, they stress that I have won various teaching awards or that I became a full professor at an unusually young age. These accolades, presented by a clear authority figure, seem to improve any low, stereotype-based expectations the students may bring to the class.

We can also choose to rebel against low expectations that others set for us. Research has found that approaching high-stakes performance situations by telling ourselves that we're excited, rather than telling ourselves to simply calm down, lowers our anxiety and improves our performance. If we fear a backlash, we can frame the upcoming task as an opportunity to learn and improve rather than dwelling on our anxiety. Rebels know to expect the most out of everyone, including themselves.

I made the conscious choice to harness this rebel spirit (rather than succumbing to stereotype threat) in the fall of 2010 when I was asked to teach in the same executive education program in which I had previously received the comment about my supposedly too-tight clothes. I agreed, but after seeing the list of who else would be on the teaching team—all incredibly accomplished men, with many years of teaching and consulting experience—I felt nervous. I was the only woman, I had a weird accent, and I was clearly younger than the other instructors (not to mention the executives I would be teaching). But as I walked to campus for the first class in the program, I decided to focus on the fact that it would be a great learning opportunity for me. I told myself to be excited to be part of such an accomplished teaching team rather than stressed. Ultimately, the program went well, and I eventually became a regular member of the team.

When we fight stereotype threats and reframe situations by focusing on opportunities rather than potential problems, we make personal gains by embracing challenging situations that we would otherwise shy away from. But fighting a stereotype threat also has an added benefit: Our behavior, once we are part of the action, can motivate others to follow our lead. Our examples and stories can change how others think, often in powerful ways.

In February 1966, twenty-three-year-old Roberta "Bobbi" Gibb reached into her mailbox in San Diego and eagerly tore open the letter she found from the Boston Athletic Association. She was expecting to see her race number for the upcoming Boston Marathon. Instead, she found that her request to compete had been denied because women were not allowed to race. Women, the letter said, were not "physiologically able" to run the race. Gibb was a lifelong runner who had been training for Boston for two years. On the day of the marathon, she showed up at the starting line, the hood of her sweatshirt pulled over her head to disguise her gender. When her fellow runners figured out that she was a woman, they encouraged her, and she lifted the hood. The press got wind of the news, and soon spectators were seeking her out and cheering her on. Gibb finished ahead of two-thirds of the men in the race and found the governor of Massachusetts waiting to congratulate her at the finish line. In 1972, partly inspired by Gibb, Boston Marathon officials opened the race to women.

Examples are powerful. The daughters of working mothers grow up to benefit from their mothers' choices in their own careers, despite the old attitude that women who stay home to take care of their children are better, more devoted mothers than those who work. Women raised by working mothers are more likely to hold managerial roles than women whose mothers stay home full time, research shows. They also earn more money. In the United States, for example, the earnings of daughters of working mothers were 23 percent higher than those of daughters of stay-at-home moms. As for the sons of working mothers, their mothers' choice of work had no effect on their employment, but, as adults, they were more likely than sons of stay-at-home mothers to share in the chores and child care.

At Harvard Business School, the issue of having a diverse set of role models was discussed a few years ago in relationship to our curriculum, which is heavily based on case studies. In 2014, women comprised about 20 percent of case study protagonists. A case study, in a way, conveys to students who should be in leadership roles. With this realization, the HBS dean of the faculty, Nitin Nohria, encouraged the faculty to seek out more cases with females and minorities as main characters.

People who are brave enough to call out discrimination, despite the fear of how it may affect their career, can have an especially potent effect. In an October 2017 *New Yorker* article, journalist Ronan Farrow reported allegations that Hollywood movie mogul Harvey Weinstein had sexually assaulted multiple women. In the weeks that followed, new accusations of sexual harassment and abuse against other powerful, high-profile men surfaced. When actress Alyssa Milano urged women to share their stories using the #MeToo Twitter hashtag, thousands of women did so; at its peak, the hashtag was used half a million times in tweets in just a day. At first, the tweets were coming from women in Hollywood. But they were soon joined by women in the media, then in the art world, in comedy, in politics—in all walks of life. When a few women had the courage to speak up, others were no longer afraid.

We all have opportunities, big and small, to change attitudes. When I was visibly pregnant with my second daughter, Emma, I could sometimes be seen on campus doing jumping jacks. People who walked by smiled. Others asked me what I was doing. "I am breaking common stereotypes," I told them.

IN 2009, EILEEN TAYLOR, DEUTSCHE BANK'S MANAGING DIRECTOR AND GLOBAL head of diversity, found herself staring at some puzzling internal data: Female managing directors were leaving the firm. The post involves stress and long hours, so it seemed possible that these women were leaving due to work-life balance issues. But when Taylor dug deeper, she found that this was not the case: They were leaving because they were taking better positions elsewhere—and after being passed up for promotions. If Deutsche Bank was neglecting the needs of promising employees and losing them as a result, that was clearly a problem that could not be ignored, Taylor realized.

Companies that can maintain and expand leadership roles for women, as Taylor wanted Deutsche Bank to do, reap large benefits. Using data from 1992 through 2006, Cristian Dezsö of the University of Maryland and David Ross of Columbia University looked at the size and gender composition of executive management teams of most of the companies in Standard & Poor's Composite 1500 list, a group that reflects the U.S. equity market. The researchers found that, on average, female leadership generated an additional $42 million in firm value, all else being equal. The study also found that firms with a particular focus on innovation experienced larger gains when women had positions in the executive ranks.

In a study of 2,360 companies using data from 2005 to 2011,

researchers at the Credit Suisse Research Institute found that businesses with at least one woman on their board had lower net debt to equity, higher average returns on equity, and better average growth. Gender diversity isn't just a laudable goal; it also makes bottom-line business sense.

But the benefits of more women in the workforce go beyond financial performance, surfacing in every level of an organization, including in the quality of ideas and decision-making. My own research shows that gender diversity helps companies attract and retain more talent by providing a more stimulating workplace. When a potential candidate learns that a company has a gender-diverse workforce, he or she puts more effort into getting the job.

Eileen Taylor took action, spearheading an internal sponsorship program called Accomplished Top Leaders Advancement Strategy, or ATLAS, that paired women leaders at Deutsche with women mentors from the bank's executive committee. Research on the careers of both whites and minorities shows a common thread among people of color who advance the furthest: a strong network of sponsors and mentors inside their organization. Developmental relationships are important for everyone climbing the organizational ladder—but especially so for women and minorities. When DuVernay needed to hire directors for OWN's *Queen Sugar*, she sought to hire only female directors. "I always say if *Game of Thrones* can have three seasons of all male directors, why can't we have three seasons of all women directors?" said DuVernay in an interview for *Hollywood Reporter*. All the directors chosen for the first season of the show had directed one film that had been in competition at a film festival but had not been able to find a job that would allow them to direct an episode of television. And, after *Queen Sugar*, all of them ended up getting booked for other pilots or TV shows.

Taylor's initiative at Deutsche Bank raised the visibility of women leaders and connected them with powerful advocates. A third of program participants won larger roles with the firm; another third were deemed ready to move up when positions became available. Since ATLAS launched in 2009, the number of women managing directors at Deutsche Bank has grown by 50 percent.

The effort was worth it. Research shows the benefits of diversity in organizations, nations, communities, and groups. A 2009 analysis of data from 506 firms found that those with greater gender or racial diversity had higher sales revenue, a greater number of customers, and higher profits. Another study of management teams found that those that had more diverse work and educational backgrounds came up with products that were more innovative. And analyses of international data show that nations thrive by many measures, from business to medicine to art, after opening their borders to travel and immigration.

People who live in more diverse geographic areas and interact with people in other regions also reap benefits from diversity. Telephone calling patterns reveal that interaction with different geographic regions—or social network diversity—is associated with greater economic prosperity in a community. Similarly, correlational evidence indicates that U.S. cities with a greater share of foreign-born inhabitants are more financially solid. And in competitive trading markets, ethnic diversity encourages more care, less bias, and greater accuracy in judgments, which in turn prevents price bubbles.

For the most part, this data is correlational—showing that more diversity is related to better outcomes—but it does not allow one to conclude that greater diversity is the *cause* of those better outcomes. Laboratory experiments, though, have shown the causal effect that diversity has on performance. Given the constraints of the lab, these studies focus on smaller groups. But it's clear that homogeneous groups are more vulnerable to narrow-mindedness and groupthink. Diversity, by contrast, has been found to produce more innovation and better decisions in both cooperative and competitive contexts, and to strengthen teamwork.

Despite the compelling evidence behind it, diversity often fails to take hold for the simple reason that homogeneous teams can *feel* more effective. We all tend to seek out comfort and familiarity, and this often translates into choosing to work with those who are like us. The feeling of comfort and ease in homogeneous groups was well captured in a 2008 study of fraternity and sorority members at Northwestern University in Chicago. Membership in these groups conveys a strong sense of identity, much like affiliation with a religious or political group, and can thus intensify a sense of internal similarity among members, while deepening a sense of separateness from outsiders. In this particular experiment, 132 sorority members and 68 fraternity members were asked to solve a fictional murder mystery. Each participant wore a color-coded nametag with the name of their Greek house and had twenty minutes to study the clues and pinpoint the likely suspect out of three possible individuals. Next, each student was assigned to a team of three with two other members of their fraternity or sorority. Each team had a total of twenty minutes to discuss the case and come up with an answer. Five minutes into the discussions, a fourth team member joined each group. This new member was either from the same Greek house (i.e., someone like them) or a different house (i.e., someone who was likely different).

After a team named the suspect they'd agreed on, each member answered questions about various aspects of their team's interactions. More diverse groups—those that included a person from outside their sorority or fraternity—judged the interactions within the team as less effective than did the groups of insiders. The diverse groups also showed less confidence in their final choices. This supports what we knew to be true: That members of homogeneous teams easily and readily understand one another, and collaboration on such teams flows smoothly, creating a feeling of good progress. Dealing with outsiders generates disagreements and friction, which naturally does not feel productive. Yet the subjective experiences of the team members did not match reality: Adding an outsider actually *doubled* a group's chance of solving the mystery correctly, from 29 to 60 percent. Working in a diverse group was uncomfortable, but the outcomes were better.

In fact, contrary to our intuition, greater diversity produces better outcomes exactly because it *is* harder to work among a mix of perspectives. Part of the reason we associate homogeneity with greater performance is our preference for information we can process easily, a bias that psychologists have named the fluency heuristic. Easy-to-digest information seems truer or more beautiful—which explains why we often appreciate songs and artwork more as they become more familiar. And when we face opinions we disagree with, discomfort is only one issue. We may also believe that disagreement will make reaching our goals more difficult and time-consuming. Again, this belief is misplaced. Think of working effectively in a group as being like studying (or exercising, for that matter): No pain, no gain.

Businesses can help to dilute the power of stereotypes, but only if their leaders are thoughtful about it. Even seemingly benign decisions, such as which magazines are kept in a reception area, have been found to shift perceptions of an organization's stance on diversity. Whether women and minorities feel accepted depends on many workplace cues, from physical environment to offer letters. For instance, the language used in recruiting documents directly influences application rates. Masculine language in job advertisements ("dominant," "competitive," etc.) lowers the appeal of these jobs for women, not because women worry that they lack the skills, but because they feel they do not belong. Such cues can set off stereotype threat and shape ideas about a company's views toward a particular group.

In addition to making changes to workplace cues, managers can confront stereotypes by increasing minority representation within the organization. Increasing minority representation not only increases the value placed on diversity in the eyes of potential recruits, it also aids in the development of role models—a strong predictor of success for stereotyped individuals.

It's important to remember that we tend to overestimate the amount of conflict a diverse group will experience. In one study, researchers instructed MBA students to act as if they were co-managing various four-person teams of interns and to imagine that one of these teams had asked for more resources. They were shown photos of the members—four white men, four black men, or an even split. Next, they were given a transcript of a group discussion and asked to rate the team on various factors. Everyone read the same transcript, yet participants viewed teams of four white men and four black men as having the same amount of relationship conflict, and diverse teams as having more. Believing that these teams would experience greater conflict led the participants to be less likely to give additional resources to mixed-race groups.

Such beliefs prompt leaders to make bad decisions when it comes to diversity, whether they are hiring, building teams, or encouraging collaboration. Fearing tension, they balk at adding diversity to a group. Rebels understand that conflict can lead to growth and that disagreement is a feature rather than a flaw.

IN JUNE 2014, THE SAN ANTONIO SPURS WON THEIR FIFTH NATIONAL BASKETBALL Association championship in sixteen seasons. The team was often described as "the United Nations of Hoops." The oldest player, thirty-eight-year-old Tim Duncan, had been with the Spurs for about as long as his youngest teammate had been alive. Other players hailed from the Virgin Islands, France, Argentina, Canada, Italy, Brazil, and Australia. In fact, more than half the squad came from outside the United States, making the Spurs much more geographically diverse than the other teams in the league. They were also the first NBA team to have a female assistant coach, Becky Hammon.

The Spurs' superb head coach, Gregg Popovich, and top-notch players were obviously key to the team's success. But a diverse culture also played a role. Popovich, the son of a Serbian father and a Croatian mother, made it a point to learn about his players' backgrounds and to try to speak to them in their native tongues. Players spoke English most of the time to ensure that no one felt left out, but occasionally the international players would switch things up, boosting both camaraderie and tactical advantage. Two French players, Tony Parker and Boris Diaw, turned to their native language when they needed to communicate quickly on the court. The two Australians on the team, Patty Mills and Aron Baynes, often spoke to each other in their own dialect. In teamwork, diversity encourages members—whether they're in the majority or the minority—to search for new information and novel viewpoints, and to process that information more deeply and accurately, which leads to better decision making and problem solving.

Just being exposed to diversity changes the way we think. In a 2006 study, undergrads at the University of Illinois were assigned to work in three-person same-gender groups on a murder-mystery task in which sharing information was the key to success. Some of the groups had only white members; other groups had two white members and one nonwhite person (Asian, African-American, or Hispanic). Information was shared among all members of a group, but each was also given key clues to the mystery that only he or she had. To correctly identify the murderer, members had to share all the information they collectively had during their discussion. The diverse groups were more successful. Being with others who are similar, the results suggest, leads us to think that we all have the same information, which discourages engagement.

Differences in beliefs and personal preferences also bring benefits. In one study, 186 people who identified as either a Democrat or a Republican worked on the same murder mystery task I just told you about and decided who they thought committed the crime. Next, each person wrote an essay about their suspicion in preparation for a meeting with another group member. Participants were told that their partner disagreed with their opinion; their task was to change his or her mind. Half of the participants were told their partner supported the opposing political party, and half were told the person supported their own party. The results showed that Democrats didn't prepare as well for meetings with Democrats as they did for meetings with Republicans, and the same pattern was true for Republicans. In general, people who anticipate joining ethnically or politically diverse groups are more thorough in their preparation.

Whether we are trying to solve a murder mystery, come up with creative solutions to complex problems, enter new markets, develop new products, or improve workflow, diversity can challenge our thinking in constructive ways. Even before we begin to interact with others in a diverse group, the simple fact of diversity promotes better preparation, more creativity, and deeper thinking by encouraging us to consider a range of viewpoints. We may not enjoy the decision-making process as much because of the greater effort required, but in the end, we'll usually reach a better outcome than a less diverse group would have produced.

When organizations and their leaders commit to diversity, the benefits are deep and wide. But increasing diversity in an organization often requires leaders to fight attitudes and practices that are holding their employees back. Rebels help their organizations reap the benefits of greater diversity by focusing on how to best leverage differences. Rebels recognize that initiatives to increase or effectively manage diversity often fail because they treat the issue as a problem rather than as an opportunity. Rebels know that to effectively leverage differences, their organizations should work beyond race and gender. In the rebel mind, all differences matter. Diversity is not a quota system; it's a long-range vision for growth.

When Ava DuVernay was starting her new career, she spent a lot of her energy trying to figure out how to break into the film-making business. She sought out people who could advise her, give her support, and show her the way to success. Eventually, though, she realized that in doing this she was wearing a "coat of desperation" and would be better off making her own films, with her own ideas, on her own budget. "I think there have been cracks made in the glass ceiling by women who can get close enough to hit it," she told *Time* magazine. "But I'm mostly bolstered by folks who create their own ceilings." By following their dreams, women and minorities can change their organizations and inspire others to do the same. By finding a way to ignore the barriers that others may create for them, intentionally or not, rebels like DuVernay create their own ceiling, one set only by their own potential.

6

COACH CHEEKS SINGS THE NATIONAL ANTHEM

A TALENT FOR AUTHENTICITY

No one man can, for any considerable time, wear one face to himself, and another to the multitude, without finally getting bewildered as to which is the true one.
—NATHANIEL HAWTHORNE, *THE SCARLET LETTER*

On the night of April 25, 2003, twenty thousand eager basketball fans streamed into the $267 million Rose Garden arena in Portland, Oregon, for the third game between the Portland Trail Blazers and the Dallas Mavericks in the first round of the NBA Western Conference playoffs. The Blazers had won thirteen of fifteen games against the Mavericks in Portland, but the Mavericks already owned a 2–0 lead in the best-of-seven series. The first two games had been played in Dallas, and now the Blazers were back on their home court.

Excitement and tension were high, but the raucous crowd quieted for the singing of the national anthem. Thirteen-year-old Natalie Gilbert would do the honors, as winner of the Trail Blazers'

"Get the Feeling of a Star" promotion. She had woken up with the flu that day, but the aspiring Broadway star knew the show had to go on. Gilbert stood before a massive American flag, all dressed up in a black-and-white sparkly prom dress, rhinestones glittering on her neck, her blond hair pulled up in a topknot. Facing the thousands of amped-up fans and millions of TV viewers, she took a last look around the arena, raised the microphone, and began to sing in a mellow alto.

"O say can you see . . ."

At first, Gilbert showed the poise of a pro, but when she hit the second line she stumbled, singing "starlight's" instead of "twilight's." She broke off and nervously chuckled, then tossed her head from side to side, trying to shake off the mistake. But she couldn't. She raised her right hand and covered her face with the mic as embarrassment set in. The music continued, but Gilbert, shaking her head, appeared on the verge of tears. The crowd's encouragement was for naught: She had lost her composure. Out of ideas, she looked to her right, then behind her, searching for her father, Vince, but with no luck. Gilbert was all alone. In just a few excruciating seconds, her dream had turned into a nightmare.

Blazers head coach Maurice Cheeks, standing near the bench in a gray suit and tie, had been focused on the game—one of the biggest of his coaching career. But he quickly strode over to Gilbert. The forty-six-year-old coach gently put his arm around her, helped her raise the mic, and began singing the words at Gilbert's side. She regained her confidence, no longer alone. Cheeks gestured to the crowd, leading the twenty-thousand-strong choir in a patriotic sing-along. By the end, the voices of players, coaches, and fans soared as one behind "the home of the brave."

The Trail Blazers lost that night. They fought hard to win the next three games, tying the series, but fell in the seventh game. Yet Cheeks is remembered less for those nail-biter wins and losses than for his moment as an on-court savior. Ministers praised him as the very definition of a Good Samaritan. Gilbert called him her "guardian angel."

"I never thought about doing it before I did it," Cheeks told the *New York Times*. "I just saw a little girl in trouble and I went to help her. I'm a father. I have two kids myself. I'd have wanted someone to help them if they could."

IN 2005, PATRICIA FILI-KRUSHEL, AN EXECUTIVE VICE PRESIDENT AT AOL TIME Warner, was about to deliver an important speech to her staff. For months, she had been working to bring flextime to the company. More and more people, she thought, valued flexibility in their work, and she worried that AOL Time Warner was in danger of losing the war for talent because they didn't have a flextime policy. But she was having trouble getting colleagues to take the idea seriously—many worried that flextime would be abused. So Fili-Krushel had decided to run a flextime pilot program with her own group of about five thousand employees. In the speech, she was going to explain the pilot to the entire staff. She needed and wanted to make the strongest case possible.

But she was also thinking a lot about her teenage daughter, who had been struggling that year. Fili-Krushel was planning to hire a therapist to work with her daughter, and she had also sought permission to work from home during the coming summer so that they could spend more time together. "Should I mention this to the staff?" she asked herself. It would be risky. Her employees might judge her for her daughter's problems, wondering if perhaps she was to blame for having focused more on her career than on her child.

Fili-Krushel took the stage and outlined the value of flextime for employees. Using flextime, she said, would not keep them from getting ahead. Taking a deep breath, she explained that, although this wasn't the reason she was advocating for the program, she would be the first employee to take advantage of it. She needed to be with her daughter. "We are all human beings," Fili-Krushel said, "and things happen in life we can't always control." Fili-Krushel's flextime pilot turned out to be a success. The program was eventually rolled out to other groups in the company, and it ultimately helped with hiring and retention. Fili-Krushel's worries about being judged gave way to a strong sense that her openness had resonated with her staff.

We all hesitate before making ourselves vulnerable, fearful of being judged by others, but these worries are usually misplaced. Opening up wins us trust, perhaps even more so when it involves showing weaknesses—whether an off-key voice, as in the case of Maurice Cheeks, or a personal problem, as with Fili-Krushel. Revealing our deepest emotions takes courage, which inspires emulation and admiration in the people around us, and allows them to connect with us more quickly and more profoundly. Rebels understand all of this. They are willing to stand "naked" in front of others.

Sharing personal information is key to developing and maintaining strong relationships. When we do, our peers trust and like us more, and also feel closer to us. In addition, self-disclosure makes us feel (and appear) more real. For one study, my colleagues and I invited college students to the lab and paired them up for computer chats. Participants asked to disclose their flaws got a more positive response from their partners. Next, during a game that required trust, the participants who disclosed their weaknesses outperformed their more circumspect peers. Even a star stands to gain from the occasional slip. When Jennifer Lawrence was named Best Actress for her role in *Silver Linings Playbook* at the 2013 Academy Awards, she tripped and fell as she climbed to the stage in her pink ball gown. She looked mortified, but the crowd gave her a standing ovation. "You guys are just standing up because you feel bad that I fell," she joked in her acceptance speech. "That's really embarrassing."

Psychologist Elliot Aronson has identified what he calls the "pratfall effect." In one of his experiments, Aronson trained a paid actor to act as a quiz-show contestant. Students listened to the recording of the actor answering a series of extremely difficult questions and getting almost all of them correct. He then described his highly successful academic career. For some students, the recording ended. For others, it continued, and the students could hear the actor knocking over a cup of coffee on himself. The students who heard the spill judged him to be more likable. We find it hard to relate to people who are highly competent, but we tend to warm to those who are flawed—because we know that we are, too. The psychologist Joanne Silvester has found that job candidates who admitted past mistakes during interviews were actually more appealing to employers than those who covered them up. When we own our blunders, people are impressed.

In May 2015, I saw this happen in person, when Intuit cofounder Scott Cook delivered an unexpected sort of commencement address to the graduating MBAs at Harvard Business School, his alma mater. Cook was following in the footsteps of many other distinguished business leaders, including Facebook COO Sheryl Sandberg. Cook, who now serves as the chairman of the executive committee of Intuit, had earned an MBA from HBS in 1976. He worked as a brand manager at Procter & Gamble and then with the corporate-strategy consulting firm Bain, taking on assignments in banking and technology. A few years later, Cook and his wife, Signe, moved to Silicon Valley when the software explosion was at its peak. He was in his early twenties. One day, the two were sitting at their kitchen table when Cook saw Signe writing out checks, one after the other. Cook started thinking that there had to be a simpler way to pay the bills. Why not create software to handle household finances? That question eventually led to Intuit Inc. and the creation of leading financial software products like TurboTax, Quicken, QuickBooks, and Mint. Starting from nothing in 1983, the company is now a $5 billion giant with over eight thousand employees.

Nine hundred and eight members of the MBA Class of 2015 were awaiting their well-deserved degrees after two long years of classes, group projects, and internships (and yes, a lot of parties at the end). With their families and friends, they were sitting under a warm sun and blue sky on the Baker lawn of the HBS campus, ready to hear an inspiring speech that would assure them that they could do pretty much anything if they applied themselves. But then something unexpected happened. Cook spoke to them about his failures.

"I realized I was holding the company back," he said. "I could feel in my gut that there were a lot of duties I had to do that I didn't enjoy, nor was I good at doing them." Cook recalled that when his limitations as a chief executive first dawned on him, Intuit was flying high: a market leader expanding into the UK after a successful IPO. And yet the man at the top worried that he was in over his head, that he didn't have the skills the company needed at the helm, and that he didn't know how to tackle its most pressing problems. Cook ultimately decided to step down. It was a decision he should have made much earlier, he told the crowd. He had failed to develop as a leader, and he had let the company down.

As the only person in the company who didn't receive a performance review during his time as CEO, Cook had sought out an executive coach and asked for a 360-degree evaluation. The results were poor. But rather than hiding them, he shared the feedback with employees. "I went to colleagues and said, 'This is what I've heard. I'm going to fix it. Please help me,'" he told the HBS students. That a person at his level was willing to admit to his flaws and even ask for help from people below him on the corporate ladder was, needless to say, uncommon. After receiving a long, warm applause, Cook was swarmed by graduates who wanted to hear more. Such is the power of authenticity.

In a recent study, a team of Harvard researchers demonstrated that it is also a good idea to show weaknesses in the context of "pitch" competitions, where entrepreneurs give "fast pitches"—short presentations of a minute or two—before a panel of investors. The investors then judge the entrepreneurs and award capital to the winners. The study focused on one actual pitch competition. In it, after entrepreneurs had made their presentations, but before the results were revealed, they listened to a recording of what they believed to be a fellow competitor's pitch and were told that they would be asked to evaluate this competitor. Some listened to a recording in which the entrepreneur only discussed successes. For example, the entrepreneur stated: "I have already landed some huge clients—companies like Google and GE. I've had amazing success, and in the past year I have single-handedly increased our market share by 200 percent." Other entrepreneurs listened to the same recording but then heard the speaker reveal her failures: "I wasn't always so successful. I had a lot of trouble getting to where I am now. . . . When I started my company, I also failed to demonstrate why potential clients should believe in me and our mission. Many potential clients turned me down." When they heard the entrepreneur describe her successes *and* her failures, rather than only the former, listeners felt less envious and more motivated to work hard to improve their own ventures.

Discussing failure in the classroom can also be inspiring and motivating to students, and research has shown that it usually results in higher grades. For example, the following details are worth mentioning when we study a genius like Einstein: As a boy, Albert Einstein saw his father struggle to provide for his wife and children, moving the family from place to place as he looked for work. Having to change schools was difficult for Albert. Not only did he constantly feel out of place, but he was always playing catch-up in class. It's not just success that inspires others to greatness. Sometimes, in fact, it's just the opposite.

About four hundred freshmen and sophomores at a low-income, mostly nonwhite high school were asked to read stories about Einstein, Marie Curie, or Michael Faraday. The stories, each just eight hundred words, focused on one of three themes. "The Story of a Successful Scientist" was about great accomplishments—winning Nobel Prizes, publishing groundbreaking papers, or pioneering new fields of study. "Trying Over and Over Again Even When You Fail" focused on intellectual and professional struggle, including failed experiments. "Overcoming the Challenges in Your Life" covered personal ordeals, such as dealing with poverty or discrimination. Six weeks after the students read the stories, the researchers asked the teachers how the students were doing in science class. The answer was that students who had read about struggle—whether intellectual or personal—now had higher grades than their peers who had read about achievements. The differences were especially pronounced in students who weren't getting good grades to begin with, suggesting that this exercise may be most beneficial to those most in need of help. Understanding the scientists' struggles helped the students see them as role models.

In another study, researchers found that exposing firefighters to case studies of experienced firefighters who committed errors brought better performance in a post-training task as compared to case studies where there were no errors. And in research I conducted with colleagues, we examined data from seventy-one surgeons who completed more than sixty-five hundred cardiac procedures over the course of ten years and found that surgeons learned more from others' failures than from others' successes, and that this vicarious learning reduced patient mortality.

In early 2016, after posting a revised CV on his professional website, Princeton University professor Johannes Haushofer became a kind of folk hero of failure. In this "CV of failures," he listed the many positions and awards for which he had applied and been rejected. When asked about the revision, Haushofer gave a simple explanation to the *Washington Post*: "Most of what I try fails, but these failures are often invisible, while the successes are visible. I have noticed that this sometimes gives others the impression that most things work out for me. As a result, they are more likely to attribute their own failures to themselves, rather than the fact that the world is stochastic, applications are crapshoots, and selection committees and referees have bad days."

We are always looking for ways to hide—whether by covering up aspects of our personality, keeping our emotions to ourselves, or concealing our fears and flaws. But vulnerability helps us create stronger connections with others. Listening to Maurice Cheeks's voice as he led Gilbert through the anthem, you'd have never mistaken him for a great singer. Nobody cared. The audience joined in because of the connection he had made. We worry that rejection awaits those who reveal their true selves. To connect, we try our best to appear perfect, strong, intelligent, and polished, without realizing that this strategy often has the opposite effect.

WHEN I FIRST ARRIVED IN THE UNITED STATES, BACK IN 2001, I SHARED A BOSTON apartment with two roommates, both Americans, who were just a few years older and who had been living together for two years. The day I moved in, they invited me to join them for dinner. "We were thinking of taking it easy and just ordering Chinese," one of them told me. "That's what we often do on Sundays."

"Sure," I said. "That would be great." Chinese is not my favorite, but I was pleased to be asked to join them and didn't mention it. Chinese takeout became a Sunday tradition in our apartment, and one that I grew to dread. I vividly remember the night my roommates added spicy chicken feet to the usual dishes. "There's not much food on the foot itself, but you can eat the tendons off the bones," my roommate pointed out. I couldn't bring myself to put anything on my plate. Eventually, my roommates served me. I slowly played with the food, taking small bites and swallowing almost without chewing. *This*, I thought, *isn't working.*

It may seem harmless to fake it, especially in a context as relatively unimportant as what to order for dinner. But it's not—our self-esteem, job performance, and relationships all take a hit. Small challenges seem bigger. We hesitate to speak up. Our health suffers. The more inauthentic we feel, the higher our stress, the lower our sense of well-being, and the more prone we are to burnout. Think about a time in your personal or professional life when you behaved in a way that made you feel untrue to yourself. My colleagues and I asked participants in a study to write about such a moment. We asked another group to write about their last visit to the grocery store, an experience we assumed would be somewhat neutral. After writing about inauthentic behavior, participants felt more anxious and less moral than those who wrote about their last visit to the grocery store. They wanted to clean themselves.

There are other, subtler costs of pretending. I often see people in organizations claiming to know things that they don't. In a meeting, for instance, the more seasoned employees may use obscure acronyms, and the new recruits nod to signal that they are following the discussion, when, in fact, they are not. They do so to make a good impression. But, interestingly, when we are praised for behavior that is inauthentic, our self-esteem suffers. In one study, a group of college students first answered a questionnaire that measured their self-esteem and then took one of two tests. One group took a test that could not be completed without the students pretending to understand several fake vocabulary words, such as "besionary." The second group took a test in which no pretending to understand words was necessary. Once they completed the test, students in both groups received praise for their performance and then answered questions about their self-esteem again. Those who had pretended experienced a loss in their self-esteem, while the others experienced gains.

Inauthenticity can also make it tougher to land a job. Research conducted by Celia Moore of Bocconi University and her colleagues found that 92 percent of job candidates actively misrepresented themselves in interviews. That behavior has consequences: Those who are inauthentic, deflecting questions about weaknesses and concealing their personalities, are less likely to be hired. Much better is the path Anne Hathaway's character chose in *The Devil Wears Prada*: She lands a job at an elite fashion magazine despite admitting she is neither skinny nor glamorous and has little interest in fashion.

And if you're trying to raise money to launch a new business, it's best to be real. In a field study, my colleagues and I looked at data from 166 entrepreneurs participating in a fast-pitch competition. The three judges, experienced private investors interested in funding start-up ventures, filled out a brief scorecard after each pitch. At the end of the event, they deliberated before choosing ten semifinalists who would be invited to participate in the competition's final round. After making their pitch, entrepreneurs, at our request, answered two questions designed to reveal how much they were being themselves when presenting: "Reflecting on the pitch you just delivered, to what extent do you feel you were being authentic?" and "Reflecting on the pitch you just delivered, to what extent do you feel you were being genuine?" When their responses were authentic, not just telling judges what they wanted to hear, the entrepreneurs were given higher ratings by the judges and had over three times higher odds of being one of the winners.

Inauthenticity also works as a drag on motivation. I showed this in a study that will send a shiver down the spine of any Boston Red Sox fan. My colleague Maryam Kouchaki of Northwestern University and I recruited a group of Red Sox fans and gave half of them Red Sox wristbands to wear. The other half was stuck with

New York Yankees wristbands. Then we had everyone put their dominant hand in a bucket of ice and measured how long they could last. The longer they endured, the more we'd pay them. Inauthenticity worked against those wearing the Yankees wristbands. Their times were lower.

This is also true for "social pain," the discomfort we experience when we feel excluded or rejected. In another study I ran with Kouchaki, we primed participants by asking them to recall a time when they felt either authentic or inauthentic. Next, we had them play a computer game called Cyberball, which involves tossing a virtual ball with two pre-programmed "players." At first, the pair tossed the ball to each other and to the study participant. Then, suddenly, the pair started tossing the ball only to each other. Participants primed to feel authentic experienced much lower levels of psychological and physiological stress. Authenticity gives us the courage, energy, and confidence we need to rebound from negative experiences.

It's also easier to be around. People can tell when we're being inauthentic. In fact, they register that inauthenticity in their bodies. When someone hides his feelings, those who interact with him experience a rise in blood pressure. This physiological response helps explain our discomfort around people who seem "fake."

This response is so strong that we actually prefer honest boasting to the dreaded "humblebrag," those phony complaints that provide an opportunity to brag about luck or talent. In other words, the friend who can't stop complaining about what a bad job she did applying to grad schools, now that she can't keep up with all the acceptance letters she's received. My research shows that people disapprove of humblebragging even more than outright bragging. Nonetheless, it survives, even thrives. Having received the mixed message that it's impolite to brag *and* not safe to share our *actual* challenges with others, we fear being rejected and judged—and end up being rejected and judged.

When Bottura opened Osteria Francescana in 1995, he met with considerable opposition from tradition-bound Italians. "It was more than resistance," the chef told me. "They were actively fighting against us. They wanted to see us dead because they didn't want me to touch their grandmothers' recipes." Bottura struggled to keep the restaurant alive in the early years. He persisted, though, in part thanks to lessons from his experience in the summer of 2000, when he worked at El Bulli, often described at the time as the best restaurant in the world. El Bulli chef Ferran Adrià taught Bottura that he had to stay true to himself. "Right away, I realized that it wasn't just about technique," Bottura told me. "What changed me was the message of freedom that Ferran gave me, the freedom to feel my own fire, to look inside myself and make my thoughts edible." He added, "Everybody looked at Ferran as the master of technique. To me, the most important focus of what he did is freedom. He gave us freedom to express ourselves in any way."

Part of freedom is expressing oneself honestly. Even pretending to be happy can take a toll. I thought about this recently when I was visiting London's Victoria and Albert Museum, whose collection of decorative arts and design is the largest in the world. Two of the 4.5 million objects really got my attention: statues of Heraclitus and Democritus, Greek thinkers known as the "weeping and laughing philosophers." Fittingly, Heraclitus looked sad and melancholic, while the cheerfulness on the face of Democritus brought a smile to my own. As many studies have found, we prefer people who appear happy. In research on speed dating, for instance, participants who appeared positive provoked uplifting emotions in others and were deemed better candidates for a second date. Yet we're not always going to be in a Democritus-like mood, and to pretend otherwise is folly. Dozens of studies, on populations ranging from students to working adults, show that inauthenticity exacts heavy costs on physical and emotional health. Among the negative consequences: sleep deprivation, headaches, and chest pain. Of course, for some of us, smiling at work isn't a matter of choice. When we board a plane or a bus, for example, we generally expect to be welcomed by flight attendants or bus drivers who are happy to see us. The problem is, sometimes they're really not.

Across two weeks, seventy-eight bus drivers working for a company in the northwestern United States took surveys before work, after their shifts, and just before they went to bed. They were asked about their sleep, their moods during and after work, and whether or not they had put on a "performance" or a "mask" that day. In the results, emotional acting was associated with insomnia, anxiety, and distress, and it also increased the likelihood of conflict at home. Meanwhile, drivers who reported behaving authentically—either by not faking smiles at all or by smiling because they felt genuinely happy—had much better sleep quality.

Doctors and nurses are no strangers to pressure, but one fascinating study shows that having a safe space to express real feelings can make a big difference. Psychologist Alicia Grandey of Penn State and her colleagues collected survey data in different health care units in a large Australian hospital. One of their measures was the extent to which members of a medical team felt free to express real feelings to colleagues when the group was not dealing with patients or otherwise in the public eye. The idea was to capture how much of a climate of authenticity existed in a given group. When such a climate was present, members were better able to cope with tough situations such as mistreatment by patients and their families. A climate of authenticity within a team, in fact, gave members a chance to replenish their emotional resources and recover from the harm of surface acting.

Authenticity is a rule at Osteria Francescana. Once a week, Bottura asks team members to cook a dish from their own culture for the rest of the staff. This tradition allows the cook to tell his or her stories, and it also reveals different ways of using the same ingredients. One morning, as workers polished dishes and cutlery, an intern with a degree in art history showed them pictures of paintings and talked in detail about the ideas behind the brush-strokes. Why did he do this? Because Bottura had kept asking him to be himself and bring more of himself into work. Bottura pushed other interns to do the same, as well as everyone else working at Osteria. And as each member of the staff found their way to be unique, in the kitchen and in the front of the house, the dishes at Osteria became more refined and delicious. In 2001, one of Italy's most prominent food writers got stuck in traffic on his way from Rome to Milan and stopped in at Osteria Francescana for a meal. A rave review followed. Within a year, the first Michelin star arrived. It was only the beginning.

IT'S A CURIOUS REALITY THAT MOST LARGE ORGANIZATIONS MANAGE THEIR EM-ployees based on weakness. Just think about how performance reviews typically work. Gaps between ideal behaviors and actual ones are identified, and feedback follows. Thanks to feedback, the employee gains a sense of where he's failing and then starts to think about making improvements. It's true that feedback sometimes covers strengths, but none of us escape the negativity bias, or the tendency for negative information, thoughts, emotions, and experiences tend to make a more lasting impression on us. When we give feedback to others, we often focus on the problems that performance reviews identify, rather than on words of praise or encouragement.

Even outside of work, when we think about self-improvement, we tend to focus on weaknesses. Consider the usual suspects in New Year's resolutions: "get healthy," "lose weight," "spend less," "get organized." These goals have the feel of a negative job review: You're just not cutting it. A study conducted by psychologists Andreas Steimer of Universität Heidelberg and André Mata of the

ISPA Instituto Universitário revealed one of the primary reasons that we tend to focus on weaknesses as opposed to strengths. Participants were told to list a personality trait that they really liked (a strength) and another that they really disliked (a weakness). Next, they answered questions aimed at determining how changeable they believed these traits to be. The results showed that people generally believed their weaknesses to be more malleable than their strengths.

In fact, we've got it backward: We improve faster in areas where we are strong than in areas where we are weak. Research on self-efficacy shows that we are more motivated toward self-improvement when we are confident of results and more likely to think that our efforts will produce good outcomes when we focus on our strengths rather than our weaknesses. One of the best reasons to focus on our strengths is that doing so encourages us to be authentic and allows our true selves to shine. Think of how coaches work with professional athletes: They might do some work on "weaknesses," but mostly they build on areas of tremendous skill.

A study conducted decades ago unintentionally proved this idea. In the 1950s, the Nebraska School Study Council commissioned statewide research that included a test of a method for teaching rapid reading to tenth graders. Before the course, the students were reading, on average, about 90 words per minute. After it, they had improved to about 150 words per minute. But there was a group who had made much larger gains: the students who were strongest at the outset. Before any training, these super readers were covering 300 words per minute. After the course, they jumped to about 2,900 words per minute. Some of the greatest gains in human development may come from investing in what people naturally do best.

In 2013, Deloitte decided to get rid of its performance management system. Deloitte is one of the "Big Four" accounting corporations and the world's largest professional services network, with more than $35 billion in revenue and 244,000 employees. Their old process was in many ways typical. Managers set objectives for each employee and then rated the employees on how well those objectives were met. These evaluations formed the basis for annual ratings that were set at "consensus meetings," where counselors represented employees to discuss where each of them stood in comparison to their coworkers. There were preset categories for the ratings, which were required to conform to a forced distribution. This is what determined any changes in compensation.

Company leaders worried that the company was failing in the ultimate goal of developing stronger employees and leaders. In addition, the performance review cycle—which included filling out forms, participating in meetings, and doing the actual ratings—took about 1.8 million hours a year. Most of this time seemed to be consumed by discussions of ratings rather than being used productively to talk to employees about their performance and potential. Deloitte replaced the system with one aimed at investing in employees for the long term. There would still be performance reviews, but they would be streamlined. The new system redistributed time and energy to coaching, more timely feedback, and career guidance. The emphasis across all these activities would be on strengths, not weaknesses. Each employee would be assigned a coach to help him or her discover and apply strengths and make sense of feedback.

In 2014, Deloitte ran a small pilot to test the new system. Six hundred U.S. workers participated. The initiative was such a success that the company soon ran a larger pilot on about seven thousand people. Data from the two pilots indicated that participants performed better, felt greater commitment to the organization, and became more energized in their work. These trends became more pronounced the longer the employees participated in the new system. The data also found that one predictor of job performance stood above all others: playing to strengths. By the end of 2017, about 85,000 Deloitte employees were working under the new process.

In a multiyear study of team performance Gallup conducted involving more than 1.4 million employees working in 50,000 teams across 192 organizations, high-performing teams and lower-performing ones responded to statements related to purpose, pay, and opportunity. A small group of items explained most of the variation between the two types of teams. The most powerful was a measure of applied aptitude: "At work, I have the opportunity to do what I do best every day." Teams whose members chose "strongly agree" as a response to this item were 38 percent more productive, 50 percent more likely to have low turnover, and 44 percent more likely to have high customer satisfaction scores.

But the introspection of a firm like Deloitte is rare. As organizations grow, they often lose sight of what made them successful in the first place: their employees. In a survey I conducted of about 280 students who attended executive education classes at HBS, I found that larger organizations were less likely to treat investing in people as a priority. It can be easy to forget about all the talent in the room, especially as a company grows and demands that its top leaders grow with it. Focus turns to investments in other markets, products, or services, and in new technologies and equipment. All the while, potential investments in employees are neglected—and huge opportunities are squandered.

According to Gallup research, people who use their strengths daily are six times more likely to get satisfaction out of their job and report less stress and anxiety. Research by the Corporate Leadership Council found that when managers focus on an employee's weaknesses, his or her performance *declines* by 27 percent, whereas a focus on strengths boosts performance by 36 percent. Similar data from Gallup suggests that employees develop better relationships with their managers and are more likely to improve and feel energized at work when their bosses focus on their strengths. When strengths are brought to the foreground, the employee's focus shifts from worrying about what others think they should be to becoming the best version of who they truly are.

It can be incredibly empowering to figure out what we're good at. We are stuck in our own heads 24/7, but we don't often *see* ourselves or take the time to examine our strengths. In a study I conducted with Julia Lee of the University of Michigan, Dan Cable of London Business School, and Brad Staats of the University of North Carolina, Chapel Hill, participants provided us with contact information for various people in their professional and personal networks, including family members, friends, and coworkers. We reached out to the people the participants had listed and asked them to write a story about a time when they had witnessed the participant at his or her best and to share it with us. Each participant received five to ten stories that were overwhelmingly and often unexpectedly positive. Consider this narrative about a boss, with names changed for privacy reasons: "Laura has good forethought for business and does anything and everything she can to help keep us employed. In 2012, when Hurricane Sandy hit the East Coast, here in Florida we did not really think much of it. But Laura was obviously worried that it would impact her business, because a lot of our accounts receivables are in the NYC/New Jersey areas. She ended up borrowing from her retirement savings to keep the business going. I even suggested that maybe she could let the couple of part-timers go, but she responded that the people there always gave their best, so she wouldn't want to do anything less for them. It took about six months to get things back on track, but we all managed to keep our jobs thanks to Laura."

We gave half of our participants the narratives about them and asked them to read through them and identify the strengths the stories highlighted. We then divided participants into teams and had them engage in tasks that would allow us to measure their performance. Those who had read about their strengths before the exercise were less concerned about being socially accepted by their team members, and, as a result, their teams exchanged more information and achieved higher performance. This is the power of self-reflection: It instills the confidence we need to accomplish our goals.

Back in 2011, the Indian IT company Wipro was experiencing some tough issues in its business-process-outsourcing division. The company was spending a lot of money training people, only to see them leave within two months. To understand why, my colleagues Dan Cable, Brad Staats, and I talked to the employees. Workers told us that the organization was asking them to strip away their identities and not allowing them to play to their strengths. So we conducted a field experiment designed to encourage self-reflection and measure its effects. We had some of Wipro's incoming employees go through a new onboarding process where we asked them to spend a designated half-hour thinking about what was unique about them, what their strengths were, and how they could bring out more of themselves authentically at work. Seven months later, these employees had found ways to tailor their jobs to their strengths—for example, they used their own judgment and words when answering customer calls instead of strictly following the firm's script. They were more committed to their jobs, performed at higher levels, and were more likely to still be at Wipro—all thanks to a half-hour reflection exercise. In another study at the company, we asked a group of employees who were going through training to spend their last fifteen minutes at the office each day reflecting, in writing, on the lessons they had learned that day. Over the course of a month, reflection increased performance on the final training test by an average of 23 percent.

Self-reflection can have significant effects over time. When Rachael Chong was working as a young investment banker, she participated in a volunteer opportunity with a group of other bankers in which they all helped to build a house in the Bronx. One day, as Chong, who is five foot two, was slowly hauling lumber across the construction yard, she realized that this task was not exactly making the best use of her strengths or of those of the other bankers. Why, she wondered, are bankers building houses when they could be using their unique skills to build financial models for nonprofits that desperately need that type of help? Fired up, she spent several months looking for an alternative way to volunteer her skills, but came up empty. A year later, Chong moved to Bangladesh to help launch the U.S. affiliate of BRAC (Building Resources Across Communities), one of the largest nonprofit organizations in the world. Eleven college students had come along to serve as BRAC volunteers. The students learned about microfinance and worked on projects pro bono. More important, they developed a deep, lasting appreciation for helping others. By watching the students, Chong realized that "a good experience opens a mind to possibilities of how much you can achieve as an individual," she told me when I interviewed her. "When you volunteer, you may think, am I really making a dent in big problems? A good volunteer experience would lead you to feel—yes!" Chong started thinking that volunteering could be an activity that empowered people, inspiring them to do more. For this to happen, they would have to be involved in activities that energized them, work they believed they were good at.

In time, Chong founded Catchafire, a firm that connects professionals who want to donate their skills with nonprofit and social enterprises that need help. She borrowed the name from a Bob Marley album. Songs like "Stir It Up," Chong says, provide a nice parallel to what volunteering should be about. "It's about finding fire in yourself," she says. Volunteering, in her mind, should help people find their spark and make the best use of their passion.

"I SAW THE ANGEL IN THE MARBLE, AND I CARVED UNTIL I SET HIM FREE." THIS IS how Michelangelo Buonarroti, the legendary artist behind the Pietà in Rome and the David in Florence, described the process of sculpting in a 1547 letter to famed Italian humanist Benedetto Varchi. For Michelangelo, sculpture was a process in which the artist allows an ideal figure to be released from the block of stone in which it slumbers. All of us possess such ideal forms within ourselves—our signature strengths. Our task is to find ways to sculpt work and life to bring out our uniqueness.

Every day, we have opportunities to be "naked" in front of our colleagues, to make ourselves vulnerable, and to be more open about discussing our mistakes. We can also make time to reflect on what our signature strengths may be so that we can make use of them more often. There is no need to wait for a nudge from the boss. We can start the process ourselves. But leaders have an important role to play.

Mellody Hobson is the president of Ariel Investments, a Chicago-based money management firm. When she first joined the company right after graduating from college, at twenty-two, she was given license to be herself. As she told me, "I received precious and unforgettable advice on my first day at work from Ariel's founder and CEO John W. Rogers Jr. He said to me, 'You are going to be in rooms with people who make a lot of money and have big titles. But it does not mean your ideas are not as good or even better. I want to hear your ideas. It is incumbent on you to speak up.'" Hobson has told that story many, many times since then because to hear it is a gift, she believes. Last year, in the process of hiring a person who is now part of the company's research team, Hobson told the candidate she expected her "to be a source of spark in the conversation and a source of difference to really push us, and to say the uncomfortable thing." If you want to see this type of attitude in the organization, Hobson believes, you can't be shy about letting people know. When we play to our strengths and find ways to be authentic at work, we feel more committed to the organization we work for and experience more joy in our pursuits.

There's a video I like to show to my students that opens with a little boy strutting through a backyard, toting a ball and bat and wearing his baseball cap.

"I'm the greatest hitter in the world," he announces. Then he tosses the ball into the air. A swing—and a miss.

"Strike one!" he yells.

Undaunted, he picks up the ball and again says, "I'm the greatest hitter in the world!" He tosses the ball in the air, only to whiff again.

"Strike two!" he cries out.

The boy carefully examines the bat and the ball. He spits on his hands and rubs them together. He straightens his cap and says, once again, "I'm the greatest hitter in the world!" He throws the ball in the air. He swings. He misses.

"Strike three!"

He pauses, confused. Then he exclaims, "Wow! I'm the greatest pitcher in the world!" And he smiles. This is the smile of finding your strength.

7

THE SECRET OF STORY

THE TRANSFORMATIVE POWER OF ENGAGEMENT

To win in the marketplace you must first win in the workplace.
—DOUG CONANT

It's 6:36 a.m. I've boarded a plane at Boston's Logan Airport and am waiting anxiously in my seat. The pilot comes on to make an announcement, and I sigh with relief: The heavy snow that was expected has been downgraded to just a few flakes, so our flight is on schedule. I'm headed to Newark for a full day of teaching. As the final few passengers take their seats, a flight attendant begins the boarding announcement: "Ladies and gentlemen, the captain has turned on the fasten seat belt sign. If you haven't already done so, please stow your carry-on luggage underneath the seat in front of you or in an overhead bin."

She continues on, about emergency exits and smoke detectors, but my thoughts turn to the classes I'll be teaching. I am planning a group exercise for forty executives, and I wonder whether the directions are clear enough. The plane door closes and the flight attendant launches into another announcement: "Ladies and gentlemen, my name is Jennifer Capstone, and I'm your chief flight attendant. On behalf of the captain and the entire crew, welcome aboard United Airlines flight 343, nonstop service from Boston to Newark." As she tells us about the flight time, altitude, and speed, my mind again wanders. I scribble a few notes on the day's first teaching session. The flight attendants position themselves for their safety demonstration. I look up for a moment, but my gaze quickly returns to my notes. Soon, we're airborne. A few other announcements drift by during the flight, but none really register. It seems we've barely reached peak altitude when the plane starts to descend for landing.

I make it to my class with plenty of time to spare, and I begin with an exercise where I auction off a $100 bill to my students. I explain to them that both the highest and second-highest bidders will have to pay for their bids, but only the person with the highest bid will win the money. Bids start at $5, and go up $5 at a time. I don't allow them to talk to one another, and I ask them to just shout out their bids. As I start the auction, many students raise their hands when they want in. The price of the bids is fast increasing, and when we get close to $100, just two of the executives keep on bidding: They seem to realize that the lower bidder will be stuck having to pay, so neither is willing to drop out. They end up bidding well over $100 for that $100 bill. The highest bid? $360! (The second highest was $355.) This turns out to be a good way to begin a discussion about common errors that affect our decision-making. The auction, in fact, shows the students that our decisions are often irrational. In the end, I don't pocket the money I made. I give it back to the group so they can buy themselves some drinks after class. I am not cruel.

At 5:00 p.m., I'm sitting on my return flight to Boston. "Ladies and gentlemen, the captain has turned on the fasten seat belt sign . . ."

From the time they are hired, flight attendants learn a variety of procedures that they must follow to the letter. They are trained to deal with everything from medical emergencies to hostile passengers, and they know how to use every piece of emergency equipment on the plane, from the first-aid kit to the life rafts to the fire extinguishers. These measures are vital to the safety of everybody on board. And it is certainly helpful to know how to access and use the oxygen mask in case of an emergency, or to be reminded to turn off electronic devices that could interfere with the flight. But all of this safety information rarely registers with me when I am on a plane, as I'm sure is the case with most passengers. As a customer, then, I'm *less* safe when I tune out during these announcements than I would be if they weren't so scripted and I was actually listening.

And imagine what these announcements are like for the flight attendants. Repeating the same exact words on every flight, using the same exact hand movements, they show a group of strangers how to fasten their seat belts and the right way to put on a life jacket. Almost mindlessly, they point to each of the exits and remind passengers not to smoke in the lavatories. And they can probably tell from the faces of those onboard that their words and gestures are not capturing anyone's attention. With so much of their job scripted, it's bound to get both boring and frustrating.

The quandary of the flight attendant is a familiar one, faced by workers in every kind of job. Most people don't show up for their first day at a new job feeling unmotivated, frustrated, and uninspired. Rather, they are excited to get started, ready to meet new colleagues, hopeful they'll make a good impression. Yet the honeymoon period typically soon comes to an end. Data that my colleagues and I have collected from a wide range of industries reveals that people feel high levels of energy, commitment, and excitement in the first few days of their new jobs, followed by a noticeable drop within the first year. It doesn't matter whether it's a first job or how many alternatives they had to choose from; the decline seems inevitable. Excitement turns into boredom. The desire to bring one's best self to work slackens into a tendency to just go with the flow. After announcing that the captain has turned on the "fasten seat belt" sign for the hundredth time, the thrill is gone.

Since 1998, the Gallup Organization has been studying engagement at work by surveying millions of employees across industries and nations. According to data collected by Gallup in 2016, only 32 percent of U.S. employees feel involved in, enthusiastic about, and committed to their jobs. Almost 20 percent are actively *dis*engaged, the label Gallup uses to refer to employees who are not just unhappy at work, but are busy *acting out* their unhappiness. These are people who, every day, slowly undermine their organizations and the attitudes of their coworkers. The results of a study led by consulting firm Towers-Watson portrayed an even bleaker situation. Only about 15 percent of employees, according to the findings of their research, are fully engaged; 65 to 70 percent of employees are moderately engaged; and 15 percent are totally disengaged. The global average is even worse, according to Gallup's 2016 survey: Across 142 countries, only 13 percent of workers feel engaged with their work.

Disengagement is expensive. It hinders commitment, retention, productivity, and innovation. Engaged employees, Gallup finds, perform 20 percent better than their disengaged counterparts, and they are three times more creative. Gallup estimates that disengagement costs the American economy up to $550 billion per year in lost productivity. Companies with a highly engaged workforce—Google, say, or Recreational Equipment, Inc. (REI)—are 22 percent more profitable and 21 percent more productive. They also have 37 percent lower absenteeism, 41 percent fewer defects, 48 percent fewer safety incidents, and lower turnover (25 percent lower in high-turnover organizations and 65 percent lower in low-turnover companies). Particularly alarming is that the problem increases with growth. According to Gallup, employees in large companies are less engaged than those in smaller ones.

Disengagement isn't just rampant at work. In a survey of nearly one million American K–12 students, Gallup found that only half considered themselves "engaged," while 29 percent answered "not engaged" and 21 percent "actively disengaged." The same problem plagues our personal lives. I recently conducted a survey of more than a thousand people in the United States who reported being in a romantic or close relationship and found that *over 80 percent* felt the relationship was, more often than not, a cause for worry and frustration rather than energy and joy. We are facing a crisis of engagement in our lives.

"Can I pretend to have your attention for just a few moments?" That's Marty Cobb, a Texas-based Southwest Airlines flight attendant, launching into the safety announcement during a 2014 flight to Salt Lake City. "My ex-husband, my new boyfriend, and their divorce attorney are going to show you the safety features of the Boeing 737 800 series," Cobb continues.

"It's been a long day for me. To properly fasten your seat belts, slide the flap into the buckle; to release, lift up the buckle. Position your seat belt tight and low across your hips, just like my grandmother wears her support bra."

"If you're traveling with small children, we're sorry," Cobb continues. "If you're traveling with more than one child, pick out the one you think might have the most earning potential down the road."

Passengers on the flight are giggling, which means they are paying attention. Cobb ends the announcement with a spin on the customary invitation: "If there's anything at all we can do to make your flight more enjoyable, please tell us . . . just as soon as we land in Salt Lake City. And if there's anything you can do to make our flight more enjoyable, we'll tell you immediately. We're not shy at Southwest."

Cobb is not the only Southwest flight attendant who diverges from the standard announcements. David Holmes, a former computer programmer and personal trainer, became known as the "rapping flight attendant" after his performance on a 2009 Southwest flight to Las Vegas went viral. (Sample rhyme: "We won't take your cash. You gotta pay with plastic. If you have a coupon then that's fantastic.") And Southwest flight attendant Jack Sullivan is known for impersonating Elvis, complete with sunglasses and scarves.

When Colleen Barrett served as Southwest's executive vice president from 1990 to 2001, one of her priorities was to encourage workers to be themselves on the job. Unlike other airline executives, she didn't require employees to carefully follow scripts, as long as they covered all the legally required information. To this day, Southwest encourages employees to welcome and entertain passengers in their own authentic ways. The company's recruiting and hiring practices were created based on the belief that authenticity and humor help people thrive during times of change, stay creative even when under pressure, work with greater energy, and remain healthy in the process. This philosophy has helped the company achieve high passenger volume, profitability, and customer satisfaction. Southwest has low turnover and a near-perfect safety record. "We have always thought that your avocation can be your vocation, so that you don't have to do any acting in your life when you leave home to go to work," Barrett has said.

What Southwest has created is a workplace where engagement is high. In a context in which routine can trap employees in mindless repetition, Southwest leadership respects human nature and allows employees to decide how to best do their work, so long as what they do is aligned with the company's main objective: safety for everyone. With this approach, it's not just the employees who stay engaged—the passengers do, too. Engagement can do great things for employees, leaders, and organizations. When we are committed to the organization and energized by our work, productivity is supercharged, ideas are more creative, relationships are stronger, the organization is more successful, and customers are more likely to be satisfied with the company's products and services. I still smile when I think about a comment I once heard from a Southwest flight attendant after a landing: "As you exit the plane, please make sure to gather all of your belongings. Anything left behind will be distributed evenly among the flight attendants. Please do not leave children or spouses."

WE ALL DELIGHT IN BEING ENGAGED. IT'S SO MUCH BETTER TO START A FLIGHT WITH a rap than it is to hear the same tedious announcement we've been subjected to many times before. One of the funny things about human nature, though, is that we tend to succumb to habits, like conformity, that aren't good for us. We are social animals, with a strong desire to be accepted by others, and conformity gives us comfort. But it also reduces our level of engagement, whether in our jobs or in our relationships. Except for the most rebellious among us, we have a strong preference for the status quo. In an organization, this preference can lead to various standard practices that may play an important role in day-to-day operations but that can also leave us feeling stuck, and make everyone around us feel stuck.

The annals of business are full of tales of companies that struggled to keep their workforce motivated in the long term and ended up with employees who were either frustrated or checked out. When Doug Conant became president and CEO of Campbell's Soup Company in 2001, he arrived at corporate headquarters in Camden to find that the parking lots were surrounded by barbed wire, the walls needed a paint job, and the floors needed new carpets. Campbell's had been struggling financially, and the problems had taken a toll on everyone. Employees described headquarters to Conant as a "prison." It had been clear that the company was in serious trouble since the end of the 1990s, when senior management had raised prices, and sales began falling as a result. By 2001,

Campbell's share price had sunk to half of the high it had reached in November 1998. To correct the error made by raising prices, Campbell's management cut costs, slashing advertising spending and laying off about four hundred employees. As Conant noted, "They had to cut costs to the point where they were literally taking the chicken out of chicken noodle soup, and the product was no longer competitive." The downward spiral continued.

The pride that employees had once taken in working for Campbell's also suffered. The company started in 1869 and grew steadily over the years. By the early 1970s, it had gone international and become one of the largest food companies in the world. In the United States, the Campbell's brand turned iconic, as Andy Warhol signaled with his pop-art soup cans. Many Americans could hum the "Mm, Mm, Good!" advertising jingle. A bowl of Campbell's Tomato Soup (one of the firm's best-selling products) and a grilled cheese sandwich had become quintessential comfort food, almost as American as baseball and apple pie.

Soon after arriving, Conant announced that his top priority was to increase employee engagement. Many company executives scoffed, believing that Campbell's faced more pressing issues. Rather than investing in its people, some doubters said, the company would be better off continuing to cut costs. Other critics believed the company had to invest in its product portfolio and marketing efforts. But, in Conant's words, the firm had "a very toxic culture." The management system had gone off the rails, and employee morale was abysmal. To turn around the company's prospects, Conant believed he needed to start with its twenty thousand employees.

The problems Conant saw in the company's workforce were confirmed by the results of a survey he asked Gallup to conduct in 2002. The goal was to assess the level of personal commitment employees felt toward the company and its goals. The survey results were dismal, among the worst Gallup had ever seen in Fortune 500 companies. More than 60 percent of Campbell's employees reported they were not engaged in their work, and over 10 percent reported that they were actively disengaged—that is, they were so unhappy at work that they were actively undermining the efforts of the few people who were actually performing. As for those in top management positions, over 40 percent operated in a state of being "tuned out," with little interest in contributing to the company's work and goals.

To take action, Conant first got moving—literally. He wore a pedometer on his belt and put on a pair of walking shoes, whether at the company's New Jersey headquarters or at production plants in Europe and Asia. He set the goal of logging ten thousand steps each day and having meaningful interactions with as many employees as possible. Conant also introduced a series of meetings he called "One-Over-Ones," so named to convey a sense that everyone was in it together. These meetings began with a regular review between an employee and his or her manager. Then the employee and manager would be invited in to meet with Conant and the head of human resources. The conversation was purposely kept informal and candid. Both the manager and their direct report could ask questions, discuss whatever issues were on their minds, and propose ideas—in fact, they were encouraged to do so. The meetings gave managers and employees the opportunity to approach the CEO with any question or idea. By including four people rather than the usual two that are present in a performance review, One-Over-Ones extended the reach of the discussion. Conant and the head of HR got access to more information than they would have by only talking to their direct reports. And, at the same time, the CEO's vision made its way down throughout the company.

These two initiatives—Conant's walks and the One-Over-Ones conversations—showed employees that they were truly valued. Conant also started sending out personalized notes, up to twenty per day, thanking employees for their successes and specific contributions. He spent about an hour each day writing these notes by hand. A staffer helped him find success stories he could thank employees for at all levels of Campbell's. Why handwritten notes? Because more than half of the workforce didn't use a computer. In his ten years with the company, Conant sent more than thirty thousand handwritten thank-yous, which recipients hung in their offices or above their desks.

Conant had the razor wire surrounding the building removed and the weeds and overgrowth cleared. He had estate-fencing installed, and the curbs painted. Then he started to fix the inside of the building: updates to the carpet, décor, and paint. Conant wanted to give employees visible signs of a turnaround, a better future for themselves and for the organization. To reinvigorate employees, Conant believed, the company needed to eliminate barriers, whether razor wire or departmental silos, that held back ideas and conversation. As a result of Conant's changes, employees were happier. Performance and retention started to improve. Engagement started to rise. And now that employees were more fired up for the workday, they offered ideas that improved product quality and led to innovations, like easy-to-open pop-top cans and new shelving systems for supermarkets that would help customers find the soup they wanted.

At the management level, Conant was ruthless. According to Gallup's research over the years, managers are key to building and maintaining employee engagement. When people quit, in fact, they're not quitting their jobs, they're quitting their bosses: Managers account for at least 70 percent of the variance in employee engagement. In Conant's first three years, he pushed out over 300 of the company's top 350 leaders. To replace those who had been fired, he promoted about 150 people from within, and for the rest, he brought in high-performance leaders from other companies. By 2009, Campbell's was doing much better than the S&P Food Group and the S&P 500. Between 2001 and 2011, the company's total sales and revenue grew about 24 percent. The revenues of Standard & Poor's 500 firms declined nearly 10 percent, on average, in the same period.

Both analysts on Wall Street and investors gave Conant full credit for Campbell's turnaround. From a psychological perspective, Conant became a model of how to inspire employees and release their talents by bringing to the company three ingredients of employee engagement: dedication, absorption, and vigor. In his walkabouts and in the One-Over-Ones, the CEO made employees feel that their work and contributions to the organization were valued. It was clear that he cared about their development and their satisfaction.

When we feel that the work we do matters, our dedication deepens. The changes Conant made to the physical environment removed distractions so that employees could focus on their jobs. When our attention is focused, we reach a state of absorption and time passes quickly. The handwritten notes also likely made a difference. When we receive expressions of gratitude, my research shows, we are more likely to persist when the road gets tough. As energy and mental resilience increase, we experience vigor. Bring together dedication, absorption, and vigor, and employees are highly engaged. When Gallup surveyed Campbell's employees in 2009, the results were quite different than they had been in 2002: 68 percent said they were actively engaged by their work, and only 3 percent reported being actively disengaged. Conant proved that employee engagement had been the main problem at Campbell's and the key to a turnaround.

Think about the times when you've most felt engaged. Maybe you were attending a concert and found your mind bouncing with creative ideas, captivated by the music. Perhaps you sat down at your desk and started writing after attending an inspiring lecture. Maybe you struck up a conversation with a stranger on the subway and felt like you could have talked for days. When we are engaged, our happiness, our outside-the-box thinking, and our productivity all increase, and the organizations we work for benefit as well. In one field study my colleagues and I conducted at Morning Star, the tomato-processing company in California, we asked harvesters to watch a short video in which a colleague told them about the positive impact their work had in the factory. Then we surveyed Morning Star employees, and those who had seen the video indicated feeling more engaged at work than those who hadn't seen it. Their productivity was also higher: They achieved a 7 percent increase per hour in tons of tomatoes harvested in the weeks after watching the video. In a follow-up study, a similar message increased not only participants' engagement and performance, but also their creativity.

For organizations, lack of employee engagement negatively affects quality, productivity, customer satisfaction, and financial outcomes. According to a study by Dale Carnegie Training, for instance, billions of dollars are lost each year to employee turnover, and companies with engaged employees outperform those with employees who report lack of engagement by over 200 percent. Lack of employee engagement is linked to higher healthcare costs and lost productivity, according to Gallup.

The positive effects of being engaged extend beyond the workplace. College students who report feeling engaged have been shown to be more likely to pass their exams. When students are energized by what they are learning, they perform better academically. In close relationships, engagement and passion lead to longer commitments, greater happiness and satisfaction, and a stronger willingness to work together in the face of adversity. In parenting, engagement leads to greater trust between parents and children, greater commitment to the family, and more joy in family dynamics.

In this book, I've introduced you to the talents that we see, again and again, in rebels: novelty, curiosity, perspective, diversity, and authenticity. What is fascinating, though, is what binds all these "talents" together: They are all paths to engagement. The talent for novelty allows us to fight the boredom that comes with routines and traditions. The talent for curiosity allows us to combat the tendency to stick with the status quo. The talent for perspective allows us to rebel against our narrow focus when we approach problems or decisions, which usually includes only one view—our own. The talent for diversity allows us to defy the stereotypes that are so ingrained in human nature. The talent for authenticity allows us to be honest about our preferences, emotions, and beliefs.

At their core, rebels are *engaged*. They have abundant energy and mental resilience, they invest in their work and in their personal relationships, and they persist even when the road gets tough. They feel inspired by and passionate about what they do and who they know—and they inspire those around them. Thanks to their engagement, rebels are successful. And yet, as individuals and members of organizations, we struggle to understand how to boost engagement. Doug Conant arrived at a failing soup company and successfully turned it around by walking the floors, repainting the walls, having honest conversations with his staff, and saying thank you again and again. Yet this is not the only way of achieving engagement and reaping its many benefits.

A GREEN-SKINNED ALIEN WITH THREE EYES, THREE-FINGERED HANDS, AND AN OB-long head with pointy ears and a single, club-tipped antenna stared up at me from the ID badge I'd been given to wear for the day. My name appeared on the badge alongside a warning: "A stranger from the outside!" It was a sunny spring day in 2017 in Emeryville, California, north of the Bay Area, and I was at Pixar Animation Studios, a large complex with baseball and soccer fields, lush gardens, a 600-seat amphitheater, tennis courts, and a swimming pool. At the heart of the campus is the two-story Steve Jobs Building:

218,000 square feet of space for hundreds of people to work, eat, and play. After being ousted from Apple in 1985, Jobs bought Pixar (which was called Graphics Group at the time) from Lucasfilm and remained the firm's largest shareholder and CEO until Disney acquired the company in 2006. In front of the Jobs building stands a statue of the company's mascot, Luxo Jr., a desk lamp with human emotions from Pixar's first short film, created in 1986.

Jobs oversaw the construction of the building from the smallest details to the big picture. It was Jobs who came up with the idea of having a very large atrium that every Pixar employee would have to pass through each day, enabling random encounters and conversations. The atrium, built with a mixture of steel and brick for an industrial feel, has lots of natural light, life-sized versions of Pixar characters, and a display case for the company's multiple Oscars, Golden Globes, and Annie Awards. The building's décor changes regularly to feature whatever Pixar film is coming out that year and to showcase off-screen employee artwork. The Jobs building also houses Pixar's main restaurant, Café Luxo, which offers wood-fire pizza, a burrito bar, daily specials, and free fountain drinks. The building also has a mailroom, a free cereal bar, a gift shop, and plenty of lounging areas. The only bathrooms on the first floor of the building are in the atrium—a compromise from Jobs, who reportedly suggested at one point that the atrium's floor have the only bathrooms for the whole main building. Having only one set of restrooms creates more opportunities for people to run into one another, ask questions, and exchange ideas.

In 2016, I had become interested in visiting Pixar after meeting Ed Catmull, a cofounder and the company's president. Pixar has had an unprecedented run of highly acclaimed, successful movies. Yet, as Catmull explained to me when we first met, Pixar probably has about the same failure rate as other studios. The difference, in his mind, is that the failed Pixar films were not released. He listed other Pixar films that had drastically changed over time. In *Rata-*

touille, for instance, only a single line from the initial script made it into the final version of the film. In its first version, *Up* was about a floating castle in the sky. Catmull described the revisions that took place on the subsequent incarnations of the film: "The only thing left was the bird and the word 'up.' In the next version, there was a house that floated up and landed on a lost Russian dirigible. In the next version, the bird laid eggs that conferred long life." No Pixar movie ever starts out as well written, funny, and heartfelt as what we see in theaters. Each one goes through all sorts of changes along the way. Rather than calling these digressions "failures," Catmull describes them as "just things that we tried."

Along with animated filmmaking, Pixar has mastered the art of engagement. The company's movies appeal to audiences of all ages, from children to adults. A child may laugh at the unexpected roles that characters take on, like toys that talk, while an adult may be impressed by the ability of the writers to cover complex topics with humor or by the sheer ingenuity of it all. Pixar movies touch a wide audience, captivating viewers from beginning to end. What is it about Pixar's storytelling that keeps everyone so engaged? And what might the rest of us learn?

The studio is one of the most successful in the world, with fifteen Academy Awards and an average international gross of over $600 million per film. Moreover, unconventional plots and ideas are in the company's DNA. The Pixar universe includes a world of talking cars (*Cars*), an elderly man whose house floats to South America thanks to thousands of balloons (*Up*), a rat who wants to be a chef (*Ratatouille*), and the emotions residing in a young girl's brain (*Inside Out*). I watched every single Pixar movie again before visiting the campus and was glued to my seat, at times laughing out loud. I was struck by how fully *transporting* the stories are.

But even the best storytellers may not get engagement right on the first try. Meet Pete Docter, the director of *Monsters, Inc.*, *Up*, and *Inside Out*. Docter, who started working at Pixar in 1989 when he was twenty-one, the day after he graduated from college, comes across as a cartoon character himself. He's impossibly tall, with a reed-thin torso, bendy arms, and eyes full of wonder. His colleagues once compared his narrow head to a pencil eraser. After starting at Pixar with limited responsibilities, Docter soon began to take on larger roles in writing, animation, sound recording, and music. As one of the three key screenwriters behind the concept of *Toy Story*, he created Buzz Lightyear partially in his own image, pausing to check the mirror while he drew the character.

Next he was charged with directing *Monsters, Inc.* Not only would this be his directorial debut, but he would be only the second person to direct a Pixar film after Pixar cofounder and chief creative officer John Lasseter had helmed the first three. *Monsters, Inc.* is set in a factory run by two monsters, James P. (Sulley) Sullivan and Mike Wazowski, whose work involves generating the screams of frightened children, which are needed to power the monster universe. With his blue fur, large frame, and leonine roar, Sulley (voiced by John Goodman) comes from a generation of kid-scarers. His best friend and coach, Mike (voiced by Billy Crystal), is a lime-green, potato-shaped monster with one all-seeing eye. Monsters who scare kids for a living, Docter thought, was a promising hook for engaging an audience. But at an early test screening, viewers began checking their watches about fifteen minutes into the movie. Disaster.

This was a difficult time for Docter, personally. For years, he had been single-mindedly devoted to Pixar. But he had recently become a father and found himself focusing on something other than work. He felt a great emotional connection to his son, Nick, the little creature who had entered his life, and wanted to make sure he took good care of him. As he struggled to figure out how to fix his movie, Docter had a key insight: Sulley, too, needed someone to care for. Sulley was solely focused on his career, and the audience was having trouble empathizing with him.

Revising the story, Docter introduced Boo, a pig-tailed two-year-old girl with big brown eyes and dark brown hair, whom Sulley saves from the clutches of his and Mike's biggest rival, Randall. Over the course of the (revised) movie, Sulley and Boo grow ever closer as Sulley and Mike help her out of one tight spot after another, all while trying to evade Randall. At one point in the movie, Boo runs away and is captured by Randall, who tries to use her in an experiment to forcibly extract screams for the growing energy crisis. But Sulley comes to the rescue. As he transforms from being "all work and no play" to caring for Boo, Sulley becomes a character audiences can relate to.

The most engaging stories have this type of deep emotional core. As a main character faces challenges, he reacts to them in authentic ways and exposes his vulnerabilities. The character might not be totally sympathetic, but if his reactions and emotions seem real, the audience will begin to care deeply about what happens to him, almost as if his story is their own. "The main character is like a surrogate for you, the audience member," Docter told me. "They're learning and discovering information at the same time you are, so that by the time the film ends, you feel like you've gone on the same emotional journey the character has." As Docter sees it, Sulley's emotional connection to Boo saved the movie, both at the box office and in the eyes of critics.

This same idea—emotional connection—can be used to spark engagement at work. At Campbell's, Conant created an emotional connection with his employees by getting to know them and celebrating their contributions. Or consider the analytics software giant SAS, whose founder and CEO, Jim Goodnight, promotes emotional engagement by giving workers plenty of freedom. When people are free to make choices at work, they feel more authentic and in control, my research finds. Employees often welcome this sense of freedom as a true gift, as it makes them look at their relationship with the organization as emotional rather than just transactional. At SAS, it's not uncommon to see employees at the company gym long after the traditional lunch hour—or to see Goodnight himself getting a haircut on campus in the middle of the afternoon.

Stories, as Pixar understands them, become memorable in a way that resonates with people when they appeal to some fundamental truth about human nature—even if monsters, clownfish, robots, or cars are standing in for humans. Think back to a recent movie or novel that moved you. What triggered your emotions? The magic typically happens when we see a character's vulnerabilities or imperfections. When a story feels authentic, we connect. Similarly, in organizations, we feel engaged when we are encouraged to be authentic by leaders who exhibit the same freedom. Organizations can encourage employees to bring more of themselves to work in small and big ways. At Pixar, for example, animators can decorate their office space however they like. The result? One animator's space is decorated like a tiki cabin. Another has a second floor built on top of the first. And several cubicle-like spaces have been converted into tiny duplex houses. The whimsical decorating is actually beside the point. It's what it says about the people who work there, the freedom they feel, and the relationships—real, emotional relationships—they build.

PIXAR PRESIDENT AND COFOUNDER ED CATMULL HAS A LARGE, BRIGHT WORKSPACE on the second floor of the Steve Jobs building. Windows overlook green lawns, and toy versions of characters from my favorite Pixar movies fill the shelves of his office. When we met, Catmull sat on a couch in his office across from me, dressed in a colorful short-sleeved shirt and jeans. He told me that, despite all the signs of comfort and whimsy I saw around me, Pixar had experienced real trouble. In 2013, seven years after being acquired by Disney, the studio had gone through some tough times. Film budgets were rising, the DVD market was shrinking, and production costs were soaring. Pixar management was also increasingly feeling that a key aspect of the company culture—employees' willingness to speak their minds freely—was not what it used to be.

"A hallmark of a healthy creative culture is that its people feel free to share ideas, opinions, and criticisms," Catmull said. He went on to note that when a creative group draws on unvarnished perspectives of all its members and the collective knowledge, decision-making stands to benefit. Candor is key to effective collaboration, says Catmull. "Lack of candor leads to dysfunctional environments," he told me. This belief has been at the core of Pixar's culture since the company was founded. At its inception, Pixar formed a group called the "Braintrust," which consisted of four or five Pixar creative leaders who oversee development on all movies, meeting every few months to assess progress and challenges. Catmull described the Braintrust in simple terms: "Put smart, passionate people in a room together, charge them with identifying and solving problems, and encourage them to be candid." The whole idea behind the Braintrust is that members should speak freely, arguing without fear of conflict, with the interests of the company in mind. The group has no authority, so when members evaluate a movie in production, the director can decide whether or not to follow any of their specific suggestions.

In the 2010s, Pixar was expanding and growing, so it hired more and more people. The new recruits were excited, sure, but the talent in the room was usually pretty intimidating and left them nervous about sharing their own ideas. Executives decided to try something bold to improve the situation. In early 2013, Catmull and a few other managers began planning a special day, Notes Day, during which Pixar would shut down to elicit honest feedback from its employees. Notes Day was an expansion of the spirit of the Braintrust. Catmull and other executives at Pixar wanted to bring the same style of safe sharing to the entire organization. For Notes Day, employees were invited to brainstorm ways to improve the company, drawing on topics and problems they themselves had identified. So that employees would feel comfortable offering candid feedback, managers were excluded from Notes Day.

Notes Day was inspired by a widespread practice among studios of screening in-progress films for executives, who offer written suggestions and criticisms, or "notes." At most studios, directors are generally encouraged, if not required, to follow the direction of these notes. But Pixar decided to handle notes differently. All employees are invited to screenings at the very early stages of a film, long before a story line is finalized, and everyone is welcome to give notes. Moreover, directors do not have to use the notes they receive; the notes are merely suggestions. Pixar's version of the practice is more like crowdsourcing.

Notes Day applied the same principles to the overall practices of the company, as opposed to a specific film. One initial goal of Notes Day was to solicit ideas from employees on how to lower costs by 10 percent. Pixar executives asked employees to prepare themselves for Notes Day by imagining they'd been transported four years into the future and to answer the following questions: "The year is 2017. Both of this year's films were completed well under budget. What innovations helped these productions meet their budget goals? What are some of the specific things we did differently?" Questions were sent out to all employees, generating over four thousand responses on more than one thousand unique topics, such as reducing implicit gender bias in Pixar films, shortening production time, and improving the workplace.

Out of the thousands of responses, executives chose 106 issues for employees to discuss in separate sessions. The sessions were spread across three buildings on Pixar's main campus, and employees could choose for themselves which sessions to attend. Trained internal facilitators led each session, which culminated with specific proposals, brainstorms, or best practices. The group also assigned certain members to be their "idea advocates"—those who would help advance their suggestions. After identifying their recommendation, employees were treated to hot dogs and beer. Out of the 106 topics, the company immediately started working on 21. Some were small changes, like implementing a faster, more secure way of delivering film cuts to directors. But even the smallest changes added up to something bigger. "They were changing Pixar—meaningfully and for the better," Catmull said. And improving efficiency may not have been the most notable benefit. "I believe the biggest payoff of Notes Day was that we made it safer for people to say what they thought," Catmull writes in his book *Creativity, Inc.* "Notes Day made it OK to disagree."

In the years that followed, Pixar saw the benefits of its Notes Day candor. It released two successful films in 2015, *Inside Out* and *The Good Dinosaur*, then *Finding Dory* in 2016, followed by *Cars 3* and *Coco* in 2017. *Inside Out* was one of Pixar's most successful movies, with an adjusted net profit of about $689 million and the best opening weekend of all time for a film using an original idea rather than existing characters.

The company, Catmull told me, has always recognized that conflict is a key aspect of creativity. With a smile, Catmull told me a story about the late Steve Jobs, Pixar's chairman—a story that Catmull also recounts in detail in his book, *Creativity, Inc.* Catmull once asked Jobs what happened when people working with him disagreed with his point of view. Jobs's answer was simple: "I just explain it to them until they understand." Though their relationship was no different in nature, Catmull developed a clever solution to voice his opinions. In the twenty-six years they worked together, Catmull told me that he and Jobs never had an angry argument, but they did disagree quite often. "I would say something," he told me, and Jobs would "immediately shoot it down because he could think faster than I could." Catmull would then wait about a week or so and reach out to Jobs. "I'd call and give my counterargument, and he'd shoot it down again." Catmull would wait another week and call again. "Sometimes this would go on for months," he told me. "In the end, [Jobs] would say, 'Oh I get it, you're right,' or I would realize he was right. And the rest of the time, we didn't reach consensus; he'd just let me do it my way and wouldn't say anything more about it."

Jobs had a reputation for being difficult and demanding, and no one would say he was an expert in conflict resolution. Catmull clearly had to work hard to make sure his boss heard his voice. But it's notable that neither Jobs nor Catmull took the disagreements personally or allowed them to create barriers to collaboration.

In the creative process, tension and conflict need to be embraced for good ideas to emerge. A sense of conflict triggers exploration of novel ideas. For instance, the sense of disorientation and conflict people experience when reading a short story that seems absurd has been shown to enhance their desire to learn novel information. People experiencing conflict have been found to generate more original solutions to difficult situations than individuals who are in a more cooperative mood. Similarly, when members of a team experience conflict, they tend to scrutinize and deeply explore alternatives, which leads them to novel insights. In my own research, I find that when people are asked to meet goals that appear to be at odds—for example, "create an original product cheaply"—their ideas are more innovative than when they have to meet only one of those goals.

When people disagree constructively, their ideas improve. At Ariel Investments, the Chicago money-management firm, constructive dissent is actively encouraged by assigning devil's advocates to meetings and other dialogues. The devil's advocate is charged with poking holes in the decision-making process. During the financial crisis of 2008 and 2009, the devil's advocate became a key feature of Ariel's research process. One person would follow a stock; another was instructed to argue the opposite. Each person tried to represent their opinion constructively while being open to debate. Mellody Hobson, the company's president, regularly opens team meetings with a reminder to those attending it: They don't have to be right; rather, they simply need to voice concerns and be willing to disagree to help the team make the right decisions.

Most of us fear conflict, and understandably so. Conflict stirs up negative emotions and makes us feel vulnerable. But when expressed constructively, conflict allows us to explore new possibilities, arrive at surprising solutions, and gain important insights into ourselves and others. Without conflict, there would be no Pixar movies. How could there be a *Finding Nemo* without Nemo getting lost? *Up* would lose its power if seventy-eight-year-old balloon salesman Carl Fredricksen, the main character, hadn't lost his wife and grown bitter. Insights and innovations seldom arise when we're feeling satisfied with the status quo. Rather, they come from the energy that's created when we crave change. In storytelling and organizations, as well as in our personal lives, conflict leads to engagement. Different perspectives work to heighten our attention.

Rebels embrace tension and conflict. "Ideas only become great," Catmull told me, "when they are challenged and tested." The right amount of conflict makes for a good story and a more rewarding life.

IN 1996, PIXAR STARTED WORKING ON THE SEQUEL TO *TOY STORY*, THE STUDIO'S first full-length picture. At the time, Pixar's second feature, *A Bug's Life*, was still in production. As Catmull recounts in a *Harvard Business Review* article on how Pixar encourages creativity, the company had enough technicians to mount a second project, but its proven creative leaders—those who succeeded with *Toy Story*—

were busy finishing their work on *A Bug's Life*. So a new creative team was put in charge, made up of people who had never run a film production.

The original concept for the sequel seemed solid. Woody, a cowboy doll, is excitedly anticipating a trip to Cowboy Camp. Finally, he'll have quality time alone with Andy, the boy who owns him. Woody is one of Andy's favorite toys. At the same time, Woody is worried about what will happen to the considerably less responsible toys in Andy's room while he's gone. But these worries are forgotten when Woody faces a major crisis: His arm is ripped, and the injury keeps him from going to Cowboy Camp. Another crisis soon follows: A toy collector kidnaps Woody and takes him to his apartment, where a new group of toys is introduced. Among them is a Cowgirl named Jessie, a horse named Bullseye, and a mint-quality doll named Stinky Pete. They explain to Woody that they are all toys based on *Woody's Roundup*, a TV show from the 1940s and 1950s. Now that Woody has joined them, the *Woody's Roundup* toys can all be sold to a museum in Japan, doomed to spend the rest of their lives separated from children by thick glass.

As part of the process of making an animated movie, storyboards are drawn early on, and these initial storyboards are then edited together with dialogue and music that is only temporary. These make up the "story reels," as they are called in the business, which are typically rough, but help illuminate problems that need to be solved in the film. Next come new versions of the reels, each typically improving on the previous one. But that was not the case for *Toy Story 2*. The initial idea was creative enough, but the reels were not getting better. By the time Pixar began animation, the reels were not where they needed to be. "Making matters worse," Catmull writes, "the directors and producers were not pulling together to rise to the challenge."

The problem was that the story was too predictable: It did not allow the audience to imagine what might happen next. At a key moment in the story, Woody faces an important decision: whether to leave his home to travel to Japan or attempt an escape from the collector's apartment and go back to Andy. As *Toy Story* fans well know, Woody and Andy have a deep connection—after all, Woody is Andy's favorite toy. This makes Woody's choice too predictable: Clearly, he'll want to go back home to be with Andy. When viewers can predict how the story will unfold, there's no drama, and they will disengage.

Pixar faced the challenge of introducing unpredictability—that is, making the audience come to the realization that Woody had a tough decision to make and it was unclear which option he would choose. But the team working on the movie was unable to come up with a solution to the challenge. Luckily, the team working on *A Bug's Life* finished up in time to take over the leadership driving the creative efforts for *Toy Story 2*. They were now on a very tight deadline, as the release date for the sequel could not be moved. Having eighteen months to work on the film would have been an aggressive schedule. At that point, only eight months were left for the job.

They created a scene called "Jessie's story" in which Jessie, a cowgirl doll, sings an emotional song to Woody to explain why she does not want to escape, but rather is willing to go to Japan. In the song called "When She Loved Me," Jessie reveals that she had been the favorite doll of a young girl, but once the girl grew up, she got rid of her. Jessie is convinced that losing someone you love is far worse than never having known that person in the first place. By going to Japan, she believes, Woody can avoid the heartache of being discarded by Andy when he grows up. And then there's the sad story of Stinky Pete. Left behind on a shelf with no chance to ever play with a child, he would also prefer to be in a museum. After all, at least he'd have a long life. Plus, as Jessie and Stinky Pete make clear, if Woody returns to Andy and his friends, he dooms the *Woody's Roundup* toys to life inside the collector's dark boxes, as he wouldn't ship them to Japan except as a set.

All of us can relate to the fears that grip Woody and his new friends. Suddenly, Woody's choice is no longer predictable, and the audience is engaged. When a Pixar movie starts, it's difficult to predict where it's going or how it will end. This is true of the most engaging stories in general—they are full of surprises. Docter gave me an example of creating surprises and unpredictability from *Toy Story*. At some point in the film, the creative team wanted to make use of the rocket strapped to Buzz Lightyear's back. But they wanted to do so in a way that was unexpected and surprising to the audience. Sid, a boy living next door to Andy's house, is rather sadistic, as he enjoys torturing toys. For instance, in one scene of the film, Sid puts a mask on as if he were a surgeon, and starts "operating" on his sister's doll. He ends up removing the doll's head and replacing it with that of another toy, and then he returns the mutilated doll to his sister, saying, "All better now." Once the surgery is over, Buzz observes, "I don't believe the man's ever been to medical school."

Buzz and Woody are trapped at Sid's, though, and have to devise an escape plan. By that point, Sid had taped Buzz to a fat firecracker, as he was planning to blow him up as he'd done with other toys. Earlier, Sid had tried to burn Woody on the grill, so Woody, being close to fire, had put a match in his holster. The storytellers thought the match could be used to light the firecracker on Buzz's back and bring Woody and Buzz "flying" back home. But they realized that the audience would see that coming. So instead, Woody lights the match, only to have it blown out by a passing car. All seems lost until Woody remembers the power of the sun. He uses the reflection of Buzz's helmet to light the fuse, and off they go.

Organizations can use unpredictability to improve engagement. The thank-you notes at Campbell's both surprised and motivated employees. As another example, an HBS study of the freelancer contracting site oDesk (now renamed Upwork) found that surprise incentives resulted in greater employee effort than higher pay. Harvard Business School researchers posted a data-entry job on oDesk that would take four hours. One of the postings offered $3 per hour for the job; the other offered $4 per hour. People with past data-entry experience were hired at either the $3 or $4 rate. But some of those who were initially told they'd be paid $3 were later told that the hiring company had a bigger budget than what they expected: "Therefore, we will pay you $4 per hour instead of $3 per hour." The group initially hired at $4 an hour worked no harder than those hired at $3. But those who received the surprise raise worked substantially harder than the other two groups, and among those with experience, their effort more than made up for the cost of the extra pay.

Surprises quench our thirst for the new and feed our curiosity, making us wonder what could happen next.

AT THE END OF MY DAY AT PIXAR, I WALKED PAST THE DESK WHERE I HAD PICKED up my badge and smiled at the Buzz Lightyear statue. The people who created him, and characters like him, had held my attention all day. I didn't want to leave. When we are engaged, time flies, and life and work take on a different, deeper meaning. The passion and engagement of the Pixar employees I'd observed that day reminded me of a story I once read about President Kennedy visiting NASA back in 1962. This was not long after his famous speech about going to the moon, at the height of the Cold War. He saw a janitor who he noticed was fully immersed in his work, sweeping the room the president was touring. "Hi. I am Jack Kennedy," the president said to him. "What are you doing here?"

Without any hesitation, the janitor gave him an answer: "I'm helping put a man on the moon, Mr. President."

8

BECOMING A REBEL LEADER

BLACKBEARD, "FLATNESS," AND THE 8 PRINCIPLES OF REBEL LEADERSHIP

Every man shall have an equal vote in affairs of the moment.
—FIRST ARTICLE IN THE CONSTITUTION GOVERNING THE PIRATE SHIP OF THE LEGENDARY BLACK BART

In the deep heat of an early eighteenth-century summer, a crew of pirates was sailing off the Virginia coast when a lookout spotted a merchant ship to the south. The pirates launched their attack, rocking the merchant ship with a cascade of musket balls and grenades. When a wounded helmsman abandoned the merchant ship's wheel, the vessel swung around, drifting out of control. The pirates boarded, swinging axes and cutlasses. Behind them came the captain, his face clouded by smoke. Sashes holding daggers and pistols crisscrossed his large chest. Black ribbons flapped in his braided beard. The most feared pirate of his era had taken another ship.

Blackbeard was a notorious English raider who terrorized sailors around the West Indies and North America in the early 1700s. Sometimes he plotted sneak attacks; sometimes he relied on trickery, such as flying the home flag of the targeted ship before hoisting his own at the very last moment. After first targeting the man at the wheel, the pirates would snare their quarry with grappling hooks, pull it closer, and leap aboard. When the attack was over, they made hostages of the passengers and crew, and went through the cabins looking for gold, silver, and jewelry.

We usually associate pirates with violence, theft, and mayhem. That's all true, but their ships were also forward-looking in a number of surprising—and instructive—ways.

On the open sea, a merchant ship was a floating dictatorship. With the blessing of the vessel's owner, the captain treated crewmen as he saw fit, often harshly. Sailors were beaten, overworked, underpaid, and sometimes starved. Morale was low. Dissent was punished as mutiny. Pirates, by contrast, practiced a revolutionary form of democracy. To keep the ship running smoothly for months on end and to discourage revolt, pirates elected their captain democratically, limited his power, and guaranteed crew members a say in the ship's affairs. They also elected a quartermaster, who in addition to his primary duties—settling minor disputes and distributing supplies and money—served as a check against the captain's authority. Except in the heat of battle, when the captain took full command, no one man ruled the others. Captain and crew took a vote on everything: where to go, from whom to steal, how to steal it, where to go next, the fate of prisoners. With enough votes, the crew could demote or even dismiss the captain. They could maroon him on an island or dump him into the sea. And when the rules were disputed, it was a jury of crewmen who decided the matter, not the captain. As Bob Dylan sings in "Absolutely Sweet Marie": "To live outside the law, you must be honest."

Any pirate could lodge complaints or concerns without fear of reprisal, as crew members were protected by "articles"—essentially, a constitution drafted for each ship. The articles were democratically formed and required unanimous agreement before an expedition launched. They set the rights and duties of the crew, rules for the handling of disputes, and incentives and insurance payments to ensure bravery in battle. Pirate ships developed highly detailed schemes to compensate injured crewmen. That the crew elected and could depose their leaders stood in dramatic contrast to the tyrannical rule common on most merchant vessels. After capturing a ship, raiders would ask their prisoners if they might want to switch sides. Given the relative freedom and power that pirates enjoyed, and the spirit of antiauthoritarianism and self-governance characterizing their endeavors, it was not uncommon for merchant sailors to seize the opportunity. As they sailed the high seas, pirates picked up mariners from different races, religions, and ethnicities, which made for a cosmopolitan lot. The democratic nature of the ships and the pirates' defiance of custom meant blacks were welcomed as equals. Slavery was easy to find on the mainland, but at sea, black pirates had the right to vote, were entitled to an equal share of the booty, could bear arms, and were even elected captains of crews that were predominantly white. The goal was competent, hardworking deck hands: Skin color didn't matter. Pirates even raided slave plantations and ships for better crews. Blackbeard's ship was arguably more democratic than America was at the time. "[P]irates constructed [a] world in defiant contradistinction to the ways of the world they left behind," writes historian Marcus Rediker.

There's another surprising detail about Blackbeard, whose real name was Edward Teach. Yes, he braided his beard and tied the braids with black ribbons. Yes, he stuffed slow-burning rope under his hat to make himself look more menacing. Yes, he had a reputation as a ruthless cutthroat. But Blackbeard did not kill a single man during his career at sea. He captured other sailors but did not take their lives. The image he cultivated for himself and his crew was a brilliant bit of eighteenth-century marketing that won him glory and riches—and did not require the loss of lives.

BACK IN THE 1950S, THE SOCIAL PSYCHOLOGIST ROBERT FREED BALES RAN AN experiment in which he divided a cohort of college students into groups of three to seven members. He was interested in studying group interactions. The groups, which had no appointed leader, met for several hours to make decisions and solve assigned problems. The students didn't know one another, but they had something in common: They were all men in their sophomore year at Harvard. Despite the initial lack of group structure and the fact that the members were very much alike, Bales repeatedly found that a hierarchy developed smoothly and quickly in each group, often within minutes. It would arise from simple behaviors, such as how much people talked, which signaled status, influence, and good ideas. Bales's results suggest that even when members seem to be of equal footing, hierarchies based on status—the respect, influence, and prominence that members enjoy in the eyes of others—take shape.

Across the globe, groups and organizations rely on some form of social hierarchy to instill order and efficiency. In groups, leaders naturally emerge from interactions, and a few central people gather most of the status. Organizations take the shape of a pyramid, with fewer people at the top than at the bottom. Both human and primate societies rely on this stratified structure. Watch children as young as four years old play together, and you'll see hierarchies develop. When organizations attempt to dodge or suppress hierarchy, they usually fail.

Hierarchies have certain benefits: They satisfy a common psychological need for order; make it easier for people to learn about one another; and can work well when coordination is needed to produce a product or service. But hierarchies have powerful consequences, and not all of them are good. Resources and power tend to be distributed unequally across members of the organization and outsiders based on role. An idea from a talkative group member is judged more valuable than a less talkative colleague's same suggestion. Groups overestimate the performance of high-status members and underestimate that of low-status members, giving the skills and competence of the former an unfair sheen.

Hierarchies, then, can be costly and ineffective. Part of the problem is that groups often fail to grant status based on merit, and the wrong people end up at the top—a situation that leads to poor decisions and performance. Steep hierarchies have been linked to lower job satisfaction, morale, and motivation; reduced employee loyalty; and more stress and anxiety among workers. Because people often do not feel at ease bringing concerns to their bosses, hierarchy can also suppress dissent. One study of over fifty-one hundred Himalayan mountain expeditions found that groups with participants from more hierarchical countries—in Africa, Asia, and the Middle East, for example, as compared with Western Europe and the United States—were less likely to survive the trek. Organizations that lack steep hierarchies are sometimes called "flat organizations." I prefer "rebel organizations." A rebel organization—be it a pirate ship or a restaurant like Osteria Francescana—exemplifies the rebel talents we've discussed in this book. It avoids the traps of routine and complacency.

If you are ever in Berkeley, California, and feeling hungry, stop in at Cheese Board Pizza, which is part of a worker-owned collective that has no explicit status hierarchy. The shop serves just one type of pizza daily. If today's toppings are red pepper, onion, feta, tapenade, and parsley, expect something entirely different tomorrow. It may sound quirky, but it works: In 2016, Yelp users rated Cheese Board the best pizza place in America. (It sure tasted that way when I visited.) The shop's democratic spirit may be part of its success. Since 1971, the collective, which includes a cheese shop (the original business) and bakery, relies upon "a shared work ethic, high standards, and the strong emotional connections among the group," according to its website. Employees run the business and share in the profits.

A flatter structure may work for pizza joints, where roles and tasks are fairly predictable, but what about at larger, more complex ventures? Just a few months after I visited Cheese Board, I wrote a Harvard Business School case study about Valve Software, which, in addition to genre-busting games such as Half-Life and Counter-Strike, counts among its successes the dominant platform for distributing PC games, Steam. Valve is a private, self-funded firm whose per-employee profitability is higher than that of Google, Amazon, or Microsoft. Valve employees arrive at decisions through argument and persuasion. When you want to make a case for a new project, you just need to find enough people to build a team to start working on it. Sure, some employees are better at persuading their colleagues than others. (If they have a good track record, this works in their favor.) But no one has the formal power to tell anyone else what to do. The firm has been boss-free since it launched in 1996.

Before founding Valve, Gabe Newell and Mike Harrington worked at Microsoft. The experience set them on a different course, like merchant sailors who take a chance with the pirate ship. Newell and Harrington made the conscious choice to create a flat organization that would give employees maximum flexibility. "This company is yours to steer—toward opportunities and away from risks," Valve's employee handbook explains. "You have the power to green-light projects. You have the power to ship products." Employees choose for themselves what project to work on, which is why desks at Valve are on wheels and why you only have to unplug to join a different team.

When you give freedom to employees, Newell believes, you liberate their talents and creativity. Self-management builds pride in the work and commitment to the company. And yet, most CEOs don't see (never mind act on) these benefits. Newell told me that people who join Valve from other firms or industries often suffer culture shock. A section in the employee handbook advises new hires on "how not to freak out." Valve's ideas have been tried in other companies, albeit in less radical ways. In the late 1940s, Toyota gave its employees total control over the assembly line so that even someone at the very bottom of the pyramid could halt the production line if he spotted a problem. The company soon reaped the benefits, in terms of product quality, productivity, and market share. Competitors adopted the method on their own assembly lines, with similar success, ultimately giving Japanese cars a reputation as among the most reliable and well built in the world. Under this new system, each employee had a clear way to contribute to the organization's goals. Realizing they had to overcome their fears of losing some control in order to meaningfully engage their employees, managers gave them a voice and their trust. As a result of gaining responsibility and taking ownership of their performance—Toyota employees solved problems faster.

According to a study of over 800 employees, those with a strong sense of ownership in their organizations are more committed, satisfied, and productive. In one study, my colleagues and I asked over 750 employees from various organizations to think about their current job. Some were asked to write about an idea, project, or workspace that they felt they personally owned. The rest were asked to write about how they spend their days at work. After everyone answered a few other unrelated questions, we presented them with an opportunity to help the research team by participating in a five-minute survey without extra pay. The people primed to feel a sense of ownership were more likely to say yes. By flattening the power structure, ownership of problems and ideas becomes shared, rather than concentrated in the hands of a few, and workers thrive.

You may or may not be interested in starting a business, but we all face a choice in life: how to best structure our relationships with others. We can let our job title, our accomplishments, or a booming voice take the lead. Or we can choose to organize our lives so that every person in it "shall have an equal vote in affairs of the moment"—the first article that governed the pirate ship of Welsh pirate Black Bart, known as the most successful pirate of the Golden Age of Piracy, based on ships captured.

REBEL LEADERSHIP IS NOT JUST FOR PEOPLE WHO THINK OF THEMSELVES AS LEADERS. And you don't need a staff of people working under you to be a rebel leader. Rebel leadership means that you prefer working in a rebel organization and that you support your organization in that mission. Rebel leadership means fighting our natural human urges for the comfortable and the familiar. We have an innate desire to be accepted by others and thus regularly conform to their views, preferences, and behavior. We rarely question the status quo. We easily accept existing social roles and fall prey to unconscious biases like stereotypes. It's human nature to stay narrowly focused on our own perspective and on information that proves us right. By contrast, rebels know themselves and are aware of these limitations, but they don't believe there are limits on what they can accomplish.

Like the pirates, rebels follow their own "articles." I call these the Eight Principles of Rebel Leadership:

1. SEEK OUT THE NEW

In a large room, men and women sit at individual desks, positioned in a row and equipped with screws, pliers, a hammer, and a few other tools. Conveyor belts deliver parts. Workers look down, intent on the job of piecing together the components that will become a completed typewriter. This is what the assembly lines at Olivetti looked like in the 1950s.

As we discussed, when he took over his father's business, Adriano Olivetti extended lunch breaks so that workers could eat lunch for an hour and then "eat culture" for another hour. Guest speakers included philosophers, writers, intellectuals, and poets from across Italy and the rest of Europe. If workers preferred to read, they could visit the factory library, which was stocked with tens of thousands of books and magazines. Meanwhile, the company prospered.

Chef Bottura has his own home library. He keeps an extensive collection of records, art books, installations, and paintings, all sources of inspiration. His kitchen creations, in fact, often find their roots in art and music. The dish *Almost Better than Beluga*, in which pearls of black lentil are placed in a caviar tin layered over dill-flavored sour cream, references the René Magritte painting *This Is Not a Pipe*. For *Beautiful Psychedelic Veal, Not Flame-Grilled*, Bottura found inspiration in the work of Damien Hirst. While he was listening to Thelonious Monk one night, Bottura came up with *Tribute to Thelonious Monk*: black cod served with daikon white radish and green onion, in squid ink, after the jazz great's keyboard.

At Bottura's restaurant, contemporary art surrounds you—from works by Maurizio Catellan to Carlo Benvenuto to the world-famous *Capri Battery* of Beuys. Even the staff bathroom doubles as a small gallery. Music plays in the kitchen and in the front of the house at every hour of the day, other than during service (there is no music playing while customers are dining). Inspiration is everywhere.

This embrace of the arts by people in two very different lines of work demonstrates the first principle of rebel leadership: Always look for the new. The rebel is voracious, with interests that are wide-ranging. A new interest does not need a justification in the moment, for it might lead to a larger insight down the road.

I've always been interested in motorcycles, particularly in their engines and in motorcycle racing. Growing up, I'd go to local races, and every Sunday afternoon I'd sit down with my dad and brother on the couch for our weekend ritual: watching motorcycle races on TV. I still remember the first time I visited a racetrack. Nestled in the Tuscan hills about nineteen miles northeast of Florence, l'Autodromo del Mugello is the jewel of Italian motorsports. The three-mile-plus track has fifteen turns. Fans hoisted the colors of their favorite teams. Sitting on a hillside, I watched motorcycles tempting the edge of calamity on dangerous turns. Fans cheered loud and long, but the sound that stuck with me was that of the engines.

Today, I smile whenever I hear that familiar roar. There is nothing practical behind my interest in motorcycles. But it's something that inspires me. My interest in motorcycles once led me to interview riders in MotoGP, the premier motorcycle-racing World Championship, which consists of eighteen different races across fourteen countries and four continents. It was fascinating to hear them talk about how they keep their focus, even when it's raining. The same interest led me to the desert at the outskirts of Dubai to interview people working at stores renting quads. I'm always looking to know more about motorcycles, from learning about models I've not tried in the past or reading about how different companies design them. Who knows where else this slightly odd interest may take me. I'm not worried.

Speaking of racing, there is a famous story about Juan Manuel Fangio, the legendary Argentine driver who dominated the early years of Formula One racing. Well into the 1950 Monaco Grand Prix, he was blazing into a blind corner when, for no apparent reason, he slammed on the brakes. It turns out that he had caught a glimpse of the crowd as he came into the curve and realized that he was seeing the backs of everyone's heads, not their faces. Just the day before, Fangio had seen a similar photograph from 1936. They were looking away because, around the corner, there was a crash. The pieces fell into place: Fangio stopped, saving himself from joining the pileup. Even situations that we've experienced many times in the past or routes that look familiar can come across as novel if we approach them by focusing on what seems new.

2. ENCOURAGE CONSTRUCTIVE DISSENT

October 18, 1962, was a chilly night as Attorney General Robert Kennedy took a seat in the front of his car. A driver was behind the steering wheel, and the chairman of the Joint Chiefs of Staff, the director of the CIA, and six other officials, all high-level, were crammed in the room left in the front and the back. They had decided to take Robert Kennedy's car rather than a limousine or two to avoid raising any suspicion. The car left the State Department for the White House, where Robert's older brother, President John F. Kennedy, was waiting. A few days before, President Kennedy and his team had learned that the Soviet Union was installing nuclear-armed missiles in Cuba—missiles with the potential to kill 80 million Americans within minutes. The United States and the Soviets were on the brink of war, and the time for a decision had come.

One of the most remarkable details about President Kennedy's management of the Cuban Missile Crisis was what he sought from his advisors: disagreement. A year and a half before, he had supported an ill-conceived secret operation to unseat Cuban leader Fidel Castro, a fiasco remembered as the Bay of Pigs. In its wake, the president ordered a review of the decision-making process, which produced a series of changes. First, each member would take the role of a "skeptical generalist," approaching a given problem in its entirety, rather than focusing only on one department's perspective (usually their own). Second, to encourage freewheeling conversations, the members would use settings free of any formality, with no specified procedures or formal agenda to follow. Third, the team would be divided into subgroups that would work on different options and then come back together to discuss them. Finally, Kennedy sometimes would have his aides meet without him to keep them from simply agreeing with his views. These changes, Kennedy believed, would stimulate debate, challenge assumptions, and clear a path for the best plan to emerge on its merits. All of the measures were aimed at defeating what psychologists call "groupthink"—the tendency for members of a group to agree with one another, which quiets dissent and suppresses alternatives.

The men in Robert Kennedy's car had divided into subgroups, with one working on a position paper that argued for a military strike and the other for a blockade of the island nation. They then swapped papers, applying merciless scrutiny in search of the superior strategy. "There was no rank, and in fact we did not even have a chairman . . . the conversations were completely uninhibited and unrestricted," Robert Kennedy would comment. In the end, the blockade in combination with deft diplomacy led to the removal of the missiles and prevented a nuclear conflict with the Soviet Union. The rebel understands that a certain amount of tension is healthy, that discomfort leads to striving. Rebels seek out diverse perspectives and experiences. Knowing when to listen is just as important as knowing when to speak up.

At Ariel Investments, the practice of assigning someone to play devil's advocate during meetings to challenge the consensus and raise different perspectives produces better decisions. At Pal's Sudden Service, when a new idea is proposed—adding an item to the menu, for example, or a change in workflow—the idea is tested in three stores at the same time: one that supports the idea, one that is against it, and one that is neutral. At Catchafire, when Rachael Chong interviews new hires, she looks for people who disagree with her. She describes decisions the company has made or ones it is grappling with and looks for people who think differently from her and the rest of her team. A study of seven Fortune 500 companies revealed that the most successful top management teams were those that encouraged disagreement in private meetings.

Alfred Sloan, chairman of General Motors from 1937 to 1956, once concluded a meeting with executives discussing a critical, high-stakes decision by saying, "I take it we are all in complete agreement on the decision here . . . Then I propose we postpone further discussion until our next meeting to give ourselves some time to develop disagreements and perhaps gain some understanding of what the decision is all about." This is rebel talent.

3. OPEN CONVERSATIONS, DON'T CLOSE THEM

At Pixar, when writers and directors are working on a story, there is a premium on developing creative solutions. Group leaders encourage a technique they call "plussing." The point of plussing is to improve ideas without using judgmental language. You add to, or "plus," what has been said. Instead of criticizing a sketch, the director might build on a starting point by saying, "I like Woody's eyes, and what if we . . ." Someone else might then jump in and add her own plus. The idea resembles the "yes, and" principle of improv. People listen, respect the ideas of others, and contribute their own. This type of collaborative atmosphere requires great effort to maintain. We all seem to feel an urge to judge others and their ideas. Sometimes our disapproval takes the form of silence—"the death pause," as Pixar's Ed Catmull describes it.

The rebel keeps an open mind, understanding that communication drives insight, and that closed conversations generally fail. Dissent is welcome, but only when there is shared respect and everyone feels they are on the same team. So many things can close a conversation—laziness, distraction, someone who talks too much or not enough, a cutting comment or slavish politeness—and the rebel resists them all. Rebels solicit honest feedback and new knowledge by sparking new conversations—even difficult ones—and sticking with them even when the going gets tough.

When James E. Rogers was the CEO and chairman of Cinergy (which then merged with Duke Energy), he conducted anything-goes listening sessions with groups of managers, which alerted him to issues that might have otherwise not reached his desk, such as complaints about unequal compensation. He also invited feedback on his own performance, even asking employees for an anonymous letter grade. His communication skills needed work, he found out, and so he worked on them. Crew members on pirate ships could bring concerns to their captains without fear of reprisal. When conversations are open, a ship runs fast and nimble.

4. REVEAL YOURSELF—AND REFLECT

Soon after becoming CEO of the Campbell Soup Company, Doug Conant got to know his senior executives in one-on-one meetings. As Conant put it, he talked about "what's important to me both in and out of work, what I look for in an organization, how I operate, why I do what I do, and much more." His goal? To convey a full picture of who he was, what he was all about, and what he wanted to accomplish as CEO. "If I do what I say I'm going to do," he told the executives, "I guess you can trust me. If I don't, I guess you can't." Conant considered this approach to be key to an effective and healthy working relationship. "I explain[ed] that my goal is to take the mystery out of our relationship in a personal way as quickly as possible so that we can get on with the business of working together and doing something special," he told me. Rebels understand the power of showing themselves—and knowing themselves. They don't hide who they are or pretend to be someone they are not. They encourage others to find and express their strengths.

Coach Maurice Cheeks had prepared to lead his team to victory, not to sing the national anthem in front of over twenty thousand fans. But when he saw a young woman struggling, he stepped in and sang with her. Nobody cared that he couldn't carry a tune. Before her time at AOL Time Warner, Patricia Fili-Krushel was hired by WebMD Health to work as chief executive. As the leader of WebMD, Fili-Krushel met with a group of engineers in Silicon Valley, all men. When they asked her right off the bat what she knew about engineering, she made a zero with her fingers. "This is how much I know about engineering," she told them. "However, I do know how to run businesses, and I'm hoping you can teach me what I need to know about your world."

We are all quick to judge ourselves and our colleagues, but it is so much better to learn to focus on strengths, not weaknesses. We are quick to judge our coworker for blowing a deadline rather than praising him for his meticulous attention to detail. We comment on the sloppy way our partner loaded the dishwasher rather than thanking her for cooking dinner. Too often, our focus is on where others are falling behind rather than on their successes.

Most organizations fall into the same trap, but some get it right. Mellody Hobson took to heart the advice she got from Ariel Investments CEO and founder John W. Rogers Jr. when she joined the firm to speak up and be herself. Hobson credits her success in part to her ability to stay authentic as she climbed the corporate ladder.

Once we're in touch with our talents, the thrill of potential takes hold. When Greg and I attended improv comedy classes, we each at our own pace became more comfortable in our skin. Chef Bottura followed his passion for cooking when he decided to leave law school, though he knew he would disappoint his father—at least at first. He reached fame by cooking Italian food in a way that inspired him and that was entirely unique to him. He faced years of resistance. But he could not stop himself from doing what he loves and being who he is.

5. LEARN EVERYTHING—THEN FORGET EVERYTHING

The legendary UCLA basketball coach John Wooden would open the first practice of every season by having his players practice putting on their socks and lacing their shoes. If the players got blisters from improperly laced shoes, they wouldn't move as well. If they couldn't run or jump to their potential, they would lose rebounds and miss shots. And if they missed rebounds and shots, the team would lose. Master the fundamentals, Wooden figured, and the team would prosper.

Rebels know the limits of their knowledge, and that mastering the basics is a lifelong project. But a rebel is not a slave to the rules either. Sometimes you return to the fundamentals only to discover a strategy that is very different—and better. In most fast-food chains, a new employee receives about two hours of training per process before starting on the line. At Pal's Sudden Service, training for new workers averages 135 hours and can span six months. With a strong foundation, employees perform at a higher level and are well positioned to think of improvements. Leila Janah, CEO and founder of Samasource, spent years learning everything she could about providing aid to the developing world and working for organizations, such as the World Bank, that operate with this goal in mind. In time, she started to wonder whether giving people aid (such as money, clothes, and food) was the most effective way to reduce poverty. It wasn't, she decided, and created a company that helps poor people by giving them jobs, not aid.

Consider another of Bottura's signature dishes, whose name is a mouthful in itself—*Le cinque stagionature del Parmigiano Reggiano in diverse consistenze e temperature*, or "the five different ages of Parmigiano Reggiano in five different textures and temperatures." The dish was first imagined twenty years ago, starting as an experiment with textures and temperatures. The twenty-four-month-aged cheese is made into a hot soufflé, the thirty-month-aged cheese is made into a warm sauce, the thirty-six-month-aged cheese is made into a chilled foam, the forty-month-aged cheese is made into a crisp, and the fifty-month-aged cheese is transformed in an "air." It is a celebration of what *stagionatura*, or aging, does to a wheel of Parmigiano. By exploring fundamental questions of how the cheese behaves, Bottura ended with a dish that had never been experienced before. "If you want to innovate," he often reminds his team, "you need to know everything, then forget everything."

6. FIND FREEDOM IN CONSTRAINTS

In April 1970, an explosion rocked the moon mission of Apollo 13. The service module in the spacecraft supplied the command module, where crew members would spend most of their time during the voyage, with electrical power and oxygen. Five and a half million pounds of explosives and two tanks of liquid oxygen were in the service module. Tank No. 2, ten feet below the astronauts' couches, had a crack in its wiring—something neither NASA nor the crew realized before launch. Nineteen hours into the flight—Apollo 13 had completed four-fifths of her outward voyage and was 200,000 miles from Earth—the cracked wires became exposed. When the crew turned on the fans in the oxygen tanks before going to bed, a spark between the cracked wires ignited a fire. The explosion severely damaged the spacecraft, leaving the three astronauts with a dwindling oxygen supply. On the ground, a team of engineers had to come up with a way to clean the air using only the equipment on board in a very short amount of time. The remarkable constraints and pressure drove them to a completely novel solution: They figured out a clever way to use the square air cleaners located in the command module in the round receivers of the lunar module. Who says that a square peg can't fit in a round hole?

Rebels work through constraints to the freedom on the other side. Human nature introduces some of the most formidable challenges: bias; a preference for the status quo; blinding self-regard. Rebels are aware of these constraints and fight against them. Research tells us that when we're faced with constraints, we dedicate our mental energy to acting more resourcefully and doggedly, and surpass expectations—or better. In 1960, Dr. Seuss made a bet with Bennett Cerf, the cofounder of Random House, that he could write a whole book relying on only fifty different words. Though challenging, the bet resulted in *Green Eggs and Ham*, a classic that's beloved in my house (and maybe yours) and Dr. Seuss's bestselling book.

Constraints, then, can open our minds and drive creativity rather than hinder it. Poetic masterworks spring from the boundaries of verse and rhyme. Masterpieces of Renaissance art started as commissions in which the painter was bound to adhere to narrow specifications on subject matter, materials, color, and size. In our own work, constraints take many different forms, from tight budgets to standardization. If you ask a team to design and build a product, you might get a handful of good ideas. But if you ask that same team to design and build the same product within a tight budget, you'll likely see even more creative results. Research examining how people design new products, cook meals, and even fix broken toys finds that budget constraints increase resourcefulness and lead to better solutions. While we all need resources to perform our jobs, scarcity can sometimes spur innovation.

7. LEAD FROM THE TRENCHES

The sixteenth-century French pirate François Le Clerc was incredibly successful—so successful that, recently, he nabbed the #13 spot on Forbes's list of highest-earning pirates. (Yes, Forbes made a list of top-earning pirates.) Legend has it that Le Clerc was a "lead from the front" pirate, often the first to board an enemy ship. This trait cost him a leg, and henceforth he was known as "Jambe de Bois" ("Peg Leg"). He went on to lead a fleet of ten vessels and over three hundred men. Why were so many other pirates willing to follow Le Clerc into battle, even after he lost his leg? Because he fought beside them.

In the TV show *Undercover Boss*, executives go undercover as entry-level employees in the companies they lead. There are almost always some unpleasant surprises. In one episode, Frontier Airlines CEO Bryan Bedford discovered major flaws in company operations when he joined the front lines, from employees having only seven minutes to clean a plane between flights to agents shifting between checking in patrons to loading luggage, by hand, in 104-degree heat. By being in the trenches with their own employees, the executives see the problems in their businesses and how they are experienced, and they also better understand what working in the organization entails for their employees.

Rebels know where the action is, and that's where they want to be—not up in a tower or secluded in a corner office. The rebel knows that the best way to lead is from the trenches. Rebel leaders are comrades, friends, and fellow enthusiasts. Napoleon would not have spent all his time in the executive suite. Chef Bottura is often found sweeping the streets outside his restaurant, unloading deliveries, and cleaning the kitchen. In Navy SEAL teams, as I've learned from naval officers who have attended my classes at Harvard Kennedy School, this hands-on philosophy is ingrained in candidates from the first day of training. Indeed, naval officers are taught to lead by example in everything they do. You'll find them at the head of the pack during runs and swims.

In a survey I conducted of over seven hundred employees, I found that the most respected leaders are those most willing to get their hands dirty. When I asked the employees to think about leaders they don't respect, they zeroed in on managers removed from the nitty-gritty. When an organization is flat, it's not just good for the leader, of course. One study of group assignments found that the more control a single member had, the worse the team did as a whole. When talking about Osteria Francescana, Bottura uses "we" rather than "I." He also shares meals with the staff, plays soccer with them in the afternoon, and constantly checks in when he's traveling. When he is not in Modena, they miss him, but the team does not falter just because one member is away.

8. FOSTER HAPPY ACCIDENTS

After World War II, a flood of veterans enrolled in the Massachusetts Institute of Technology. To accommodate this new population and their families, MIT built Westgate West, a maze of one hundred low-rise housing units for families on the far western edge of campus. A pair of psychologists were interested in knowing more about the social network in the housing complex, so they asked residents to list their three closest friends. The people listed most often as best friends tended to live in a first-floor apartment, right at the bottom of the staircase. Forty-two percent said one of their best friends was a direct neighbor. Friends are the people you bump into.

When Steve Jobs needed a new home for Pixar back in the 1980s, he bought a dilapidated Del Monte canning factory. The initial plan was to create separate spaces for each department (animators, computer scientists, etc.), but instead he decided to configure the old factory as one large space, centered on an atrium. He put employee mailboxes in the atrium, as well as the café, gift shop, and screening rooms. (He even considered putting the only restrooms there, but changed his mind.) Jobs believed that separating the groups, each of which had its own unique culture and approach to problem solving, would discourage idea sharing.

These fruitful connections happen not only by designing workspaces differently, but by designing teams differently. Bottura's two sous chefs are Davide di Fabio and Kondo Takahiko. The two not only differ in their origins (Italy and Japan), but also in their strengths: one is more comfortable with improvisation, and the other is obsessed with precision. Bottura believes that such "collisions" make his kitchen more innovative. Too often, leaders believe that success depends on hierarchical command and control. Rebels, on the other hand, know the value of happy accidents. They believe in workspaces and teams that cross-pollinate. The rebel realizes that a mistake may unlock a breakthrough.

One day at Osteria Francescana, Takahiko dropped a lemon tart . . . and Bottura transformed it into the now famous dessert "Oops! I Dropped the Lemon Tart." The story of how the dish was created found its way into his book, which I happened to pick up one day at a bookstore in Massachusetts. Which, eventually, brought me to Modena to watch as Bottura's dishes, and the stories behind them, were ferried from the kitchen out to the hungry customers, all waiting in anticipation, ready to be astonished.

CONCLUSION

RISOTTO CACIO E PEPE

You should always keep the door open to the unexpected.
—MASSIMO BOTTURA, OWNER AND CHEF, OSTERIA FRANCESCANA

Shortly after four a.m. on May 20, 2012, the ground began to buckle. Bricks fell to the ground, and the sounds of shattering glass filled the air. The windows of parked cars caved in. The walls of churches, schools, and residential homes started to give out. The power failed, leaving entire towns in darkness. Mobile phones didn't function.

A magnitude 6.0 earthquake had hit the Emilia Romagna region in Northern Italy, affecting the historic cities of Bologna, Ferrara, and Modena. As dawn broke, the aftershocks were still not over, but the extent of the damage was already clear. Large cracks ran from the top to the bottom of many apartment buildings. The streets were filled with architectural remains. In one of the towns shaken by the earthquake, a centuries-old clock tower was sheared in two, with one half collapsing into rubble and the other half standing precariously. In another town, the battlements and towers of an imposing fourteenth-century castle had crumbled into dust. Many households were left with no water. In yet another, the town hall was severely damaged, and the public-school buildings had collapsed. Nearby, the roof of a beloved chapel had caved in, leaving statues of angels and saints exposed to the sky.

Emilia Romagna sits at the top of the Italian boot, stretching from the Adriatic Sea on the east coast all the way to the Liguria region on the west coast. In the south of the region, castle-capped hills, green fields, and breathtaking views of the forested Apennine peaks are dotted with remote, sparsely populated villages. In stark contrast, the north of the region is pool-table flat: The landscape mainly consists of the fertile farmlands all across the Po River valley. Emilia Romagna is considered Italy's gastronomic heartland. Modena's balsamic vinegar, Parma ham and Parmesan cheese, and Bologna's meat ragù, lasagne, and mortadella are all Italian icons.

The region also boasts an unusually rich architectural and artistic heritage. There are medieval castles, Romanesque churches, Christian mosaics, and striking Renaissance palaces dating back hundreds of years, when the region was a patchwork of city-states, each independently governed by local dynasties with a lot of power. The damage to this heritage from the quakes was extensive. More aftershocks occurred throughout the day. Fearful of staying in weakened buildings and damaged homes, hundreds of people spent the night in their cars, while others took shelter in tents. Nine days later, with the worst seemingly over, people found themselves searching through debris for the second time, after a 5.8-magnitude earthquake shook the same region, bringing down buildings damaged by the previous quake. Many lives were lost. Countless homes had been leveled. The earthquake damage was estimated at more than $15 billion.

The earthquakes also threatened an entire industry: that of Parmigiano-Reggiano cheese. Parmigiano-Reggiano was first produced in the Po Valley by Cistercian monks as large wheels of cheese that could be easily stored and sustain pilgrims on their long journeys. Today, official Parmigiano-Reggiano can only be made in a few provinces in Emilia Romagna. The cheese must be produced in a very specific way that includes what is fed to the cows that produce the milk. Experts check the quality of wheels of Parmigiano-Reggiano by tapping the rind with a little hammer created just for the job. At a retail price of some $15 a pound in Italy, and even more abroad, Parmigiano-Reggiano is one of the most expensive Italian cheeses. Wheels of Parmigiano-Reggiano are key to the region's economy. Every year, the area produces over three million wheels of Parmigiano-Reggiano, generating about $2.3 billion in consumer sales. Many Italian banks still accept interest payments in Parmigiano.

The cheese is aged in humidity-controlled warehouses, which were hit hard by the earthquake. Hundreds of large wheels of cheese—each as big as truck tires—fell from twenty-three-foot-high shelves, tumbling to the floor like books in a bombed-out library. All in all, about 400,000 wheels of Parmigiano-Reggiano from thirty-seven factories were damaged. These damaged wheels could not be sold as usual, threatening losses in the hundreds of millions. Cheese producers started to worry they'd have to close the doors on businesses their families had tended for generations. In the span of nine days, the tremor had placed an entire industry in danger.

MASSIMO BOTTURA HAD ALWAYS FELT A SPECIAL CONNECTION TO PARMIGIANO- Reggiano. For most big dinners in the house where he grew up, his father brought home some of the cheese to be used as an ingredient in pasta sauces and ravioli or tortellini, eaten in big chunks as appetizer, or grated on pasta. Bottura would steal pieces of it while his mother and grandmother were cooking. The taste was intense and complex. Even today, Bottura considers a piece of Parmigiano and some fruit to be the perfect snack.

When Bottura learned about the damage the earthquake had done to his beloved wheels of Parmigiano-Reggiano, he wondered if there was something he could do to help. He couldn't stop thinking about it and decided to focus on what he does best: developing new recipes.

What if he came up with a new dish that had this almost magical cheese as the star? He wanted to devise a recipe for a dish that would be delicious, but simple enough for almost anyone to make. If Parmigiano-Reggiano was the star of the dish, he reasoned, those who were interested in cooking it would buy cheese from the damaged wheels.

Then he started experimenting. Bottura thought about traditional dishes that are made with just a few ingredients unique to a specific region. One of Rome's traditional dishes seemed to fit the bill: a classic pasta dish called *cacio e pepe* (pasta with cheese and pepper). It can be made in minutes with four of the most basic ingredients: salt, pasta, black pepper, and a type of cheese often used in Italian cooking called Pecorino Romano. Pecorino is a sheep's-milk cheese with a sharp flavor that has been made in Campania, a region in southern Italy, since ancient times. *Cacio* is the local Roman dialect word for Pecorino Romano. Bottura saw a parallel in what Pecorino meant for Campania and what Parmigiano-Reggiano meant for Emilia Romagna. So he decided to give this traditional recipe his own creative spin. Instead of the usual Pecorino, he would use Parmigiano. And instead of pasta, he would use rice—another product greatly affected by the earthquake. He called the dish *Risotto Cacio e Pepe*.

Though the traditional *cacio e pepe* recipe calls for only a few ingredients, the way the dish is prepared elevates it to an elegant creamy twirl of noodles that makes your palate sing. For Bottura's new dish, he opted to prepare the risotto with a Parmesan water, instead of the usual stock. He grated some Parmigiano-Reggiano and soaked the shredded cheese in a pot full of water. He brought it up to a boil, turned the heat off, and then stirred until it became creamy. He then stored the creamy mixture in the refrigerator overnight. By the next morning, the liquid had separated into three different layers. There was a milk protein at the bottom; a thick, viscous broth in the middle; and a cream of Parmigiano at the top. He toasted some rice, and then he started adding the Parmigiano broth until the rice was ready. The dish was finished with the cream of Parmigiano from the top layer. The recipe, as Bottura described it, "borrowed an iconic Roman spaghetti dish . . . and transformed it into an Emilian symbol of hope and recovery."

But that, alone, would not solve the problem. There were so many wheels of damaged cheese, and they could be saved only if they were sold soon. Bottura and the consortium of Parmigiano-Reggiano producers decided to sponsor a one-day event when people across the globe could make *Risotto Cacio e Pepe* at the same time. So, they organized an online fund-raiser: On October 27, 2012, people were encouraged to make the new recipe or a dish of their own featuring Parmigiano-Reggiano.

This special night kicked off at eight o'clock on a major Italian food show, broadcast live via the Internet from the Salone del Gusto, a biannual gastronomy exhibition held in Turin. Over a quarter of a million people had dinner "together" that night. Some of them got together with friends and family and ate Bottura's dish at home. Others ate it at restaurants. Still others devised their own Parmigiano-Reggiano concoctions. The event gathered a lot of attention, not only from people living in Italy, but also from people abroad—from New York City to Tokyo—who wanted to help save one of Italy's culinary treasures. In the end, all 400,000 wheels of damaged Parmigiano-Reggiano were sold. No one lost a job. No cheese makers closed their doors. An industry was rescued by a recipe.

WHEN BOTTURA IS IN MODENA, HE WORKS AT THE RESTAURANT, VISITS THE LOCAL markets, and goes to farms to check on his suppliers. Dressed in his chef's whites, he preps dishes, carefully plates them, tastes pretty much everything that leaves the kitchen, expedites between the front and back of the house, chats with the staff, and works with his team on new recipes. The same month might find him in Tokyo, Melbourne, New York, Rio de Janeiro, and London, returning between each trip to cook at Osteria Francescana. The year the earthquakes struck was also the year that Bottura's restaurant won its third Michelin star, so it was an especially busy time, with a surge in customers, requests for speeches from conference organizers, and constant inquiries from the media.

And yet, when so many wheels of his dear cheese were damaged, he made time to help. Indeed, this is part of a pattern in his life, which continued in 2015, when he started an initiative called Refettorio, which uses leftovers to feed people who do not have access to good food. His first Refettorio was in Milan. The ones that followed occurred in Brazil, Spain, New York, and in other parts of the world where Bottura found the time to travel. Each time he organized a Refettorio, he created menus using leftover ingredients from big ongoing culinary conferences or other cooking events and served his creations to children and homeless shelters in the area.

Somehow, with Bottura, there always seems to be time for more, for sucking the marrow out of life and making the most of every moment. On the evening I worked the front of the house at his restaurant, the doorbell rang about forty-five minutes into the dinner service. The restaurant was full, and Beppe, surprised, went to see who it was. As he opened the door, the bass rumble of a Ducati motorcycle filled the room. The rider, who had a boy of about ten years old perched behind him, asked, "Table for two?" He revved the engine again. And then there was laughter: It was Bottura, who was spending part of the day with a kid who had asked to meet him through the Make-A-Wish Foundation.

We tend to think that the more we have to do, the less time and mental space we will have for other tasks. This is a matter of basic logic, and it is hard to imagine life being any other way, right? But it turns out this is wrong. When we are fully engaged in our work and in our lives, we actually have the energy to accomplish more. Bottura, who often plays a game of soccer out on the street with the staff before dinner starts, has discovered this. This is another secret of the rebel: What seem like tangents, or doing extra—or helping someone when it seems that there is no time—become paths to a more vibrant life. Doing more gives us more.

Psychologists are catching up with this rebel insight. Cassie Mogilner of the University of California in Los Angeles and her colleagues have shown that when we give our time to others, we actually feel less time-constrained. Of course, giving time to others gives us a "connected" feeling and brings us meaningful experiences. But people who give time, Mogilner's research shows, also feel more capable, confident, and useful. They feel they've accomplished something and, as a result, that they can accomplish more in the future. I've seen a similar effect in my own research. I recruited participants to work on a data-entry task, and I deliberately made some of them busier than others by giving them more work to complete in the same amount of time, telling them that they would be helping a researcher's project by doing so. The participants who got more work done within the same allotted time, and thus were objectively busier, felt less time constrained, and were more willing to take on more.

Perhaps this explains the almost magical quality I sensed when I was with Bottura and the other remarkable people I met during my research for this book. In their joy of doing—in their total engagement with life—their recipe for success turned out to be rebelling against time itself.

EPILOGUE

REBEL ACTION

The way to get started is to quit talking and begin doing.
—**WALT DISNEY**

On a chilly day in the late 1970s, a teenage Massimo Bottura was sitting in the passenger seat of his father's blue Alfa Romeo. His older brother was outside, standing next to a gas pump, filling up the tank. As he was waiting, Bottura decided to have a look at a little red book his father kept in the car: a beat-up edition of the *Michelin Guide*. A decade and a half later, in 1986, Bottura went to speak with his father, who was not happy that his son had decided to leave law school to try his hand at being a chef. He reminded his father of the book he'd discovered in the car that day. "You'll see, Dad, someday I'll have a Michelin star, too!"

Taking the first step wasn't easy for Bottura. He had long looked up to his father, who didn't want him to become a chef. He didn't have the experience or skills that many told him he would need. He didn't have connections. But he had an idea—breaking with the traditions of Italian cuisine—and a lot of passion for it. And so, even in the early years, when tradition-bound Italians criticized his cooking, he refused to give up.

In your own journey toward embracing your rebel talent, you

may also find that the hardest part is getting started. For help, visit www.rebeltalents.org, where you will find a variety of resources and tips to set you on the right path.

WHAT TYPE OF REBEL ARE YOU?

In the years I've been studying rebels, I've realized that they come in many varieties. They behave in different ways, and need different approaches to develop their talent. Understanding what I refer to as your Rebel Quotient is an important first step. On www.rebeltalents.org, you'll find a free assessment to determine which rebel ingredients come most naturally to you and where you have the most room to grow. Are you the kind of rebel who speaks your mind to a charismatic boss who's on the wrong track? Or are you the kind who is more apt to recognize what's new in a project you've completed a dozen times before? Being rebellious is uncomfortable. But becoming more aware of your own rebel profile will help you become more comfortable with the uncomfortable.

It's hard to bring out the rebel inside of you on a regular basis. After all, being a rebel means fighting against elements of human nature. But it can also be incredibly exciting and satisfying: Even small changes in your approach to work and life can produce powerful results. You'll find concrete tips based on the habits and strategies rebels rely on regularly—and some stories about how those techniques can pay off.

REBEL WAYS TO KEEP LEARNING

Rebels value learning and stay humble. As Bottura told me when I first met him, "When you think you know everything, you've stopped growing. . . . Keep your eyes open and ask questions." To help you in your continuous learning, www.rebeltalents.org also includes stories and case studies of other rebels who I hope will inspire and teach you. You'll also find links to research on rebel talents, which—like a Bottura menu—keeps evolving over time.

THE WAY FORWARD

Fortunately, Bottura's father lived long enough to see him receive that first Michelin star, in 2001. It was just the beginning of an amazing journey. In December 2001, about a month after receiving the honor, Bottura gave a commemorative T-shirt to each Osteria Francescana team member as a Christmas gift. Printed on the T-shirt was the date when the first Michelin star arrived, a Michelin star symbol, and the sentence: *Ma dove vuole arrivare questa pasta e fagioli?* (Where do these pasta and beans want to go?) They had traveled far. In fact, Bottura went well beyond his initial promise to his father. He had reached for the stars and eventually got three of them from Michelin.

Like Bottura and the other characters you met in this book, rebels go about their work and life a bit differently: They break rules and bring about positive change in the process. They smile at life and feel fulfilled. There is no better time for rebel action than now.

ACKNOWLEDGMENTS

Great things are done by a series of small things brought together.
—VINCENT VAN GOGH

In February of 2016, *Harvard Business Review* approached me to see if I was interested in being part of an experiment to test ideas about what a digital "article of the future" might look like. "Experiment?" I thought: "I am in." In the end, the feature included videos, case studies, and even a live event in San Francisco, all focused on the idea that acts of rebellion could be positive and productive. The enthusiastic response we received kindled my desire to write the book you hold in your hands today.

At HBR, I worked closely with Senior Editor Steve Prokesch, who held my hand through the process, asking insightful questions, giving candid feedback, and making everything I wrote more compelling with his thoughtful edits and clever suggestions. I am so grateful for all of his outstanding help. Thank you also to HBR's Scott Berinato, Amy Meeker, Sarah Cliffe, Amy Bernstein, Gretchen Gavett, Tina Silberman, Karen Player, Kate Adams, Amy Poftak, and Editor-in-Chief Adi Ignatus. Their creative ideas, encouragement, and willingness to try new things were thoroughly invigorating. I want to express my gratitude to the entire HBR organization.

When I first wrote *Rebel Talent*, the ideas were clear in my head. Or so I thought. I was getting ready to submit the manuscript and shared it with a journalist, Gareth Cook, for a look. I ended up rewriting every chapter thanks to his incredibly helpful feedback and ingenious guidance. I wrestled through each idea in the book with him, and I am grateful for his patience, high standards, and rare ability to shape ideas into much better ones. I thought I had met a book doctor, but I ended up working with an astoundingly curious and sharp "idea coach" who cared about the project as much as I did. Thank you, Gareth, for seeing the potential in my ideas, for pushing me (so, so) hard to make them better, and for keeping me on track despite all the uncertainty about where this adventure would take me.

A big thanks also to my agent, Max Brockman, who saw promise in this project when the book was just a notion. Max provided insightful advice as I chose the right publisher, and he was a pleasure to work with even when my decisions gave him a headache.

I was joined in this journey by my brilliant editor, Jessica Sindler, at Dey Street, who read through many drafts of this book and always found ways to strengthen it with her thoughtful feedback and careful edits. Jessica's excitement for the book kept me motivated throughout the process, and I feel fortunate to have found her.

I owe an enormous debt to my friend, the writer and editor Katie Shonk, who read every chapter many times and suggested edits that made the writing much clearer and more compelling. Her wise advice along the way was invaluable, and her willingness to provide so much help speaks to the kind attitude I have benefited from over the many years I've known her.

The research and stories reported in this book are based on many hours spent reading papers and books, hundreds of interviews, countless plane rides, dozens of visits to organizations around the globe, and thousands of conversations with colleagues, executives and friends. I am fortunate I've had the opportunity to collaborate on the research mentioned in this book with such exceptional scholars: Linda Argote, Dan Ariely, Emma Aveling, Silvia Bellezza, Ethan Bernstein, Alison Wood Brooks, Daniel Cable, Tiziana Casciaro, Tiffany Chang, Giada Di Stefano, Molly Frean, Adam Galinsky, Evelyn Gosnell, Adam Grant, Paul Green, Brian Hall, Karen Huang, Laura Huang, Diwas KC, Anat Keinan, Tami Kim, Ata Jami, Li Jiang, Maryam Kouchaki, Rick Larrick, Julia Lee, Joshua Margolis, Julia Minson, Ella Miron-Spektor, Bill McEvily, Mike Norton, Gary Pisano, Jane Risen, Ovul Sezer, Juliana Schroeder, Maurice Schweitzer, Morgan Shields, Sara Singer, Brad Staats, Juliana Stone, Thor Sundt, Leigh Tost, Mike Yeomans, Kathleen Vohs, Cameron Wright, Evelyn Zhang, and Ting Zhang. The research that brings so much joy to my life is thanks to all of you—to the dedication you have for science, your unsparingly honest feedback, your seemingly bottomless well of creative ideas.

For raising questions about rebels I had not thought about, and for providing a delightful environment in which to work, I am extremely thankful to my colleagues in the Negotiation, Organizations and Markets Unit at HBS: Max Bazerman, John Beshears, Alison Wood Brooks, Katherine Coffman, Ben Edelman, Christine Exley, Jerry Green, Brian Hall, Leslie John, Jenn Logg, Mike Luca, Deepak Malhotra, Kathleen McGinn, Kevin Mohan, Matthew Rabin, Joshua Schwartzstein, Jim Sebenius, Guhan Subramanian, Andy Wasynczuk, and Ashley Whillans. I am so lucky to have an office on the same floor as you, and to have the opportunity to keep on learning from you.

The inspiration for this book came from the many rebels I've met throughout the years. I am especially grateful to Chef Massimo Bottura, his wife, Laura Gilmore, as well as Giuseppe Palmieri, Alessandro Laganà, Enrico Vignoli, and the rest of the remarkably talented and joyful crew at Osteria Francescana. I am thankful to Ed Catmull at Pixar for spending a big chunk of his birthday to speak with me; his keen intellect, thirst for learning, and contagious humility are the perfect combination for a truly engaging conversation. I am also grateful to Captain Sully, Scott Cook, Greg Dyke, Doug Conant, Rachael Chong, Pete Docter, Andrew Gordon, Dan Scanlon, Jonas Rivera, Jamie Woolf, Patricia Fili-Krushel, Leila Janah, Mellody Hobson, Andrew Roberts, Peter Leeson, Riccardo Delleani, and all of the other remarkable people who generously made themselves available for interviews and on-site conversations. Their wealth of knowledge, innovative insights, and approach to life left an indelible impact on my thinking.

For help connecting to rebels, I thank Gianni Lorenzoni, Sally Ashworth, Gareth Jones, Bruno Lamborghini, Avi Swerdlow, Anthony Accardo, Mike Wheeler, Taylor Luczak, Sarah Green Carmichael, and Kathleen McGinn.

I also want to acknowledge the precious help I received from research associates and fact checkers, who worked under time pressure with much good cheer, including Susan Chamberlain, Rijad Custovic, Ivan Dzintars, Annisha Simpson, Cam Haigh, and Leoul Tekle. Jeff Strabone's careful work on the Notes likely drove him crazy, but I am grateful to him for being so attentive and precise. Alex Caracuzzo, Jeffrey Cronin, Barbara Esty, and Rhys Sevier, who are all part of Baker Library Services at HBS, worked their magic in finding information on anything I asked about, whether it was a history of the New York's Hippodrome Theater, or details on the techniques used across the centuries to cut diamonds. Thank you for being so responsive to my dozens of requests, even when many of them had "last request" in the subject line. Along the way, I was aided enormously by my faculty support specialist, Meg King, who not only patiently read various drafts of this book but also dealt with all sorts of last-minute requests with such graciousness. Without Meg's support, my life at work would be complete chaos.

I refined many of this book's ideas in classrooms, with hundreds of executives. I am thankful for their insightful feedback and comments, which shaped my thinking as I learned more about rebel talent. For the many opportunities I had to be in front of executives in Executive Education Programs at HBS, I owe a large debt to David Ager, Cathy Cotins, Jim Dowd, Pam Hallagan, Deborah Hooper, Ani Kharajian, Beth Neustadt, Carla Tishler, and many HBS colleagues who gave me the privilege to share my ideas in the classroom.

When I was ready for feedback, Judith Schaab, Carmen Reynold, and Gary Pisano were generous with their time and attentively read every page. I know how precious your time is, and I appreciate that you spent some of it offering ways to improve the manuscript. Thanks also to Elizabeth Sweeny, who read so many versions of the Introduction that I lost count, and yet still always had ideas on how to sharpen it.

At HarperCollins, I want to thank Lynn Grady, Ben Steinberg, Kendra Newton, and Heidi Richter for their innovative plan for bringing the secrets of rebel talent to a wide audience.

I am also indebted to my HBS Research Director, Teresa Amabile, as well as HBS Director of Research Jan Rivkin and HBS Dean Nitin Nohria for being such stalwart supporters of my work. This book would not exist without their devotion to my research over the years, and their insistence that I always aim higher. Special thanks also to Steve O'Donnell, who graciously keeps an eye on my spending: Steve, this year I promise not to blow my budget.

Writing a book with three children under the age of five was not always easy and it would not have been possible were it not for the peace of mind that comes from knowing they were in great hands when I could not be with them. I want to give a special thanks to the people who took good care of my little ones. I am grateful to Glenda and Mena Chavez, for the love you have for our family, and for the sweetness you brought into our home. Thanks also to Jayla Chavez, who often spent her days off school with us, making the little ones laugh, and being a wonderful role model for them.

My mother deserves my deepest gratitude. I can't believe I am still asking you favors as an adult, after all you've done—and that you are willing to fly across the ocean many times a year to pitch in. I couldn't have written this book without your generous help. Thanks to my brother, Davide, my sister, Elisa, and my father, not only for allowing me to "borrow" Mom for long periods of time, but also for being so understanding and supportive of the work that I do.

Last but not least . . . I am forever grateful to my wonderful other half, Greg Burd. I broke many rules while working on this book, from staying up late to filling many of our conversations with research ideas: You are more than a good sport. Greg, thank you for your grace, your steady encouragement for any project I take on, and your generous partnership at home. You are the biggest reason why I keep smiling even when the pages are blank. I feel so lucky to have met you, and am reminded of this whenever I look at the three wonderful little rebels we brought into the world together.

January 3, 2018
Cambridge, Massachusetts

NOTES

INTRODUCTION: *MARCIA!*

ix **Introduction epigraph:** Jane Kramer. (2013, November 4). "Post-Modena," *The New Yorker* 89, no. 35 (November 4, 2014). Retrieved from www.newyorker.com.

ix **Story of Osteria Francescana:** Personal interviews with Bottura, June 7 and 11, 2016; Personal interviews with staff at Osteria Francescana during May and June of 2016. Two-day visit at the restaurant, July 26–27, 2016.

1. NAPOLEON AND THE HOODIE

1 **Chapter 1 epigraph:** Retrieved from AZ Quotes, http://www.azquotes.com/quote/1428582 (accessed November 29, 2017).

1 **"40 centuries look down upon you":** David Chandler, *The Campaigns of Napoleon* (New York: Simon & Schuster, 2009), p. 224.

1 **Story of Bonaparte:** Ibid.; Andrew Roberts, *Napoleon the Great* (New York: Penguin, 2015); Andrew Roberts, *Napoleon: A Life* (New York: Penguin, 2015); Alan Forrest, *Napoleon's Men: The Soldiers of the Revolution and Empire* (London: Hambledon and London, 2002); Stephanie Jones and Jonathan Gosling, *Napoleonic Leadership: A Study in Power* (Thousand Oaks, CA: SAGE Publications, 2015). Personal interviews with Andrew Roberts, summer 2017.

5 **Bonaparte also fought in the trenches:** Ralph Jean-Paul, "Napoleon Bonaparte's Guide to Leadership," *Potential2Sucess*, http://potential2success.com/napoleonbonaparteleadership.html (accessed November 17, 2017).

5 **a job usually performed by a corporal:** Will Durant and Ariel Durant, *The Age of Napoleon*, vol. 11 *The Story of Civilization* (Ashland, OR: Blackstone Audio, 2015).

6 **the subject of a case study:** Francesca Gino, Bradley R. Staats, Brian J. Hall, and Tiffany Y. Chang, "The Morning Star Company: Self-Management at Work," Harvard Business School Case 914-013, September 2013 (revised June 2016).

8 **rules governing many social interactions:** Marco F. H. Schmidt, Lucas P. Butler, Julia Heinz, and Michael Tomasello, "Young Children See a Single Action and Infer a Social Norm: Promiscuous Normativity in 3-Year-Olds," *Psychological Science* 27, no. 10 (2016): 1360–1370.

8 **the stocks or pillory in the center of town:** Gary Ferraro and Susan Andreatta, *Cultural Anthropology: An Applied Perspective* (Belmont, CA: Wadsworth Publishing, 2011).

10 **fourteen-karat gold:** Walter Lord, *The Good Years: From 1900 to the First World War* (New York: Harper and Brothers, 1960).

10 **cheaper, functional equivalents:** Thorstein Veblen, *The Theory of the Leisure Class* (London: Macmillan, 1965 [1899]).

11 **common in the animal world, too:** Gibert Roberts, "Competitive Altruism: From Reciprocity to the Handicap Principle," *Proceedings of the Royal Society B: Biological Sciences* 265, no. 1394 (1998): 427–431.

11 **attract mates and raise their status:** Amotz Zahavi and Avishag Zahavi, *The Handicap Principle: A Missing Piece of Darwin's Puzzle* (New York: Oxford University Press, 1997); Alan Grafen, "Biological Signals as Handicaps," *Journal of Theoretical Biology* 144 (1990): 517–546.

12 **told Bloomberg TV:** Doug Gross, "Zuckerberg's Hoodie Rankles Wall Street," *CNN*, May 9, 2012, http://www.cnn.com/2012

/05/09/tech/social-media/zuckerberg-hoodie-wall-street/index.html (accessed November 27, 2017).

13 **my research shows:** Silvia Bellezza, Francesca Gino, and Anat Keinan, "The Red Sneakers Effect: Inferring Status and Competence from Signals of Nonconformity," *Journal of Consumer Research* 41, no. 1 (2014): 35–54.

17 **in front of an audience of peers:** Francesca Gino, "When Breaking Rules Pays Off: How Nonconforming Behaviors Increase Confidence and Engagement," Working paper, 2016 (available from author).

18 **their personal lives outside of work for a few weeks:** Ibid.

18 **an experiment:** Ibid.

19 **powerful, research says:** Gerben A. Van Kleef, Astrid C. Homan, Catrin Finkenauer, Seval Gündemir, and Eftychia Stamkou, "Breaking the Rules to Rise to Power: How Norm Violators Gain Power in the Eyes of Others," *Social Psychology and Personality Science* 2, no. 5 (2011) 500–507.

20 **what the experimenter might think:** Adam D. Galinsky, Deborah H. Gruenfeld, and Joe C. Magee, "From Power to Action," *Journal of Personality and Social Psychology* 85, no. 3 (2003): 453–466.

20 **ignore situational pressure:** Jacob B. Hirsh, Adam D. Galinsky, and Chen-Bo Zhong, "Drunk, Powerful, and in the Dark: How General Processes of Disinhibition Produce Both Prosocial and Antisocial Behavior," *Perspectives on Psychological Science* 6, no. 5 (2011): 415–427.

20 **a more socially acceptable emotion:** Sally D. Farley, "Attaining Status at the Expense of Likeability: Pilfering Power Through Conversational Interruption," *Journal of Nonverbal Behavior* 32, no. 4 (2008): 241–260.

2. THE DOG NAMED "HOT"

23 **Chapter 2 epigraph:** Raymond Chandler, *The Long Good-Bye* (Boston: Houghton Mifflin, 1954).

26 seven married women greet them: These examples are also mentioned in Ovul Sezer, Michael I. Norton, Francesca Gino, and Kathleen D. Vohs, "Family Rituals Improve the Holidays," *Journal of the Association for Consumer Research* 1, no. 4 (2016): 509–526.

27 improve group performance: Tami Kim, Ovul Sezer, Juliana Schroeder, Jane Risen, Francesca Gino, and Mike Norton, "Group Rituals Increase Liking, Meaning, and Group Effort," Working paper, *Open Science Framework* (2017), https://osf.io/xcun3/ (accessed November 17, 2017).

28 they even copy their mistakes: Derek E. Lyons, Andrew G. Young, and Frank C. Keil, "The Hidden Structure of Overimitation," *PNAS* 104, no. 50 (2007): 19751–19756.

29 higher levels of fidelity than preschoolers: Nicola McGuigan, Jenny Makinson, and Andrew Whiten, "From Over-Imitation to Super-Copying: Adults Imitate Causally Irrelevant Aspects of Tool Use with Higher Fidelity Than Young Children," *British Journal of Psychology* 102, no. 1 (2011): 1–18.

29 folding T-shirts: Francesca Gino, "Taking Organizational Processes for Granted: Why Inefficiencies Stick around in Organizations," Working paper, 2016 (available from author).

30 sticking with a status quo position: William Samuelson and Richard Zeckhauser, "Status Quo Bias in Decision Making," *Journal of Risk and Uncertainty* 1 (1988): 7–59.

30 the idea of potential gains: Daniel Kahneman and Amos Tversky, "Prospect Theory: An Analysis of Decision under Risk," *Econometrica* 47, no. 2 (1979): 263–291.

31 Italian Commedia dell'Arte: Sources used for the history of improv: Keith Johnstone, *Impro: Improvisation and the Theatre* (London: Routledge, 1987); Steve Kaplan, *The Hidden Tools of Comedy: The Serious Business of Being Funny* (Studio City, CA: Michael Wiese Productions, 2013); Jeffrey Sweet, *Something Wonderful Right Away: An Oral History of The Second City and The Compass Players* (New York: Limelight Editions, 2004); and Kelly Leonard and Tom Yorton, *Yes, And: How Improvisation Reverses*

"No, But" Thinking and Improves Creativity and Collaboration—Lessons from The Second City (New York: HarperBusiness, 2015).

33 a second look at the snakes: Alfred Edmund Brehm, *Brehm's Life of Animals: A Complete Natural History for Popular Home Instruction and for the Use of Schools*, trans. R. Schmidtlein (London: Forgotten Books, 2015 [1864]).

33 friends and threats in our environment: Wojciech Pisula, *Curiosity and Information Seeking in Animal and Human Behavior* (Boca Raton, FL: Brown Walker Press, 2009).

33 unfamiliar things: Adele Diamond, "Evidence of Robust Recognition Memory Early in Life Even When Assessed by Reaching Behavior," *Journal of Experimental Child Psychology* 59, no. 3 (1995): 419–456; Jennifer S. Lipton and Elizabeth S. Spelke, "Origins of Number Sense: Large-Number Discrimination in Human Infants," *Psychological Science* 14, no. 5 (2003): 396–401.

34 genes linked to novelty seeking: Specifically, the genes are DRD4 exon 3 gene alleles 2R and 7R. Joel Lehman and Kenneth O. Stanley, "Abandoning Objectives: Evolution through the Search for Novelty Alone," *Evolutionary Computation* 19, no. 2 (2011): 189–223. See also Wojciech Pisula, Kris Turlejski, and Eric Phillip Charles, "Comparative Psychology as Unified Psychology: The Case of Curiosity and Other Novelty-Related Behavior," *Review of General Psychology* 17, no. 2 (2013): 224–229.

34 northeast Tennessee and southwestern Virginia: Gary P. Pisano, Francesca Gino, and Bradley R. Staats, "Pal's Sudden Service—Scaling an Organizational Model to Drive Growth," Harvard Business School Case 916-052, May 2016 (revised March 2017).

36 a Japanese bank: Bradley R. Staats and Francesca Gino, "Specialization and Variety in Repetitive Tasks: Evidence from a Japanese Bank," *Management Science* 58, no. 6, (2012): 1141–1159.

36 a list of facts: Brent A. Mattingly and Gary W. Lewandowski Jr., "The Power of One: Benefits of Individual Self-Expansion," *Journal of Positive Psychology* 8, no. 1 (2013): 12–22.

36 accomplish new things in the future: Brent A. Mattingly and Gary W. Lewandowski Jr., "An Expanded Self Is a More Capable

Self: The Association Between Self-Concept Size and Self-Efficacy," *Self and Identity* 12, no. 6 (2013): 621–634.

36 the act was anonymous: Timothy D. Wilson, David B. Centerbar, Deborah A. Kermer, and Daniel T. Gilbert, "The Pleasures of Uncertainty: Prolonging Positive Moods in Ways People Do Not Anticipate," *Journal of Personality and Social Psychology* 88, no. 1 (2005): 5–21.

37 after seeing the film: Ibid.

37 skiing, hiking, or dancing: Charlotte Reissman, Arthur Aron, and Merlynn R. Bergen, "Shared Activities and Marital Satisfaction: Causal Direction and Self-Expansion versus Boredom," *Journal of Social and Personal Relationships* 10 (1993): 243–254.

38 relationship satisfaction: Kimberley Coulter and John M. Malouff, "Effects of an Intervention Designed to Enhance Romantic Relationship Excitement: A Randomized-Control Trial," *Couple and Family Psychology: Research and Practice* 2, no. 1 (2013): 34–44.

38 nine years later: Irene Tsapelas, Arthur Aron, and Terri Orbuch, "Marital Boredom Now Predicts Less Satisfaction 9 Years Later," *Psychological Science* 20 (2009): 543–545.

38 they shared novel activities: K. Daniel O'Leary, Bianca P. Acevedo, Arthur Aron, Leonie Huddy, and Debra Mashek, "Is Long-Term Love More Than a Rare Phenomenon? If So, What Are Its Correlates?," *Social Psychology and Personality Science* 3, no. 2 (2012): 241–249.

38 the relationship as exciting: Arthur Aron, Christina Norman, Elaine Aron, Colin McKenna, and Richard Heyman, "Couples' Shared Participation in Novel and Arousing Activities and Experienced Relationship Quality," *Journal of Personality and Social Psychology* 78 (2000): 273–284.

41 describe who we are: Brent A. Mattingly and Gary W. Lewandowski Jr., "Broadening Horizons: Self-Expansion in Relational and Nonrelational Contexts," *Social and Personality Psychology Compass* 8 (2014): 30–40. See also Brent A. Mattingly and Gary W. Lewandowski Jr., "Expanding the Self Brick by Brick: Non-Relational Self-Expansion and Self-Concept Size," *Social Psychological and Personality Science* 5 (2014): 483–489; and Kevin P. McIntyre, Brent A. Mattingly, Gary W. Lewandowski Jr., and Annie Simpson, "Workplace Self-Expansion: Implications for Job Satisfaction, Commitment, Self-Concept Clarity and Self-Esteem Among the Employed and Unemployed," *Basic and Applied Social Psychology* 36 (2014): 59–69.

41 **no matter how tough the road:** Mattingly and Lewandowski, "The Power of One: Benefits of Individual Self-Expansion."

3. THE VANISHING ELEPHANT

43 **Chapter 3 epigraph:** Leo Hardy, *Paranormal Investigators 8: Harry Houdini and Sir Arthur Conan Doyle* (New York: Pronoun, 2017).

43 **"supreme in size and extravagance":** July 1917 issue of *The Green Book Magazine* (p. 788).

44 **Houdini story:** William Kalush and Larry Sloman, *The Secret Life of Houdini: The Making of America's First Superhero* (New York: Atria Books, 2007); James Randi and Bert Randolph Sugar, *Houdini: His Life and Art* (New York: Grosset & Dunlap, 1976); Kenneth Silverman, *Houdini!!! The Career of Erich Weiss* (New York: HarperCollins, 1996); and Daniel E. Harmon, "Houdini—The Greatest Showman of All?," *New York Times*, November 1, 1981, p. D4.

45 **"this strange appearance":** Adam Smith, *Selected Philosophical Writings*, ed. James R. Otteson (Exeter, Eng.: Imprint Academic, 2004).

47 **Houdini remembered:** Kalush and Sloman, *The Secret Life of Houdini.*

47 **a car for the masses:** Willy Shih, "Ford vs. GM: The Evolution of Mass Production (A)," Harvard Business School Case 614-010, August 2013 (revised November 2013); and interviews with Ford employees, May 4, 2016.

48 "has failed to master change": National Research Council, *The Competitive Status of the U.S. Auto Industry: A Study of the Influences of Technology in Determining International Industrial Competitive Advantage* (Washington, D.C.: National Academies Press, 1982), p. 27.

49 curiosity, research suggests: Alison Gopnika, Shaun O'Grady, Christopher G. Lucas, et al., "Changes in Cognitive Flexibility and Hypothesis Search Across Human Life History from Childhood to Adolescence to Adulthood," *PNAS* 114, no. 30 (2017): 7892–7899; Laura E. Schulz and Elizabeth Baraff Bonawitz, "Serious Fun: Preschoolers Engage in More Exploratory Play When Evidence Is Confounded," *Developmental Psychology* 43, no. 4 (2007): 1045–1050; Maureen A. Callanan and Lisa M. Oakes, "Preschoolers' Questions and Parents' Explanations: Causal Thinking in Everyday Activity," *Cognitive Development* 7, no. 2 (1992): 213–233; Alison Gopnik, "Scientific Thinking in Young Children: Theoretical Advances, Empirical Research, and Policy Implications," *Science* 337, no. 6102 (2012): 1623–1627; and Cristine H. Legare, "The Contributions of Explanation and exploration to Children's Scientific Reasoning," *Child Development Perspectives* 8, no. 2 (2014): 101–106.

50 Story of Greg Dyke at the BBC: Greg Dyke, *Inside Story*; Georgina Born, Uncertain Vision: *Birt, Dyke and the Reinvention of the BBC*; Rosabeth M. Kanter and Douglas A. Raymond, "British Broadcasting Corporation (A): One BBC," Harvard Business School Case 303-075, February 2003 (revised July 2005); Rosabeth M. Kanter and Douglas A. Raymond, "British Broadcasting Corporation (B): Making it Happen," Harvard Business School Case 303-076, February 2003 (revised July 2005); and Peter Killing and Tracey Keys, "Greg Dyke Taking the Helm at the BBC (A)," IMD Case, IMD-3-1353, January 2006.

53 were also put in place: Rosabeth M. Kanter, *Confidence: How Winning Streaks and Losing Streaks Begin and End* (New York: Three Rivers Press, 2006).

53 **a group of 170 students:** Alison Wood Brooks, Francesca Gino, and Maurice E. Schweitzer, "Smart People Ask for (My) Advice: Seeking Advice Boosts Perceptions of Competence," *Management Science* 61, no. 6 (2015): 1421–1435.

54 **many questions or just a few:** Karen Huang, Michael Yeomans, Alison Wood Brooks, et al., "It Doesn't Hurt to Ask: Question-Asking Increases Liking," *Journal of Personality and Social Psychology* 113, no. 3, (2017): 430–452.

54 **information about themselves:** Ibid.

55 **engaged in small talk:** Todd B. Kashdan, Patrick E. McKnight, Frank D. Fincham, and Paul Rose, "When Curiosity Breeds Intimacy: Taking Advantage of Intimacy Opportunities and Transforming Boring Conversations," *Journal of Personality* 79 (2011): 1067–1099.

55 **in existing relationships:** Todd B. Kashdan and John E. Roberts, "Trait and State Curiosity in the Genesis of Intimacy: Differentiation from Related Constructs," *Journal of Social and Clinical Psychology* 23 (2004): 792–816. See also Todd B. Kashdan and John E. Roberts, "Affective Outcomes and Cognitive Processes in Superficial and Intimate Interactions: Roles of Social Anxiety and Curiosity," *Journal of Research in Personality* 40 (2006): 140–167.

55 **when we respond to a provocation:** Todd B. Kashdan, C. Nathan DeWall, Richard S. Pond Jr., et al.,"Curiosity Protects Against Interpersonal Aggression: Cross-Sectional, Daily Process, and Behavioral Evidence," *Journal of Personality* 81, no. 1 (2013): 87–102.

56 **excuse transgressions:** Diane S. Berry, Julie K. Willingham, and Christine A. Thayer, "Affect and Personality as Predictors of Conflict and Closeness in Young Adults' Friendships," *Journal of Research in Personality* 34, no. 1 (2000): 84–107.

56 **behavior and learning that it inspires:** Todd B. Kashdan, and Michael F. Steger, "Curiosity and Stable and Dynamic Pathways to Wellness: Traits, States, and Everyday Behaviors," *Motivation*

and Emotion 31, no. 3 (2007): 159–173. See also Jaak Panksepp, "The Primary Process Affects in Human Development, Happiness, and Thriving," in *Designing Positive Psychology: Taking Stock and Moving Forward*, ed. Kennon M. Sheldon, Todd B. Kashdan, and Michael F. Steger (New York: Oxford University Press, 2011), 51–85.

56 the top of the glass: Susan Engel, "Children's Need to Know: Curiosity in Schools," *Harvard Education Review* 81, no. 4 (2011): 625–645. Susan Engel, *The Hungry Mind: The Origins of Curiosity in Childhood* (Cambridge: Harvard University Press, 2015).

56 Scott Cook Innovation Award: Personal conversation, May 2015.

58 living in Turkey: FTN News, "General Manager of The Ritz Carlton Istanbul," https://www.youtube.com/watch?v=jmcQdy4DgdE (accessed November 17, 2017).

60 between efficiency and innovation in 1991: James G. March, "Exploration and Exploitation in Organizational Learning," *Organization Science* 2, no. 1 (1991): 71–87.

60 Olivetti story: Adriano Olivetti, *La biografia di Valerio Ochetto* (Rome: Edizioni di Comunità, 2013); Adriano Olivetti, *Le Fabbriche di Bene* (Rome: Edizioni di Comunità, 2014); Pier Giorgio Perotto, *P101: Quando l'Italia inventò il personal computer* (Rome: Edizioni di Comunità, 2015); interview with Riccardo Delleani, CEO of Olivetti, May 15, 2017; and interview with Bruno Lamborghini, May 17, 2017.

63 "T-shaped" employees: Sources for the story: Morten T. Hansen, "IDEO CEO Tim Brown: T-Shaped Stars: The Backbone of IDEO's Collaborative Culture," *Chief Executive*, January 21, 2010, https://chiefexecutive.net/ideo-ceo-tim-brown-t-shaped-stars-the-backbone-of-ideoaes-collaborative-culture__trashed/ (accessed November 28, 2017); and Haluk Demirkan and Jim Spohrer, "T-Shaped Innovators: Identifying the Right Talent to Support Service Innovation," *Research-Technology Management* 58, no. 5 (2015): 12–15.

63 curiosity and innovation abounds: Spencer Harrison, "Organizing the Cat? Generative Aspects of Curiosity in

Organizational Life," in *The Oxford Handbook of Positive Organizational Scholarship*, edited by Gretchen M. Spreitzer and Kim S. Cameron (Oxford: Oxford University Press, 2011).

64 people sell handmade goods: Lydia Paine Hagtvedt, Karyn Dossinger, and Spencer Harrison, "Curiosity Enabled the Cat: Curiosity as a Driver of Creativity," *Academy of Management Proceedings* (2016): 13231 (and working paper).

64 their company's call center: Spencer Harrison, David M. Sluss, and Blake E. Ashforth, "Curiosity Adapted the Cat: The Role of Trait Curiosity in Newcomer Adaptation," *Journal of Applied Psychology* 96, no. 1 (2011): 211–220.

65 Google story: Interviews with members of the People Innovation Lab at Google (Jennifer Kurkoski and Jessica Wisdom), May and August 2015; and Saman Musacchio, "What Google's Genius Billboard from 2004 Can Teach Us About Solving Problems," *Business Insider*, July 22, 2011, http://www.businessinsider.com/what-google-can-teach-us-about-solving-problems-2011-7 (accessed November 17, 2017).

66 the most curious candidates: Scott Simon, "Solve the Equation, Get an Interview," *National Public Radio*, October 9, 2004, https://www.npr.org/2004/10/09/4078172/solve-the-equation-get-an-interview (accessed November 28, 2017).

66 exact times of the day that this occurs?: Here is the solution, in case you are curious. After 12 o'clock, the minute hand races ahead of the hour hand. By the time the minute hand has gone all the way round the clock and is back at 12, one hour later (i.e., at 1 o'clock), the hour hand has moved to indicate 1. Five minutes later, the minute hand reaches 1 and is almost on top of the hour hand, but not quite, since by then the hour hand has moved ahead a tiny amount more. So the next time after 12 that the minute hand is directly over the hour hand is a bit after 1:05. Similarly, the next time it happens is a bit after 2:10. Then a bit after 3:15, and so on. The eleventh time this happens, a bit after 11:55, has to be 12 o'clock again, since we know what the clock looks like at that time. So the two hands are superimposed exactly twelve times in each twelve-hour period. To answer the second part of the puzzle, you have to figure out those little bits of time you have to keep adding on each hour. Well, after 12 o'clock, there are eleven occasions when the two hands match up, and since the clock hands move at constant speeds, those eleven events are spread equally apart around the clock face, so they are 1/11th of an hour apart. That's 5.454545 minutes apart, so the little bit you keep adding is in fact 0.454545 minutes. The precise times of the super-positions are, in hours, 1 + 1/11, 2 + 2/11, 3+ 3/11, all the way up to 11 + 11/11, which is 12 o'clock again.

67 **"questions, not answers":** Jeremy Caplan, "Google's Chief Looks Ahead," *Time*, October 2, 2006.

68 **"have them stay":** "Cognition Switch: What Employers Can Do to Encourage Their Workers to Retrain," *The Economist*, January 14, 2017, https://www.economist.com/news/special-report/21714171-companies-are-embracing-learning-core-skill-what-employers-can-do-encourage-their (accessed November 28, 2017).

69 **expression turns negative:** Robin Hornik, Nancy Risenhoover, and Megan Gunnar, "The Effects of Maternal Positive, Neutral, and Negative Affective Communications on Infant Responses to New Toys," *Child Development* 58, no. 4 (1987): 937–944. Susan C. Crockenberg and Esther M. Leerkes, "Infant and Maternal Behaviors Regulate Infant Reactivity to Novelty at 6 Months," *Developmental Psychology* 40, no. 6 (2004): 1123–1132. See also: Robert Siegler, Nancy Eisenberg, Judy DeLoache, and Jenny Saffran, *How Children Develop*, 4th ed. (New York: Worth Publishers, 2014).

69 **openly with their colleagues:** Amy Edmondson, "Psychological Safety and Learning Behavior in Work Teams," *Administrative Science Quarterly* 44, no. 2 (1999): 350–383.

70 **apply their new knowledge:** Satya Nadella and Jill Tracie Nichols, *Hit Refresh: The Quest to Rediscover Microsoft's Soul and Imagine a Better Future for Everyone* (New York: HarperBusiness, 2017).

70 **challenge existing practices:** Ed Catmull, "How Pixar Fosters

Collective Creativity," *Harvard Business Review,* September 2008, https://hbr.org/2008/09/how-pixar-fosters-collective-creativity (accessed November 28, 2017).

70 **an online training program for the firm:** Personal conversation with Spencer Harrison, March 17, 2017.

71 **the Vanishing Elephant trick:** Lydia Paine Hagtvedt, Karyn Dossinger, and Spencer Harrison, "Curiosity Enabled the Cat: Curiosity as a Driver of Creativity," *Academy of Management Proceedings* (2016): 13231 (and working paper).

74 **not actually invented by Houdini:** Victoria Moore, "The Yorkshire Man Who Taught Houdini to Make an Elephant Disappear," *Daily Mail*, July 31, 2007, http://www.dailymail.co.uk/news/article-471954/The-Yorkshire-man-taught-Houdini-make-elephant-disappear.html (accessed November 17, 2017).

4. THE HUDSON RIVER IS A RUNWAY

77 **Chapter 4 epigraph:** Chesley B. Sullenberger III, with Jeffrey Zaslow, *Highest Duty: My Search for What Really Matters* (New York: William Morrow, 2009).

77 **Sully story:** Interview with Sullenberger, April 25, 2017; Sullenberger and Zaslow, *Highest Duty: My Search for What Really Matters*; Chesley B. Sullenberger III with Douglas Century, *Making a Difference: Stories of Vision and Courage from America's Leaders* (New York: William Morrow, 2012); and National Transportation Safety Board, Aircraft Accident Report, adopted May 4, 2010, https://www.ntsb.gov/investigations/AccidentReports/Reports/AAR1003.pdf (accessed November 28, 2017).

78 **Sully said:** Sullenberger and Zaslow, *Highest Duty: My Search for What Really Matters*, p. 209.

78 **Air Traffic Control:** "Cactus" is the radio call sign for US Airways flights. The airline chose it after it merged with the former America West Airlines.

83 **Flight 1549 was no different:** Interview with Sullenberger, April 25, 2017.

84 the modern world: Giora Keinan, Nehemia Friedland, and Yossef Ben-Porath, "Decision-Making Under Stress: Scanning of Alternatives Under Physical Threat," *Acta Psychologica* 64, no. 3 (1987): 219–228.

85 we broaden our perspective: Ting Zhang, Francesca Gino, and Joshua Margolis, "Does 'Could' Lead to Good? On the Road to Moral Insight," *Academy of Management Journal* (2018, in press).

86 a group of study participants: Ibid.

87 a vascular stent: Interviews with three surgeons at a major hospital in Boston, April–May 2015.

88 blood clotting and even death: Susan Mayor, "Drug Eluting Stents Are Safe for Licensed Indications, FDA Panel Says," *BMJ* 333, no. 7581 (2006): 1235.

88 what role expertise might play: Bradley R. Staats, Diwas S. KC, and Francesca Gino, "Maintaining Beliefs in the Face of Negative News: The Moderating Role of Experience," *Management Science* (2017, in press).

89 "tactical military aviation," he's said: Carl Von Wodtke, "The 'Miracle on the Hudson' Was No Miracle; It Was the Culmination of a 35-Year Military and Airline Flying Career," *History Net*, September 7, 2016, http://www.historynet.com/sully-speaks-out .htm (accessed November 28, 2017).

89 must be kept alive: Interview with Sullenberger, April 25, 2017.

90 landing planes: Ruth Kanfer and Phillip L. Ackerman, "Motivation and Cognitive Abilities: An Integrative/Aptitude-Treatment Interaction Approach to Skill Acquisition" *Journal of Applied Psychology* 74, no. 4 (1989) 657–690.

90 had learning goals: Don VandeWalle, Steven P. Brown, William L. Cron, and John W. Slocum, Jr., "The Influence of Goal Orientation and Self-Regulation Tactics on Sales Performance: A Longitudinal Field Test," *Journal of Applied Psychology* 84, no. 2 (1999): 249–259.

90 "control over relevant outcomes": Joachim I. Krueger, "Return of the Ego—Self-Referent Information as a Filter for Social Prediction: Comment on Karniol (2003)," *Psychological Review* 110, no. 3 (2003): 585–590. See page 585.

90 two hypothetical investment options: Staats, KC, and Gino, "Maintaining Beliefs in the Face of Negative News: The Moderating Role of Experience."

91 power aggravates the problem: Adam D. Galinsky, Joe C. Magee, M. Ena Inesi, and Deborah H Gruenfeld, "Power and Perspectives Not Taken," *Psychological Science* 17, no. 12 (2006): 1068–1074.

92 power over other people: Leigh Plunkett Tost, Francesca Gino, and Richard P. Larrick, "Power, Competitiveness, and Advice Taking: Why the Powerful Don't Listen," *Organizational Behavior and Human Decision Processes* 117, no. 1 (2012): 53–65.

92 taking most of the airtime: Leigh Plunkett Tost, Francesca Gino, and Richard P. Larrick, "When Power Makes Others Speechless: The Negative Impact of Leader Power on Team Performance," *Academy of Management Journal* 56, no. 5 (2013): 1465–1486.

92 a lot of room to others' perspective: Deborah Britt Roebuck, *Communication Strategies for Today's Managerial Leader* (Cambridge, MA: Business Expert Press, 2012).

92 contribute whenever appropriate: Juliana L. Stone, Emma-Louise Aveling, Molly Frean, et al., "Effective Leadership of Surgical Teams: A Mixed Methods Study of Surgeon Behaviors and Functions," *The Annals of Thoracic Surgery* 104, no. 2 (2017): 530–537.

93 the detriment of patients: Amy C. Edmondson, "Speaking Up in the Operating Room: How Team Leaders Promote Learning in Interdisciplinary Action Teams," *Journal of Management Studies* 40 (2003): 1419–1452.

93 a snowy flight out of Minneapolis: Interview with Sullenberger, April 25, 2017.

94 both Friday and Saturday night: Interview with Giuseppe Palmieri, July 7, 2016.

95 when we weigh ourselves: Daniel Gilbert, "I'm O.K., You're Biased," *New York Times*, April 16, 2006, http://www.nytimes.com/2006/04/16/opinion/im-ok-youre-biased.html (accessed November 28, 2017).

95 a dangerous enzyme deficiency: Peter H. Ditto and David

F. Lopez, "Motivated Skepticism: Use of Differential Decision Criteria for Preferred and Nonpreferred Conclusions," *Journal of Personality and Social Psychology* 63, no. 4 (1992): 568–584.

95 college admission decisions: Ibid.

97 had certain events not occurred: Hal Ersner-Hershfield, Adam D. Galinsky, Laura J. Kray, and Brayden G. King, "Company, Country, Connections: Counterfactual Origins Increase Organizational Commitment, Patriotism, and Social Investment," *Psychological Science* 21, no. 10 (2010): 1479–1486.

97 do better in the future: Rachel Smallman and Neal J. Roese, "Counterfactual Thinking Facilitates Behavioral Intentions," *Journal of Experimental Social Psychology* 45, no. 4 (2009): 845–852.

97 the unpredictability of life: Laura J. Kray, and Adam D. Galinsky, "The Debiasing Effect of Counterfactual Mind-Sets: Increasing the Search for Disconfirmatory Information in Group Decisions," *Organizational Behavior and Human Decision Processes* 91, no. 1 (2003): 69–81.

97 that was pivotal in their lives: Laura J. Kray, Linda G. George, Katie A. Liljenquist, et al., "From What Might Have Been to What Must Have Been: Counterfactual Thinking Creates Meaning," *Journal of Personality and Social Psychology* 98 (2010): 106–118.

98 people who became their best friends: Ibid.

98 the experience of being *in*experienced: Ting Zhang, Tami Kim, Alison Wood Brooks, et al., "A 'Present' for the Future: The Unexpected Value of Rediscover," *Psychological Science* 25, no. 10 (2014): 1851–1860.

98 recruited expert guitarists: Ting Zhang, "Back to the beginning: How rediscovering inexperience helps experts advise novices." Working paper, 2017 (available from author).

99 relatively cheap lasers: Thomas W. Overton and James E. Shigley, "A History of Diamond Treatments," in *The Global Diamond Industry: Economics and Development*, vol. 2, ed. Roman Grynberg and Letsema Mbayi (Basingstoke, UK: Palgrave Macmillan, 2015).

100 Story of InnoCentive: Karim R. Lakhani, "InnoCentive.com

(A)," Harvard Business School Case 608-170, June 2008 (revised October 2009).

101 over 300,000 registered solvers: Ben Shneiderman, *The New ABCs of Research: Achieving Breakthrough Collaborations* (Oxford: Oxford University Press, 2016), p. 134.

101 an astrophysicist: Thomas M. Koulopoulos, *The Innovation Zone: How Great Companies Re-Innovate for Amazing Success* (Mountain View, CA: Nicholas Breale, 2011), p. 97.

101 closer to the problem: Karim R. Lakhani, Lars Bo Jeppesen, Peter A. Lohse, and Jill A. Panetta, "The Value of Openness in Scientific Problem Solving," *Harvard Business School Working Paper* No. 07-050, p. 11, http://www.hbs.edu/faculty/Publication%20 Files/07-050.pdf (accessed November 17, 2017).

101 another project: Oguz Ali Acar and Jan van den Ende, "Knowledge Distance, Cognitive-Search Processes, and Creativity: The Making of Winning Solutions in Science Contests," *Psychological Science* 27, no. 5 (2016): 692–699.

102 evidence that confirms our views: Teresa Garcia-Marques and Diane M. Mackie, "The Feeling of Familiarity as a Regulator of Persuasive Processing," *Social Cognition* 19, no. 1 (2001): 9–34; Arie W. Kruglanski, "Lay Epistemo-Logic—Process and Contents: Another Look at Attribution Theory," *Psychological Review* 87, no. 1 (1980): 70–87; Charlan Jeanne Nemeth, "Differential Contributions of Majority and Minority Influence," *Psychological Review* 93, no. 1 (1986): 23–32; Claudia Toma and Fabrizio Butera, "Hidden Profiles and Concealed Information: Strategic Information Sharing and Use in Group Decision Making," *Personality and Social Psychology Bulletin* 35, no. 6 (2009): 793–806.

102 the nearby neighborhood of Karaköy: Aslı Çekmiş and Işıl Hacıhasanoğlu, "Water Crossing Utopias of Istanbul: Past and Future," *ITU Journal of the Faculty of Architecture* 9, no. 2 (2012): 67–88; Walter Isaacson, *Leonardo da Vinci* (New York: Simon & Schuster, 2017).

103 a bridge based on Da Vinci's design: Doug Mellgren, "Da Vinci

Comes to Life 500 Years On," *The Guardian*, November 1, 2001, https://www.theguardian.com/world/2001/nov/01/engineering .internationaleducationnews (accessed November 17, 2017).

103 **Story of Jessica Rosval:** Interviews with staff at Osteria Francescana, July 26–27, 2016.

104 **what we know is sharply limited:** Tenelle Porter and Karina Schumann, "Intellectual Humility and Openness to the Opposing View," *Self and Identity* (2017): 1–24.

104 **Story of dish *Camouflage*:** Interviews with staff at Osteria Francescana, July 26–27, 2016.

104 **different from the present:** Ethan Kross and Igor Grossmann, "Boosting Wisdom: Distance from the Self Enhances Wise Reasoning, Attitudes, and Behavior," *Journal of Experimental Psychology* 141, no. 1 (2012): 43–48.

5. UNCOMFORTABLE TRUTHS

107 **Chapter 5 epigraph:** George Bernard Shaw, *Pygmalion: A Romance in Five Acts* (New York: Penguin Books, 1957).

107 **Story of Ava Duvernay:** Interview with Tendo Nagenda, November 8, 2017; Interview with Avi Swerdlow, November 3, 2017; Katherine Schaffstall, "Ava DuVernay Unsure How 'Wrinkle in Time' Will Be Received," *Hollywood Reporter*, October 9, 2017, https://www.hollywoodreporter.com/news/ava -duvernay-unsure-how-wrinkle-time-will-be-received-new-yorker -festival-2017-1046858 (accessed November 28, 2017); Kristal Brent Zook, "Queen Ava," *Essence*, March 1, 2017, https://www .questia.com/magazine/1P3-4318030261/queen-ava (accessed November 28, 2017); Dale Roe, "'Selma' Director Talks Motivations, Revelations," *Austin American-Statesman*, March 15, 2015; Loren King, "Ava DuVernay's March; 'Selma' Director Could Make History, Becoming the First African- American Woman to Get an Oscar Nod for Directing," *Boston Globe*, January 4, 2015; Manohla Dargis, "She Had a Dream: How This Woman Brought Martin Luther King's Epic Story to the Big Screen," *Observer*,

December 14, 2014; Joelle Monique, "Ava DuVernay on Walking into a Room 'Like a White Man'," *Vice*, July 6, 2017, Brittany Jones-Cooper, "Ava DuVernay Shares the Perks of Being a Red-Hot Director in Hollywood," *Yahoo Finance*, October 4, 2017, Ashley Lee, "Ava DuVernay's Advice on Hollywood: 'Follow the White Guys, They've Got This Thing Wired,'" *Hollywood Reporter*, July 18, 2015; Arianna Davis, "How Oprah & Ava Duvernay's Queen Sugar Has Transformed TV," *Refinery29*, June 19, 2017.

114 I give my students a little test: The test is known in the psychology literature as "Implicit Association Test." To learn more, you can read the paper that first introduced the test: Anthony G. Greenwald, Debbie E. McGhee, Jordan L. K. Schwartz, "Measuring Individual Differences in Implicit Cognition: The Implicit Association Test," *Journal of Personality and Social Psychology* 74, no. 6 (1998): 1464–1480.

115 form primitive stereotypes: Gary D. Levy and Robert A. Haaf, "Detection of Gender-Related Categories by 10-Month-Old Infants," *Infant Behavior and Development* 17, no. 4 (1994): 457–459.

115 softness as female: Mary Driver Leinbach, Barbara E. Hort, and Beverly I. Fagot, "Bears Are for Boys: Metaphorical Associations in Young Children's Gender Stereotypes," *Cognitive Development* 12, no. 1 (1997): 107–130; Marsha Weinraub, Lynda P. Clemens, Alan Sockloff, et al., "The Development of Sex Role Stereotypes in the Third Year: Relationships to Gender Labeling, Gender Identity, Sex-Typed Toy Preference, and Family Characteristics," *Child Development* 55, no. 4 (1984): 1493–1503.

115 boys as being rough: Cindy Faith Miller, Leah E. Lurye, Kristina M. Zosuls, and Diane N. Ruble, "Accessibility of Gender Stereotype Domains: Developmental and Gender Differences in Children," *Sex Roles* 60, nos. 11–12 (2009): 870–881.

116 gravitate to people just like us: William G. Graziano and Jennifer Weisho Bruce, "Attraction and the Initiation of Relationships: A Review of the Empirical Literature," in *Handbook of Relationship Initiation*, ed. Susan Sprecher, Amy Wenzel, and John H. Harvey (New York: Psychology Press, 2008); Miller McPherson, Lynn

Smith-Lovin, and James M. Cook, "Birds of a Feather: Homophily in Social Networks," *Annual Review of Sociology* 27 (2001), 415–444.

116 people similar to us: Angela J. Bahns, Christian S. Crandall, Omri Gillath, and Kristopher J. Preacher, "Similarity in Relationships as Niche Construction: Choice, Stability, and Influence Within Dyads in a Free Choice Environment," *Journal of Personality and Social Psychology* 112, no. 2 (2017): 329–355; Silke Anders, Roos de Jong, Christian Beck, John-Dylan Haynes, and Thomas Ethofer, "A Neural Link Between Affective Understanding and Interpersonal Attraction," *PNAS* 113, no. 16 (2016): E2248–E2257.

116 backlash, researchers have found: Laurie A. Rudman and Peter Glick, "Prescriptive Gender Stereotypes and Backlash Toward Agentic Women," *Journal of Social Issues* 57, no. 4 (2001): 743–762; Rudman and Glick, "Feminized Management and Backlash Toward Agentic Women: The Hidden Costs to Women of a Kinder, Gentler Image of Middle-Managers," *Journal of Personality and Social Psychology* 77, no. 5 (1999): 1004–1010.

116 the backlash can be especially strong: Madeline E. Heilman, Aaron S. Wallen, Daniella Fuchs, and Melinda M. Tamkins, "Penalties for Success: Reactions to Women who Succeed at Male Gender-Typed Tasks," *Journal of Applied Psychology* 89, no. 3 (2004), 416–427.

116 "the right way for a woman to speak": Alice Hendrickson Eagly and Linda Lorene Carli, *Through the Labyrinth: The Truth about how Women Become Leaders* (Cambridge, MA: Harvard Business Review Press, 2007), p. 102.

117 respective national industry: China Gorman, "Why Diverse Organizations Perform Better: Do We Still Need Evidence?," *Great Place to Work*, February 18, 2015, https://www.greatplacetowork.com/blog/238-why-diverse-organizations-perform-better-do-we-still-need-evidence (accessed November 17, 2017); Vivian Hunt, Dennis Layton, and Sara Prince, "Why Diversity Matters," McKinsey & Company, January 2015, http://www.mckinsey

.com/business-functions/organization/our-insights/why-diversity-matters#0 (accessed November 17, 2017).

117 better financial performance: Lois Joy, Nancy M. Carter, Harvey M. Wagner, and Sriram Narayanan, "The Bottom Line: Corporate Performance and Women's Representation on Boards," *Catalyst*, October 15, 2007, http://www.catalyst.org/knowledge/bottom-line-corporate-performance-and-womens-representation-boards (accessed November 17, 2017).

117 accelerates economic growth: Organization for Economic Cooperation and Development (OECD), *Gender Equality in Education, Employment and Entrepreneurship: Final Report to the MCM 2012*, p. 17, http://www.oecd.org/employment/50423364.pdf (accessed November 17, 2017). See also Stephan Klasen and Francesca Lamanna, "The Impact of Gender Inequality in Education and Employment on Economic Growth: New Evidence for a Panel of Countries," *Feminist Economics* 15, no. 3 (2009): 91–132.

117 as much as 21 percent: Anu Madgavkar, Kweilin Ellingrud, and Mekala Krishnan, "The Economic Benefits of Gender Parity," *Stanford Social Innovation Review*, March 8, 2016, https://ssir.org/articles/entry/the_economic_benefits_of_gender_parity (accessed November 17, 2017).

117 even if this wasn't the case: Susan Ware, *Holding Their Own: American Women in the 1930s* (Boston: Twayne, 1982).

118 low-, medium-, and high-priced: David Neumark, Roy J. Bank, and Kyle D. Van Nort, "Sex Discrimination in Restaurant Hiring: An Audit Study," *Quarterly Journal of Economics* 111, no. 3 (1996): 915–941.

118 the reviews of women: Kieran Snyder, "The Abrasiveness Trap: High-Achieving Men and Women Are Described Differently in Reviews," *Fortune*, August 26, 2014, http://fortune.com/2014/08/26/performance-review-gender-bias (accessed November 17, 2017).

119 Story of Ann Hopkins: Ann Branigar Hopkins, *So Ordered: Making Partner the Hard Way* (Amherst: University of

Massachusetts Press, 1996); Joseph L. Badaracco Jr. and Ilyse Barkan, "Ann Hopkins (A)," Harvard Business School Case 391-155, February 1991 (revised August 2001); Joseph L. Badaracco Jr. and Ilyse Barkan, "Ann Hopkins (B)," Harvard Business School Supplement 391–170, March 1991 (revised July 2001).

120 **good managers are typically male:** Arnie Cann and William D. Siegfried, "Gender Stereotypes and Dimensions of Effective Leader Behavior," *Sex Roles* 23, nos. 7–8 (1990): 413–419.

121 **the men get more credit:** Heather Sarsons, "Gender Differences in Recognition for Group Work," working paper, November 4, 2017, https://scholar.harvard.edu/files/sarsons/files/full_v6.pdf (accessed November 17, 2017).

123 **not the case for women:** Victoria L. Brescoll, "Who Takes the Floor and Why: Gender, Power, and Volubility in Organizations," *Administrative Science Quarterly* 56, no. 4 (2012): 622–641.

123 **incompetent and unworthy and are penalized:** Victoria L. Brescoll and Eric Luis Uhlmann, "Can an Angry Woman Get Ahead? Status Conferral, Gender, and Expression of Emotion in the Workplace," *Psychological Science* 19, no. 3 (2008): 268–275.

123 **took the same test:** Steven J. Spencer, Christine Logel, and Paul G. Davies, "Stereotype Threat," *Annual Review of Psychology* 67 (2016): 415–437; Steven J. Spencer, Claude M. Steele, and Diane M. Quinn, "Stereotype Threat and Women's Math Performance," *Journal of Experimental Social Psychology* 35, no. 1 (1999): 4–28.

124 **leaders, negotiators, entrepreneurs, and competitors:** Laura J. Kray and Aiwa Shirako, "Stereotype Threat in Organizations: An Examination of Its Scope, Triggers, and Possible Interventions," in *Stereotype Threat: Theory, Process, and Applications*, ed. Michael Inzlicht and Toni Schmader (New York: Oxford University Press, 2012), pp. 173–187.

124 **pain created by dental work:** Martina Amanzio and Fabrizio Benedetti, "Neuropharmacological Dissection of Placebo Analgesia: Expectation-Activated Opioid Systems versus Conditioning-Activated Specific Subsystems," *Journal of Neuroscience* 19, no. 1 (1999): 484–494.

126 **strides in their academic journey:** Robert Rosenthal and Lenore Jacobson, *Pygmalion in the Classroom: Teacher Expectation and Pupils' Intellectual Development* (New York: Holt, Rinehart and Winston, 1968).

126 **improves our performance:** Alison Wood Brooks, "Get Excited: Reappraising Pre-Performance Anxiety as Excitement," *Journal of Experimental Psychology: General* 143, no. 3 (June 2014): 1144–1158.

127 **Story of Bobbi Gibb:** Shanti Sosienski, *Women Who Run* (Berkeley, CA: Seal Press, 2006); Tom Derderian, *Boston Marathon: The History of the World's Premier Running Event* (Champaign, IL: Human Kinetics Publishers, 1996); Bobbi Gibb, *Wind in the Fire: A Personal Journey* (Boston: Institute of Natural Systems Press, 2012).

128 **devoted mothers than those who work:** Kathleen L. McGinn, Mayra Ruiz Castro, and Elizabeth Long Lingo, "Mums the Word! Cross-National Effects of Maternal Employment on Gender Inequalities at Work and at Home," Harvard Business School Working Paper, No. 15-094, June 2015 (revised July 2015).

128 **Weinstein had sexually assaulted multiple women:** Jia Tolentino, "Harvey Weinstein and the Impunity of Powerful Men," *New Yorker*, October 30, 2017.

129 **Story of Eileen Taylor of Deutsche Bank:** Interviews conducted with Deutsche Bank employees in February and March 2013.

129 **that reflects the U.S. equity market:** Cristian L. Dezsö and David Gaddis Ross, "Does Female Representation in Top Management Improve Firm Performance? A Panel Data Investigation," Robert H. Smith School Research Paper No. RHS 06-104, March 9, 2011, https://papers.ssrn.com/sol3/papers.cfm?abstract_id=1088182 (accessed November 17, 2017).

130 **a more stimulating workplace:** Work in progress in collaboration with Dan Ariely (of Duke University) and Evelyn Gosnell.

131 **organizations, nations, communities, and groups:** Adam D. Galinsky, Andrew R. Todd, Astrid C. Homan, et al., "Maximizing the Gains and Minimizing the Pains of Diversity: A Policy

Perspective," *Perspectives on Psychological Science* 10, no. 6 (2015): 742–748.

131 and higher profits: Cedric Herring, "Does Diversity Pay?: Race, Gender, and the Business Case for Diversity," *American Sociological Review* 74, no. 2 (2009): 208–224.

131 products that were more innovative: Katrin Talke, Søren Salomo, and Alexander Kock, "Top Management Team Diversity and Strategic Innovation Orientation: The Relationship and Consequences for Innovativeness and Performance," *Journal of Product Innovation Management* 28, no. 6 (2011): 819–832.

131 travel and immigration: Dean Keith Simonton, "Foreign Influence and National Achievement: The Impact of Open Milieus on Japanese Civilization," *Journal of Personality and Social Psychology* 72 (1997): 86–94.

131 prosperity in a community: Nathan Eagle, Michael Macy, and Rob Claxton, "Network Diversity and Economic Development," *Science* 328, no. 5981 (2010): 1029–1031.

131 more financially solid: Gianmarco I. P. Ottaviano and Giovanni Peri, "The Economic Value of Cultural Diversity: Evidence from US Cities," *Journal of Economic Geography* 6 (2006): 9–44.

131 prevents price bubbles: Sheen S. Levine, Evan P. Apfelbaum, Mark Bernard, et al., "Ethnic Diversity Deflates Price Bubbles," *Proceedings of the National Academy of Sciences* 111, no. 52 (2014): 18524–18529.

132 fraternity and sorority members: Katherine W. Phillips, Katie A. Liljenquist, and Margaret A. Neale, "Is the Pain Worth the Gain? The Advantages and Liabilities of Agreeing with Socially Distinct Newcomers," *Personality and Social Psychology Bulletin* 35, no. 3 (2009): 336–350.

133 the fluency heuristic: Ralph Hertwig, Stefan M. Herzog, Lael J. Schooler, and Torsten Reimer, "Fluency Heuristic: A Model of How the Mind Exploits a By-Product of Information Retrieval," *Journal of Experimental Psychology: Learning, Memory, and Cognition* 34, no. 5 (2008): 1191–1206.

133 an organization's stance on diversity: Geoffrey L. Cohen and Julio Garcia, "Identity, Belonging, and Achievement: A Model, Interventions, Implications," *Current Directions in Psychological Science* 17, no. 6 (2008): 365–369.

133 they feel they do not belong: Danielle Gaucher, Justin Friesen, and Aaron C. Kay, "Evidence That Gendered Wording in Job Advertisements Exists and Sustains Gender Inequality," *Journal of Personality and Social Psychology* 101, no. 1 (2011), 109–128.

134 within the organization: Valerie Purdie-Vaughns, Claude M. Steele, Paul G. Davies, et al., "Social Identity Contingencies: How Diversity Cues Signal Threat or Safety for African Americans in Mainstream Institutions," *Journal of Personality and Social Psychology* 94, no. 4 (2008): 615–630. See also Steven J. Spencer, Christine Logel, and Paul G. Davies, "Stereotype Threat," *Annual Review of Psychology* 67 (2016): 415–437.

134 success for stereotyped individuals: David M. Marx and Jasmin S. Roman, "Female Role Models: Protecting Women's Math Test Performance," *Personality and Social Psychology Bulletin* 28, no. 9 (2002): 1183–1193.

134 additional resources to mixed-race groups: Robert B. Lount Jr., Oliver J. Sheldon, Floor Rink, and Katherine W. Phillips, "Biased Perceptions of Racially Diverse Teams and Their Consequences for Resource Support," *Organization Science* 26, no. 5 (2015): 1351–1364.

134 Story of the San Antonio Spurs: María Triana, *Managing Diversity in Organizations: A Global Perspective* (New York: Routledge, 2017), p. 15; National Basketball Association, "NBA Tips Off 2013–2014 Season with Record International Player Presence," *NBA Global*, October 29, 2013, http://www.nba.com/global/nba_tips_off_201314_season_with_record_international_presence_2013_10_29.html (accessed November 29, 2017).

135 the key to success: Katherine W. Phillips, Gregory B. Northcraft, and Margaret A. Neale, "Surface-Level Diversity and Decision-Making in Groups: When Does Deep-Level Similarity Help?" *Group Processes & Intergroup Relations* 9, no. 4 (2006): 467–482.

136 who they thought committed the crime: Denise Lewin Loyd, Cynthia S. Wang, Katherine W. Phillips, and Robert B. Lount Jr., "Social Category Diversity Promotes Premeeting Elaboration: The Role of Relationship Focus," *Organization Science* 24, no. 3 (2013): 757–772.

136 more thorough in their preparation: Ibid. See also Samuel R. Sommers, Lindsey S. Warp, and Corrine C. Mahoney, "Cognitive Effects of Racial Diversity: White Individuals' Information Processing in Heterogeneous Groups," *Journal of Experimental Social Psychology* 44, no. 4 (2008): 1129–1136.

136 rather than as an opportunity: Research by Martin Davidson of the University of Virginia finds that organizations that rely on traditional approaches to manage diversity are generally ineffective, and that those that focus on leveraging differences are more successful in the long term. See Martin N. Davidson, *The End of Diversity as We Know It. Why Diversity Efforts Fail and How Leveraging Difference Can Succeed* (Oakland, CA: Berrett-Koehler Publishers, 2011).

137 she told *Time* magazine: Steve Lee, "Time Reveals 'Firsts: Women Who Are Changing the World,' a New Multimedia Project," *LGBT Weekly*, http://lgbtweekly.com/2017/09/07/time-reveals-firsts-women-who-are-changing-the-world-a-new-multimedia-project/ (accessed November 28, 2017).

6. COACH CHEEKS SINGS THE NATIONAL ANTHEM

139 Chapter 6 epigraph: Nathaniel Hawthorne, *The Scarlet Letter* (Cambridge, MA: Harvard University Press, 2009).

139 Story of Coach Cheeks: Ira Berkow, *Autumns in the Garden: The Coach of Camelot and Other Knicks Stories* (Chicago: Triumph Books, 2013). Video of the singing: https://www.youtube.com/watch?v=q4880PJnO2E.

141 a Good Samaritan: Ira Berkow, "Proper Praise for Cheeks's Saving Grace," *New York Times*, May 11, 2003, http://www.nytimes.com/2003/05/11/sports/sports-of-the-times-proper-praise-for-cheeks-s-saving-grace.html (accessed November 17, 2017).

141 "guardian angel": Elizabeth McGarr, "Natalie Gilbert," *Sports Illustrated*, August 2, 2010, https://www.si.com/vault/1969/12/31/105967059/natalie-gilbert (accessed November 17, 2017).

141 Story of Patricia Fili-Krushel: Kathleen L. McGinn, Deborah M. Kolb, and Cailin B. Hammer, "Traversing a Career Path: Pat Fili-Krushel (A)," Harvard Business School Case 909-009, September 2008 (revised June 2011); personal interview with Fili-Krushel, September 22, 2017.

142 feel closer to us: "Improving Relationships, Mental and Physical Health By Not Telling Lies," *Medical News Today*, August 7, 2012, http://www.medicalnewstoday.com/releases/248682.php (accessed November 17, 2017).

142 paired them up for computer chats: Li Jiang, Maryam Kouchaki, and Francesca Gino, F. (2017). "Attribution of authenticity: Powerful people benefit from self-disclosure of unfavorable information." Working paper (available from authors).

143 "That's really embarrassing": Lauren Sher, "Jennifer Lawrence Trips on Her Way to Collect Best Actress Award," ABC News, February 25, 2013, http://abcnews.go.com/Entertainment/oscars-2013-jennifer-lawrence-trips-on-her-way-to-collect-best-actress-award/blogEntry?id=18587011 (accessed November 17, 2017).

143 "pratfall effect": Elliot Aronson, Ben Willerman, and Joanne Floyd, "The Effect of a Pratfall on Increasing Interpersonal Attractiveness," *Psychonomic Science* 4, no. 6 (1966): 227–228. See also Robert Helmreich, Elliot Aronson, and James LeFan, "To Err Is Humanizing Sometimes: Effects of Self-Esteem, Competence, and a Pratfall on Interpersonal Attraction," *Journal of Personality and Social Psychology* 16, no. 2 (1970), 259–264.

143 those who covered them up: Joanne Silvester, Fiona Mary Anderson-Gough, Neil R. Anderson, and Afandi R. Mohamed, "Locus of Control, Attributions and Impression Management in the Selection Interview," *Journal of Occupational and Organizational Psychology* 75, no. 1 (2002): 59–76.

143 Story of Scott Cook: Personal interviews with Scott Cook in May 2014, May 2015, and October 2016.

145 evaluate this competitor: Karen Huang, Alison Wood Brooks, Brian Hall, et al., "Mitigating Envy: Why Successful Individuals Should Reveal Their Failures," Working paper, 2017 (available from authors).

145 results in higher grades: Xiaodong Lin-Siegler, Janet N. Ahn, Jondou Chen, et al., "Even Einstein Struggled: Effects of Learning About Great Scientists' Struggles on High School Students' Motivation to Learn Science," *Journal of Educational Psychology* 108, no. 3 (2016): 314–328. A 2012 study in Taiwan found similar results: When students read about scientists' struggles, they saw them as individuals (similar to them) who had to overcome obstacles; when they read about achievements, they saw scientists as special people with rare, innate talent. The students in this study who read about struggles performed better on a task in the laboratory. Huang-Yao Hong and Xiaodong Lin-Siegler, "How Learning About Scientists' Struggles Influences Students' Interest and Learning in Physics," *Journal of Educational Psychology* 104 (2012): 469–484.

146 there were no errors: Wendy Joung, Beryl Hesketh, and Andrew Neal, "Using 'War Stories' to Train for Adaptive Performance: Is it Better to Learn from Error or Success?," *Applied Psychology* 55, no. 2 (2006): 282–302.

146 reduced patient mortality: Diwas KC, Bradley R. Staats, and Francesca Gino, "Learning from My Success and from Others' Failure: Evidence from Minimally Invasive Cardiac Surgery," *Management Science* 59, no. 11 (2013): 2435–2449.

147 a simple explanation to the *Washington Post*: Ana Swanson, "Why It Feels So Good to Read About This Princeton Professor's Failures," *Washington Post*, April 28, 2016.

147 wanted to clean themselves: Francesca Gino, Maryam Kouchaki, and Adam D. Galinsky, "The Moral Virtue of Authenticity: How Inauthenticity Produces Feelings of Immorality and Impurity," *Psychological Science* 26, no. 7 (2015): 983–996.

149 questions about their self-esteem again: Murad S. Hussain and Ellen Langer, "A Cost of Pretending," *Journal of Adult Development* 10, no. 4 (2003): 261–270.

149 misrepresented themselves in interviews: Celia Moore, Sun Young Lee, Kawon Kim, and Dan Cable, "The Advantage of Being Oneself: The Role of Applicant Self-Verification in Organizational Hiring Decisions," *Journal of Applied Psychology* 102, no. 11 (2017): 1493–1513.

149 a fast-pitch competition: Francesca Gino, Ovul Sezer, Laura Huang, and Alison Wood Brooks, "To Be or Not to Be Your Authentic Self? Catering to Others' Expectations and Interests Hinders Performance," Working paper, 2017 (available from authors).

150 any Boston Red Sox fan: Francesca Gino and Maryam Kouchaki, "Feeling Authentic Serves as a Buffer Against Rejections," Working paper, 2016 (available from authors).

150 either authentic or inauthentic: Ibid.

150 when we're being inauthentic: Sebastian Korb, Stéphane With, Paula Niedenthal, et al., "The Perception and Mimicry of Facial Movements Predict Judgments of Smile Authenticity," *PLoS ONE* 9, no. 6 (2014): e99194.

150 a rise in blood pressure: Emily A. Butler, Boris Egloff, Frank H. Wilhelm, et al., "The Social Consequences of Expressive Suppression," *Emotion* 3, no. 1 (2003): 48–67.

150 even more than outright bragging: Ovul Sezer, Francesca Gino, and Michael I. Norton, "Humblebragging: A Distinct—and Ineffective—Self-Presentation Strategy," *Journal of Personality and Social Psychology*, 114, no. 1 (2018): 52–74.

151 candidates for a second date: Marian L. Houser, Sean M. Horan, and Lisa A. Furler, "Dating in the Fast Lane: How Communication Predicts Speed-Dating Success," *Journal of Social and Personal Relationships* 25, no. 5 (2008): 749–768.

152 inauthenticity exacts heavy costs: Ute R. Hülsheger and Anna F. Schewe, "On the Costs and Benefits of Emotional Labor: A Meta-Analysis of Three Decades of Research," *Journal of Occupational Health Psychology* 16, no. 3 (2011): 361–389.

152 before they went to bed: David T. Wagner, Christopher M. Barnes, and Brent A. Scott, "Driving It Home: How Workplace

Emotional Labor Harms Employee Home Life," *Personnel Psychology* 67, no. 2 (2014): 487–516.

152 a large Australian hospital: Alicia Grandey, Su Chuen Foo, Markus Groth, and Robyn E. Goodwin, "Free to Be You and Me: A Climate of Authenticity Alleviates Burnout From Emotional Labor," *Journal of Occupational Health Psychology* 17, no. 1 (2012) 1–14.

153 the ideas behind the brushstrokes: Personal interview with Davide di Fabio, July 26, 2016.

154 ISPA Instituto Universitário: Andreas Steimer and André Mata, "Motivated Implicit Theories of Personality: My Weaknesses Will Go Away, but My Strengths Are Here to Stay," *Personality and Social Psychology Bulletin* 42, no. 4 (2016): 415–429.

154 our strengths over our weaknesses: Albert Bandura, "Self-Efficacy Mechanism in Human Agency," *American Psychologist* 37, no. 2 (1982): 122–147.

154 unintentionally proved this idea: Donald O. Clifton and James K. Harter, "Investing in Strengths," http://media.gallup.com/documents/whitepaper--nvestinginstrengths.pdf (accessed November 17, 2017).

154 Story of Deloitte: Francesca Gino, Bradley R. Staats, and Paul Green Jr., "Reinventing Performance Management at Deloitte (A) & (B)," Harvard Business School Case 918-020 and 918-021, 2017; interviews conducted for the case throughout 2016 and 2017.

156 performance by 36 percent: Corporate Leadership Council, "Building the High-Performance Workforce: A Quantitative Analysis of the Effectiveness of Performance Management Strategies," 2002, http://marble-arch-online-courses.s3.amazonaws.com/CLC_Building_the_High_Performance_Workforce_A_Quantitative_Analysis_of_the_Effectiveness_of_Performance_Management_Strategies1.pdf (accessed November 17, 2017).

157 focus on their strengths: Susan Sorenson, "How Employees' Strengths Make Your Company Stronger," *Gallup News*,

February 20, 2014, http://news.gallup.com/business journal/167462/employees-strengths-company-stronger.aspx (accessed November 17, 2017).

157 **family members, friends, and coworkers:** Julia Lee, Francesca Gino, Daniel Cable, and Bradley R. Staats, "Preparing the Self for Team Entry: How Relational Affirmation Improves Team Performance," Working paper, 2017 (available from authors).

158 **I talked to the employees:** Daniel Cable, Francesca Gino, and Bradley R. Staats, "Breaking Them in or Eliciting Their Best? Reframing Socialization Around Newcomers' Authentic Self-Expression," *Administrative Science Quarterly* 58, no. 1 (2013): 1–36.

158 **lessons they had learned that day:** Giada DiStefano, Francesca Gino, Gary Pisano, and Bradley R. Staats, "Making Experience Count: The Role of Reflection in Individual Learning," Working paper, 2017 (available from authors).

159 **Story of Rachael Chong:** Personal interview with Rachael Chong, April 27, 2016.

160 **Story of Mellody Hobson:** Personal interviews with Mellody Hobson, November 4, 2014, December 8, 2014, and August 9, 2016.

7. THE SECRET OF STORY

163 **Chapter 7 epigraph:** Travis Bradberry and Jean Greaves, *Leadership 2.0* (San Diego, CA: TalentSmart, 2012).

166 **across industries and nations:** Gallup Organization, *First, Break All the Rules: What the World's Greatest Managers Do Differently* (New York: Gallup Press, 2016). Questions were simplified for younger participants. They included "At this school, I have the opportunity to do what I do best every day" and "I have a best friend at school."

168 **be themselves on the job:** Kevin Freiberg and Jackie Freiberg, *Nuts! Southwest Airlines' Crazy Recipe for Business and Personal Success* (New York: Broadway Books, 1996).

168 Barrett has said: Source of the quotation: "Southwest Airlines' Colleen Barrett Flies High on Fuel Hedging and 'Servant Leadership,'" http://knowledge.wharton.upenn.edu/article/southwest-airlines-colleen-barrett-flies-high-on-fuel-hedging-and-servant-leadership/ (accessed November 29, 2017).

169 Story of Doug Conant at Campbell's: Personal interview with Doug Conant, October 10, 2017; Douglas Conant and Mette Norgaard, *TouchPoints: Creating Powerful Leadership Connections in the Smallest of Moments* (San Francisco: Jossey-Bass, 2011); "Keeping Employees Engaged in Tough Times: An Interview with Douglas Conant, Former CEO of Campbell's Soup Company," *Harvard Business Review*, 2011, https://hbr.org/2011/10/keeping-employees-engaged-in-t (accessed November 29, 2017).

170 "no longer competitive": Robert Reiss, "Creating TouchPoints at Campbell Soup Company," *Forbes*, July 14, 2011, https://www.forbes.com/sites/robertreiss/2011/07/14/creating-touchpoints-at-campbell-soup-company/#72e2f2792c41 (accessed November 17, 2017).

170 "a very toxic culture": Conant and Norgaard, *TouchPoints: Creating Powerful Leadership Connections in the Smallest of Moments.*

173 in the same period: : CapitalIQ database, accessed November 20, 2017 (copy available from author).

173 dedication, absorption, and vigor: Engagement is a state that is broader and different from another state you may be familiar with: flow. Flow, a concept first described by psychologist Mihaly Csikszentmihalyi, is the holistic sensation we experience when we are completely absorbed in an activity, even with no promise of an external reward for doing so. Flow and engagement both are states of absorption, but conceptually, they are different. Flow is activity-specific, while engagement is more pervasive. Flow is often conceptualized as a peak experience. Engagement, instead, is a pattern that people carry over several domains. Those who are likely to experience engagement at work are also more likely to be engaged at home, research suggests.

173 **expression of gratitude, my research shows:** Adam Grant and Francesca Gino, "A Little Thanks Goes a Long Way: Explaining Why Gratitude Expressions Motivate Prosocial Behavior," *Journal of Personality and Social Psychology* 98 no. 6 (2010), 946–955.

174 **after watching the video:** Productivity data was measured as tons of tomatoes harvested per operating hour—calculated by dividing the tons harvested by a harvesting team during the shift by the number of hours the harvesting team operated that shift. The number of shifts for which we captured data following the intervention varied by harvester, as the harvest season end is dictated primarily by the onset of fall temperatures and rain, which varies across the state. Consequently, the number of post-intervention records collected varied by harvester—from 1 to 26, with a mean of 13.06. The full paper is here: Paul Green Jr., Francesca Gino, and Bradley R. Staats, "Seeking to Belong: How the Words of Internal and External Beneficiaries Influence Performance," Harvard Business School Working Paper 17-073 (2017). http://www.hbs.edu/faculty/Publication%20Files/17-073_9e2b9c23-cac0-4dcc-86ae-aaa2d32698d1.pdf (accessed November 17, 2017).

174 **pass their exams:** Wilmar B. Schaufeli, Isabel M. Martínez, Alexandra Marques Pinto, et al., "Burnout and Engagement in University Students: A Cross-National Study," *Journal of Cross-Cultural Psychology* 33, no. 5 (2002): 464–481.

175 **Story of Pixar:** Personal interviews with with Ed Catmull, Dan Scanlon, Jonas Rivera, Jamie Woolf, and Andrew Gordon conducted during a visit at Pixar, March 31, 2017; personal follow-up interview with Pete Docter, September 13, 2017; Ed Catmull with Amy Wallace, *Creativity Inc.: Overcoming the Unseen Forces That Stand in the Way of True Inspiration* (New York: Random House, 2014); David A. Price, *The Pixar Touch: The Making of a Company* (New York: Vintage, 2008); Lawrence Levy, *To Pixar and Beyond: My Unlikely Journey with Steve Jobs to Make Entertainment History* (Boston: Mariner Books, 2016).

184 exploration of novel ideas: Li Huang and Adam D. Galinsky, "Mind-Body Dissonance. Conflict Between the Senses Expands the Mind's Horizons," *Social Psychological and Personality Science* 2, no. 4 (2011): 351–359; Ella Miron-Spektor, Francesca Gino, and Linda Argote, "Paradoxical Frames and Creative Sparks: Enhancing Individual Creativity Through Conflict and Integration," *Organizational Behavior and Human Decision Processes* 116, no. 2 (2011): 229–240.

184 learn novel information: Travis Proulx and Steven J. Heine, "Connections from Kafka: Exposure to Meaning Threats Improves Implicit Learning of an Artificial Grammar," *Psychological Science* 20, no. 9 (2009): 1125–1131.

184 a more cooperative mood: Carsten K. W. De Dreu and Bernard A. Nijstad, "Mental Set and Creative Thought in Social Conflict: Threat Rigidity Versus Motivated Focus," *Journal of Personality and Social Psychology* 95, no. 3 (2008): 648–661.

184 leads them to novel insights: Bianca Beersma and Carsten K. W. De Dreu, "Conflict's Consequences: Effects of Social Motives on Postnegotiation Creative and Convergent Group Functioning and Performance," *Journal of Personality and Social Psychology* 89, no. 3 (2005): 358–374.

184 appear to be at odds: Ella Miron-Spektor, Francesca Gino, and Linda Argote, "Paradoxical Frames and Creative Sparks: Enhancing Individual Creativity Through Conflict and Integration," *Organizational Behavior and Human Decision Processes* 116, no. 2 (2011): 229–240.

185 Story of *Toy Story*: Ed Catmull, "How Pixar Fosters Collective Creativity," *Harvard Business Review*, September 2008, https://hbr.org/2008/09/how-pixar-fosters-collective-creativity (accessed November 28, 2017). Personal interview with Ed Catmull, March 31, 2017.

189 greater employee effort than higher pay: Duncan S. Gilchrist, Michael Luca, and Deepak Malhotra, "When 3+1:4: Gift Structure and Reciprocity in the Field," *Management Science* 62, no. 9 (2016): 2639–2650.

8. BECOMING A REBEL LEADER

191 **Chapter 8 epigraph:** John Reeve Carpenter, *Pirates: Scourge of the Seas* (New York: Sterling Publishing, 2008).

191 **the legendary Black Bart:** Within the span of his three-year-long career, he captured more than 400 ships. For comparison, Blackbeard captured about 120 of them in a two-year span. Articles like this one were quite common on pirate ships.

191 **Sources for the pirates' story:** Charles Johnson, *A General History of the Pyrates* (Seattle, WA: Loki's Publishing, 1724); Colin Woodard, *The Republic of Pirates: Being the True and Surprising Story of the Caribbean Pirates and the Man Who Brought Them Down* (Orlando, FL: Mariner Books, 2008); Marcus Rediker, *Villains of All Nations: Atlantic Pirates in the Golden Age* (Boston: Beacon Press, 2004); Peter T. Leeson, *The Invisible Hook: The Hidden Economics of Pirates* (Princeton, NJ: Princeton University Press, 2009); multiple conversations with Peter Leeson, spring 2017.

192 **a constitution drafted for each ship:** Peter T. Leeson, "An-*arrgh*-chy: The Law and Economics of Pirate Organization," *Journal of Political Economy* 115, no. 6 (2007): 1049–1094.

193 **Marcus Rediker:** Marcus Rediker, *Between the Devil and the Deep Blue Sea: Merchant Seamen, Pirates and the Anglo-American Maritime World, 1700–1750* (Cambridge, MA: Cambridge University Press, 1987), p. 267.

194 **three to seven members:** Robert Frees Bales, *Interaction Process Analysis: A Method for the Study of Small Groups* (Chicago: University of Chicago Press, 1950; reprinted 1976).

194 **see hierarchies develop:** Elizabeth Gellert, "Stability and Fluctuation in the Power Relationships of Young Children," *Journal of Abnormal and Social Psychology* 62 (1961): 8–15.

194 **they usually fail:** Harold J. Leavitt, *Top Down: Why Hierarchies Are Here to Stay and How to Manage Them More Effectively* (Cambridge, MA: Harvard Business Review Press, 2004).

195 **a less talkative colleague's same suggestion:** Henry W. Riecken, "The Effect of Talkativeness on the Ability to Influence Group Solutions of Problems," *Sociometry* 21 (1958): 309–331.

195 the former an unfair sheen: Muzafer Sherif, B. Jack White, and O. J. Harvey, "Status in Experimentally Produced Groups," *American Journal of Sociology* 60, no. 4 (1955): 370–379.

195 poor decisions and performance: Chester I. Barnard, *The Functions of the Executive* (Cambridge: Harvard University Press, 1968).

195 more likely to die: Eric M. Anicich, Roderick I. Swaab, and Adam D. Galinsky, "Hierarchical Cultural Values Predict Success and Mortality in High-Stakes Teams," *PNAS* 112, no. 5 (2015): 1338–1343.

196 according to its website: Cheese Board Collective, "The Cheese Board: A Worker-Owned Collective Since 1971," http://cheeseboardcollective.coop/about-us/about-main/ (accessed November 17, 2017).

196 Story of Valve Software: Ethan Bernstein, Francesca Gino, and Bradley R. Staats, "Opening the Valve: From Software to Hardware (A)," Harvard Business School Case 415-015, August 2014.

197 committed, satisfied, and productive: Linn Van Dyne and Jon L. Pierce, "Psychological Ownership and Feelings of Possession: Three Field Studies Predicting Employee Attitudes and Organizational Citizenship Behavior," *Journal of Organizational Behavior* 25, no. 4 (2004): 439–459.

197 think about their current job: Maryam Kouchaki, Francesca Gino, and Ata Jami, "It's Mine, But I'll Help You: How Psychological Ownership Increases Prosocial Behavior," Working paper, 2017 (available from authors).

200 Formula One racing: Martin Williamson, "Monaco Grand Prix 1950: Fangio Escapes the Pile-Up," ESPN, http://en.espn.co.uk/f1/motorsport/story/12022.html (accessed September 25, 2017); Gerald Donaldson, "Monaco Smart Win for Fangio—1950," http://www.f1speedwriter.com/2012/05/grand-prix-de-monaco-1950-juan-manuel.html (accessed September 25, 2017).

201 the front of his car: Sources for the story: Robert F. Kennedy, *Thirteen Days: A Memoir of the Cuban Missile Crisis* (Boston: W. W.

Norton & Company, 1971); Ernest R. May and Philip D. Zelikow, eds., *The Kennedy Tapes: Inside the White House During the Cuban Missile Crisis* (New York: W. W. Norton & Company, 2002); Arthur M. Schlesinger Jr., *A Thousand Days: John F. Kennedy in the White House* (Boston: Houghton Mifflin Company, 1965).

202 **quieting dissent and suppressing alternatives:** Irving L. Janis, *Victims of Groupthink: A Psychological Study of Foreign-Policy Decisions and Fiascoes* (New York: Houghton Mifflin, 1972).

202 **Robert Kennedy would comment:** Kennedy, *Thirteen Days*, p. 36.

203 **disagreement in private meetings:** Tony L. Simons and Randall S. Peterson, "Task Conflict and Relationship Conflict in Top Management Teams: The Pivotal Role of Intragroup Trust," *Journal of Applied Psychology* 85, no. 1 (2000): 102–111.

203 **"what the decision is all about":** Tim Hindle, *Guide to Management Ideas and Gurus* (New York: Bloomberg Press, 2008); "Alfred Sloan," *The Economist*, January 30, 2009, http://www.economist.com/node/13047099 (accessed November 29, 2017).

203 **a technique they call "plussing":** Personal interview with Ed Catmull during a visit at Pixar, March 31, 2017.

204 **anything-goes listening sessions:** Boris Groysberg and Michael Slind, "Leadership Is a Conversation," *Harvard Business Review*, June 2012.

204 **what I do, and much more:** Personal interview with Doug Conant, October 10, 2017.

205 **in Silicon Valley, all men:** Kathleen L. McGinn, Deborah M. Kolb, and Cailin B. Hammer, "Traversing a Career Path: Pat Fili-Krushel (A)," Harvard Business School Case 909-009, September 2008 (revised June 2011); personal interview, September 22, 2017.

206 **lacing their shoes:** Andrew Hill with John Wooden, *Be Quick—But Don't Hurry: Finding Success in the Teachings of a Lifetime* (New York: Simon & Schuster, 2001).

205 **can span 6 months:** Gary P. Pisano, Francesca Gino, and Bradley R. Staats, "Pal's Sudden Service—Scaling an Organizational Model to Drive Growth," Harvard Business School Case 916-052, May 2016 (revised March 2017).

206 with this goal in mind: Francesca Gino and Bradley R. Staats, "Samasource: Give Work, Not Aid," Harvard Business School Case 912-011, December 2011 (revised June 2012).

206 "five different textures and temperatures": Personal interviews during visit at Osteria Francescana, July 26–27, 2016.

207 the moon mission of Apollo 13: William David Compton, *Where No Man Has Gone Before: A History of Apollo Lunar Exploration Missions* (Washington, D.C.: U.S. Government Printing Office, 1989).

208 surpass expectations—or better: Irene Scopelliti, Paola Cillo, Bruno Busacca, and David Mazursky, "How Do Financial Constraints Affect Creativity?" *Journal of Product Innovation Management* 31, no. 5 (2014): 880–893.

208 Forbes's list of highest-earning pirates: Kris E. Lane, *Blood and Silver: A History of Piracy in the Caribbean and Central America* (Oxford, Eng.: Signal Books, 1999).

208 Yes, Forbes made a list of top-earning pirates: "Top-Earning Pirates," *Forbes*, September 19, 2008, https://www.forbes.com/2008/09/18/top-earning-pirates-biz-logistics-cx_mw_0919piracy.html#521a37307263 (accessed November 29, 2017).

208 lead to better solutions: See: Irene Scopelliti, Paola Cillo, Bruno Busacca, and David Mazursky, "How Do Financial Constraints Affect Creativity?" Ravi Mehta and Meng Zhu, "Creating When You Have Less: The Impact of Resource Scarcity on Product Use Creativity," *Journal of Consumer Research* 42, no. 5 (2016): 767–782.

210 their three closest friends: Leon Festinger, Kurt W. Back, and Stanley Schachter, *Social Pressures in Informal Groups: A Study of Human Factors in Housing* (Stanford, CA: Stanford University Press, 1950).

210 Del Monte canning factory: Personal interviews during a visit at Pixar, March 31, 2017.

210 team did as a whole: Jennifer L. Berdahl and Cameron Anderson, "Men, Women, and Leadership Centralization in Groups Over Time," *Group Dynamics: Theory, Research, and Practice* 9, no. 1 (2005): 45–57.

CONCLUSION

213 Conclusion epigraph: Jeff Gordinier, "Massimo Bottura, the Chef Behind the World's Best Restaurant," *New York Times Style Magazine*, October 17, 2016, https://www.nytimes.com/2016/10/17/t-magazine/massimo-bottura-chef-osteria-francescana.html (accessed November 29, 2017).

213 Sources for the earthquake story: Nick Squires, "Earthquake Strikes Northern Italy Killing Six," *Telegraph*, May 20, 2012; Elisabetta Povoledo, "Thousands Are Homeless in Deadly Quake in Italy," *New York Times*, May 21, 2012; "Another Earthquake in Italy Hits Almost Same Spot as Previous One," *Tripoli Post*, May 29, 2012; Andrea Vogt and Tom Kington, "Earthquake in Italy Kills Five and Razes Centuries of History," *Guardian*, May 21, 2012; Tom Kington, "Wheels of Misfortune: Race to Save Parmesan Toppled by Earthquake," *Guardian*, May 23, 2012; interviews with locals, July 2016 and May 2017.

219 less time-constrained: Cassie Mogilner, Zoe Chance, and Mike Norton, "Giving Time Gives You Time," *Psychological Science* 23, no. 10 (2012): 1233–1238.

EPILOGUE

221 Epilogue epigraph: Jayson DeMers, "51 Quotes to Inspire Success in Your Life and Business," *Inc.com*, November 3, 2014, https://www.inc.com/jayson-demers/51-quotes-to-inspire-success-in-your-life-and-business.html (accessed November 29, 2017).

INDEX